Deliver Me From Evil

The memoirs of Thomas, First Earl of Strafford

For Phil Hewitt
with thanks for all
your help.
T. G. Stanton
5th May 2017.

A Novel by

T. G. STANTON.

Deliver Me From Evil

For information address mickiedaltonbooks@lycos.com

First Printing March, 2017

ISBN: 978-0-6480021-4-7

Published by The Mickie Dalton Foundation
NSW
Australia

Contents

Dramatis Personae.

Thomas Wentworth, later Earl of Strafford.

Sir William Wentworth, Baronet, Thomas's father.

Henry Clifford, later Earl of Cumberland, Thomas's school-friend, and brother-in-law.

Christopher Wandesford, Thomas's school-friend and colleague in Government.

Margaret Clifford, Henry Clifford's sister, and Thomas's first wife.

George Radcliffe, Thomas's friend and colleague in Government.

Sir Arthur Ingram, Thomas's close business acquaintance and entrepreneur.

Sir John Savile, one of Thomas's enemies, a Yorkshire magnate.

Lionel Cranfield, later the Earl of Middlesex, the Treasurer.

Richard Weston. Replaces Cranfield as Treasurer.

Sir Edward Osborne, a friend of Thomas's and his Vice-President on the Council of the North.

George Villiers, Duke of Buckingham, James I's 'favourite', and then Charles I's best friend.

Charles I, King of England from 1625.

Queen Henrietta Maria, Charles's wife.

Arabella Holles, daughter of Earl Clare, Thomas's second wife and mother of his son William and daughters Arabella and Anne (Nan).

William Laud, rising clergyman and ultimately Archbishop of Canterbury, Thomas's close colleague and friend.

John Pym, one-time Parliamentary colleague of Thomas, and later his bitter enemy.

Denzil Holles, Arabella's brother, Thomas's colleague in early Parliaments, later a supporter of Pym, but then of Thomas again.

Elizabeth Wentworth, nee Rodes, Thomas's third wife; mother of his son Thomas and his daughter Margaret.

Philip Mainwaring, Thomas's secretary in Ireland.

Richard Boyle, Earl of Cork, Thomas's chief enemy in Ireland.

Francis Annesley, Lord Mountnorris, another enemy in Ireland.

Richard de Burgh and his son, Ulick, Earls of Clanricarde in Ireland and St Albans in England, also Thomas's Irish enemies.

James Butler, Earl of Ormonde, Thomas's friend in Ireland.

James Ussher, Primate of All Ireland, and Archbishop of Armagh.

Algernon (Algie) Percy, Earl of Northumberland, a friend of Thomas's.

Lucy, Countess of Carlisle, Thomas's mistress, and Algie's sister.

John Lesley, Bishop of Raphoe, a friend of Thomas's in Ireland (not to be confused with Henry Leslie, Bishop of Down, or John Leslie, Lord Rothes, or Alexander Leslie, Scots General).

Lord Traquair, King Charles's Commissioner in Scotland for the Bishops' War.

Lord Hamilton, Scots friend of King Charles; member of the English Privy Council.

Alexander Leslie, General of the Scottish Army.

Bulstrode Whitlock, one of Pym's colleagues and Thomas's prosecutors.

John Glyn, one of Pym's colleagues and Thomas's prosecutors.

Lord Digby, MP, one of Thomas's prosecutors who later supports him.

Richard Lane, Thomas's leading Counsel.

Thomas

I wasn't a good man; I can see that now. Mind you, I thought I was pretty good at the time, trying to do what I thought was honourable, endeavouring to be honest. At least I didn't attribute all my deeds to God, like that hypocrite Oliver Cromwell. On the other hand, I don't think I was an entirely bad fellow, either, but I recognise that a lot of people perceived me, and still do, as always acting entirely in my own interests. I don't think they can be right about that, but then I suppose I would say that, wouldn't I?

After all, the very last scene of my life could hardly be said to have been in my interests, yet it was a piece of theatre I had crafted completely, and almost unwittingly, on my own. True enough, there were hundreds, if not thousands, of people who were very anxious indeed to have a part in that play, but if it hadn't been for what I wrote to the King at the end, they might have been deprived of the opportunity.

However, that all comes later, much later. Before we start, I must tell you that in preparing this account of my life, I have called upon a number of the people I knew, some of them friends, some of them anything but, who are up here too. They have contributed, as best they can, and in their own words, what happened, and what they thought about me at the times of which they write.

Why am I writing this now? Many serious books have been written about me. The authors have either liked me or loathed me. I want to set the record straight. I want to show people the real me. I hope I can.

This is my story.

Thomas. 26th March, 1628. Westminster.

My hands are slick with sweat. My knees are locked with tension. Despite all the speeches I have made in Court, and those I have previously made in the Commons, I have never been so deafened by the thunder of my heart-beat sounding in my ears. The House is packed; I think every single MP must be here on this rather gloomy day, the chamber barely lit by the wintry sun outside.

If I had to hold notes they would be useless; they would be stuck together with perspiration. My fingers are trembling so as to make moving from one page of notes to another almost impossible, but I do not need notes. I've learned what I shall say like an actor reciting the longest of Shakespeare's soliloquies.

Charles I is desperate for money. That is to be the subject of the eloquence I pray for. Six days ago he opened this, his third Parliament. He set the tone for it at once, by telling Lords and Commons that if we did not grant him the supply of funds he needed and wanted, he would take it in any event by those other means which God had placed in his hands. Some of my fellows interpreted this as a threat, but he wouldn't think of threatening anyone. In fact he more or less said as much at the end of his speech. He told us: "Do not take this as threatening, for I scorn to threaten any but my equals".

How insulting! We know well enough that we have only one King in England so he has no equals here. He thinks his word – "I want this or that, and you will give them to me" – is all that is required, no matter how tactlessly that word is expressed. Having rather stunned and shocked most of the House, he withdrew, and left us to our debate on his speech.

My moment is today. I know exactly what my strategy is.

A stocky MP with an extraordinarily high-pitched voice at last opens the debate on the matter of supply. There are several speeches from others, most in favour of refusing the King what he wants. There are only one or two for the King's cause, and they are weak and ineffectual.

Then the Speaker calls upon me. "Thomas Wentworth, Member for Yorkshire".

How did I get to this position? How did I get to be the kind of man who stands up in the House of Commons to make a speech such as mine will be?

I need to take a look at those questions from the beginning.

In The Beginning.

Thomas. 8th October, 1599. Rotherham.

I have never seen so many people milling about, and the noise is tremendous.

"Who are all these people, Father? Where have they come from?"

Sir William Wentworth grasps my hand more tightly, and drags me along in his wake as fast as my six-year-old legs will carry me. "They are the people of Rotherham, and from the surrounding villages and farms and hamlets. And ...."

"Do people live in little bits of ham, Daddy?"

"What are you on about, boy?" He sounds a bit crusty, but he is a loving Father, kind and gentle, but firm in his handling of me and the other children.

"Hamlet. Isn't it ...."

"A hamlet is a very small collection of houses, maybe five, or ten."

I am puzzled. "But Daddy, if a piglet is a small pig, why isn't a hamlet a small ham?"

Sir William stops, and looks at me affectionately. "Now Thomas, you have to stop thinking like that. People who take your words apart are called lawyers, like your Grandfather Atkinson. And you don't want to become one of those, whatever you do! Now come along, or we shall be late." We start off again, picking our way carefully between the people, wicker crates of chickens stacked on the ground, cow-pats, and horse droppings.

"Why have they all come here?"

"It's Rotherham market day. See that woman over there? She's selling bread, and that one's got a barrow full of turnips and vegetables. And there, behind those hurdles, the farmers have brought their cows and sheep to market to sell."

I stop in my tracks, and Sir William loses his grip, having to come back for me. "Why is that man sitting on the ground Daddy? And what has happened to his legs? Why are they stuck through that plank?"

"Thomas, that is a very naughty man. He is a robber and a thief. He is in the stocks – that's the plank of wood. Actually it's two planks, and they trap his legs so that he can't get out. The Justices of the Peace have made him sit there for three days to teach him not to steal again, and to warn other people not to steal either."

"What is a justitches?"

"Will you please stop asking questions for a minute? I'll tell you about Justices when you are old enough to understand."

"That's what my sister always says – that I'm too little to understand."

"When did she say that?"

"When I asked her why she goes to wee-wee sitting down and I do it standing up."

"Quite right too. And a very bright answer considering she's only seven herself."

I will not give up. "But why has the man got apple squashed in his hair, and clods of mud on his face and clothes?"

"Because the local folk, especially the ones he robbed, throw things at him."

"That's not fair. He can't throw anything back. Look. His arms are in those other planks."

"I think you really will have to be a lawyer after all. Anyway he should have thought of that before he started stealing."

"Where are we going?"

"I told you. I'm taking you to see a friend of mine to play with his son whilst I go to the Quarter Sessions and ...."

Suddenly a stentorian voice shouts out from across the other side of the street: "Wentworth!!" To our right a large man on a large black horse is glaring at Sir William. Immediately my father transfers me from his right to his left, as though to protect me from the newcomer. He takes my hand again, so hard it hurts.

"Wentworth, I say!!" The man shouts again. He is a very big man indeed, bigger even than Father, and looks even more gigantic astride his horse. Until now I have always thought my Father the tallest man in the world. The man is dressed in burgundy coloured velvet with gold slashings in the sleeves, and a large earring. His broad hat is of the same hue as his knickerbocker suit, surmounted by two or three large feathers. He whips his steed's neck with the reins and moves across the street towards us. The contrast between this magnificent if frightening personage and my father's rather puritanical black costume is startling.

"Have you nothing to say, Sir?" shouts the man.

"Should I have anything to say to you, Sir Thomas? You sound as though you expect me to know what you think I might say. I'm no mind reader. You may be given to shouting loudly in the street, but I am not."

The man laughs, and shouts again. "You always were a pusillanimous clod, Wentworth. And now you're interfering with my tenants, damn your hide."

Looking down at me, my Father must be able to see that I am quite terrified. Determining to try to keep the peace, he replies gently: "I haven't the slightest idea what you're talk – yelling – about."

"That blaggard Holt. You've been lending him money."

"I don't deny it, but he's no blaggard. He's a good man, an excellent farmer, and a kind neighbour. Last year when my daughter Anne fell in the village pond, he dived in and rescued her."

"Good man be damned. He's a peasant. And if you're lending money to scum like him you can't be much better."

Father smiles. "Sir Thomas, we are both Justices of the Peace, we are not setting a peaceful example, and we...."

"Peaceful example be buggered. I haven't finished with you. I'll see you on the Bench later." He spurs his horse away.

I am trembling: "Father, no-one is ever going to do anything like that to me. I'll thrash the man who tries".

Father smiles: "Well, son, you're a bit on the small side for that yet. Come on, I'll not leave you now. I'll take you to Court and you can sit at the back."

The Court seems huge, and is full of people of all sorts and shapes and sizes. Before the cases start my Father and the nasty man are up on the bench, and appear to be talking angrily to each other; at least, Sir Thomas seems angry. He shouts very loudly, "A turd in your teeth, Wentworth, you're a rascal, a villain, and a coward who dares not draw a sword. I sent you a challenge a while ago, but you were too afraid to accept it."

My Father is rather quieter, but I can still hear him. "You're wrong, Sir Thomas. I am not afraid but we are ..."

Suddenly he grabs my Father's collar, hits him in the face and then pushes him off the Bench, holding onto his ears and pulling Father about by them. Papa tries to pull him off, but as Reresby has so firm a grip on his ears this just makes his pain worse and he cries out. Their retainers leap forward to join in the quarrel, daggers drawn and clearly ready for use. Two other justices seize Reresby and pull him away as three others come between the servants and command them to sheath their weapons.

Pandemonium rules for a while, until the magistrates call the watch and the constables. At last calm prevails, but in the most frigid atmosphere. Father gets up. He is shaken, but he does not retaliate. I am even more determined that no-one will ever treat me like that.

Father is in no fit state to hear any cases; he comes to the back of the Court and takes me home. He is bleeding from the ears; the skin is torn where the lobes join the jaw-line. He tells me the man is Sir Thomas Reresby. That is my earliest memory.

* * * *

As we go home I ask Father what had happened, but I am too young to understand. Some years later he told me that Reresby and he had quarrelled a couple of years before about the ownership of some farm land. At least, Reresby was suggesting that by lending money to his tenant, Holt, my Father was pretending that he was the owner of the farm Holt rented in Sir Thomas's manor in part of Hooton Roberts. After the quarrel, Reresby sent his uncle to our house to ask Father if it were true that he had said he wanted to fight a duel with Reresby. Father sent the uncle back with a message that he had no intention of fighting, and had said nothing of the sort. He bore Sir Thomas no malice, and as far as he was concerned the quarrel was over and done with.

The two men did not see each other again until the Court Session. A prisoner had escaped and there was some difficulty about empanelling a jury, and Reresby made these problems an excuse for challenging Father to a duel. He declined to fight, and Reresby hit him. Papa was never a bold fighting type, but the two magistrates who rescued him were so appalled at what had happened that they reported it to the Star Chamber. This was a very strict and powerful Court which dealt particularly with the prosecution of rich and mighty people, and Reresby was fined 1000 pounds. That was an enormous sum of money.

He was also removed from the Commission of the Peace so he could no longer sit as a magistrate.

I learned a lot from this. First, rich and powerful people can't just do what they like and get away with it (unless they are very rich and powerful indeed). Secondly, it is better to be peaceful and law-abiding (like Father), if you could. Thirdly, if you use the law properly you can make other people do what you want, and stop them doing things you don't want. Father had said to me earlier that day that I shouldn't become a lawyer, but it was a bit of a joke, because Mum's Father was a lawyer, and most young men of the landed classes went to the Inns of Court to learn about the law even if they didn't want to be advocates. So when I was fourteen and was sent off to the Inner Temple, I was very happy about it. If you think you can run two manors and manage a lot of farms and tenants without some knowledge of the law, let alone go into politics, you need to think again. I was not to be content with just two manors.

Around the time Dad told me all about Reresby something else happened which taught me the value of knowing the law. Thomas Gargrave was my Uncle; he was married to Dad's sister. He was arrested for murdering one of his servants. He must have done it because no-one in their right mind would do what he did otherwise. When the case came to Court, he refused to plead Guilty or Not Guilty. He wasn't tried for the crime after all. No. He was punished for refusing to plead. The Sheriff and the constables laid him out, and slowly heaped heavy slabs of stone on top of him, and he wasn't fed either. Gradually he starved, or was crushed, to death, or both. It took days. Most people gave up long before that and entered a plea. But not Uncle Thomas Gargrave. He stuck it out to the bitter end.

Why did he do that? He knew that if he was tried and found guilty he would hang, and if he was hanged, all his land and all his goods and money would be forfeit to the King. But if he died under this punishment for not pleading, his fortune would be safe for his family.

Still, you might say he wasted his breath if he hadn't had it all squeezed out of him. He was in financial trouble when he was killed, and his land fell into the hands of a grasping swindler called Sir Arthur Ingram. You'll hear more of him later.

* * * *

I was born in London on Good Friday, 13th April, 1593. It wasn't too bad. My mother had already had my older brother (but he died soon after I appeared), and my sister Anne, so she was getting quite good at it. She needed to be; she was going to have another eight babies in the next sixteen years. And they all lived. I don't think she lost any in child-bed, as it used to be called.

My mother was an Atkinson, daughter of Sir Robert, a pretty wealthy chap with thousands of acres of land at Stowell in Gloucestershire, and most of those acres packed with sheep, and most of the sheep producing lots of wool to be spun and woven by the people (peasants we called them), who lived in the hovels and cottages in the hamlets and villages on those acres. Sir Robert's carts trundled the lanes round his acres collecting the wool and the cloth and taking it to the markets, and sometimes to Bristol to be shipped to France and Spain, and the American colonies. Some of the ships were Sir Robert's too, and all the money from all those enterprises came back to him. So, yes, he was a pretty wealthy chap. He was also a barrister of Lincoln's Inn, with a house in Chancery Lane.

And he was my grandfather. Of course, I didn't know that then, when the midwife stuck me on my mother's lovely nipple for the first time. But my mother, Anne, was Sir Robert's only child, his heiress. I didn't know that either. Of course, one day Sir Robert would die, and leave a fair slice of it to my mother. Then she'd leave it all to me to manage for her, and I'd be good at it. When she died I'd give a proper share to my siblings, which I did, which shows, as I said at the start, that I wasn't all bad.

Good Friday is the day of the ultimate sacrifice. What sort of omen will the 13th of April prove to be for me?

I was christened Thomas Wentworth on 22nd April, 1593 in London. St. Dunstan's in the West is a funny little London church in Fleet Street. Inside it is a very holy place, calm and peaceful, and it's difficult to remember that a few yards away, just beyond the oak doors, hundreds of people and dozens of carts, wagons, and carriages, are shouting and milling about.

I was christened there nine days after coming into the world. Everyone in Tudor England believes in God, and for many people the way you are supposed to worship Him and pray to Jesus is a passion. People have been dying for it in England for the best part of this century after King Henry parted company with the Pope. All this dying for faith or religion – well, for religion, anyway, since if the people stopped to think about it they'd see that their faith is all the same – wasn't going to stop for a long time. It may not do me a lot of good either, but how can a baby in a christening gown in St Dunstan's know that?.

Why did this happen in London, when our home is in Yorkshire, at Wentworth Woodhouse, where my father is lord of the manor? Well, as I say, my grandfather is a pretty wealthy chap, and he could afford a nice house in London, in Chancery Lane. We were staying there when my Mother realised I was on my way. We always went to St Dunstan's when we stayed at Grandfather's.

It is a tall and narrow house with a winding stair up the middle. It is built of dark grey bricks set between grey oak beams. London burns coal from Durham and Newcastle. The smoke from the coal fires is turning London black.

Thomas. September, 1601. Well, Yorkshire.

He is fair haired, with a golden skin, and he's an inch or two taller than me. He is quite different from me, since I am quite pale, and my hair dark, almost black. He is the first person I see as I walk into the garden of the strange looking house. What is strange is that, although it is a Tudor house of black oak beams and white plaster, there seems to be an awful lot of black oak, and only small spaces of white. It is the home of Dr John Higgins. He runs it as a small school for sons of the gentry.

edge of the lawn. Like me he is dressed in grey clothes with a small lace collar. He is engrossed in a book, and taking no heed of his surroundings. On the other side of the path is a knot garden of low box hedge; the dark green leaves are highlighted by the tiny red berries. It is odd that I notice that, because I'm not much interested in nature and plants and flowers. I can only put this impression down to the effect that what happens next has on me.

As I watch him, two larger boys come running along the path behind him, and quite deliberately cannon into him as they pass. He's knocked off his feet and falls over the box hedge into the knot garden. His book drops on the path and one of these bullies stamps on it. They run on, laughing and shouting: "Swotty Wandy! Swotty Wandy!"

I look around. No-one else is in sight. I walk swiftly to the boy, step over the hedge, and crouch down beside him. "Are you alright?"

He rolls over onto his back. "Alright, I think." He has a blob of mud on the end of his nose, and his hands and knees are muddy too. He wipes the mud from his nose with the back of his hand, so I take my handkerchief from my sleeve and offer it to him. He wipes his nose and hands with it and gives it back. "Thanks," he says.

"What was that all about?"

"What was what all about?"

"Them bowling you over like that!"

"Oh, that! Nothing really. Happens all the time. To me, anyway."

I remember old Reresby hitting my father, and how I had promised myself that I should never let anyone do anything like that to me. "And what was it they shouted at you? Sounded like Swotty Wandy."

The boy laughs in an oddly sad sort of way. "That's it. They knock me about because I'm no good at sport. No, they call me Swotty because I'm always wandering about with my head in a book."

"I'm Thomas; Thomas Wentworth."

"And I'm Christopher Wandesford. You can call me Kit if you like. That's what my Father calls me." We shake hands. "Do you have any friends?"

"No. I only got here last night. You can call me Tom, if you like. No-one else does." I get up and cross the hedge to pick up his book. The spine is broken and some pages fall out. I pick them up, go back, and give him the sorry bundle. "Is that a school book?"

"No, it's mine, I'm glad to say. I can't think what the Head would do if it was his. I've been here three weeks. We've both got a friend now. That's if you want to be friends with me." He smiles shyly as he says this. I grab his hand again. "We'll always be friends! And I won't let those idiots bully you again!"

"Don't be silly. You're not as big as me, and they're even taller."

I let go of his hand and stand as tall as I can. "Well, I'm not afraid of them. I'm not afraid of anybody. Anyway, if we're friends we can beat them together."

"How?"

"I don't know. But I'll think of something." I look at him again. Why do small boys always want to know how old other small boys are? Well, I do, so I ask him.

"I'm nine. How old are you?"

I had been so ashamed that this boy was at least an inch, maybe two, taller than me, but now I know that I am his junior by a year! "I was eight in April. But I'm going to be taller soon!" Christopher laughs.

Christopher. 1601. Well. Yorkshire.

Boys of eight make lots of rash statements and promises, but the promise of friendship from this Thomas - Tom - was one that was to last, and bring me enormous benefits. If I hadn't been sent to Dr Higgins' school at Well I might never have met him, nor Henry, of whom more later. Well, maybe I'd have met Tom, because it turned out he only lived a few miles from us, and his Father and mine had known each other a long time.

Dr Higgins was the Dean of Ripon Cathedral, and an acquaintance of my Father's. The good Doctor accommodated a few boys for tuition at his home in Well, which was about fifteen miles away from Ripon. He was as unlike a priest or Dean as anyone could imagine – over six feet tall, with massive shoulders and a barrel of a body, he looked more like one of the wrestlers who toured the country taking on all comers at the fairs. Even so, he was a kindly man and Godly, but it was a foolish pupil – or adult, come to that – who got on the wrong side of him. He had an odd saying, too. When faced with a recalcitrant and guilty student who played the unlikely innocent he would shout: "Do you think I'm deaf, dumb, blind *and* silly?" All the boys knew this phrase by heart.

****

A few days after the incident in the knot garden Thomas and I were playing catch on the lawn. I was calling him Tom by then. Behind him the windows of the Headmaster's study overlooked the grass. Tom had taken it upon himself to try to get my limbs and muscles to coordinate and to see if I could develop an eye for a ball. That all sounds very altruistic, but as the years went by I found that much of what Tom stood for was altruistic, especially where an underdog – like me – was concerned. Actually, I wanted to be able to play the games my friend liked. I wasn't averse to sport; I just couldn't do it. We'd been playing for about ten minutes with quite a hard ball and I was beginning to get the hang of it – good thing as this was the third day in a row we'd been practising. Then I caught sight of the two boys who had knocked me down. I'd known them some time, and I'd told Tom that their names were Chesworth and Clifford. Chesworth looked strong, with ears that rather stuck out. He was taller than me, but not as tall as Clifford. They were coming our way and laughing. I was sure they had some little scheme to annoy us, or at any rate me. Still, I pretended to take no notice.

I threw the ball to Tom and one of the boys – the one called Clifford, a tall, slim chap - leapt in between us, seized the ball, and threw it to Chesworth. I was surprised when Tom ran up to him and said: "It's our ball. Give it back."

"Say please!"

"Please give it back."

"Sod off." And with that he pushed Tom hard in the chest and Tom fell flat.

I heard Clifford say: "You didn't have to do that, Chesworth. We were just going to nick their ball!"

The red mist came down. Where did my normal timidity go? I shouted out: "Chesworth. You're a flea-ridden bully." And I stuck my tongue out.

Chesworth threw the ball at me as hard as he could. I ducked. There was a crash of broken glass. Chesworth was running towards me. Suddenly I was afraid. I started to run but had hardly moved when the loudest voice I had ever heard shouted: "Chesworth! Come here at once!" Chesworth stopped, and I fell over. I looked round and up and there, looking through three small, broken, diamond-shaped panes in the latticed window was the face of Dr Higgins. "All of you, come to my study immediately!"

Two minutes later, Thomas and I, Chesworth and Clifford, were standing in the study. Higgins stood in front of us with his back to the fire. I could see his cane grasped in both hands behind his back. "What was that all about?"

Chesworth replied: "Just a bit of fun, Sir?"

"I do not find three broken pieces of my window fun, Chesworth."

Chesworth made his first mistake. "It was these two, Sir. They were playing with their ball."

"Do you think I'm deaf, dumb, blind and –"

" – Silly." Chesworth made his second mistake.

Dr Higgins roared again: "First you break my window, then you lie to me – yes lie, Chesworth – I saw you throw the ball; and then you dare to poke fun at my idiosyncrasies?"

Clifford said: "We're sorry about the window."

"You are part of this bullying enterprise, Clifford."

To my own amazement I stepped forward. "Excuse me, Sir, but Clifford only caught the ball. He didn't push Wentworth over or break the window."

Higgins looked at Tom. "Is that right, Wentworth?"

"Yes, Sir, and he didn't like it that Chesworth pushed me over. I heard him say so."

Chesworth, standing next to Tom, whispered: "I'll get you for this, runt."

Higgins told me, Tom, and Clifford to leave. He ordered Chesworth to remain for what he called a little gentle improvement session with the cane. As we walked off down the passage to the accompaniment of the swish of the cane and the squeals of Chesworth, Clifford grabbed me by the shoulder. I thought he was going to hit me, but Tom pushed him off, and snarled: "Leave him alone!"

Clifford was shocked. "Look," he said, "I was just going to thank him for sticking up for me like that. Specially after we've been so rotten to him in the past." He turned to me. "It was really decent of you."

I laughed. "Say no more. Anyway, I can't help it. I'm addicted to telling the truth."

Tom then introduced himself and me, and that is how we met Henry Clifford.

Thomas. The same day.

Today Kit and I have some real fun when that chap Chesworth, who bullied Kit and broke Dr Higgins' window, gets caned. We also make friends with the other one, who's called Henry. He's a Lord! His father is the Earl of Cumberland.

Later, in the dining room, when I am sitting down to eat, Chesworth passes the back of my chair, and leans down to say: "Watch out, Wentworth. I'll see to you."

I grasp his sleeve. "See if I care. You won't ever touch me." As he moves away I smack him as hard as I could on the site of the gentle improvement. He cries aloud, and tears spring from his eyes. He never touches me or Kit after that. I think that if I ever come across him again, it would be an interesting time.

Thomas. March, 1603. Well.

It is a beautiful early spring day; tiny buds are breaking out on the trees in the garden. I can see them from the classroom window where we take our lessons. Young Master Trenchard, a pole-like stooped figure, Dr Higgins' assistant, is trying, hopelessly in my case but with more success in Christopher's, to inculcate into us some semblance of Euclid's geometric genius. Suddenly, Dr Higgins bursts into the room with an extremely uncharacteristic turn of speed.

He comes to an abrupt halt by Trenchard's desk, and raises his hand for silence, a somewhat pointless exercise as you could have heard a pin drop; none of us has ever seen the Doctor move so fast or seem so disturbed. Or is he excited? Perhaps both.

"Master Trenchard; boys. I bear the gravest news. Please stand." We do so. "Queen Elizabeth is dead." Henry faints. Two of the boys sit down involuntarily. I am stunned. Gloriana, as the Queen was so widely known, has been on the throne longer than any of us can remember - nearly four times as long as I have been alive. Come to think of it, she was on the throne when my father was born.

The headmaster goes on: "There is good news too. King James VI of Scotland is now our King. There will be no war to establish the succession." I don't know what he means, but some of the boys cheer, and Higgins holds up his hand again. "The Queen is dead. Long live the King." We all shout that out too. He speaks again. "There will be church services all over the country. Some have already taken place in London and towns the news has already reached. I have to help organize a celebration of the life of the late Queen and our thanks to God for King James at Ripon Cathedral. I shall close the school for two weeks, from Saturday. You must all send letters to your parents telling them that you will be home soon."

Class is dismissed. Henry has recovered. He says that he couldn't get a letter home in time. His father, the Earl, is away visiting some of his properties in Cumberland. I tell him that Christopher and I will be travelling home together as we are neighbours, and he could come and stay with us at Wentworth Woodhouse. I've never had a friend to stay at home before. I just hope my parents will understand. I also hope that one day Henry will take me home with him. I've not met an Earl yet.

"Sir!" I catch up with Dr Higgins in the corridor. "Yes, Wentworth, what is it?"

"Sir, what did you mean by 'there will be no war to establish the succession'?"

"Ah! We must have more history lessons. Learning Latin and Ancient Greek is all very well, but you young gentlemen need to understand how this country works. Why, you may be in the Queen's – I mean the King's – government one day. But, to answer your question: the Queen had no children. If she had, the eldest son would be King. That is what usually happens. But as there is no child, the Queen had to choose her successor, and she chose James, who is the 6th King of that name in Scotland. Parliament is happy with her choice, and there is no other contender."

"Contender, Sir?"

"Yes, Wentworth. Contender. Someone who sets himself – or come to that, herself – up as a claimant to the Crown."

"Would a woman do that, Sir?'

"Not very likely, but fifty years ago some very powerful men put up a young lady – Lady Jane Grey- to be Queen instead of Queen Mary. Those men – and the unfortunate young woman – who probably had no choice in the matter – were beheaded for their pains."

"I bet it was painful, too, Sir."

Higgins laughs. "Not quite what I meant, boy."

"I hope you didn't mind me asking, Sir."

"Don't apologise, Wentworth. Nothing I like better than a question which shows someone has actually been listening to what I say." With that he whirls his gown about and strides away. I go in search of Henry and Christopher.

****

The three of us travel to Wentworth Woodhouse by carriage, which we hire. Well, Henry hires it, and Kit and I give him a coin or two towards it. Henry seems to be much better off than we are, and he is generous too. Spring is further advanced, and as we move gradually from North to South Yorkshire, the weather improves by geometric progressions (I know what they are now). It had been unseasonably warm in Wells and Ripon, but as we pass near Barnsley, temperatures soar.

Boys and girls sit on gates and styles as we pass along chalky white roads from which dust rises under the wheels of our carriage. The horses drawing the vehicle are, for the most part, chestnut or darker, but frequently, by the time we reach a staging post, they look more like dappled greys. We, inside the contrivance, are often little better; dust clogs our nostrils, hair and eyebrows. By the time we disembark at a wayside inn or town tavern to spend the night, even we, boys of ten in my case, and twelve in the case of Kit and Henry, are glad to get out of our clothes, and wash ourselves down in the ewer and basin of water in our rooms.

The sun blazes down every day, and we take it in turns to sit next to the coachman. Brambles grow in profusion by the roadside, and I, for whom blackberries are a passion, cannot wait for the end of summer to pick them.

These are dangerous times, for the war in Ireland, fomented in large part by Philip the Spanish Beelzebub, is largely over, and discharged and unpaid soldiery hang about the lanes and byways of England, as well as footpads and highwaymen. We are unharmed, however, as Henry's Father, the Earl, always has Henry shepherded by two extremely violent retainers, who carry firearms, daggers and swords, which are far less threatening than the appearance of the men bearing them. As luck would have it, however, their martial skills are not called upon, and they follow the carriage peaceably enough on their horses.

The only folk frequenting the highways are people going about their lawful business, or destitute beggars. These beggars are, of course, breaking the Poor Laws, but most of them are so pitiful that we give them small coins. I am very moved by the sight of these people, especially those who have their wives and children with them, and I resolve that, if ever I have the opportunity to do anything to alleviate the terrible sufferings of the really indigent, I should do so.

We take two uneventful days and a night to reach my Father's house, but for three quite young men who have never made such a journey, unaccompanied, before, it seems like an enormous adventure; and it is the start of a superb holiday which lays the foundation of two of the most important friendships of my life.

Thomas. April, 1603. Home.

Henry, it turns out, is the same age as Kit, and is an inch or two taller than me. Two years have passed since I arrived at the school in

Well, and I have actually grown so that I am now two inches taller than Kit. Otherwise we look much the same as before, but Henry is better looking than either of us, and he has all the arrogant charm of a young aristocrat. His bullying days are over. He is unfailingly polite, and when I say he has an easy, arrogant, charm I mean he has that air about him which, whilst being extremely pleasant, nevertheless means that he does not expect, indeed could not imagine, that you would not do as he asks. I must learn to be like that.

He is dark-haired, but not as dark as me, and like me he is fit and athletic. Like Kit, he likes books for their own sake, and has started to write verse, and sing. My interest in books is virtually non-existent, and I read them only for the ideas and practical help they provide. Henry is really good at mathematics, and my life at school would be very miserable indeed if I did not have him to lean on when it comes to numbers.

My parents welcome Henry, thank goodness. In fact, I think they are delighted to have an Earl's son in the house. Mother will be the envy of the neighbours, and Father, who is quite ambitious, sees it as a definite step up the ladder to have a new connection with the nobility. I say new; that's not really correct. This is his only connection with the nobility.

We have a wonderful holiday, riding over the country round about, walking, talking – frequently fantastical talk about what we would do and how rich and famous we should be one day – and learning new things. One day we are passing one of Papa's woods when we hear men chopping trees down. They are using big axes with long handles. I know these men. They are some of our farm workers. Father is a good Master, and the men are friendly to me and my brothers, so Henry and I stop and ask them if we can have a go with their axes. They show us how to hold and swing them. It is hard work, and soon we have large blisters on our palms, but I love it. The men do not let us have a try at chopping the trees down – we are too small – but they let us chop up into logs the trunks of trees already felled.

Thomas. Summer, 1604, Londesborough.

Did I say that the holiday in 1603 was wonderful? Well, the summer vacation in 1604 was even better.

The Earl, Henry's Father, had some wonderful hunting country, and although I had often been hunting and hawking on my Father's lands, the riding and sport around the Londesborough Estates was in an altogether higher class. We hunted deer, with hounds, and with bow and arrow, and hawked for game birds. We even went after stags with flint-locks, but that wasn't much fun. The guns were so inaccurate, and heavy, and the noise usually did us more harm than the shot did the deer.

It was during this holiday that hunting became my favourite recreation, especially hawking.

Henry was a wonderful host, and at his home I found out just how cultured he was. He loved books and writing for their own sake, and he was even learning to play the lute. I liked music, but I never had any pretensions to musical skill, but Henry – he was a musician.

He also had something else. He had a sister. Margaret. She was as tall as me, and fair unlike Henry, and, as an eleven year old like me would think, she was probably pretty. But she was a girl, and we didn't play with her. I danced with her though. The Earl had a dancing master for his children, and when I was there on holiday I was included in the dancing lessons too. Just as well. The Earl said you couldn't get on in society, and especially not in its upper levels which whirled around the King and Queen, if you couldn't dance.

Margaret. Summer, 1609, Londesborough.

My brother, Henry, has brought that Wentworth boy here again for the holidays. I think he's been here nearly every year. Sometimes Henry goes to his home in South Yorkshire. He's called Thomas. He's well-mannered, but he's clearly not a real aristocrat like my Father. When he first came to stay with us, about five years ago, I suppose, he had quite a thick Yorkshire accent, whereas Father has a Southern way of speaking. But then Papa's family have been Earls since about 1250, and have mixed with Royalty, or fought them, all those centuries. I don't think Thomas's Father can be a fighting type, from what I've heard. He seems to be a bit timid compared to his wife. Thomas talks about his Mother as though she's the strong one in their house.

My Father is the one with the power here. Mum is much less forceful, but they're both lovely. Papa says he would be an even more powerful man if we weren't so poor. That's a bit daft really. We've got all this land and this huge house, and more lands and another home in Cumberland, and more land in other places, and a house in London. We've got loads of servants, and there are farmers renting land from Dad, so the money rolls in. He's just too extravagant. He keeps us "poor" as he calls it. I expect he hopes to marry me off to someone rich one day. Someone who can help him get back up the ladder to influence with the King and all the really rich men, like the Earl of Newcastle.

Thomas gets on well with my parents, and he and Henry are great friends. They both go to university now, and when they're not at college, they are studying law in London. Thomas goes to the Inner Temple, I think. All this education at Cambridge and in London is changing his accent. He almost sounds like one of us now. He says he doesn't really like books, but then he says: "If you want to be a great man, you need to know the law." Sometimes he talks as though he thinks he's a great man already.

They - Henry and Thomas - go riding together, and hawking, and sometimes they let me go with them, but that's not much fun for me. Boys are odd. Perhaps they think that girls come from another planet. Do they ever wonder why their parents are together and do things together?

Mind you, they are changing. I see Henry looking – staring sometimes – at one of the maids who is really quite pretty, and other girls in the street if we go to York, or even in the village.

And Thomas, well, sometimes he just seems to be unable to take his eyes off my chest. He didn't do that last year, so he's beginning to take some notice of me. But then I only had very small bumps there last summer; this year they're not small at all. I rather like them. My nipples are very sensitive. I stroke them when I'm in bed. Sometimes I think it would be nice if Thomas did it for me. After all, he's quite good-looking in a dark sort of way. His hair is very black, and he has lovely long hands and sensitive looking fingers, which would be just right for touching my even more sensitive buds. I wish I could just ask him.

****

Henry and Thomas are playing tennis on the grass today. It's a new game. Some people have indoor courts and hit the ball around the walls or something. Father says that's what the old King, Henry, used to do. He says that was about a hundred years ago!! Anyway, the boys are playing on the lawn at the back of the house, where the terrace is, and where I am sitting. Henry is very good at all games, and always beats Thomas. What is amazing though, is how determined Thomas is. He really doesn't like to lose, and fights every inch of the way. You'd think he'd get fed up with being beaten, but no, he comes back for more every day.

Anyway, I'm sitting there watching them run about and get all sweaty, and suddenly Henry hits a really wild ball, and it soars over the wall – well, sort of stone banisters really – along the front of the terrace. The ball bounces straight to me, and I catch it and stand up and run along the terrace and round the bushes at the end of the grass where Thomas is. He comes running after me, shouting: "Margaret, don't be rotten. Give me the ball. I'm going to beat Henry this time."

I'm almost out of breath as I disappear behind the bushes and come to rest against a wall. "You can't beat him; he's too good."

Then Thomas rounds the corner, and I hide the ball behind my back. "Give it to me."

"If you don't say please, you'll have to take it."

"Right." And he puts his arms round me feeling for the ball behind me. Then he stops, and this really weird look comes over his face, and he just looks at me. Slowly his face comes towards me, and he kisses me, and pulls me by the waist towards him. I was out of breath from running, but it's not that which is making me pant now. This kiss is so exciting. Why do we have to wear these stiff fronted dresses? The front of mine is like a board. I can feel my nipples pressing against it. I wish I could feel them pressing against Thomas. I want him to feel them doing it too.

"What's going on round there?" Henry is coming our way. I push Thomas away just as Henry appears. "Come on, Margaret, give us the ball." So I hand it to Thomas, and run my hand down his shoulder and arm as he turns away. I don't want him to think I wanted to push him off.

I think he understands. As he walks off with Henry he turns and smiles at me. His face and his expressions are quite stern and forbidding most of the time, but when he smiles he is transfigured. It sounds silly, but when it happens it makes me think of that bit in the Gospel when Jesus goes up the mountain with St Peter and someone, and Moses and Elijah come to Jesus, and his face is lit up. Not that I'm saying Thomas is like Jesus. He can be quite frightening when he wishes, and he's far from perfect.

Thomas. 1609. Londesborough.

I'm on holiday at Henry's home again. It is a very large, sprawling place, three storeys with four large windows either side of the front door, and nine on the other two floors, one being above the door on each floor. It has a yellow stone front. The back and sides are brick. Henry says it's only twenty years old. It's built in an H layout, surrounded by beautiful gardens. It must be five times the size of our home at Wentworth. Ours has a stone ground floor, and bricks above that.

I played tennis with Henry yesterday, and kissed Margaret behind some bushes in the middle of the game. She's getting really pretty. That kiss has been on my mind most of last night and all day today. I've been with a couple of whores in Cambridge, and another one when I've been living down at the Temple – in fact I've been with that one more than once – but I enjoyed kissing Margaret more just once than going all the way with those women. The other business is all so quick and somehow it doesn't seem to me like something a fellow should be paying for. I'm at St John's College and Kit is at Clare College, so we can meet often in Cambridge. You can't take women into your rooms, and when I'm at the Temple I stay at Grandfather Richard's, and I can hardly take girls back there either, so harlots it has to be.

I wonder if I'll get the chance to kiss Margaret again. There's a stiffness inside my codpiece just thinking about it. People keep on about sin, but I'm sixteen now, and some chaps I know are married and get it whenever they want it. I really have to wrestle with my conscience over all this. It's enough to make you wonder what God's plan really is, when he gives a bloke a willy, surrounds him with pretty girls, and then the priests tell you "you can't use it".

I must try to think about something else. Like the law. I really enjoy studying at the Inns of Court. All these fantastic lawyers I see and hear! I've got to learn to talk like them. I see them in Westminster Hall. Some of the cases are small and boring, but when it's a murder, or a divorce in one of the big society families – they usually have to get an Act of Parliament – the way the barristers argue with each other, and with the judge, it is pretty exciting. Best of all though, is when they question and cross-examine witnesses and catch them out lying. I'm going to learn to do that. I'm going to have my own court one day – be a judge or something.

Kit and Henry are studying law too. It's very fortunate for me that they are at Gray's Inn, and I'm only half a mile away at the Inner Temple. We go to the eating houses and taverns together, and have a lot of laughs. We also go to the Hall at Gray's Inn. We were all talking about it at dinner the other night. It was a bit of a special dinner because Henry had just heard that he had got his BA.

Henry was full of it. "Now that's behind me I expect to be called to the Bar next year."

I said: "If you want to be a great man, you need to know the law. That's why I'm studying it too." Everyone laughed and the Earl leaned towards me and said, kindly really, I hope; "That sounds a bit pompous, Thomas."

Margaret patted my hand under the table. "I'm sure Thomas will be a great man one day, won't you Thomas?"

The Earl laughed at us. He's a very amiable man, but can be curt. He's big, with a florid face from hunting and the wine he drinks at dinner. Margaret looks nothing like him. There I go again. I've got Margaret on the brain.

Talking of brains, I've seen the Attorney General, Sir Francis Bacon in action in the Courts. He must be one of the cleverest men in the country; or even the world. I've seen him talk about law at the university too. He does special lectures sometimes. He believes in the Divine Right of Kings. He thinks the King should rule and Parliament should be obedient and do what he wants, which is mainly to give him the money to get on with governing. I don't know whether I agree with that. I feel that the King should listen to the things Parliament tells him. That's what it's supposed to be there for; not just filling up the King's coffers. At least, that's what some of the other lecturers tell us. I think I agree with that. But I'm sure that in the end it's the King who has to be in charge.

When dinner was over, we – I mean Henry, the Earl, and I – rose from the table to go and smoke a pipe or two. Well, the Earl smokes, and Henry tries to, but I don't care for it. This tobacco stuff that Raleigh brought back from America is proving to be very popular. Anyway as we got up from the table and the ladies went off to do some embroidery,

Margaret pulled me aside: "Come to my room later." I couldn't think of anything to say. What did she mean by later?

Today I learn what she meant. After dinner tonight Henry and I go out for a stroll. Too much venison and trout make it essential to walk it off before bed. And then we play a few games of cards with the Earl when we get back, so it's about midnight when I walk as quietly as I can along the corridor to my room. Margaret's door opens. She sees it is me and pulls me into the room.

She is cross. "You didn't come to me when I asked you the other night."

"I couldn't; it was too late. When they'd had a smoke the Earl wanted a few hands of cards, and then he challenged me to a game of draughts, so...."

Margaret is imperious. "I said later, didn't I? I didn't care how late."

"I didn't know what you wanted. I don't usually go into girl's bedrooms late at night."

"Oh, Thomas, don't be a dunce. You want to as much as I do."

I understand, and she's right. Now I know that she wants me to kiss her again, and I do. It is even better than the other day. This time Henry isn't coming round the corner. I can feel her body through her nightgown, and she makes me put my tongue in her mouth. How she makes me do that I don't know, because I've never done it before, but she opens her mouth under my lips and it just seems like the right thing to do. We both give a little moan.

She pushes my doublet off my shoulders and I let it drop to the floor. Now there is only my shirt and her nightdress between my chest and hers, and I can feel these small things pushing into my breast. I slide my hand up between us and find I'm clasping her breast now, and the thing that was pushing into me is a nipple, and it is getting harder.

Margaret moans again, so I slide my other hand down her back and begin bunching up the nightgown until I can feel the skin of her thigh against the backs of my fingers. She then grabs the hem and, breaking away from me, whips it over her head.

There she is. Naked. I thought she was pretty. Now I know she's stunningly beautiful. I am pole-axed, like a bullock at the meat market. But she knows what to do. She comes and kisses me again, and lifts my hands to her breasts, and I come back to life. Suddenly I realise that if I don't get my breeches and hose off I shall burst, and as I start to push them off, Margaret undoes the fastenings on my shirt. Now we are naked together.

She takes my hand and starts to pull me to the bed, but then breaks away and locks the door. I grab her hand and pull her onto the bed.

****

I am in paradise, but Margaret is still moving beneath me. I feel I have let her down, but before I can say so, she says: "It's lovely Thomas, and it'll get better".

"When? Tomorrow?"

"No, silly. In about half an hour." And she is right. At the end she starts to make a loud noise, and then bites down on my shoulder to keep herself quiet.

Will there ever be another holiday like this one?

Margaret. 1609. Londesborough.

I've never made love with anyone before now, and now I'm doing it with Tom (nearly every night, and as often each time as we can do it), I just can't get enough. I've no-one to compare him with, of course, but I am sure he is a very tender and affectionate lover. He seems to worry – well, perhaps not worry, but be concerned – that I am really enjoying our love-making, and when we finish I just feel so fulfilled, satisfied, relaxed, overjoyed, and....... There just aren't enough words.

It's supposed to be wrong to enjoy sex. They say it's wrong for girls, anyway. The Puritans are pretty miserable about it, but I don't think it can be all that wrong, because most of the ladies at Court seem to have new lovers all the time. And I hear strange stories about the King spending lots of time with handsome young men. Father says King James sometimes seems to take more notice of these youths than he does of the wise men on the Privy Council. Still, I know what Tom and I are doing is wrong because we're not married. I'm looking forward to being married. Then I won't have to worry about whether having sex is wrong. And the amount I like to do it means I'd be worried all the time. Nor would I be worried about getting pregnant!

It would be fantastic if I could marry Tom.

Henry Clifford. 1610. All over the place!!

This has been the most incredible year. I was admitted to the Bar as a member of Gray's Inn in June – at the same time as Kit Wandesford - and on 25th July I was married to my lovely Frances. She is Robert Cecil's daughter, and he is the Secretary of State, the most powerful political person in the Kingdom. We were married in Kensington, and soon afterwards we came to Paris, where we are living, and I am studying at a French academy. I'm a Lord because I'm an Earl's son, so Frances is a Lady anyway, but she is also a Lady because her Dad is an Earl too – the Earl of Salisbury.

This connection has given the family a leg up. If only we had some money!! Thomas will be called to the Bar next year, and I think he will do well. He works really hard at making speeches. He studies all the arts of rhetoric, and his Yorkshire accent has gone a bit, but he has this earthy country way of talking, and it mixes strangely with the things he's learned about Demosthenes, Cato, Cicero, and all those old orators. Mind you, when Tom wants to make a point, he can be very forceful and persuasive, but he has a violent temper sometimes, and then he doesn't even try to persuade people. He just tells them how things are. Not many can stand up to him then.

Now how have I got onto all that? Ah yes, the family money. It made me think about Tom because his Dad has money, and he's only a knight – Sir William Wentworth. So if Tom does well at the Bar or whatever he goes into he'll be really rich, I should think. I don't know if I'll ever be like that. You can't make a lot of money or get far in politics by playing the lute and writing poetry! And those are the things I care for.

I miss him. He was my best friend at school and College, and I saw a lot of him in London. Mind you, sometimes, during the holidays he spent with us at home, I thought there might be something between him and Margaret. The way they looked at each other, and often seemed to have just been whispering to each other, even though you couldn't catch them doing so, must mean something.

Thomas. October 1610. Inner Temple.

I've been back at Grandad's for a week and lectures and dinners start next week. It's a funny old system, becoming a barrister. You qualify by eating a number of dinners each term, as though your appetite is what has to be tested, and not your brain, let alone your knowledge of the law. But I'm working hard at the books, and going to all the lectures, listening to as many cases as I can, and I've even taken part in mock trials three times. I was prosecuting a murder once, and lost – the "defendant" got off. Another time I was defending a farmer who was in debt with a mortgage. He hadn't been paying enough, but I showed that the lender had been calculating the interest wrongly, and much too high, so the farmer had to pay half the arrears, and could stay on his farm.

They set these test cases with all the facts in them. The lecturers and Judges who work out the facts don't tell you things like "the interest is wrong." You have to work that out for yourself, plan your legal arguments, and your questions. Great fun, but goodness gracious, was I nervous. When I was presenting my case I was on my feet for about an hour, and my legs were rigid with nerves. When I finished I couldn't sit down at first as my knees wouldn't bend. I hope I get over that soon. As it is, I have visions of finishing an argument, bowing to the Judge, and then toppling over sideways and disappearing between the benches.

Talking of getting over things, I had a letter from Margaret this morning. She tells me everything that's going on. Her parents were glad I was able to stay with them again during the Long Vacation, and that she enjoyed seeing me, and all that sort of thing. There is never a hint of what we get up to together. She tells me that her Mother looks at her letters before they are given to the post, but she occasionally manages to slip a little note in before the letter is sealed. She only does this when I'm at College, or here in London. We wouldn't want anyone at home finding out about us. I'm jolly glad my Grandfather doesn't check my mail.

The note with today's letter said: *"Darling Thomas, (or should I say Daring Thomas), We're in luck again. No babies this time!! Love and kisses (in those special places) from Margaret".*

Thomas. Christmas 1611. Paris.

This has been an incredible year! And not just for me. The Prince of Wales has been causing quite a stir. I haven't met Henry Stuart, of course, but I caught sight of him once when I was near the Palace in Whitehall, and another time when I'd gone out of the Temple for a walk at lunch-time, and he came riding up to the Tower. When he'd gone in, one of the guards (for a bribe, of course) told me that he goes there quite often to talk with Sir Walter Raleigh, who's been locked up there for years. Hardly anyone thinks he deserves to be a prisoner, but no-one's making a fuss, although to many he is a hero. This is not helping to make King James popular; in fact, quite the contrary.

Prince Henry is so very different, and seems to have absorbed the mood of the people. I waited outside the Tower for him to emerge, and as he did so I heard him remark to his equerry: "No-one but my Father could have such a bird in such a cage." Since that weird Spaniard, Guido Fawkes, and his friends, tried to blow up the King and Parliament six years ago, any kind of talk that might be thought treason has virtually disappeared, but I suppose that if you're a Prince and don't say it too loudly, you can get away with it.

Prince Henry's tall and very good-looking, with reddish hair. They say he is very straight-forward and honourable. He must be pretty clever, too, to admire and be acceptable company for Raleigh. Apparently the King wanted him to marry a girl from the Spanish Royal Family, but he says he won't have a Catholic in his bed, and he's told the King he wants to marry a Protestant. And what about his sister!! She's a blond beauty. How did old King James – pursy and fat old King James – as he called himself once, apparently – get such lovely children? Because he has a most beautiful wife, that's how. Queen Anne comes from Denmark and she is stunning. Nearly all the ladies at Court wear these low cut dresses, but few of them have the bosom to display that the Queen has. Did I say display? I mean flaunt. She takes no chances that you might not notice.

I have heard a rumour about Henry and Elizabeth – that's the daughter, the Princess – and it's this. They're not really James's children at all. People say that the Queen is rather indiscreet about her admirers (lovers would be nearer the mark), and there are several handsome men about Court who have been said to have done a lot of "admiring" at one time or another. On the other hand Henry and Elizabeth's little brother, Charles, is certainly the King's son, if my opinion means anything. He's small, and neat, which the King probably was before he became "fat and pursy" and old. They say he's shy, and not as bright as Henry, so it's just as well he's not going to be King when his Father dies. I don't think I believe the rumour anyway. Queens have their heads chopped off for adultery.

Mind you, if it is true that the Queen takes lovers, you can hardly blame her. The King is not at all lovely. He smells badly, so they say, and looks dirty. He's often the worse for drink, and falls over, or falls off his horse. If he's not cuddling up to and stroking his handsome young companions, he goes out hunting (which is when he falls off), and pays the Queen hardly any attention at all. He has a particular favourite at present, a Scot called Carr – Robert Carr – who is not much more than a peasant really; it's said he can't read or write, yet the King apparently takes his advice, and a few months ago created him Viscount Rochester. If that doesn't show what the King's perve – I mean preferences – are, I can't imagine what does.

Yet on the other hand, almost at the same time as a Peasant became a Peer of the Realm, the King had the first Authorised Version of the Bible published. He'd commanded the Bishops and Divines at the Universities to get together and perfect a translation of the Scriptures because there were too many home-made versions going around. It has become a very popular book already, and no wonder. It is beautifully written, and most of it reads like poetry, the language is so powerful. It is a supreme Protestant achievement. Even the Puritans are starting to use it.

Which brings me back to Elizabeth. She may be going to marry the Elector Palatine from Germany. He's a Calvinist, and leader of the Calvinist Princes of Germany, so he's opposed to Spain and the Emperor of Austria, and that will be a very popular wedding, if it happens.

That's why it is a good year for the country. Why has it been good for me? First, the whole family took a step up the social ladder early in the year. Not a very praiseworthy step, but a step up nevertheless. And this is why.

King James is hard up. King James is always hard up. In fact, according to Dad, even Queen Elizabeth was hard up, and there was no money in the kitty when James came to the throne. It's a bit odd really, because as far as I can see, as I ride up and down from Yorkshire to Cambridge and London and back, most people in the country are doing very well. Now the war in Ireland is a fair way behind us there don't seem to be so many beggars and foot-pads about

To get money, the King has created a new rank of the nobility. It's called a baronetcy. It's not as low as a Knight – and Father was one of those already – and it's not as high as a Baron, let alone a Viscount or Earl. Anyway, you can buy a baronetcy direct from the King – well, his finance people – and Father bought one for five thousand pounds. He was one of the first men to apply for one. Now he is Sir William Wentworth, Bart. I'm his eldest son, so when he passes on, I'll be a Bart, too. So it's a bit commercial – not like being made an Earl for winning a battle or doing some other heroic thing for the King – but it means the Wentworth family move in better – or perhaps I should say wealthier and more influential – circles than before.

It also means that he was able to take me to Court and present me to the King. That's when I saw the Queen. She must be about thirty-five or so, but she is still rather beautiful.

The baronetcy and going to Court has meant that at University and at The Inner Temple I get treated with a bit less contempt than I used to. So many of the law students are from the real upper classes – blue blooded aristocrats, even if they are often just the younger sons of the peerage – that even now they look upon me as some sort of country bumpkin. My Yorkshire accent doesn't help, but I have a feeling that one day my voice and my accent are going to be pretty important in this Kingdom. Being the son of a baronet made me feel a lot easier in all this exalted company when I was called to the bar, which happened half-way through the summer.

And this step up has led to something even better for me. I just couldn't believe it. About a month after becoming a fully qualified barrister, I arrived home for the holidays, and after dinner the first night, Father called me into his library, and gave me another glass of wine. When we sat down he opened the conversation. "As you know, Thomas, things are a bit different now that I've obtained this baronetcy."

"Yes, Father."

"And you are eighteen, and have a profession."

Where is this going? Why is he telling me things I already know? "Yes Father."

"I have decided it is time you were married."

Dear God, what about Margaret? I don't want to get married yet. My mouth has gone so dry I could drink a lake. I say nothing.

"I have therefore been to see a gentleman whose daughter, I think, would make you a very suitable wife, and at the same time take the family's social position considerably higher."

Oh God, Papa, I'm thinking, you're supposed to love me. How can you do this to me? I don't want to marry someone I've never even seen. I know what it's like to have sex with someone I really like – love even. And you know how you've brought me up. We're not exactly Puritans, but profligate promiscuity isn't what our family does after marriage. Don't sentence me to a life of fucking - or not fucking - someone I don't even like!

Unaware of my thoughts, Father continues: "The man indicated that he approved, and has recently written to tell me that he has informed his daughter, who appeared to be quite joyful at the prospect."

No, Father! No! She must be desperate, and old, and ugly, with buck teeth, no hair, and a flat chest. I emit a very slight groan, but Father doesn't seem to hear it, and goes on.

"And the beauty of it is that we already know the family quite well and you know them very well. Lord Henry Clifford will be your brother-in-law, and I am sure the Earl of Cumberland will be a very good father-in-law. I think the young lady's name is ...."

"Margaret!!" I leap out of my chair and rush to embrace my Father. We are quite an affectionate family, but I excel myself in kissing his old face.

****

What else does this incredible year do for me? Well, on 22nd October my family and I go to Londesborough. Margaret and I are married in the Earl of Cumberland's private chapel by the Earl's private chaplain. Margaret's family are all there, except for Henry. He is already in Paris with his wife. Margaret is stunning in a yellow velvet dress, very modest as to the neckline, and revealing little of the charms I know it hides. My brother William stands with me in the chapel, and has custody of the ring. I am so nervous I drop it when the priest hands it to me to put on Margaret's finger.

There is a banquet in the great hall. The hall is far from full, as only the two families are there. Nevertheless, the Earl has spared no expense with the food and the wine. Looking around at the opulence and the splendour, it is hard to imagine that he thinks he is poor, which is what my darling tells me he believes. There are twelve courses, and at least a glass of wine with each. The Household Steward acts as butler, and in addition to him there is a servant behind every chair to top up goblets, and serve more food. My mother tries to restrain Father, but he eats as though he's never had food before, and does not pretend to be impartial to the wine, either. However, he is not drunk, and no more the worse for wear than the Earl, brother William, and one of Margaret's aunts.

I notice that Margaret eats only small amounts from each plate, and is sipping her wine. Once I even see her distract her aunt (the tipsy one) and empty her glass into auntie's. I decide to take it easy myself. I fancy that one way or another I might have quite a heavy night ahead, and there will be dancing after the dinner, before the heavy goings on. A very full stomach does not seem like a good idea.

I dance with Mama, and Margaret's Mother, her sister, my sisters, and, of course, Margaret. I am desperate to get to the bedroom, and when Margaret whispers "holding your hand and dancing is just not good enough," I am nearly overcome. She looks so innocent, and has a sort of nervous seriousness outwardly that must make her Mother think she is dreading what she'll find out when I got my breeches off. What an actress!

Apart from that I hardly remember anything about the ceremony, even though I concentrated on it very intensely at the time. I cannot recall a great deal about the banquet afterwards, either.

Neither of our families feel the need to put us to bed, though my little brother George accompanied us to the bedroom door. How anyone ever puts up with people ensuring that the marriage is consummated I'll never know. Unless you are a sexual athlete from a Roman orgy, nothing could be much more off-putting to someone who has no experience and does not know what he's doing, particularly if the lady were not his personal choice. It must be even worse for the girl, who is, at least in theory, expected to be a virgin, and know nothing about sex.

Anyway, as I say, we were spared that. I don't think either of us could convincingly have acted innocent virginity and inexperience.

I may not remember a lot about the wedding and the banquet, but what followed I recall very vividly.

Where was I? Oh yes. My wedding day in October. I am waiting for the dancing to end. And it does. Both families take us up to our bedroom..... and leave us there. Was there a four poster bed with hangings? Curtains at the windows? A carpet on the floor? I had eyes only for my wife. If any two people have ever got undressed faster than Margaret and I do then, their clocks must have been going backwards. It is two in the morning when the dancing ends and we close the bedroom door. I am naked two seconds later, and so is Margaret.

Suddenly we are still. We stare at each other. "Father in Heaven, thank you," I think. "Can anyone have ever been happier than I am now? Thank you."

A tear rolls down Margaret's cheek, but she is smiling; and incredibly beautiful. My penis is priapic. We both start to speak at once. "Margaret...." "Thomas ...." And we laugh. I start again. "Margaret." She waits. I move a pace towards her, reach out and put an index finger on each nipple. She quivers, and puts her hand on my cock.

I smile. "You are so lovely, and I love you so."

She smiles, wickedly. "You are so handsome, ... And big. And I love you." And she strokes it. This is like the first time all over again. I think I'm going to come on the Turkish carpet.

"We can do this any time we like now."

"Yes. And as often. And anywhere we like."

I laugh. "But not in front of the servants. Nor your Mother."

"She isn't the prude you seem to think. As far as I can make out she likes these things" (giving it another stroke) "as much as I do."

Another stroke and I moan loudly. Margaret takes her hand from me and puts both arms round my neck, leaps into the air, clasps her legs round my waist, and settles herself onto this thing of mine. "So make me happy Thomas."

And I do. All night.

****

The year is still not over. Margaret and I have a seemingly inexhaustible appetite for each other. Sometimes I can barely stay awake during the day, and if I go to the bedroom for a snooze, as often as not Margaret comes and finds me, and sleep comes a poor second to a much more satisfying pastime, no matter how tired I am.

At the end of November Father dragged me off to Royston in Hertfordshire where King James was holding Court. I don't know how it happened – maybe Papa parted with more cash – but this time when I was presented to the King, he knighted me. 'Arise, Sir Thomas Wentworth." I liked it. Another little step up. Mind you, knights are pretty common, and I didn't perform any act of valour for it, as I should have had to if we had King Arthur on the throne. I was very nervous about being knighted, not least because the King's hand was very shaky, and I feared he might stab or behead me by accident.

Maybe he was nervous too. Or just old. Or just drunk.

There was a ball, and a masque – the Queen is mad on them, and they cost a fortune – no wonder the King has no money – and Dad and I went. My Mother and Margaret were at home, so I was without my loved one for the dancing. We all had to wear masks, which made it all a bit intriguing. In most of the dances you line up and dance with the lady opposite you, and keep changing partners at the end of each sequence of steps. There were pavanes and sarabandes, gavottes and country dances, and I was glad I had had lessons at Henry Clifford's.

****

"It is time your education was completed." Father is formal. We are in the library after dinner. It is not a large room, but the walls are lined with leather bound books, and the fire crackles in the hearth.

"How can it be, Papa? You've always told me we never stop learning."

He smiles. "That may be true, Son, but there's a formal part of your training as a Gentleman still left undone."

I swallow nervously. I've been through school with Dr Higgins, I've been to Cambridge and got a degree, and I'm a qualified Barrister. I've learned to dance, ride, fence, and help Dad manage our estates. What else have I got to do?

"So I'm sending you on a tour of Europe, to learn French, foreign customs and ways, and see the remarkable achievements of civilizations even older than our own. Of course, many of them are Roman Catholics, and the fact that they aren't English is a disadvantage to them, but they have wonderful architecture, splendid works of art and music, and in the South, much tangible Roman history. You will enjoy it."

"Is that an order, Papa, or a statement?"

He laughs. "It's my hope for you, Thomas. So many young men from good families make this tour nowadays, that with our improving financial and social position, it would be remiss of me not to insist that you have this experience."

"Henry – you know - Lord Clifford – he's staying in Paris with his wife. Margaret and I shall be able to stay with them for a while. Wonderful!"

"Yes, I was aware that your friend is there, and certainly you should be able to stay with him, but .... Well ..."

"Well what?" I smell a rat.

"Well, I have spoken with your Mother about this, and she ... we feel that it would not be wise for Margaret to accompany you." Father is grave.

"How long will I be gone?"

"At least a year, maybe two or more. The reasons ...."

"Damn it all, Father, I can't leave Margaret for that long. We've only been married six weeks. We love each other." I am furious.

"As I was saying, the reasons are that if she is with you, her presence will interfere with the studying I expect you to do ...."

"Studying?" I swear under my breath, but he hears it anyway.

"That's enough of that Thomas. Yes, studying. I have appointed a tutor to accompany you. He's Charles Greenwood of University College, Oxford, and ..."

"Look here, if I've got to go abroad without my wife, the last thing I want is to be ordered around by some old fart from Oxford!"

"Did I say he was old? He's only a few years your senior, and you will like him, of that I am sure. You're 18; he's about twenty-four, I think. And as for 'ordering you around', as you quaintly put it, if you can talk to me the way you have been for the last few minutes, young Master Greenwood doesn't stand a chance." Father is quiet but fierce.

I am ashamed. He is still my dear old Papa, and I have just been unforgivably rude. "Sorry Father. It's all a bit of a shock."

"I forgive you, Thomas. I should not have been happy when I was young, being torn from your Mother after so short a space." Probably not, I think; after all, look how many babies you two have made. "Still, you will not be leaving until 20th December, so you have another three weeks to do your duty."

"What duty's that, Dad?"

"Why, getting me a grandson, of course. And that's the other reason Margaret should not go with you. If you perform this duty ...."

I interrupt. "Trying for an heir is no duty Dad."

He laughs. "I rather thought not. But anyway, your Mother says that if you succeed, it would be quite wrong to have dear Margaret gallivanting about Europe if she is pregnant. And we hope she will be."

I can see the force of that. Come to think of it, why isn't she expecting already? It's not as though we haven't been trying. "Maybe Mama is right. But it'll be really hard, leaving her behind."

A knowing smile lights Father's face. "I know, my boy. So you'd better make the best use of those three weeks before you get on the boat."

I run from the library as fast as I can, looking for Margaret. She won't want to waste a second.

****

"He wants you to do what?"

"He wants me to go to Europe for God knows how long. To complete my education!!"

"Listen Thomas. You're not going to defy your Father, are you? And I wouldn't want you to. He's a good man. You love him. I love him. He's kind to me. He treats me like a daughter." Margaret sits on the bed. "I'm not daft. I know he wanted you to marry me because I was a good catch dynastically, and I know he didn't know we were already in love. But some fathers in his position treat the daughter-in-law as just another addition to their property and estates."

"I know, darling, but even so, leaving you for a year or even more is .... Well, frustrating, to say the least. And that's just the sex."

"How romantic!! You could say 'the lovemaking'." Margaret smiles to show she's joking. She's wonderful. She holds out her hand. I take it. She pulls me to the bed. "Come on. We've got three weeks to banish frustration for a while. If we get it right, by the time you leave I'll be pregnant and you will be so worn out you won't feel frustrated for ages."

Margaret stands and starts to unfasten my shirt. "Thomas, if you're the hammer, I'm the tongs. Let's go to it."

****

So now it is the end of this fantastic year, and here I am, as I said before, staying with Henry in Paris. He has a beautiful stone house, with intricate carvings on the outside and quite stunning ornate moulded stucco work decorating the walls and ceilings inside. I miss Margaret badly, but Henry is good fun and company as always, and I like his wife, Frances. They have a large house, which is just as well. They have about twenty servants and gardeners and ostlers and maids and chefs and cooks, and Father had me bring a similar number of folk to look after me and Charles Greenwood.

Dad was right about Charles. He is very mild-mannered, almost shy, and we get on very well. He won't have any nonsense from me, because he is authoritative in his quiet way. He has already started teaching me French, but in Henry's home I get little chance to practice it. We shall leave here in a few weeks and then, in the country, I should meet plenty of people who speak no English, so it'll be interesting to see how I cope. I've told Charles he mustn't nurse-maid me!

We go to the theatre together, but I don't understand the French dialogue much. The French also have this new art form; they call it the ballet. Non-stop music with dancing; and what dancing! It's not like ordinary dancing, with a partner or partners. It's all leaping about and twirling round and very intricate footwork. I don't know if it will catch on. Still, I like it, and really admire the skill of the dancers, and how fit they look. No fatties on their stage!!

Sometimes Henry and Frances come with us. He is getting known in fashionable Parisian circles, and gets invited to dinners and balls, so I am now included. I just wish Margaret were with me. Some of the ladies are very beautiful, and, if I say it myself (and I shouldn't) some of them are clearly interested in me, but all their attentions do is make me yearn more for Margaret.

I find myself thinking about her a lot, and wondering when I shall hear from her.

I write to her every couple of days, but it takes a courier at least two days to get to the coast, and a day across the channel if the wind permits, and then a day or two to get to London, if she's there, let alone Yorkshire. I've been here a week, so a letter from my love should arrive in a day or two.

I wonder if she's expecting a baby yet. She ought to be; we nearly wore the hammer and tongs out that last three weeks.

Margaret. March, 1612. Yorkshire.

Dearest Thomas,

I am always so glad to get your letters. Today I had three!! As I did not get one for two post days, and there are rarely any on Sundays, I had not seen one for five days. I was frantic and fed up, to put it mildly. It is good that you are happy, still, in Orleans, and that your French is coming along well. I shall have to try to learn some so that we can speak it at home and hardly anyone will know what we are saying.

This is the last time you need ask if I am expecting that baby. You have been gone three months now, I've just started a third course (what a curse), and there is no chance I'm pregnant. We'll just have to start again when you come home, and I can't wait for that. It's eighty-nine nights since you made love to me. Do you remember how to do it? More importantly, do you remember how to do it the way I like it?

Anyway, that's enough of that; if I go on about it I shall get either excited or depressed!

So you like the cathedral in Orleans better than Notre Dame. I must say from the sketches you have sent the Paris one looks extremely – well, heavy I suppose would be my word for it, but the Orleans one is light and airy looking. You are very lucky to be seeing all these places. I don't suppose I shall ever get to go abroad, especially if I do have that baby, or babies!! I've only ever been to my Father's houses in London and Yorkshire and Cumberland, your home (ours now) and your Grandfather's house in Chancery Lane.

By the way, I went down to London with your parents recently and we saw a new play by Shakespeare. 'The Tempest'. It was really strange, all about a shipwrecked King and his daughter, and a deformed creature named Caliban. The King is called Prospero, and somehow he reminded me of your Dad. Not that he can do magic or anything, like that, but your Dad certainly knows how to Prosper. Sorry, that's a terrible joke, isn't it?

Anyway (sorry, I've used that word before), I noticed on the way back from London that your Dad seemed rather tired. He bucked up when we got home, and when I asked him if he was well, he laughed and said, in that jokey way he has of taking off the servants: "Eh oop, lass, there's nowt wrong o' me being back in Yorkshire won't see right." Even so, I'm still a bit worried about him. Your Mother is well, and doesn't seem worried about Papa, but she is such a strong type you can't always tell what she's thinking.

How much longer are you going to be in Orleans, and where are you off to next? I hope you're being careful of all those Maids in that town. They can't all be saints.

Remember I love you,

Your Margaret.

Thomas. 2nd April, 1612. Orleans.

I've just read a letter from Margaret. She says she didn't get a letter for seven days. Yet I write to her nearly every day. Letters from here to Yorkshire must be able to find their own way by now. It's the weather. Sometimes when what I've written reaches the coast it waits on a boat for a week for the wind to change so that the vessel can get out of the harbour.

And that letter upset me a lot. Little does Margaret know it but she really hit the nail on the head with what she wrote about the Maids of Orleans. She's not the only one who's been missing our sex-life, and last night I went out on my own for a drink in a tavern. It was a clean and warm inn (*auberge* here), and a good bit better than some I have seen in France. It wasn't very different from an English Inn with a low beamed ceiling and smokey walls.

My French is really getting quite good (Charles Greenwood has been working me rather hard and getting me into lots of conversations with French people), so I was able to order a meal, and actually get what I thought I'd asked for, which was roast *'mouton avec legumes et pommes de terre'*. Yes, potatoes!! I did not realise that those roots which Raleigh brought back from the Americas had got to France as well as England.

I had just started on my second glass of a really fine claret when a girl brought my dinner. She was slim, with blond hair and a superb bosom, and at first glance I thought she looked like Margaret. She was wearing a kind of local costume, with a black dress over a white shirt thing, which was very low cut, and as she put my dinner on the table she leant over in front of me so that I could examine her charms at very close quarters.

I have been a very good boy up to now, and had not strayed like a lost sheep, nor a randy ram, come to that, but the sight of this sensuous girl was more than I could bear. I might be nineteen soon, but I had never been in a situation like this before, and did not know what to do. From the way she smiled at me I thought – or at any rate hoped – that she liked the look of me as much as I liked the look of her. My French deserted me for a moment and I asked her in English if she would like a glass of wine too. She smiled again and looked mystified.

I then managed to ask the same question in French. "*Oui, monsieur*," sounded like exquisite music when she said it. I was about to call to the patron for another glass when she pushed my hand down and said she would fetch it, which she did, and then came and sat with me. How she did not get into trouble I did not then know, but it turned out that the patron was her Father, and he was a very 'understanding' man.

What we talked about I cannot now say, but talk we did, and she even helped herself to some of my dinner. Then she took my hand and led me out of the inn for what I thought was going to be a stroll, but after we had gone a couple of hundred yards she turned up an alley, turned again at the end of it, led me back to the rear of the tavern, and up the back stairs to her bedroom. She was not shy, but she wasn't brazen either, and we made love beautifully four times over the next few hours.

I don't know how it is possible to feel so happy, excited, and guilty all at the same time, but that is how I felt. Today all I really feel is the guilt, but I don't know if I have the strength to stay away from her for the rest of my sojourn in Orleans, nor how I shall cope with any other willing ladies I may meet in the rest of this tour. This is the first thing I have done since Margaret and I married that I have not been able to tell her about. And I don't think I ever shall be able to. How would I feel if she told me something like this? I don't even want to think about it.

Of course, when I got up this morning, I looked pretty awful, even if sated, and Charles Greenwood, alert and attentive as ever, wanted to know where I had got to last night. I told him I wasn't tired, walked further than I meant to, got lost, and only came in at dawn. Well, at least the last bit was true.

Thomas. June, 1612. Saumur.

My darling Margaret,

Today is our last in this lovely old town on the Loire. I wanted to stop here because it is the home of Philippe Duplessis-Mornay. Do you remember me talking about him at home? He is a Protestant, and was a great help to Henri IV, the last French King, who was stabbed to death eight years ago. Philippe drafted the Edict of Nantes, which was supposed to give religious toleration to the Huguenots, and he had supported Henri when he was the Protestant King of Navarre, but he was rather betrayed when Henri became a Catholic to get his hands on the French Crown.

Even so, Mornay is a well respected elder statesman in France, and I wanted to meet him. Charles came with me. We found him to be a very sad and rather disillusioned man, and he's losing his sight. He had a huge library, and we talked a lot about his books – he's written a great deal – and his religious and philosophical views. I had a feeling he was glad to have someone different to talk to, so I'd like to think we left him happier than we found him, but I probably flatter myself.

He let me buy some of his books, and I now have quite a collection of French works, including plays, and not just Protestant religious tomes, but even some Catholic ones. You know me – wanting to see both sides of everything.

Heavens, don't I write serious letters? When I compare your funny and light-hearted outpourings with my diatribes and lectures, I can't help wondering what pleasure you can get out of reading this tripe at all.

But then you know what I'm like, and you tell me you love me, so I can't be all that bad. How could the loveliest wife in the world love a really bad man?

Next stops, La Rochelle and Bordeaux. Writing every day is not so easy now we are on the road, but I am still writing as frequently as I can. However, I may not be able to write at all in Bordeaux. After all, it is where the very best claret comes from, and I may be unable to see the paper. Let alone write on it.

All my love to my love,

Thomas.

Margaret. August, 1612. Yorkshire.

Dearest darling Thomas,

I have just received your letter from Carcassone. I love the sketch you sent me of the town and its fortifications. Your drawings are getting better and better, but then you are getting quite a lot of practice. It surprised me that you said that the countryside round there "does much resemble Yorkshire." I thought it was really hot down there, not far from the Pyrenees, and all rocky. Still, you've seen it; I haven't, so you must know what you're talking about.

And you're going on to Avignon and Arles!! How I wish I were with you!! I'd love to see all those Roman ruins and Roman pillars. I'd quite like to see your Roman column again, too. What do I mean by "quite"? I'm desperate to see it, let alone feel it. It's been nine months now. Can I wait much longer? It's driving me mad.

And who's a clever boy then? Not only speaking fluent French; you can write Spanish, too. I showed that Spanish page of your last letter to a lady from Spain who is working as one of my Mother's maids at the moment. She said it was almost perfect, and very easy to understand. Can you speak Italian too? You'll have to become a diplomat.

On second thoughts, you're the last person who could be a successful diplomat. You say exactly what you think, and when you tell a fib, it is written all over your face that "I am not telling the truth." I think that's one of the things I love about you. It will also make it rather difficult for you to go into politics, which is what I think your Dad wants you to do. He's always talking at dinner about how he hopes to get you a seat in Parliament.

Must put the quill down now. Your Mother is calling me. We're off soon in the carriage to go to York for a few days. Your Father is going to see his Doctor. He still seems to be tired a lot, and looks a bit grey in the face.

I don't think it's anything serious, but I just hope the treatment is not more blood-letting. I don't see how having all your blood let out can make you well. Still, what do I know?

I Love You With All My Heart.

Your Margaret.

Thomas. Avignon. September, 1612.

Dearest darling Margaret,

Charles and I arrived here two days ago. It is a very old town, and some of the streets are even narrower and more winding than those in York. They don't have the half-timbered houses we have there. You know how they lean towards each other and it looks as though you could reach across the street and eat the breakfast off the plate of the man in the house opposite? Not here. The houses are close, but go up more vertically.

You can still see the neighbours getting dressed, though, if they don't pull the shutters, and if you look. Of course, being a good husband I never would look. So how do I know what I might see if I did look? Charles tells me, of course. He's still a bachelor, and not averse to pretty women. He's not so keen when the neighbour is a fat old man, but when choosing a place to stay you can hardly knock at the house opposite and ask what sights are to be seen through the bedroom window.

Back to the real sights of Avignon. There is a narrow stone bridge across the river, and seven years ago three of its arches were swept away by huge floods. There's a little chapel on what's left of the bridge, the chapel of St Benezite, who was allegedly told in a dream by an angel about 500 years ago that he had to get the bridge built. Some of the bridge has been washed away before, and rebuilt. I suppose they'll try to mend it again one day.

It's been a very religious city in the past. There's a huge palace which nine Popes lived in for a hundred years or so when Rome wasn't safe for them. The town I like best near here is Orange. It is a fantastically old place, and has an amphitheatre from Roman times which is in remarkably good condition. Charles and I stayed there for a few days and had a very interesting day exploring.

We went into this amphitheatre and sat on the terraced seating – all stone. Then I went down onto the stage area, leaving Charles back at the top. I waved to catch his eye, and then I said, in an ordinary voice, not a stage voice: "Can you hear what I'm saying?" He answered; "Perfectly." What amazing architects and builders those Romans were!! Some of their old roads you can still see in England are much better than the muddy tracks we dignify with the name of The King's Highway.

We get invited to dinner by some noble or other worthy in nearly every town we stay in. Tonight we will eat with the Bishop of Avignon, even if he is a Catholic. Catholic food tastes every bit as good as Protestant fare, I'm glad to say. Now that I can speak the language so much better I enjoy myself, but not as much as if you were here.

All my love,

Thomas.

Thomas. November, 1612. Lyons.

Darling Margaret,

Why did we come to Lyons? Charles and I had such a wonderful stay in Provence, and a beautiful journey up the Rhone. The weather was kind, but cooling as the autumn came on, and then it deteriorated drastically. It seems to rain nearly all the time. This is a big city, but somehow dull, without the charm of all the small towns and cities we have stayed in, nor the excitement and culture of Paris.

Even so, the cuisine is wonderful, and so is the wine. We think they send good vintages to us in England, but I'm sure they keep the best wine here in France. And of course, it is so much cheaper than at home, because here we are not paying tunnage and poundage on the imported barrels. I am trying hard not to become a drunken sot!!

I know I say it in nearly every letter, but I do miss you dreadfully, and wish you were with me. Charles is good company, and we've met many interesting and amusing – and challenging – people, but none of them is a soul mate for me as you are.

We shall be in Lyons and exploring round about for another few weeks, and then we plan a trip down the Rhine, so I'll have to try out some German.

I am glad to read that you and Mother and all my brothers and sisters are well, but it's a great shame Dad seems to be no better.

We wrote about castles and fortresses in recent letters, do you remember? Well, we have visited nearly every castle and fortification wherever we have been, and in chess parlance I am just about castled out. If I'm not a world expert on towers and redoubts and salients I must be pretty close to it!! I could bore a portcullis to death.

I am going hunting in an hour or so with our host and his son. Frankly I can think of better things to do in this rain. With the ground being so muddy, riding may be risky, but I can only appear churlish by refusing to go. Wish me luck!!

Write soon.

All my love,

Thomas.

Margaret. Yorkshire, November, 1612.

Dear Thomas,

I have only just opened your letter from Lyons. It took three weeks to get here – one end of the month to the other!! This is only a quick note to tell you that your Father is not at all well. He will not take to his bed, but he falls asleep in the drawing room, in the garden if he sits down, and last night he even fell asleep at the dinner table. Fortunately we had no guests, but your poor Mother was – is – so worried. I am doing all I can to help her.

I don't know how to tell you all that without worrying you, but I could not bear to upset you by not telling you, either. Fortunately some of your brothers and sisters are too young to realise there is anything wrong, but William and John – you know how sensitive they both are – are not taking it very well. I try to cheer them up, but it is hard.

I hope you enjoyed hunting in the rain!! And that you did not fall off your horse.

There is another very shocking piece of news. Henry, the Prince of Wales, has died!! Princess Elizabeth was supposed to be getting married to the Elector Palatine from Germany just then – the beginning of this month – and the wedding had to be put off. The whole country is in serious mourning. Henry was so popular. Your Father was down in the dumps for days and I don't think the shock helped his health at all.

Write soon!! Sorry this isn't one of my normal silly chatty missives.

All my love, dearest Thomas.

Margaret.

Thomas. Lyons. 10th December, 1612.

My Darling Margaret,

The news about my Father is dreadful, and that about Prince Henry is devastating, but I cannot do anything at the moment. I did not fall off my horse while hunting, but I got completely drenched, there was a cold wind riding back to the Chateau, and by the time I got indoors I was chilled to the bone. I was stupid. Instead of getting into a warm bed, I changed and went down to dinner.

In the night, I was sick and going at the other end too, and shivering, and I've been ill ever since. I can get up now for a few hours at a time, but am still off my food and only fancy broth and hot drinks. The weather is worse, and the Mistral – it's a terrible wind which whistles down the country at this time of year – has come early, so it is really freezing here now. If only it would warm up a bit I might be feeling better sooner.

As it is, Charles and I have decided to cancel the journey on the Rhine, and I shall come home as soon as possible to see Dad – and you of course. Please give Father a hug and a kiss from me – you'll do it so much better – and Mother and all the little pests too. I am so glad you are being good to Mum and Will and John.

I love you and am dying to hold you close and kiss you over and over – and all over.

I am yours, through and through.

Thomas.

Thomas. 10th March, 1613. Yorkshire.

Looking back, I can hardly describe how difficult I found the next few weeks after that last letter to Margaret. First, I was still unwell, and couldn't even make a start for home for another week. Secondly, I was, obviously, rather worried about my Dad. Thirdly, because of that, I wanted to get home as quickly as possible.

I had a choice between going on a horse, slowly, or in a carriage (slower), or by ship, which could be a bit faster or slower than the other two, depending on the weather. If the wind keeps blowing you back into harbour it can take ages, and when you get out to sea it can blow you in the opposite direction to the one in which you wish to go.

Charles Greenwood and I could have taken a boat from Lyons down to Marseilles, and then a ship from there, westwards through the Mediterranean, round Spain and Portugal, through the dreaded Bay of Biscay, round Brittany, and then into whichever English port the wind then favoured. On a ship you don't have to keep on looking for a bed for the night, and with luck the vessel keeps on going through the night, but sea voyages are a lot more risky than land journeys, and your chances of ending up in Heaven instead of Hampshire are greatly increased.

We decided to go by horse and coach as fast as we could. Bearing in mind it was winter, the roads were appalling, and most of them were deep mud, we were anything but fast most of the way. Our train of servants with all the baggage – greatly swollen during this Grand Tour by all the books, statues, pictures and other things I had bought – had to follow at an even more leisurely pace. Then the wind imprisoned us in Honfleur Harbour for a week, delaying our departure.

We eventually reached Wentworth Woodhouse at the start of March, soon after the delayed wedding of Princess Elizabeth to the Elector Frederick had been celebrated.

I was shocked at the state I found my Father in. He was a pale shadow of the man I had left fourteen months before. He had never been a fat man, but, rather, somewhat stocky; now he was very thin, and very tired nearly all the time. It was the saddest part of my life so far, and I cannot write about it as if I were back in that time. Here was a man I loved dearly, and he was fading away before my eyes. Even so, he had not lost all his old fire, and had a real rant about the tremendous expense of the Royal Wedding and the masques and parties that followed it, saying that when the King did not have two groats to rub together, he should have kept things simple.

Dad is a died-in-the-wool Monarchist, so this came as a bit of a shock to me, but the cost of the marriage certainly figured large in what folks talked about that winter – much larger than the supposed advantages of an alliance with a small Protestant German state.

This topic livened him up for a little while, but then he lapsed back into lethargy. I got so miserable about it that one day I did something which seemed unforgiveable at the time, and still is, really, although it had a temporarily good effect. I said to him: "Father, when you are so ill, how do you go on? Wouldn't you rather be with Jesus?"

He was silent for a little. "No, son. I don't want to die." And he began a fight back. He began to get up more, walk about the estate a bit, talk to us (that was a great thing), and eat a bit more.

Margaret. 15th March, 1613. Wentworth Woodhouse.

Thomas has been home a week, and it has been heaven. I think we have made love more times than we did even in the week after our wedding. I have missed him so much, and it was so obvious how much he missed me. If I don't get pregnant now, then I never shall.

And we are doing some different and exciting things. All because of a book!! A few weeks ago I was in my Father's library at Londesborough, where I'd gone for a family visit for three weeks. I was looking for something to read, and wandering along the shelves behind Dad's writing table. The drawers in this desk have always been locked. I had never been able to open them when I was little, and once Dad had told me very sternly when he spotted me trying one: "If you open that drawer, you'll never go to Heaven." He never smacked me; he wasn't that kind of Father.

As I passed behind the desk this time, I did what I always did: put out a hand idly and tugged at the drawer-handle; the same drawer Papa had seen me try to open years ago. To my astonishment the drawer opened, and I saw it contained some books. I could see two were in French, one in Italian, and one looked as though it might be from China.

As I picked up the Chinese one I glanced down the room to check that the door was quite shut. It was. I then opened the book, roughly in the middle. Astonishment turned instantly to shock. I was looking at a hand-painted picture of a young woman on her knees with the penis of the man standing in front of her in her mouth!! I turned the page and there was one of the same girl lying on a bed with the man crouching on top of her, facing towards her feet, doing something with his tongue between her legs, whilst she had his prick in her mouth.

I shut the book with a slap, and was then worried if anyone had heard. I slipped the book back in the drawer. I left the library fast.

A little later I realised I had found nothing to read, and would therefore have another chance to look at this naughty book. Nobody was in the library, the drawer was still unlocked, and I stared at its pictures for a good quarter of an hour, my heart hammering away all the while. I then recalled what I was there for, and found a play by Marlowe, and took that away. Despite daily library visits I never found the drawer open again.

I couldn't wait to try out what I had learned on Thomas, even though I was a bit worried about what he might think.

Thomas, 16th March, 1613.

This has been a marvellous week. When I got home the family were so pleased to see me, and I them, that there was a real party atmosphere. I gave them all small presents I had acquired for them – small but not necessarily inexpensive. The amethyst and diamond earrings and necklace I bought Margaret cost me a small fortune, as did the tiny devotional Italian oil painting of Jesus with John at the Jordan which I gave my Mother. It is supposed to be over two hundred years old.

My Father was up, and gave me a hug, and I was disturbed his formerly stocky strong arms had become so thin, and weak; he could not even stand for very long. He was almost hanging himself on me, like a sash. Tears ran down both our faces. In fact tears were running down all our faces, except little brother Matthew, who always seems to have a different way of behaving from the rest of us. He actually poked his tongue out at me.

I gave out the presents, and there were more tears, except from Matthew, but even he liked his present, a model of a French Castle with a drawbridge and portcullis that work, and a moat you can fill up.

I had a present for Smeaton, the steward, and summoned him to receive it. He is a tall, slim, almost gaunt, figure, with straight and long grey hair. He is fiercely loyal, and devoted to the family. I gave him a set of French wine-glasses. Tears rolled down his face too. Then he announced that dinner was served. Brother William helped me assist Dad into the dining hall, and as I moved around the table to my chair, Smeaton took my arm, and said, very quietly, "The household and the estate staff would like to greet you on the terrace in the morning, Sir Thomas."

"How nice. Make it eight-thirty, Smeaton." I had a gold French coin for each of them.

Margaret was very gay, and so was I. Soon all tears were forgotten, and happy chatter and laughter reigned.

We all retired to the music room and Mother played the spinnet, and we sang for a while, until my Father announced that he was done for, and had to go to bed. Margaret rose quickly, saying she was tired too, and would see Father up to his bed, and then go to bed herself. My brother William went with her and Dad, and a few minutes later William returned. Margaret did not.

My sister Anne then played a few more tunes, and by this time I felt the need to join Margaret in the bedroom. I kissed everyone and left. I have never run up the stairs so fast, tired though I was.

Thomas. March, 1614. Yorkshire.

And so we went on for another year, thoroughly enjoying each other, sad that we were not yet parents, yet not unhappy that pregnancy was not interfering with our love-making.

Yesterday I rode into the village, to the blacksmith's, to get my hunter shod. I got back at noon, handed the horse over to the groom, and went round to the terrace. I was delighted to see Father walking on the lawn. I vaulted the balustrade and ran down to meet him.

I smiled. He looked at me very seriously. "A messenger came from York. The King has called Parliament. I want you to stand as a Knight of the Shire. Do you good to get into politics."

"Why didn't you tell me before?"

"I had to take some soundings; send letters to some friends and neighbours; see what they thought."

"Couldn't you have asked me first?"

"Not a chance, lad. You and Margaret are inseparable – and I'm very glad about that – lovely woman, just lovely – but if I'd asked you you'd have said no, and you know me; I've never been the sort of parent to force you to do anything you didn't want to do."

I was livid. "You made me go on that tour. How do you know I won't say no anyway?"

He smiled now. "Because I know you, Son. You love me and you're too considerate to hurt me by refusing when I've set it all up for you. You know how proud I am of you, and I'll tell you something else: you'll love it. There's a powerful streak in you, and once you've seen real power being exercised you'll want a share."

My anger faded fast in the face of this flattery and seduction. Papa was right. I just knew it. I smiled back, rather sheepishly. He spoke before I could.

"And you don't need to leave that lovely wife behind either. You can stay at the Earl's place in London. You'll be able to see Henry and Frances, won't you?"

"Yes. Henry's been back from Paris for some months. You've really thought all this out, haven't you?"

"I have. You've got a pretty good chance of being elected, as everyone I spoke to was keen. They know I'm not fit to stand. It's time a Wentworth made a mark on Yorkshire."

"Very well, Father. I'm a marked man. I shall do my damndest to hit the bulls-eye."

Margaret. 15th March, 1614. Yorkshire.

This week ends on a slightly less than happy note, in a sense. At lunch Thomas tells me his Father wants him to go into politics!

We are all sitting down to lunch in the dining room. It is a fine day and the sun is shining in the windows, and there are daffodils on the lawn. There is not a lot of talking as everyone seems to be hungry, including even my father-in-law, who has been out walking in the garden. Suddenly Thomas gets up from the table, goes to the side-board, and brings back a couple of bottles of wine, which I see are already uncorked. He pours wine into everyone's glass – even the smaller children's, but not too much in their case – and, still standing, proposes a toast to the new Knight of the Shire for Yorkshire.

One of the boys asks what a Knight of the Shire is, and another asks who it is. Sir William laughs, and so does Lady Wentworth. Thomas is majestic (I know I'm married to him and very biased, but I have to say that he can – does – look very imposing when he wishes). "A Knight of the Shire, Philip, is a Member of Parliament, and the new one, Matthew, is – me!!"

There is uproar. Everybody talks or shouts at once, but eventually young William says; "But you haven't been elected yet."

Old William laughs again. "Don't you worry about that, Will. Your big brother will be the next MP. I've made sure of that."

Before I could utter a word, Thomas turns to me, and kisses me. "The election is next week, and we shall be off to London the following week."

"But I'm not going to be an MP, Thomas. I'm not sure I want you to be one either."

"I've decided I'm going to be the greatest in the land, and with you at my side, I can do it." He says this with a smile, but then I can see that he was only half joking, and with that, I want it for him, and for me.

I'm thinking our lives will change forever. Will they, though? If they do, will it be for better, or for worse? That's why I'm not entirely happy about it.

Henry Clifford. 14th April, 1614. Cumberland House, London.

Thomas and Margaret have been here a week. Margaret and Frances get on so well. Thomas and I are very lucky fellows. Mind you, I'm luckier than Thomas at the moment for two reasons. First, Frances and I have a daughter now, whereas Margaret has had no babies yet.

Secondly, I am with both these lovely ladies a great deal, whilst Thomas is off to Westminster nearly all the time, and I'm sure I'm having more fun, dining with the girls, taking them to the theatre, walks in the parks and fields around London, and boat-trips on the river. Even so, Thomas comes home in the evening – and that's pretty late – absolutely full of politics and what's going on in Parliament.

Mind you – golly, I really should stop using that expression – so boring to keep repeating oneself – I'm not sure he really understands what is supposed to be going on. From what he tells us at dinner – and repeats to me in the study afterwards, but with more detail – I get the impression that no-one in the House of Commons agrees with anybody else about anything.

Thomas says: "How can they do any government's business like that? The King doesn't seem to have any kind of gathering of like-minded MPs to support him, and even the MPs who oppose him aren't organized; they just obstruct."

All this shows me a Thomas I haven't seen before. He's always been quite a serious sort of chap, but never really had any sort of focus. I knew he wanted to look after the underdog, like that time he helped sort me and that bully Chesworth out at school, but it was all ..... well, sort of woolly, I suppose. Now I can see that he is forming ideas about how politicians ought to act and combine if they want to get anywhere. I'm not sure he sees it like that, but the other night, after dinner and over a glass or two of cognac, he was chundering on about the chaos in the Commons, and nothing getting done, and how he would do it.

I just couldn't help ribbing him about it. "Thomas, go on like this and you'll be running the country one day." And I laughed.

Thomas just stared back for a moment. "You know, Henry, if the King gave me the chance, I think I'd like that."

Margaret. 22nd April, 1614. Cumberland House, London.

Thomas and I have been here with Frances and Henry for over two weeks now. The time has gone so quickly, because Henry is a marvellous host, and takes us ladies to every sort of entertainment he can think of. I'm impressed with Frances, too. She has a very good housekeeper, and an even better cook, but she oversees everything with such flair, and she is so polite to the servants. She doesn't command them imperiously, or rudely, ever, and always says "Please would you do this, and that," and she almost always thanks them afterwards.

I've noticed, though, that she has a manner about her that makes her requests seem like commands, in the sense that it wouldn't occur to anyone to say "no." When Thomas and I have a house of our own, I'm going to try to run it the same way. All the staff here seem happy, and willing, and I'm sure it's the way they are treated. Thomas's Mother works in much the same way, but she's not quite as kind, nor does she take the interest in the servants' welfare the way Frances does. Frances knows if their children are ill, visits their rooms, and even their homes if they live out.

There's another thing that amazed me at first. Most people give their servants Sundays off to go to Church as long as there are enough of them about to do the basic tasks for the day, and an afternoon off every couple of weeks, and a week or weekend once a year. But Frances and Henry give most their staff an afternoon off every week!! As well as Sundays. No wonder they're happy!! And they never seem to leave. But then why would any of them want to go and work anywhere else?

All this is quite different from the way my Papa behaves. He doesn't ask the servants anything. He just tells them: "Fetch this," or "Do that'. He's not rude. It's almost as though he doesn't know that the servants are people. You don't say to a chair "Please may I sit down?" The chair is there to sit on, so you sit on it. Father is the same with the servants. They're there; he pays them; he uses them as he wishes. I don't think he knows whether they have feelings or not.

But then there's something else here at Henry's that makes me want to laugh or cry by turns. And that's Frances's baby. She is such a sweet little thing called Alice. And Frances loves her so much! She even feeds her herself, instead of getting in a wet-nurse. I don't think I know of any other woman in society who does it. It looks so lovely and peaceful when she does it. I know Henry sees her do it, but of course Thomas doesn't; it's not the sort of thing you do in public. Well, our sort don't, but I have seen the farmworkers' wives feeding their babies in the fields at home. The wife of one of our tenants even had her baby in the field last harvest time. Anyway, those baby things are what make me laugh and feel so gay. So what is it about Alice that makes me want to cry?

Well, Frances has this nasty habit of keeping on saying things like: "It's such a shame you don't have a baby yet:" or: "I expect you'll have your own lovely little Alice person soon." I'm beginning to wonder if I ever will. It's not as though Thomas and I don't try. We love trying, and wear ourselves to a frazzle trying nearly every night, and nothing is happening.

Even though Thomas is out at Westminster watching the parliamentary proceedings – he says he hasn't made a speech yet – comes home late, and then sits up late telling Henry about it, he still wants to make love to me when he comes to bed, and I'm usually dying for him to as well, even if he has to wake me up. And if he doesn't one or other of us makes the first move when we wake up in the morning.

They say ladies ought to take it easy in the day if they want it to work, so I don't rush about, and none of the trips Henry arranges for us are too energetic, so it can't be that – you know – too much violent exercise.

That's enough of that. Let's think about Thomas. He's changed a bit since we came here and he went into Parliament. He seems more thoughtful a lot of the time, and he says some very provoking things about other MPs and the way the Commons does its business – or fails to. What really seems to get to him is the waste of time.

Last night at dinner he was furious. "The King called this parliament because he needs money to run the country. Most of the Members are cross because they say he's not running the country, and won't listen to their 'grievances', as they call them, so they won't vote for any taxes or loans to help him run the country. Then the people who support the King say he can't do anything about their grievances and running the country until he gets the money. No-one gives an inch, and meanwhile the country goes to the dogs."

Henry laughed: "Thomas, go on like this and, as I told you the other night, you'll be running the country one day." And we laughed.

All except Thomas. He looked around at the three of us with an expression I've never seen on his face before. "And as you know, Henry, if the King gave me the chance, I'd do it."

He is definitely not joking now. The trouble is I can't really see him as a politician. He's just too truthful about things. He is very clever – well, I'm bound to say that, aren't I – so he might get on well to start with, but I'm sure he'd end up upsetting too many people. It might all end badly.

Thomas. 23rd May, 1614. Cumberland House.

This Parliament is likely to drive me mad. It's like a bear pit, with the noise and fighting, even if it is only in words. It's been going on for two months, we haven't passed a single Bill, the King's been down here three times and made speeches which don't help at all, and we haven't voted him any taxes, loans, or subsidies. I've heard him called The Wisest Fool in Christendom, but no-one, wise or foolish, can run a kingdom without money.

How is the King foolish? Well, for a start he took steps to keep out of their seats men who, he knew, opposed him. They weren't unreasonable men, and they knew how things work. Instead all those seats have been filled with hot-heads, and there have been interminable debates about unfair elections as a result, which get the King's business nowhere.

As far as I can make out, he wants to do everything in accordance with the law of the country, just as Queen Elizabeth did, but hasn't taken the trouble to get anyone on his side. She used to get some of her Privy Counsellors into the Commons so they could guide debate and organize voting, but James just comes to the House and lectures us in his fine academic style. He says things such as; "Never King was in all his time more careful to have his laws duly observed and himself to govern thereafter than I," and – and this was incredible – "The evidence of a King is chiefly seen in the election of his officers, and in filling places, not to choose those whom he favours most, but to have every one according to his abilities".

What made that so incredible is that he has cloth-head Carr – now Earl of Somerset, would you believe! – as his right-hand man. It's as though the King can't avoid saying one thing and doing exactly the opposite. They say Somerset sits in on all the Privy Council Meetings, says nothing, and no decisions are taken. He then goes off privately with the King, and they come back to announce their policy. If Somerset ever has his head cut off, it'll be hard to find a brain inside it.

I've got to do something, but what? I'm definitely not a republican – as some of the wilder sort say they are – and I'd die for the King if it would help, but this way of carrying on makes me feel more sympathetic to the opposition. I've met some MPs who are of a like mind. Two of them are particularly impressive, and have very high principles, even if they are not quite the same as mine. One is John Eliot, and the other is John Pym. They are not leaders – or not yet, anyway. The big wig in the House is Sir Edwin Sandys. He's a major merchant in the City, so he's quite different from me and the other two; we're all country landowners.

Sandys may be taking the lead, but he hardly sees things straight. He said the other day that the King was out to make us bondmen or slaves, which is just ridiculous. The King doesn't even have an army. He's in no position to force anybody to do anything.

I've even been in Court listening to how cases are conducted, and at the King's Court picking up hints and gossip. I heard the Lord Chief Justice, Sir Edward Coke, state his view of the Law, which is that the King is subject to it just like everyone else. "The King is under the Law" is what he said. And guess who he said it to? The King: face to face. If anyone else had said it they'd be in the Tower by now. You can get away with a lot in a Court of Law, it seems to me, especially if you're the Judge, but talking like that to the King himself somewhere else seems to go a bit too far. Henry VIII would have had his head off in no time. I suppose there'll be some kind of confrontation between the King and his lawyers on one side and the opposition lawyers on the other side, if this sort of argument goes on.

This Parliament is going to be dissolved soon: I can feel it. It's not called the Addled Parliament for nothing, since it is certain nothing can hatch out of it. Heaven knows when we shall have another, but if I get in again I'll be more vocal than this time – I haven't said a thing so far - but I don't think I shall endear myself to the monarch, even though I only want to help him. Criticism – even if it's constructive – doesn't seem to go down well with people in power.

Talking of which, try as I might, and as much as I like trying, I just don't seem to have the power to make Margaret pregnant, and it clearly worries her. I'm even beginning to think that maybe my musket fires the wrong sort of balls. And how many men want to think it might be their fault? This is doing neither of us any good. At least we're on the same side and don't fight with or blame each other over it.

Thomas. 1st June, 1614. London.

Today I have a letter from Father.

My Dear Thomas,

I do enjoy your letters. It is very good of you to write me such interesting reports of the House. It is not so good to read that you and Margaret are still having no luck in the off-spring stakes. These things can take time. Look at Genesis and the story of Abraham, and think of Luke's account of Zechariah and Elizabeth, and continue to say your prayers, as your Mother and I pray for you.

I am not at all sure that what is being said about the decline in West Country trade is entirely accurate. As far as I can make out, merchants all over the country are doing well, and much wool is being shipped from Yorkshire to the markets in Europe, so I cannot see why the excellent broadcloth being woven in Devon, Cornwall, and Somerset, should not be selling just as well. Frankly, I fear it may be some kind of deceit on the part of men like Pym. I know you think highly of him, and I have never met him, but what I read in the pamphlets and some of the cartoons and lampoons that circulate make me suspicious of him and his motives.

He and his kind are against taxes for the King, and what better way than to say that they just don't have the money to pay tax down in Calne or wherever it is he sits for? I know you think the King shouldn't have the revenue if he doesn't redress grievances and has advisers like Carr, but you are not against the King in principle. I fear that may not be the case with Pym. You need to be wary of him.

And talking of being wary, I have heard that Arthur Ingram is MP for Romney. Now he is a Londoner of a sort, but he has quite a bit of property up here in Yorkshire, and he has a rather unsavoury reputation, so keep clear of him.

I have also heard a rumour that a young fellow called Villiers has appeared at Court, and seems to be vying with Carr for the King's affections. I suppose I'm getting old and intolerant in my old age, but when I think back to the King's peculiar tastes I marvel. There was that fellow James Hay who came down from Scotland with him; he wasn't odd, as far as I know,but what did he do to deserve being made a Viscount? Still, I understand he is doing very well as a diplomat, but when you think of that sodomite Philip Herbert being made Earl of Montgomery, and Carr being made Viscount Rochester and now Earl of Somerset, it makes you wonder.

I believe Carr's only claim to fame was to fall off his horse and break his leg when jousting at a Royal Tournament, right in front of the King, who was so fascinated by his good looks that he arranged for his treatment by physicians. Gossip has it that the sure route to Royal favour these days is a predilection for sodomy.

It is all beyond me. If that sodomy business is true, why on earth was there all that fuss about Carr stealing the Earl of Essex's wife, and the rest of that scandal? I suppose these men are just like weather-vanes (I nearly wrote cocks, but that seems too near the mark in this context), so they turn to the front or the back according to where the best offers are coming from.

I am glad to hear that Parliament has been dissolved and that you will be home soon. Your Mother and I are looking forward to seeing you and Margaret again. Mother is well, and you could say 'mothering' me. I am still not too fit myself, and it worries her a lot, I can see. Most days I have very little energy, and the physician doesn't seem to be able to do me any good, either.

Kiss Margaret for us. Much love from your Mother, and of course from me.

Dad.

****

What Father says in that letter about James's favourites is important. I must try to remember, when I get into power (and I shall), that having favourites is no way to run a government: ability and statecraft are what count..

Thomas. 24th September, 1614. London.

We are staying at grandfather Atkinson's house in Chancery lane. Margaret and I travelled down to London in early September so that I could undertake some cases in the Courts during Michaelmas Term, for which I had been briefed in York. Trying cases in Westminster Hall is, well, trying, to say the least. The crowds mill about at the back, and voices can be heard from the cases going on on the other side of the partitions. This means you have to raise your voice, which just adds to the din, and almost everyone ends up shouting. If the judge is hard of hearing – and some are – it is either not funny, or extremely amusing when he doesn't understand what is going on.

Some of the judges can just be witty.

Juryman._ My Lord, can I be excused from sitting in this case?
Judge. Why?
Juryman. Because the Missus is conceiving a baby today, and there's no-one else at home.
Judge._ Don't you mean she is *having* a baby today? Well, whichever it is, I think perhaps you ought to be there.

I have taken Margaret out to the theatre a number of times, and we saw some bear baiting in a park on the other side of the Thames in Southwark, but Margaret thought it was disgusting, and we stayed only a few minutes. I'm not too keen on that sort of thing myself. At least with hunting the stag has a chance of escape, and often does, but the bear is chained up, and as many as six dogs torment him at once. I have to say I was very glad when the bear picked up one dog by the back legs and used it like a club to beat a couple of others away, and dispatched all three of them. We did not wait to see what happened in the end.

I had three briefs from Yorkshire, and picked up another couple from London Attorneys. Four went to trial, of which I won three, and the other one settled on very good terms for my client. His ten acre field had been squatted on by a neighbour. We got the field back and 30 pounds in damages, and the neighbour had to agree to pay all my client's legal costs. These results were very promising, and another two London solicitors said they would instruct me in future battles.

In fact today one of these attorneys is talking to me about another brief outside the Courts, when I see Margaret hurrying towards me followed by a man I recognise as one of my Father's servants from home. I excuse myself from the legal discussion, promising to contact the solicitor soon. I nod to the servant, and take Margaret's hands which are held out towards me as she runs.

"Oh Thomas, I ..." Margaret is breathless.

"What is it, my darling? And what is Isaac doing here?"

"I could not let him come to find you on his own." Margaret is terribly distressed, but not tearful, despite looking as though she has been. I put my arm around her, and turn to Isaac.

"What is it, Isaac? What brings you to town?"

Isaac is a groom, and an excellent horseman. I see that he is filthy with dust. He was obviously sent here for speed, rather than one of the usual messengers. I begin to apprehend something dreadful.

Isaac removes his cap and turns it in his hands. "Sir Thomas, Lady Wentworth sent me. It's yer Father, Sir; Sir William is .... is dead. Ah'm sorry, Sir."

Margaret starts to weep. "Dear Thomas, I am so sorry too. Isaac arrived at Chancery Lane only two hours ago. I gave him a drink and a bite to eat, and then we came straight here." She puts her arms about me.

I am stunned. My Father is dead. Can I take this in? When Margaret and I left for London he seemed rather fitter than he had been for some time. We even walked in the parkland and fields of his estate a few times only four weeks ago. How can he be dead? He was not a bold man, but he was wise, and loved us all so. I know I shouldn't say it, but he loved me especially because I was his eldest son. He didn't love the others less, but there was a deep bond between us. We used to talk for hours about the estate, the tenants, local politics, national politics, religion and faith – so many things. I am going to miss him; in fact I'm missing him already. Who will give me wise counsel now?

Margaret puts both hands to my face gently and strokes my cheeks, and I realise I have been in a trance for a minute or more. I still have my arm around my wife, and poor Isaac is standing there like an earthenware statue, he is covered in so much dust.

Margaret is solicitous. "Let us go home, Thomas. Isaac and I came in the carriage. We can be home soon, and we can talk about it all."

I have tears rolling down my face. I see that Isaac now has tears coursing down his face too, making channels in the dirt. Neither of us is sobbing, but Margaret is, and we are attracting some attention from people going in and out of Court. We walk to the carriage, and make for Chancery Lane. On the way Isaac tells me it took him three days to ride from Yorkshire, using eight horses, and riding as hard as he could. Indeed, one of the horses actually died under him, a mile or two outside Nottingham, where he stayed one of the nights.

Margaret is rather concerned about him, and has the housemaids prepare a bath and the cook a meal for him, after which she sends him to bed.

Thomas. 29th September, 1614. Yorkshire.

Isaac and I reached Wentworth Woodhouse yesterday, having left London the day after he arrived. The journey took us five days. I'm not up to Isaac's feats of long-distance riding, even though I am no bad horseman myself. He was tired anyway from his previous ride, and slept for nearly twenty hours. I had told him to stay in London and travel up with Margaret and the other servants when he was rested. He would not hear of it.

"Ah doan't lark Lun'on, Sir, an' be best Ah ride with ye, Sir, to mek sure t'horses is well cared fur." Isaac's Yorkshire accent is broad and strong. I shan't try to write it again. Perhaps it can be imagined!!

My Mother is strong and doing remarkably well. She always was stronger than Father, but they were devoted, and I'm worried she will fragment soon. Her usually serene face looks care-worn, and she has more grey hair. She tells me about him.

"He seemed to grow worse as soon as you and Margaret left for London, Thomas. I don't think he wanted to say anything; he wanted you to get on with your life, but he must have known the end was near. Two days after you went he did not get up in the morning and stayed in bed until the end."

"What about the others?"

"Your brothers and sisters have all been very good, and done as much to help and comfort me as they can. Except Matthew, of course, as usual."

"I'll have a stern word with him, Mother."

"I don't think there's any need for that. I said 'as usual' because Matthew is the one who's normally naughty and a nuisance, but this time he hasn't been naughty. Just the opposite. He's stayed in his room, barely says a word, and rarely comes down to meals. He has been so quiet and upset by losing his Father. I never knew he was so fond of him. It's as though all the rebelliousness has gone out of him."

"So he hasn't been much comfort to you, then?"

"No, but then I haven't been much help to him either. If you have a word with him, it had better be a kind one. Try to find a way to bring him back into the family, if you can."

"Do you know what killed Papa? Did the Doctor say?"

"Oh dear, you know how vague they can be! It seems your Father had a cancer on his liver. It grew very slowly, and that is why he's been ill for so long. There was nothing the physician could do. In the end William died very peacefully, in his sleep. Then I sent Isaac to find you."

Now it is Mum's turn to cry, silently, and with great dignity, like everything she always does. I hold her close, and kiss her hair through her bonnet.

"And how is young brother William doing?"

"You saw him at dinner last night."

"I know I did, but he's even quieter than you and gives little away."

"Well, we've left the running of the estate to Smeaton the last few weeks, so William hasn't had to do much there. He's been dealing with Peter, sorting out papers and legal things until you got home."

Peter Man is the family solicitor. "I shall have to go into York to see Peter. I need to see him anyway, to tell him the results of the cases he sent me to London with. I'll take William with me." I start into one of my trances again, but snap myself out of it. "How did Smeaton manage, then? He must have found it hard with Father lying in bed. He never did anything without his agreement."

"That's the trouble, dear. He relied on Father for orders, and now he's gone it's clear Smeaton really doesn't have the skills or personality to manage the estate, or even to decide how it should be done, let alone do it. He needs help."

It suddenly hits me. I've got to do all this from now on. Smeaton will look to me for instructions. My word will be the one that runs the parks, the farms, the tenants, labourers and other servants from now on. How much of it is there? I need to see Peter Man sooner than I thought. Am I going to panic?

No. Panic is not going to help, and it's not what I feel. What I feel is the need to get on with things. Quickly. Mum must be able to hear the wheels and cogs and ratchets whirring and grinding in my head.

"I'll need to get a new steward."

Mother bristles. "You are not going to get rid of Smeaton, I hope; not after all these years. That is not how we do things here, Thomas."

"I know that, Mother. I have no intention of abandoning Father's kind ways - nor Smeaton, come to that. We shall have to find him a special project, and put him in charge. I shouldn't want him and the new steward fighting over territory."

"I have the very thing. You remember how your Father talked last year, before he became really ill, of creating a new lake by damming the stream below the south pasture, and stocking it with fish? Well, he was talking to Smeaton about it again only a month ago."

"And if there's one thing Smeaton knows about, it's fish and fishing. That's just the job, Mum. I'll ask Peter about finding a new steward."

Then Mother drops another burden on my shoulders. "Whilst you were away we had another tragedy, I'm afraid. Anne's husband died three weeks ago. He was just lying in bed, cold and still, when she woke up in the morning next to him."

"Christ help us. She must have been really shocked. Had he been ill?"

"She was in a dreadful state. No-one knew he might be ill. His heart must have given up. He was only thirty-four."

Anne is my elder sister. She's five years older than me, and has two lovely young boys, my nephews, George and William. William is named after his Father, Sir William Savile. Anne is only twenty-six, and little George is six, and William four. Then this one hits me too: I'm head of the family, so these boys are my wards, and in addition to being their guardian, I'm also *pater familias* to eight of my brothers and sisters who are still under twenty, and now I have to take care of Anne. Thank heavens brother William is old enough to be off my hands, and that Dad gave him his own estate a while ago.

Before we can say anything further a small personage with a mass of fair curls cannons into my legs, clasping me firmly round the thighs, and shouting "Fly me! Fly me!!" It is another George. This one is my youngest brother. There are too many Williams and Georges in this family, or there were until my Father and my brother-in-law passed away.

"Fly me! Fly me!" So I pick him up by left wrist and left ankle and whirl him round until he is flying through the air at my waist height, his arms and legs stretched out. He is whooping with glee. He is five years old. I love him dearly, and Mother tells me he worships the ground I walk on. How am I going to deal with all this? I'm only twenty-one myself. Tomorrow I shall be burying my Father. Meanwhile George is shouting: "I'm an eagle; look, Mummy, I'm an eagle."

Margaret. 11th October, 1614. Wentworth, Yorkshire.

We buried Sir William nearly two weeks ago. It was a quiet day, although neighbours, family and friends came from far and wide, and Holy Trinity Church was full. The sun shone too. Lady Wentworth was very dignified, and no longer shedding tears. She is a fine looking woman, and was clearly something of a beauty when young, but much childbirth, and the worry of her husband being ill for a long time and then dying have taken their toll. Her face is thinner, and her hair is quite grey now.

Thomas was stern, as he so often is in public. In the Church he stood for a long time gazing at the tomb of his grandparents, which his Father had had built. It's one of those sarcophagi with prone statues of the departed lying on the top. He spoke to me afterwards about getting one done for his Father, and eventually his Mother, but I pointed out that the Church is quite small and you need to leave some room for a congregation.

He smiled at that. He hasn't done too much smiling for the last fortnight. Even our lovemaking had taken on a different character. Instead of the usual passion we engender, he seems to be using it more as a source of comfort. He's so gentle and slow. I think I love him more.

This makes me think of his parents, too, some of the time. They had twelve off-spring! Twelve!! How do you do that? I still haven't got one, and there's no sign of any either. And they were - they still are - all so healthy. Only one child died. Most of the women I know lose about one in two of their babies. It can be even worse for the lower classes; they live in such squalid conditions, some of them.

And Thomas is so good with these children. Someone has to keep them in order; he's rather strict and bossy but he's also kind and makes time for them, and plays with the little ones. I think he has a favourite. It's George, who is rather a sweetie,with a face like a cherub, and masses of honey coloured curls.

John is dark and very quiet, but he always was, and hardly ever seems to come out of the library except to eat or go to bed. We don't see a lot of William either, as he lives on his estate most of the time, but he comes over at least once a week to see Lady Wentworth, and to talk business with Thomas. They are off to York tomorrow to see Peter Man, the lawyer. I haven't met him yet, but I imagine Thomas thinks highly of him. He must think quite well of Thomas too, if he's prepared to brief him to handle cases in London and here at the Assizes.

Going back to the boys and girls, I have to say that Matthew can be a little beast. He really seems to resent the fact that Thomas is now head of the family and in a position to tell him what to do, and in his case, even more, what not to do. He can be so naughty and defiant. For the first few days after I got home, he hardly emerged from his room, and I know Lady Wentworth worried about him. Thomas tried everything to get him to join the family at meals and cheer up, but I think Thomas missed the point here. He's not very good at working out how others think and feel. He was going on the basis that Matthew was sad about losing his Father.

But having noticed how Matthew reserved his real rudeness and sullen attitude for Thomas, I had this idea that he was just very cross about Thomas being in charge, so that whatever he suggested, to Matthew it was an order to be flouted. I knew he liked riding, and I'd heard Thomas ask him to join him for a canter or a hunt more than once, but he always said "No." Then a week ago I asked him, and he was down the stairs dressed in his riding clothes in a few minutes. He's been a lot better since that ride, which was fun.

Thomas. 12th October, 1614. York.

William and I rode into York this morning and we're sitting in Peter Man's study. He practices from his rather lovely town house, which is in a row of Tudor buildings with overhanging upper storeys. The study is panelled in oak, with a few oil paintings, and furnished with the latest dark oak furniture, which is very heavy, and with quite a lot of carving. He has four clerks in an adjoining room who do all his copying and engrossing of documents and deeds.

He's about forty, I think, and tall, and academic looking, with dark hair, rather short and swept straight back from his forehead. His dress is sombre and plain, black, with white collar and modest lace cuffs. He wears a fairly thick gold chain round his neck, with a jewel, a dark yellow citrine, suspended from it on his chest. Apart from this sole item of decoration, his appearance is rather puritanical, but it is obvious that his whole outfit is expensive and beautifully made in an unostentatious way.

He is not a puritan, however. His simple elegance goes with the elegance of his mind. He's a fine lawyer, and my Father trusted him implicitly, which is an excellent recommendation. William has also reported to me favourably on Peter's services whilst I was away in London.

We start with my giving Peter an account of the cases I did for him at Westminster Hall, and then we get down to the real business of the day; Father's Estate. Peter does not beat about the bush.

"Apart from the two original family Manors at Gawthorpe and Woodhouse, there's the one at Harewood, and another –Thorneton Risborough - which Sir William acquired about the time he purch – um – I should say ....."

I laugh. "'Purchased' will do well, Peter. After all, that is the truth of how he came to be a baronet. Let's start as we mean to go on. I shall always tell you the truth and I expect you to give me the best advice bluntly and fearlessly."

"Thank you, Sir Thomas. I am far from inexpensive, as you will find out, but I hope you will always find the fees reflect the quality of the advice I give, and of the work I do."

"No false modesty there, then Peter." And we all laugh.

"So, there are now four manors, all in Yorkshire, as well as some farms elsewhere, and a large tract of sheep grazing, which I think came through your Mother. That is in Gloucestershire, as you know. All these lands are let to good tenants, apart from the home farms at Woodhouse and Gawthorpe, which are kept in hand. The rents are substantial. What is more, they are always paid. Your Father was a fair landlord, his rents were not extortionate, and he chose good farmers, who recognised that if they failed to pay, their chances of getting equally good land from equally fair men were, let us say, somewhat remote."

"I intend to continue with Dad's policies. I can never understand why some landowners would rather try to maximise their rents even if it means land remains untenanted for months." I pause. "Is there any money?"

William leans forward. "There's about three hundred pounds in coin in the treasure chest in the library, and I think Mother has some cash with which she supplies the housekeeper."

Peter produces a ledger from the corner of his desk, and flicks to some recent entries. "I hold about a thousand pounds of your Father's, and here I keep an account of the money he has out on mortgages. There are fourteen of those, for a total of 68,000 pounds. One is in default at present, and we are endeavouring to foreclose, but the rest are paying the interest regularly." He looks at William, and then turns to me. "Currently, Sir Thomas, the income from your Father's Estate is 6,130 pounds per annum. You are a wealthy man. On the other hand, you have your Mother to care for, and extensive family responsibilities."

I cannot help smiling. "You know, Peter, we have a shepherd at Woodhouse, and two farm-workers at Gawthorpe, each of whom have eight children and an ancient parent living with them, and all they have is their rent-free cottage, a small vegetable plot, a small paddock for a cow or pig or two, and a few chickens, and we pay them about twenty-five pounds a year. As you say, I am a wealthy man. I shall never forget that I owe it to my Dad, though."

William is sad. "And all that is after he set me up in some style."

"We are very lucky to have had such a father." I actually have to dry my eyes with my kerchief.

Peter changes the subject. "I've been thinking about your letter asking if I could help find a new steward." He hands me a piece of paper. "That is the address of Richard Marris. I have met him and he comes highly recommended. He is looking for a new position because his last employer decided, a couple of months ago, to take a bigger role in running his own estates. You, I think, are too ambitious and will be too busy, to want to do that."

How right he is.

****

Wealthy man!! I should say so. Just think. If the cottage and vegetable garden and paddock are worth five pounds a year, those men are on about thirty pounds a year, and probably not as much as that. They are, of course, just about the bottom rung of the economic ladder, the beggars and tramps being beneath even their feet. So if the lowest paid men earn 30 pounds a year, my income is two hundred times what theirs is, and that is without thinking what the house I live in would command in rent. I'm glad I don't have to pay rent for it!

Yes, I am a wealthy man. I'm ambitious, too, as Father was, but he was cautious and timid, whereas I feel bold and determined to get what I wanted. What couldn't I do, where couldn't I rise to, if I put my mind to it?

Should I be worried about the family finances, particularly that I have to find "portions" for my three young sisters of 2000 pounds each? No, I don't think so, for that will only be when they are adults or married. This doesn't worry me, then. Dad took me into his confidence early on, and even discussed how his estate should be disposed of when he died. Does anyone suppose he didn't talk to me about his daughters, my sisters? Of course he did. He recommended that at the right time I should assign to them one or more of the mortgages, or set aside money from the rents and keep it for them.

A bold man - a man like me – sees every difficulty as a challenge and each problem an opportunity, and that is exactly how I see things. What is on my mind is how to get wealthier, and how to become a bigger landowner than I am already. The best way to do that in Jacobean England is to get into government. Well, let's face it, it always has been. The Ministers of His or Her Majesty's Government never stay poor. Power and wealth will enable me to help the poor.

I do have one worry, though. Margaret still isn't expecting.

Thomas. 10th November, 1615. Westminster.

Back in June last year I wrote about a letter from my Father about Robert Carr, Earl of Somerset, and what a clot he was. Things have moved on a lot since then. This is the story.

Father's letter refers to James Hay, the Scot. As Father said, Hay had been made Lord Doncaster. I'd met him in Parliament; he, of course is in the House of Lords, unlike me, in the Commons. He's a very nice chap, red-haired, tall, good looking, and very kind and helpful to me. I've even been to dinner at his house in London. Although he seemed to be a favourite of the King's when he got down to London, he clearly wasn't "the one." The King was surrounded by the English now, and Hay did not want the Scots to be backed into a corner, or swept out of Court altogether. His plan was to find another Scot to whom the King might take a fancy, and Hay could then make sure that Scottish influence did not die out. That was where Robert Carr, who was a friend of Hay's, came in.

As Dad said, Carr was thrown by his horse (or the other fellow's lance) charging about in the lists. His leg was broken, but not irreparably, and the King, taken with his good looks, actually went down from the stands. Being even more impressed close up, he ordered his own doctors to care for this young Adonis, visiting him every day, and giving him everything he wanted. By the time he was up and about, Carr and the King were bosom pals, in more ways than one.

Carr was as thick as the oak timbers of a man o' war, but the King, even so, tried to teach him Latin and politics. That was a wasted effort, because dear Robert's brain never did improve! But he was now the favourite, and somehow indispensible to every decision the King had to make.

But the King's gifts to his Robert were not just of the intellectual kind. No. Carr received money, and rings, a large house, and the rents on various properties and farms. The worst thing was when some kind of fraud was perpetrated, and poor old Raleigh, still pining away in the Tower, had his castle and land at Sherborne in Dorset taken away and virtually given to Carr.

Dear Robert was also made Viscount Rochester, giving him more land in Kent, and was already a Gentleman of the Bedchamber. Not inappropriate, perhaps, as most of the King's business was being transacted there.

So dear Robert became a Privy Councillor, and that really meant something. He was appointed Keeper of the Signet, a really glorified private secretary, which must have urinated from a great height over the Earl of Salisbury, the Secretary of State, and very talented and generally upright men like him. Not that I'm saying Salisbury and his ilk were perfect and incorruptible, but they generally had the King's and the country's good at heart. That was not the case with a favourite whose position – I use the word in both senses – is itself a form of corruption. It leads too easily to the giving and receiving of bribes and "rewards."

In 1612, Salisbury died anyway, leaving Robert Carr in undisputed control of the King, and therefore of the country. Perhaps that is a trifle unfair. The King was in charge, but because he procrastinated and relied so much on bad advice, he had effectively delegated control to Carr.

Carr wasn't too dangerous for a while, as he had an assistant named Overbury. Thomas Overbury was clever, and worldly, and experienced in diplomacy, and could keep Carr from real disasters. Until, that is, they fell out. Fell out seriously. Indirectly the cause of their quarrel was a woman. Frances Howard was the daughter of the Earl of Suffolk, and she was married to Robert Devereux, Earl of Essex. Essex was a good and intelligent man, so it is difficult to understand what it was that Frances found so attractive about dear Robert Carr, apart from his looks, his only good point. But she did. Whatever Robert may have been up to in the bedchamber with the King, he clearly wanted to get up to something else with Frances.

And they probably got up to it, because the next thing was that Robert and Frances wanted to get married. Of course, that meant she had to get a rather trumped up divorce from her husband, who was not happy about it, but the King's favourite could get anything he wanted. The trumped up nature of the divorce was extremely shameful.

By some means the King forced Essex to agree that he was impotent. Essex was not a lucky chap. He was only a couple of years or so older than me, and at twenty-four he was compelled to admit that he couldn't get it up. I can't think of anything more humiliating, especially if it weren't true. I was worried about the possibility I might be sterile as Margaret was not getting pregnant, but at least we kept that between ourselves. But impotent!! No, I didn't have to worry about that.

I can see the King's reasoning, and why Carr and his Frances would want it to be impotence, because a divorce pure and simple would not have allowed these illicit lovers to be married in the eyes of the Church. But impotence meant that Essex could not have consummated the marriage, and that meant it was void, and could be annulled. Hey Presto! Frances had never been wed, and a Church wedding with

Robert was on, if the Commission appointed by the King pronounced the annulment.

Not only was Essex unlucky in losing his wife to another Robert. When he was about 12 his Dad, yet another Robert, had his head removed at the request of Queen Elizabeth for treason. Mind you, he deserved it, having marched into London with a small army to try to take over her Kingdom.

Now, as I say, Sir Thomas Overbury was clever. He realised that if Robert married Frances, he would fall into the powerful clutches of the Howards, and poor old Overbury's lucrative career as Robert's *eminence gris* would be over. Gossip was that Overbury governed Carr, and Carr governed the King; not a situation many men would be happy to lose. Robert and Overbury quarrelled about Easter time 1613, and Overbury vengefully promised to let the cat out of the bag about Robert and Frances, and put the divorce out of their reach if he lost his perquisites.

Some say Thomas Overbury then did something to defy the King, but he was probably framed by Carr or Frances's uncles. He ended up in the Tower of London for it. He died in the Tower pretty quickly, so the annulment went ahead, and the lovers married. Frances even turned up dressed as a virgin to marry the man she'd been rutting with for a year or so. This sort of behaviour is totally against God and the Bible, and God plays a serious part in most people's lives, so having it the topic of common gossip in the streets and markets does a King and his reign no good at all.

That is why I shall ensure that none of that sort of tittle-tattle arises about me.

The Howard clan then owned Carr, and took over and pursued government policy. This policy was to give the Howards the important offices of State, and even more money than they already had.

The annulment case was heard by eight Bishops, including Archbishop Abbott, and he and three others thought dear Frances was lying. The King ordered the Bishops to give a verdict favourable to Frances and Carr, appointed two more compliant Bishops to make sure they did, and told Abbott he was to keep all the details secret, but that isn't how these things work out.

The King gave it all his seal of approval!! Having been married to the Earl of Essex, Frances was a Countess, and the King couldn't let his favourite marry her when he was only a Viscount, now could he? That is how dear Robert became Earl of Somerset. It was all corrupt.

This vile story affected my thinking – particularly about power and the way to govern. You have to keep your nose as clean as possible.

Thomas. 14th December, 1615. Yorkshire.

Nearly the shortest day!! And another twelve months of making love to Margaret and her gorgeous body, and she still isn't pregnant. I have to say I am really quite depressed about it. I am already rich, and intend to get richer, but I have no heir of my loins. True, I have a gaggle of brothers, to any one of whom I could leave everything, but it will probably go to William, as he is the next eldest.

I expect he would be quietly capable, but I'd really like to give it all to George, except that he is still only a child. John is clever and studious, but I don't think he would put himself out to look after the family fortune, nor the family, come to that. He'd rather sit in the library and read. The others are all too young, just like George.

Ah well!! I'll just have to keep plugging away, as one might say. Not that it's a hardship. Goodness knows how many times Margaret and I have had sex, but it always seems like the first time, apart from the fact it gets better and better.

Richard Marris is making great progress. He's the new steward Peter Man recommended. He started here at the beginning of February. He is authoritative but fair to the tenants and the labourers, and has demonstrated a deep knowledge of the land, soil, cattle, sheep, and crops. He is also interested in trees and the forests, and tells me we should be ready to exploit any rise in the demand for timber for the navy. I hope I am going to be able to rely on him. Already we don't seem to be just Master and Servant. I must introduce him to Christopher Wandesford soon, and see what Kit makes of him.

I'm going to need good men like them about me. I had a worrying visitor a few days ago: Sir John Savile. (Yes, he is related to Anne's deceased husband, after a fashion). That he came to see me was odd in itself. Men in his position don't usually call on men younger and not as wealthy. They send for us. So what is his position?

Well, he's rich. His interests in the wool trade hereabouts are vast. His sheep on the moors and elsewhere are almost as thick and numerous as the snow-flakes in winter. So he makes money from sheep, from their wool and from their mutton. He sends about half the wool to markets where yarn and cloth manufacturers buy it, and he sends some of the sheep and lambs to the livestock markets where the butchers and other farmers and landowners buy them. And he rakes in the coinage.

When the sheep have been shorn, the moiety of fleeces Sir John has not sold goes to the homes of the shepherds and his other labourers and farm workers where their wives and daughters spin the wool into yarn. This yarn goes into the cottages of his own weavers, and the houses and hovels of those who live in Leeds where he has a huge labour force. He sells the cloth in the markets, and exports it to France and Spain, and puts some of it into tailoring shops in Leeds which he owns. And he rakes in more coinage.

Then he takes this money to land agents and lawyers acting for deceased folks' estates, and he buys those estates. He puts more of his sheep on those estates, and rakes in more money, and buys or builds more of Leeds. And then rakes in even more coinage. He also grows a lot of wheat and other crops and makes money from that, as well as from rents on the properties he owns.

Do I dislike him for this? Not at all. I can learn from him. He has made his way in the world, as I intend to. He is wily, and shrewd. Do I dislike him at all? No. I can't say I do. My Father did not care for his company, and was wary of him, so I suppose that has influenced me. Sir John comes from a spur of the great aristocratic Savile family, but it is a spur with a spike to it. Two generations back one of the noble Saviles – Sir Henry - took a fancy to one of the maids. Not just an ordinary fancy, either; not the sort where the Lord of the Manor, feeling horny, takes a tumble in the hay with a farm girl. This Savile was besotted.

He installed the maid in a cottage, and apparently treated her like a lady, except in one respect. He would have married a lady. But then he was married already, and besides, he could not marry a maid so far beneath his station in society. Married or not, the maid presented him with a fine son, of whom Sir Henry was very fond. When he grew up, having been christened a Savile, his Father gave him an estate, and bought him a knighthood to go with it. That knight was Sir John Savile's Father.

That is how this branch sinister of the Savile clan came into existence. Being a legitimate scion of the illegitimate branch, even a generation later, has embittered Sir John. This makes him sinister in both senses of the word. He felt he could look down on my Dad, who was not as rich, nor as well connected. Believe me, being bastard aristocracy like Sir John is better than being mere landed gentry, like Dad. Or me, come to that. For example, when that oaf Reresby hit Father and challenged him to a duel, Savile was one of Reresby's supporters, and when Dad got Reresby punished in Star Chamber, Savile went about Yorkshire spreading the most awful slander about Dad bribing the judges. A lot of people believed him. I'd have sued him for defamation, but Dad wasn't that sort.

Father got his own back, though, even if he didn't intend to. He did it by marrying my sister Anne to another Savile; one of the real old untainted Saviles. Then Dad capped it all by marrying me to Margaret, the Earl of Cumberland's daughter. Her brother Lord Henry is one of my best friends; now Sir John has to look up to me, or at any rate to be respectful to my wife, and treat me with some care.

On the other hand I have to be careful how I treat him. He's not just rich; he is very powerful politically in the West Riding. So many people are dependent upon him for their farm, their job, their shop, or other ways in which their livelihood means they cannot do without him, that he controls votes at elections, and power amongst the Justices of the Peace, and influence with many local lawyers. If he says to his cronies and friends "Don't buy from so-and-so," or "that man is an outcast," the victim may well be doomed.

Savile is about sixty, and I am twenty-two. He has a good head of white hair, and a beard cropped short. He's about the same height as me, and slim for the most part, but has a protuberant pot belly. They say this is due to his fondness for ale, an odd taste for a gentleman, since it is the mead of the labourer, but it takes all sorts. Myself, I prefer wine – good wine at that – but I take little of it. By contrast Sir Arthur Ingram is a vintage wine connoisseur. Unlike me, Sir Arthur drinks two bottles at a sitting, and frequently more.

I do not know him well. I first came across him in Parliament last year. He was MP for Romney. I find him very pleasant and helpful. Cynical friends like Henry tell me that is because I am gentry, and Arthur would like to be gentry too. He hopes to rise in the ranks by getting to know and help people such as me, and gain entry to higher circles that way. Not that I am in the highest circles, of course, but

Arthur is rich, getting richer, and aiming for power and influence. He is great friends with the Howard family, which includes the Earls of Northampton and of Suffolk - well, that is what he says – but I doubt that they would say he is their friend, more likely an acquaintance with whom they do business. Suffolk is the Lord Treasurer, but that doesn't stop him spending more than his income, as so many of these really rich and powerful people do. As a result he borrows heavily from Sir Arthur.

It seems there is nothing Arthur likes more than having the powerful in his debt. That is how he came to be an MP. Lord Northampton, as Warden of the Cinque Ports and one of the great landowners, controls the elections in many of his boroughs, and Romney is one, so he put Arthur into that seat. Arthur can be expected to vote the way the Howards tell him.

Why do the aristocracy look down on him? Because his father was in the cloth trade in Leeds, and went to London to pursue that line of business. Arthur followed him into it, and got pretty rich doing so. He then started buying up lands from the Crown (one of the ways the King finances his government), and then selling them back to the King, usually at a profit, a few years later. He then uses the money he makes to buy more properties, from which he gets rent and other income, and lends that to people like Northampton and Suffolk. The interest rate for this sort of loan is usually about 10 percent, so Arthur does very nicely, thank you.

I am learning a lot by watching how Arthur goes about things, but I hope not to adopt all his methods. One of his favourite tricks is to buy a property for a substantial deposit, the balance to be paid later. Then, having got the property and the rents from it, he delays paying the balance of the price, and waits for the vendor to sue him. He then uses his wealth to run them ragged through the law courts. He also gets his wealthy "friends" to put pressure on such people.

What makes this strategy so successful is that he seeks out men who are virtually bankrupt, and who are anxious to sell their estate to pay off their debts. This means that Arthur can offer them a good price, but as he only pays part of it, and never pays the rest, he actually gets the land for far less than it is really worth.

But back to Sir John Savile, and what he came to see me about. He had sent a servant over from Howley Park one morning, with a note asking if he could call on me the next day. I scrawled on it that I should be delighted, and suggested lunch at noon.

He arrived on horse-back with a servant, who took the mounts to our stables and was fed in the kitchen. I asked Mother and Margaret to keep the children occupied and to take lunch in the dining room, and I ordered mine and Sir John's served in my study. Sir John greeted Mother and Margaret with a slight bow and a few pleasantries, and then the ladies made for the dining room with the children, and we went into the study and our .... What did I expect? Just social banter? From Sir John? Hardly. Whatever he said he'd come to talk about, there would be business or politics, or both, in it somewhere.

We ate, and we talked of hunting, and the price of wool, and Sir John drank two jugs of beer with his food, and I had one small goblet of wine. I was beginning to wonder whether he had turned up just to be sociable after all, and then it happened.

Margaret. 14th December, 1615. Yorkshire.

I met a reptile a few days ago. Not a real one. Just a man who seemed like one. Sir John Savile. We exchanged only a few words when he arrived to see Thomas. They didn't have lunch with me and Mother-in-Law. They ate in Thomas's study.

I didn't see Sir John go, but immediately afterwards Thomas came running, yes, running, into the drawing room and took me back to the study. He was so excited.

"Margaret, I think I'm about to step onto the ladder!!"

"What makes you think so?"

And then he related this conversation he had had with Savile.

Savile. I suppose you must have turned your mind to some public office some day, Thomas. No point in my keeping on calling you Sir Thomas and you calling me Sir John. We know who we are, don't we, young fellow?

Thomas. We do indeed, John. *(A pause).*

Savile. Well, what about it?

Thomas. What about what?

Savile. Public office! I just asked you....

Thomas. I know you did. But surely everybody thinks about it?

Savile. *(With a laugh).* I hope my ploughman doesn't.

Thomas. You know the old chant kids do with the plum stones? Tinker, tailor, soldier, sailor, rich man .... Don't you think they say that even in the shepherd's hut? Even the shepherd's children know it's only men with public office get to be the rich ones. If they're not rich already.

Savile. But if *they* think about it it's just a dream. But for the likes of you, it can be true. I mean, take me. I've been *Custos Rotulorum* here in the West Riding for .... Oh, I don't know; must be years now.

Thomas. Is it worth it?

Savile. Worth what? The effort? Definitely. The pay is paltry, I grant you that, but then I pay a clerk to do most of the grind for me, and he's happy with a quarter of the fees I get. But that's not what makes it worthwhile.

Thomas. *Custos Rotulorum.* Keeper of the Court Rolls. Not exactly the pinnacle of excitement there.

Savile. But that's where you're wrong. Verily I say unto thee – I just love these phrases out of the new Bible, don't you? Verily, verily, I say unto thee, the record keeping is a bore, but what about the things you find out? I know the details of every serious quarrel between anyone of importance which has gone to Court for miles around. No crime of any seriousness for which men of standing have been tried – doesn't matter whether they were convicted or acquitted – escapes my notice. That knowledge is power, Thomas.

Thomas. Don't tell me you read all the records yourself!

Savile. You're damned right I don't. But I give the clerk an extra pound for every useful case he draws to my attention. It makes him very assiduous, and nearly doubles his pay some years. He does all the reading and just gives me a summary.

Me. Very interesting.

Savile. Yes, isn't it? I wanted you to know about it because I'm thinking I may give it up soon.

Thomas. Doesn't sound like you, John. But anyway, why tell me?

Savile. I thought it might suit you, with your barrister's training and the cases you've tried.

Thomas. But don't the holders of jobs like this one sell the place to the next fellow to take it?

Savile. True, and you can give me half a year's fee if you wish, though I'm not in a position to sell you this place. You have to be appointed. *(He smiles).* And you can sell it back to me if I ask for it. *(He chuckles).*
Thomas. *(He roars with laughter).* Well now.
Savile. I'll put your name forward.

Thomas paused. I shook my head. "And?"

"So we stood and shook hands. I didn't know whether to take him at face value or not. I thought he was obviously joking about letting him have the job back. Soon he called for his servant and departed. Straightaway I sought you out, Margaret."

I was stony. "He's up to something".

"Why do you say that? You've never met him before today. And that was only for a few moments."

"Thomas, I've never met a snake, but I'll know one when I see one, and he, believe me, is a snake. You'd better find out more. Go and see Peter Man. I bet he knows something."

Thomas. 21st December, 1615. Yorkshire.

Today is the shortest day. I'm acting on Margaret's advice of a few days ago, and I'm sitting once again in Peter's chambers. I'm telling him what I told Margaret about Sir John Savile.

"I can't tell you anything now, Thomas. I'll have to look into it. Savile's reputation is unsavoury, to say the least. I can't understand why he should want to give up being *Custos Rotulorum*, but perhaps he is just fed up with it, as he suggests. At the moment I cannot see how it can harm you to accept his recommendation for the office, and it doesn't sound to me as though you promised to give it back to him later, even if he thinks you did."

"Very well. I'll accept."

Peter nods. "And as soon as I have news, I'll let you know what I've heard. In the meantime, be very careful what you say to him and everyone else about this, and whatever you do, don't make him any promises about anything."

"My dear Dad used to say 'My lips are as tightly closed as a bull's arse in fly time,' but he used to say it about some men's wallets."

As soon as I get home, I go up to see Charles Greenwood in his study. He stays here a lot of the time helping to educate my brothers, and teaching the younger girls to read and write. He and I became good friends whilst we were on my Grand Tour four years ago.

"Charles, I want you to do something for me."

"Anything which is not illegal, Thomas."

"Can you find some excuse to call on Sir John Savile at Howley Park, and see if you can find out a) why he is giving up the post of Keeper of the Records, and b) why is he offering it to me?"

"Delighted, Thomas. In fact I wanted to go to see him and his library. There's a book by Francis Bacon I'd like to read. Sir John may have a copy."

"Why didn't you tell me you wanted it, Charles? I'd have bought it for you."

"I know you would, and I don't know why I didn't think to ask you, but it's as well I didn't or I wouldn't have an excuse to go and see him for you, would I?"

"Very true. What's it about?"

"It's called "The Advancement of Learning," and as a teacher I ought to read it."

"Will you enjoy it?"

"I'm not sure. Bacon is a genius, and some of his work is wonderful but I'm told the King said of one of Bacon's books that it is like the peace of God, since 'it passeth all understanding'".

Thomas. 23rd December, 1615. Yorkshire.

Charles comes into my study. It is a very cold day, and he stands before the fire warming himself. He is so excited. "Thomas, I have it."

"He told you what this Keeper of the Records business is about?"

"What?"

"Yesterday you told me you'd arranged to see Sir John Savile to find out why he wants to give up the job and give it to me. You went to see him this morning. Why are you so excited if he didn't tell you anything?"

Charles gathers his wits. Then the light dawns. "Oh, that! No, the point is he had the new Bacon book .... And he's lent it to me!!"

"Well, that's very nice for you, I'm sure. But what about me? What about *Custos Rotulorum?"*

Charles is downcast, looking at the floor, which is constructed of the finest, wide, dark oak, planks. "Sorry, Thomas. I'm a sinner. I was putting myself first. I didn't do very well there, I'm afraid."

"Come on Charles, I don't think you'd know how to sin if you had Satan for a teacher. What happened? Here, have a brandy, and we'll try to cheer you up. So, what did he say?"

"Nothing much. He's a wily old bird, and no mistake. I tried to be subtle, and make out that it was the book I'd come about, but he saw through that straight away. 'I tell Sir Thomas about the *Custos Rotulorum* post just a week ago, and you're round here today asking to borrow a book? And you're a tutor in his house? Do I look as though I was born yesterday?' he says.

"I say: 'But Sir John, I haven't asked to borrow the book. I just wanted to know if you had it.' Then he takes me by the arm and leads me into his library. 'I don't read 'em', he says. I just buy 'em and put them in here for show. Bastow', he shouts, and a dusty little man appears at the other end of the library. 'Get this gentleman that new book by Bacon. I'm going to lend it to him, whether he likes it or not.' So he takes me by the arm and takes me back to the other room. 'So is Thomas interested in the job or not?'

"I can see there's no use trying to fool him – I just don't have any acting talent – so I say: 'I don't know for sure, but I think he must be or he wouldn't... er .well ... er ...he wouldn't....'

"Sir John laughed. '... or he wouldn't have asked you to find an excuse to come here. I can guess what he wants to know. First, why I'm going to retire from the post, and secondly, why I'm offering to get the job for him. Well, I'll tell you something young feller. If Thomas thinks there's a catch, he's wrong. There's nothing else to tell.'

"So that's it, Thomas. We're no further forward than a week ago. Sorry."

I pace the room. After a bit I say: "Not entirely true, my friend. We are further forward because we now know just how subtle and clever Savile can be. I shall accept the job, and thank him for it, but I shan't trust him; no, not at all."

I see that Charles is carrying this famous book, and I feign interest when he shows it to me. I never did like heavy reading, and as I have no interest in teaching, I have to draw on my poor theatrical skills for this pretence. Fortunately Charles soon departs for his room to make a start on the turgid prose of famous Francis, and I sit down at my desk to compose a letter to Sir John accepting his offer and thanking him for it. I shall send it over to him tomorrow.

Thomas. 7th January, 1616. Yorkshire.

A letter from the Secretary of State arrives today. I have the position of *Custos Rotulorum* for Yorkshire, and a salary of 300 pounds a year. Not a bad sum, but nothing to get excited about. What excites me is having my foot on the ladder of official appointments. This post also brings me into a bit more contact with Sir Arthur Ingram, who is Secretary of the Council of the North, a pretty important position. He bought the job from the previous incumbent, I am told, for five thousand one hundred pounds. That is how these offices change hands, but the King's approval has to be obtained. In Arthur's case approval was, in truth, a foregone conclusion. The Exchequer was so empty that he was supplying it with money on loan, or getting other wealthy men to do so. He either gets interest on his own loans, or a commission or backhander from the people who lend the money for putting them in the way of the opportunity, and from the Treasury for finding the cash.

Sir Arthur obtained an even more important post. He was appointed Cofferer to the Royal Household. However, he didn't last all that long in that exalted position. He was so unpopular with the courtiers because of his trade background, and his rather shady reputation, that he was drummed out of office.

He told me that this was a rather severe blow for him. "I have never had such a setback, Thomas. I was doing so well with the backing of the Howards, but I fear they are on the way down. As you know, Carr is, or was ..."

"Carr? You mean Somerset?"

"Yes, the Earl of Somerset. He was the King's favourite, and now there's a new one. George Villiers. I've been lending money to his backers, so now I have a foot in both camps. If the end is nigh for the Howards, I'll be on the right side with Villiers' sponsors. If he proves to be a power behind the throne, I should be safe."

I could not help smiling. "You'll be safe anyway, won't you, Arthur? You're one of the biggest landowners in Yorkshire now, and you have property in many other counties too. And what about the alum industry? You seem to be in it in a very big way."

"So I should. There's a lot of wool in Yorkshire, and lots of textile making. That's where my father started. You cannot have a successful woollen trade without the alum. When you soak the raw wool ...."

"... in a mixture of alum and water it softens the fibres so that they can be dyed more easily. I know that. That's why I'm interested in investing in alum, too. There's a quarry of it on the coast between Whitby and Robin Hood's Bay." Sometimes Arthur annoys me by stating the obvious. It's a rather patronising habit he has.

Thomas. 10th January, 1616. Yorkshire.

I open a letter from Peter Man. He writes:

Dear Thomas,

My enquiries about Sir John Savile have borne fruit. I am not sure that they show why he has offered you the post of Custos, but it is probable that it has something to do with a scandal which is apparently brewing and the Court case which I am told is likely to follow. It will be no ordinary Court case; it will go to the Star Chamber.

It seems that a few months ago Sir John insulted a fellow member of the Justices' Bench at the Assizes last Hilary term, and then threatened him with violence. It follows that if he is convicted he would be forced out of office anyway. It looks so much better for him to have resigned before there is any trouble.

Unfortunately I have not discovered why he helped arrange for you to step into his shoes, nor why he asked you, even in jest, to hand him the job back if he should want it. We shall just have to wait and see.

I realise that I haven't told Peter that I already have the job. I write to tell him immediately, and hand it to his messenger who is waiting in the hall to see if I have any response for him to take back to his Master. I can't help noticing that Savile and Reresby, who beat my Father, are very similar men. Reresby was fined by the Chamber. Perhaps Savile is hoping that, having given the post away, it cannot be taken from him later if he gets it back from me.

Thomas. Palm Sunday, 1616. London.

The first Law Term of the year has ended. I have been down here for some weeks representing clients and also dealing with litigation involving my Savile nephews' inheritance; that is, my sister Anne's boys. I shall be going home in a day or two. It is not often that I have been away from Margaret, consequently remaining celibate, for so long.

Margaret. October, 1617. Yorkshire.

Thomas has been away in London. He writes to me two or three times a week. I'd rather have Thomas. His letters are no good in bed. Thank God he's home now for a while. His letters give me news about life in the city and his cases, but it is the city news which is so fascinating. Thomas has been writing to me about a new star in the King's firmament. Every letter for the past few weeks has related more of this saga, and today, after Church, we sit talking about it.

Thomas is excited as he tells me. "This story is so corrupt even the clergy are involved, and you may find that hard to believe, but it's true. It starts with Robert Carr, the Earl of Somerset."

"You always said he was stupid, not wicked."

"He's not been so wicked, but his wife and the people who back him have been. What brought the corruption out into the open was the revelation that Sir Thomas Overbury, Carr's former friend, hadn't just died in the Tower; he'd been poisoned and his beloved, Countess Frances was behind it. The four assassins she hired were caught and tried for murder, and this let all the sordid facts about Frances and Carr become common knowledge."

"So did these men inform on the Earl and Countess, then?"

"Yes, Margaret, they did. Eventually Frances and Robert went on trial before the House of Lords, and were sentenced to death, but the King reprieved them, and banished them to live on their country estates."

I shake my head. "That hardly sets an example, does it? I think I remember something about this."

Thomas smiles. "Of course you do. It was the dominant topic of conversation two years ago. The damage all this did to King James and the Crown was huge. The Earl of Essex, Frances's first husband, is a puritan, so he is very popular with a large slice of the population. He's a war hero from Holland's fight for freedom from Catholic Spain."

"Of course. He was forced to 'admit' he was impotent. "

"Exactly, and now the King's being seen as ignoring murder by his favourites. He seems to be blind to all of this. He can't see that he's alienating his subjects. Their sense of justice and fair play – looking after the underdog is an English passion – means that all their sympathies were with the Earl of Essex, and now they think the Earl and Countess should have their heads removed."

I am mystified. "What's all this got to do with – what did you call it? 'A new star in the King's firmament'?"

Thomas holds up his hands in a gesture which seems to acknowledge that he has rather lost his thread. "What made it easier to get rid of Carr is the fact that a new pretty lad has hove into King James's view. His name's George Villiers. He's the King's new favourite."

"Where did this George spring from, Thomas? Have you met him?"

Now Thomas shakes his head. "No, I haven't met him yet – only caught sight of him. Where did he spring from? A lot of powerful people, including Archbishop Abbott of Canterbury and the Earl of Pembroke, were opposed to the hold Carr had over King James. How to get rid of Robert Carr? Well, what about finding a new pretty boy for the King to be besotted with? So that is what they did."

I laugh. "Seems to me to be a strange and immoral occupation for an Archbishop."

Thomas laughs too. "Villiers comes from a gentile but poor Leicestershire family. He had so little money that these powerful backers bought him some fine clothes. Then they took him to Cambridge where the King was peregrinating around the country with his Court, living off the local gentry.

"In Cambridge George landed a part in a play the King went to see. It wouldn't have been difficult for George to get the part, because his backers were funding it, but to be fair to him he could probably have got the role anyway. Why? Because he has what nearly all successful male actors have: tremendous charm; reasonable intelligence; a slim athletic figure, and fantastic good looks."

"You'd think that would make him a ladies' man."

"Well, I understand he's not averse to them, but none of them can give him what a flirtation with the King can offer."

I shudder at that. "That's disgusting!"

Thomas laughs at me a bit. "Don't be naïve, dearest. It is disgusting, but some men will do whatever it takes to get rich and powerful. The poorer they are to start with, the more they are prepared to do. And don't forget it's the King who's truly disgusting. Rumour has it that poor old James was smitten at first sight. Unlike Carr, George didn't even have to break his leg to attract the Royal attention. His handsome person was all it took. He was summoned into the King's presence, and the love of James's life was born."

"The Archbishop and Lord Pembroke got what they wanted, then."

"Not straight away. They had to gild the lily a little more, so they bought George even more clothes, and a job which would keep him near the King. Not much of a job; just a Cup-Bearer. But it did the trick. The positive side was that the clothes and the job brought George even more of the King's favour; the negative side was that it attracted the ire of Carr and his coterie."

I think about that for a moment. "I suppose even if Carr is unintelligent, he'd have enough brains to see Villiers as a threat to his power over the King, and therefore over everyone else."

"That's it precisely, Margaret. He did everything he could to belittle his rival in the eyes of the King, and picked quarrels and daily struggles for supremacy of a surprisingly petty nature. Of course that may have been because, lacking any subtlety or real cunning, he could not come up with any cleverly devious way of keeping Villiers out of the picture."

"You'd think the Howards would have done that for him."

"Yes, that hadn't occurred to me." Thomas ponders that for a space. "Be that as it may, whoever thought up one of his tricks made a big mistake. I was there so I saw this for myself. It was a big banquet at St James's Palace. Somerset had placed all his cronies on the Royal Table with the King. He'd also filled up all the seats on the other tables above the salt. When George Villiers came in, there was no important place for him, so he sat quietly in an empty seat at the far end from the King's dais. He didn't have to sit there long. The King saw him, sent a steward to fetch him to the top table, and when he came up, told one of Somerset's friends to give George his place, and go and sit in the humble seat from which George had just come."

I cannot help laughing at that. "That just shows Somerset hadn't spent enough time reading the Gospels. Wasn't that Jesus' parable? Wait for the King to exalt you; don't seek the best place for yourself; sit below the salt instead. King James probably didn't realise what an insult he'd given Somerset and his friends, but the signal his action sent to the whole dining hall was; 'Watch out; George Villiers is about!'"

Thomas stands and starts pacing about in the way he has, waving his arms about as he talks. "That's the bull's-eye, my love. From then on the decline of Somerset was guaranteed, and the rise of Villiers set in stone. Once the involvement of Somerset and his Frances in the poisoning of Overbury in the Tower was broadcast, Somerset was doomed. He was swept aside in favour of Villiers."

"So what has happened now, Thomas?"

"Once a man becomes a power at Court, he becomes a power in most other fields. Villiers was knighted about this time last year. I doubt anything can stop him taking not just Somerset's mantle, but most of his other garments too. Already a few men at Court are seeking favours from George. That's where the power comes from. If George scratches their backs, he can be sure that they will do the same for him in the future.

Thomas runs his hand through his hair in a medidative fashion. "These events have made a great impression on me. I realise if you really want to do something for King and Country, and be able to go on doing it, you have to keep your nose clean, try as hard as you can to be honest, and maintain a reputation for integrity. Don't foster friendships which may bounce back on you. Don't make a pretence of what your policies are. Stick to what you believe in; make it hard for anyone to call you a hypocrite justifiably. And try to do what you think is good for England, not just for yourself. What's good for a King is usually good for the people, and vice versa, and what is bad for either usually leads to revolution and civil war."

I smile at my husband. "I hope you manage to abide by all those rules yourself, Thomas, if - when - you get to be a power in the land."

Thomas smiles too. "Well, I'm not perfect, but I hope I can keep most of them most of the time. It's odd though. Although King James never seems to perceive just how seriously he breaks all these rules, even though he preaches them himself, I do hope he doesn't pass these awful practices on to his son, Charles. If the Prince of Wales inherits them he'll reap the whirlwind, and if I support him, so will I."

I know Thomas would like to be a power at Court, but he is so blunt and honest – well, I wouldn't say he wasn't, would I? – that I can't see him scratching anyone's back. Not in a pleasant fashion, anyway, but he might lacerate them if they get in his way or do what he thinks is the wrong thing, though.

Thomas. 23rd December, 1618. Wentworth Woodhouse.

A couple of months ago I asked Charles Greenwood to come and stay with us for a few months to give me some extra help with legal matters and the running of my estates. That would give Richard Marris more time to go round the farms, check the boundaries and fences, confer with the tenants, and find out why some rents are seriously in arrears.

I do not care just to turn farmers and tenants out when they have been good workers. If they are ill or have been injured somehow, and cannot work, they cannot find the rent. I prefer to see if we can come to some arrangement enabling them to pay what they owe over a period. That way I keep a good tenant, which is better than taking on someone new who may turn out to be no use and not able to pay at all. It has worked well, and Smeaton, who is acting as Bailiff, has had far fewer arrears cases to report.

It is always pleasant to have Charles's company. He must feel at home here, because at the beginning of the month he asked me if he could have a friend to stay.

Margaret and I were very happy to agree.

"His name is George Radcliffe. He comes from Overthorpe ..."

"Another Yorkshireman then."

"Yes, and another lawyer, too. He was called to the bar at Gray's Inn earlier this year. He's very bright; he was my pupil for a year or so. I think he will do well as a barrister, as he has a devious mind!!"

"Truly, Charles? Then I shall have to try to find him some work."

Radcliffe arrived three days ago. He has a manservant with him. At dinner we have found him witty and charming, and rather religious. He makes many allusions to Jesus and the Gospels when he talks. He comes out riding and walking. He is of medium height, looks fit, and is clean shaven. As we both had Charles as our tutor at different times, we had quite a bit in common.

He is a widower, and he is only twenty-seven. I should hate to lose Margaret that early in life; in fact I should hate to lose her at all. That's a morbid thought.

It's going to be quite a large gathering for Christmas Day, as my Aunt, my Mother's sister Mary, is coming for a few days with her husband, Sir Francis Trappes, and two of their children. I understand one of them, Anne, is rather lovely now.

Margaret. 5th January, 1619. Wentworth Woodhouse.

It is Twelfth Night tonight, and I have organised a party. Well, there are so many people staying here, or coming this evening, that it will be more like a ball, but I don't want it to be as grand as that. I just hope everyone will be happy and relaxed. They will all go home tomorrow, apart from Charles Greenwood. He'll still be working here. It has certainly been a happy time so far. Our cooks have done a splendid job with the food, and despite the wine flowing freely, no-one has been drunk or objectionable in any way.

I've been particularly taken by George Radcliffe, though I find him very formal. He has been so kind to my sister-in-law, Anne, and I suggested to Thomas that he should talk to her about letting George try his hand at some of the legal problems arising from her late husband's estate. Thomas kissed me and said: "How often we think along the same lines. I've been wondering whether to do that. I've enough to do with Court cases, Parliament, and all our own affairs. In fact, I've been so impressed by his grasp of the law when we have talked about our estate, and I've a good mind to ask him to do some work for us, too."

"Then you'll have to ask Peter Man to brief him and see what happens. You're so busy with your thumbs pulling plums from so many pies, Peter won't be sending you to London much longer."

"How right you are, Margaret."

"There's another thing. You know how prettily your cousin Anne has turned out."

Thomas smiles. "Any relative of mine is bound to be attractive. Anyway, what has that to do with George Radcliffe?"

“You can be so blind about some things, Thomas. Haven’t you noticed how he always seems to be looking at Anne, or talking to her, or making sure he sits next to her at dinner?”

“Actually, no I haven’t. Are you scheming, you old matchmaker?”

“Oh! Get away from me Thomas. I’ll wager he sits next to her tonight, and doesn’t give her much chance to dance with anyone else, either.”

Thomas laughs. “Well on the first point, I heard you talking to the housekeeper about the table plan, so I know you’ve put them together. As old Higgins used to say, ‘Do you think I’m deaf, dumb, blind, and silly?’ And what about the second point. What do I get if you lose the dancing bet?”

“I have to make love to you once tonight.”

He laughs again. “Fair enough. And what do you get if I lose?”

“You have to make love to me twice. Then I win either way.”

I am Moving Up.

Thomas. 30th September, 1619. London.

Yesterday I arrived back in town for legal and other business when the new term starts. Today I go to the Palace in the hope of being noticed and picking up the latest gossip. I am lucky. I pick up a great piece of gossip, and am then noticed by the subject of it.

When I say gossip, I don't mean rumour or scandal. This item is true. Villiers is now Earl of Buckingham!! He is still charming, and very friendly, and anxious to help people who are willing to help him, but he seems to have no political motives. He is not yet a power behind the throne, or even in front of it, as Somerset was, but it is coming, I am sure. His influence just seems to come from the fact that the King is charmed by him, and will give him anything he wants, either for himself or for anyone who asks his help.

As I'm wandering about in one of the ante-chambers, he comes in, and notices me. I have no idea how he knows who I am, but someone may have pointed me out to him. Come to think of it now, I saw Sir John Savile in another room earlier. He was very pleasant but it was probably Sir John who manoeuvred the Earl in my direction, judging by what happens. Rumour (and I mean rumour) has it that Savile is a sycophant of Buckingham's, though he probably thinks he is the Earl's friend! Margaret was right. I don't trust Savile. He is a snake, as she said.

Buckingham comes up to me with a slight and polite nod of the head, and I make him a rather deeper bow. He must be over six feet tall, slightly taller than me, very fair, and very handsome indeed. He is beautifully dressed in a regal blue velvet doublet over a startlingly white linen shirt with ornate lace cuffs and collar. No wonder the King loves him. Women must gasp with anticipation!! Heavens, it sounds as though I love him myself. Not a bit of it, but I fail to see why a man should not appreciate a person of beauty, no matter what the sex.

Villiers. Sir Thomas, is it not?

Me. It is, My Lord. I trust you are well.

Villiers. I am, I am. And you?

Me. I should be better if I had a position at Court, My Lord.

Villiers. Then you must let me know if any particular place might suit you, and I'll raise the matter with His Majesty.

Me. You are too kind, My Lord.

Villiers. Too kind? Too kind, Sir Thomas? Can one be too kind? Perhaps not. But I should be grateful if you could see your way clear to doing me a kindness.

Me. If I can, it would be an honour.

Villiers. Your neighbour, Sir John Savile, has asked me to remind you to honour a promise he says you made him some time ago.

Me. A promise to do what, My Lord?

Villiers. A promise to do with the post of Custos Rotulorum for Yorkshire, I believe. You are the *Custos,* are you not?

Me. I am, My Lord. When Sir John resigned from the position, he offered to put my name forward and then I was offered and accepted it. I recall no promise.

Villiers. No promise. No promise, you say? Sir John tells me that when he arranged for you to get the Custos-ship, he asked you to resign in due course if he wanted the position back. He says you agreed.

Me. My Lord, I am embarrassed. If I tell you the truth so that we can both act with honour in this matter, I shall probably risk offending you and Sir John.

Villiers. You need have no fear of telling me the truth. I know from Sir John that his enemies caused him a great deal of trouble in Star Chamber to such an extent that he felt it prudent to hand over his office as Custos until the air had cleared and he could resume it.

Me. Then I must disabuse you, My Lord. Sir John is an ambitious and arrogant man who ....

Villiers. *(He smiles charmingly and disarmingly so that I cannot possibly take offence).* And you are not Sir Thomas?

Me. *(I cannot help laughing).* I am indeed, but I hope that I am not also unscrupulous and hot tempered. Savile's hot temper is the cause of the trouble. He apparently assaulted a fellow magistrate, Sir Edmund Sheffield, who was President of the Council of the North at the time, and in other ways brought disrepute on the office of *Custos,* which is why Sir Edmund referred the man to the Star Chamber.

Villiers. Interesting. Interesting. It never occurred to me to ask Sir John to be specific as to who these enemies were, nor why they were his enemies.

Me. And you will be aware My Lord, that in his judgment on the case, Lord Ellesmere ...

Villiers. The late Lord Chancellor.

Me. Indeed, the Lord Chancellor. In his judgment he said that Savile was disorderly and passionate in his behaviour, which ill became a man in his position.

Villiers. I wasn't aware of that. Savile did not mention it. Didn't mention it. Are you suggesting that he misled me?

Me. You must draw your own conclusions, My Lord, but it seems to me that the conduct which took him to the Star Chamber and which caused him to resign and led to my getting the post, makes him singularly ill-suited to that post.

Villiers. And the promise? The promise to let him have the office back?

Me. There was no such promise, My Lord. I recall that he made a joke about my doing so, but he laughed, I treated it as a jest, and I promised him nothing.

Villiers. Thank you, Sir Thomas. One might be forgiven for thinking that it would be inappropriate to restore a hot-tempered, unscrupulous and disorderly man to so important a position.

Me. Indeed, My Lord.

Villiers. Hmmm. I must apologise if I have given any offence by raising this matter with you when I was not in possession of all the facts ... not in possession of all the facts.

Me. No offence taken, My Lord, and I know none was intended. You would have had no reason to doubt or question Savile's word.

Villiers. You are gracious, Sir Thomas, and I shall be more circumspect another time.

Unlike Margaret, he doesn't always know a snake when he sees one. He walks away, greeting and chatting with place-seekers and fortune hunters as he goes, and charming all. I dare say I shall have to watch out for the reptilian Savile henceforth. So should the Earl.

It will also pay me to keep my eye on this Earl of Buckingham. He is, as I say, on the verge of being a real power with the eye and ear of the King. He has not only supplanted Carr, Earl of Somerset. He has also seen off the Howards in the shape of the Duke of Suffolk and the Earl of Nottingham. They were Carr's backers, and used him to gain control of the government after Robert Cecil died in 1612. After Carr's disgrace, Suffolk's wife tried to foist onto James an effeminate fool called Monson. This act of procurement was not a success, but it made Villiers see the red mist.

It also made him take his first political step, although whether he saw it like that is another matter. He sought out Sir Arthur Ingram. Ingram is another reptile. . He may have started out as a barrow boy in London, but he has a big business now, and is a member of the Guild of Drapers and Haberdashers. His particular talent is as a go-between in financial matters, and he was well-known to serve the Howards in that capacity. His loyalty is not as developed as his monetary acumen.

Approached by Buckingham for information, he therefore had no difficulty in revealing that there were certain irregularities in the way Suffolk, as Lord Treasurer, discharged his duties. Buckingham then went to Lionel Cranfield, a senior figure at the Treasury, and between them he and Lionel persuaded the King to set up an inquiry. This inquiry was held in Star Chamber. It found that Suffolk had declined a pension from Spain but acquired one for his wife for a thousand a year; he had his builder paid from the Treasury for work at his homes; from which large sums had gone missing for which he had no explanation, and similarly with money which was supposed to go towards the Irish debt. The Earl of Nottingham was by that time senile, but the corruption in the Admiralty, which had enriched him, was laid at his door as Lord High Admiral. He and Suffolk were dismissed from their posts, and Suffolk was smacked with a huge fine.

The fate of Nottingham was especially humiliating, since he had been the commander of the English fleet which (with the assistance of the weather) had defeated the Spanish Armada thirty years before.

As I see it, nothing now stands in George Villiers' path to control of the King and government policy if he wants it. It seems like blasphemy to me (though Kings don't get prosecuted and in any case James is Head of the Church) that the King is supposed to have said that "Christ had his John, and I have my George." I heard that from Arthur Ingram. He told me that the King came to the christening of one of his sons some years ago and said this to the guests!!

I suppose Arthur Ingram's about fifty or so now. He has a reputation as a fixer and a crook, and this extends even to his matrimonial adventures. Everything is money to him, it seems. After his first wife died, by whom he had had children, he married a young widow, Mistress Holyday. Of course, I did not know him then, but this is what I have been told. Arthur had been knighted by the King in July 1613, 'for services to the Crown', mainly consisting of lending money, or finding men who could lend it and getting them to do so.

Knighthood raised his status above tradesman, even if it couldn't make him a gentleman, but this enhanced status meant he could look around for a new and profitable wife.

Apparently Mistress Holyday was a pretty and rather delicate creature, with one very attractive feature so far as Arthur was concerned. Her deceased husband had been a rich merchant in London, and had provided her, on his death, with an inheritance of sufficient capital to produce an income said to have been three thousand pounds a year. How did he get her to marry him? He could be sly and wily in business and politics; perhaps he could turn these talents into charm if he needed to.

He would definitely have needed to, since he must have been over forty then, and he was never what you could call handsome, or even attractive, but short, corpulent, and coarse. She, on the other hand, had apparently been besieged by a host of admirers, and it was said that in picking Arthur she had chosen the worst of them. They were married in September 1613.

The new Lady Ingram did not have much luck. Within nine months she gave Arthur a son, and then died four months later. But Arthur was three thousand a year better off. He had all the luck; but then he made a lot of it, even if the making was not a choice way of carrying on.

Over the years he had lent a lot of money to Sir Edward Grevile. Now Edward was a real gentleman from an old family with estates in Warwickshire. He owed money to others as well as Arthur. And Edward had daughters, including one called Mary. Arthur told Edward he would buy his estate for 21,000 pounds, and marry Mary. He should have paid more for Edward's land, but Arthur had knocked off the dowry in fixing the price, so he did very well.

He let Sir Edward go on living in the house and grounds, but Arthur enjoyed the rents from most of the farms and other properties on the estate. Fortunately for Mary she and Arthur were happy, and she had more children for him.

I do not criticise Arthur for getting married and remarried in rapid succession. That is how things are, especially in the upper classes. Rich men do not look after their own children on a day to day basis. That is what a wife is for, and if you lose one, you look around for another. What varies from case to case is how much cash is involved, and whether it is more important than any other factor.

Thomas. 1st November, 1619. Yorkshire.

I have been home a month.

"Your father is dead, Sir Thomas."

I do not move. I might not have heard. I stand leaning, palms down, on the stone balustrade, looking out from the rear terrace of the house over the Yorkshire landscape. One foot is thrust forward, knee bent, the other leg straight. The servant might have thought I look much as a sea captain must look on the poop deck of a galleon. Not that Smeaton would really know what a sea captain looks like. He's only ever seen a galleon in some of the pictures in the big house. He's never seen the sea, but he has been to Sheffield twice. Some of the people in the village have never been out of it.

He decides to try again; "Sir William is dead, Sir Thomas."

I straighten and turn to the old steward with a distinctly unemotional expression. "He's been dead for eight years, Smeaton."

Smeaton gives a little bow. "Sir," he says.

I move to him and put a hand on his shoulder, and smile, sadly. I pause. "Why did you feel you had to remind me he is dead?"

"The way you were standing, Sir. You looked like you expected the Master to come walking up here through those fields, and the park, just like the old days."

"Then you must have been reading my mind." I look away from Smeaton, and back across the park and the fields beyond. That was exactly what I had been thinking. How I wanted my father to come striding, or riding, as he was wont to do, across that park. He was only about forty-four or so. That wasn't old. How could he have been taken from me so soon?

Tears roll down Smeaton's cheeks. "Sir William was a fair Master, Sir Thomas."

"He was a good father, too. Too good in many ways. Even if he left me eight brothers and sisters to feed, and a mother to care for."

Smeaton dries his eyes on his sleeve. “And you’ve had the Lady Anne to look out for, and her two children; and her a widow three months before your Father died.”

This makes me laugh, short and sharp. “Why, what a Job’s comforter you are Smeaton. As if I could forget my big sister and her brood!” I run my fingers through my short, dark hair. I begin to stride back towards the house.

Smeaton, somewhat shorter than my five foot eleven, does his best to keep up, but his rather rotund figure and fifty-nine years makes this a struggle. “Sir,” he pants, “shall I call the staff into the Hall so that you can tell them the er, the er....”

“...the news?” I slow down as Smeaton comes up and I say, “Yes, do that. I’ll speak to them as soon as I’ve seen my mother.” I stop, and catching Smeaton by the arm, look him straight in the face. “Smeaton, I’m not still grieving for my father. But I do still miss him. And now I could do with his wise counsel.”

Smeaton starts crying again. “I know, Mast... Sir Thomas. I haven’t been steward here, and a servant before that, for nigh on forty year without knowing you’re a close family.”

I turn aside to wipe my own eyes with my sleeve. I can’t bring myself to use a handkerchief in front of even so loyal a servant. “Thank you, Smeaton. My father and grandfather counted on you. I count on you, too, even with Mr Marris here.”

Smeaton goes off in search of the staff. I stand still a moment, staring at the Tudor house as though never before had I seen the oblong stone blocks rising to the red bricks of the first floor, with large rectangular windows. With a sense of wonder I find myself thinking the same thoughts I had when Dad died: “This is all mine now. All this Manor of Wentworth, and the one at Gawthorpe too.” I recall that I blushed with shame. “By God, Thomas,” I recall muttering to myself, “how can you say that? Your Father only dead a few days and all you can think about is the money?” As I do so another little voice whispers to me: “But you have to be realistic, don’t you, Thomas?”

Entering through the double doors from the terrace I make straight for my Mother’s bedroom. I had never had the heartlessness to ask her to go to live in the dower house next to the Church in Hooton Roberts, which Father had had built twenty-one years ago. As I run up the oak staircase I stumble as another old thought struck me: I was only twenty-one when Dad died! I recall thinking then: "How am I to do it all? A Mother, nine brothers and sisters, and two nephews to provide for, and four manors to run from which to secure enough of a living for all of us! With Dad dead I really need to retrieve my digit from the fundamental orifice."

Mother is sitting by her window, reading. She looks up.

"Mother, I am on my way. I have been appointed a member of the Council of the North!!"

"Why Thomas, your Father would have been so proud of you! So very proud. And so am I. But why has this come about? Or should I ask how it has?"

I am slightly shocked. Mother's question is one I had not yet considered. I scratch my head, then my chin, and begin to stride about the room. "I'm not sure. I've worked quite hard at being Keeper of the County Records, and I've kept my eye on the clerks who help me. I think I have a fair reputation for honesty locally, and I'm known to work hard."

"Nobody gets these places without some kind of patronage or influence from on high, my son. Who is watching out for you?"

"I really don't know. Perhaps.... You know Mother, you've surprised me. You're more political than I thought."

"Thomas, your Father may not have got far politically – well, to be honest he never tried. But he was very wise and knew all the nuances of the system. I could hardly be married to him all those years without learning something, now could I?"

I smile. "No Mother, you couldn't. And yes, Mother, Dad was wise. I've always missed him, but being on the Council without him behind me will be so hard. I shall be sorely in need of his guidance."

"You will, Thomas, but you have Charles Greenwood and Christopher Wandesford to talk to, and they are sensible young men."

"You're right, Mother; between the three of us we must have almost as much in the way of brains as Dad did." I pause. "I wonder. If I have a patron, it might be Buckingham. He might have put my name forward as a quid pro quo for letting him see that Savile is an untrustworthy reptile."

"Perhaps. I fear you may have acquired an enemy there, Thomas."

"That's what Margaret thinks."

****

Then I go down to tell the staff, all gathered in the hall as Smeaton promised, that I am now on the Council of the North, and we may have a larger number of important visitors to deal with in future. I shall rely on them to care for the strangers within our gates.

The Council is a body appointed by the King to rule the Northern half of England for him. Because he is two hundred miles or so away in London the King needs men he believes he can trust to carry out his policies, keep the peace, and be able to deal effectively with emergencies. If it takes a messenger, or a team of them, two or three days to get to London with a message, and another two or three to get back with the King's orders, without such men a real disaster could occur in the meanwhile.

Mother says she's proud of me. Father might well have been proud of me if he had still been amongst the living. Although I am pleased to be on the ladder, I'm far from satisfied. I want – or rather, lust after – a place at Court. I go there often enough – in fact, as often as I can. I'm getting known, but not sufficiently. Perhaps, in many ways, I do myself few favours.

I'm not fashionable. I have my hair cut the way I want it to look. Everyone else has theirs done to ape Prince Charles or Buckingham. I'm a bit too puritanical for that. I favour black clothes with a little white linen showing, and very little gold and jewellery. Most courtiers go about looking like a dummy out of a goldsmith's shop – and that's just the men!

I don't mean I am a Puritan. I belong to the Church of England, but I'm not really enamoured of High Church ritual. It seems a bit too much like Popery to me, but that seems be the emerging trend. No, I don't dress in style, and I don't worship in style. And I can see that I annoy people, especially a lot of important people.

I lack that easy-going way of talking to people I don't know well. Upper-class people have ways of speaking, phrases they use, expressions, which are instantly recognisable to those in the know. They use them, and if you don't respond in the right way, with the same sort of mannerisms, they know you're not one of them, and then they treat you differently. They then use subtle ways to humiliate you, and to let you know that you're not quite good enough. Well, that's how I feel.

The graduations of society are numerous, and largely to do with property and wealth, or the lack of it, as well as sheer 'class', which is what most of the real aristocracy possess - Dukes and Earls from families whose ancestors have been Dukes and Earls for generations.

The mistake I'm making is to think that I'm as good as they are, and to try to demonstrate that that is so. I tell people about my family, and the claim (or myth or legend, it may be) that I am descended from John of Gaunt. It is boring. And vain. And looks like inferiority making a cloak for itself. I can see that. For the most part people take little notice, but occasionally someone lets me know they've heard enough; that they are fed up with it. One Lord told me: "If you were King you'd be so insufferably high and mighty, I'd become a rebel!"

Getting onto the Council of the North is not exactly getting high and mighty, but Arthur Ingram has been its secretary since 1612. What he doesn't know about money and business and property up North isn't worth knowing. He's been Controller of Customs for the Port of London since 1601. Men don't get big salaries for these jobs. Their task is to make sure the customs dues and taxes are paid for the King, and they are expected to reward themselves by taking a percentage of the revenue they collect. It is a system open to all sorts of corruption, and men like Ingram can make a fortune out of it. And he does.

As Arthur was so embroiled in the financial chicanery surrounding Parliament and the King, he **was** able to prevent the suppliers of goods and services from swindling the King. He knew how to do that, and how to profit from it, too. Any one who wanted to do business with the Court, from selling meat to the cook or bedding to the housekeepers, had to go through or be paid by Ingram or his minions. To keep him sweet they supplied him for free with most of what he wanted, or just added to their bill the amount of any bribe they paid him.

Of course, the Court soon got fed up with having this working class *nouveau riche* merchant sucking up to everyone, and being so lacking in subtlety with his manners and his sharp practices, that he was sent packing. Did he vanish from sight? Not at all; he used the money he had made to buy property and develop it, and become richer still. Over the years I expect I shall learn a lot from him.

Henry Clifford. March, 1620. London.

Thomas has been here quite a lot lately. He is a hive of activity all on his own. He is desperate to get some sort of office under the Crown. He may be a Member of the Council of the North, but he says he wants a really important post down here in the capital. Mind you, I don't think he goes about it in quite the right way. He's not sufficiently suave, or even diplomatic.

What he tells people is whatever he thinks. The fact that it might upset them never seems to occur to him. Let's take an example.

There's a rather low life money broker at Court. His name is Sir Arthur Ingram.

It seems his father was some sort of tradesman in York, and Arthur came down here to make his fortune. His methods of doing so are, to put it mildly, rather suspect. I came upon him and Thomas recently. They were talking about Thomas's desire to buy into the peerage, apparently something Arthur Ingram knows how to arrange – provided some of the silver sticks to his own palm. Being an Earl's son, I find this kind of talk rather odious, and it annoys me that Thomas indulges in it. On the other hand I recognise that if he wants to get on, he has little choice.

Anyway, I wanted to change the subject, so I asked Ingram how his litigation with Sir Edward Waterhouse was going. How anyone can boast about conduct which is little better than criminal, I do not know, but that is what Ingram did. He explained that he had been buying a lot of property in Yorkshire, and had agreed to buy two manors from Sir Edward. There were some problems over the title deeds, and Ingram, who had taken possession of these manors, and was enjoying the rents and other income from them, used these problems as an excuse to delay paying most of the 6000 pounds purchase price.

Sir Edward was already hard up, which is why he wanted to sell in the first place, and his finances just went from bad to worse whilst Arthur held on to the property, the income from it, and the purchase money. Arthur was very proud of his conduct. He clearly thought this was the right way to conduct business. Thomas was clearly appalled. He told Ingram, in front of me, that haggling over the price after the deal had been struck, and trying to beat the seller down, was dishonest and dishonourable, and conflicted with his own sense of justice and fair play.

Fortunately Ingram has boot-leather for skin, so he laughed, and told Thomas that if he wanted to get rich, he'd have to learn, and Arthur would be the one to teach him. Unfortunately not everyone is as tolerant of Thomas's forthright utterances, and he will make enemies, and lose friends.

Mind you (I wish I could stop saying that), Thomas has made some very good friends at Court, and I don't just mean me. Archbishop Abbott thinks highly of him, largely because their religious views are similar. Sir George Calvert, another MP, like Thomas, for Yorkshire, and now one of the Secretaries of State, is close to him. Lord Doncaster is a friend, and so is his wife, Lucy; she was a Percy, a sister of the Earl of Northumberland. Lucy was and is the most beautiful woman at Court, and I cannot help noticing that Thomas seems rather interested in her, even if he is married to my sister, Margaret. Not that he does anything about it. Not yet, anyway. But I digress.

Back to Sir Arthur Ingram. Thomas might learn a lot about making money from him, but he would have to abandon his principled approach to business, and his desire to deal honestly with his neighbour, as the parable calls our fellow man. That would be a pity.

Thomas may be stiff and lacking in warmth to those he does not know well, but his frankness and candour are what make him what he is, and are such a refreshing change from the oily front presented by those who tell you what they think you want to hear, and not what they really think. Thomas is a formidable character, and you know exactly where you stand with him.

Margaret. 9th September, 1620. Yorkshire.

Thomas arrived home from London yesterday. He was exhausted, but that did not stop him talking about Parliament and Government, and his anxiety to get back into Parliament. We sat at dinner, just the two of us. I could not bear to have to share him with anyone else when I had not seen him for weeks. I had had the servants lay our places close together, with a pentangle candelabra near us, shedding what I hoped would be a romantic glow.

Romance was not what occupied Thomas, however. He was full of encounters with Buckingham, and his gradual engrossment of the power of the state on behalf of the King. He was full of praise for the changes in Prince Charles, who, he told me, was becoming more confident with each passing day, but remained a contemplative, reserved, and somewhat hesitant character.

"Undoubtedly his friendship with Buckingham is working these changes. Before Charles's brother Henry died, he was so shy, whilst Henry shone like the handsome beacon he was. The favourite is so easy-going, and charming, he is not awed by anyone, and the Prince looks up to him and goes about with him, so to some extent he is put at his ease too. This makes him easier to talk to, and the readier to enter into conversation."

I was intrigued. "Why should the heir to the throne be shy? Who is likely to worry him, or be condescending to him?"

"Difficult to say. His brother was such a young god, with so much energy, spirit, and sheer joy about him, Charles must always have been in his shadow. Henry was so popular, too. Charles is too diffident to attract that kind of adulation. There's something else, too."

"What's that?"

"I'm not sure, really, but I just get the feeling that he doesn't trust people."

I smiled. "But you just said he looks up to Villiers. You don't look up to people you don't trust."

"True, but that's different. To Charles, Villiers must shine like the sun."

This time I laughed. "Then Charles can only be a planet. Not very encouraging for the man who is born to be King,"

Thomas paused, and looked at me thoughtfully, before saying: "You're right. Perhaps, when he is King, he's going to need someone bigger and more decisive than Villiers to help him."

"And I wager you know just the man, and he's sitting right opposite me at this table!"

Thomas laughed in his turn. "Don't be silly, Margaret."

"Don't tell me I'm silly, Thomas. I know you. Who wants the best place he can get at Court? Who thinks constantly of the best way to run Yorkshire and the country? Who has ideas about getting the most out of the King, Lords, and Commons, for the benefit of the country? And who honestly thinks that no-one could do it all better than he can?"

Thomas looked very serious: then he slowly smiled. "Sometimes, my love, you know me better than I know myself."

"I haven't known you for weeks, Thomas. Take me to bed."

And he did, but he fell asleep as soon as he lay down.

Thomas. 9th September, 1620. Yorkshire.

I'm having the most marvellous erotic dream. I'm lying on my back. I can feel long, soft, warm hair floating across my thighs and the V of my groin. Lips are wrapped around my member, slithering wetly up and down, up and down, while a tongue glides over the head of it so exquisitely that I shudder with the sheer pleasure of it. I am in one of those odd states when I know I am asleep and I know I'm dreaming, and I do not – do not – want the dream to end. This tongue is imparting so elemental a pleasure that it has a likeness to some sort of torture, and I shudder again, and again. And then again. And it wakes me.

It is Margaret's hair on my thighs. It is Margaret's mouth inflicting this incredibly enjoyable torture. As I open my eyes I can see that her beautiful buttocks are near my face, and her knees are either side of my waist, and I can feel her nipples pressing into my stomach. I want to seize her and make love to her. Yet I don't. I want her to go on doing this until I can take it no longer, and come gloriously. My dick feels like a skittle held upside down, with the thick end at the top, she has aroused me so.

I feign sleep for a minute, and another, and a fourth and fifth. I cannot keep it up. Her quim is so near my face, I just raise my head slightly and lick it. She is wet; excited. She emits a sigh somehow, but doesn't take her lips from me. Maybe I only feel the sigh. I lick slowly with long strokes, and stick my tongue in deeply. I lift my hands off the sheets, and slide them, palms up, between her body and mine, and hold her breasts, and run my thumbs round her nipples, which harden further.

I begin to moan. My body stiffens as I feel the beginnings of orgasm, and I think she will recognise the signs and stop. It is more than I can do to stop her, and she goes on, manipulating me in the warm sanctuary of her mouth, and I flood into her.

She turns around, and smiles at me. She is so beautiful. I think: "I'll make her pregnant this morning; I could make love to her all day." And I go straight back to sleep.

An hour or so later, and I wake, and Margaret is gently playing with me, and stroking herself – stroking what she calls her Parliament. She's been calling it that for some time now; in fact, since I got into the House of Commons again. When I asked her what she called it that for she said: "Thomas, you're a Member now, and I want my Member in my Parliament."

I need no prompting. I kiss her nipples; I assist her with the stroking; and I introduce my member to the House as soon as she's ready. Please God I make her pregnant this time!!

Thomas. 12th December 1620. Yorkshire.

A few days ago the most awful news began to spread through England. It was about the King's beautiful daughter Elizabeth. At the start of 1614 she had married Frederick, Elector Palatine of Germany. In 1619 in Hungary the people had risen up against the Austrian Empire and its Emperor. They didn't want to be ruled from Vienna any more. They wanted to be free and to have their own king in Prague. They asked Frederick to be their monarch, and Frederick accepted. His principality, the Palatinate, was on the Rhine, and a long way from Hungary, so he had to go there.

The English people are delighted. Frederick is a Protestant standing up to the most powerful Catholic ruler in Europe, if not the world: the Emperor of the Austro-Hungarian Empire. The national wish is for an English Army to go to Europe to fight alongside Frederick and his Hungarians. However, King James does not want a war. For one thing he knows wars are very costly. Secondly, he knows that even if the people want war, they would not want higher taxes to pay for it, and Parliament, if called, would not vote for more tax. Thirdly, he wants to marry Prince Charles into the Spanish Royal Family, believing that he would then, with the help of the Spanish King, have enough clout to secure a peace between Frederick and the Emperor.

In the end all this daydreaming on both sides came to nought, because on 20th November 1620, at the Battle of the White Hill outside Prague the Emperor's army defeated Frederick's forces utterly. That was the news which made us all so sad. But it didn't mean that the King will send an army, or that Parliament and people would pay for it, even if that is what they say they want.

****

All that is not so remote from my story as it may seem, since it is in fact quite significant. It shows me that politics, and politicians, can be quite stupid. One side wants to do something they do not want to have to pay for, and the other side wants to try to get the same result by a different means that costs little, and neither side will listen, and no-one will give way. It is a dialogue of the deaf. No-one can admit that the other chap's idea might be better, and working together is hardly ever tried. This discovery will make a difference to the way I try to do things if I ever get to have any power.

****

However, I am cheered up by the fact that the King has called for a new Parliament to be elected, and I am to stand as a candidate again. I've asked Sir Arthur Ingram to help me. I know that wily old bird Sir John Savile will do all he can to defeat me, so I need a wily old bird of my own to make sure I win. I have another good card in my hand: Sir George Calvert will be the other MP for Yorkshire if we get in, and he is a Secretary of State, one of the most important people in the land. On the other hand, whilst he comes from Yorkshire, he hasn't been here much for a long time as his office requires him to live in London and travel about with the King. That may mean that local voters do not pay much attention to him.

None of that bothers Sir Arthur. He says he can drum up a large mob to shout for me and Calvert on the hustings. He also tells me to ask the Sheriff – who has to summon the freeholders to vote – to be firmer than usual in telling the people to vote. He also wants the Sheriff to tell us which men don't turn out for us. I think that may be going a bit too far, but as there's little point in owning a dog and barking myself, I do what he says, even if this dog might come back to bite me.

The hustings from which the candidates make their speeches, and seek the votes of the electorate, are noisy, and can be violent, places. Violence is common.

In Yorkshire, for example, if I were speaking in Ripon, say, or Rotherham, my supporters would be there, shouting for me and Calvert, and cursing Savile and any other candidate. And then a bunch of thugs from Savile's side might tear in and start clubbing my supporters, and an affray would get going until the constables and the Sheriff show up. The next day, Savile or one of his colleagues might be speaking in Hallam, and my men would go and attack his people. When I say clubbing, that is exactly what I mean; all these bruisers carry big sticks and clubs and worse weapons, and the bloodshed can be frightful.

And it isn't just violence. Some big landowners like me – well, not like me - pay people to vote for them, and some – as I've said before – threaten their local people with losing their farm if they do not vote the right way. None of the ordinary farmers can afford to fight a big landowner, like an Earl or someone with a huge estate (and I am getting that way myself) through the Law Courts, so these threats can be very real.

I don't go in for that myself as I am always interested in small people getting justice, and I cannot bring myself to be that big a hypocrite.

Thomas. 31st January, 1621. Westminster.

The State Opening of Parliament is today. King James rode down on his horse with Prince Charles, the Prince of Wales. It was a splendid sight, though nothing like as grand as a French King would have; after all the French monarch barely needs to seek the approval of his *Parlement* for anything, and is not answerable to or likely to be criticised by it, as our King is. The royal pair was accompanied by a score or so of armed retainers in royal livery.

It is splendid, too, that he brought the Prince with him. He'll have to run the Kingdom eventually. It's a good idea to give him some idea of how to go about it.

On the way to St. Stephen's Hall the King did something he doesn't usually do; he waved to his subjects and blessed them. It was a common touch he rarely displays. I may not be a top-of-the-tree aristocrat, but I don't see myself as one of the people either. Even so, I can see the advantage from a political perspective of making the people think you love them, especially when you are the ultimate power in the country. I hope that is a lesson not lost on Charles.

However, what follows in Parliament is no guarantee that he will learn anything, unless it is how not to do things. The King talks in a relatively kind way to the Peers and the Members, but he is patronising, almost like a gentle father lecturing a wayward son on his behaviour. He is pedantic. He'd probably like to give them a book like the one he wrote for the instruction of his deceased son, Henry, the *Eikon Basilike*. He just tells us what he expects of us, and nothing about what he will do for the people. He speaks of the tragedies being enacted in Europe, and seeks our support (more like a demand, in truth) for his foreign policy. Then he asks us for unstinting aid, by which he means plenty of money.

I am a loyal subject, and believe in the over-ruling power of the Monarchy, but I am not at all impressed by this performance, even though I shall do what I can to smooth his path with Parliament. Still, I am quite nauseated when that sycophant, Francis Bacon, stands to praise the King and tells us all to remember our duty to this wonderful King of ours, and to revere him in a fitting manner. If my own feelings are anything to go by, and if I am any judge of how both Houses receive this tripe, the King has done himself no favours at all, and fulsome Francis will have fuelled the flames.

How many of these men, Lords or Commons, have any real idea what is going on in Europe, or what to do about it? Clearly they are upset about the fate of Frederick and Princess Elizabeth, and hate to think of the consequences for the Protestant states if the Emperor and the Spanish King win more battles such as the White Hill, but they have no solutions except a war they do not wish to pay for. Many are also very worried by the way England's trading position is going from bad to worse. The country's finances are diabolically poor, and that makes it hard for the King to get taxes, and difficult for the MPs to vote for them even if they wanted to (which they do not), and virtually impossible for the people to pay them.

There are more discharged soldiers in the streets and byways, some begging, and some turning to more violent and desperate measures to feed themselves. Poor people are everywhere. I am rich, but I cannot help them all. I do what I can on my estates, but I am resolved that when and if I get any real power, I shall see what I can do to make the Poor Laws work as they should.

All these problems are just driving the King and Parliament further and further apart. The King says his policies don't work because he is given no loans or subsidies. He says he hasn't had any for nine years. The Parliament says his policies are stupid so they won't give him any cash. Obstinacy on both sides rules the roost. Sitting down to negotiate a way forward never seems to occur to anyone.

The King wants a marriage between Prince Charles and the Spanish Princess, as he thinks if Spain is his ally, he will be able to get them to halt the war against the Protestants in Germany, Hungary and Holland,. That would be an inexpensive policy, if it worked. The last thing Parliament, and come to that, most of the country, want is anything to do with Spain at all except to send an army to fight the Catholic powers. Even if the King agreed, no-one would give him the money for a well-equipped army.

After the Opening Ceremony, and the King and Prince have departed, I decide to talk to my friend George Calvert about these things, and what might be done. "Were you impressed with the King's Speech, George?"

George ponders; he is not ponderous; he's small and neat, with brown hair worn fairly long, and a pointed brown beard, but he always ponders. I suppose you don't normally get to be a Secretary of State if you don't. "The King's right, of course. We have no power to make him do anything. And starving him of money to carry out his policies makes him resent having to have any sort of democracy at all."

"We just don't seem to have any control over what the Commons do."

Unusually quickly George comes back with: "We need a leader of the House. It was different under Good Queen Bess. She attracted a group of MPs who followed her lead and her policies and .... er ...."

"Manipulated?" I suggest.

George laughs. "That's somewhat Machiavellian, but let it serve. We have a number of clever men who could do the same sort of manip – let's say organising – it sounds better – the conduct of the King's business in the House."

"But even so, Elizabeth was always short of money. Well, that's what my Father always used to say."

George acknowledges that with a nod or two. "Yes, but she avoided calling Parliament as far as she could, and when she did so, she was so seductive with them. She might harangue old Salisbury and other ministers in private and in Council, but she never talked down to Parliament or the people. She had the knack of striking exactly the right note."

"You'd expect that from a skilled harpsichordist."

"Indeed you would. Maybe that's why she got more harmony than King James manages. But back to business. As I said just now, we need a leader to knit together those who support the King." That is what I shall try to do. It will be hard. Somehow I shall have to seem to be on the side of the House at the same time as I persuade it to do what the King desires. I can see myself getting crushed between these two massive rocks if I fail.

Thomas. 5th February, 1621. Westminster.

A few days ago, being worried about Roman Catholics and some Puritans, the House resolved that everyone has to attend a communion service in St Margaret's Westminster, and take the sacraments. Anyone who fails to do this will be excluded from the House. We think this will help ensure the safety of the Kingdom.

A couple of days later we passed a law that no Catholic should be in or near London, but must retire to his home in the country-side, and not move more than five miles away from it. On top of that we decided that no Catholics should come within ten miles of Parliament, or the Courts of the King and the Prince of Wales. This is bound to cause trouble; the King raises money by selling indulgences to the wealthy Catholics excusing them from attending the Church of England.

Parliament's purpose with these new laws is to guarantee that we do not see men of all faiths and none sitting in Parliament, but only those who follow Jesus in the way we think we are all supposed to do. Any advanced degree of toleration would shock Jacobean England to the core.

Thomas. 15th February, 1621. Westminster.

The first sessions of this 1621 Parliament hardly do the Members any credit. The first ten sitting days are mostly taken up with debating our Parliamentary privileges, and what we see as the King's attacks on them. He had assured us at the opening ceremony that we had Freedom of Speech in the House, and all our privileges were safe with him. We nurse our grievances as if they were sick children. We spend days deciding how to put our worries to the King, instead of just doing it.

Sir Edward Coke, a famous lawyer, large enough and with red hair to remind me of portraits of the last King Henry, tells the House that "The Prerogatives of Princes grow daily, but the liberties of subjects stagnate, and if once they are lost, they are in danger of never being regained".

All the time the House fails to consider properly the King's request for money. Yet on the question of Spain, he had explained to us, via the Lord Chancellor, that he had spent 100,000 pounds of his own money on help for the Elector Palatine, and 30,000 on ambassadors to try to negotiate. He also told us he had costed sending a military force to help Frederick and Elizabeth; the first year would cost 300,000 pounds, and if Parliament would not vote the money, he could not afford it.

We have a debate about the gradual rise and fall in the value of money. Trade is bad, and the country seems to be poor. The landed gentry in the House (including me) complain that there is not enough money in circulation, and that the price of land is falling, and our rents with it. I can vouch for that. I don't think I have ever been so hard up in my life. A ridiculous and trivial, reason for the disappearance of the currency in England is the fashion for jewellery, and gold ornamentation and gold thread on clothes, because gold bullion and coins are melted down to adorn the apparel of the rich!

A serious cause of this lack of cash is what we call the "Balance of Trade." In 1620 we sold only 1,100,000 pounds worth of goods abroad, but imported 1,300,000's worth.

At last we have a serious debate about money for the King and the government of the country! It is mixed up with our grievances. It is said that the greatest grievance is the King's need for money, and Parliament must find some for him. Without that, the loss of the Palatinate would be certain, and someone says that "foxes have holes, but the King's daughter, Elizabeth has no place where to lay her head." However, it is pointed out that an army of at least 25,000 foot and 5,000 cavalry would be needed. No wonder the King could not afford it.

Parliament would have to be generous. A small subsidy would be like a plaster which covered only a tiny bit of a huge wound, and would do no good.

In spite of a lot of talk to that effect, the House steers clear of being generous. Instead of giving an adequate subsidy or two for war to help the Elector and Elizabeth, and another to relieve the King's needs, the House gives two smaller subsidies "as a free gift and present of the Love and Duty of his subjects."

Calls for three grants, or enough to enable the King to take some realistic action, are rejected.

Thomas. 17th February, 1621. Westminster.

Yet another attack on Catholics!! Both Houses, Lords and Commons, have the Lord Chancellor deliver a Petition to the King. He is asked to take it seriously because it comes from both Houses, and is based on Law and Religion. Parliament is worried about the Papists flocking together, especially in London; bearing arms; practising their religion openly; spreading their corrupt faith, chiefly through their priests and the Jesuits; and their increasing numbers through their avoidance of the Law and its Penalties.

The King's reply is that any existing licences for Catholics to be excused Church of England worship would be looked into by the Privy Council; that he believes that disarming the Papists is already happening; that only foreign ambassadors could hear Mass, and if English Catholics attend these ceremonies they should be arrested; and, finally, that whilst the laws against the priest and Jesuits should be enforced, he does not believe, any more than the late Queen Elizabeth did, that men should be made to die for their religion.

We have more fun in the afternoon. The conflict between the different Law Courts, and their different jurisdictions, is the subject of debate. The Common Law Courts have different rules and different remedies, and apply the law in different ways. This can have comic results, if those results were not so expensive and disastrous for the litigants. Mr Fuller and Mr Hall had a dispute about land. Hall sued Fuller in the Court of Wards. The Court found in his favour, ordered Fuller out, and sent him to prison for disobeying the Court order.

At the same time Fuller sued Hall in the Courts of Chancery, and that Court gave judgment for him, ordered Hall out, and sent him to prison for disobeying its order. So both men are in the Fleet Prison!! This is a system of Justice?

Margaret. 21st February, 1621. London.

Thomas says I have been insufferable the last few days. He's joking, of course, but in a way he's right. I haven't been able to resist poking fun at him about George Radcliffe. I told him right at the start that something would go on between his cousin Anne and George, and it has. Soon after that Christmas party of ours three years ago George was invited to stay at the Trappes' home in Harrogate. A few months later he was at a house party at their other home in Nidd.

He's got a busy legal practice in London now, when he isn't in Yorkshire doing work for Thomas's sister Anne (not to be confused with the cousin!) and her boys, and he's doing more and more for Thomas. Christopher Wandesford has more or less replaced Charles Greenwood, who has moved on to other things, so between them George and Christopher, Richard Marris, and Peter Man are more or less running our estates and business affairs for Thomas, whilst he deals with politics and the North, and looks out for more opportunities for business and acquiring more land. I do admire his ability to get other people to do things for him and let them get on with it. I have a horrid feeling as time goes by he will find it harder to do that, because he does like things done his way, and to have his hand on the details. These four men do what he wants. Others may not be so willing and loyal.

George has been lucky to be making a good living in the law in London and up in York, because up there he was able to see cousin Anne regularly

But I digress. The point I want to make is that today was George and Anne's wedding in Harrogate. We should have been there, but Thomas is just too busy to get away and go all the way up to Yorkshire, and North Yorkshire at that. I dare say it would have been lovely, but Harrogate will be so cold now. It's bad enough down here, but just thinking about going back to the snow and ice makes me shiver.

I really shouldn't tell Thomas "I told you so" quite so often.

Thomas. 26th February, 1621. Westminster.

I was a very busy boy last week. The Commons has been considering the uses and abuses of the licensed trade in liquor. Many MPs have been worried that there are too many unlicensed and disorderly Inns and Ale-houses around the country. Behind some of this is the resentment of the granting of Patents by the King for cash. Once upon a time the responsibility for controlling the licensed trade was in the hands of the local magistrates, but the King granted a Patent to Sir Giles Mompesson to regulate the Inns. This had led to much corruption of which, it was suggested, Sir Giles was the beneficiary.

It was alleged he had been charging inn-keepers fees for building a new room on their inn, or a new staircase, or any other improvement.

He was supposed to enforce the licensing laws against disorderly houses, and take action in respect of Inns and ale-houses which had been opened without permission. What he was said to do, was to take bribes from the owners of such inns, and then take no action against them, even when other inn-keepers complained. He was also said to be charging exorbitant amounts for granting licences to build new inns.

He defended himself as best he could against these allegations, including saying that he was entitled to do some of it under an old law of Edward VI's from the 1550s. He came unstuck, though. When it was put to him that he had threatened a magistrate named Drake who had closed down an ale-house where the owner-brewer had plotted the murder of a guest staying in the tavern, he denied it. He denied he had granted the murderous publican a new licence, and when Drake objected to that and took the brewer to Court, Mompesson threatened to make his life a misery. This was a course he was said to have taken with anyone who objected to his unscrupulous and criminal behaviour, and with which he succeeded.

How did he come unstuck? What he did not know was that I had been given the letter in which he had threatened Drake. Making his life a misery was his euphemism for having him beaten up, or even assassinated, a practice he was alleged to use frequently. I insisted the letter be read to the House.

The House has to decide what to do with this villain, but today we learn that he had issued no fewer than 3500 writs against inn-keepers, and had had about a hundred of them outlawed. Bearing in mind that an outlaw was, as the name suggests, outside the law, he could be killed by anyone! Pretty drastic for merely having refused to pay bribes to Sir Giles, you might think.

Margaret. April, 1621. London.

Thomas has been so worried, although hardly anyone but me would know it. That snake, that ghastly Sir John Savile, has been trying to get the House of Commons to declare that the election of Thomas and our friend George Calvert was fraudulent. What a hypocrite! He started this nonsense in February, about a week after the King opened Parliament.

So Parliament set up the Committee of Privileges to look into it.

From what I can make out, and what I hear everywhere, Savile was bribing anyone he could think of to vote for him or his candidate, yet he complains because, he says, Thomas asked the Sheriff to word the summonses to vote very powerfully so that men knew they had to vote. What is wrong with that? I'm only a woman and don't even have the vote, but surely, if you have a chance to take part in an election which may express your views and wishes, isn't it only right that you should do so?

If you don't, how can you complain if the King's policies are not what you want, if you have no MP to speak for you? If they are what you want, shouldn't you vote for someone who can support them?

Still, I have to admit that perhaps – and I only say perhaps – Thomas should not have told the Sheriff to let him know who did not give their support. Of course, this is the problem with the way the voting is organised. On polling day, the men go to the village green or a square in town, and they have to hold up their hand for the candidate they fancy. That means that anyone can see who voted for whom, and the one who didn't get their vote may send some toughs round to give them a pasting.

Maybe one day women – well, upper class women - will get the vote, and we'll have voting on bits of paper so nobody knows who voted for this man or that.

Anyway, Thomas tells me that it is all over now, and the Committee decided he and Calvert had done nothing wrong, and that Savile had done the right thing in reporting what might have been an abuse. Clever really, to leave honour satisfied on both sides.

We had Calvert to dinner the other night. Considering he is so small, he contrives to look extremely elegant, a description usually reserved for taller men. He was not happy about the way things are going in the House. "I just don't seem to be able to hit the right note about the King's need for money, do I, Thomas?"

Thomas, as usual, was blunt. "That's not the problem. The Members just do not like the King's foreign policies. Until he agrees to send soldiers to fight on the Protestant side they will not help. Even so, they did vote him some subsidies."

George laughed. "Just about enough to put on two of those masques the Queen loves, but hardly enough to secure an alliance with Spain, which he wants, or a war against Austria, which they want."

"You're right, George, but I shall go home to Yorkshire to make sure that the money that has been voted is raised promptly there. I don't see how the people can hope for fair and competent government if they do not co-operate with the King and pay the taxes honestly."

I chimed in. "But won't the MPs see that as just bowing down, knuckling the forehead, to the King? The way I see it, they think that if they pay the piper, they ought to call the tune."

George laughed again. "Margaret has more brains than many of our colleagues in the House, Thomas. How will we men fare if women are educated, get the vote, and can enter Parliament?"

I hated Thomas's reply. "There are some things I prefer not to contemplate." But then he improved it a bit; not much, but a bit. "I have enough trouble dealing with the problems we already face than the ones beyond the horizon." I had to punish him for that, by not letting him make love to me that night. Well, I said "no" for ten minutes or so. If I'd held out much longer I'd have been as unhappy as it made him. Sometimes it would be nice if I didn't love him and enjoy sex quite so much.

Next week we shall go home and Thomas will make speeches telling the people in Rotherham and other towns to give the subsidies happily to the King if they want good government to last.

Thomas. April, 1621. Yorkshire.

Back home for a short while and very busy making speeches, and seeing people who matter; not much time for people who don't. Well, everybody matters, really, especially those who can vote, but there are very few people who truly count if you want to be successful in politics. You can always tell when a politician is conversing with someone who matters, because he looks interested. When he talks to someone who doesn't matter, he looks animated when he is speaking, but when the nobody speaks, a sort of glass screen comes **over the politician's eyes**, and you know at once that he's not really taking any notice. Unless you tell him how wonderful he is, of course.

What do I learn as soon as I get back here? Why, that Sir Arthur Ingram is buying a large estate called Temple Newsam, just outside Leeds, for 12,000 pounds. He's buying it from the Duke of Lennox, who was given it by King James. Of course, Lennox is the King's cousin, and a Scot, so James favours him, as he seems to favour most of his own countrymen. Come to think of it, the fact that George Villiers is not a Scot but still became the favourite, ousting Somerset and all comers, is yet another tribute to his looks, his skill, and his tenacious grip on the Royal Household.

Temple Newsam is a huge estate, including two coal mines and some other land. Rumour has it that Sir Arthur intends to build himself a palace on this new estate of his. The rumour is almost certainly true. I heard it from Peter Man, my solicitor, and he is rarely misinformed.

But 12,000 pounds? Where does Arthur get the money? I spent 1,500 on some land at Kirkby Malhamdale in 1618, but there was more money about then than now. And I bought the manor at Ledstone for about 5,000 pounds in 1617, and rebuilt the house in what I hope has been a stately fashion, but 12,000 all at once? It would be incredible if I did not know Arthur's business methods.

Thomas. May, 1621. London.

Back in the city again. The weather is warmer and the streets stink. It is a shame that the centre of power has to be here. Life would be so much more pleasant and kinder on the nose if Parliament met in a building in the fields of Yorkshire. I'd accept a field in Sussex or Northampton, or far away Devon! Never mind. I wasn't forced to come here. I volunteered, didn't I?

It's been a very busy few weeks. At home I met with deputations of fishermen from Whitby and other places on the coast, makers of knives and forks from Sheffield, and spinners and weavers from all over the county. They are very worried about trade. We should be worried about it, and them too, in Parliament. The wool and cloth business is one of the country's biggest exporters. If we don't do well there, the King's subsidies and taxes are a lost cause.

Even the cutlery people matter. They have been famous for three hundred years, since Edward III carried a Sheffield knife all the time, and left it to someone in his Will. The steel they make and the quality of their knives seem to be getting a fine reputation everywhere, not just here, but in Europe too. I'm told some of it even goes across to America, to these colonies in Virginia, because no-one there makes any of these things.

The fishermen's labours are an important source of food, especially in winter when there are no crops, and all the edible cattle have already been killed. This subject cropped up in the February sittings. It emerged, as a result of my talks with the fishermen, that many of them sail all the way to the fishing grounds off Newfoundland on the other side of the Atlantic. They may be away for weeks on these hazardous enterprises. They pack their catch in ice, and sail home to sell the fish in the London market at Billingsgate, and in Grimsby, Whitby, and Hull (good Yorkshire ports, those), Great Yarmouth, and ports and harbours on the west coast.

I speak in the House about all these things. I point out that the services of the fishermen are extremely important, and their trade and their prices should be protected. This is not just because of the food they produce. They are marvellous seamen, able to turn out for the navy in time of war, and their small trawlers are useful as auxiliary vessels, for harassing enemy shipping, and as fire ships to be sent amongst enemy fleets, as was done against the Armada.

Regrettably, too many of my Parliamentary colleagues care for nothing but their own money-making schemes and scratching each others' backs to concern themselves with what is in the best interests of the country, let alone the people on the bottom rungs of the ladder. Consequently such matters are ordinary Commons business, and do not usually arouse much passion. Not so with questions of religion. Nor with money.

The King always needs money. He cannot run the country without it. Despite my best efforts to get MPs to open the nation's purses (not just their own) Parliament refuses him any more taxes, loans or grants. They still want him to go to war with Spain (for being Catholic, basically), but won't give him the funds for an army. The King tries to raise cash by selling monopolies, and the House pursues Francis Bacon and a couple of others for being involved. Those others have been obliterated, but Bacon is on trial over the scandal. Poor Francis; the House in hot-bloodied pursuit of a victim is a shocking sight. I hope it isn't one I come to know myself.

The victims on the religious side are the usual suspects, the Papists and the Puritans. The Catholics are always in trouble because they do not go often enough to the services of the Church of England, but every now and again the same charge is levelled at the chapel and meeting-house worshippers. The member for Tavistock in Devon, John Pym, recently supported the making of a new law to enforce proper observance of the Sabbath Day. Its target was the Catholics; the object was to make more of them attend 'our churches', not 'theirs'. As usual, it also aimed to have fewer games (such as football and wrestling) and other entertainments on Sundays.

A Mr Sheppard, an unpleasant looking man with a predatory nose and a pock-marked face, whose constituency I can't recall, was outraged that we did all we could to fence the Roman worshippers in, but left the Puritans (who go to the 'wrong churches' too) alone. Being a devoted Protestant myself, of a Low rather than High Church order, with few truly denominational preferences, I much resented this attack on fellow Protestants, as Pym did. Albeit they may be Puritans, I cannot see that they represent any kind of threat to England. They have no Pope, no King of Spain, willing, indeed anxious, to reduce me and my compatriots to the status of Popish satraps.

Mr Sheppard's views outraged me in turn, and I vented my feelings in the House. "The Puritans are not an enemy. They have no desire to enslave England as yet another Spanish colony, or bind it with superstitious hocus pocus. For the most part they are honest Protestants, as we are, hard-working and loyal. Another Member may well say that we do not make mousetraps to catch Puritans, and maybe he thinks we should, but his views do nothing but offend our Protestant friends, and give comfort to those who would forfeit the religious freedom we value."

But back to finance. Not only does the Commons fail to get King James to attack Spain: he inflames them even further by continuing to sell weapons to the Spanish from the Royal Armouries and Arsenals. The fact that this gives employment and income to the country and to many people employed in the industry is ignored. Can Parliament accept that with a good, if disgruntled grace? After all, he is the King. No. Happily for the House and the King a whipping boy – almost literally - has appeared.

A bankrupt lawyer recently published a pamphlet making fun of the King and Queen of Bohemia, Fredrick and Elizabeth. Not a very tactful thing for him to do, when you recall that Elizabeth is James's daughter, and the darling of the Protestant cause, here and in Europe, but a really stupid thing for him to have done when you know that he is a Roman Catholic.

In the petty way of many politicians the Commons decides it has to punish this unfortunate, if very misguided, fellow, because it cannot punish the King. He was to be hauled before the House and tried by it in its capacity as a Court. The King then makes the situation even worse by taking the matter over himself. As a result one of the most tumultuous debates I have so far witnessed takes place. I use my legal training to argue in my speech that the King was legally entitled so to act, and that the Commons could not and should not take the matter any further.

This hardly increases my popularity in the House, but I am attracting attention. Perhaps the Monarch may receive reports that I'm not opposed to his policies, and support them whenever I feel it right to do so.

It is now Whitsun, and the King has called for the adjournment of Parliament. A large number of members is totally opposed to this move. They want to be able to go on taking the King to task over money, and Spain. The atmosphere during this debate is only marginally less toxic than during the debate about the punishment of the Catholic lawyer. I try to pour oil on the waters, and to calm the rather savage breasts of those endeavouring to keep the House in session.

"It was undoubtedly wrong of this Catholic gentleman" (there were sudden yells of "Gentleman? Traitor rather!"); "...very well – I agree with the Honourable Member that the man is a traitor to have spoken so of our beloved Princess Elizabeth and her husband, the Elector. But she, the Queen of Bohemia, is our venerated King's daughter, and if he feels it proper to overlook such treachery, is it for us to seek revenge on her behalf?

"Let us consider what it is we are really complaining about. Are we so desperately anxious to punish a foolish man for being a Catholic, and for speaking his mind in a partisan, Catholic way? Are we not speaking our minds in a Protestant fashion? Do we only do so because we have the freedom and privilege of the House to protect us? Or are we rather protesting against the King because he has not rectified all our grievances?

"What are those grievances? That he sells the rights to monopolies in goods, such as soap and cloth, to people who will fill his coffers, without which he cannot govern? That he chooses not to victimise the followers of sects, Roman or otherwise, whose religious practices are not ours? Does it lie with us to criticise him for taking money from those who can pay and are willing to do so, when we refuse him loans and taxes and grants? Is he not the Father of the nation, and are not we all, Anglicans, Catholics, Puritans, all his subjects, and does he not care for all?

"If we fail to do as he wishes, is it right for us to moan that he does not do what we desire? He is our benevolent ruler and guide. If we do not do our duty by him, how can he do his by us, if we withhold the means by which he might do so?

"Gentlemen, we are debating the adjournment of the House. Let us not fall out with our Monarch. Let us not depart with a mistaking, a misunderstanding, a rift, between us and the King, and between the King and his people.

"We have before us a dozen or so excellent Bills to consider, some proposed by the King and his officers, and others of our own suggestion. All are worthy to be passed. Instead of consuming the time in rancorous debate achieving nothing, or 'signifying nothing', as the playwright says, let us do some honest business, and please His Majesty with our endeavours, rather than aggravate him with our intransigence."

I feel that this is the best and most important speech I have yet made, and certainly the longest. Quite how successful it is, is not for me to say, since other older and wiser heads than mine speak to similar effect. Suffice it to say that the House does calm down, and a lot of good work is done before we go away for the summer.

Thomas. July, 1621. Wentworth Woodhouse.

I've been spending a lot of time since that Parliamentary episode learning as much as I can about foreign affairs. I've met men who have extensive experience abroad as ambassadors and emissaries to various European Courts, and the complexity of foreign dealings never ceases to amaze me.

Hardly any event in India, say, or China, or the Americas, affects England at all, save in matters of trade, and that not significantly. The King, it is said, wants to have the Spanish Infanta for a wife for Prince Charles. The Spanish King Philip would be glad indeed to have England for an ally in his war with the Dutch. At home this policy is deeply unpopular because of the English hatred of Catholics and Spain. In fact, it isn't the King's policy at all now.

If there were a Spanish match and alliance, and the English sided with Spain against Holland, there would be a serious disadvantage.

Holland is a Protestant country. So is England. Holland is the only ally Frederick and Elizabeth have found in their struggle with the Holy Roman Empire. England would be incandescent with fury if the King took us to war with the Dutch. On the other hand, the Dutch are our greatest trade rivals, their ships and navy competing with ours on every sea and ocean. Many of our merchants outside Parliament want Dutch vessels sunk, but those same merchants are well represented in Parliament, and totally averse to paying taxes for war!

These and similar arguments rage throughout England, with Parliament moaning about monopolies, and lack of war against Spain, and the King bewailing the lack of money, the failure of Parliament to grant taxes, and its interference, as he sees it, in foreign policy, which he regards as his province alone.

There are many acrimonious debates, in which I normally side with the King whilst trying to mollify his Opposition, but my words usually fall on deaf ears. I try saying what I hope has a Biblical flavour, about trampling on the King's favour like squeezing olives for the oil but letting it all run away. These debates repeat themselves in an endless procession, doing no good to either side. There is little point in my going into detailed descriptions of them; suffice it say that there is no war, which pleases King James, and there are no more taxes which doesn't, but keeps Parliament happy, whilst it bemoans the fact there is no war.

Thomas. August, 1622. Stratford.

Parliament resumed last November, adjourned for Christmas, started up again after the holiday, and the quarrels between the King and both Houses, especially the Commons, go on unabated. If anything they are getting more and more vitriolic. It is so bad that even an overture for peace from one side makes the other more intransigent and unreasonable. I still try for calm and reason, but I have had no more success than the year before.

I have been busy in London for my sister's boys, and I have been busy in Yorkshire on my own behalf. My estates grow and prosper.

I returned to London last month and I had a fever, and this running of the bowels from which I seem to suffer from time to time. The summer was so hot that Margaret and I decided to move into the country nearby where the smell of the kennels in the city streets, the putrefying fish at Billingsgate and the meat at Smithfield markets could cause no offence. We rented a small and elegant house in Stratford. It is a rather lovely small village in the flat Essex countryside a few miles to the west of the city.

We took to walking in the lanes and woods, and riding in the fields and over the commons. Sometimes we dressed in shabby clothes and went out like farmers or workers, walking to an alehouse and having a drink or two, and dining on whatever fare might be on offer. It was romantic, laughing and joking with each other, and sometimes with the locals. I don't think the locals were fooled much. Neither of us were as grubby as we should be if we really worked in the fields or on haystacks, and hedging and ditching, but they took it in good part, and the innkeepers and their servants seemed not to mind the tips we gave.

We walked home hand in hand like man and maid, or with our arms around each other, neither being fat enough to make that impossible. And of course, the touch and feel of my beloved so close and so happy led to the inevitable when we got to bed – which was as soon as we got indoors. Nipples, and breasts, and legs, and skin, and softness, and at least one hard thing, and blessed release, and relief, and kissing and stroking and then more of .... Well, you know what I mean.

And it was there, in that bed, a few days ago, that the greatest tragedy that has ever befallen me occurred. Margaret died. Yes, God in His Wisdom (if that is what it was, I think heretically every now and again) took her from me.

We had not been in the Stratford house longer than a few weeks when she began to feel unwell. She became very hot and sweaty, and sometimes seemed not to know me or make any sense. I sent for a physician, who said it was a fever, and bled her. It did no good. I sent for another, and he bled her. Since all illnesses seem to be different, I do not understand why these medical men think – and apparently believe – that taking someone's blood away is going to do them good. I resolved not to let her lose any more blood this way.

I sat with her, and slept by her side constantly. We relied on fervent prayer together. At times I could not hide my despair, and I strode up and down the room and round the house and back into the room, and on my return found Margaret praying alone, if she were not sleeping fretfully, or mumbling incoherently in the grip of the fever. The servants brought our food, and I fed her myself when she was too weak to hold a cup or a spoon. God knows I tried to be cheerful for her sake, but I was cold and dead inside, try as I might to keep hope alive. In our eleven years together neither of us had ever been seriously ill; I felt I could not bear it, but somehow I did. Perhaps our prayers gave me strength even if they didn't help her.

Eventually the day came when I had to send a manservant for the village Rector, and he came to give my beloved her last Communion, in which I joined her, kneeling by the bed. I knelt, not just out of piety, but because I was exhausted with the vigil and weak from fear of losing her. It may seem wrong, inappropriate, to dwell on it now, but we had continued to enjoy the fullest conjugal bliss right up to the onset of her illness. Despite being an MP, a landowner, and on the council of the North, and having many interests, there had been no-one whose company I enjoyed more, and whose companionship was more dear to me.

Henry, Lord Clifford. October 1622. Yorkshire.

I was very much saddened by the death of my sister Margaret. Our marriages and affairs of state and estates kept us apart in fact but not in spirit and affection. I know from her letters that she and Thomas were very happy, and so it always seemed whenever we saw each other.

But Thomas has not just been saddened; he has been devastated. His letters to me are such outpourings of grief as I had never imagined he had the sensibility to compose. I feel for him deeply. It would be different, perhaps, if he had more intimate friends to whom he could turn for comfort and company, but he doesn't. He is possessed of few friends. He has me, of course, and Christopher Wandesford (we three were boys at school together) and George Radcliffe, but those two are not close, as far as I am aware. I suppose that, apart from being friends of Thomas's, Christopher and George have one thing in common: each is married to a cousin of his.

Why do I not think of Thomas in terms of sensibility? God knows he was sensitive enough to Margaret and cared for her endlessly in her sickness. I think it is because until one knows him, he seems distant, even arrogant. He cannot tolerate fools or foolish talk. He can't make light, or what is known as 'polite', conversation, but is usually serious in the subjects he picks, even though he can be witty about them. I was thrust into his company at school, and learned his virtues and his loyal qualities first hand.

Thomas almost never speaks diplomatically. He says exactly what he thinks, even if it causes offence. I do not think he causes offence intentionally. (If he wishes to be insulting, of course his directness makes his intent perfectly clear). It is just that he expresses himself precisely so that his meaning is as clear as daylight, and if the cap he describes fits the people he is talking to well, then wear it they must. This is not the way to charm your path to others' hearts.

Of course, he has not the comfort of children from my sister. As her fate shows, and the Bible tells us, we none of us know when God will summon us home, and God forbid that Thomas should die a widower. He still helps his sister Anne and all his other brothers and sisters, and Anne's two boys. He has amassed a fortune and seeks to make it grow larger and larger. What would happen to them, and to that fortune?

I have to reconcile myself to the idea that, miserable as he is at present, he must look for another wife. Is that disloyal? I think not. If my darling were taken from me, could I care for my daughter as a woman devoted to me would do, should I choose wisely? Could I live the celibate life of a monk, but surrounded in society by women? Not a hope. If I were to die now, would I want my wife to live on as a widow? How could I be so selfish? She is still young and beauteous, and I should be glad, up in Heaven, to think that life with me was enjoyable enough that she would be happy to risk another marriage. She would not make a good nun, and I should not wish it upon her.

And Thomas is a mere twenty-nine years old. He is vigorous, fit, and strong, and from the hints Margaret used to drop, and the alacrity with which they used to retire to bed together, exceeding lusty. But then if my sister Margaret was as keen on conjugal relations as I am, this lustiness was a shared interest. She loved him too well to want him to be miserable.

No. I fancy Thomas will not remain single long.

Christopher Wandesford. November, 1622. Yorkshire,

My wife Alice and I, having spent some weeks in London for Margaret Wentworth's funeral, and I in keeping Tom company, have returned home at last. We have been very sad. Tom always spoke of Margaret as a most obedient and loving wife, but that almost makes light of her virtues. She was in fact a tower of strength to him. She was intelligent. She easily held her own in a discussion of the issues of the day with me and Tom, George and Anne Radcliffe, and Henry and Frances Clifford when we all dined together.

Tom has changed since her death. He was always serious and proud, although he could be very entertaining. Margaret's passing has humbled him somewhat. He is quite different from the bold, confident orator who proposed the toast at my wedding to Alice Osborne. Like me and Tom, Alice is off-spring of a Yorkshire gentleman, and as it happens, one of his cousins. He is different from the joking, generous man who accepted the role of godfather a year or two since to our eldest son. Then he never seemed to need anyone but Margaret, and me, Henry, and George, but above all Margaret.

Come to think of it, it must have made both of them sad that when he could be godfather to a child of mine, they could not beget one of their own. The pride I take in these sons of mine is almost a passion. I know Tom would dearly love to have a son, or any children, but particularly a son. He is so adamant about building up his family's status, his family's fortune, his family's reputation, that it only makes sense if he has "an heir of his own body," as the old saying goes. By contrast, I have hardly anything to leave anyone, except the debts my Father burdened his estate with, and which are the reason I am poor by comparison.

Now he seems to be so lonely, and depressed. He rouses himself in company to make jokes and appear to be jolly, but there is none of the spirit that used to move him and delight the rest of us.

Thinking about 'the rest of us', it occurs to me that we are quite a disparate bunch: Tom, mainly so serious, consumed by ambition, rich, and getting richer; Henry, son of an Earl, rich and a Lord, fairly idle, good humoured, and given to music and poetry; George, poor, like me, but, unlike me, very religious, extraordinarily intelligent, and very lawyer-like, methodical and organized. And me; pretty quiet, almost shy, reluctant to think a bad thought or utter a bad word about anyone.

I suppose the biggest contrast is between me and George. He can be very interfering (a trait I find it odd that Tom should tolerate, when he himself likes to get his own way), pedantic, and, believe it or not, quite likely to let all sorts of cats out of the bag; almost a gossip really, one might say. Except when he's doing a case, or negotiating one. If his opponents can guess what he's thinking then, they must be very clever indeed. However, that side of him is more than off-set by his frank talk; he is always brave enough to say what he thinks. That may be one reason why he and Tom get on so well; you always know exactly where you stand with both of them.

Thomas. 19th March, 1624. Westminster.

I'm back in Parliament again as MP for Pontefract in Yorkshire. That devil Savile and his son are MPs for the county. No-one ran against them. I've still got a large number of business interests as well. I need to keep busy, since I still miss Margaret so much, and to be frank, I still want to "get on." One of the businesses is the alum trade, which I have mentioned before. Sir Arthur Ingram is, as I have said, also in this game. It is a curiously complex business. It is known as the alum farm, and we are the farmers. The King farms out to us the right to dig up this special soil and we pay him rent for the right to produce the alum for the wool and cloth trades. We have people dig up the ground in which the alum is found, and we get others to process it for us to sell to the cloth manufacturers.

The trouble is that the King (or someone on his behalf) tells us how much alum he wants us to produce, and sometimes it is more than we can manage. And the rent we pay can be high. Ingram is in this Parliament too. He tells me he has been paying 9,000 pounds a year to the King for his share of the farm. I'm not that far into the trade, but we make money out of it most of the time.

A couple of years ago, Arthur was not doing so well, though. He has friends in all the high places because he does so many people favours. One of his pals is Lionel Cranfield. He is the Lord Treasurer, and one of the most powerful men in the kingdom. He was elevated to be Earl of Middlesex in 1622, just about the time Arthur was having trouble with the alum farm. These two have been doing business together for ages, mainly lending money to hard up members of the aristocracy and gentry.

Ingram, swapping favour for favour with Cranfield, got him to persuade the King to lower the amount of alum he expected Arthur to produce. As a result, Arthur now represents Lionel in the House of Commons. It has been a very interesting day.

Arthur has presented a report on trade to the House. It is the Earl of Middlesex's report. Arthur got a shock. Middlesex turns out to be rather unpopular. MPs are exposing the report as a cover for a new book of customs dues Lionel has imposed, and the House says these rates will decimate the economy (just a bit of exaggeration here, perhaps).

Arthur then asked the House to raise a lot of tax for war with Spain. As usual, the Commons wants war with this Popish neighbour, and the Duke of Buckingham and the Prince of Wales are clamouring for it, but the members do not want to pay. I'm not keen on the war myself, and I have no desire to ask my constituents to pay more taxes for it.

What emerges in this debate is that Middlesex has fallen out with Buckingham. At first sight that seems odd, because Lionel got where he is today by being an acolyte of Buckingham's in the first place. Buckingham is no fool, as Robert Carr was. He plays his cards (and the King) very skilfully. He sees people like Lionel Cranfield rise, and that is good so long as they do not oppose him, but if they cross him, they are doomed. Lionel has made two mistakes.

First, he has spoken out against the Spanish war, which means he has set himself against the policy Buckingham and the Prince of Wales espouse. The fact that his view is also the King's does not help him, since the King is putty in George Villiers' hands. His second offence probably looks even more serious to Villiers. Cranfield, sensing that he has been losing influence with him, has tried to get another pretty boy into the King's embrace. This young man, Arthur Brett, is a relative of Lionel's. Other people have tried this tactic, as I have mentioned before. Indeed that is how Buckingham got there in the first place.

But no-one can repeat that trick with Villiers in control, and the King getting into his dotage. Brett is sent packing, and Cranfield is doomed. Even so, he might not be in so much danger if Buckingham had not seen the virtue of sacrificing him in an attempt to assuage the hatred Parliament feels towards Villiers himself. This is an amazing side of Buckingham's mind and talents. Whilst his idea of any kind of policy is farcical, he is extraordinarily astute at making use of people, playing one off against another, and taking personal advantage of any opportunity that comes his way. If he could do that for the benefit of the country, England would be much the richer.

Talking of better shape reminds me that my finances are on the mend. The last three or four years have been pretty tough. My sister Margaret was 19 in 1621, and sister Elizabeth a year later. They were entitled to 2000 pounds each under Dad's Will, and parting with that when I was also shelling out for my younger brothers' education was far from easy, even though Father had set it aside for them. But that isn't their fault. I have been spending quite large sums on buying more land over the last few years, there are large country houses we live in at our four main manors, and of course, I have to have accommodation when I'm attending Parliament. They have to be repaired, maintained, and staffed with domestics, gardeners, grooms, and all the rest. On top of that the country has been in recession for the last three years, which has meant that rents have fallen. With a bit of luck they will pick up soon.

But to revert to Buckingham and Cranfield: George Villiers was, of course, a Duke, and Lionel was only an Earl. That difference mattered. On top of that, George was the King's favourite, and the Prince's hero. Lionel did not stand a chance. George persuaded the King to let the Earl of Middlesex be impeached by Parliament.

He was accused of fraud and abuse of his position as Lord Treasurer over the customs farm. I've already written about the alum farm. The customs farm was similar. The King has no effective civil service which could collect and administer taxes and duties for him. What he does is lease to rich men like Cranfield, and Sir Arthur (and me), the right to collect the tax and customs duties, in return for ready money in pretty large amounts. The farmers are expected to collect more tax than they pay over in rent to the King. They are also supposed to pay over to the Treasury a large percentage of what they collect. The system is rife with corruption.

The farmers, in many cases, keep more than they should, and falsify their accounts to cover themselves. The case against Cranfield was that he knew what was going on, and took advantage of it. A man called Dalison short-changed the King by over 13,000 pounds, but still managed to get into debt to Cranfield for a lot of money on loan. Lionel then 'bought' Dalison's land and property from him, allegedly to pay off his debts for him. That may even have been true. The fact that he was also selling baronetcies didn't help him.

The trouble for Cranfield was that Arthur Ingram was also involved in all this, and when he was called to give evidence, he shifted any blame which should have attached to him onto Cranfield's shoulders. And the odd thing was that Dalison's land had ended up in Arthur's hands. More Ingram luck? Or was it just that as Buckingham had been gradually falling out with Cranfield ever since he had been made Earl of Middlesex, Arthur's betrayal of Lionel made little difference?

Even so, although it might be said that Arthur helped Buckingham by giving evidence against Cranfield, it did him no good, because Buckingham saw him as part of Cranfield's gang of crooks.

In a curious, shameful, way, I admire Arthur Ingram for an ability I have never had, and do not think I could ever acquire. He could trim his sails to any wind, and tell any tale that suited. Had he supported Cranfield at the trial, he might have shared his fate, and be fined and banished from all power and influence. As it is, he now has no patron to protect him from his own rivals.

But nothing is likely to stop Arthur from going on making money, getting rich, and acquiring more and more land. He is just too cunning.

Thomas. July, 1624. Yorkshire.

Two very interesting things have happened. One has a big effect on me, and the other slightly less so. The lesser one is, however, extremely unfortunate for Arthur Ingram. The first thing is related to Buckingham. You remember that I wrote that Cranfield was doomed because he had spoken out against the Spanish War? He was also speaking for peace with Spain. That, of course is the King's policy; he doesn't want war at any price. Why is this bad for me? Because I have been taking the same line, in other words, supporting the King, and in a small way it follows one could say I am critical of the Duke and the Prince by implication.

This means I am now *persona non grata* with the Duke, and to some extent with the Prince. Life is going to get a lot tougher. I have to review my position. Do I continue to support the King, and advocate peace, or change sides and talk about war, and hope to win Buckingham's approval again? If I were sensible, I'd go with the Duke and the Prince. That is definitely what Arthur would do. After all, the Duke is the King's favourite, and James is hardly likely to protect me against his beloved. And James is old, and not well, and likely to pass away and leave the Prince as King in the not too distant future; anyone who thinks that Charles would abandon his own policies and Villiers for me should be caged as a lunatic.

The second thing that has happened is that Arthur has lost his share of the Alum farm. In spite of having Middlesex, the Treasurer, as his erstwhile patron, it has been discovered that Arthur embezzled a huge amount of money from the Crown in respect of the alum farm rents and profits. His lease of the farm has been forfeited, but fortunately for him he has been able to negotiate a "composition" with the King. In other words he has agreed to pay 20,000 pounds compensation, and in return the King will not pursue him any further, or have him prosecuted.

No wonder he was able to find 12,000 for Temple Newsam two years ago!! And more cash to start building his palace.

The effect these events have had on me is to show me just how profitable these financial farming practices are. I have decided that somehow I have to get into them in a big way, whether it is an alum farm, an English customs farm, or even an Irish one. Imagine getting into all three!!

Arthur would still be essential to such a venture because he has all the right contacts, and knows so much about how it all works. For some legal reason I don't yet understand, the farmers (or their contractors) have to make the alum at 8 pounds a ton, but are allowed to sell it for 24 pounds. That is a huge profit. The wages of the workers make little difference to the profits. Most of them are paid about 8 pounds a year. How does anyone live on that? Only with the greatest difficulty.

The process and the materials are cheap. The alum is not hard to dig, and it just gets mixed with urine. Imagine earning your living by going from house to house collecting piss!! But then in London, the night soil men come round in the morning collecting the shit and taking it out to the market gardens for manure. I suppose they do that in other towns, like Leeds, and Bristol, but I've not been too interested in that.

I must bide my time and ask Arthur to help get the farm when an opportunity arises. There's no point in worrying about it now; a new lease is already being granted to someone else.

George Radcliffe. 29th March, 1625. Yorkshire.

James VI and I is dead. The news reached here yesterday, and the bells have been tolling in all the Churches. Long live King Charles. I feel sorry for James. He was, by all accounts, highly intelligent and learned, but he just had no real political intuition. If he could see what he should do, he had insufficient self-control and authority to make others do it, especially his favourites. He must have been quite worn out by what Charles and George had been doing over the Spanish business. He'd failed to unite England and Scotland and establish a single religious atmosphere based on tolerance, which was his desire.

He was no tyrant, and had had no inclination to be one. He had done no harm, but he had achieved little or nothing good, either.

How will King Charles fare? Buckingham has done James no good. God forbid that matters should go on in like manner under Charles with Villiers in charge!!

Christopher. May, 1625. Yorkshire.

King Charles seems to be making a very conscientious start to his reign; long may it continue. A week ago he issued writs for the summoning of Parliament, so elections have been held. Thomas stood, hoping to represent this shire. Our neighbour, Sir Thomas Fairfax, who was a candidate too, has been a great help to him, and with Sir John Savile as his opponent again, he needed a lot of help. Yesterday was election day, and what a day it was! Sir John was up to his tricks, as usual.

In the days before the election he had bribed, with drink or coin, or both, many of the workers in the cloth trade around Leeds and Halifax to support him, and they rioted. Quite what he hoped to gain from a riot I am not sure, unless he anticipated that if his support was violent, our voters – I say "our" because I have been campaigning for Thomas – might stay away from the meetings and the ballots.

Then yesterday, when all the 40 shilling freeholders who intended to vote gathered in York to do so, Savile struck again. Somehow he started up a rumour, aimed at Thomas's likely voters, that the election might last half the week, so some of them left. When they had gone, a crowd of Savile supporters, with a mob from the taverns, charged into the voting area shouting for him to be elected. Fighting broke out, and the Sheriff cleared the area to prevent further violence.

How it happened I do not know, but Thomas cornered the Sheriff in the Guildhall, and the Sheriff, when he emerged, declared that Thomas and Fairfax were the winners. Savile was furious, and the city and countryside are buzzing like a hive with gossip that Thomas persuaded the Sheriff to decide in his favour, or worse – blackmailed him or bribed him. Thomas will not talk about it. Parliament is due to be opened in about three weeks.

I marvel that Thomas feels he can afford to go. His income is at full stretch, or so he says, and he has spent freely on being elected for the county, though I am told Savile has spent more. He will cause Thomas more grief shortly, I doubt not. I do not imagine the new Lady Wentworth will be anxious to see Thomas leave for London.

Thomas. 20th June, 1625. Yorkshire.

Dad died eleven years ago. I was twenty-one, and William was nineteen. John was sixteen, and both of them were at St John's College Cambridge. They went on to study, as I did, at the Inner Temple. Fortunately, Father had given William his own estate, and had made some provision for the others, but I still had to support them for quite a while. Five of my brothers were under eleven, and I had to pay pretty much the whole cost of educating them, and it was not cheap, since I wanted all of them to be cultured, as befits a gentleman, and anyway, that was Dad's wish too. He had made some provision for all of the boys, but it was not enough.

So I sent George, Mathew, and Philip to University College, and I paid for John to go to Italy on the tour six years ago. Two years after that I supported Michael and Robert to live and finish their education in France. And now John is dead. It is hard to believe, as he is – was – so young. On the other hand he was such a quiet fellow, preferring books and study to lively company and sport or politics, that his absence is not as noticeable as the loss of William or George (my dearest brother) would be.

How can you be dead at twenty-seven? He had not married; in fact I think he had never had a girl, and would not have known what to do with one. But if John could not be dead at twenty-seven, how could Michael have died two years ago, and even younger? I wish I had known Michael better, but he was much younger than I, and I was away on business and politics, and with Margaret, so that I had little time for him, or the other younger ones. Success certainly comes at a price. Should any of us bother?

My finances seem in such a mess. Yet if I sit down and think about it rationally, things are not so bad. I owe about 7,000 pounds, but as I could clear that with two years of my income (if I had nothing else to spend it on), I can hardly say that I'm on the verge of bankruptcy. I am still trying to get a decent Crown appointment, with a good salary and the chances of private profit that go with it, but I have had little luck.

If I didn't buy other land and property I should not owe as much as I do, but the property I buy produces more income. There are many who would like to be in my shoes, with my wallet. Kit Wandesford and George Radcliffe would be delighted.

I live well. I have about fifty servants who run my country houses at Wentworth Woodhouse, Gawthorpe, Harewood, and Ledstone. Feeding fifty costs a good deal, and when any of my brothers and sisters come to visit, there may be sixty people in the house. According to the housekeeper's account book, food alone costs about 1,500 pounds a year, and on top of that there are clothes for the household, tools for the farms, and fodder for the horses, and for the cattle in the winter. I spend a fortune travelling to and staying in London to attend the Courts and Parliament. And, joy of joys, I am married again.

I was very low and miserable for a long time – or so it seemed to me – after Margaret's death, but after a year or so I decided I must find another wife, and try once again to have some children. I had little luck at first.

I flirted with a daughter of a rich City merchant for a time, hoping to get her 25,000 pounds of dowry. It was not an inappropriate match as her father is a knight, and very respectable, but it came to nothing. Then I made an approach to young Lady Exeter, the daughter of the Earl, and that fizzled out too. I do not know why.

Thinking the third time might be luckier, I made suit for a cousin of Margaret and Henry's. She is the widow of the late Earl of Dorset. Her maiden name was Lady Anne Clifford. She is about thirty-four, so it was not a good prospect for any hope of begetting an heir and other children, but she has plenty of money. She is quite attractive, too, and if she had Margaret's appetite for love-making, it might have been a good match. But it did not get that far. And then I found out what my problem was – or should I say wasn't?

It was in September last year that I was telling Henry Clifford about my approach to Lady Dorset, when he said: "Well, old boy, you don't stand much chance there. Not with what people are saying about you."

"What are they saying?"

"That you are impotent."

"What absolute rubbish. Henry, you know it's rubbish. Margaret and I could barely keep our hands off each other ..."

"And certainly not when you were bare. I know, Thomas, I know; sometimes Frances and I could hear the two of you through the bedroom walls, and it would set us off. Not that that was a hardship. But you and Margaret never had any children did you?"

"No." I felt embarrassed.

"You've not even got any bastards, either, have you?"

"Certainly not! Not that I know of, anyway." I didn't feel as confident as I tried to make that sound, not because I do have bastards, but because I could see where this was going. And that's where it went.

Henry stated it clearly. "Well, maybe you can get it up, but maybe your powder and shot are no use. To be blunt perhaps your emissions are ...."

"Alright Henry, I get the picture. The women or their fathers don't want me because they think I can't get anyone pregnant. But that's not fair, because Margaret didn't get pregnant either. It could have been either of us with the wonky apparatus."

"That's it, Thomas."

"But how does that apply to your cousin Anne of Dorset. She's a bit old to have a baby anyway isn't she?"

"Is that one of your seduction lines, Thomas? I don't recommend you use that as an argument for marrying you. In any case, I dare say she would love to have a child of her own."

"It's alright for you to take the piss out of my situation, Henry, but I'm serious. What am I to do?"

Henry was contemplative for a while. "I'll give you a tip. You know the Earl of Clare? He's not very old aristocracy like Dorset, or my family, but he is rich, and he has rather a sweet daughter called Arabella. She's ..."

"Ugly and fat? And older than your cousin Anne?"

"How crude and ungallant you can be, Thomas! Actually, I understand she is only just 16, and when I saw her with her father a few months ago, I thought her extremely pretty. I'll go a stage further than giving you a tip. Frances and I are having a small house party at Skipton Castle next month, and I'll ask Frances to invite you. Clare and his family are coming anyway."

"I was not being crude and ungallant, my friend. I was just slightly taken aback that you should be shying me away from your cousin and acting as a matchmaker."

"Nothing altruistic about it, Thomas. First, we are old friends, and I should love to see you happily married again. But Anne has some sort of a claim to the Earldom or one of the family titles and much of what goes with it. Frankly, I should not relish having someone with your energy and abilities becoming enamoured of Anne and increasing her chances of taking it all away from us, especially if you get her with child!"

October saw me at the house party at Skipton. It was a grand place, and Henry's artistic temperament, and the artists, actors, and musicians he gathered about him ensured the twenty or so of us who were invited had a very entertaining time. Clare and his wife and daughter came, and she proved to be most beautiful indeed.

She had the thickest, most abundant and shimmering auburn hair I had ever seen. It curled entrancingly almost to her waist. Her blue, almost violet, eyes, had a luminescence about them that was, to me, irresistible, encircled as they were by long dark lashes. She was not exactly shy, but had a ladylike reserve which much became her youthfulness. I cannot say it was love at first sight, but at the end of our stay, it had been more than enough for me to ask her father if I might call upon them. He agreed, but I felt that he was somewhat reluctant, partly because of the rumour about my abilities as a stud, and partly because of the differences in our ages, as I was thirty-one. On the other hand I could sense that he was tempted, because I was not a bad catch, either in terms of class and status, or income and estate.

I was invited to visit them at Haughton Hall, which is the main family estate at Bottamsall in Nottinghamshire, and went there in November. There were not many guests, so I could enjoy Arabella's company alone, walking in the grounds, or sitting in the library. It was a chaste courtship. There was none of that sudden outburst of passion which had distinguished my pre-marital flirtation and mutual seduction with Margaret.

She curtseyed and I bowed when we met in the morning, and I kissed her hand, as I should have done with any other lady. When we walked in the grounds she occasionally took my arm, and once or twice she even let me hold her hand. And when the family and I parted for the night, we went through the bow, curtsey, and kiss with which we had graced the morning.

I was charmed to discover that she was well-educated, and when she learned that I had spent much time in France, she spoke to me in French. When I told her I could speak some Italian, she surprised me by conversing in Italian, too. She exuded gaiety, with a light and delightful laugh, and her voice, as Lear remarks, was ever soft, gentle, and low. Certainly it is 'an excellent thing in woman'. Even nagging is not nagging in a quiet and melodious voice; and Arabella never nags. The Earl of Clare is a Holles, a very well-respected political family. It follows that Arabella is even well-informed about political matters.

When I left I was invited to visit their other family seat at Clare Place in Nottingham in December. At the end of that sojourn, I chanced to be alone in the library with her. Her parents were saying goodbye to a couple of other guests. I was nervous. This was not bold Margaret; this was a shy young girl from whom no clues as to her affections or sexuality had emerged.

We were sitting before the fire, and on the same sofa. I was already holding her hand. We had been talking about hunting, and the paintings in the house, and her wish to have been to Italy, and being perfectly pleasant, but my mind was not on that, and I suspect she knew. If her intelligence did not tell her so, her intuition would have done. Suddenly, I could restrain myself no longer.

I raised her hand to my lips and held it there for some little while, longer than ever before. I kissed it several times, then lowered it and spoke: "Lady Arabella, you cannot, I think, be indifferent to the fact that I have fallen in love with you. I should be ... I cannot ... I wish you to be my wife, and if you could, in due course, find it in your heart to say yes, I should like to speak to the Earl about it very soon."

"Yes."

"Yes? But you haven't had any time to think, and have never given me any sign, except perhaps that you do not find my company uninteresting."

"Sir Thomas, I need no more time. If my father did not find the idea of you as a son-in-law tolerable he would not, I assure you, have invited you here twice. Please speak to him as soon as you can. I should very much like to be married, and I should very much like to be married to you. I cannot say that I love you, but I am sure love will come. I am also sensible of the fate of girls in our class who do not marry someone they like when they get the chance. Their fathers or mothers marry them off to someone they choose, and a life of misery and boredom, or both, is all they can look forward to."

"You are not very ..."

"Flattering, Sir Thomas? No, but like you I can be blunt and honest. I find you very handsome, forthright, and ambitious, and I know I can support you in your endeavours. I am in no doubt that love will come, and if you truly love me it will come quickly."

I was amazed by this speech. That this little thing could express herself so clearly and well – far better than many of my colleagues in Parliament – quite took my breath away for a moment, but that gave me the opportunity to consider the essential truth of what she had said. "Then we shall make a good team, Madam, and I shall speak to your father in the morning."

I rose from the sofa, still holding her hand, and she rose too, and standing on tip-toe, to my even greater surprise, kissed me gently on the lips, and then turned away, and said goodnight. I could not move as she left the room in her graceful way. Graceful she was. We had danced together much at Skipton, to Henry's musicians, and when not dancing with her or another, I had barely been able to keep my eyes from her.

In the morning, when the servants were packing my things and loading the carriage, I asked to speak to the Earl, and he took me into the library. He is tall, with thick iron-grey hair, rather stout, and stern, but not altogether unkind. He poured wine for us both, and came straight to the point. "You wish to marry Arabella, I suppose."

"Yes, my Lord, I do. She is beautiful, cultivated, charming and ..."

"Yes, yes, I know all that. I've lived with her for sixteen years. Let's get down to business. You want a dowry for her?"

"Well, it is customary in ..."

"Yes, of course it is. I wasn't born yesterday. Well, I propose to make 6,000 pounds available with her. It's take it or leave it; I do not indulge in haggling, and it is my best offer."

I cannot hide the fact that I had hoped for more, but I was not in a mood to haggle. I was inflamed at the thought of Arabella in my bed, and I loved her, and (mercenary and shameful thought) 6,000 would almost clear my debts. "I should not insult you by seeking to haggle, sir; nor would I wish you to think that I expected you to pay me to take your daughter away. I have told her that I love her, and I tell you the same. Your consent is vital to her happiness and mine."

The Earl was, if anything, even more blunt that I am. "I should hope so too. Anyway, I hope you will both be very happy, but don't come complaining to me if you are not. Marriage is a chancy business at the best of times, let alone when you are old enough to be her father. And let's face it, I just hope that you are in working order, and that you will be a father. I hear rumours."

"Groundless, I assure you," I replied with rather less confidence than I felt.

And so Arabella and I were married on 25th February this year of Our Lord 1625. And are we happy? I am ecstatic, and I think Arabella is too.

****

A month after our wedding, King James died. He was carried off by an ague, and Charles became King, and our ruler, whilst being largely ruled himself by Buckingham.

The Prince and Villiers had, eighteen months or so before James's expiry, been to Spain in a vain attempt to seduce the Infanta and the Spanish court into a dynastic marriage. It was a dismal failure, not to say a disaster. Buckingham was said to have behaved appallingly, insulting everyone, and even persuaded Charles to invade the Royal Gardens to speak to the Infanta, as a result of which she was terrified and the prospects of marriage, flimsy to start with, vanished completely.

The Prince and his favourite had returned to England in shame over there, but to acclamation from the King's subjects, who had not wanted a Spanish marriage or Queen in the first place. There was feasting in the London streets, which was understandable. Less so was the way the London mob greeted a terrible tragedy which occurred not long after Charles got back to London. At a hall in Blackfriars, where a huge Catholic congregation had assembled to hear a firebrand Jesuit preach, the floor collapsed and many people fell from the upper floor to ground level, at least a hundred died, and many more suffered terrible mutilation, losing legs and arms. The mob stood around, doing nothing to help them, and jeering and abusing them.

The King and Buckingham then tried for a French Princess for Charles. This proposition was almost as unpopular with the masses as was the idea of a Spanish Queen being thrust upon them. After all, we have been fighting the French on and off for ever, and in one case for about a hundred years almost continuously. I spoke out against it in the House, and locally, although I temper my remarks to some extent. After all, the French and Spanish hate each other more than the French hate us and we them, and the French have not sent an Armada to invade us as the Spanish did almost forty years ago. That being so, there was some logic behind the Royal thinking. But why can't the King have an English wife, or even a Scottish one?

The last King Henry had six wives, and four of them were English, and it was the English girls who gave him children, a son and a daughter, unless you count the daughter born of the Aragonese Princess. The memory of Queen Mary is not that fond in the bosom of my countrymen after all the Protestant hangings and burnings she instituted. Charles ought to find himself a girl like my Arabella.

Whilst the negotiations for Charles to wed the French Princess were afoot Buckingham organised (for want of a better word) an expeditionary force to fight the Spanish, but it was another inspired disaster, only worse, since this time many men died. How Charles can remain devoted to this totally incompetent nemesis of his is quite beyond my comprehension. Whenever Parliament met I spoke out against these so-called "Royal" policies, which were, in truth, just adventures of Buckingham's vanity, supported by our new King. Of course, this was just about the worst thing I could possible do if I want advancement at Court. With Buckingham in charge of the King and the country, I could get nowhere of any significance.

****

I am back in London for the opening of the new Parliament. When I arrived in Westminster I learned that Savile had presented a petition to the House to have my election set aside on the grounds that I had forced the Sheriff to declare in my favour. Of course I deny that.

Granted, I sought the Sheriff out after the disgraceful riotous and drunken conduct of the mob Savile is proud to call his electorate, but I merely told the Sheriff he had to do something, for having cleared everybody away from the hustings and the courtyard where the voting was taking place, he had prevented anybody being chosen as MP for the county.

Did I bribe him? Did I blackmail him? Did I bully him – something I am said to excel at? I decline to defend myself against these scurrilous suggestions, but I was there and Savile wasn't, so the Sheriff did the only sensible thing and declared that Fairfax and I had won the seats.

That did me no good at all when I walked into the House. I was unaware of the rule that when an inquiry is afoot as to the validity of an election, the Member whose seat is disputed is suspended until the result of the inquiry is known. As soon as I walked onto the floor of the House to take my seat, Sir John Eliot, one of the greatest orators we have, caught the eye of the Speaker. Dressed entirely in black, without a shred of colour, he was scathing of my presence.

His voice is marvellous. There are no better voices on stage at the Globe. "Mr Speaker, if we ignore our own rights and privileges, it hardly behoves us to criticise others outside the House who would take away the benefits of free Parliaments. What greater disgrace or contempt can be shown the House than that of the Member for Yorkshire who has just entered it. There has been no greater affront since Cicero declaimed against the invasion of the Senate by a non-member.

"But stay; did I say 'Member for Yorkshire'. I crave the pardon of the House, Mr Speaker, for this man is no member but an interloper. I call upon you to have him expelled!"

And expelled I was. Immediately. I have never been so humiliated. I have tried to familiarise myself with the rules and procedures of Parliament, but clearly I have more home-work to do. I shall not make a mistake like that again.

****

I almost forgot. King Charles married Princess Henrietta Maria of France ten days ago in Canterbury. Instead of a Spanish Catholic Queen, we have a French Catholic Queen. There have been no riots about that so far, but it will not take the people long to be in some turmoil about it, not now the French King and his grey eminence,

Cardinal Richelieu, have resumed persecution of French Protestants. I suppose war with Spain will not be enough for Buckingham. He'll want to attack the French as well soon. And to think that this French marriage and the treaty that goes with it were rushed through in the teeth of the feelings of the people and Parliament!

Royal policy goes from bad to worse. At least James was wise enough to be able to exercise some influence over his favourite's whims, but Charles sees no fault in his George at all. Already I hear rumours that the royal marriage does not go well. It seems the Queen is jealous of Villiers, who is rude to her relations and French friends and servants. The King takes his side, not hers, and dismissed her servants when, as Catholics, they spurned the English Protestant servants. He replaced the French ones with English.

Christopher. July, 1625. Yorkshire.

I am exhausted. Another election, and this one a whirlwind of a campaign, but thankfully very short. Tom came back from London in what must have been one of the fastest journeys ever, saying he had been turned out of the Commons, and an MP for the county had to be chosen all over again. This time there were no riots, and no violence of which I am aware. The Sheriff didn't need to be told what to do, and at the hustings Tom was chosen as the MP almost unanimously. If I am tired he must be nearly dead, or will be by the time he arrives back at the Commons.

Sir John Savile must have had apoplexy at being defeated like that.

There is an outbreak of the plague in London, Tom tells me, and Parliament is meeting in Oxford, so that is where he will go. The King and Buckingham have gone there too, with the Court, which has undergone a number of sudden changes since James's death.

First, Charles is elegant, polite, distant, and always conscious of his dignity. He has a studied, practised air and posture. He never forgets he is a King for an instant, unlike his father, who was scruffy, dirty, smelly, and crude. James was undignified, and familiar. He never put on an act. With him what you saw was exactly what you got. He told you exactly what he thought, so you did not need to "read" him. With Charles it is almost impossible to guess, let alone know, what he may be thinking, or what his feelings are. This, of course, is what I am told. I have never met this King.

He also splashes less money about than James was wont to do, so the Court has become less corrupt, there is less vice and wantonness (at least, in public), and austerity or correctness of behaviour is the order of the day. This is not surprising, since Charles is rarely at ease, standing on his dignity and trying very hard to be and look every inch "The King." This naturally imposes a straitened atmosphere, and many courtiers are unhappy at this change. They delighted in the bawdiness, the luxury, the money, the intrigue, and they haven't enjoyed losing it.

I've heard all this from Tom, and Henry Clifford, and others who've been to Court. Even Sir Arthur Ingram has remarked on it. Of course, it makes no difference to Tom. He's disgusted by blatant corruption, and the appointment to high office of totally incompetent men, just because they are friends of Buckingham's. He has no time for extravagant masques, public flirtations, and private liaisons.

Thomas. 15th August, 1625. Wentworth Woodhouse.

I arrived in Oxford a week ago, and went straight to the Hall where the Commons is sitting. It is like a bear pit every day. The Speaker is only just able to control the business of the House. MPs from all over the country, but especially from the South and West and the harbour towns of Dover, Portsmouth, Plymouth, and Falmouth, are furious at the press gangs roaming the streets and dragging away the menfolk, without regard to anyone's family obligations. With no man in the house, there is no money, and the women cannot pay the rent. With no home, they are thrust onto the streets, often with small children. They are forced, as a result, into whoring and other crimes. Last week, the House was told, a woman was hanged in Bristol for stealing a loaf for her children, and was feeding the smallest at the breast as she was taken to the gallows.

But she was from the lower classes, so the house did not get as surly about that as it did about the billeting of soldiers and officers on some of the Members and their rich friends. There is uproar about that. Quartermasters rove the countryside requisitioning food, horses, uniforms, and arms for the soldiery, which adds to the chaos, and the fact that these things are done for Buckingham's vanity makes it all much worse. If anyone in the House thinks Villiers is to be trusted to fetch a victory at Cadiz after the fiasco and the loss of life at Walcheren two years ago, they are keeping very quiet about it.

Of course, that is despite the desire of Parliament for the war with Spain!! I am still trying to persuade the house to give the King the money supply he needs, and in return get the King to remedy grievances. It is amazing that he has been given anything, but I reckon that from his point of view, what he has been granted just looks insulting.

Almost from time immemorial Parliament has granted the monarch the right to tunnage and poundage on all foreign trade for the rest of his life as a matter of course, and has not fettered that right with restrictions. This Parliament has granted this King these Customs dues for one year only, and stipulated that he cannot increase the rates by his decree. That is for the running of the Kingdom. And money for the war? 140,000 pounds!! How can anyone, let alone Buckingham, fight a war with a treasure chest as tiny as that? Yet, as I say, hate Buckingham as they may, they want war.

Lack of Parliamentary logic doesn't stop there. The country wants war with Spain because the Elector Palatine and his wife, Charles's sister Elizabeth, have been driven out of their home by the Emperor of Austria. Granted, the King of Spain and the Emperor are related, and they both owe fealty to the Pope. Granted, Spain fights on the side of the Emperor, but this fight is on land in Northern and Central Europe. None of the MPs seems to grasp that fighting sea battles with Spain (as they wish our navy to do) will never force the Austrians to restore the Palatinate to Frederick and Elizabeth, or help the Bohemians, where the war started.

I might not have tumbled to this idea myself if I had not chanced to meet Sir Thomas Roe, one of our most experienced diplomats, who explained it to me, and said that he had had discussions with some well-placed generals who hold the same views. As a result, I find myself in something of a paradoxical situation. On the one hand, I hate the idea of war, and of Buckingham being in charge of it. On the other, my natural inclination is to support the King. In the debate I said: "If we deal with our grievances, and the business of the country, then we can do what is necessary for the King, and I shall do as much as any man".

In any case, Parliament can now do nothing. The King dissolved it on the 12th. It only met for a few weeks. I am back home.

The last straw for the King was when it became known that the Marriage Treaty with France broke a promise Charles had made to the people. He gave his assurance that, whilst the Queen and her family could follow Catholic rites, there would be no softening of the laws against the practice of those rites by English Catholics. The Treaty contained a secret provision that was intended to make life easier for the recusants, and when this was revealed Parliament went wild.

Will Buckingham's expedition to Cadiz achieve anything? I doubt it very much.

Thomas. October, 1625. Wentworth Woodhouse.

News has reached me here that the King may soon call another Parliament. It will be his second. If it is more successful than the last it will be a miracle despite what Buckingham has now persuaded the King to do. The law is that the Sheriff of a County cannot be one of its MPs, because it's the Sheriff's duty to announce the winner at the election, and he can hardly declare that he himself is the winner.

Christopher Wandesford called on me with the revelation that I have been appointed Sheriff of Yorkshire, by the King, at the request of Buckingham.

"But why me, Kit? I know I have spoken out against the Spanish War, and Buckingham's policies – if that's what they can be called – but I am far from being one of the real troublemakers in the House."

"Villiers cannot brook any sort of criticism, and the King won't hear his friend denigrated to the slightest extent. Certainly you are not the worst of the opposition, Tom, but you are getting a name for yourself. You speak your mind openly and honestly. Indeed, when shown Villiers' list of proposed Sheriffs, the King apparently said: 'Ah, Wentworth. He's an honest gentleman'. Whether he meant it or was being sarcastic, I cannot say, but I suspect it was the former."

I was downcast for a moment, and Kit sympathised. "It's a shame, I grant you, but it gives you more time at home with Arabella, which you won't object to, I'm sure. It is not as though you have been married to her so long you can be tired of her charms already."

That made me laugh. "Far from it, old chap. And I must look on the bright side, mustn't I? It'll do me no harm to stay at home for a while, consolidating my position in the county, doing my duty, and keeping, as far as I can, quiet and cool. After all, it's my aim not to fight against the King's prerogatives and powers, and never to do so outside Parliament. No man is strong enough to stand against the King outside Parliament."

Christopher was very serious. “Certainly not. That is why we have to fight to protect our privilege of free speech in the House. Without that we dare not utter a word of reproach to the King about Buckingham or anything else.”

I asked him who else was on the list, and he told me as many as he could recall, and one was Sir Edward Coke. The penny dropped. “The King has taken me and Coke and the others out of the running for a Parliament by making us Sheriffs, and he thinks that will shut us up, and silence the opposition. Doesn’t Buckingham realise real hot-heads are just waiting to take the lead in the Commons? Coke and I and a few sensible types may have spoken firmly against Royal policy, but we were keeping the cork in the bottle.”

Now Kit was biblical. “Jesus warned against putting new wine in old bottles. The likes of Sir John Eliot will burst this Parliamentary bottle asunder. There’s one major subject for debate in this Parliament, and that is the removal of Buckingham. No money for the King will be forthcoming unless he yields to that.”

“Charles will never, ever, do that. He would rather go without the money, and keep his George.”

Thomas. December, 1625. Wentworth Woodhouse.

Buckingham’s venture to Cadiz was a complete and utter failure. The fleet left England in October. It turned out that the canvas and rigging on many of the navy ships had not been renewed or overhauled for thirty years. The food and water supplies were inadequate, and much of what there was was rotten, largely due to the corruption which always seems to accompany the provisioning of the army and navy, and partly to the unsavoury conditions in which the food was kept.

I received a letter from an officer with whom I was well acquainted. He was adjutant to Sir Edward Cecil, the Commander of the army expedition. He wrote:

Dear Wentworth,

I am barely able to find the words to describe the futility of the venture from which I have just returned. Before we set off Cecil was elevated to Viscount Wimbledon. He was, of course, chosen by Villiers. He was not a completely inappropriate choice, as he is a very experienced soldier, but he has never commanded anything as large as the force now at his disposal. I felt throughout that his diffident personality gave him little sway over his subordinates.

When we reached Cadiz many of the ships' captains were too frightened to make any serious effort to capture Spanish ships, and some simply turned tail and ran before the wind. In their favour I do not think some of them could be blamed, since their vessels were merchantmen and colliers from Newcastle and the North, and the crews had never been in a battle before, and had been press-ganged to serve.

Nevertheless, some of the Navy ships made it into Cadiz harbour and, having weathered a heavy bombardment from the fort at the entrance, managed to land some marines who succeeded in storming and taking the castle. This triumph enabled the main army to land, but thirst and a shortage of water – the poorest of planning to land an army with nothing to drink and little to eat – induced the soldiers to raid the local wine-cellars; they became hopelessly drunk, and had to be sent back to the ships, achieving precisely nothing!!

We then took to sea again, Wimbledon intent on intercepting a flotilla of treasure ships bringing gold and silver bullion from Spanish Mexico, but the old rigging was beginning to fall apart. It could not possibly stand the strain of fast sailing to catch a fleeing vessel, and certainly not the major stresses of a battle. To make matters worse, we ran out of food, and were throwing men who had starved to death into the sea! On my ship the water for the men was so foul by then that even the ship's cat would not drink it.

Before we reached English ports we were caught in a storm, and lost more men and a couple of small ships. Who do we have to thank for this? Why, our Lord High Admiral, of course, our George, Duke of Buckingham.

Sir John Eliot, one of the wisest, but now one of the most inflammatory of our MPs, changed from being a supporter of Buckingham's to feeling much about him as I do. He was Vice-Admiral for Devon at the time of this travesty. He told the House that starving men died in the streets of Plymouth and the nearby villages of Devon and Cornwall when the remnant of the Cadiz fleet came home. His part of the country was the heart of the English navy, and proud traditions and seafaring heritage were in their sailor's blood. He said; 'Our honour is lost, our ships are sunk, and our men have perished, but not by the sword or the cannon, but by those we trust. The Lord High Admiral is a cancer in the King's estate, the moth in his goodness, the rust that enters in."

Thomas. March, 1626. Yorkshire.

Kit called on me again last week. He had been in London, taking some of my Sheriff's reports to the King and Buckingham. I have been sending copies to Buckingham as well as His Majesty because it is essential that, if I am ever to be rehabilitated at Court, I restore my reputation with both of them.

"Your reports are well received, Tom. They both remark that, as far as a Sheriff can, you are following government policy, supporting the raising of revenue for the Treasury, dealing efficiently with prosecution of those who avoid paying, and pursuing the Catholics for fines for non-attendance at Protestant services. They seem to be well pleased, from what I hear."

"Splendid news, Kit. Let's hope it does some good. There's not so much call for me to stand up against the King in this role as there is as an MP. Mind you, I could have been Sheriff and an MP if I were prepared to be more devious than I am."

"Devious, my friend?" Kit smiled at that. "No-one can be as straightforward in what he says as you are, and be devious at the same time."

"You cannot judge from what I say what goes on in my head, Kit. You have no idea what devious schemes are afoot there. In any case, I'm talking about others' deviousness, not mine. One of my fellow Sheriffs of equally recent appointment, and also with me in the last Parliament, suggested I should secure his election here in York, and he would do the same for me in, well, let's say Gloucester, Hereford, or Bury St. Edmonds. It's only in our own counties that we cannot be Sheriff and MP."

"It is certainly devious, but clever, even so. And you turned him down?"

I nodded. "As you know, my every inclination is to try to do good for myself – yes, I make no bones about that – and the Kingdom, by working with the King, not against him. There is a much better chance of doing that from a position of power and influence than by being his ranting enemy."

Kit, always very alert and attentive, was suddenly more so. “Then there is an opportunity to do just that which may arise soon. You know about Lord Scrope?”

“Of course I know Scrope. You can’t be on the Council of the North for a few years and not know its President. And I am the Vice-President.”

“That’s not what I asked, Tom. I know you are the VP. Of course you know Scrope. What I said was ‘do you know about him?’”

“I’ve heard that he’s under pressure from the Commons because he goes easy on the Catholics. I am trying to pursue them and he is letting them get away with it.”

“That’s it, Tom. He is supposed to be considering resigning. You’re Vice-President. You’re the obvious choice to replace him. Why don’t you write a letter to the King now, asking for the job?”

“Do you think I’m back in his good books sufficiently to do that yet?”

“Nothing ventured, nothing gained. The worst that can happen is that he says ‘No’. How can you lose by it?”

That stopped me. How indeed? So we sat down and I dictated to Kit, and he made some useful points, and I then wrote out a version for dispatch. It hardly seemed appropriate to send the King a letter in someone else’s hand asking for the most important job north of the Wash.

That is not the only star above the horizon. Arabella is pregnant!!

Denzil Holles. March 1626. Westminster.

Dear Thomas,

I was at the opening of Parliament, and I regret to say that King Charles has done it again. He has offended all but the most devoted Peers and MPs. Here, as best as I could note it down, is what he said:

‘You may remember that in the time of my Blessed Father you persuaded him, and me, to break off the Treaties with Spain. We did as you wished. Now that you have everything you wanted, and seem to think that I have gone so far with you in war against the Spanish that there is no retreat left open to me, you start rolling your own dice and making the rules of the game as you go along.

'I pray you, make no mistake and do not deceive yourselves: this is not a Parliamentary way, nor is it a fitting way to deal with a King. Sir Edward Coke has told you that it is better to be killed by a foreign enemy than to be destroyed in battle at home. For my part, it is better for a King to be invaded and almost destroyed by a foreign army, than to be despised by his own subjects.

'Remember that the power to call, permit the sitting, and the dissolution of a Parliament is entirely in my power. If I find the fruit of a Parliament good, I shall let it sit; if I find it evil, it will not continue a moment longer.

'Remember also, that if this Parliament persists in the errors of the last one, and you delay doing as I ask, you deepen those errors and make your position and mine irreconcilable. By contrast, if you mend your ways cheerfully, and consider the distressed state of Christendom, and the desire you and I have to aid our beloved sister Elizabeth and our brother Frederick, and the parlous state of the affairs of this Kingdom because of the war, you will do yourselves honour, and I shall be encouraged to go on with Parliaments.'

Isn't that arrogant? Verily, I understand that kings may be entitled to be arrogant, but it is not an auspicious beginning to a plea to us to open the nation's coffers to him, is it? Does he think this was diplomatic? It was so offensive to most of us – Lords and Commons – that even those who might have spoken up for the King were too cowed to say a thing.

How could he say to us: "Now you have everything you wanted"? Has he not heard that the thing we want above all else is the end of rule by favourites in general, and Buckingham in particular?

What good does he think Parliaments are to us if we cannot ask for what we want with some expectation of getting it, but have to dig deep in our purses for Buckingham to waste as he wishes? And all that manure about being despised by his subjects; respect has to be earned, or doesn't he know that? Probably not; he just thinks we should show respect no matter what he and Buckingham do.

With the affection of your brother-in-law, and my love to Arabella,

Denzil.

Thomas. 7th June, 1626

The early Parliament of 1626 went very badly for Charles, the Lords and Commons, and, of course, the people. Nothing of note was done. Perhaps the only positive thing to come out of it was that as no money was voted, the people were spared the necessity of paying the taxes. However, if the nation doesn't pay any tax, it can hardly complain if it gets nothing it wants. And if you wish to balance the books, why would you go to war at every available opportunity? There is no more expensive pastime in the universe.

That is the trouble for Charles. He has to have war because Villiers wants it. The people want it too, but not with Villiers in command, so they would not pay, even if they wanted to. It might be different if Charles were better at explaining why he needs the money, and at coaxing it out of Parliament, as Queen Elizabeth used to do, rather than demanding it as of right. Of course, she had favourites too, like Essex and Leicester, but she did not let them run her or the country. They were her servants, not her masters.

Even so, I can see that because she was good at calling elections, and getting Lords and Commons to do her will, she encouraged an expectation that that is how things would be. Her father, King Henry, well, he would never have let anyone, let alone Parliament, forget that he was in charge. Persuasion was not his way either, any more than it is for Charles, unfortunately, but Henry was magnificent, huge, majestic, clever, very cunning, and overawed everyone, so it worked for him. It doesn't work for Charles. He is small. He is very dignified, and gracious, but no-one could pretend he's majestic. He looks more like an ambassador from Spain.

Arabella. Yorkshire. 9th June, 1626.

Could anyone burst with joy and happiness? I believe so, and it will be Thomas if he goes on as he has yesterday and today. He is charging about the house, and into the village, he tells me, grabbing hold of anyone he sees, and telling them that I have given him a son!! He even ran into the inns and taverns, threw gold coins on the counter, and told the landlords to serve all the customers at his expense. Then, of course, when this got out, there was a stampede for the ale-houses.

He has been sending messengers, grooms, and servants out by horse to all the neighbouring seats of the gentry announcing this event. Anyone would think I have done the greatest thing since the Virgin Mary!!

But a virgin I am not. In February last year, after our wedding and the celebratory dinner and dancing, Thomas and I were put to bed by our families. Thomas's brother George was there. I have never been so embarrassed or nervous in my life. Here I was about to embark on a voyage I knew nothing about, having been told very little by my mother or anyone else. In fact I have no idea whether my mother enjoyed sex or not. Perhaps if she had, she would have been more informative. However, at least she did not tell me I should hate it.

I was going to bed a man whose appearance before me had always been fully clothed. I had seen dogs, and cattle and sheep doing this 'thing' that I was, I knew, now expected to indulge in, but they seemed to get little pleasure from it. Would it be the same for me? Would I have to stand silently bent over as a mare does when serviced by the stallion, motionless except for the impetus his thrusting induces?

I need not have feared. Thomas came to my rescue. He spoke to my father as our families stood around the bed; "I am not a callow youth," he said. "I have run this course before, and would spare Arabella any indignity she might feel at being watched as she runs it for the first time. Please be so kind as to leave us to ....er ..." My new husband very delicately left the last words unspoken, but my father seemed to acquiesce gladly, and gestured for everyone to leave the room. Someone called "Good luck!!" and someone else giggled, but the door shut and my blushes were now a private matter.

****

No. I am not a virgin. The sight of blood on the sheet next morning did not deter me. We had made love three times that night, and I started on his body as soon as I awoke next morning. We have continued like that ever since, until my swelling belly, full of the baby, made ordinary lovemaking rather difficult, and uncomfortable for me. And Thomas was so considerate, and we pleasured each other with our hands and mouths - how astounded I was when he taught me that - and the night before William was born he came into me from behind, so softly and stroked my clit (he calls it) with one hand round my tummy and the other on my breast, that we both came and then fell asleep, until I was woken by the baby's kicks and then the start of the birth.

I shan't go into that. I dare say what happens is familiar to most people. When I told Thomas last December that I was with child, he was so happy he cried, and was afraid to make love to me, so I had to take him to bed and show him that it was just what I needed and wanted. I have never seen him so happy as he was at the thought that we really were going to have a child, and that, despite the rumours, he had fathered it!! At least, I had not seen him so happy until yesterday and today.

We shall have him christened William after Thomas's father, and every few minutes Thomas starts pacing about saying, and even shouting: "I'm a Father. My lovely wife has given me William. I have an heir at last!!" Or words to that effect, and in as many combinations as you can think of. I'm still in bed of course, but the servants tell me that The Master cannot even sit to his dinner for more than a few minutes before having to get up and shout the news to someone he has probably told ten times already.

I know that Thomas is said to have a cold and hard image in public, and in business, but that is not what I see at home.

There is only one small blot on my landscape at this time; Thomas will be leaving home next week for London and Parliament. For my sake and the baby's he doesn't want me to go with him, though I know he would like me there for his own happiness. He says that London is an unhealthy place for little ones, and as Margaret died there, he does not want it to be the scene of more grief. I should be distraught if we lost this gorgeous little boy, and I think Thomas might lose his reason.

Thomas. 10th June, 1626. Yorkshire.

I am a father. I made a baby, after all these years!! I have the most wonderful, beautiful, soul-mate for a wife. I'm sure I'm a new man. I have never known such joy, such sublime content.

At the same time I'm still me. Ambition still drives me on, but I am getting nowhere. I ought to be like Sir Arthur and other time-servers, and speak up for the Royal policies, but I am still me. I have to say what I think, what I believe. My period of keeping my opinions to myself is at an end. I was not appointed President of the North. The snake, as

Margaret used to call Sir John Savile, has found the ear of Buckingham again. Clearly I have not.

Savile is cunning, no doubt about it. It turned out to be true that the King wanted Scrope out of the job, and hoped to appoint a replacement who would please the Commons, but Savile got to Buckingham, advised him to persuade the King to leave Scrope where he was, and – and this is the bit that really hurts – appoint him, Savile, as another Vice-President!

My situation is worse than ever. Scrope knows I applied for his position, so there's no love at all lost between us now, and of course, having kept him in the job, Savile has become his right-hand man. He's not only added to his power in the county by this move. He has also secured the grant of a charter for his town, Leeds. This is important, since it gives the town its own measure of self-government, with all the opportunities that affords its leading lights – not least Savile himself – to make more money by fair means or foul.

Where does that leave me? Shall I take Savile on at his own game? Shall I sit quietly for another few months or years hoping the sky will clear? I don't think I can do that. I was doing pretty well in Parliament last year, and had a lot of support from the patrician landowners, not just here at home, but in many parts of the country, and I shall just have to reassert myself in that role. I may be wrong, but I felt that Coke and I were leaders of the House. If I can win that reputation back, perhaps the King will see that I'm not so much an enemy as an ally he ought to embrace.

I have to go into opposition, and see where that leads me.

George Radcliffe. July, 1626. York.

Today I have seen Thomas as angry as I have ever known him. It is hardly surprising. He was sitting in office as *Custos Rotulorum*, presiding over the Court, when a messenger, dressed in Savile's livery, approached the bench, and sought permission to hand him a letter. Thomas invited him to come forward and took the missive, breaking the seal. He asked the Court's indulgence whilst he read it, and his face turned red with passion, but he kept a grip on himself as he rose to his feet.

His restrained stateliness and powerful voice dominated the gathering. "My Lords and Gentlemen, I have just received, even as I sit here, His Majesty's command depriving me of this office of *Custos* in the Commission of the Peace. I shall, of course, dutifully and cheerfully obey. Still, I could wish that my successor had chosen some other time and place for the delivery of this dismissal. This Court is not the arena for humiliation of its President, nor a theatre for the showing of poorly contrived insults which do nothing to enhance the dignity of this Court and its proceedings.

"Nevertheless, as they chose this feeble method of trying to disgrace me in the opinion of the people of Yorkshire, I shall endeavour to erase it, and maintain the reputation I hope I enjoy amongst you of an honest gentleman, which I might otherwise lose if I behave otherwise. There are too many amongst us who value honesty not at all. I do not wish to be one of them.

"Many may think that I could have stayed in this seat if I had kept my opinions to myself, but to buy my place with my silence is a price I am not prepared to pay. I am not told of any wrong that I have done, but of this I am certain: I am not guilty of those 'virtues' which have given my successor this post."

He then left the Court with all the magnificent dignity of which he is possessed. As I hurried after him I heard whispers from all sides: "Wentworth blames Savile!" "Savile and Wentworth are at it again!" "Sir John has had his revenge!"

Thomas is not a swearing and cursing man, but as I came up to him on the steps of the Court as he awaited his carriage he was uncharacteristically crude. I have no need to reiterate the language he used, but to say that he made it clear he is not terribly fond of Sir John or Buckingham puts it as mildly as I can. My efforts at sympathy fell on deaf ears, but at least he did not take his temper out on me. I just let his anger subside as we got into the coach and started for Wentworth Woodhouse.

When he was calm, he turned to me. "How was London, George? How was Parliament?"

Thomas did not need to know about London. "Parliament does not improve, Thomas, unless more chaos is what is needed."

"Eliot is leading the impeachment of Buckingham, isn't he? How is that faring? I remember Arabella's father telling me in February that we would see some real hobgoblins in the Commons without Coke and me to keep a lid on the pot."

I chuckled. “He was right, but don’t get me wrong. Eliot is a fine speaker; orator even. That isn’t enough though. As you said before, attacking the favourite will get nowhere with the King.”

“But with impeachment the King has no role to play,” Thomas said. “He doesn’t have to sign it or assent to it in any way. If Parliament upholds the charges, and a majority votes for it, he is doomed. This is so ironic. Old King James told Charles and Buckingham that they would have a bellyful of impeachment when they used it to get rid of Cranfield, you remember?”

“I remember Villiers sacrificing his friend Cranfield. He’d made him Earl of Middlesex not long before. If you have friends like Buckingham you have no need of enemies. What is that old saying? ‘Greater love hath no man than this, that he lay down his friends for his life’? Mind you, some of our lawyer friends in London told me they think the impeachment is badly drafted, and can’t succeed.”

“Then Eliot is a fool and has done his cause no favours.” Thomas was judgmental. “The King will never let his friend Villiers be impeached. He’ll get no money from this Parliament, and will dissolve it.”

Thomas, August, 1626. Wentworth Woodhouse.

The King has dissolved Parliament again! He gets nothing out of Parliament, and Parliament gets nothing from him. It is a waste of everyone’s time. Yet he cannot govern without it because he cannot run the country without money. He must have money. What will he do to get it?

It follows that the impeachment of Buckingham is as dead as a shot duck floating in the lake. The news from Westminster is that the atmosphere between the King and his Parliamentarians is dreadful. The country will go to the dogs at this rate.

Henry Clifford. April, 1627. London.

Thomas has surprised us all. Amazed us is more accurate. A little while ago he was telling his friends that he would not tangle with the King unless driven to it, and not even then except in Parliament. Well, there is no Parliament, and he has tangled with the King so decisively outside the Commons that he is in prison for it.

He is in the Marshallsea. If you have to be in prison, it's not a bad place to be, and George Radcliffe is there with him, so he has congenial company. Indeed it is a prison for gentlemen, in truth, and there are plenty of gentlemen there at present. Would you believe they are, most of them, imprisoned for debt?

Mind you, it is a special kind of debt. Last year the King could not get the Commons to give him any money, so he decided to take it. He issued Royal Proclamations ordering the aristocracy, the gentry, and wealthy merchants to lend him what he wants. People are up in arms about it all over the country. Well, I say up in arms, but no-one is actually carrying his musket about with evil intent. The proclamations are the subject of meetings and speeches, some pretty wild. Everyone is clamouring for another Parliament, but what good that will do, judging by the last two, is difficult to imagine.

I was up at Wentworth Woodhouse a week ago with Frances, visiting Arabella, who, as you might guess, is not too happy with Thomas two hundred miles away in prison. She told us she is expecting again. I have come to see Thomas, to tell him Arabella is well, and I want to find out why he has chosen incarceration.

We are out for a walk with George Radcliffe. Yes, we are out for a walk. The country hereabouts is fairly flat, and the prison is just west of Southwark, and within an easy stroll of the Thames. The prisoners at Newgate Jail would hardly recognise this as a prison at all. Because it mainly houses men from the upper classes, and because most of them are wealthy, they can eat as they wish, they can have proper beds, and fires, and books, and lamps or candles by which to read them. And they are allowed out for walks, like this one. Because they are gentlemen their word that they will make no attempt to escape is accepted, and they don't.

Thomas is adamant. "Why should I try to run away, Henry? I'm here because I shall not pay this 'loan' to the King. Loan? I have to say I think that's a joke. He is forcing men to make a loan because he cannot raise any revenue, since there is no Parliament to grant him taxes, and every time he calls one, the mood of resentment over grievances is so strong that MPs will give him nothing. How can he pay back a loan? What can he pay it back with?"

"Have you heard that people are calling it the Forced Loan?"

"Yes. A couple of new prisoners arrived yesterday. They said that's what it is popularly known as."

"But why have you chosen this course, Thomas? Only a few months ago you were saying ..."

"I know: that I would only stand up to the King in Parliament, and even then only if forced to. Well, I think this Forced Loan has forced my hand. I am not just talking about a principle. I am standing firm on it, come what may. My conscience will not let me do otherwise."

I find it incredible, not that Thomas will abide by a principle, since that has ever been his way, but that he will run the risks. "You stand no chance of getting back into favour at Court like this, Thomas. The King's heart is so inflamed by this business, he vows he will never forget it, will bear the memory against all the defaulters, and punish them severely. Your health may not stand imprisonment for long. You know you are of a nervous disposition. Freedom to move as you will has always been essential to you."

"You think I do not care about that? And that I have not seen Arabella and little William for weeks? Of course I care. Yes, I may never recover my standing with the Court, though goodness knows it has been at a low ebb these many years, but I am taking a calculated gamble. Tell me, though, how is Arabella? Is our new child flourishing *en ventre sa mere*?"

"She is the picture of very rude health for a lady of her quality, old fellow, and sends you her love, and this package of letters which I would ask you to read later. You spoke of a gamble? What gamble is that?"

"Let me ask you a question first, Henry. How do men speak of me now?"

"Very well, for the most part. There are, of course, a few who think you are just a trouble-maker, but the majority say you're the leader of the landed men and the aristocracy in Yorkshire, and elsewhere. Your quarrel with Savile has boosted your standing vastly, because people see you as representing them against the trade interests of men like Savile, who's no better than a wealthy merchant, and not truly nobly born into the bargain."

"Precisely. It's not as though I can't afford to pay the loan; none of the gentlemen in here with me is that hard up. Part of my gain from gambling is that these same men, and many outside, will see me as a sort of martyr for their cause. They live on the rents and produce from their lands and their tenants. Most of them are not at Court, and have no hope of gain from the King. They do not get charters for their towns or villages, as Savile did for Leeds, increasing his wealth. My lands and my money are mine, not to be taken by the King when and if he chooses, and these men feel the same about theirs, unless an act of Parliament says so."

I see now where Thomas's argument is heading. "And Parliament doesn't say so. They feel, as you do, as I do, that if the King can help himself to what he wants, the rights and privileges of the gentry, of England, will be gone forever. If enough men resist the loan the King must call an election."

"And I shall be back in the House, and shall lead it again, but not like a trouble-maker, as you put it, Henry. I hope that with men like Coke I shall be able to secure redress of our grievances, and persuade the Commons that we really do have to give the King some money, but in the proper, lawful way. My other possible gain is that the King will realise that I can help him if he will employ me properly, and that forcing me into opposition is not in his interests."

I point out that the huge risk is that the King will never employ Thomas in any truly important office. He might also be kicked off the Council of the North.

"Precisely. That is why it is all a gamble."

I ponder this a while. "But you cannot stand for Parliament in prison, nor when you are still Sheriff."

"My office as Sheriff ended with imprisonment, so that obstacle is out of the way. I don't think the King will keep us in prison for long, as this time he'll appreciate that if he does, the House will be full of more hot-heads, the election will be seen as rigged, and his chances of getting any money will be gone."

That makes me smile. "Do you think he will get his taxes and grants even then?"

Thomas becomes very serious. "He may not. After all, I am here on the King's command. There has been no trial. I have not been found guilty of any crime. Many men have paid up in the face of being put in prison without a hearing. Some of my wealthier tenants or their sons have been conscripted into Buckingham's army as punishment for refusing to pay. There is enormous resentment of this new style of government which has hardly been seen in England since Magna Carta."

I nod. "And remember the five knights, imprisoned for refusing to pay the loan, as you are, with no trial, but solely on the King's warrant. Their application for *habeas corpus* was rejected by the Judges who ruled that it did not run in the case of 'His Majesty's special command'. Have you heard that the King dismissed the Lord Chief Justice for advising him that he was acting illegally? And that old Archbishop Abbott has been stripped of his powers, if not of his actual office, for his comments?"

Thomas looks shocked. "No, I have not. What is he supposed to have said?"

"He told the congregation in Canterbury Cathedral that when he heard about men being called to arms because they would not pay, he was reminded of King David sending Uriah into the front line of the battle to be killed so that David could take his wife, Bathsheba, and bed her. Abbott got into more trouble for refusing to licence a priest to publish a sermon saying that it was the Christian duty of the citizen to pay what the King demanded, even if he did so illegally.

"Buckingham and the King liked this sermon as it made the case for what the King was doing. When Buckingham tackled Abbott about this, the old man said: 'I cannot agree to this, nor with Sibthorpe. If I do, and the next day the King commands me to send him all my money and my goods, I must obey him. Sibthorpe bases himself on weird interpretations of Apostolic Succession. He's wrong. The apostles never demanded money with menaces, and neither does the Church'."

Arabella. October, 1627. Dartford, Kent.

We now have two children. Anne was born a week ago, and I am with Thomas here in the country, and very happy. July was hot, and August hotter. London was a cauldron, and Thomas and the other prisoners were being boiled alive. A few of them wrote to the King to ask permission to move into the country, still on terms of imprisonment, and still on their honour not to abscond. Their petition was granted, and they were housed in some pleasant dwellings here in this village.

Thomas immediately sent a messenger to ask me to join him, so William and I, with a few servants, travelled here by easy stages. I was seven months gone, and rather large. The journey was not pleasant for me, though William thought it a great adventure. Anne is well, and I love feeding her. I do not favour giving my little ones to wet-nurses, as my milk is for my children. God made it so.

I know why a lot of ladies of my station in life employ these nurses. It is because they stop having their monthly courses while they have a baby at the breast, and this stops them getting pregnant. They treat themselves – or their husbands treat them – just like breeding cattle. Neither I nor Thomas thinks like that.

In any case, we rediscovered after William was born that sex when I am not pregnant is a lot better than when I am. I just wish that I were ready for some lovemaking now, but I am not quite recovered from the birth. I do long for it so, and I can tell that Thomas is getting quite desperate. He loves it that my nipples have grown larger and darker as a result of feeding William, and that they are doing so now with Anne. He gets so randy; I bring him off with caresses and licking, which gives him relief, but he hates my being left out of it, and I am almost as desperate as he is, but I am still too sore to let him do anything about it.

Still, there are plenty of things to occupy us. He gets letters from his solicitor, Peter Man, and his steward, Peter Marris, and he tells me what is going on on our lands. He is very angry about some tenants who've been forced to go in the army, and sympathises with others from this part of the country and the South of England who have had Buckingham's troops billeted on them. They even have to feed these soldiers, since the King does not.

Thomas tells me the Forced Loan has raised about 290,000 pounds, which is a lot, but less than half of what the King expected. Thomas thinks Parliament will have to be summoned again. He is looking forward to that, but I am not. It just means, as far as I'm concerned, that he will be away from home, and me and the children, for another long period. It was bad enough when he was in the Marshallsea. I just hope he doesn't end up in prison again, as he is bound to speak out against Buckingham. My feelings get so mixed up.

Part of me really resents it that he puts me and the children at risk of losing him, and of being persecuted by the King's servants, yet at the same time I love him for his courage and standing up so firmly for what he knows, or believes, to be right, and he makes me so proud.

How do I know he will speak out about Buckingham? Well, last week, my brother Denzil came to dinner. He's good-looking with the same auburn hair and blue eyes as mine, but he looks like a man, not a girl. He and Thomas get on very well, and both are opposed to what the King lets his favourite do. Denzil was talking to Thomas at the table. "Can you believe it? Villiers is still fighting the French on an island near La Rochelle. He thinks he could help the Protestant Huguenots defend themselves against Louis's army. Thirteen is an unlucky number. Well, having Louis XIII on the throne is certainly unlucky for you if you're a French Protestant."

"Maybe, but Protestant though I am, through and through, I can't see how we can help them much. Villiers still has us at war with Spain, and he can't get enough cash from Parliament for that, let alone a simultaneous war against France."

Denzil leapt in again. "And what a crazy policy. What was the idea behind getting Charles to marry Henrietta Maria if not to get us a powerful ally who hates the Spanish as much as we do? How does Villiers think he can – we can – afford to fight the two most powerful countries in Europe at the same time?"

"God alone knows, Denzil. It's not as though the people are really behind him over these wars. They may want to assist the Huguenots, but the quarrel is really about two things. Villiers lent King Louis some ships which are being used to fight the Huguenots, and not Spain and the Emperor. That has angered King Charles. The second thing has angered Louis: Charles has broken the marriage treaty and is not allowing more tolerance for Catholics. Besides, I do not suppose Louis has forgiven Villiers his outrageous flirtation with his Queen when he was in Paris as an Ambassador a year or so ago. On top of that the fuss about the conduct of Buckingham's troops and sailors around the southern ports is growing."

"I don't think 'fuss' is a good word for it, Thomas. It suggests that they are having an unjustifiable moan. It is really serious, let me tell you. You don't feel it so much up in Yorkshire, but down in Kent, Sussex, Hampshire, Devon – in fact all along the South coast - there is uproar."

Thomas laughs. "But this is Dartford, Denzil, and Dartford is Kent. We do hear the news here."

Denzil seems not to hear, and is, in any case, unstoppable when in this mood.

"Trade is virtually non-existent. At home wagons get waylaid by bands of hungry soldiers looking for food, and clothes, and bedding. And abroad, because the Spanish navy is out looking for our merchant ships, fewer are sailing. Although we're supposed to be on good terms with the Dutch because they are helping Frederick and Elizabeth try to get their Palatinate back, that doesn't stop their ships attacking ours over exports, and ours doing the same to them. Nobody can sell anything."

I decide to make a comment. "But that only affects the merchants, doesn't it? Are there enough of them to cause uproar?"

Both men look at each other and then at me. They smile, but I can tell they are serious. Thomas says: "That is not the worst of it, Arabella."

Denzil interposes. "Not by any means, dearest sister. Farmers can't get a decent price for their sheep and cattle, if they have any left after the army and navy have taken what they want."

"But the King pays them for it, doesn't he?"

"Unfortunately not. He just doesn't have the money, and Villiers doesn't control the troops."

It is odd that most of the time, when talking of the Duke, Denzil and Thomas call him Villiers instead of Buckingham, as though his title means nothing to them. "So we have many farmers and their labourers on the side of the merchants. And then Villiers, with the King's warrants and orders, billets soldiers and officers on the gentry, and expects them to feed these troops, and they don't get paid either. So now we have the gentry on the side of the farmers and merchants. But it doesn't stop there. Some of the officers make love to the ladies of the house, or the servant girls, and the soldiers do the same in the fields with girls from the farms and villages, and some of these women get raped. Parliament is unlikely to vote much war tax in these circumstances."

Thomas takes a turn. "I've heard it said that in some villages the number of unmarried mothers is rising fast, and that a chicken that hasn't been stolen by the army is a very rare bird."

"So it is Thomas, so it is. One of my farmers was on his way home from market with a pair of new boots and he was set upon for the boots by two sailors, whilst a third stole the eggs his wife was carrying home. People are furious with the war and Villiers. If you are elected when Parliament is called, you'll have a busy time of it, and no mistake."

"And talk I shall, have no fear, brother Denzil," Thomas replied. "But I have nothing against the King. He's just a fool to let himself be controlled, perhaps even bullied, by an idiot like Villiers."

Now I know. Thomas will put himself in the forefront of the struggle to preserve the liberties of England.

Thomas. 27th December, 1627. Dartford.

Today is a good day, and it started last night, when Arabella felt really well, and we were able to make love in whole, not in part, for the first time since Anne was born.

Then today I was released from imprisonment, and Arabella and the children and I must return to Yorkshire as soon as possible. It is obvious the King will shortly call for a Parliament, and I must be at home to organise my re-election.

It is impossible to believe that the King thinks a new Parliament will do him any good when he clings to Buckingham. Buckingham took the army to relieve the Huguenots in La Rochelle, and it was a complete disaster for us, for him, and for the Huguenots. I had a letter from a friend the other day saying that "Buckingham has returned with no little dishonour to England, excessive charge to our treasury, and great slaughter of our men."

On the 29th of last month Denzil wrote to me about this saying; "Since England was England it received not so dishonourable a blow." At the beginning of November the ships brought home the tattered remnant of Buckingham's Army (if that is what it could be called). I had a visit at Dartford from one of the commanders, Sir Edward Conway, a charming but very military man, soon afterwards.

He told a harrowing tale. Buckingham set sail with about 100 ships and 6,800 soldiers in June. This fleet arrived off the Ile de Re, an island which guards the entry to La Rochelle Harbour, on 10th July. "It was a good plan to start with. If we could take the two forts on Re it would be very hard for the French to keep us out of the harbour. Buckingham had listened to and taken the advice of his generals."

I could not help myself: "That makes a change. I thought he never listens to anyone".

Sir Edward chuckled, and continued: "One of the Forts is the Fort de la Pree, and the other is St Marin, which is the one he chose to attack first. We landed not far away on the 12th, and the French attacked us ferociously straight away. We were nearly thrust back into the sea. When you think how ill-equipped and trained our men were, it is quite amazing that we didn't all drown, but they fought very hard and we got ashore. Buckingham was hoping that the Huguenots would help, but they did little."

"They may have been afraid that they would fare much worse at the hands of the King if they did."

"True, Sir Thomas. Anyway, we got to St Martin and started the siege on the 17th. I can only say how much one has to admire the courage with which the garrison fought and kept us out. We made little progress. After nearly two months I made a note in my diary. It read: 'The army grows weaker every day; our victuals waste, our purses are empty, ammunition consumed, the approach of winter grows, our enemies increase in number and power; and we hear nothing from England'."

I was appalled. "But didn't you get any supplies or reinforcements?"

"Yes, we had one small flotilla arrive with a few hundred equally inadequate soldiers, some food, clothes, and ammunition and gunpowder, but it was not enough. Then, to add insult to injury, a French fleet arrived outside the fort and unloaded reinforcements and supplies for them. The morale of our men was devastated."

"It seems the whole expedition was a mistake and hopelessly planned, Sir Edward."

"That's an understatement, though as I say, Buckingham's original idea was good, and I have to admit that when he decided we had no alternative but to retreat and withdraw from the island, he conducted the evacuation from Loix, at the other end of the island, very competently. It won't save him though. We boarded ship on 30th October but with only 3000 men – that's less than half the Army which left England five months earlier."

Sir Edward is right, of course. Villiers may now be doomed. Denzil is likely to be elected for Dorchester, where he lives, and I should get in for the county again. I cannot believe the King and Villiers will find many friends in the Commons.

Thomas. March, 1628. Westminster.

My brother-in-law and I are back in Parliament. Perhaps I should say a bit about Denzil. He takes after his father, the Earl of Clare, in being opposed to Buckingham, which puts them both at odds with James and Charles, although I understand that when young, Denzil was one of Charles's chosen companions and friends. He's about the same height as me and dark haired too, but his beard is just a small dot under his lower lip, whilst mine is a pointed one much in the style of the King's. All three of us have a full moustache.

The Earl's family have estates in Cornwall, as well as at Haughton in Northampton, and when Denzil married Anne, his father gave him property in Cornwall. Her father, Sir John Stanhope, settled Dorchester Priory on them, and that is where, in the main, they dwell. He first became in MP in 1624, but I did not know him well. Indeed, he did not make much of an impression in the House then. He was MP for the constituency of Mitchell, which was near the Cornish family estate.

I began to know him better when I courted Arabella, his sister, and since our marriage we have become firm friends. He is of a keen intellect, well educated at University and in Gray's Inn, and such a treasure of a son to his father as I hope William grows to be for me. Not, I hasten to add, that William is not a treasure to me already, but he is too young yet to make any kind of a mark on anything but his parents' hearts.

Denzil began to show some heart and spirit in the 1626 Parliament, speaking out against Buckingham and his Spanish war policy. He has an unerring eye and instinct for foreign affairs, and sees clearly that where the Duke leads, shame for England and the monarchy will follow. However, he and I differ over these policies in one major respect. He is more violent in the expression of his opinions, and seems to care little for the monarch, whoever he may be, whereas I endeavour to speak more moderately, with a view to bringing the King and people closer together, to heal rifts rather than dig them deeper. Despite that we gain a great deal from our discussions and the ideas we can bounce off each other.

I hope that we are able to work together in this Parliament. Denzil is MP for Dorchester this time, and I again for Yorkshire, as we expected. He is as opposed to the continuance of the wars with Spain and France as I am, so we have to try to get rid of the Duke. Bearing in mind the King's devotion to him, this task will take all the patience and skill of pushing the proverbial pea up-hill with our noses, but it has to be attempted. It is a bonus that we have Sir Edward Coke here to help us, as he is not Sheriff of his County now.

Buckingham deserves, even more thoroughly than previously, to be removed; he has further humiliated us all by sending his brother-in-law, Lord Denbigh, back to La Rochelle recently, in another futile venture to assist the Huguenots. The same sort of ill-chosen rabble passed muster for an army, and, of course, after the retreat of October, their morale was at its nadir. The sailors would not attack Richelieu's moles and booms across the harbour entrance, and the fleet turned back having achieved nothing apart from the depletion of yet more of the King's tiny store of bullion.

Now the troops are ashore, and so are many of the sailors. There is pandemonium all along the South Coast, with more rapes, robberies, murders, and foul deeds of every conceivable variety. The men have not been paid for months, and rumour is rife that Buckingham is planning yet another expedition against France, for his constant desire is for a mighty victory to wipe out the memory of all his shameful defeats and failures. He is like an insane gambler who thinks that having lost his fortune at the tables, he will, with one more roll of the dice, cover himself in gold and glory. The trouble is, he is not playing with his own fortune, but ours – the nation's. It is not his life that is at risk. It is those of the poor benighted souls who have to go and fight for him.

It is not as though all this money and lives lost have done the French Protestants any good. Louis pursued his policy of starving out the citizens of La Rochelle, and entered the gates of the city in triumph some weeks before Christmas. That, of course, as Denzil is fond of saying, just adds to England's shame.

My Career Begins.

Thomas. 26th March, 1628. Westminster.

Six days ago King Charles opened this, his third Parliament. He set the tone for it at once, by telling us that if the House did not grant him the money he needed and wanted, he would take it in any event "by those other means which God has placed in my hands." He'd already done this once with the Forced Loan. Some of my fellows interpreted this as a threat, but I do not see it that way. I'm sure Charles thinks only in terms of what he believes to be the Divine Right of Kings to rule, and the obligation of the rest of us to be obedient, do what he says, and pay up.

This means he wouldn't think of threatening anyone. In fact he more or less said as much at the end of his speech. He told us: "Do not take this as threatening, for I scorn to threaten any but my equals".

How insulting! We know well enough that we have only one King in England, so he has no equals here. He thinks his word – "I want this or that, and you will give them to me" – is all that is required, no matter how tactlessly that word is expressed. Having rather stunned and shocked most of the House, he withdrew, and left us to our usual debate on his speech.

No-one was taken off balance by Sir Edward Coke rising to his full magisterial height and immediately putting a Bill before the House calling for the protection of the citizen from imprisonment without trial. Moderate as I wish to appear, even I could not object to that, having so recently been incarcerated with him and George Radcliffe and others, in an arbitrary fashion, in the Marshalsea for non-payment of the Forced Loan. Coke's method was ill-chosen, but I decided to keep my powder dry until a more opportune moment came.

That moment is today. I know exactly what my strategy is; I have been discussing it with Sir Edward and Denzil. What we intend to do is persuade Parliament to present a Bill of Rights to the King. There's another man in the House who merits watching, and whom we expect to support us. He is John Pym. He's almost a farming type from Somerset. He's been in Parliament before as MP for a place called Calne in Wiltshire. He is no more a friend to the Duke than Denzil and I. He's the Member for Tavistock now. He's small and rotund, rather like

Ingram. He's very astute, a brilliant political strategist, and several years older than me.

I stand in the centre of the benches along the wall of St Stephen's Hall. I have chosen this position because I can be easily seen from every part of this huge room. I feel all the weight of being an MP for the largest, and by no means the least, of the counties. The murmur of the voices of other members and the Speaker seems to come from off stage in the darkness, as though this were a theatre, even though the space is hardly lit by wintry daylight.

Sir Francis Seymour, from a very old aristocratic family, at last opens the debate on the matter of supply. He harkens back provocatively to what the King said a week ago, repeating much of what the Royal Speech contained on this subject, giving his reasons at some length for voting no money, and ending: "If his Majesty shall be persuaded to take what he will, what need have we to give?"

There was uproar, with shouts of "Hear, Hear," "That's telling him," and more besides until the Speaker makes himself heard above the din and members settle down again. Someone with the courage to speak up for the King then asks us to forget all that, and come to agreement and make peace – in other words, give in and vote the money!

The Speaker then calls Sir John Eliot. There is absolute silence. His authority hangs over from the last Parliament, and the attempted impeachment of Buckingham. He is very powerful, and his oratory can inflame almost anyone, but that is not what we need just now. I must wrest control of the House from him and his followers, and find a surer path for it to follow. Sir John tears into the Royal – or should I say Buckingham's – policies. He refers to those who have spoken of the oppressive conduct which many of them and their constituents have experienced.

He says, in effect, that we should not concentrate on the trees, but on the wood. "In this dispute it is not just our lands, our goods, and our chattels which are at risk, but everything which, as Englishmen, we call ours. These rights, to a fair trial, to a jury of our peers, to *Habeus Corpus*, our freedom of speech in this House to give voice to the concerns of the men of our cities and counties, and to decide here, with the King, Lords, and Commons in Parliament assembled what taxes we shall pay, and what advances and grants we shall make the King for the government of the country, are the privileges that made our forefathers free. We acquiesce in their removal at our peril, and that of all generations to come."

There is thunderous acclamation for that; fortunately he has not proposed any insurrection or violent course be adopted.

Then another Court acolyte, Sir Benjamin Rudyard, a weak fellow, catches the Speaker's eye, and in a weak voice and weaker speech, asks the House to trust the King, and aim for unity with him. He says there is a crisis of confidence, and asks: "Men and brethren, what shall we do? Is there no balm in Gilead?" Steeped as we all are in the Bible, this offers no solution, and he is greeted with a sullen silence.

And that is when the Speaker calls upon me. "The Member for Yorkshire."

Me. Mr Speaker. This is the third Parliament in which I have had the honour to represent the county of York, this time with my colleague Thomas Fairfax. When last this House met, we were asked to grant subsidies to His Majesty for war with France to assist our Protestant brothers, the Huguenots. His Majesty declined to remedy our grievances - we denied him the subsidies. Instead, he forced loans from those who would pay.

A Member. Stole, more like. Mr Speaker, I refused to pay and went to prison.

Me. True Mr Speaker, the Honourable Member and I were imprisoned, with many others, in the Marshalsea and elsewhere for that refusal.

A Member. And is it put to good use, this forced loan? *(General laughter and scornful comments greet that interjection).*

Me. It might as well have been thrown in a pit. Villiers, our glorious Commander in Chief, our ...

A Member. He may be **your Villiers**. He's certainly not mine!

Me. I stand corrected. Members need no reminding that the Duke of Buckingham attacked La Rochelle, was defeated, and achieved nothing but the loss of much of his ill-provisioned Army.

A Member. That was no Army. It was a rabble.

Me. Aye, a rabble, but none the better for being led, or perhaps I should say misled - by Buckingham. *(A chorus of "Right, Yes, True, Hear Hear" is my reward for that).*

A Member. And he followed it up by sending Denbigh there with another rabble and no result at all.

Me. It is our privilege in this House to lay our grievances before His Majesty and seek to unburden our country of the yoke Buckingham has laid upon it.

A Member. He should be impeached.

Me. Let us not move too fast, Mr Speaker. We are fortunate to have a good and noble King, but the advice His Majesty gets and the Counsellors from whom he gets it are not always of the best.

A Member. What course does the Honourable Member suggest, then? They say King James liked to have his arse licked. Is that to be tried again?

Me. Mr Speaker, I leave that to him who suggests it, and resent the suggestion that our rightful King, King Charles, might welcome such advances. No, Gentlemen, we should address the King regarding our grievances in a way which will advise His Majesty on those courses which, to us, seem fit. We must make it plain that forcing loans from the people contrary to the will of this House is bad; that billeting troops on unwilling folk to induce them to pay is unacceptable; that imprisoning people, including Members of this House, without trial, for refusing to make these "Loans" is the ultimate interference with those liberties guaranteed by Magna Carta. When the loyal subject is deprived of his fundamental liberties, then as Sir Francis Seymour said, what need have we to give when the King's Ministers will take what they like regardless? The way to make this approach to the King is by a private Bill, to which he can assent.

Pym. The King has made it clear that he will not countenance any measure Parliament puts forward if it goes any further than Magna Carta. Yet we must have protection against the forced loans, and the ravishing of our daughters by the soldiers billeted on the people.

Me. This has not been done by the King, under the pleasing shade of whose crown I hope we shall ever gather the fruits of justice, but by counsellors who have extended the prerogative of the King beyond the just symmetry which makes a harmony of the whole. *(I hear whispers of "he means the Duke").* The sovereign and the subject, though both be innocent, both are injured and both need a cure. The Privy Council has taken from us all means of supplying the King.

A Member. It is the King we must control.

Me. Mr Speaker, by one and the same thing - bad advice - have King and people been hurt, and by good advice must they be cured. Let us trust in the goodness of the King and he shall not refuse us, with God's help.

A Member. God's help may be hard to come by when His Majesty will not even let us worship as we will.

Me. Mr Speaker, I speak not of worship and religion, but of the administration of the realm. The blame for current ills is not with the King but with his administration. This remonstrance must concentrate on four crucial grievances. It must seek an end to imprisonment without trial, the means by which many of us were imprisoned recently; un-parliamentary taxation, such as the Forced Loan, which is why we were imprisoned; forced billeting of troops in our homes, when the old law is clear, 'that no man shall be forced to accommodate soldiers, except inns, and the innkeeper shall be paid'; and impressment to fight abroad. Many of us know this was used instead of imprisonment to force payment of the loan, because we have seen our neighbours marched off to the army or navy because they would not pay. Let us hope that we shall carry their Lordships' House with us, so that His Majesty may see that the wisdom of both Houses is expressed without disadvantage to King or People.

Speaker. The member for Tavistock.

Pym. Honourable Members would do well, Mr Speaker, to heed the words of the member for Yorkshire. It is not seemly - indeed it is not sensible - to confront the King with yet more grievances on top of those which have already been addressed to him.

Me. True. It were better to concentrate on a limited number of substantial complaints than to offer His Majesty so many criticisms that for very weariness we shall tread the olive and lose the oil. Let us first satisfy the King with a competent sum of Revenue and then present our humble request to him to consider our views. The greatness and power of His Majesty is our prop and ought to be dear to us.

A Member. As like as not he'll take the money and give nothing in return.

Me. This House has the sense to see that such an attitude confronts the King at the outset leaving no escape for either side. The Bill I have proposed is a middle way with a better prospect of success. This motion should be put.

Denzil. I second the motion.

Coke. Mr Speaker, kindly put the motion.

Speaker. All those in favour say "Aye." (There is an overwhelming roar of *"Aye."*) All those against say "Nay." *(A very few mutter "Nay.")* The Ayes have it.

There is a loud chorus of, "A Bill of our Rights, yea, yea, forward with the Bill" and other shouts, which go on for some time. A number of us then carry the Bill up to the House of Lords, where it is passed after a short debate, and where the King gains little more support than he had in the House below.

Thomas. June 1628. Westminster.

From Parliament the Bill of Rights was taken to the King, who received it graciously enough, considering he was aware that along with the Bill we should, in due course, seek the dismissal of Buckingham. He told our deputation that he gave his word as King that he would observe its provisions, but he declined to commit himself to any particular cure of our complaints. He said that should satisfy us 'without additions, paraphrases, or explanations'.

The House was not at all happy with this message. We all wanted it done in the form of a Bill, which when signed, would make it an Act of Parliament, with the force of law.

To sweeten this medicine we told him we would give him five generous subsidies if he agreed to this, a suggestion I had put before the Commons.

By June his military situation was so desperate that he seemed prepared to do as we asked, but then he suggested the words "The King wills that right be done according to the laws and customs of the realm." He tried tenaciously to hang on to his right to put us in prison without trial, saying the foundations of the Kingdom would crumble without it. In response to criticism of the Duke he tried to forbid us to lay any scandal or aspersion upon the State, the Government, or any of his ministers.

We were not prepared to accept his kingly word. Surely he did not think that we could accept a form of words which rested on the law as it already stood, and on the customs of the land? According to him, that gave him the right to the billeting, the taxation without representation, imprisonment without trial, and so on, but those phrases of his would not bind him.

As for allegations about Buckingham, the King got just what he did not want: another bitter attack on the favourite followed.

Does the King think we were all born yesterday? Perhaps that is what he thinks. He obviously doesn't think a lot about the rights of ordinary Englishmen. What he thinks about is his Divine Right, which means, in simple terms, he can do just as he likes. We knew what we wanted, and that was the old Norman French words for the assent to a private bill, namely *'soit droit fait comme est desire'* or 'the law should be as is desired'.

On top of all the abuses of our rights that are the subject of the Bill of Rights and money, we are being plagued with religious abuses too; at least, that is what many members and their constituents allege. This is a topic I do not want to be drawn into, as it detracts from the more pressing arguments about billeting, press-gangs, and so on. Further, although the writing is on the wall that there will probably be increasing troubles about worship in the future, they are not already on our doorstep, as the Forced Loan has been.

The main sign of the worship troubles which may come is what has happened to poor old Archbishop Abbott, for whom I have great respect. His objection to the Forced Loan is well known, and he is not now popular with the Court for that, but his toleration of the more Puritan forms of service is his undoing.

A fat little red-faced bishop, the Bishop of Bath and Wells, is making a name for himself. Because of his desire for more ceremonial enrichment of church services, he has a growing reputation with the King and the Court. Strong as my faith in Christ is, I am not that concerned with how other people worship as long as I am allowed to worship in my own style. This Bishop, William Laud, is very firm in his desire that all should worship in a style which, although not Roman, requires rich vestments for the priests, gold crosses on altars, particular kinds of music, and orderly parades of priests and choirs in the aisles of the Churches. He wants 'the beauty of holiness' to be observed by the eye as well as experienced spiritually; for him the two go together.

This sort of thing is anathema to the more Puritanical elements of society, and trouble is brewing. Some people are imprisoned for their views by the Church Courts. Where Archbishop Abbott was tolerant, and did not pursue such matters with any vigour, Laud is implacable. As the King's views on worship are similar to Laud's, this Bishop is bound to come out on top, at any rate for a time. He started in a nasty way, by hounding Abbott, after it became known that Abbott had written a tract which said: "When I beheld that some were to be imprisoned, I thought this was a somewhat new world, but I swallowed my own spittle and spoke not of it to anyone."

The contrast is astonishingly clear, since Laud is not a man to keep quiet about anything to do with what he regards as 'his' Church. Having the ear of the King, and many of the clergy being of a similar mind and taste in worship, he has persuaded the monarch that Abbott should be prevented from exercising his office. The Archbishop is, in effect, suspended from duty now, partly on the issue of liturgy and ritual, but to a considerable extent for his denunciation of the Forced Loan, which had aggravated Charles enormously. Another sign of the times is the appointment by the King, almost certainly on Laud's advice, of Dr Montagu to the See of Chichester. This rigidly austere cleric has published some books expressing views very similar to Laud's, which have been roundly condemned by Parliament.

Passion about religious questions runs so swift, that I am determined to avoid them. I say not a word in Parliament about worship. Some of these 'faith' arguments are so trivial. One side says the altar should be at the far east end of the Church; the other says it should be a Communion Table in the nave right in front of the choir, or at the top of the steps – if there are any – into the chancel. How can anyone get really furious about this? Does anyone know exactly where in the dining room above the tavern the Last Supper was actually served? Isn't the idea of the bread and the wine being the symbol of Christ's sacrifice the important thing?

Even so, I am Puritan enough to dislike too much pomp at Church. One priest told me that in Durham Cathedral "The Sacrament itself is turned very nearly into a theatrical performance, and the congregation is seduced with pleasant music, glittering pictures, and histrionic gestures".

Bearing in mind my speeches on the Bill and the Petition of Right, I dare say the King will look even less favourably on me than he has in the last year or so. He will be well aware of my role in opposing the Duke and the royal policies. He knows that in March, when Sir John Coke, Secretary of State, demanded arrogantly that the House should vote money before there was more discussion of our grievances, I spoke powerfully for a delay of two or three days. I told the House that unless we were sure of our liberties and privileges we could not grant subsidies; we needed these rights secured and confirmed so that we could give in a happy spirit. I'm sure the King will have hated that.

Even when we were prepared to offer the King the five subsidies, I maintained forcibly that I should not agree to them unless our fundamental liberties were guaranteed by the Bill. That captured the mood of my colleagues. The King was furious, and sent a message on 12th April that we had broken faith with him after what had seemed an excellent start, and the nation could not afford to put one new fighting ship in the water without the money. A couple of days later he appeared in the Commons himself to tell us that he would observe the rights of his subjects, but would not sign the Bill, and thus make it an Act of Parliament.

I took the lead in the Lower House debating this for another two weeks, and we still gave the King no money. We all hoped that delay would make the King see reason, or at any rate yield what we wanted. On the 28th Charles sent another promise to obey the law, but there was still no sign of his agreeing to our Bill.

I always try to express myself moderately and get the House to behave moderately too, but I do not want to weaken our stance by making it look as though we are about to yield. I tell the House that the Bill contains all we want, but not to forget that while we want cast-iron assurances from the King on our liberties, we have no desire to alter the balance of power between the sovereign and his subjects. Again we refuse him the subsidies he asked for, and he replies that he would sign a Bill giving effect to Magna Carta and all the other old Acts about the freedoms of the people, but he would have nothing added to that.

Fortunately Sir Edward Coke comes to the rescue by suggesting we put the Bill forward in the form of a Petition of Right. If the King accepts that, he would be shackled by it as if it were an Act of Parliament. Of course, I support this, the House goes for it, and so do the Lords, for a while.

The King then sends the Lords a letter promising there would be no imprisonment without trial, and the Lords are softened up by that, although it goes nowhere near far enough. The peers tell the Commons that if we go any further we would interfere too much with the King's prerogative powers.

I cannot put up with that; once again I speak to the House in firm terms. Later I pen a letter to George Radcliffe. After customary enquiries as to his health and his family's, I set out the text of my speech:

'We have put to one side the Bill which we debated for securing the just, fundamental, and vital liberties of the King's subjects. We are now reduced to a Petition of Right, which is as low as we can possibly go and yet retain the honour of this House, and keep faith with those trusts for which we are accountable to the people.

'Now, unless the Lords co-operate with us in this, the sinews which allow us to move will be severed, and the stamp of approval which validates our actions will be removed. If Lords and Commons join together, this Petition will make history, as the record will show. If Lords and Commons are separated, our labours are as useful as glass hammers.

'There are, therefore, two expedients we must use in this business. First, we must not weaken our Petition in any way, not by a tittle or a jot, either in whole or in part. Secondly, we must win the coalition of both Houses in this endeavour. If we fail in either of these objectives, we destroy our own efforts.

'Our minds and our intentions are made up; we desire no new liberty for the subject; we have no wish to diminish the just and lawful prerogative power of the Crown; we seek to lessen no power of His Majesty to punish the criminal; we desire only to protect the innocent, since without fair trial, and with arbitrary imprisonment, there can be no peace for the innocent.

'Mr Speaker, with your leave I move the House that we may end this conference with good manners towards their Lordships, and persuade them not to take any further votes on these matters until we are nearer agreement with them. In doing so let us again profess our equal care with them to carry this Petition whilst preserving the sacred rights of the Crown undiminished.'

When I had finished, Sir John Eliot was doubtful about dealing with the Lords in this way. He thought the strategy was good, but if we pandered thus to the Lords, we were just playing second fiddle to them. He seemed to imply that I was being hypocritical.

Someone else actually said as much. I was angered by that, since all I was trying to do was use moderate methods to bring both Houses and the King together. If Lords and Commons could not work together, we stood no chance with the King.

Dear George, I am your affectionate friend,

Thomas.

I was beside myself with joy when the Lords agreed with the Commons.

The Petition was taken to the King on 26th May, and the hot-heads were incensed when he tried to avoid dealing with it. As a result the King once again got just what he did not want: the allegations about Buckingham were revived. Even Sir Edward Coke, definitely not a hot-head, rose in the House and called the Duke 'the cause of all our miseries, and the grievance of grievances', and yet another bitter attack on the favourite followed.

The King was misguided if he still expected us to rely solely on his word. When he gave his assent to the words "*soit droit fait comme est desire*" on the Petition on 7th June the Commons immediately renewed the allegations against the Duke and the demands for his dismissal.

****

I have placed myself in a double bind. The King may think that I was the foremost promoter of the Petition, which is true, and that I am also immoderate in my advocacy of it, which is untrue, and certainly not my intention. Conversely, many in the Commons (like Eliot) may see me as doing everything I can to preserve the King's prerogative, despite my working so hard to get the Petition endorsed by the Lords and accepted by the King. In some situations if you are not seen as on the lunatic fringe in favour of a policy, you are seen to be against it.

During the last three weeks of Parliament the House vents its fury on the fact that the customs have never been voted to the King, and the customs rates never approved. Many MPs are saying that continued collection of these taxes by the Crown is illegal, and that the money taken should be refunded. Lumping that together with the attack on Villiers, and the attack on that silly sermon, it is hardly surprising that Charles halted the sitting. I do not contribute to that debate.

Whilst that argument rages I have a very unexpected visit from Richard Weston, the Treasurer who succeeded my friend Cranfield, Earl of Middlesex. He sees me at my London home. He is an exceedingly suave and subtle gentleman, but I feel there is something untrustworthy about him, though I cannot define it. "The King and I have been talking about you, Sir Thomas. I've been aware for a long time that you have, until the last couple of years, always supported the Crown, and most royal policies. During those years the King's attention has been drawn to the fact that, although you are in the front line of the battle over the liberties of Englishmen, and of Parliament in particular, you are never extreme, but combined your advocacy of the Petition of Right with attempts to get the Commons to supply the King's financial needs."

"If you, My Lord Treasurer, have pointed these slight virtues out to the King, I am most grateful."

"Sir Thomas, I'm on your side, because you, like me, favour peace, not war with Spain. Even the Duke of Buckingham begins to see that if he wants to fight France, he needs peace with Spain. We can help each other. The King makes you an offer to join his ministry in due course, and I am here to summon you to an audience."

Arabella. 20th June, 1628. Westminster.

I've been in London for a few weeks with Thomas. I left William and Anne in the care of their nanny at Wentworth Woodhouse. It has been marvellous. Thomas has been so energetic, not just in the House of Commons, but also in the bedroom. I think it is because he is so excited by his part in the debates, and the success he had over the Petition.

Yesterday capped it all. We had a visit from Richard Weston in the morning, and Thomas was closeted with him in his study for a long while. When they came out, I invited him to stay to luncheon, and he kindly did so. He seems extraordinarily pleasant for as important a being as the Treasurer, and as straightforward and honest as Thomas. I think they like each other well. They are of similar height and colouring, but Weston is not as powerful-looking as my husband. Conversation over the meal was friendly and general, about our children, the forthcoming hunting season, our homes and estates, his family; all that sort of thing. I picked up no sense of what the men had discussed, and as they did not drop any hints, I did not care to ask. If they wanted me to know, they would say so.

About half-past-three Weston left. As soon as the footman closed the door behind him, Thomas seized my hand and dragged me, laughing, up to the bedroom. He slammed the door behind us, grabbed me round the waist and kissed me until I was breathless. I was quite as excited as he was, but I could not wait to find out what lay behind this sudden passion, so I pushed him away a little – only a little.

"What is it Thomas? What has happened? What did Weston say?"

He kissed me again, and again I had to break off. "Tell me, my love, or that will be the last kiss."

Thomas laughed at that, and said: "Oh no it won't, lovely one. When you hear what he said you won't be able to stop kissing me!"

"Are you being beastly, husband? Or are you going to tell me?"

"I am to have an audience with the King early next month. I am offered a position under the Crown. We are on our way, Arabella!"

I pushed my hands against his chest again. "Is this one of your silly jests, Thomas?"

"Far from it. He even gave me this note from the King."

He held it up for me to read, which I did, aloud. " 'You are to come to the Palace of Whitehall on 17th July'. It's unbelievable." And I threw my arms about his neck and kissed him voraciously. "So you are to be a friend of the King."

"Hardly that, my love. Apart from Villiers I think Charles has no friends. I fancy Villiers would not let anyone else get close enough to the King to become his friend. The Duke will have no rivals, actual or potential. Even the Queen is not allowed to get close to him."

"I cannot say that you don't let me close to you, husband." I kissed him again, and with my left hand fondled him through the cloth of his breeches. He was as hard as a cudgel already. He returned the compliment by unlacing my dress as fast as he could, and kissing and nibbling my breasts and sucking and biting on my nipples.

I had just released his weapon from his clothes when he pushed me back on the bed, threw up my skirts and petticoat, and plunged himself into me. I was already sopping wet, but this suddenness was a surprise as he is normally so tender and attentive to my wants. To my surprise I found I was as keen and eager to start with the main course as he was, but he was too rash, too out of control, like a young man having his first maid, and after no more than twenty powerful strokes and thrusts he came with a loud shout, leaving me gasping and unsatisfied on the brink of my own climax.

Even so, I was glad for him, knowing that he would not leave me like that. His lovemaking has been very strong these last few weeks. If it is not excitement, as I suggested just now, then it must be the rush of whatever humour it is fires men up for the battles they have on hand, whether of the soldiers' violent kind, or the politician or lawyer's intellectual one, especially when they have planned and won their vote or their case.

He did not leave me like that. Thrice he did not leave me like that.

****

How we found the strength to get dressed and go down to dinner later I do not know. Fortunately our romp went uninterrupted by the servants.

Naturally, as we ate we returned to the forthcoming audience with the King, and I raised a new thought with him. "Thomas, if the King is pleased with what you have been doing in his cause, even though you have also been working with Coke and Eliot and the others, won't they see your going over to the King as some sort of betrayal?"

It turned out not to have been a totally new thought to my husband; I might have expected that. "You're probably right; I've been thinking much the same myself. It's John Pym I shall have to look out for. He's a very wily parliamentarian."

Thomas. 20th June, 1628. Westminster.

John Pym had supported me in the March debate about the Bill of Rights. He is another fat little chap, and whilst he may not be unlike Bishop Laud in many ways to look at, they are totally unalike in matters of faith and politics. First, he is a staunch Puritan; secondly, he holds the Royal Court in contempt. He has no time for the Crown and Buckingham, but that hadn't stopped him being the Receiver of Rents for Crown Lands in Hampshire, Wiltshire, and Gloucestershire earlier in his career.

He comes from a Somerset family, and his father, Alexander, seems to have been the first to establish any claim to fame (as opposed to infamy - one ancestor had been heavily fined by Henry VII for supporting the pretender Perkin Warbeck), by becoming a JP and a well respected barrister of the Middle Temple. He - Alexander -had just been elected MP for Taunton when he died in 1585, when John was about one year old, so he's about eight or nine years my senior.

Unlike me, Pym went to Oxford, and like his father, he studied law in the Middle Temple. He first entered Parliament for Calne in 1621, and for Chippenham and then Tavistock in 1624, which is when I first came across him. Like me, he supported the supply of subsidies to the King then, but in his case that may have been a reflection of the fact that the collection of the King's rent for three counties was up to him. He is an extremely hard worker, very conscientious, completely convinced of the correctness of his own point of view, and quite oblivious to anybody else's. He has no discernible sense of humour, and cannot learn or remember his own speeches, whether in Parliament or in Court, but has to read them from his own unintelligible notes.

That makes it sound as though he would be a terrible and hopeless politician, but his mastery of parliamentary procedure gives him a huge advantage over many of his opponents, as anyone who falls foul of him quickly discovers.

He became passionate about religious questions in the Parliaments of 1625 and 1626, being extremely severe about the toleration of Catholics. Pym also savaged Richard Montague, Bishop of Chichester, for 'inclining and reconciling the people, as much as he can, to popery', as he put it. He was equally passionate about the impeachment of Buckingham, and was a prime mover in this, doing much to bring up to date the knowledge and practice of this antiquated procedure.

Pym was also the man behind the attacks on the priest who had delivered a sermon in favour of the Forced Loan. John Pym would be a frightful man to be anyone's nemesis.

Thomas. 26th June, 1628. Westminster.

Debate about the dismissal of Buckingham raged for a while. Charles would not tolerate the attacks on his favourite; today he prorogued the sitting until the autumn. Fortunately for him, I had helped persuade the House to grant the subsidies just before he did so.

Nothing could illustrate more clearly how misconceived the King and Buckingham are in what passes for a foreign policy and what would please the people than the announcement of a new attempt to rescue the Protestants of La Rochelle. More wasted money? More dead soldiers? More military disgrace? Only ambitious officers looking for pay, promotion, and plunder would fancy another such enterprise.

Charles I. 17th July, 1628. Whitehall Palace.

The Queen and I are sitting in our private audience chamber. It is a relatively small room for a palace, particularly one built by Cardinal Wolsey for himself when he was Archbishop of York. In his day it was known as York Place. There are two modestly throne-like chairs on a small dais. Apart from some of my beloved pictures on the walls – I can see a Michaelangelo, a Holbein, and a da Vinci opposite me – and some long, rich, velvet curtains at the large windows, there is no other furniture.

It is almost noon, and I am sitting back in my chair, legs crossed, and for me I am fairly relaxed. I prorogued Parliament three weeks ago, so at least those aggravating MPs are not causing me any anguish for a while, though I wish they had given me more money.

Henrietta Maria is leaning forward in her seat to look at me earnestly as she speaks. She is quite a lovely little thing, if truth be told, and it is a shame I do not love her, but her jealousy of my great friend, George, is more than a little off-putting. Her English has improved enormously in the three years we have been wed, and I do rather care for her French accent, which is as attractive to hear as I find her face and figure to look at now that she is no longer a child, but I find it very annoying that she tries to advise me on what to do. That is what she is doing at the moment, and we have that man Wentworth arriving in a few minutes. I am beginning to wonder why I asked her to join me this morning.

Queen. Is this wise Charles? If what the Speaker tells us is to be believed this man - this Wentworth - he is a trouble-rouser. He says the most terrible things about what you are doing. He is causing trouble.
Me. My dear; first I think you mean he is a rabble-rouser, and second he does not say terrible things about me or what I have been doing, but about what is being done in my name.
Queen._ So I hoping – sorry, so I hope. In France if he said anything against the King he would lose his head.
Me. But this is not France, and I am not Louis. In France, the Estates - what we call Parliament - are withering. The Kings call them

less and less frequently. In England, Parliament grows stronger all the time. Henry VIII spent all the money his father had saved, and more besides. He didn't dissolve the monasteries just because he fell out with the Pope. He destroyed them so he could spend their money and sell their land. Queen Elizabeth and my Father had repeatedly to call Parliament to ask for money. I am too poor to do otherwise.

Queen. But a King should be able to do as he likes - it is his right.

Me. And so it is, my love, but a wise King wants to carry his people with him so that they see that he acts only in the commonweal.

Queen. Commonweal?

Me. He must act in the whole country's interests. He should listen to the people through the voice of Parliament, but he alone should decide what is done.

Queen. But this Wentworth, he wants to be telling everyone what you should be doing.

Me. And that is exactly why I have commanded him to attend upon me! When he tells people what I should do, they listen. When he tells them what they should do about their grievances, they listen. But he is not disloyal to me. He's not disloyal to the throne. There is an old English saying; If you cannot beat them, join them. Well, a King can't join the opposition, but he can invite its fighters to join him.

Queen. That is what you will ask this Wentworth? To join you? It is a monstrous gamble. And if he will not serve? What if he wants to rule? What then? You may live to regret it, Charles.

Me. He may live to regret it. He may die because of it. Think of all those who died for having served the Tudors. Wolsey, More, Cranmer, Cromwell - all Thomases - just like Wentworth - even the best bloom of the flower of chivalry - Walter Raleigh - imprisoned and beheaded.

Queen. Treason is something for which men ought to be beheaded.

Me. But was it treason? Wolsey knew no greater crime than failing to achieve a policy on which the King had staked his all in a game in which the Pope held all the Aces. Thomas More was beheaded because he couldn't hide his conscience from the King. Cranmer was burnt alive because he refused to hide his from Queen Mary.

Queen. And Raleigh - he was executed by your father, I think?

Me. He was, after many years in prison under Elizabeth, and a disastrous voyage to South America, which failed to fill my father's coffers.

Queen. So, if this Thomas Wentworth fails you will execute him?

Me. I doubt that I am the executing kind, Henrietta, but even if I were, the danger to my servants comes not only from me. Look at how the House of Commons seeks to destroy George Villiers.

Queen. The Duke of Buckingham. Yes, you love him, but you know Charles, even though you are my husband and my King, that I cannot see him as you do. You love him, but you do not love me, and I am your wife.

Me. Enough, Henrietta! I have told you before not to speak to me like that. I am your husband. I am also your King and obey me you shall.

Queen. I try, Charles, I try, but sometimes is very hard. I do not want to see you turn from me to love some other Minister. And Villiers is not even good at the job - at least, that is what they are saying in the Commons - that is what this Wentworth is saying in the Commons.

Me. I am not choosing Wentworth for love - I am choosing him for fear of what he may do if I don't. He is a powerful speaker, and carries men with him, as he did over the Petition of Right. I need men like that working for me. In any case, you know that George wants to continue the war with France ...

Queen. That just shows how stupid he is.

Me. I shall ignore that. He wants to continue the war with France, but he is thinking now that we should make peace with Spain.

Queen. Wentworth has been saying for years you should make peace with Spain. He doesn't want war with France, because it costs too much.

Me. How on earth do you know that?

Queen. You dismissed all my French servants and ladies in waiting, Charles. You replaced them with ladies chosen by you – or by Buckingham, is more like. These ladies are married to men who know, or are the daughters of great lords. They talk. I listen. So, this Wentworth, he makes the Duke come up – you say up, or round?

Me. Round, probably.

Queen. The Duke is coming round to Wentworth's way of thinking?

Me. So am I. I cannot afford to fight two of the world's most powerful nations at once. Wentworth may have been right all along. I'm told he works very hard at any job he is given, as he has done on the Council of the North.

Queen. So there are three reasons to use him. He is eloquent and persuades people to agree with him, he is efficient, and on this point about war he persuades Buckingham. *Peut etre* he will not be so bad after all.

Me. Precisely, and on top of all that, he seems to be a pretty honest gentleman. I hope I may profit from his counsel.

Queen. And I may counsel you also?

Me. I'm not so sure about that. I'll have to think about it. What would people say if a woman busied herself with politics?

Queen. Have you forgotten the glory to which Queen Elizabeth, a mere woman, raised this realm?

Me. You are right my dear. "A mere woman, but with the heart of a King" was what she said. Sometimes I forget that you have the blood of Kings of France and Holy Roman Emperors in your veins.

Queen. My mother ran France after my father was killed, until Louis was old enough to take the reins. I am still not sure you should have this man, Charles.

At this moment there is a knock on the door and the Chamberlain steps inside the room when I answer. He bows and says: "Your Majesty - Sir Thomas Wentworth seeks admission."

"Then admit him."

The Chamberlain bows again, goes out, comes back, and announces Wentworth with another bow. I know I am King and am supposed to love all this flummery, but sometimes it just wastes time when I want to get on with the business of the country. Still, if I am to preserve the dignity of the monarchy – so diminished by my Father's vulgarity - I have to put up with it whether I like it or not.

Wentworth comes in. He is tall, and rather good-looking in a threatening way. He is dressed entirely in black, apart from a plain square white collar; I can see no jewellery. He does not seem at all abashed at appearing before me. He bows and kneels. "Your Majesty, you honour your humble servant beyond measure."

Henrietta gasps in sarcastic disbelief. I cover her hand with mine to stop her saying anything, and keep it there. For my part, I cannot think this arrogant looking man really thinks of himself as humble. Perhaps he is not quite as honest as I have been told. Perhaps I am unjust, though. There are every few courtiers who do not flatter me. I observe that he has a slight Yorkshire accent.

I wave my other hand in a gesture indicating that he should rise.

Me. I'm told your speeches are provocative, Sir Thomas. Humble men do not customarily provoke.

Wentworth I seek your pardon, Sire, if aught I say offends. Your Majesty's Court is not often in Yorkshire and I haven't had much chance of learning Courtly Language, and saying one thing and meaning something else. If my speeches give the impression that I -

Me. Do not trouble to explain your speeches to me, Sir Thomas. A dozen courtiers a day endeavour to do so, every day that Parliament sits. I think they will make me mad. Kings are by their very nature suspicious - they need no lessons in paranoia.

Wentworth Then Your Majesty will know that I am Your Majesty's loyal servant and -

Me. That you are critical of the manner and style of government, not of the fact that I am the governor? Yes, I know all that even if others do not.

Wentworth. Then, Sire......?

Me. Then Sir Thomas, will you turn your oratory to good effect in my cause? Will you advise and guide me, and present my policies to Parliament and the people so they see, so they learn, that they are my first care under God?

Wentworth. Why me, Your Majesty? There are other orators in the Commons.

Me. There are, but they are not moderate in their expression. Eliot is one of them, and I have a mind to have him locked in the Tower for the way he speaks about the Duke, and our policies. Such men have never supported the idea that the King needs money to govern, as you have done. Many of them want war with Spain and France, but I cannot afford it, and you have always wanted peace with Spain. Even the Duke is beginning to see that two wars are folly. Will you serve or not, Sir Thomas?

Wentworth. Your service shall be my constant and thorough study, Sire. I vow to devote all my care and diligence to the well-being of Your

Majesty and your subjects. *(He kneels).* At your right hand, I would lay down my life in that service.
Me. I pray that you will not have to do so, Sir Thomas. It is not often that I have to ask a man twice to accept preferment. Do I have to ask twice if you will accept the title of Baron?
Wentworth. I doubt that you will ever again have to ask me twice to do or be anything in your service, Your Majesty. I am overwhelmed and more grateful than I can fairly say.
Me. I suspected you might say you felt humbled by it, Sir Thomas, but I dare say your ambition lies higher than a mere barony, and that there is no promotion you would consider too high for you. Have you considered a title?
Wentworth. It would be false if I pretended I have not thought of it. Sire. Would you find Baron Wentworth of Wentworth Woodhouse, Newmarch and Overly, acceptable?
Me. If it is acceptable to you, it is to me. You will have to write it, and I shall not. If you don't find it cumbersome, why should I? That is all.
Wentworth. Your Majesty.

With that he bows, making a flourish with his broad-brimmed black hat, and backs out of the room. I find I am still holding Henrietta's hand, which is a fairly unusual occurrence.

John Pym. 1st August, 1628. Westminster.

I'm walking along a corridor in the House, between the Commons and the Lords, accompanied by Sir Harry Vane. When Parliament is sitting, he is MP for Thetford in Norfolk, though in the past he has normally been MP for Carlisle. Harry is a bright fellow, though I suspect he may be going deaf. He is very much on my side in the struggles with the King and the Duke, but does not make this public as he has profitable offices under the King, some of them going back to James's time.

He is a big man, with a sportsman's florid face, a huge moustache and a small beard. There is something almost piratical about him. Unlike me, he dresses in the height of fashion. Most people do if they hope to get on at Court, since the King sets the pace for the tailors, and men copy him as a form of flattery. As might be expected, we are discussing the political problems as we go.

Vane. The situation is getting serious, Mr Pym. Bishop Laud's power increases all the time and the King espouses his doctrines for reform of the Church. We're getting nowhere so far as ridding ourselves of the Duke goes. And now there is talk of peace with Spain!

Me. I'm tempted to say "Don't speak of Laud to me" and dismiss him with the contempt he deserves, but he's dangerous. A little, low, red-faced man of mean parentage he may be, but he's not without worldly wisdom. He has the King's ear, and the King listens. These religious questions are what concern me most. But Laud's efforts to bring the Country to a state of High Church Orderliness, and this talk of a new Prayer Book, may play into our hands.

Vane. True. Two nights ago, I was in a Tavern not a mile hence when I heard talk of it. One man said "The way Laud goes about his business is fit to cast himself and God in the role of the worst tyrants in the world".

Me. Yet King Charles is Laud's master so he should share the blame. And share it he must if the rumours are true.

Vane. Rumours?

Me. Have you not heard? Not even in your tavern? But no, I suppose it has not yet percolated so far. Rumour has it that when the Archbishop of Canterbury is dead, the Bishop of London, our unlovable William Laud, will be the new Archbishop, our new Primate of all England.

Vane. Then God help those of us of a Puritan turn of mind. Laud is, as you say, dangerous, and rises too quickly for my liking in the councils of the King and the Church. He was Bishop of St David's for a few years, then Chaplain at the Chapel Royal, then Bishop of Bath and Wells for a year, and elevated to London last month. If he reaches the very pinnacle of the Church he'll make life impossible for Puritans.

Me. We must count on it - the help of God and the people's fear of Popery and High Church. The King fails to understand these matters. He can't govern the country forever without money from Parliament. He cannot expect the House of Commons to vote Taxes and Subsidies which they fear will be used against them and their religious consciences. If we - if I - can so manage the next Parliament as to keep those fears for their religion, unjust taxes, arbitrary imprisonment and so on in the forefront of their minds, then we shall make it impossible for the King to control Parliament. And in the end we may be able to control the King.

Vane. Right now he's controlled by his advisors, including Laud.

Me. 'Controlled' is too strong a word - the King knows his own mind. The difficulty is that he seems unable to take good advice, but to prefer the bad sort from those not fitted to give any, like Buckingham.

Vane. And to put cap it all, the Queen is a Catholic. The talk in the Taverns is clear - the Catholic Queen is behind many of the causes of discontent.

Me. Yes, but a change in the King's counsels may be coming. Have you heard that the King has raised Thomas Wentworth to the peerage?

Vane. Sorry, I missed that. What did you say?

Me. The King has raised Wentworth to the House of Lords.

Vane. My God!

Me. Yes. To the House of Lords, and what's more, to high office. He is soon to be appointed Lord President of the Council of the North. Some say he may be appointed Lord Treasurer, though I doubt that will happen. We must watch him closely.

Vane. That we must; he's a powerful speaker, an able administrator, and absolutely fearless.

Me. Aye, fearless. That may yet be his undoing. He has principles, and he stands by them. I fancy we shall find him unyielding when what is politic conflicts with those principles. He can't afford to make too many enemies of the rich and powerful. The poor and powerless don't count. His policy may be to help the lower orders, but they command no majorities, and pay no armies.

Vane. His principles!! What have principles to do with politics?

(We are standing at the end of the passage, and as Vane says that, who comes out of a door on our left but Wentworth? He speaks in his usual arrogant fashion.)

Wentworth. What have principles to do with politics Sir Harry? Much, I hope, for without the one the other is a short route to chaos.

Me. Didn't Sir Thomas More say that any man who puts himself forward for public office is automatically unfitted for it?

Wentworth. So he did Master Pym, yet the three of us have not been backward in putting ourselves forward, have we? But it is only by adopting some principles and sticking to them that we have any hope for the future. Promise of office should be a spur to better things, not a recipe for greed and corruption.

Me. Are you without greed and corruption My Lord - what is it now - Baron Wentworth of Wentworth Woodhouse, Newmarch and Overley? And tomorrow, perchance, Lord President of the North? What other titles await you?

Wentworth. Why, Mr. Pym, if I didn't know you better I should say you were envious. I'm as fond of money as any man and I do not expect to go out of politics poorer than I came in, but my greatest ambition is to serve His Majesty and the people well, and to shelter the poor and innocent from the proud and insolent.

Vane. Much good may the poor and innocent do you if the proud and insolent, as you call them, are against you, my lord. Your persistent attacks on men in the highest places will embarrass the King and all who desire a quiet life. Your victims will ultimately return to haunt you.

Wentworth. I attack only those whose corruption undermines the power of the King, or oppresses the poor. Having served in three Parliaments I can see it's far safer that the power of the King should increase than the people should gain advantage over the King. His power may prejudice a few particular people, but if they get power over him it draws everything to ruin. It's like a schoolroom in which the pupils gain ascendancy over the Master, who can no longer teach, whilst the pupils can no longer learn.

Me. Yes, My Lord, and so to get your own share of power you've gone to the House of Lords and left the Commons, but whilst you may leave us, we shall never leave you whilst your head is still on your shoulders.

(I am really annoyed when Wentworth laughs at that).

Wentworth I care naught for your threats, Master Pym. They are the essence of pride and insolence. Is the Commons so wonderful a place? I believe if I walked into a chamber full of Members of Parliament and shouted "Fly at once, the secret is out," many would be killed in the stampede for the door.

Vane. And what secret is that?

Wentworth. Why, Sir Harry, they all have a secret - even you, I dare say. But I jest. I don't share the King's prejudice against Parliaments in general. I object only to the behaviour of certain Parliaments in

particular. I do not forget that I was a member of the Lower House, and now I am a member of the Upper.
Me. Have you rejected your old opinions, then, that it is better for King and Parliament to agree than for one to try to gain the supremacy over the other?
Wentworth. I still hold that view. If the King had honoured the grievances of the Petition of Right, and if the Commons had granted him the Revenue he needed, we should not now be in this present ghastly pass.
Vane. But the King would not listen.
Me. And he should listen. Parliament is a vital part of the state and the King should use it to learn the needs of the country.
Wentworth. I agree, but recent Parliaments have confused legitimate needs with unjust demands. They've thrown away the chance of offering sound advice to the King on the mood of the people.
Me. Do you truly think you can help the King to take more notice of the people, My Lord?
Wentworth. If the King governs justly for a time, he'll gaiin the affections of the people, and the past will be forgotten. I tell you this, gentlemen, if the people think that if Parliament gains power over the King, Parliament will listen to the people, they shall be much mistaken.

(Wentworth turns smartly away and strides off down the corridor).

I am not finished, however. "You must be happy for your friend on his elevation to the Lords, too."

That stops him. He turns. "And which friend is that, may I ask?"

"Why, My Lord, surely you have written to congratulate Sir John Savile on being created Baron of Pontefract."

Wentworth is clearly shocked. "We pronounce it Pomfret in Yorkshire," which I find a pretty feeble retort, and now it is my turn to laugh.

Thomas. 24th August, 1628. London.

Buckingham has breathed his last. News came by the fastest horsemen from Portsmouth to the King; Villiers was stabbed to death there yesterday. The news spread like a flood through the cities of London and Westminster. The King will be distraught, but Parliament is rid of one of its most serious problems, and the people are celebrating in a manner verging on the riotous. There are bonfires everywhere, the taverns and inns are full to overflowing, bells are even being rung in some churches, and not the death toll either. Such gaiety and rejoicing has not been seen for many a year. I heard one old man say he's seen nothing like it since the Armada was driven off.

Apparently what happened was this.

Lieutenant John Felton was one of the Duke's officers during the invasion of the Ile De Re. He had had no pay, he had been deprived of his ambition, and he would get no plunder. Last year, when the army was retreating from St Martin to Loix, the commander of Felton's group of soldiers was shot dead, and he took command. As a result he expected to be promoted to his late superior's rank, but Buckingham passed him over. On returning to England he had no position and little money. What he saw as betrayal by Buckingham worked on his mind in depressed isolation.

He bought copies of the Parliamentary speeches which were aimed at the Duke in the House. These inflamed his passion to revenge himself and the country on this 'cause of all the evils the kingdom suffers, and the enemy of the public', as one of the speeches called Buckingham, and as some sermons repeated. One of these speeches was found in Felton's hat. He said he put it there in case he was slain before he could explain himself.

Buckingham was being accommodated by a Captain, the reception rooms of whose house were swarming with people that morning because there was gossip (quite untrue, as it turned out) that La Rochelle had been relieved. Army and navy officers were worried that, if it were true, they might lose the chance of another campaign in France, and refugee Huguenots who were convinced the story was just a rumour, were all there clamouring for Buckingham's attention.

Felton had no trouble insinuating himself into the clamorous crowd, and stabbed the Duke straight through the heart as he moved from one room to another. None of us who had spoken against Buckingham and wished to be rid of him had foreseen this result of our efforts. I cannot say that any of us were sorry, but it was not the end we had expected.

I'm far from sure what is going to happen to me now. Will Buckingham's removal ease my path or make it more difficult? If I do not go up the ladder, who will? If it is someone else, will they tread on my fingers to make sure I do not get any higher? Not that I am really very high yet. I may be a Baron, but I have no important office. I am not a member of the Privy Council, so my opportunities of impressing the King with anything I may say or do are pretty remote. Still, I must stick to what I believe in. Much as I want power and riches, I do not want them at any price.

My philosophy of government is practical, and so, I hope, are my principles. I do not want war with the Austrians over the Palatinate and Bohemia. The country can't afford it; we can't win with the size of army we can raise; the Emperor has a well-trained and experienced army already, even if they were given a mauling for a few years by the Swedes under Gustavus Adolphus. I despair of seeing what we could gain by victory anyway. Sorry as I feel for the French Protestants, fighting Louis XIII is a waste of money and men for the same reasons.

The war with Spain must be terminated as soon as possible. It harms our trade, and the nation will never be prosperous if we go on with it.

Our prosperity depends on stability at home, and that in turn depends on the liberties of the subject and the peaceful ownership of our properties. Those are the things for which I fought so hard nursing the Petition of Right through Parliament and having it accepted by the King. If we manage all these elements, we can put the economy of England on a sound footing. With stable finances we can have good government, and the King, the fount of all justice under God, can shelter the poor and innocent from the rich and insolent, as I have said before.

At the moment the King tries to govern the country, and Parliament tries to govern the King and the people, and it just does not work to have two rival overlords. For me, the King has to be the ruler. The Crown has the power to appoint or dismiss ministers. The King has his Privy Council from which to seek advice. When it comes down to it, Parliament is little more than a debating chamber with no power to do anything except obstruct policy by withholding money. At least, that is what it usually does. I have to try to make King and Parliament function together, but if that is impossible, the King must be the ultimate authority.

I know people like Pym and Eliot, and even Denzil, think my view is naïve, but I hope it is pragmatic. I may secure surer results by saying and doing what I mean than by making shady deals to agree to things I do not believe in so that I can get my own way on something else. I fail to see how that sort of bargain can be a matter of principle.

Thomas. 5th December, 1628. London.

It is three months and two weeks since Felton assassinated the Duke of Buckingham. I have wondered for much of that time what would happen to the murderer in the end. I recorded earlier that when news of the Duke's death spread there was great rejoicing all over the country, except in the King's private world. A neighbour, Sir John Hippisley, told me that it was he who whispered the news of Buckingham's murder to the King in the Royal Chapel when the King was praying. The King showed no emotion, but at the end of the service retired to his bed where he was distraught with grief for days on end. How the peal of bells and the people's gaiety must have clashed with his tears and sobs!! Will he ever get over it?

The people's joy did not quickly vanish as so many public demonstrations of feeling do. Wrong as Felton's crime was, there was an almost heroic aspect to it, since he rid the nation of an incubus that no other method had succeeded in doing. Immediately after the killing he appeared before the crowd in which he had been concealed, and publicly acknowledged that he was the perpetrator. It seems that he believed he would be praised for his actions, but he was arrested at once, hauled before the magistrates, and sent to London for questioning.

Did he act alone? Were there accomplices? The Privy Council was very anxious to know these things.

Felton was fortunate that the Petition of Right had been accepted by the King, since it forced the prosecution (backed by the Privy Council) to apply to the Courts for permission to rack and torture him for details of the accomplices he was suspected of having. The Judges stood firm, denying the request, and stating that torture was contrary to the laws of England. It pleased many of us, me, Sir Edward Coke, Eliot, and others, that our insistence on the Petition should have borne fruit so very soon.

In the meanwhile public joy at Villiers' death continued. A priestly Oxford scholar wrote that Felton had saved England and the King from

Buckingham's corruption. An unknown hand penned some doggerel the first couplet of which recited:

'The Duke is dead, and we are rid of strife
By Felton's hand that took his life'.

Felton was tried two weeks ago. Curly haired, rather handsome, and surprisingly gentle-looking, he was hanged a week ago today, on 29th November. He was fortunate not to have been drawn and quartered. This was not the end of the extreme vexation the King suffered from the aftermath of his favourite's death. The murderer's corpse, taken from Tyburn to Portsmouth there to hang in chains as a warning to other malefactors, has become instead an object of the veneration normally reserved for the relics of a saint.

I have been rather luckier. I've been told that I am shortly to be appointed President of the Council of the North, and because of that, I am to be a Viscount: Viscount Wentworth of Wentworth Woodhouse, Newmarch, and Oversley. (The King was right; that is a ridiculously long name, but it would look very silly to try to do something about it now). I've only been a Baron for five months and now I'm a Viscount, so how high can I go, and how quickly?

How I came by this promotion to President and this elevation to another rank of the peerage is due to my having dealt, at last, with Savile of Pontefract. For some time I had been approached, as a member of the Northern Council with tales, and in some cases with evidence, of Savile's taking bribes and indulging in other dubious conduct. I had been able to do little about these matters during Buckingham's lifetime and his patronage of my old enemy, but once he was gone, I sent all I had against Savile to the Privy Council. The complaints were upheld, and he was removed from the office of Vice-President. The President, Lord Scrope, was in the pockets of Savile and the Duke, and without them he was finished, too.

The vacancy had to be filled, and I was the King's choice. Has all this happened in five months? I can hardly believe it; I have waited so long.

I shall have a salary of 2000 pounds a year. I am buying more land than I am selling, spending more than I receive, but increasing the amount of property I own as a result. In due course rents will balance the books.

Arabella. 30th December, 1628. York.

I am the wife of a Viscount. I am the wife of the President of the North. I'm a very contented woman. I have a handsome, clever, powerful, rich, husband, and two adorable children, William, and Anne (we call her Nan). I love Thomas very much. He tells me I make him happier than he has ever been, but if I am honest with myself, being Viscount and Viscountess Wentworth, and he President of the Council, play a great part in his happiness.

We are trying hard to make another baby, a past-time I have no objection to at all. Indeed, the fact that success is eluding us for the time being is not so much a worry for me as the fact that without being pregnant we can go on trying for so much longer, and that is a pleasure and anything but a worry. Should a lady enjoy it quite so much? Perhaps I am no lady.

Today I have been enjoying Thomas in a quite different fashion. I went with him to hear his speech opening the Council of the North as its new Lord President. Old Scrope has gone. He was tired and almost past it, and Savile's stooge into the bargain. In his place the North now has a President who is young, dynamic, ambitious, and beholden to no-one except the King – and me, he would say!

As best as I can recall, this is what he said:

"I come before you all today as the most grateful man in the world. I think you can see that for yourselves. The great trusts you have placed in me are their own testimonial. Even when I was treated by others like a deadly disease you dared to clasp me to your bosoms again. What greater confidence or warmer affection could be placed in the scales to weigh my good fortune?

"In the other scale let us put the free bounties I have received from my gracious Master, His Majesty the King. Let us weigh what has happened to me in the space of a year. Then I was like a bird cast out of the nest, and then in prison. Now I am back on my own Yorkshire soil, amongst the companions of my youth, my house honoured, and I entrusted with the rich endowment of this office, a barony, and the title of Viscount.

"Am I not a lucky man? Can you show me so sudden, so strange a variation in private fortune? Tell me, was anyone ever so extravagantly rewarded? Was such credit ever given to so great a

debtor? Thus I am faced with an obstacle before I begin, from owing more both to King and people than I shall ever be able to repay.

"Yet in an effort to make good my indebtedness to you all, and to the King, I swear that throughout my ministry in this office I shall devote all my care and diligence to the well-being and joint interests of sovereign and subject.

"I am well aware that of late some ill-disposed persons have tried hard to separate those interests. They try to represent the interests of the King and his people as though they were opposed to each other, with different objectives. That is a wicked and corrupt concept, a monstrous suggestion. We cannot all be the head of the family, or all its limbs. Princes should be kind fathers nurturing their subjects like children, protecting their freedoms; the sober and respectable rights of the people should be precious in the eyes of the King. The King's government should shelter and shade the people that they may live in comfort and peace.

"The King's subjects, on the other hand, should be solicitous to protect the prerogatives of the Crown, for it is the authority of the King which is the keystone of the arch of government, and without it the whole structure falls apart, into a heap of broken walls, foundations, and battlements. The strength and beauty of our system of government would be lost.

"This system of love and protection descending from monarch to people, and of obedience and loyalty ascending from them to him is what should always pass between a King and his people. The faithful servants of King and people, the ministers, the Members of Parliament, and the Lords, should weave these elements together, and labour and study hard to maintain the rights and duties of both without enlarging or diminishing either, and, by observing the old traditions and customs, strangle any chance of dispute at birth.

"Anyone who tries to separate the interests of King and people shall never be able to restore them to their former glory and good order.

"Let us work together to maintain that sense of order. Gentlemen, I call upon you to support me in the efforts I shall make to serve both you and the King. I ask you to put your private interests to one side, to join hands and hearts with me and with each other, so that we may go on cheerfully as one man in the service of the public. My own life I

dedicate to that end, I do assure you. Here and now, before you, I offer myself as an instrument for good for the use of every man. He that uses me most has the greater part of my heart, even though he be the least significant man in the Council's jurisdiction.

"Having said which, His Majesty has instructed me to say this: he will no longer tolerate numerous applications to the Courts in London designed to take away the right of this Court to deal with local matters. That procedure has led to endless strife between the Council of the Welsh Marches and the Chancery Court on the one hand, and the Court of King's Bench on the other. It is a procedure open, in effect, only to the rich who can afford lawyers to argue endlessly in one Court after another, and so deny the more humble subject any justice anywhere. Neither the King nor I have any quarrel with the jurisdiction of the Common Law Courts, but we shall not let those Courts take away the powers of the Courts set up by the Monarch for specific purposes in different areas of the country.

"The King is the fount of all justice in the Kingdom, and he has endowed this Council of the North with all his power. The Court of this Council is a shelter for the poor and innocent from the rich and insolent.

"It is my greatest ambition above any earthly thing, to serve His Majesty and you acceptably and fruitfully. I challenge you to give me your help as best you can; indeed, I demand it of you. You will not as friends, you may not as Christians, you cannot as lovers of your country, deny me this."

When he sat down there was a stunned silence for a moment, and then loud applause and cheers echoed around the room. I was so proud of him, but I wondered about the wisdom of using his saying about 'poor and innocent and proud and insolent' so publicly. Many of the Lords and 'gentlemen' on the Council, and many of those in the galleries, are amongst the proudest and most insolent you could wish to meet, and very far from wanting the poor and innocent whom they victimise to be protected or sheltered by anybody.

But then that is Thomas all over. He says exactly what he thinks and means what he says, and I'm not sure he always thinks of the consequences. He had enemies enough in the last two Parliaments when he was opposed to the Court and to Buckingham and his policies. Is he going to start making enemies on the other side now he is working for the King? He has enough trouble with the Saviles; I dare say most of the gentry there today realised all that stuff about Thomas being treated like a deadly disease and a bird cast out of the nest was aimed at them.

I think he's bound to be a pretty aggressive and demanding bird in the nest when we get to bed tonight, he's so pumped up and full of himself. So he should be; I think he's wonderful.

Christopher Wandesford. 20th January, 1629. York.

Tom has lost no time. He wants a Council he can control. Who better to help him do that than me and George? He has made some other appointments to make sure his policies are followed. Since all Presidents of this Council have always appointed their friends and supporters to sit on it, one might be forgiven for thinking that nepotism was rife in the North. In fact one would usually be right, but in Thomas's case, he picks men who have ability: they are not noticeably "Yes men," either. I can hear someone say, "Well, Kit, you are one of them so you're bound to approve of his choice".

I suppose so, but no-one can question that George's ability is proven. He has a very successful practice in London and up here. He's been Tom's right hand legal man for years now, and for other members of the Wentworth family. I had a letter from Denzil the other week saying his Father, Earl Clare, has now taken to getting his solicitor to brief George. You don't get that kind of work if you're no use in Court.

Even his spell in prison in the Marshalsea and Dartford with Tom eighteen months ago did his career no harm at all. It may even have done him some good on both sides of the political divide, since no-one could deny that he was a man who stuck to his principles, and it gained him a lot of publicity. He was lucky there, though, in a strange way, because if he had been imprisoned after trial and found guilty, his Inn would probably have had to disbar him. Barristers with criminal records are not permitted to appear in Court.

Not only has Tom put us both on the Council; he persuaded the King to appoint George as his Attorney-General in York, so he is the Council's lawyer. A better one the King would be hard put to it to find, but what will old enemies like Savile think?

Being friends with Tom has certainly been advantageous to me, and to George. He helped me be chosen as MP for the town of Richmond, Yorkshire in 1625 and again in 1626 for Thirsk, when I helped Eliot with the attack on Buckingham. Tom thinks the impeachment was not wise; I have come to agree with him that what the Commons needed was patience and courage to find a proper cure for all the wrangling between King and Parliament. Concentrating on the wrongs done to individuals should not blind us to the necessity to save the ship of state first, and then go after the captain who ran us on the rocks.

That was the attitude I adopted when I sat for Thirsk in the 1628 Parliament. Tom is right. We have to work with the King, not against him. Yet sometimes I have to wonder at Tom's methods. Recently George told me that "Tom loves justice for its own sake." Yet something happened last week that makes you wonder whether what he really enjoys is discomforting 'the proud and insolent', as he calls them.

The Court of the Council had assembled, and was waiting for Tom, as Lord President, to enter. In he came, preceded by certain officers and the Sheriff bearing the Council's mace. Everyone stood and doffed their caps, and bowed. These formalities are not so much to honour the President as to acknowledge that he is the King's representative and the personification of justice on the King's behalf. The Presidential party, in ceremonial regalia, proceeded down the middle of the Court, between the benches on either side, crowded as they were with bowing, hatless men. One man stood tall, his scarlet hat jauntily perched on his head, right by the centre aisle, not two feet from Tom. This arrogant young fellow was Henry Bellasis. Some say he was prompted to this display of discourtesy by Tom's own disdainful and autocratic manner, and that Tom's affronted reaction was a personal one.

I do not see it like that. I believe Tom was affronted on the King's behalf, but I thought what he did was inappropriate. He stopped, took Bellasis by the forearm, and commanded him to bow and remove his cap on the instant. Bellasis smiled, and did nothing. Tom immediately called the constables and had him arrested, taken to the jail, and then sent forthwith to the Star Chamber in London to answer for his behaviour.

Whilst I accept that what young Henry did was extremely offensive, I fancy that I should have dealt with him rather differently. I should have snatched off his cap, thrown it on the ground, stood on it, told him I believed his Father would have brought him up better than that, and walked on. I expect that would have raised a laugh at his expense, and that would have been the end of that. As it is, Tom has definitely established himself as a President not to be trifled with, but he has also made an enemy or two. Henry will not enjoy being held in custody until his case is heard, nor will he and his Father, Lord Fauconberg, welcome the fine or other penalty his foolish conduct merits.

These two are well-known, well-connected, and quite well liked in the North. They have been friendly with Tom in the past. Indeed, when Tom got me my Parliamentary seat at Thirsk, he did so by using his influence with Fauconberg, in whose gift that town is. That influence with the Bellasis family will be lost now; and any influence they may have elsewhere will be used against Tom, not for him.

Of course, Tom has shown, without any shadow of a doubt, that he fears no-one, on the Council or outside it. It may be that is due to his wealth and his enormous sway as a mighty landowner, but in my view he would probably be the same in any event as Lord President even if he were relatively poor. He is arrogant, but determined to do the right thing so far as lies in his power.

He has established a commission to look into the operation of the Poor Laws here in the North. That will not be too popular, to put it mildly, bearing in mind that the rates to help the poor, build work-houses and so on, come from the rich. He has also laid out policies to keep an eye on the performance of the Justices of the Peace. That is part of his plan to make sure that justice is available for all. That will not please those landowners who use their position on the bench to oppress those whose lands they have taken, or wish to take.

We shall have some exciting times, I can see.

Arabella. 10th February, 1629. York.

Thomas and the children and I are still up North, and I have just come in from the town. I go straight to the library, where I find Thomas working with Christopher and George Radcliffe. Thomas looks up.

"Thomas, I must tell you?"

"Where have you been, my love?"

"I've been to the dressmakers and the furriers. I thought I told you where I was going."

"So you did, but I forgot."

Radcliffe smiles at me. "I thought you usually send for these people to attend you here."

"I do, but it's so cold I thought a walk would brace me up a bit, and I went to see if some new, warm clothes I ordered were ready for a fitting. Then I went to select some fur for a new coat. But I have something I must tell you."

"The snow is still thick on the ground, and it's been there four weeks now. No sign of a thaw. You'll need the furs, dear." Thomas comes from behind the desk and places a chair for me before the fire. "What sort of fur did you ...."

"Never mind that, Thomas. I picked up the most amazing piece of news in the dressmakers. I met the Dean's wife. She said the Bishop told her husband that he has heard from the Bishop of London that it's all over the City."

Kit laughs. "What is all over the City?"

"About Frederick and his boy."

"Frederick? You mean the Elector Palatine?"

"Yes, Thomas, that Frederick. He was on a boat sailing from somewhere near Haarlem to another town when the boat sank. He was badly injured, and they say he might die."

"And the boy? What's his name?" Thomas asks. All three men are standing in front of me now.

George speaks before I can. "I think he's a Frederick too. Or was, if he didn't recover."

Thomas nods. "That's it. Frederick Henry. I think he's about fifteen. The King will be sad if he has lost a nephew." Thomas is quite stern. "But it's a good thing Frederick and Elizabeth have two more boys; Charles Louis and Rupert. Otherwise they'd have no heir; not that they've got much to inherit now Frederick has lost Bohemia and the Palatinate."

I am intrigued by what has just been said. "What about an heir to the English throne? She could be our Queen if Charles has no children."

George chimes in. "And her son could be our King, if something happened to her."

Thomas's mood changes. "No more talk of that. Next you'll be imagining the death of the King, and that's treason even to speak of it. But until the King and Henrietta have some children, and preferably some boys, Elizabeth is next in line."

"Then we must pray that they beget some soon, husband, or a new Queen Elizabeth would have us fighting in Europe for Charles Louis' lands and titles."

The men all mutter at once. "God forbid."

Denzil Holles. 20th April, 1629. King's Bench Prison.

I have a visit from Thomas today. He is, of course, in the House of Lords now, so we are not working together in the Lower House any longer, and I cannot work even there until I get out of here. In fact, I am fairly certain that we shall be working together in no sense at all soon. He is more and more part of the Court faction, and I am still part of the opposition. Our ships are drifting further and further apart. This may be a prison, but my room is dry, I have reasonable furniture (mine, of course), and as I have money I am treated well. There is even a fair sized barred window, but I have an oil-lamp alight. The damp squalor in the part of the jail occupied by the poor is dreadful.

Thomas is well aware of the fracas – almost an affray – in the Commons on 2nd March, but is anxious to hear the details from me, principal actor in the drama as I was.

"Parliament had only been sitting for a few weeks, and the main debates were all about religion and money. There's so much strong feeling about all this church ceremonial – what some are calling Arminianism – and the House is largely against it."

"It's the doctrine Laud favours."

"Yes, Thomas, and it's odd that you favour him. Friendship with him will do you no good."

"I hardly know the man, but from what I've read of his sermons and pamphlets, he has very similar views to mine on the role of the Monarch, and of the Church in supporting the King, and of the King supporting the Church. Remember what King James said when the Scots and Puritans wanted to get rid of the Bishops? No? Perhaps you are too young."

That annoyed me a bit. "I'm not that much younger than you, Thomas, but tell me anyway."

"What he said, Denzil, was 'No Bishop, no King!' He knew the one depended on the other. So why do you believe that being friends with Laud will do me no good? The gossip is that he will soon be Archbishop of Canterbury."

"Because it makes you look pro-Catholic. Soon after the King opened Parliament a member called Rouse told the House an Arminian is the spawn of a Papist, and if you look closely, you will see an Arminian reaching out a hand to a Papist, and a Papist to a Jesuit, while the Jesuit gives one hand to the Pope and the other to the King of Spain. You can't afford to throw in your lot with the Catholics."

Thomas is magisterial: "If the House thinks that is what Laud is doing they are much mistaken. He and I have little time for the Pope and his flock, and my desire for peace with Spain is due, not to a love of Rome, but of saving us from the expensive disasters Buckingham was wont to inflict upon us. Heaven knows, the Commons doesn't trip over its own feet in the rush to fill Charles's war chest, does it?"

That stopped me a bit; Thomas has, as usual, exposed the hypocrisy of the Commons for what it is.

"The point is that Laud is going up the Church ladder much too fast for our liking. There'll be no stopping him until he has homes in Canterbury and Lambeth Palace. I doubt the people will put up with it, even if the King – and you – might like it."

"I cannot say I like it, but I prefer to have him as an ally in supporting the Crown than on the other side, Denzil."

"You mean on my side, then. Be careful how many enemies you make, Thomas. If he is your ally, then so are Bishops like Montague at Chichester. They take this idea of the Divine Right of Kings too far. I always thought your idea was that the King and Parliament should work together, but if Montague is right, the King doesn't need Parliament at all. He can just do exactly as he likes."

"I don't think that, Denzil, and well you know it. What worries me though, is that the way the Commons – and you – behaved in March will make the King think he should never deal with a Parliament again."

I began to get angry. "That wasn't about religion. Anyway, what do you expect. It was about money."

Thomas is calm. "I know that. When I was in the Commons last year we were going to grant the King his Tunnage and Poundage in the customary way at last, but when the King prorogued Parliament to stop the attack on Villiers the chance was lost. That was what the main debate was about at the beginning of March and ..."

I am angrier still. "You hardly need to remind me what it was about. I was there; you weren't."

"So tell me."

I restrain myself. "Very well. The money and the religious matters are tied up to some extent. Sir John Eliot told the House we should not vote the King his Tunnage and Poundage and the right to set the rates himself unless he has a religious policy that suits us. There was a great deal of sympathy for that. The next day the Speaker read out a message from the King ordering us to keep to subjects we understood. Well, bloody hell, you can …."

"No need to swear, Denzil. You know I do not care for it. And I can – what? - imagine how the members reacted to that? Yes, indeed I can."

"They were furious, and insulted. Fancy suggesting that they didn't understand their own religion, and the practice of it! Many of them read the Bible every day, and are regular Church-goers, even if they don't all go to the same type of Church. Some shouted angrily that telling us what we could and could not discuss was another infringement of freedom of speech in the House and that the Petition of Right wasn't even a year old yet. There was chaos."

Thomas was thoughtful. "It was certainly not a wise message. I wonder who advised the King to send it."

"Who cares; it was probably his own idea. Anyway, the next day, 2nd March, the Speaker had another message from him, telling him to prorogue the House again. Speaker Finch tried to rise from his chair, to adjourn the House, but I ran across the chamber with Ben Valentine and William Strode, and we grabbed his arms and forced him back down and a couple of us sat on his lap. Finch was in tears."

"I'm not surprised. And then you put those motions before the House?"

Denzil laughed. "We were almost robbed of them by Eliot, yet he had drafted them. He was so mad with rage at Finch telling the House to adjourn, that he tore up his notes and threw them in the fire, saying that the King was stopping us debating them."

Puzzled, I say: "So how were they put forward?"

"I had them off by heart, and recited them, and the clerks wrote them down. First, no-one should make innovations in religion, or encourage Popery or Arminianism; secondly, no-one should advise or help the King on the collection of Tunnage and Poundage without Parliamentary sanction, and thirdly, no-one should pay it; and anyone who did any of these things was a capital enemy of the Kingdom and Commonwealth."

"So Parliament could have them executed, Denzil?"

"Exactly."

"And then what happened?"

"Your friend Christopher Wandesford was one of those who voted against the motion, but we had a majority. A week later the King dissolved Parliament, and ..."

"What did you expect?"

"... and his guards came to the House and arrested me, Eliot, Valentine, and Strode, and a few others. We were taken before the Court. Eliot refused to make any defence or apology, and told the Judges that 'being but a private man, I will not trouble myself to remember what I may have said or done as a public man' and they sent him to the Tower. We say what the Judges did was illegal."

Thomas nodded. "But laying hands on Finch like that to hold him in his chair was an assault. Not just that, but an assault on the Speaker! Assault is a crime, Denzil. If a peasant had done it he would have been hanged, flogged, or branded. Didn't any of you apologise?"

"Of course not! We didn't regret what we'd done. We had nothing to be ashamed of; in fact we were pretty proud of it."

"And here you are."

"Yes Thomas, here I am. All of us were fined, and some were sent to prison. A few were allowed out on bail as long as they behave themselves, but I told the Judges that I would rather be the subject of His Majesty's mercy than of his power. One of them asked me: 'Don't you mean you'd rather be the subject of his mercy than of justice?' And I said: 'I say of His Majesty's power, My Lord. His justice and his mercy should be the same thing.'"

Thomas laughed at that. "Very noble. In fact almost what More is supposed to have said to Thomas Cromwell. Cromwell told him that if he would not acknowledge Henry as Head of the Church, he was threatened with justice, and More is said to have replied: 'Then I am not threatened.'"

"So here I am, in prison."

"What will you do?"

"I shall try to make peace with the King. I may need your help."

"We shall see. I must go. Arabella sends her love."

"She's a good sister. I hope she is well. Give her mine."

Thomas nods. "By the way, did you hear the sad news about the Queen?"

"No; what has happened to her?"

"Fortunately nothing happened to her, but she was pregnant. It seems to prove that it is true, and not just Court gossip, that the King and Queen are actually in love with each other now. Unfortunately, she had a baby son, and he died an hour later."

"But we have no heir to the throne. Charles has no brother, and his sister is tied up in Europe fighting the Emperor and Spain. If she becomes Queen it'll cost the country a fortune."

"Then Charles and Henrietta will just have to keep on trying, won't they, Denzil."

Thomas. November, 1629. York.

The King has made me a Privy Councillor! Now I can really serve him, advise him, and achieve much for him, and the country, and let us make no mistake, for me too. I'm a Viscount, a Privy Councillor, and President of the Council of the North. Can I go yet higher? (I always seem to be asking that question). I think so. I want to be the King's right-hand man as Buckingham was, but I'll be better than the Duke. I know I have my own interests, but I can put the King and the country's needs before mine, and that is how I shall rise, too.

Many men in my position use the money they collect for the Crown on their own business. They 'borrow' it. They often deliberately fail to pay it into the Exchequer when it is due. They rip off more than the percentage they are entitled to for collecting it, and some do not even keep accurate records of what they do collect, so that they can keep a huge chunk secretly, and still take their slice of what they are good enough to hand over to the King!

That, of course is what Sir Arthur Ingram used to do (or perhaps still does). I do not do this and have no intention of starting. Certainly I borrow the money and use it to buy property, invest in the alum industry, and things of that sort, but I pay it over in full when it is due. I do not take more than I am entitled to, but I must admit that when I took over collection of the recusancy fines I arranged to double what I was entitled to as my cut, because I was doing it so efficiently, and the

King's revenue increased sharply. Money is coming my way, and money is power.

Power may be coming to me, but that old bastard - no swearing, Thomas - Savile still manages to annoy me when he can. There's this business of draining Hatfield Chase. It's a marsh, and many local people live and work there. They like it, even if I would not, and they know how to make a living out of it, unpleasant as that might seem. Now Savile and a gang of speculators want to drain the marsh, reclaim the land, and evict the people. They'll then divide the land up between themselves, and keep it some of it.

They have the backing of the King. I dare say this is the idea of one of his advisers, or perhaps Savile got the idea from a Dutchman, Cornelius Vermuyden, and sold it to His Majesty. Be that as it may, the King wants the scheme to go ahead because he has three manors covering a vast area there, and has some hunting grounds too. He thinks if the land can be improved he'll be able to sell some off, and make better use of what's left.

I'm all in favour of improvement and better finances, but ignoring the rights of the poor is just the sort of behaviour I cannot abide. I don't suppose anyone has told the King that the poor will be badly affected. Jesus was right; the rich should help the poor, not victimise them. To make matters worse, these men have hired this Vermuyden to do the work for them. He's a famous engineer from Holland, building dykes and canals to keep the sea out, so he knows what he is doing; no doubt about that. He did some work for the King at Windsor a while ago.

But this marsh is common land, and he has no right to do the work, and his paymasters have no right to ask him to do it. All the rights to these commons rest with the locals. They are up in arms about it, sometimes literally, Vermuyden says. He may be right, but it was one of the local fenmen who was killed in a violent encounter, not a developer. What makes matters worse, and helps provoke the riots, is that Vermuyden wasn't even employing local labour to dig the channels and ditches, and build the embankments. He brought over a hundred or more of his compatriots from Holland, which just rubbed the locals' noses in it; not only will their common land and the living they make from it be lost, but they are not even earning anything out of the work.

No-one in Yorkshire is ignorant of the rivalry between me and Savile and they know it is far from a friendly affair, so these fenmen came to see me, and asked for my help. I thought the law was on their side, so I agreed. Can I pretend the fact that I could spike Savile's guns at the same time was not a factor? Hardly.

There was another bonus. Three of the men had been with the fenman who had been killed in the fight. They told me that the local people had been marching to the place where a channel was being dug as part of the work when they were set on by a group of Dutch workers. The fenmen fought back, but were outnumbered, and disorganised. The Dutch, however, had a leader who shouted some orders, and they could hear he was English.

They said he was dressed and spoke 'like a gent'. One of the men followed this gent home to see where he went. When he told me it was to the manor house in Wroot, I knew it was my old bullying enemy from school, Chesworth. It made sense for him to have become an acolyte of a cad like Savile. I could not investigate this myself, but accompanied the men to see a local magistrate, and helped them interest this Justice of the Peace in their story. One of my lowly companions told the magistrate that he had seen Chesworth strike the fatal blow which killed their friend. The others were unable to say that was so.

The crime was investigated, and eventually Chesworth was charged with leading an affray, and with murder of the fenman. I could not resist sending Christopher to watch the trial and report to me. Chesworth's feelings at seeing the victim of his schoolboy bullying rejoicing in his downfall would be worth knowing. The judge directed the jury that they could not convict Chesworth of murder on the evidence of one man, with no corroboration, so he was acquitted on that count, but the jury upheld the evidence of the fenmen on the affray charge, and Chesworth was found guilty and sentenced to three years in prison. It was not a happy time for him.

That's all been going on for some while. A few weeks ago I took the fenmen's case to the Council; now I'm its President. If the case comes before me, should I hear it? Probably not, but I don't think I'll be able to resist the chance to put Savile's nose right out of joint.

The trouble is the King's interest in the drainage project, and the fact that some of the Privy Council support him. I shall have to be very careful.

Arabella. 31st May, 1630. York.

There is great rejoicing throughout the nation. Two days ago the Queen was delivered of a healthy baby boy. Let us pray he lives. Thomas says he'd better, or we'll be fighting in Europe. I suppose it's something to do with having no heir to the throne, unless it's Charles's sister Elizabeth. If that's it would her husband Frederick be King?

We have various bits of business news from Sir Arthur Ingram today, which is why Thomas keeps in touch with him. He writes that my brother Denzil is now out of prison. He paid his fine of a thousand marks, and sent the King a petition – a very grovelling one, by the sound of it – asking to be set free, and he was.

I'm surprised Denzil didn't write to tell me about this himself, but relations between him and Thomas seem to be getting slightly strained. I know he did not really care for Thomas going over to the King's side, and leaving the Commons, and then there's been that strange business with my Father.

Someone produced a document planning some sort of plot against Parliament by the Monarchy, and my husband sent it to the Secretary of State, Sir John Coke. My Papa had a copy of it, and he got into trouble over it, but it turned out be an old thing someone had written back in King James's time, and he'd thought it ridiculous. Papa was not at all pleased, and Denzil blames Thomas.

Thomas says it was all a bit silly, because the plot needed an army to keep control of the people, and the King just doesn't have one. He's hardly got any soldiers at all. In any case, I think it's a daft idea. Armies have officers, and officers have families too; they don't want them locked up for what they think or say. And the ordinary soldiers are the same. They don't want to use a musket on their own Mothers and Fathers for their ideas. They may start off shooting other folks' parents, but when it gets nearer home, I think they'd run out of enthusiasm for it.

Still, I do think Thomas should have thought about the effect on my family, especially on my Father. Lord Clare is not likely to be well received at Court now.

Since Thomas was appointed to the Privy Council last November, he's advised the King that as the Huguenots have been defeated by King Louis, there's no need to fight France any longer. There have not been any real hostilities between us and the Spanish for some years, so peace can be made with both countries. Thomas tells the King he can't afford any more wars if he doesn't have any Parliaments, and Charles now sees the force of that.

I don't think Thomas is under any illusion the King likes him much, though. Clearly, he says, the King is grateful for his advice and the efficient way he is running the North of the Country, and getting good revenue out of the fines on the Catholics, but there is nothing very friendly in their dealings. It seems to me the King just sees him as a higher type of servant. It wasn't like that with the Duke of Buckingham and Charles; they were like David and Jonathan.

Perhaps it makes Thomas a bit sad, though he doesn't say so. He talks a lot about his plans for making the King financially independent, and making the country work thoroughly, not just for the rich, but for the benefit of the poor, too. He wants to make the Poor Laws work properly; he doesn't like the way a lot of the rich avoid paying their contribution to the rates and the upkeep of the housing and the creation of jobs for poor people.

I say 'thoroughly' because that is what he and this Bishop Laud write to each other about. They call their policies 'Thorough'. Thomas wants to make the state and its servants thorough, and Laud wants to do the same with the Church. What worries me is that there are so many Puritans who will hate Laud for all his incense and candles and robes and decorated churches, and there are so many men who think the King should call Parliament so they can make a fuss about their 'grievances', as they call them. Will these people turn on the King one day, and on Laud and Thomas for helping him? God alone knows what might happen then.

Christopher Wandesford. 16th February, 1631. London.

I'm staying with Tom in the city. Yesterday he came back from a Privy Council meeting and told me that there have been reports of food riots in Rutland. The Council resolved to take care of this sort of thing by making sure the market was well supplied with corn and bread to be sold to the poor at fair prices.

This morning Tom had me draft a letter for him to Richard Marris, his steward at Wentworth. The letter was about the price of wheat, and for once it made me question some of Tom's motives. The background to the riot in Rutland and this draft is the shortage of wheat throughout much of the country due to the very poor harvest last year.

The Privy Council was really worried that there might be a famine, so it fixed the price of wheat and other cereal crops. The sale of corn to foreign countries was banned, the amount of grain that could be used for brewing beer and other drinks was restricted. To avoid a black market in flour and bread, the magistrates were ordered to investigate anyone suspected of hoarding these basic foods-stuffs, or the grain from which they could be made. The Council went even further. It passed laws ensuring that the grain discovered was to be distributed and sold to the poor at the fixed price before anyone else could buy or sell it.

Of course, Tom is on the Privy Council and he's President of the Council of the North, and he is very much in favour of this sort of law. He worked very hard on the Commission looking into excessive fees charged by officials for doing their jobs. He not only argued that the top officers should not charge excessively for their services on top of their official salaries; he also proposed that they should be held to account for the fees their minions charged, too. That was a pretty revolutionary idea, and not the sort to make him very popular. Neither was his work on the Poor Law Commission, bearing in mind that you can't really help the poor unless you take some cash from the richer elements of society. Even if they go to Church every Sunday, one thing the rich do not care for is parting with their money to help the lower classes. Heaven knows what they think the parable about the rich man and Lazarus at his gate meant.

Anyway, it is that background, and that benevolent aspect of Tom's policies which worries me a bit. This is what the letter to Richard says:

Dear Richard,

Thank you for your last report. I am glad that all rents are up-to-date, and that there seems to be plenty of food about in Yorkshire. It is, unhappily, not the same down here. The price of wheat is astronomical. I am told that is because shipments of corn from the Irish harvest last autumn have not been delivered yet.

I want you to go around the county buying up all the spare wheat you can, get it to Hull or other ports as fast as possible, and shipped down here.

The price you pay should be much less than what it will fetch in the London markets, and we can see a healthy profit.

Let me know how you get on.

Wentworth.

I gave the draft to Tom, and he approved and signed it, as he always does . With not a little trepidation I said: "I'm not sure you should do this. You're on the Council down here, and up there, and it's your duty to see that the Order in Council stopping people making money out of the corn shortage is obeyed."

Tom looked up from copying the letter. "Is that what it looks like, Kit?"

"I'd say so. If that isn't the way it looks, why don't you explain it in the letter?"

I got one of his arrogant looks in return, but not his temper, thank the Lord. "Richard is my agent, Kit, my servant. I owe him explanations for nothing."

"Perhaps, but what worries me is not what Richard thinks, but what others may say. They are sure to work it out."

Tom was unmoved. "I do not propose to defend myself against accusations which have yet to be made. It seems to me that if I ship a lot of wheat down here, and we put it on the market, that will itself lower the price, there will be more flour and bread for the Londoners, and I shall still make some money. Is that wrong?"

"But the price is supposed to be fixed!"

"Will anyone complain if the price goes down?"

He and I are friends, but it would be chancing my arm to argue with him too much over that, so all I said was; "I just don't think it looks right, that's all."

He thanked me for the warning, but I am still far from happy about this episode. Tom is implacable with people who profit from disobeying the law, and if he had caught Savile, say, doing this, he would probably have chased him up-hill and down-dale to stop him and get the money out of him. Calling Tom a hypocrite is more than I dare do, but it is what I am close to thinking.

Thomas. 13th April, 1631. London.

I have a letter from Richard Marris who is at Wentworth.

4th April.

My Lord,

I have sent off the second of three shipments of corn today. I was pleased to hear that the first arrived safely last week from Whitby. Today's cargo left from Hull. The third will go from Hull, too, probably in about three weeks.

Buying the wheat and other grains is becoming increasingly difficult. Your fellow Councillors here are diligent in looking for evidence of black-market activity, so I have been using others to act as my agents – well, yours really – in secret so that your identity as the buyer is not known.

Not only are the magistrates and the Council to be feared. The people are very stirred up, and threats of violence, indeed of lynchings, are uttered against cheats and black-marketeers.

Am I to go on buying?

I am your obedient servant, My Lord,

Richard Marris.

I show it to Christopher. "What do you think?"

"I don't think you should get Richard to buy any more. It's dangerous."

"Did I tell him to buy in secret through undisclosed agents?" Kit mumbles "No".

"Has the price gone up in Yorkshire?"

"Not that I know of."

"Did the price go down in London when our shipments were sold?"

"A bit." Christopher looks like a startled rabbit.

I try to sound a little less aggressive. "So we have not harmed our fellow Yorkshireman and we've made life a bit easier for Londoners. Is that it?"

He is reluctant. "I suppose so."

"And we have made some money, and you and Richard have had a bonus. Is that so bad?" Kit just looks at the floor. I continue: "And when the next two shipments arrive the price in London may go down further, and we shall not be so profitable on those."

"Maybe."

"You see Kit, the reason for the order in Council was that we wanted to stop real profiteers from cornering the market in their own area and then selling the goods to the local people when they had forced the price up. I haven't been forcing the price up anywhere. I've just been getting Richard to buy what is available, and send it down here so that London can eat. How would you feel living down here with hundreds, if not thousands, of starving people from the east side of the city rampaging through the streets looking for food?"

"Pretty scared."

"Yes, pretty scared. So would I. Anyway, with luck the Irish corn shipments will arrive in London soon, and there will have been no food riots."

Thomas. 30th May, 1631. York.

I returned from London two weeks ago. Just before I left London the Irish wheat boats arrived, and the price of bread came down sharply. I wrote to Marris at Wentworth telling him this and saying: "The shortage in London is over. God be praised; gains there will be none." Of course, I had made some gains, but there would be no more.

The plague is running round the country like an affliction of rats. People are dying in large numbers, and labourers are hard at work digging pits and burying the diseased corpses in them. There is no time to make any attempt to distinguish one body from another and many families have no idea where their dead have gone. I have been working hard here with a committee I set up to try to isolate the sick from the general public, and check the spread of the disease.

It is difficult to know whether we are succeeding, as some people do not succumb to this dreadful scourge, some villages escape almost completely, and no-one understands it. Even doctors and physicians blunder about in the dark. I'm not aware of a single person who can be said to have been cured by any medicine or any of the strange and sometimes bizarre remedies these barbarous barber surgeons dream up. One of the worst is supposed to eliminate what the doctors call an evil humour which they say causes the plague. To suck this humour out they heat up glass vessels – jars or stout glasses – over a lamp or fire until they are almost red hot, and then place the open end of the vessel upside-down on the patient's body. They are already in acute distress from thirst, and the pain of the 'bubes' growing in their groins and armpits, and sometimes their knee and elbow joints. As the hot glass cools it sucks a great lump of their flesh up inside it. The glass cools down more, and falls off. The patient is left with a nasty burn and a blister, and then dies anyway. Gruesome.

I've travelled about the northern counties quite a bit to see for myself how the measures we are taking have progressed. We have done as much as we can to help the poor, who always suffer more from this sort of thing than the rich, like me. After all, they have so little to start with, and the burden on a young widow with four or five small children and her husband newly in the ground is overpowering. She has no money, and no leisure in which to go out to earn any. Does she go on the streets to beg, or worse? We have to help these people.

Doing so is tiring and a worry, but today is a good day, and different work. I'm presiding over the Council of the North. The issue is Vermuyden's drainage scheme of at Hatfield Chase. There has been a significant change in circumstances in the last few months. I have been using my position on the Privy Council to petition it and the King in such subtle ways as I can find to support the local people against this Dutchman and his backers like Savile. I persuaded a lot of the country folk affected by the scheme to write to the King and Council with their complaints. I've even had George and Kit penning letters for the farmers and others who could not write.

It has taken a year or so, but it has worked and the King has set up a Court of Sewers for Hatfield Chase. It is a sort of Commission to enquire into the problem, and he has appointed me to be its chairman.

Several farmers and others who live and work these fens appear before us. The Council Chamber is a large square, with dark oak panelling in a linen-fold pattern, heavy brass sconces in the walls for candles, and two huge crystal chandeliers at either end of the room hanging from the ornately plastered, very lofty ceiling. I cannot help wondering whether these working people have ever been in a room like this in their lives. Are they frightened? One in particular impresses me. He is a tall, strong and, for a peasant, extremely eloquent man, even if he cannot read and write. He tells us his name is Arthur Fenn – quite appropriate – and that he lives in Low Eggborough, a small village near the border with Lincolnshire. Our clerk administers the oath, reading out the words which Mr Fenn repeats.

I invite him to tell us his story.

"My Lord, I farm fifty acres just outside the village, and I lives on the farm. Corneloos Verminden and Lord Savile called a meeting about eighteen months ago. I went. They wan'ed to talk about a scheme to drain all the fens round about Hatfield Chase. At first I were in favour of it. I thought it'd make more of the land useful, if it was drier."

"What changed your mind?"

"Some of my neighbours, people in Eggborough and other villages, was gettin' very alarmed and unhappy. They'd been told as how this scheme'd be good for them, as I'd been, but as the work went on they found that Lord Savile and his friends, and Mr Verminden, was taking over a lot of the common land where they used to graze their cattle and pigs and sheep, where they could forage for firewood, and blackberries, and things like that."

"Is it important to them to be able to do that?"

"Very important, My Lord. A lot of them are poor and without them things they can pick up on the common, and keeping a few animals on it, many o' them'd starve, or die o' cold in winter. And – well – I hope you don't think me impertinent, but there's som'at else."

"Yes, Mr Fenn. What might that be?"

"Well, like I say My Lord, it may be impertinent, me being what I am and you being a great Lord and lawyer and President an' all, but isn't it the law that a man's rights can't just be took off him, like, in England?"

I cannot help smiling at that. "Certainly, Mr Fenn."

"Well then, My Lord, if that's so, and a man has a right to go on the common, like, and put his animals there, who can take it away, if you know what I mean?"

"That is the point exactly. That is what this commission is looking into, and we shall be asking Sir Cornelius and his friends how they deal with your argument."

Fenn is anguished: "My Lord, don't take agin me like that. I aint arguin' with nobody; leastways, not with you, My Lord."

"Of course not, Mr Fenn. You are not arguing with me. What I mean is, I want to see how the other side deal with what you have been saying. Have no fear. You are in no trouble." Fenn thanks me and calms down. "Was there any other point you wanted to tell me?"

"Yes, My Lord, I thank'ee." He draws a big breath and himself up to his full height. "It's the floods, My Lord."

This is what I have been hoping for. "Are you talking about the floods at harvest last year?"

"That's it My Lord. It was like this. All round the Chase and Hatfield Moors – the whole of the Isle of Axholme, you might say - we had good crops, and we was gettin' in the harvest. Well, there's many streams - like the Went and the Aire - what flows through these parts into the Don and the Trent. Normally they don't cause no trouble; well, not in September like. They can flood a bit in winter sometimes, but it don't matter too much then."

Mr Fenn seems to have lost himself a bit. "So what happened last September?"

"Well, My Lord, lots of them streams got flooded right high, and people was driven out o' their houses in Fishlake and Sykehouse, and Snaith, and their fields was washed out, and their crops was lost."

"How did you find out about this? Were you or your farm affected?"

"A couple of my fields on the edge of the farm was drowned, and a couple of cows with 'em, but we was lucky, My Lord."

"But how did you find out about the other villages?"

"I mean, we all knows about 'em now, don't we My Lord, because everyone was prayin' for 'em in all the churches back September, and you and your Council was goin' round giving money and food to the poor folks. But how I knows it then was the people. All these poor mites come off the highway into Eggborough, 'cause Your Lordship knows it runs past my village. They come off the main road seein' as how it was flooded, and they was trying to get to Knottingley or Pomfret."

"Thank you, Mr Fenn. Do go on. What were these poor people doing?"

"They was looking for places to sleep, and a bite. Loads of 'em was just women with little brats; some o' the menfolk had stayed behind tryin' to save what they could. They was all wet through, and the kids was cryin'. Some of the women, too."

"What happened to them?"

"My wife's a good woman, My Lord, and she can't watch nobody in trouble like that without she's got to do som'at. So she tells me to lay a lot of clean hay and straw in our barn, so's they can sleep there, and she sends our young Arthur off to the neighbours what hadn't been flooded too, and gets them to do the same. Sal, she ..."

"Sal, Mr Fenn?"

"That's the wife, My Lord, Sally Fenn. Well, she goes out to these poor folks and tells 'em to go to the barn, and she sends others off to the neighbours – except old Wainwright, o' course – he's too mean. And then all the women got together and makes this big cauldron of broth, and we feeds 'em, and they sleeps in the barn"

"Tell me, Mr Fenn, what caused this problem, this terrible flood?"

"First, like, I only knew about it because the women in the barn told me about it, and I could see from my own two fields that there was some problem somewhere. But next day, when the water had gone down a bit, I got a little boat I keep to row down the stream to the river for a bit o' fishin', and I goes up-stream towards them villages. An' that's when I see it."

I am beginning to get rather impatient; he talks as though he's repeating a tale in his corner by the fire in the tavern, but I restrain myself. "And what was it you saw?"

He turns and points across the Court rather dramatically at Vermuyden and Savile. Vermuyden is short, but clearly muscular, almost as though he digs his ditches and canals personally. His hair is flaxen, and hangs down straight around his head as though cut under a bowl. "I sees them men, and some others, My Lord. They was standing by the side of the stream – well – more like a lake it was, at that point – and beside them, running into the stream was this big channel what they'd dug. Full of water, it was, rushing out of the ground and into the stream. It ain't a big stream, normal like, so it couldn't cope with all this extra water, and that was what flooded it all."

"How do you know these men dug the channel?"

"A few weeks before I was on my way to Doncaster market. I were riding my old cob along the byways, across the country, when I sees this big channel being dug by lots of men, and looking over it all was these same two gen'lemen. So I goes up to 'em and takes off my hat, and asks 'em what's going on. Then I recognised 'em from the meetin' when they was setting up this drainage thingy in the first place.

"Very well, Mr Fenn, and what did they tell you?"

"Lord Savile, he don't talk much to the likes of me, but the one with the foreign voice, Mr Verminden, he knows me from afore, and tells me it's a canal – I thinks that's the word he used – to drain the Chase and the marshes, and it'll be good for everyone."

"Did you believe him?"

"Looked all pretty neat to me, My Lord, then, 'cos there weren't no rain or nothin'. There wasn't no reason to think it would all go wrong."

I have to tread carefully here. I do not want to be seen to be getting into the ring myself. I am the judge and should seem to be impartial. "Are you saying that no-one was ever worried about these drainage canals before the floods?"

Mr Fenn is alarmed again. "No, My Lord, I didn't say nothin' like that. No. There was lots of folks real worried about it as soon as they heard about the scheme. There's even some in Eggborough, people what live or 'ave land on the low-lying bit where the two streams joins up; they was sayin' that the canal would flood the streams and their houses. Then there was others what make a living in other villages getting fish and reeds and peat and stuff out of the marshes and bogs."

"Thank you Mr Fenn. Is that all?"

"Ain't that enough My Lord?"

Even Savile laughs at that, and so do I. I turn to Savile and Vermuyden. "Have you any questions for Mr Fenn, gentlemen?"

Savile rises, arrogant in his bottle-green finery and delicate lace cuffs. He sneers at Fenn. "You lost two cows, Fenn. Anything else?"

"Just a bit of wheat, like."

"My Lord, to you, Fenn. And this gentleman is Sir Cornelius Vermuyden, not Mister Verminden. Don't forget it. I dare say you are going to sue for your two cows and your bit of wheat, aren't you? Isn't that why you have come here, to bolster your claim?"

"I can't afford no lawyers, My Lord. I an't never sued no-one, and I an't going to start now."

"Your evidence is nothing but what you have been told by other people, isn't it?"

Fenn turns to me. "That an't fair, My Lord, I told you that I seen all the things with my own eyes one time or another."

I cannot help glancing at Savile with a warning look, as I say to the witness: "So you did, Mr Fenn. And it is up to me to decide whom to believe when I have heard all the evidence."

Savile is, of course, not abashed. "You made the rest up, didn't you, Fenn?"

"No I never, and you can get that gentleman – Sir Corneloos - to tell His Lordship that I seed you both by the river them two times, and what happened."

Vermuyden tugs at Savile's cloak and when he stoops to him, I can tell from Vermuyden's expression he will not lie. He has a reputation as a strict Lutheran, and I doubt he has ever lied deliberately in his life. He is an expert in his drainage profession, and I suspect he just made a big mistake here. He's not had as big a task as this one in England before.

Savile does not stop. "Now this whole area is known as the Isle of Axholme and the Hatfield Chase or Marshes, is it not?"

"Aye, it is." He adds after a pause: "My Lord."

"That's because it's boggy, isn't it?"

"Yes, My Lord."

"And it's boggy and marshy because it floods, isn't it?"

"It does that, My Lord."

"It has always flooded, hasn't it?"

"It has, My Lord."

"So nothing has changed, has it?"

"Oh yes it has." Fenn turns to me. "You see, My Lord, it flooded every couple o' year or so, but only on the low bits. I know I an't as bright as that Lordship over there, like, but we an't all stupid neither. We don't build our homes and barns and villages on the low bits what flood. We builds on the higher ground what the water don't hardly ever reach. Well, this time nearly all the houses and barns and villages went under, an' yer knows what it was." Fenn points straight at Savile "It was all that water rushin' down 'is canal, what I seed with me own eyes. We an't never had the canal before, an' we an't never had all them houses flooded out before neither."

Savile looks down at Vermuyden, who registers no reaction at all. Savile looks up again, and I ask him: "Have you any more questions for Mr Fenn, My Lord?"

"No, My Lord Wentworth, I do not."

"Or any witnesses as to the flood, and what caused it, or anything else?"

"No My Lord, I do not. Despite our history I did not expect Your Lordship to accept the evidence of ... of ... peasants like these against me and Sir Cornelius. It is a betrayal of our class." Savile sits. I am surprised by that last remark. Savile is himself disdainful of foreigners, and would have no reason to suppose I should favour a Dutchman who had only been knighted six years ago, and for what? Digging ditches?

I do not need to retire to consider my decision and that of my colleagues. I whisper to them asking if we are agreed that the evidence of Fenn and the others should be held to be true. They all agree. In fairness, I believe some of them would not dare disagree with me in any circumstances.

"I shall give judgment at once. The commission finds the evidence conclusive that the flood did considerable damage to the villages of Fishlake, Sykehouse, and Snaith, and to the inhabitants of those villages, and their crops and cattle. The flood is due to the negligent design of the defendants. We have also heard evidence that those undertaking this project to drain Hatfield Chase and its marshes have taken considerably more of the reclaimed land than the area originally sanctioned by His Majesty as their reward for undertaking the work. We have found that evidence to be true.

"I therefore order that, first, the undertakers will forthwith cut a new channel to divert the drains away from the affected villages; secondly they will submit plans to the Court showing that the new works will not adversely affect any other village or hamlet; thirdly, they will surrender all those parts of the land they have taken which are shown coloured red on the plan drawn up and put in evidence by the Court surveyor. That land will be shared amongst the villages, and will remain common land. The Court will rise."

As my colleagues and I leave the Court I hear Savile say, in a very loud voice:

"Wentworth will not get away with this, Vermuyden. We shall do all we can to delay and frustrate this judgment."

George Radcliffe. 5th October, 1631. York.

My Lady Arabella Wentworth died yesterday in the President's fine house in this city. Aside from my own wife, she was the best of women, kind, considerate, loving, and caring. The local people, to whom she ministered like an angel throughout her marriage to Thomas, are very much cast down. Thomas is in a dreadful state. I am afraid to go home and leave him. I fear to contemplate what he may do if left to himself. I shall have to stay by him until his crisis is over and he begins to be himself again.

For such an apparently hard man he weeps without shame, and trying to cheer him up seems a Herculean task at present. If anything he is in a worse pass than when Margaret died. He finds no comfort just now in the three living children she bore him, but that is understandable, because their youngest son, never a strong boy, died a few months ago, and if Arabella had not been pregnant when she fell, she might not have been carried off by the miscarriage which the fall induced.

It is a strange story. The weather has been fine, and a few days ago it was warm and sunny, and the Viscount was walking in the garden, talking to me and some other guests. Arabella called to him from the open door of her sitting room which looks out into the garden. Why she called we shall never know.

He hurried to her as he always does, and I heard her say: "Thomas, you have a wasp on your coat," and I could see her step forward to brush it off, but suddenly she stepped away again - I know not why – slipped, screamed, fell across a small table, and rolled off that to the floor.

I ran to the door as Thomas knelt beside her, and lifted her to a couch.

"What's happened?"

"She brushed an insect off my coat, and it flew at her. She tried to get out of its way, tripped over that table and fell on the floor".

Arabella groaned in pain. She was conscious. "My pains have started. I think my waters have broken." I looked down, and saw that her skirts were wet. Without any urging I ran to the hall and shouted for a servant to hasten to the doctor.

When I went back, Thomas asked me to send for a surgeon. "I have done so. He should be here soon. He is unlikely to keep you and the Lady Arabella waiting." There are definite advantages in wealth and power, though they do not stop this sort of thing occurring.

The doctor could do little except help the tiny dead morsel, which should have been a baby, leave its mother, and he did what he could to ease Arabella's suffering. She faded away over three days, and died on the 4th. The doctor offered Thomas a sleeping draught, but he is not one to indulge what he sees as 'that sort of weakness', even though I can see that in the next few days or weeks, some sound sleep is exactly what he will need.

In fact I am in much the same need myself, but at least I have not suffered the loss of my wife to add to my cares and woes. What has been causing both of us a lot of concern, if not anguish, has been the number of serious attempts that are being made to undermine the authority of the Council, Thomas's role as President, and mine as the

King's Attorney in the North. These matters come in addition to the normal run of ordinary cases, and the other duties that devolve upon us in trying to carry out the King's wishes and policies. We shall have to watch carefully how they develop, and with Arabella dead, Thomas is in no condition to watch out for anything. That is the worst woe of all.

Thomas. 9th December, 1631. Wentworth Woodhouse.

I have hardly been able to think for the last six or seven weeks. Arabella gone? I can still hardly believe it! She was such a fine woman, such a fine wife in every way: intelligent and quick like the rest of her family; an excellent mother who had presented me with my treasured son and heir and two gorgeous daughters, Nan and Arabella, of whom I am equally proud and fond. I cannot write more. Ink is likely to be blotted by tears if I go on. I loved you, my darling Arabella.

If you had not been trying to bear me another son, you might still be with me! God's mysterious ways are impossible to comprehend.

Thomas. 15th January, 1632. Wentworth Woodhouse.

To my amazement in the middle of last year the King offered me the appointment of Deputy Lord Lieutenant of Ireland. I asked for clarification.

Yesterday I received a letter from the King.

12th January, 1632.

My Dear Wentworth,

I have been giving serious consideration to the request you made for certain assurances from me about the way in which you might be allowed to govern Ireland in my name. I have discussed them with the Treasurer, Weston, and my Chancellor of the Exchequer, Cottington, and with Bishop Laud. Weston and Cottington were rather amused that, as Weston put it, you sought to impose terms and conditions upon me as though we were merchants engaged in negotiating the sale and purchase of silks and spices from India, but Laud took a different line.

He pointed out that almost ten years ago my dear Father, King James, sent a commission to Ireland to enquire into the loss of Crown and Church lands and income there. It reported that both King and

Church had been defrauded by the very people he had appointed to look after these things for him. They were, as you would expect, almost exclusively Protestant settlers of the last fifty years or so. That was unfortunate because at the time we were at war with Spain, and could not risk upsetting these people when we needed them to keep the lid on the Catholic pot, and prevent Spain being given a foothold to invade Ireland. Consequently we could not act on the commission's recommendations.

As we are now at peace with Spain and France those considerations no longer apply. Those were Laud's arguments, and the other two could not refute them. He proposed, and I accepted, that it is time to take a new broom to Ireland, and recover Crown and Church lands and income. Weston and Cottington had no choice but to acquiesce. You are the new broom.

The following are the assurances you asked for, and to which I agree:

1) You may leave Ireland to attend my Court and the Privy Council as often as you feel the need; this was the term my two money men had the most difficulty with; I almost felt they wanted you exiled to Dublin and forbidden to return, as if they do not want you near me. That is a trifle odd when they recommended you for the post in the first place, unless that is why they suggested you. The Bishop, on the other hand, was entirely behind your having this right; he mumbled something about it being essential if all is to be thorough.

2) You may deal direct with Lord Treasurer Weston on matters concerning Irish finance.

3) I shall not make any grant of lands or estates in Ireland without consulting you first, and you may give or withhold your consent as you see fit.

4) I shall not entertain any petition which would enable the petitioner to avoid your Irish Courts, nor shall I allow any appeal against any decision of yours unless you are clearly guilty of an obvious injustice or unreasonable conduct.

5) You may keep the Presidency of the Council of the North. I trust you are satisfied that your Vice-President, Osborne, is up to the task, and that you will appoint a suitable man to be your Deputy if he is not.

Your final request was that I should create you an Earl to reinforce your authority and place you on a level with men like Ormonde, Cork, and Clanricarde. I do not see the necessity to do that at this juncture. The fact that I have appointed you, and you have my unconditional backing must, in their eyes, give you all the authority you need.

I shall be obliged if you can attend to your affairs in England as soon as possible, and take up your post in Ireland, in which I wish you every success. May God Bless your endeavours.

I am your grateful

Charles R.

I am mortified about the Earldom, but content with the rest, and write immediately with my acceptance in unequivocal terms.

Thomas. 21st February, 1632. Wentworth Woodhouse.

Over the last month or so I have been obtaining reports and information about the state of the accommodation I am likely to have when I get to Dublin in due course. It seems that the Deputy is supposed to live in the Castle, although I am told that it has been neglected for so long that my last couple of predecessors have lived in houses they built or rented. I'm not at all sure I want to acquire property in Ireland. I have no idea how long my appointment might last, or whether I might be called back to London for some even more significant job.

I must give directions for repairs to be carried out, and dispatch an order for work to start immediately.

Thomas. May, 1632. Whitehall.

I've met a most interesting man from Ireland. He's one of the New English Protestants, and is Vice-Treasurer of that kingdom. Francis Annesley, Lord Mountnorris, seems a clever chap, and being so recognises (although he is not blunt enough to say as much) that if I am to be Deputy Lord Lieutenant there, I am worth cultivating. It is hardly surprising that I feel the same way about him. I can only be of use to him in the future if I choose, whereas he can be of enormous help to me now, if I can recruit him.

It shouldn't be difficult. He tells me: "I'm over here in London trying to clear my name of allegations that I've been misusing my public office and the administration for my own purposes".

"What do these allegations involve, then?"

"Oh! I don't think we need to look into them. They are false." Annesley smiles. He's almost fifty, I should say, fairly slim, with grey hair, which he wears longish, to the bottom of his neck, and a pointed grey beard and moustache, not unlike mine. "The thing is, I'm not a member of the clique of powerful Protestant nobles that runs Ireland behind the scenes, and you need to know about that. I've acted against them on the King's behalf, too."

"Well, I suppose if that's true, it explains why you might be the victim of trumped up charges."

"That's it! I'm outside the charmed circle because I report to the King against the Irish Council."

There is something sly about this chap, and I'm not sure how far I can trust him, but he must hoard a lot of dirt on these people. It would be worth a great deal to me to be familiar with all this dirty washing.

I must find out all I can about the Irish nobility, the way the administration and the government works, the army, and the Irish Treasury. Then I can make policies, and plans to implement them. I shall try to make Annesley my ally. William Laud tells me that Annesley's alleged crimes involve helping himself from the monies he collects on behalf of the King to 'commissions' to which he has no legal entitlement.

If true, this proves that he will be well-acquainted with the seamier side of Dublin life, and, if guilty, that he is someone on whom I should keep a close eye. I do not want my Irish Court to be renowned for its corruption, as those of so many of my predecessors have been.

Something else has been brought to my attention about this man. He has a foppish air. He went to live in Ireland in 1606, when Sir Arthur Chichester was Lord Deputy there. He joined Sir Arthur's household, and lived with him in circumstances of curiously close intimacy. He was rewarded with a small number of offices of state in Ireland, and – when he was only 22 – a pension!! What did he do to earn these perks? It reminds me of King James and his affection for Carr and Villiers. The mind boggles at what some men will do, and appear to enjoy, for money and advancement.

Despite that, I do not suggest there is any mere pretence of pleasure at perverse relations with other men about Mountnorris; that seemed to me to be his natural bent when I met him. I'm glad to say I was spared any of his advances. Close and loving friends I may be with Christopher and George, but I've never had any interest in or desire for other than verbal intercourse with my own sex.

Perverse tastes or not, Lord Mountnorris did not balk at marriage to Dorothea eight years ago, nor at what it takes to beget two sons, with, he tells me, another child on the way. Laud has also told me that Annesley became the owner of the Mountnorris estate in 1612 because King James had been so impressed with Chichester's reports on 'this fine young man'. The estate includes a castle with its surrounding lands. In 1628 Charles made him an Irish peer as Baron Mountnorris.

By that time Chichester was long gone, and the Deputy was Lord Falkland, who had been in office since 1622. Annesley at that time enjoyed the salary of the paymaster of the Armies and Garrisons of Ireland, and the chances of embezzlement and other perks which such posts carry. This caused him to fall out with Falkland, who tried to sail a more or less honest ship, so Annesley did all he could to stir up storms and other bad weather for the Deputy. So bad a voyage was Falkland having that in 1625 it was reported to the English Privy Council by the Secretary of State that some of the Irish Privy Council, 'amongst whom Sir Francis Annesley is not the least violent and impertinent', were making Falkland's attempts to govern almost impossible.

Far from getting Annesley punished or reprimanded, the result, somehow, was that he was promoted to Vice-Treasurer of Ireland, which simply increased his opportunities for stealing from the King. I can only imagine how Falkland felt about that; much as if a stiletto had been slid between his ribs from the rear.

But that was just the start, and it would get worse. The cause was an Irish family, the Byrnes, who had owned land in Wicklow from time immemorial, which had been the subject of legal disputes. The results had been unfavourable to the Byrnes, and they accused Falkland of being unjust towards them. The Irish Privy Council set up a committee to investigate, and Annesley was on the committee. False witnesses were called and Annesley used his position as a committee member to ensure that all findings went against Falkland, and in August 1929 Charles recalled him to London.

That was what gave rise to my being offered the government of Ireland last year, but in the intervening two years, Mountnorris and Richard Boyle, Lord Cork, ran the country for Charles as Lords Justice. This story of Mountnorris's campaign against Falkland made me determined that, much as I might make use of him now in learning the wrinkles of political survival in Ireland, and in setting up a skeleton administration there before I sailed for Dublin, I should never give him the chance to best me or take money from my – I should say the King's – Irish coffers.

I learned something else from Mountnorris: just how careful one must be about the religious divide between Catholic and Protestant. He told me that this was another cause of Falkland's dismissal. The Old English and the small but sturdy middle class – lawyers, merchants and so on – still own most of Ireland. They were content with law and order which came with English rule, and were, as a result, loyal. The difficulty was that they were Roman Catholics. The Protestants resented any favours or privileges extended to the idolaters, as they saw them. They wanted to take over their lands and rob them of any power. That's what they still want.

The Catholics can sit in Parliament and practise law, but the Protestants take every opportunity to denounce these rights. Falkland tried to steer a middle course hoping to get peace for all. He offered to be lenient with the Catholics in return for some generous subsidies. The 'rights' he wanted to sell them for the money are called "the Graces." If they could prove sixty years' title to their land they could keep it. They could hold public office. They could practise their religion.

The New English, or Protestants, were appalled. Guaranteed land rights for Catholics would stop them stealing Catholic lands, and they certainly didn't want Papal spawn holding office under the Crown. Some of the richest and most powerful New English were members of the Irish Privy Council. They had no intention of letting Lord Deputy Falkland guide this sensible subsidy raising measure through the Council. This was another reason, Annesley proudly told me, why Falkland's return to ignominy in England was engineered.

In spite of the fact that Falkland lost his job and the Catholics have not had the benefit of his side of the bargain, I am told they are still paying the subsidies into the Treasury regularly. How can that sort of loyalty be sacrificed?

Perhaps he thinks I'm grateful to him for getting rid of Falkland, and showing how Catholics should be dealt with. I am grateful, but not for that; I'm pleased he has shown me just how vital it is to prevent either side – Protestant or Catholic – from becoming more dominant than the Deputy. I shall have to work out a policy.

Annesley is not my only new contact who will be of use to me when I am in Ireland. William Railton is Clerk of the Privy Seal and Keeper of the Privy Council Chamber. He agrees to be my messenger and agent in London, to help with business both public and private, and to keep me informed. There is a difference between him and Annesley: I trust Railton; I cannot say the same of Annesley.

Thomas. June, 1632. Great Houghton, Yorkshire.

It is early summer, and the weather is glorious. I must confess that news of my promotion to Deputy in Ireland lifted my gloom to a considerable extent. And gloomy I have been since Arabella's death. She was such an angel. She made me feel so young, and I had to be young in outlook to keep up with our four children – well, four until Thomas died not long before she did. The other three, William, Ann, and little Arabella, miss her dreadfully. Dearest Arabella is only two, and by way of further confession I have to admit that I have so much business with the Council of the North, the Privy Council, and all my own interests, I hardly know her. More importantly, she hardly knows me.

This means I cannot be much comfort to her, and must seem like a stranger some of the time. I've been making an effort – not always successful – to be at home more, and get home earlier so that I see them all before Arabella's governess and the Nanny put them to bed. I find it dreadfully upsetting when Arabella rejects me, as she is so like her dear Mother. I want to love and be loved more by all the children now my lovely wife, is no more. Once or twice I've found myself on the verge of losing my temper with her, but have kept it at bay. Thank goodness I have, since I should only terrify her, and make things infinitely worse. So I cuddle her when she lets me, and we are beginning to play little games, and when William and Ann join in, she finds it much more fun. Six year old William and five year old Ann have a much better idea of what amuses a two year old than I do.

Unfortunately this cannot go on. I am commanded by the King to go to Ireland. Refusal of so great an honour is just impossible, even if that were my inclination. And it is not. There is hardly a greater honour in any of Charles's three kingdoms. He has plenty of loyal Dukes and other nobles in Scotland who would not welcome interference from an Englishman. The only higher position I can think of in England is to be one of the Secretaries of State, or Treasurer. Even so, in some ways the Deputy Lord Lieutenant of Ireland is the more important, as he is almost a King in his own right. London is too far away, with the dangers of a sea to cross, for there to be much risk of detailed instructions from Whitehall Palace or Windsor Castle arriving on a regular basis. If I agree policies with the King, and follow them, I dare say I shall be left to my own devices how I implement them.

I shall have the Irish Treasury and the collection of customs duties and taxes under my control. I shall be commander of the Irish Army, and I shall have every opportunity to advance the development of agriculture and industry there.

I cannot wait to get started, but I have been working to put my own affairs in order here in England, and arrange a deputy to run the Council of the North for me. I must test out Sir Edward Osborne, my Vice-President a bit more; I have found him very loyal and reliable so far. Perhaps I can leave the Council to him.

Fortunately Christopher and George are available to accompany me to Dublin, and will do whatever I ask. At last I shall have the chance to see that they are properly rewarded for all that they have done for me hitherto. But they are not the answer to my family problem, which is, put simply: how do I care sufficiently for the children? I have no intention of leaving them in Yorkshire. I could not bear to be without them. And there is something else. After ten years of happy marriage to Margaret, and seven years of an idyllic existence with Arabella, I am thoroughly miserable with no woman in my bed. I have no lady to grace my table, and add that undefinable magic a good wife brings to running a happy home and rearing happy children. It has been a challenge to find a replacement for either of my previous goddesses, but I think I have succeeded.

Today I am courting the very lovely daughter of Sir Godfrey Rodes. They are almost neighbours, living at Great Houghton, not very far from Wentworth. Her name is Elizabeth, and she is twenty-five. I took the precaution of speaking to Sir Godfrey before embarking on what I hope might be a successful flirtation. I wanted him to know in advance that my intentions were honourable. In any case, the Rodes family are fairly strict Puritans of very respectable repute, and should I have made any advances to his daughter without his permission, I fear that he would very likely have refused consent to her marrying me on principle.

Let's be honest, though. I may be some years her senior, but I am a Viscount, and wealthy, and likely to be more so. I have powerful posts under the Crown, and am about to take up another, even greater, in Ireland, which leaves the ones I already enjoy in the shade. I suspect Sir Godfrey sees a dynastic tie with the Wentworths as valuable, and a feather in his cap, as well as a sure foundation for Elizabeth's security, if not her happiness. As to that, it will be up to me to make her happy, and I shall do my best. I have never had an unhappy home, and have no intention of starting one now.

I was received graciously at lunch by Sir Edward and Lady Rodes, having spoken to him for an hour or two beforehand. He left me in the library for a while and went to ask his wife what she thought about having me for a son-in-law, which I thought rather unusual, but showed a lot of care for Elizabeth, and that he reposed a lot of trust in her Mother. When he returned he was smiling, shook my hand, and wished me luck in my suit.

So now Elizabeth and I are walking in the garden. She holds a pretty pink parasol as the sun is strong today, and she is rather fair, and the top of her head comes up to my shoulder. She wears a pink striped dress to match the parasol. I have my hands clasped behind my back to avoid any risk that I may hold her arm or hand or do anything else untoward before I am as sure as I can be that it would be welcome. That is hard, as she really is rather pretty. We have passed the usual pleasantries at the table, and there has been rather a silence since we came out into this walk between tall, immaculately trimmed yew hedges.

Elizabeth breaks the ice. "And your children, My Lord, how are they?" as though continuing a subject of conversation, when in fact we had not touched on it.

Me. Well, thank you Madam, and I hope playing happily at home. But may we dispense with this formality? Did your father tell you why I have come? *(How could I make such a churlish start? Do I want to frighten her to death? Surely there are some occasions when I could abandon my blunt, plain speaking approach?)*
Elizabeth. *(Who is unabashed).* Yes My Lord; to ask for my hand in marriage.
Me. Your father has been kind enough to say he will consent to my suit if it - perhaps I should say if I - please you. That you please me is clear, for were it otherwise I should not be here. And this isn't my first visit.
Elizabeth. No, My Lord, we've been honoured to receive you here many times in the last few months, but I fear our modest household may not be what you are used to. As Lord President of the North you must be accustomed to the finest of everything, and far more than my parents can offer.
Me. They don't need to offer me anything but their warm family hospitality.
Elizabeth. My Lord, I know....
Me. Come, let us end this stately dancing. I'm a man and my name is Thomas; I want to marry you, and I want to call you Elizabeth. I want you to call me Thomas.
Elizabeth. Very well, I shall try to remember to call you Thomas, My Lord.
Me. *(I chuckle).* You need more practice, Elizabeth, but if you become my wife, practice you shall have.
Elizabeth. Yes My Lord - I mean Thomas. Here in Great Houghton - here in my father's house, we don't have many lords as guests. I'm a country-woman, with no real experience of Society.
Me. But in Ireland, as my wife, the wife of the Lord Deputy, you'll have much experience of Society. That is, if you would like it.
Elizabeth. I'm not sure that I should like it, Thomas. I fancy I'm not suited to pageantry and the bustle and swirl of a busy Court. We are puritans. My pleasure is more likely to be found in tending a quiet home, and doing what I can to see that my husband is keen on returning to it - and to me - as often as he can.
Me. Then you are an unusual young lady, my dear. Most of the women at Court cannot bear to be parted from it for an evening, unless

that evening be spent in the arms of their latest lover. *(I wish I had not said that. She may be shocked. But she takes it in her stride and I admire her the more for that).*

Elizabeth. I have no taste for lovers, My Lo..., Thomas. And if I am to take on your children, and God willing, have some of my own, I shall be busy enough, and happy enough, running your household. I think you have three children; is it so?

Me. It is so. You've been making enquiry about me, Elizabeth? I'm flattered. Did you find out their names?

Elizabeth. *(She is embarrassed).* My Lord, I..... In truth, you are a celebrity here in Yorkshire now, and our neighbours are anxious to talk. Your visits here have been the subject of much gossip. But it didn't concern your children, and I do not know their names.

Me. My son, William, is named after my father. The girls are Ann - we call her Nan - and Arabella. I see them less than I like. Carving a career in politics, perhaps in anything, is strange, Elizabeth. We say we are doing it for our children, for posterity, yet we venture forth in the name of fame and fortune and leave behind our little ones just at the time they need us most. It's a paradox. And for my children, whose mother is dead, it's doubly hard. My dear, I need a wife, but it would be wrong of me not to acknowledge that my children's need for a loving step-mother is a weighty factor in this courtship.

Elizabeth. I know Thomas, I know. If I can make the children happy, I shall. And if they are happy you will be too. Your happiness shall be my first concern, and if my happiness should be yours, what need would I have of lovers?

Me. My happiness shall be your first concern, Elizabeth? Does that mean that we are to be married?

Elizabeth. If you will be my lord, Thomas, then I shall be your lady.

Me. Then I am a fortunate man. And you, My Lady, need have no fears about the Lord Deputy's Court. You need never go there unless you want to, and if domestic bliss is the happiness you seek, you will have it aplenty.

Elizabeth. I am content Thomas, and shall strive to make you so.

Me. Content? Dearest Elizabeth, you've done so much already. If only you knew how the thought of going alone to Ireland has been weighing on my mind! But now, with you, the prospect is an altogether sunnier one. Do you think you can bring some sunshine to Dublin?

Elizabeth. I shall try.
Me. Your smile will be sunshine enough. We'll have need of it. I'm told there's an Irish Bishop who constantly prays for rain. Who knows? Perhaps he spends too much time in his Cathedral to see what Irish weather is like. Perhaps he never goes out. But you and I, my darling, must go in, and I must tell your father of my good fortune.
Elizabeth. I shall not bring you a fortune, Thomas. My father is not rich, and neither his purse nor my taste will stomach an expensive wedding. I should prefer a modest family ceremony.
Me. As befits a modest lady, though in my eyes you have little to be modest about, and much to be proud of. And as for money, I have more than enough, and if a large dowry were what I wanted, your father's house is not the place I should have come looking for it. You were - are - what I wanted, Elizabeth, and I shall ensure that you want for nothing.

We go into the house. As we do so, Elizabeth takes my arm, and smiles at me. The parents are delighted, and it is clear that Lady Rodes is excited that Elizabeth has made a good match. Sir Godfrey makes it plain that Elizabeth will get a dowry of 1,000 pounds (more than I expected) and an annual allowance of 100 a year. She will also get her quiet wedding; in fact he wants it to be more or less a secret wedding. He is concerned that many will criticise me for marrying so soon after becoming a widower. He thinks it should remain out of the public eye until we are in Ireland, and I can see his point. Earl Clare and the rest of the Holles family have hardened their attitude towards me, and may be among those who say I killed Arabella. Preposterous, but I can do without scandal, and I'm sure Elizabeth would have no idea how to handle it.

Christopher Wandesford. September, 1632.York.

Almost a year ago I was writing of attacks on Tom's efforts to reinforce the authority of the Crown and the Council in the North. There are now some really serious matters affecting his efforts. First there is the case of Sir David Foulis. He's a Scot. The second is that of Sir Thomas Leighton, who is Foulis's son-in-law. The third is that of Sir Thomas Gower.

Foulis used to have a position at Court, but quite what it was, I know not. Whatever it was it must have involved the handling of Royal

Revenue, because some time ago he apparently managed to embezzle nearly 6,000 pounds, and he bought an estate with it in Yorkshire, to which he retired. When his misconduct came to light, it seems he was afraid that Tom would pursue him with his customary vigour on behalf of the Crown. Foulis embarked on an attempt to create a smoke-screen round himself by alleging that Tom, too, was helping himself to the King's cash.

Tom had been commanded by the King to enforce the very old rules under which any man owning land yielding rents of forty pounds a year or more had to pay fees to the King instead of providing armed retainers, or make a bargain with the King by paying one large sum to cancel out that feudal duty, known as Knight-Service. Crazily, Foulis started telling his acquaintances that Tom was pocketing the money, and that the receipts they were given for the lump sums had no effect on their liability to go on paying the fees each year. There were many willing ears as the gentry did not care to have to make these payments.

Sir David's surname invites the quip that he was a fool to make these allegations, since he knew the business of collecting Royal revenues, even if he had found ways of avoiding the paperwork so that he could keep the money himself. He also badly misjudged Tom, who was scrupulous about such things. Indeed, one of my tasks was the supervision of the clerks who held the cash, and entered up the books.

We reported the figures to Richard Weston, the Treasurer, on a regular basis, and Tom and I would have been as stupid as Sir David if we had tried to mislead him over their accuracy. After all, prior to Tom's appointment as President, the tally from these sources was pathetically small, and after his appointment, it rose dramatically. Why should Tom tell the Treasurer lies about his success if he did not hand over the money? Why should I cooperate in such a fraud knowing that if Tom fell, he would take me with him?

It was at this point that Sir David's son-in-law, Sir Thomas Leighton, became involved. He is the Sheriff of the county. One of his minions told him that some of the wealthy had not paid their knight-service dues. Tied in with what Sir David was saying, this fuelled the idea that Tom was stealing the money, because in fact the men in question had paid. These payments were recorded in my books.

Tom was angry. He summoned Leighton to appear before the Council, and he refused to come, on the advice of – you guessed it – Sir

David. Foulis told a crowd, including Leighton, at a banquet, that the Council of the North had no jurisdiction to command a Sheriff to appear before it. Tom was absolutely furious. His aim was, in accordance with the King's commands, to assert the power of the Council as a reflection of Royal authority, and the actions of Sir David and Leighton were a direct attack on that aim.

Fortunately for Tom and Leighton something happened almost immediately that saved the situation for them to some extent, but not for Foulis. Leighton, as Sheriff, was ordered by the law courts to recover possession of a fortified manor house. The previous owner had sold it off to pay his debts, and then refused to leave. Leighton was forced to eat humble pie before the Council and seek Tom's help in evicting this man, who was so entrenched in his old home that the Sheriff had to borrow the Council's cannon and troops to blast him out. Thus peace seems to have been restored between Tom and Sir David's son-in-law, if not with Sir David.

Foulis fled to Whitehall, and endeavoured to persuade the King that he was of such importance in the North that the King would do better to side with him than with his President. I helped Tom with a letter to the Monarch setting out his case.

Your Majesty,

I have been informed of the charges Sir David Foulis is levelling against me, and I deny them robustly. I have taken not a penny of what is due to you, the records make that plain, and I have faithfully reported all monies received as knight service fees or settlements to the Treasurer, Sir Richard Weston.

If I may be so bold, Sire, I should point out that your authority will not be enhanced by taking back into your service one such as Sir David, who is well-known to have served your Treasury so falsely in the past. Rather than that, you should make him an example of your justice, by bringing him before the Law Courts. It is the only way to deal with the presumptuousness which is common these days, that every man is as good as the King, and entitled to challenge his power. I cannot abide this attitude.

It matters not if forty or more Foulises or Wentworths are swept away as long as Royal authority remains unblemished.

King Charles took no notice of Foulis. He was not taken in by this rather nasty, tiny, and almost deformed 'gentleman.' He has left it to Thomas to sue him for slander and libel in the Star Chamber.

The third attack on the Council started a few days ago. It aims at George Radcliffe.

Thomas. 25th October, 1632. Great Houghton.

Today I am married to Elizabeth Rodes. We are staying at the house of her Father, Sir Godfrey for a few days. The wedding was a very small, quiet affair, in accordance with his wishes. It was a happy day, but the start of what should have been happy matrimonial experiences in the bedroom did not materialise. Elizabeth seems to have some fear of sex, and I did not find a way to release what I am sure is a passionate nature. I cannot bring myself to deal with that here at present. Perhaps I shall do so another time.

Even now I cannot go to Ireland yet. I still have details to settle at the Privy Council, and the Council of the North, and the arrangements for my own properties and business interests to finalise with Peter Man and Richard Marris. On top of that I cannot possible leave with the Foulis and Gower cases not finished.

George Radcliffe. 10th December, 1632. Wentworth Woodhouse.

It is rather odd, in a way, that Thomas has become so friendly with William Laud. They do not quite see eye to eye about Church services, since William is very High Church (some say almost Catholic), and Thomas comes from a less theatrical religious tradition, although he is not exactly Low Church either. However, they have met a number of times at Privy Council meetings, and found that they have very similar views about supporting the authority of the King.

This has resulted in their corresponding a great deal about their policies for the country and the Church, and they seem to agree about almost everything. As I help Thomas with his business of all kinds, including Council and government matters, and write some letters for him, I get to see quite a lot of this correspondence. They call their policies "Thorough".

We have been working on some of these letters today, but Thomas is in a strange mood. We heard this morning that Sir John Eliot died of consumption on 27th November in the Tower. He'd been sent there (illegally, some say) for the part he played when the Speaker was held in his chair in the Commons in 1629. The King hated him for his leading role in the failed attempt to impeach his friend Buckingham. His cell was as horribly damp as the one Thomas More ended up in before they chopped his head off. When we received the news, Thomas laughed and said: 'Thank God. That's one obstacle out of the King's way. And mine."

Then he became quiet and thoughtful for quite a while, and eventually said to me: "I'm rather ashamed of what I said just now. Eliot was a noble character, and stood up for what he believed in, even if it wasn't what I believed in. For a long time we were on the same side. He was too hot-headed, even if he was a fantastic orator."

"Being in the Tower for three years must have cooled him off a bit."

"Is that meant to be a joke, George? Well, he's dead cold now, alright. He never did apologise to the King, which is what the Judges ordered him to do."

"There's a lot of ill feeling about his imprisonment, Thomas, and now he's dead it'll get worse."

"You may well be right." Thomas glances at the letter we had had from London, and looks back at me: "His family asked the King to move him to a better, drier, cell, and Charles refused. He wouldn't even let them have the body back to bury it!! He's supposed to have said: 'Let Sir John Eliot be buried in the church of the parish where he died'. So he was interred in the churchyard of the Tower. That does seem so mean, and so petty."

"Yes, because it wasn't his wife or children who needed to be punished. People say the King has no heart."

"Some of the others who were arrested at the same time ..."

I interrupt: "Like Denzil Holles?"

"No, George, I didn't mean him – he made an apology and paid up his fine and got out. I meant others such as Strode and Valentine, who were involved in that assault on Speaker Finch three years ago. They are still in prison, and likely to be there for several years yet. It won't do the King any good at all."

"It won't do you any good, either, Thomas. You work for the King now."

Thomas smiles. "Then this talk must remain a secret between us, mustn't it? We live in dangerous times for public men." He pauses. "When he was young Eliot was very friendly with Villiers. They travelled abroad and about the country together, and it was Buckingham who got him the position of Vice-Admiral of Devon."

Again I interrupt. "But it was as Vice-Admiral that he became disenchanted with his friend Villiers for the disasters at Cadiz and the Ile de Re, wasn't it?"

"Yes, George, quite right. Eliot has been in prison more than once. About ten years ago, as the Navy's top man in Devon, he made a plan to catch a notorious pirate called John Nutt ..."

"Yes, I've heard of him. He plundered the South Coast for years and robbed merchant ships – even English ships – in the channel."

Thomas nods. "Well, Sir John caught Nutt, but he was a friend of George Calvert, who as you know was a friend of mine. Calvert persuaded King James to pardon Nutt, and for his pains poor old Eliot – well, not old; he was only about thirty then – went to prison for a few weeks on some trumped up charges. He was in the Marshalsea, where you and I were four years ago."

"As you say, Thomas, these are dangerous times for public men, and no-one is more public than you are becoming. Take care, because......"

There is a knock at the door, and Lady Wentworth comes in at once. As she shuts the door behind her I bow and say "Lady Wentworth." She begins to drop me a curtsey but Thomas rises from the desk, and puts a hand on each of our arms before she can speak. "Careful, George. Remember, this is not Lady Wentworth yet. That's why she knocks at the door." He winks. "This is the children's governess on probation to see if she is fit to come to Ireland with us. I asked you before to call her Elizabeth, and you, Elizabeth must, for the time being, call him Sir George."

"I'm sorry, Thomas, I forgot. It won't happen again." George actually blushes.

Elizabeth is amused. "And when the world knows I am Lady Wentworth, you must still call me Elizabeth, Sir."

"And you can forget the 'Sir' then, too. But forgive me, what did you want?"

"To give you both some important news. A messenger just came. He gave the message to me as he has to visit others in York, Halifax and Leeds as soon as he can."

"And the message, my dearest?"

"Frederick is dead; the husband of our King's sister Elizabeth is dead. He died, I gather, of a terrible fever on 29th November."

"And he had been so ill after that boating accident two or three years ago, when his son died. The King will be grieving for this loss." Thomas is thoughtful. "I must write to him expressing our sorrow. Charles Louis is now the claimant to the Palatinate, and he's still only a boy."

Thomas. 12th December, 1632. Wentworth Woodhouse.

I am President of the Council of the North, and Deputy Lord Lieutenant of Ireland too. The latter is a post which has been the death knell of many a political career. I have to consider carefully how I should exercise the power this exalted post gives me, and what I want to achieve.

It is a strange situation. I do not share Charles's contempt for Parliaments. Having been in both Houses in England I can see the advantage of a well-managed legislature, and that is what I intend to have in Ireland. The King has no idea how to manage the Lords and Commons. He thinks all he needs to do is tell them what he wants and why it is their duty to give it to him, and he will get what he wants. I know that isn't how it works.

Even so, when he dissolved Parliament in 1629 I thought it a great opportunity to get things done if we could steer clear of war, as there would be no interference from politicians. With all power resting in the King and emanating from him we could make England rich and prosperous. The King's service could become very efficient, and the more efficient it was, the more revenue could be collected, and with more money more could be done for the people, and the administration of the country.

I do not know that my colleagues on the Privy Council saw it like that. They just seemed to be happy to make policy almost on a day-to-day basis, without any long-term plan, except perhaps William Laud. He always knows where he is headed, and we were going in the same direction, and still are. For us the King and the Church stand or fall together, and that was the paramount fact on which we worked, and still is. It is the same in the King's mind, I am sure, but he sees no necessity to work for that end. He thinks that he embodies all that, so that's the end of the matter.

Other Privy Councillors, like Weston the Treasurer, and Francis Cottington, the Chancellor of the Exchequer, are very clever men, but the day-to-day routine, and making sure they keep their jobs, are enough for them, especially when they are getting richer. And they are. So am I, but money is not everything. I want power too, because it gives me the chance to do good.

We can't rely on the way things have been done before. We need to make the King's government live up to the power it enjoys but has for so long seemed unable to exercise successfully. Whilst the King has silenced Parliament, he has not silenced its members. Putting Eliot in the Tower might have shut some people up, but discontent continues to rumble throughout the land. If the actions the King takes are just and fair, and aim at pleasing the people rather than negligently alienating them, a few years of going alone without Parliament could set the country on a safe course.

I don't fool myself that we could run the country for more than a few years without summoning the representatives of the people to Westminster. That would have to be done once the King's authority has been shown to work, and work well. If we could do that the people would put all the mistakes of the Buckingham era behind them. Most people live for today, and do not seek revenge or harbour vendettas for what has gone wrong in the past. Memories are short. And once Parliament is called again, it would have to be managed. I manage the Council of the North, and I know it could be done with the whole country. With God's help it will work.

Properly managed, Parliament could do what it was always intended to do: inform the King what the people's problems are, offer solutions for him to consider, and put up the money to make the policies work. I have to make sure that the two Houses do not make war on the King by withholding taxes to try to force him to do what they want. The King would have to listen, and correct all just complaints. What happened in 1628 was stupid. I did not go along with the Forced Loan, but I was against the sort of brawl with the King which took place then. There's a world of difference between freedom to think and say what you like and act in a conscientious manner, and unrestricted licence to behave just as you please and end up destroying everything that is worth preserving.

What do others think about this? Truly, I do not care. I'm sufficiently sure of my philosophy to pay little heed to their opinions of me. If they are rich and powerful, and opposed to my ideas for taking care of the greater part of the people, I shall find ways to bring them into line, or bring them down.

To do all this I need – the King needs – a loyal band of servants who will implement our policies. He has nothing like enough, and too many are only interested in their own pockets. I think that my fellows in the Lords, and the gentlemen who are the backbone of the judiciary as Justices of the Peace, with all the functions the law and government impose upon them, will happily enforce the King's laws when they are seen to be fair, and lead to stability and prosperity. I believe they will work as hard as I do. I believe that if the King's officials had proper and adequate salaries so that bribery and corruption could be reduced, government would be more efficient, and stronger.

In addition to all that, I should like nothing better than to be the King's friend as well as one of his ministers.

William Laud, Bishop of London. 18th January, 1633. Fulham Palace.

To Thomas Wentworth, Viscount Newmarch.

My Lord,

I trust you are well, and had a good journey back to Yorkshire from our last Privy Council Meeting. I do not intend to make this a long epistle on political or Church matters. To come immediately to the point, I have the unpalatable task of warning you that a rumour is circulating in the cities of London and Westminster that you have installed a pretty young woman at Wentworth, and that she accompanies you on some of your circuits in the North, sometimes at the Lord President's House in York, and on other occasions elsewhere.

You must not think that I tell you this in any spirit of criticism or condemnation. I know not the truth of it, but as you are now not only President of the North, and must shortly take up your position in Ireland, it would ill become you to have any scandal the basis of which were true going the rounds. Of course, as a cleric, if this matter is true, you would appreciate that I could not approve of it.

Perhaps you would be good enough to let me know whether this gossip is true or false, so that I can defend you should the need arise. As you are aware the King is fairly straight laced, and might well not feel able to maintain you in office in the event of scandal.

I am your constant friend, and pray for you daily, as I do for the King and rest of the Council.

William + Londiniensis.

Thomas. 2nd February, 1633. Wentworth.

This letter is quite alarming. How these rumours get going is quite beyond me. Or is it? One may well say "Not in front of the servants," but you do not actually have to do anything in front of them. They are not stupid. Elizabeth has not been living at Wentworth continually, but has spent several periods of two weeks or so at her parents. I have been telling anybody who enquires that she is visiting with a view to seeing whether she would be suitable as a governess for the children, and whether they like her. She has accompanied me on some of my duties, but only when we have taken the children. We go to bed and wake up in separate rooms, though we do not always spend all night in those rooms.

In the main this is due to our desire to follow her Father's wishes and keep the marriage secret until we are in Dublin. However, it is partly due to the unfortunate and unhappy fact that we have been unable, so far, to establish a satisfactory conjugal relationship in bed. I think it will come, but at present I have to be patient, and am rather afraid, as I have described earlier.

I shall tell Laud this rather misleading but partially accurate tale of a young woman who is and is to be a companion to the children, and tell him the truth of it in private when I see him at the next Privy Council meeting. I sit at my desk and pen a letter to him at once.

In the meanwhile, for her sake as well as mine, I have to send her away to avoid the gossip and scandal growing out of control. I resolve to send her over to Dublin as soon as possible, with the children, to await my arrival in a few months. That should reinforce the tale that she is governess to my children, and we shall resume married life when I get there, and make the marriage public.

I wish I could go too, but with all the litigation arising out of the Foulis and Gower cases, on top of my political and business affairs, and the need to find people to take charge of them whilst I am in Ireland, I am simply not ready to do so. There's been that idiot Sheriff, Leighton, to deal with and the Gower case will probably go on for a year. Besides, I'm still advising the King as a member of his Privy Council, and the advice of which he seems to take most notice comes from me, Laud, Weston the Treasurer, and Cottington, the Chancellor of the Exchequer.

Interestingly, I had always thought of Weston and Cottington as friends, and I am sure it was their influence with the King that got me the post of Deputy in Ireland, for which I am grateful. My gratitude was tarnished, rather, when Laud told me that he had reason to think that those two were wary of my relations with the King, jealous of the sudden rise in my fortunes at Court, and had put my name forward for Ireland as a means of getting me out of the way, so that my influence with the King might be reduced. That is what the King wrote, too. Not for the first time I have been warned that this post has been the graveyard of political ambition, and that it had sentenced my predecessors, Grandison and Falkland, to oblivion. That, however, has not discouraged me.

Elizabeth. 3rd March, 1633. Dublin.

It is miserable here, cold and damp, and no Thomas! Dublin may be the capital city of Ireland but it is a poor place compared with York. I arrived from England a few days ago. The journey from Wentworth to Chester wasn't bad, but the Irish Sea crossing was rough and made me and William ill. The two girls were not, thank the Lord.

I am in quite a nice house, but I think the Deputy and his family are expected to live in the Castle. Yesterday I went there with my new Irish maid, Kathleen, who is very pleasant indeed. She had been there before, which was useful. We were shown round by the Constable, a big beefy man with black hair and moustache. He was very attentive and seemed apologetic for the state of the place.

He pointed out that the East Wall, where there are no buildings, had not been repaired for so long it had partially fallen down. The main entrance to the Castlc is on the North side with a draw-bridge, and there is a moat. He said part of it is the River Poddle. The walls form a rectangle, with a tower in each corner, and the Deputy's House is against the South Wall and in its shadow, which is a shame as the sun shines – if it does – from that side so the house never sees it. No wonder it is cold and damp.

I'm sure Thomas will be disturbed by the appalling impression all this creates. I must write and warn him of it. He is rather fastidious and likes everything to be in order, as it is at home. He will be furious that the repairs he ordered are so slow in being carried out.

Charles I. 14th March, 1633. Windsor.

A week ago I promulgated a new Commission for the Council of the North. I have been impressed with the manner in which Wentworth has restored its power and authority, and felt it only right to give the Council some firm guidance on how it should proceed from now on, and free it from interference from the Courts in London. There is little point in having a body in the North charged with looking after that region on my behalf, and then having every important decision it takes challenged in King's Bench or some other Court by an Earl or Baron who thinks the law doesn't apply to him. I know how King John felt.

Those whom Wentworth calls "the proud and insolent" love the law to control others, but have no desire to have any sort of control exercised over themselves.

Despite such problems, my four years or so of non-parliamentary government seem to have been rather successful, if I say so myself, even if I cannot claim all the credit. I have made peace with Spain and France, and peace with Spain has brought an ingenious trade agreement engineered at the Exchequer by Cottington, my Chancellor. I shall have to give him some sort of title soon, I dare say. And Weston, the Treasurer too, I suppose. This trade agreement brings in a great deal of Spanish gold and silver so that the mint is churning out coins at a great rate.

Somehow this facilitates commerce, but I do not pretend to understand how. It suffices for me to know my Kingdom and my people are getting richer, since I benefit too. How is that? Well, on every pound of bullion that is minted the Treasury gets a percentage. With the extra income from that and no wars to bleed the coffers dry, I am just able to make ends meet, and run the country at least as well as if Parliament were paying the paltry amounts it used to allow me. I use the word 'allow' advisedly since that is how it always seemed to me; just like a poor widow going to the Poor Law Magistrates to ask for a pittance for food or clothes.

My sister Elizabeth is a fairly poor widow herself now. Frederick, her husband, was a victim of the plague some months ago, so I send her and her children what I can afford, but there is no question of my going to war with the Emperor or anyone else for her sake. I simply do not have the money, I have no army, and the people would not pay to support an army in Europe even if I did. It is the old story; they say they want to fight to put Elizabeth and my nephews back on the throne of the Palatinate, but they do not want it to cost them anything.

Things looked much brighter for Frederick and Elizabeth eighteen months ago when the King of Sweden, Gustavus Adolphus, was winning battle after battle on the Protestant side, but then he was killed in combat last year, and now Spain and Austria are doing all the winning again.

The fact that England is not in this fray is excellent for trade, I am told, and that increases my income from Tunnage and Poundage. We are neutral, in effect, and English merchants trade with both sides. I recall that Wentworth was always against war, particularly with Spain. Perhaps I should have listened to his counsel – and Weston's - earlier. I cannot forgive his part in hounding Buckingham, but I should be foolish not to recognise that George's desire to fight Spain and France did no end of harm to my relations with Parliament, and the Crown's finances.

However, I must also thank God that I am His instrument for the government of England, Scotland, Wales, and Ireland, and that He has blessed these Kingdoms with peace, and prosperity, and the North with better administration and a more cultured and less tribal approach to life. I am fortunate that Wentworth plays his part in all this, and that I have had the sense to employ him.

Nevertheless, he is a man of such energy and ability he worries me. These great virtues might make a King more afraid than ashamed to employ him in the mighty affairs of state.

Thomas. 20th March, 1633. London.

I'm at Westminster for the Privy Council. Elizabeth is not with me. She is in Dublin now. I sent her there with my young brother George. I should not have brought her here anyway, as I still seek to keep our union secret for the time being, but I have told William Laud the truth of it. He was mightily relieved. He is not a cleric who tells his flock to be moral but whose private life is more like a follower of Satan. He works hard at his Christianity, but is so intolerant of denominations other than his own brand of Church of England. That is his major fault. A letter from Bess came today.

Dearest Thomas,

I miss you terribly, and the Castle is horrid; so cold at this time of year, and damp. You told me you had ordered repairs to be carried out a year ago, but it is obvious so much needed to be done that the builders have hardly scraped the surface of it. Some of the Castle walls have actually fallen to the ground, and have not yet been rebuilt. At least the Hall and other more official parts of the place are functional now, and are being decorated.

Fortunately a Mr Hall came to see me and said he was your agent for getting the repairs done, and had been ordered by you to prepare accomodation for me in a house at Killmaignham, and it is much more comfortable there. I think it will be some time before the Castle is fit to live in. Wentworth and my Father's house are not too large, and feel like homes. I'm not sure Dublin Castle will ever feel like that.

It was not a good journey here, for William and I were sea-sick, but luckily Nan and Arabella were not. I am very busy settling in and getting used to the servants. I shall write again as soon as I have time.

I love you, my dear Thomas, and long to see you again.

Bess.

Today I am shown that the King does truly appreciate what I am doing in the North. He has issued a new Commission and a set of instructions for the Council of the North; these make it clear that my Council – well, his really – is every bit as important and powerful as the Star Chamber. I regret that I shall not be in York to enjoy directly these new powers, but I can rely on Osborne to use them wisely and to write to me for guidance where he needs it. He is very loyal, reliable, and clever.

This new Commission is not something unusual. When a new President is appointed a new Commission is usually issued for his guidance. What is unusual here is the extension of the powers of the Council.

Thomas. 30th March, 1633. Westminster.

Dear Bess,

I was so relieved to get your letter saying that you had arrived safely in Dublin, despite a bad crossing. I'm sorry you were sick. I was also pleased that my letter was waiting for you. I wrote it a couple of days after you left. This will be a rather short one as I have to pen some letters to brother George and Christopher giving them directions about some of the things I want them to attend to. I hope they are looking after you and that you are not having any trouble with the servants who are so new to you. The fact that the work on the Castle is not yet complete, and that in consequence you are uncomfortable is distressing to me. I shall take steps to expedite the repairs as soon as I am with you.

I'm both glad and sad that you miss me. I miss you too. I am glad because you would not miss me if you cared little, and I'm sad to think that you may not be as happy as you usually seem. Marriage is many things, but companionship and fellowship are in the end the most important. Marriage ought to carry with it more of love and equality than anything else that there might be to worry about. I desire that it may ever be thus between us, nor shall it ever break of my part. Having said which, I must again apologise for having had to 'break' us apart by sending you away so soon after we were married. You may rest content that I shall never do that again if it is in my power to stop it.

Last night I was at dinner with Henry and Frances Clifford. Some of the ladies were very lovely and scandalously dressed - but not Frances. I should very much like to see you dressed in such a way, but only for my eyes, and in utter seclusion. I hope to be doing so in two or three months. Waiting is hard work.

Your loving,
Thomas.

Elizabeth. 10th April, 1633. Dublin Castle.

My Dear Thomas,

Your sweet letter was delivered this morning. It was dated 30th March, so it has taken almost two weeks to get here. I know I say it in all my letters but I do love you and miss you. Having your letters and your news always cheers me up. The fact that they start "Dear Bess" is cheering in itself. Do you remember how, before we were married, you used to start your letters to me "Dear Madam"? I have never told you before that that used to make me laugh; I know most men think women are silly, but I was not blind to the possibility that you might be coming to our house with a view to courtship, and I thought it an odd way to address someone with a view to affection!!

Talking of affection, and as you ask about the children, I am pleased to say they seem to be quite fond of me now. I think the fact they are young helps. William is a bit shy with me but he is very good, and does what I tell him nearly all the time. Ann is a bit more difficult, but she is old enough to remember Arabella and finds it a bit more difficult to adapt to me. Little Arabella hardly recalls her mother at all, so she is the easiest. She calls me Mummy or Mother, and so the other two are starting to do so. She is also quite a strong character and can be a bit naughty at times.

When she is I find it hard to play the wicked step-mother and smack her, and as the governess I should have no qualms about that. Fortunately I am just a pretend governess, but if the children all call me 'Mummy', soon it will be hard to keep up that pretence. It is very wet here so the children cannot go out to play, but they are all very well.

I hope we shall have one or two of our own one day. As you are in Yorkshire or London and I am over here, that is more than a bit difficult at the moment! You never complain, but I think that you feel there is something missing in our lovemaking, and I do hope that it will be better when you are here. It made me so happy to read that you hope to be here in the next two or three months.

I was amused by what you told me about the ladies at Henry and Frances Clifford's dinner. As a good puritan girl I suppose I should be shocked, and even jealous, but you wrote so wittily that I knew you could not be serious about any of them (I hope). Happily I do not think there are many ladies here to take your fancy, though my handsome husband may take theirs. If there any beauties, I have yet to see them, but then, as you know, I do not go out much.

Please come to Dublin in two months, or even one, and certainly not in three. But that is selfish, since I know you have so much to do.

I must go and put the children to bed, or at any rate Arabella. I put them down at one hour intervals. I don't think it fair to put them all to bed at the same time. Either William goes to bed too soon, or Arabella is up too late. What do you think?

You poke fun at me for forgetting to sign my last letter to you. I shall not forget this time.

Your loving Bess.

Thomas. 17th April, 1633. London.

I am still in town. For the last year or more, I've been trying to learn all I can about government in Ireland, and about its finances. Both clearly need a great deal of reform. Mountnorris has given me a lot of help. One of the main money problems is the customs farm. No; this is not an agricultural project for growing cash. It is a method of farming the collection of the customs and taxes out to a group of wealthy men who pay a lump sum to the King every year for the privilege of gathering in the revenue. On top of the lump sum, they pay the King half of the extra they collect over and above that sum, and they keep the other half. This saves the King the expense of employing people to do the work for him, and those people would not work so hard at it as the ones who aim to make a profit.

Even so, the system is hopelessly inefficient. In 1618, when George Villiers had established himself as King James's blue-eyed boy, the whole custom farm was given to him – having been taken from a group which included Arthur Ingram – for 6,000 per annum, plus half the profits. Buckingham was to have it until 1628, but after a few years the King extended it so he got it until 1635 and, would you believe it, with no provision to increase the lump sum.

Then Buckingham was assassinated in 1628, and the farm went to his widow. She went on paying the King (now Charles) 6000 plus half the profits. Like her husband, the late Duke, the Duchess used agents in Ireland to do the work for her.

I was appointed Deputy Lord Lieutenant of Ireland in mid 1631, and shortly after that a new Book of Rates for the customs was brought out, which raised the amount of revenue which could be collected. The same thing had been done in England a few years earlier. I do not claim that the Book was my work. At the same time the men who worked for the Duchess were got rid of, and a new group took over, including, as you might expect, Sir Arthur again, with a man called Cogan, and also George Radcliffe and Mountnorris.

Even though I was not yet in Ireland I strove to ensure that the customs were properly collected and accounted for. The new men had to pay the King 8,000 pounds to take up the farm, and 15,000 pounds a year plus half the profits. Out of their half the farmers had to pay the Duchess a pension, but they still made a profit for themselves of about 5,000 this last year. The King got his 15,000 plus his half of the extra, another 11,000. Everyone did very nicely, thank you.

Elizabeth. Dublin Castle. 3rd May 1633.

Dearest Thomas,

I must tell you something quite extraordinary. As you know, we usually go to Divine Service here in the Castle Chapel, but this morning I went with the Wandesfords to St Patrick's Cathedral.

Behind the altar there is one on the ugliest things I have ever seen. It is like an extremely crude Roman frieze, not beautifully carved, as they are, but as if it had been moulded out of clay or something. It also bore the most appalling colours, mainly reds and browns. After the service we enquired of the verger or sacristan what it might be. He said it is a monumental tomb for the late Countess of Cork.

It so dominates the place that it is difficult to remember that if we focus on anything it should be the cross on the altar, and Jesus, not the memorial to a lady, no matter how great or good she might have been. When you are here, I do hope you will be able to do something about it. I should not take it kindly if you had such a "tribute" to me erected in such a place.

Please come to me soon. All my love,
Elizabeth.

Thomas. 3rd July, 1633. Wentworth Woodhouse.

Your Majesty,

Once again I must express my humble thanks for the honour and great opportunity you have granted me in sending me as your Deputy to Ireland.

I desire above all else to make Ireland a good source of revenue for the Crown, and the only way to do so is to foster commerce and introduce more manufacturing. By doing so I hope to leave your Irish subjects happier than I expect to find them, but in doing so I shall do nothing to prejudice those in England.

I plan to take advantage of the Spanish navy's need for a place to stop for supplies of food and water. It is a lucrative trade. There are other schemes of which I shall make a trial, and inform you of them as they come to pass.

However none of this can work and revenue cannot be increased without your Royal authority being enhanced by a stable administration. There are many powerful nobles there whose only interest is in their own private ends. They don't give a fig for the public good. I intend to call them to heel by very firm government and bringing unbiased justice to all, rich or poor.

If I fail to make you, Sire, a more absolute master of your Irish Kingdom than any of your forbears, it will not be for want of trying. In this I must endeavour to knit the differing sections of this strange society into a quieter unity. If I succeed in these aims – and I do not intend to fail – the opportunity and means to supply your wants is there. I know you will not begrudge your humble servant some profit he may gain; unlike some, I shall not place my own interests above yours.

I am, Sire, your loyal and grateful Deputy,
Wentworth.

Is This The Head Of The Staircase?

Thomas. 23rd July, 1633. Dublin Castle.

My ship docked in Dublin Harbour today after a swift sailing from Queensferry, near Chester. Now I am at the Castle with Elizabeth and the children. The most amazing thing has just happened. A smaller ship arrived soon after we did, bearing, amongst other things, a messenger from my Deputy Sir Edward Osborne, Vice-President of the North. His dispatches include a letter saying that at last Vermuyden and Savile have finished the new channel at Hatfield Chase to stop the flooding, and have allowed the land they stole to be redistributed to the local people.

I think Savile believed he could wear me down, and keep it all, and that Vermuyden need not dig the new canal. Osborne says the whole scheme turned out much more expensive than Vermuyden had calculated, and that the extra work and the loss of the extra land has made it hardly worthwhile. Savile and his cronies will be furious. I cannot say I am sorry.

Osborne adds an interesting snippet. Vermuyden is now working on drainage projects in Somerset. I hope those poor West Country farmers are treated properly from the outset.

I've interrupted myself. I was describing my arrival in Dublin. All sorts and conditions of people from the highest to the lowest and the richest to the poorest went to the harbour to greet me, I'm told. Naturally the nobility were at the front in the best places, making it difficult for any of the ordinary folk to see anything. I dare say the cheering would have been impressive and heart-warming. However, as it turns out, I deprived them of the spectacle, not realising anyone would be there. I asked the ship's captain to have me rowed ashore before we reached the harbour, and I started to walk into town quietly with a couple of companions. I should have walked all the way, but Lord Cork somehow learnt of my disembarkation and raced from the harbour to meet me when I was about half way there. I travelled the rest of the way in his carriage.

We do not have a large gathering at dinner as I am rather tired, and anxious to go to bed with Elizabeth, something I have been unable to do since the middle of February when I put her on a ship for Dublin. I hope for much; I am as excited and inflamed as I was on our wedding night. Will absence have made the heart grow fonder? Will it have increased, or should I say created, her desire?

Unfortunately not. The night is spent much as the first was.

George Wentworth. 25th July, 1633. Dublin.

Yesterday my brother honoured me by taking me with him to call on the Earl of Cork, and Lord Loftus the Lord Chancellor of Ireland at their splendid town houses, Cork's being the more splendid of the two. It seemed to me that they were surprised and pleased that he had shown them this courtesy, and I must admit it made me feel rather important to be moving in these exalted circles almost as soon as I was off the ship. These two ruled the country between Falkland leaving four years ago, and Thomas arriving.

Today was even grander. Thomas was invested as Deputy Lord Lieutenant.

Cork and Loftus came to our apartments at the Castle to accompany Thomas to the Council Chamber. Loftus is tall, with a grey beard shaped like a spade, and he favours dark clothes of Elizabethan cut, and a large Elizabethan type of ruff. He must be about sixty-five, so he's from the age of Gloriana, I suppose; he comes from Yorkshire, and has been here for about forty years. Cork is about the same age, so they are both older than Thomas. Cork – his name is Richard Boyle – is quite flamboyant, with a bush of fuzzy hair all around his head. He was probably rather handsome when he was young. He wears a square collar, as Thomas does sometimes, but whereas my brother's is plain, Boyle's is of the most expensive and intricate lace.

Thomas walked between them, and told me to follow. I thought it a bit odd that he let them go first through all the doors as though they were more important than he is, but then I realised they were still the real power until he had been installed. When we entered the chamber Thomas bowed to the King's chair in the Presence Chamber. He told me afterwards: "This chair is the mark of the King, and where he would sit if he were there." Then someone handed him the Sword of State, and he took his seat on the rostrum next to the King's throne.

He stood again, and summoned me to step forward and kneel. I did so. He struggled to pull the sword out of its scabbard – it hadn't been used for years – touched me with it on both shoulders, and said: "Arise,

Sir George." I was so excited and so moved by this. My brother is the King's Deputy and he knighted me!!

Of course, Loftus and Cork have now stepped down from their roles as the justices ruling the country, and my brother is in charge. He told me to talk to George Radcliffe and Kit Wandesford about those two men, as they have been making enquiries regarding them. Thomas says that knowing all you can about people is the way to keep control. From what I hear, keeping tabs on these two will be hard.

The Earl of Cork is English, from Hereford. Under Queen Elizabeth he came to Ireland with her boyfriend, the Earl of Essex, and when Raleigh got into trouble he acquired his Irish estates. Raleigh was ruined and in prison, and Boyle picked up his properties really cheaply. Thomas says Cork's business methods remind him of Arthur Ingram's, which suggests he's not a very savoury character, and will do anything to get what he wants. Down in the south of the country he's known as 'the Great Earl of Cork'. He's made a lot of money, and is now one of the biggest landowners in Ireland, and wants to be the biggest. Perhaps he needs to be; he's fathered fourteen children! Yes, fourteen. I bet Lady Cork gets tired.

Richard Boyle is also pretty cheeky. When my sister-in-law Arabella died, he waited hardly any time at all before asking Thomas if he wanted to marry his daughter. Thomas was in no mood to marry anyone just then, but he didn't let the grass grow under his feet either. He realised Cork might be useful as an ally in Ireland so he suggested that Cork's son should marry Elizabeth Clifford. Elizabeth is Henry's daughter and Margaret's niece – that's Thomas's first wife. Cork's son is Lord Dungarvan. Thomas doesn't seem to miss a trick. He caused no offence by turning down the daughter, but did what he could to keep it all in the family. No wedding has taken place yet, though.

Kit and George do not have so much to tell about Loftus. They say he's a very clever lawyer, and extremely vain. They are still finding out about him.

They tell me the most dangerous man on the Council is Annesley, Lord Mountnorris. He saw off the last Deputy, Falkland, and they worry he'll do the same to Thomas. Thomas seems friendly with him; he'd better watch his back, I tell him.

"Thanks, George, but I'm well aware of what Annesley's like. I'll deal with him." Thomas is very happy today; he's heard that his friend

William Laud was made Archbishop of Canterbury when old Archbishop Abbott died. Laud is important to the King and also a Privy Councillor. This means, Thomas says, that no-one back in England can attack him without Laud telling him about it. I think it's awful that when we are all supposed to be working for the King, there are so many people just waiting for a chance to stab someone else in the back.

That's politics, I suppose!

Thomas. 26th July, 1633. Dublin Castle.

So William Laud has been raised from Bishop of London to Archbishop of Canterbury! He has done very well indeed. He came from very humble beginnings compared with mine, and mine were not that grand. I'm not sure that I entirely agree with his High Church policies and ceremonies, but as he supports the King, and his type of religion does so, and as I support the King too, it will pay me to agree to enforce William's Church policy in Ireland. Doing so will be far from easy; more of a Herculean labour.

I shall make a start by bringing from England as my personal Chaplain John Bramhall. He's a follower of Laud's. He is bound to be a good and helpful man, as he's a Yorkshireman, as I am; as all the best men are. He comes from Pontefract, where my old enemy Savile is lord. I need someone I can rely on to enforce Laud's policy for me. It will be difficult because of the intense rivalries of the different religious groups; rivalries not just of religious practice and doctrine, but spilling over into politics.

The state of Christianity in Ireland is pretty complicated. The mixture of Gaelic Irish, who are Catholic, the Old English, also mostly Catholic, the New English who are Anglican, and the other lot of New English who are mainly Scottish, and of a more puritan turn of mind, keeps the cauldron boiling nicely. The Old English and the Irish have, of course, lived side by side for four hundred years or more; at least they have the same religion. The Gaelic Chieftains had fought the Old English nobility over the centuries, as none of the Irish wanted to be ruled by them and an English King, but they are united in fearing the consequences of too many puritanical New English taking over their country.

When the Tudors re-conquered Ireland fifty years ago, they tried to impose the Church of England here and called it the Church in Ireland, but this has not been very successful. The Irish are happy being Catholic (or at least afraid not to be). The New English dislike it because they are fiercely Scots Presbyterian for the most part, and they don't want an Irish version of the English Church forced on them. To add to the confusion the Archbishop of Ireland, James Ussher, is on the puritan side of that Church, despite having come from an Old English Catholic family. The only really important Old English Earls are Clanrickard - a Catholic - and Ormonde, an Anglican.

So how does the Church in Ireland maintain a foothold at all? It did so to start with by flourishing, if that is not to extravagant a word, in towns with an Army barracks, or government establishments, and, of course, in strong Protestant plantations. That is what the counties of Ulster offered, where they weren't settled by Scots. The Church acknowledges the King as its Head, but its Articles make no mention of bishops. The tenets of its faith would have been quite acceptable to John Calvin, but are quite unacceptable to the Papists.

In strongly Catholic areas ruled by the Old English nobility the local Earl often has in his gift the appointment of more priests, and the allocation of more rectories for them to live in, than the local Church in Ireland Bishop. Because that Church has taken over so many of the old Catholic church buildings, the local Irish people see no necessity to pay for the upkeep of places of worship where their own brand of worship is forbidden, and many have therefore fallen into ruin.

The consequence of this is that much Ecclesiastical land has fallen, not into ruin, but into the hands of the aristocracy, both Catholic and Protestant, and with it the right to the tithes and the rents and profits of these lands. Richard Boyle, Earl of Cork, has even taken over some former monasteries with all that belonged to them, and he is not alone in this; he may just have done it on a bigger scale than anyone else. The College of Youghal, with all its livings, is one such, and I shall have to see what I can do about it. Boyle may come from Yorkshire, but I'm not sure he's someone to trust! How can a Church, which had been so rich when it was entirely Catholic, ever hope to succeed when it has been robbed of the greater part of its assets?

Naturally, neither the Roman Catholics nor the true Puritans care about this; from their point of view the weaker the official Church is, the better they like it and the easier it is to foster their own denominations.

This is the situation I have come here to deal with, charged as I am with reforming the ownership of Church as well as Royal lands and income, and glad to be so. The possibility of making many more enemies than friends is inherent. Yet I cannot start by making enemies of the Catholics when I need their help to get the subsidies paid. Driving them into alliance with Catholic powers such as France or Spain by persecuting them hard would be stupid. Fortunately the policy of James's reign was, and that of Charles is, one of toleration for the Pope's followers for fear of them seeking French or Spanish assistance, so I need only to follow that for a while. Imposing Archbishop Laud's new doctrines upon them suddenly would be a very short-sighted change indeed.

Having lost a lot of his flock and power to the Reformation, the Pope has aimed the Counter-Reformation at recovering them. He's been pretty successful in Ireland, keeping the vast majority of the people on his side and worshipping in accordance with his liturgy, even if they have to do it in secret and in private houses. His success is due to the number of Roman priests, monks, friars, and Jesuits in this island, estimated not very long before I got there to be well over 1000. For a theoretically banned faith, that is hardly a meagre workforce for keeping the people in line.

As it happens, I think my first target will, curiously, turn out to be the New English, since I expect them to fight very hard against Laud's reforms, and against the repossession of their ill-gotten Church and Royal lands. It doesn't help that, in addition to Archbishop Ussher, many Church in Ireland Bishops are quite strongly puritan. I shall have to get rid of as many of them as I can to make that Church Laudian in outlook. These will be interesting times, to put it mildly.

Thomas. 27th July, 1633. Dublin Castle.

Today Beth and brother George and I went to Communion at the Cathedral. Afterwards we wandered around it, having a good look at the tombs and memorials, and the architecture. At the end I walked towards the altar on my own to make a study of Lady Cork's tomb. When Beth wrote to me describing it before I left England she did not exaggerate. It is hideous.

As I stood there I muttered: "Unbelievable!"

I heard a soft step behind me and someone said: "Unbelievably good, isn't it?" I looked round and there was Boyle, Earl of Cork.

"Well, you've certainly pre-empted things having it put there, haven't you?"

"What do you mean?"

"No-one could put up a tomb to their wife there now, could they? Not even the King."

"Hurrumph!" was all the response I got to that. I really must get the monstrosity taken down. He can have it in the Cathedral, but not dominating the altar.

Later I made an inspection of the Castle. I was shown round it by the Constable, a pleasant man who has apparently been very kind to Elizabeth in my absence. He's a burly chap named Blackburn.

"This bridge we're going over leads through the West Wall straight into the main Hall." We entered through quite a small door into a huge Chamber. Blackburn continued: "This is where Parliament sits, and that's the King's throne at the far end. The four rooms in the corners are the Law Courts, Chancery, Common Pleas, Exchequer and...."

"King's Bench," I interrupt. I was pleased to see that my orders for the redecoration of this most important place had been carried out. "What's through that door on the left?"

"That, my Lord, is the prison. On the right, behind that wall, is the kitchen yard for the Deputy' house."

We went out through that yard and found ourselves in front of the Deputy's – my – quarters. From the outside they look substantial, but once inside I can see what Elizabeth had to complain about. A horribly damp feeling crept into my bones within minutes even if it is July, so I ordered Blackburn to make sure that fires are lit in every room and kept going until we can move in. I asked him to take personal charge of the repairs and the workmen, and make sure the results are satisfactory. What on earth could have permitted my predecessors to allow this dreadful state of affairs? Are the finances of Ireland so poor that its government must be carried on in these conditions?

We went out into a huge Courtyard – a parade ground really – where the artillery is stored. It is not undercover, and with the East Wall fallen down so far that children could climb over it – indeed three were playing there as we walked about until Blackburn chased them off – it would not be difficult for determined rebels to take the cannon away. I told Blackburn to get this seen to immediately. We then walked to the North side where the Council Chamber lies, adjoining the offices of the more important officials. The Chamber is long, with an equally long table running the length of it, and chairs for about sixty-five Privy Councillors. It is an impressive room, or will be when it has been repaired and decorated to my satisfaction.

Christopher Wandesford. 5th August, 1633. Dublin Castle.

"The more I think about it, the more I am beginning to realise just how much power the King has conferred on me." Thomas is pensive as we sit, after lunch, in the library, with a glass of wine.

I smile at that. "But you asked him for what you wanted, Tom, and he gave it to you."

"I know I did, but clearly I hadn't thought through all the ramifications of it. I'm almost a king here. Everyone in Ireland is accountable to me, but I am accountable to no-one but His Majesty, and ..."

I interrupt; "What about Parliament?"

Tom makes a derisive, dismissive gesture. "The King has even agreed that he will not listen to criticism or appeals from here unless I'm really overstepping the mark."

"After what you achieved in York and the North I should think he realises you need a pretty free hand if you're to restore Crown and Church lands and revenue. He must know what Ireland's nobility has done to drag down most of the previous Deputies. He can't afford to let that happen again."

Tom is thoughtful. "You're right, of course. But he must also know his writ hardly runs here any more. The idea the King has any power here at all is almost a joke. I've got the means to bring it back to life."

Now I laugh. "Well, Tom, you're not the Messiah, no matter what power the King gives you."

Tom acts as if he were cross. "You verge on the blasphemous, Kit. The point is that I not only have the right to control everything to do with government, but the King promises he won't give away any offices or grant any land or pensions; that is up to me. I'm not only a sort of Deputy King, but I am the most important patron in the land. Anyone who wants anything will have to cooperate with me. Can you imaginc just how vital that is in the web of intrigue and corruption that is Irish political life?"

"You don't need to be a Shakespeare or a Jonson to see that. And don't forget the money, will you? If all these office-seekers pay you handsomely for their appointment you will do very nicely out of it."

Tom laughs and winks. "Why, my dear Kit, how cynical you are. But you may rest assured you'll get your share."

"I do not doubt it, Tom. I am no longer the poverty-stricken wretch I used to be. You have been very generous."

He has someone else to be generous to now. Tom has added to the number of his advisers. George Radcliffe and I are no longer alone in his cabinet. Tom has brought over this sycophant from the King's Court in London. His name is Philip Mainwaring. We have all known him for some time. Tom says he's been very useful in the past because he knows a lot about foreign affairs and other government matters. How he acquired this knowledge I do not know, but Tom trusts him, even if I don't. I'm not sure George cares for him either, and in England both Laud and Chancellor Cottington told me they have no time for him.

He's rather good-looking, with chestnut hair and beard after the King's fashion, and tall and well-built into the bargain, which somehow seems to make him even more detestable. It's no use complaining though; if Tom wants him we shall just have to learn to work with him, and see how we get on.

Thomas. 10th August, 1633. Dublin.

If I get too depressed I shan't be able to do all the King has given me the authority to achieve. Why should I be depressed? Well, first, there's the weather. Everyone knows it's supposed to rain a lot in Ireland, but this is ridiculous. It has rained a good part of almost every day since I arrived here. I told Bess there's an Irish Bishop who regularly prays for rain. I can't help wondering whether he's even been here. Where has the sun gone?

The day after my installation as Deputy in the great hall, I was standing at my bedroom window when Ann came and stood at my side, and slid her little hand into mine. We stood looking out at the rain falling in a field nearby. Then she said: "Look Papa, that poor horse has no feet. It's standing on its ankles."

I hadn't really been paying attention to what I was looking at; I was miles away thinking about running this country. I looked more carefully at the horse. "It looks as though it has no feet, darling, because it's so muddy out there; its hooves have sunk into the mud right up to its fetlocks."

"Fetlocks, Papa? What are they?"

"That is what we call horses' ankles, Ann. See how difficult it is for the horse to walk. It can't just lift its feet up. It has to pull them out of the mud, and it's hard work."

It isn't just in the fields and the garden that there is ankle-deep mud, either.

True, the streets of London and York, to which I am accustomed, are cobbled to a large extent. Here in Dublin cobbles or any other sort of hard surface are rare, and the mud is thick, treacherous, and slippery. There is no form or pattern to the way in which the streets are laid out, and compared with the magnificent buildings in those English cities, Dublin is very ill provided. Some of the nobility have grand town houses, and there is the Cathedral and the very delapidated Castle, but they are the exception rather than the rule. Notable public buildings are scarce. Yes, I find this all rather depressing.

Similarly, when I enquire about any chance of some good hunting I'm told that game birds are scarcer than Unicorns, and as hawking is my preferred form of sport, I may have a thin time of it. The weather plus the lack of any recreation I really care for is, however, as nothing compared to the problems I have to face in governing the country. Still, those are challenges I can do something about, and do something I shall. I can't do anything about the weather, no matter what power the King's given me!

Of course, the first challenge is the lack of money. I had some idea about that before I ever got to Dublin, but now I'm here I see it is worse than I thought. For a start the Army is hardly ever paid. This is not England. There is no hostile native population in England, but the native Irish can be very hostile. I might feel the same if my country had been taken away from me, but I should think after about four hundred years they'd have got used to it, and adapted. They haven't. They are still pretty wild, and where they can, lead a rather nomadic life, driving their poor cattle from place to place as long as the grazing lasts.

They do not settle down anywhere for long. They don't plough the land much, and when they do it is poorly done so their crops are not much good. They use a strange small plough, and they tie the tow-rope to the horse's tail to pull it. It's hardly surprising the horse doesn't want to pull very hard! I shall have to make that illegal.

With few decent sized villages and towns, there are few tradesmen, and for an apprentice to be taken on is unusual. The conditions in which many of the people live are appalling, and I have rarely seen squalor like it anywhere in England. I shall try to get them to learn from the New English and those Old English who are prepared to work with me and my government. They will never get anywhere following the old ways of their clans.

The only solution is to attract many more English settlers to come here. Until that happens we need an Army, and an Army that gets paid.

Yes, I should like more settlers to come here. What I definitely do not want are more of the sort I find in great numbers on my Privy Council and in high office. They are arrogant - did I hear someone mutter "you can talk"? – and think almost exclusively of their own interests. They pay very little attention to the reason for the Council's existence, which is to look after the interests of Ireland as a whole. I may not have much time for the native Irish, but whoever the people are, whatever their religion, whether they are native Irish, Old English, New English, Scots, or just English, like me, Kit, George, and my new secretary, Philip Mainwaring, they are entitled to justice, to the recognition of their rights. They must be encouraged to participate in the growth of this kingdom and its trade and prosperity.

We need prosperity to increase government revenue so that the Army and Navy can be paid. When Buckingham was fighting Spain and France the Irish Army was built up to resist any foreign invasion, since Ireland is England's Achilles heel in the event of war. Unfortunately little was done to find the money to pay this Army and the Irish Exchequer is 76,000 pounds in debt. Not only that, but government income is 20,000 a year less than its outgoings, so there's no early chance of reducing the debt.

Some on the Council think we can pay the debt off by laying into the Catholics with the recusancy fines; their argument is that it is because of the Catholic Irish that we need the Army, so they should pay for it. Cork is the man most in favour of that policy. This is a point on which I agree with Mountnorris. He says if we fine the Catholics hard – persecute them – they may convert to Protestantism in large numbers. If they do, they won't have fines to pay, so how will that pay for the Army? And we need an Army here because of the threats from abroad. We can never be certain that Spain or France will not attack us again, particularly if persecuted Catholics refuse to convert. If they do convert, how can we be certain their 'conversion' is genuine, and not just camouflage? Those who fail to convert will just add to the number of hostile elements.

But there is an even more powerful argument against persecuting the Catholics. You can do it to a limited extent in England because they are the minority, but here they are the majority. The whole island could explode like a powder keg. I'd rather make the island wealthier, and collect more in tax and customs duties, and make everyone happy, than risk a Catholic revolt.

Again Mountnorris has been very useful. He has helped me over the last year or so, starting before I left England, to induce the most important Catholic aristocracy to pay their share of further instalments of the annual tribute even though the Graces were not confirmed by Falkland, and even though I may be unable to guarantee them either. They make these payments reluctantly, but they hope the Graces will be confirmed and that they will not be pursued for recusancy fines. The Graces are concessions that make life easier for Catholics. They are not law, but give them a measure of religious freedom.

I am fortunate that Annesley - Mountnorris - is still on the Irish Privy Council, for his main opponent in the battle to push through the Catholic subsidy is Lord Cork. Feeling ran so high amongst the settlers that some Protestants, led by Privy Councillor Lord Balfour, were planning an insurrection in County Fermanagh. They did not want to pay their share of the subsidy, but wanted the Catholics fined heavily instead. When I learned of this from Annesley I issued warrants for the arrest of Balfour and his rebels. That was in May, before I got here. They were tried before the Privy Council within a few days of my arrival. We dismissed Balfour from the Council and sent him to explain himself to the King. The others were ordered to apologise to the Council, and did so, and were discharged.

I wanted to demonstrate to all and sundry that no-one was to defy me or my government with impunity; the fact that I had, quite by coincidence, to start by making an example of some Protestant settlers could not have been more fortuitous if I had planned it myself. If that did not reassure the Old English and Irish Catholics that justice and fair play was for them too, it is difficult to see what would.

That subsidy has only three or four months to run. I need to secure some money for next year. I wonder if I should get more cooperation from the Catholics if I say I intend to ask the King if I can call the Irish Parliament, and let them think that I shall put the Graces before the two Houses to be confirmed and passed into law.

Christopher Wandesford. 24th August, 1633. Dublin.

Tom came to see me today, and brought George Radcliffe with him. We had arranged to discuss what we had succeeded in learning about how government, and what passes for an administration, works here in Ireland. George had been looking into the functioning of the Law Courts. "They work very much in the interests of the rich," he says. "It is hardly surprising, since most of the judges come from or are related somehow to the powerful families. It is very hard for the poor, or even the moderately well off, to win a case, even if they can get it to a hearing."

You could almost see the hair on Tom's head stand on end. "That's an impression I've been getting but I'm glad your investigations confirm it. We must work out what we're going to do about it. We did it at home through the Council of the North. I suppose ...."

"You could take more cases into the Court of Castle Chamber, particularly those between civilian parties, not just State cases," I make so bold as to interrupt. "You can hear them yourself when that's possible. I dare say that would be fairer than leaving the small men at the mercy of the judges and the barons who may control them, or pack the juries with their own retainers."

" 'I dare say', Christopher?" Thomas mimics me. "Do you doubt my impartiality then, my friend?" And he laughs at his own jest.

George asks: "So what do you think you've found out, Thomas? Anything much, after we've been here nearly a couple of months?"

"Nothing much, actually, George. If it weren't for the help I've had, and still get, from Mountnorris, I should have learned very little indeed. The Irish Privy Council seems to have some sort of secret motto; I think it goes; 'Keep the Deputy in the dark'. The Councillors pay lip-service to my having the most significant job, but try to keep me ignorant so they can go on doing whatever they wish, be it right or wrong. No wonder previous deputies have been able to achieve so little for the King. They've never truly been in control."

George responds. "We must continue to gather information, and keep each other posted on what we learn. Besides, you have Philip Mainwaring beavering away. He seems to have no trouble ingratiating himself with all kinds of people."

"Yes. His reports are more and more useful. All this is like being the captain of a ship. You put a man in the bows to take soundings with the lead, and for a long time there's no bottom at all, but if we keep on we shall get to know what secrets lie on the sea-bed."

I say: "The three of us are pretty cynical and suspicious by nature. As long as we trust no-one, and examine all possibilities, we should not get caught out. The great lords here, Catholic or Protestant, have had it all their own way for far too long, it seems to me."

Thomas claps me on the arm. "That's it exactly, Kit. Do you agree, George?"

"Most definitely. And you could do worse than make a start right at the top of the Courts. You still have to appoint a new Lord Chief Justice." George turns to me. "Have you heard about the Bushin case, Christopher?"

Tom says: "Well, I have, and that's why we need a new Chief Judge."

"No, I haven't heard about Bushin," I say, and George soon lays a well-researched story before me. "Poor Mr Bushin was charged with the murder of his wife by the Sheriff. Now Mr Bushin was not poor in financial terms, but just in the way he was treated. He owned some very nice land indeed, and the local sheriff wanted to get his hands on some of it. So did the Lord Chief Justice."

"When did this happen?"

"Oh, before Thomas arrived in Dublin. Philip Bushin was incarcerated in Dublin Castle's prison and brought on for trial before His Lordship, who closed the Court so that justice could not be seen to be done. He made sure it was not done. During this hearing *in camera* the Judge refused to let Mr Bushin's counsel call any defence witnesses. Even so, the jury clearly didn't care for the prosecution case, or the evidence the Sheriff presented; they threw it out, and found Mr Bushin Not Guilty."

"Thank God for that!" I interject, but I see George shake his head.

"That wasn't the end of it. Truth did not out in this tragic matter. Not yet, anyway. The judge was furious. He discharged the jury and brought in another one. It is not beyond the bounds of probability that the Sheriff hand-picked the new jury, or threatened them with prosecution for something or other if they found the Defendant Not Guilty this time. Of course Mr Bushin should not have been tried again when a jury had reached a clear verdict; the Rule of Law prohibits anyone being tried twice on the same charges. But that didn't matter to this land-hungry Judge and Sheriff.

"The second jury did what was required of it, found Philip Bushin Guilty, and the Chief Justice sent him off to be hanged by the neck until dead. And hanged by the neck until dead he was." Tom nods, and I am disgusted by this horror story. George goes on. "At that point rumour began to play its part. The rumour had it that somehow my predecessor, Lord Falkland, had been involved. He considered he'd been libelled. He brought an action in the Star Chamber in England against the rumour-mongers. That led to the Chamber ordering an inquiry into the way Kilmallock had dealt with the case."

Tom joins in: "I went to hear the case in the Star Chamber. I was trying to prepare myself for my duties in Dublin. Fourteen High Court Judges heard the case, and they ordered Lord Chief Justice Killmallock to travel from Ireland to appear before them to be cross-examined. He was charged with perverting the course of justice. I was appalled. He should have been charged with conniving at or even securing a judicial murder."

"How did the case against him go?" I ask.

"Well, actually. Unlike Mr Bushin, Killmallock was allowed to call his own witnesses, but they were pretty ineffectual, and hardly credible since they were all people in his pocket, one way or another. Added to that neither he nor the Sheriff told the same story, which made them both look foolish."

George joins in again. "Of the fourteen judges, two had reasons for acquitting him, but the other twelve found him guilty. Kilmallock was forced to give all the land back to the Bushin family, pay a five thousand pound fine, and stripped of his office. As a result you have to appoint a new Lord Chief Justice, now you are in Dublin."

Tom looks crestfallen. "With everything else on my mind, I'd forgotten. I was making enquiries about a new one before I left England."

George tells us: "I've been attending Dublin and other Courts to hear how various judges operated. All my researches lead me to believe Sir Gerarrd Lowther is a completely honest and upright judge. Attorneys and members of the bar of all persuasions, whether English or Irish, say he is quite the man for the job. He's from New English Protestant stock, but his reputation makes it very unlikely he would let his Protestant - even puritan - sympathies influence his conduct of trials, or his judgments. Another reason you can trust him is that, like the three of us, and even your chaplain, John Bramhall, he's a North-countryman."

We all have a chuckle at that. I add: "Won't bring Bushin back to life, though, will it?"

Thomas adds: "I'm beginning to wonder if coming from Yorkshire is as good a recommendation as I thought. After all, that's where Lord Chancellor Loftus comes from, too. I think he is another troublesome judge."

Thomas. 6th September, 1633. Dublin Castle.

My appointment of Lowther as Lord Chief Justice of Ireland has been completed. As I've indicated before, these appointments to office are usually sold, so I decided I would ask Lowther for a few thousand pounds for this one.

I told him the post was his for a certain sum, and he was happy to pay for this promotion to a lucrative position. The amusing thing was, though, that Boyle, the Earl of Cork, had pushed hard for me to give Lowther the job. He put up another candidate who was totally unsuitable. He obviously hoped that whichever of these men got the post, he could expect friendly judgments in any of his own cases. In both instances he offered me an extra thousand on top of what the successful candidate would pay. I would not have appointed the alternative man for many times that thousand, but saw no reason not to take it for giving the job to Lowther, who was my own choice in any event. I feel I can trust him not to favour Cork. I cannot afford to let that man get the better of me.

To Sir John Coke, Secretary of State.

My Dear Coke,

I have been here a mere two months but it is already clear to me that I am unable to do much to lift the revenues of this Kingdom unless I can get the King's warrant to grant licences allowing the export of Irish wool. As Secretary to the Council and the King you will be aware of the rather chequered history of the wool trade here.

Sometimes there has been no restriction on sending our wool to England, usually when it is in short supply over there, and the cloth manufacturers want it. Sometimes the Irish wool is forbidden to be sent to England because you have enough of your own. This uncertainty is bad for the economy here. You know that a few years ago the Irish merchants, and indeed some of the big landowners who have sheep on their farms, sought a provision in the Graces enabling them to send their wool to all the ports and not just to the staple ports such as London, Barnstaple, Workington, without having to get licences.

I accept that this Grace cannot be granted at the present time, if ever, but at least if I had a warrant to issue licences I could arrange some exports abroad in proper cases. The licence fees would add to the King's revenues, as would the customs duties.

Your prompt attention to this would be much appreciated. Please speak to the Council and His Majesty as soon as possible.

I am your faithful servant,

Wentworth.

Charles I. Windsor. 15th October, 1633.

My dear Wentworth,

I have read with interest your account of the enquiries you made about Sir Gerrard Lowther – now of course, Lord Chief Justice Lowther. I approve of your choice and of his appointment. I have also been considering very carefully what you have written to me about the administration of justice generally in Ireland, and I share your concerns.

I find it quite unacceptable that, as you say, a man with no significant family connections, or little money, cannot get justice in my Irish Courts. I have discussed with my Privy Council your request that the Court of Castle Chamber should be empowered to hear cases inter partes, and not just cases involving the State and the Crown. They felt, and advised me, that if you had that power, it would provide a safeguard against the too frequent denial of justice, and I agree with them and with your reasons for advancing the suggestion.

I accept your view that the prohibition on hearing inter partes cases has never been reduced to a proposition enshrined in law. However, the granting of these powers would be such a departure from what has always gone before, that I am reluctant to make it a permanent change immediately. By Order in Council, therefore, I have decided to grant this power solely for the term of your being Lord Deputy. These powers can be reconsidered when your successor is appointed.

I was particularly impressed by your argument that the most humble of my subjects would know "where to seek and have relief without being afraid to appeal to His Majesty's universal justice against the greatest subjects".

You have my blessing on this project.

Charles R.

Thomas. 27th October, 1633. Dublin Castle.

Today has been a joyful day for me, and for George Radcliffe. With Kit, he has helped me through some trying times over the last two or three years in connection with the Council of the North. There was a lot of trouble with Sir David Foulis saying that I was swindling the King by pocketing fees and settlement money from the enforcement of knight service. He wasn't just saying it in York, which was bad enough, but in London to the King and his Court. He even put it in writing in the hope of turning the Privy Council against me.

It didn't work, but that didn't stop him, either, so I sued him for libel in the Star Chamber. I was awarded three thousand pounds in damages, he was fined five thousand pounds, and sent to prison. George's legal genius was invaluable in this case. As he pointed out, I would be highly unlikely to sue Foulis for libel anywhere in the land, let alone in the King's most awesome Court in London, if I could not show the accounts of the money collected, and of its payment over to the Treasurer.

Then we had trouble with Foulis's son-in-law, Leighton. How a buffoon like him came to be Sheriff of Yorkshire I do not know, but he had to seek my help in a siege of a property he had to recover from a trespasser, so I decided not to pursue him for his disrespectful behaviour to the Council.

Then last year there was a very serious incident in a North country English Court with one of the magistrates, Sir Thomas Gower, a Justice of the Peace. During a trial he told the Court that justice could not be found in the North when the King's attorney was George Radcliffe. This was a reflection on me for having sought his appointment by the King, and on the King for having agreed. Since George is scrupulous in his application of the law, and his conduct of litigation of any and every kind, this was not to be tolerated.

The Council decided to deal with Gower for contempt of Court, but hearing of this, he escaped to London. Despite his best efforts to get the King and Privy Council on his side, he failed, was taken prisoner, and sent to York to be incarcerated for four months. Could I have let this attack on the King's attorney succeed? Impossible. The authority of my Council, its Court, and the King would be destroyed by such talk.

For George's loyalty and assistance I recently petitioned the King to appoint him to the Irish Privy Council, and with no delay whatsoever, the King agreed. I was empowered to knight him, too. I did this in a ceremony in the state rooms of the Castle this morning.

My rejoicing is heightened by a letter from the King. The jurisdiction of the Court of Castle Chamber is increased as I requested. We shall have a banquet soon to celebrate.

Thomas. 3rd November, 1633. Dublin Castle.

Last night we did indeed have a banquet, and a very happy and, I must confess, a very ostentatious occasion it was. I was determined to demonstrate that the King's Deputy is an extremely important man, not so much in his own right as in the King's, and should be treated accordingly in the King's name. If the King lives in a dignified and regal fashion, so should his Irish representative.

The food was lavish and the wine flowed richly as to price, if not as to quantity. I did not want my Court having a reputation for

Bacchanalia. I invited the Irish Privy Council and many of the Irish nobility. I did not differentiate between Catholics and Protestants. I had no desire to alienate either side of the religious divide.

I had some trouble persuading Elizabeth to attend, but she did so and sat on my right at the table. I had George Radcliffe on my left. During the course of the dinner various toasts were proposed, including one to him, our newest knight. I proposed one to Elizabeth, introducing her to the company as my wife, and saying that we had been married in England.

Although I had told her beforehand that I should do that, she was nevertheless embarrassed. She rarely drank, but she blushed at the people standing to roar their acclamation, and picked up her own glass of wine and took a rather larger sip, or perhaps two, than usual.

After the meal there was dancing, and Elizabeth danced with me, and George, and Christopher, and several other guests. I danced with Alice Wandesford and Anne Radcliffe, who was extremely happy to be called Lady Radcliffe, but I had little time for dancing with anyone else. Guests do not seem to expect the Lord President to have fun on social occasions. For a Deputy Lord Lieutenant it is far worse. They always want to importune you with some petition or scheme, or offer some favour for which they hope you will reward them with an office or pension. It can be very tiresome. During a lull in the proceedings, when the three ladies were off dancing or talking, George and Kit and I had the chance to talk together.

George thanked me yet again for his knighthood, and referred to our time together at the Council of the North. He started with a compliment. "When you think of the low state to which the reputation of the Council had sunk under Scrope and Savile and some of their predecessors, Thomas, it's remarkable how you succeeded in restoring its authority in so short a space as four years."

Then Kit threw in a critical note. "But pursuing the knighthood fines and the recusancy fines so vigorously did not result in harmony."

I must say that annoyed me. "I was doing my duty, Kit; it was what the King wanted me to do. He needed the revenue."

George joined in. "I am in no position to preach, Thomas, since as your lawyer and the King's attorney I was your right-hand man, but to some extent I agree with Kit. You are not a persecuting man where religion is concerned, but what your intentions are and how other people perceive them may be two entirely different things. That is true of much else. Look at the criticism you received for rebuilding the King's manor house at York as a fine residence for him, and for you."

I was almost angry. "Are you saying I shouldn't have done it? Are the King and his President of the North not to be fittingly accommodated, George?"

"Did I say that, Thomas? Not at all. What I am saying, and what Kit means, is that you need to think how your policies, and the way you pursue them, will appear. Goodness knows, you have spoken often enough about the need for harmony in politics and the country. You have criticised the King, privately, for seeming to ignore how the people feel about him and his aims."

"Quite," said Kit. "Just look at the Spanish marriage, the Spanish War, and the French one. You disagreed with all of that. The people weren't too happy about having a French Catholic Queen either, and some still are not."

That made me smile; I remembered thinking myself some years ago, that Charles should find himself an English girl like my Arabella. Thinking that, I looked up as Elizabeth came dancing by on the arm of the Earl of Cork. As she passed, she gave me a dazzling smile and a small wave of her hand.

That took my mind right off the conversation. She looked slightly flushed, and very happy. Had she been drinking? She was so unaccustomed to wine it would take very little to have an effect. I did not need to worry; I knew that her puritan upbringing would prevent her from getting drunk or behaving unwisely. Charming as Cork can be, I had no concern about his effect on her.

I came out of the happy reverie induced by her smile to hear George finishing a sentence: ".... and if you try to make your policies clear here in Ireland, and avoid creating divisions, you will be criticised less. Your strong rule will be the more welcome. Remember this: Kit and I are the only real friends you have here."

What wise advice that was. I reflected on the enemies I had made in England; on Pym, Savile, Foulis, Gower, and others. Even, to some extent, Arabella's father, Earl Clare, and my brothers-in-law, including Denzil – they had still not truly forgiven me for Arabella's death. I don't believe Lady Clare would let them. Doubtless there were many others.

I wondered if I could behave differently here in Ireland. I doubted it; adjusting my principles for popularity is quite impossible. A course of conduct is either right or wrong. If I think it is right and honourable when I decide to act, how can I bring myself to do the other thing, which I believe to be dishonourable? What I do may turn out to be wrong, but that's hindsight.

****

The banquet and ball ended at about two in the morning, and Elizabeth stayed up with me to say farewell to those of our guests who were not staying at the Castle. We stood at the top of the steps by the main door as hosts should, saying goodbye, waving to departing carriages, before going in. I whispered to Elizabeth that we should go to bed, and I told the guests who were still drinking and talking and dancing in the hall to go on as long as they liked. I handed a purse of gold coins to the leader of the musicians, who had been playing for hours. I do not know how they can remember so many tunes, and go on seemingly inexhaustibly for so long. Of course, they are from the lower orders of society, so would probably not ever have the nerve to say; "We're tired; can we go home now?" In any case, I dare say the amount I paid them is more than they usually earn in a year.

I take Elizabeth's hand and we climb the stairs, and as we do so she drops my hand, puts her arm around my waist, and rests her head on my shoulder. I put my right arm round her shoulders and hold her close. I see that she is still very rosy-cheeked, and smiling. I could kick myself for thinking it, but this is so unlike her normally reserved behaviour I cannot help wondering how much she may have had to drink. However, at the top of the stairs she walks ahead of me to the bedroom, and I can see that she is far too steady to be drunk.

On entering the room she dismisses her maid at once, telling her she will see to herself tonight. The maid goes, and Elizabeth starts to undress in front of me, something she has never done before. I take her by the shoulders and kiss her, and she responds, not passionately, but gently. She says: "I have enjoyed myself tonight Thomas, so much, and you do so much to make me happy."

Then she lies on the bed, completely naked, and waits for me to undress too. She lies there as still as usual, not moving, but there is a difference. For once she is relaxed, and not indifferent. I can sense it, and she is watching me instead of averting her gaze. I kiss her and she responds, and when I caress her breasts and kiss and suck her nipples, she raises her head off the pillow to watch. Her nipples respond too, which they have hardly ever done before. I can feel that she likes it. At the same time I can tell that she is still shy and reserved about this lovemaking.

When we make love it is wonderful and fulfilling and releasing, not just for me, but for her too.

As I thrust she thrusts back. She has never done that before. I am on the verge of coming, but I must not. How I control myself I do not know. I have never seen her look so beautiful. I have never heard her make so much noise, or breathe so hard and fast, gasping in fact. Normally her arms lie at her sides, as she lets me 'do it'. Now her hands are on my shoulders or stroking my back, or her finger-nails are digging into me. This is passion. Then her legs come up and her feet are digging into the tops of my thighs and buttocks, gripping me into her so hard I cannot move, and she is shuddering, and moaning, moaning, louder and louder, with an "Oh God!" And we both come, and it seems as though it's going on forever.

Elizabeth holds me there, neither of us moving as the passion subsides, and our hoarse breathing calms down, and she tells me she doesn't want me to go. No danger of that, I say. "I never expected you to call on the Lord at such a time, my love".

"That's because I never realised until now just how clever God was – is – to give us each other to do that whenever we wish. It's not sex, Thomas. It's love." And she holds me in her until I get hard again. It doesn't take long.

Thomas. 5th November, 1633. Dublin Castle.

Today is the thirtieth anniversary of Guy Fawkes' attempt to blow up King James in the Houses of Parliament. I haven't been blown up. I've been deflated. Sir John Coke has replied to my letter in September asking for permission to grant licences for Irish wool to be sold in foreign countries.

In short, the answer is "No'. The Council has no scope for letting me do this. He does not say what the King thinks. It is simple politics. The English manufacturers have been pestering the Council and the King with petitions: wool from England, Ireland and Scotland should be prohibited from being sold abroad. That is because so much of it is being sold to the Low Countries and France that they no longer need to buy cloth from England. At least he says that we can send our wool to England, Wales, Scotland, and some to the colonies across the Atlantic. He'd rather the colonies bought the woven product, though, meaning more work, more money, and more taxes in England.

He tells me I have to make sure that no wool should go from Irish ports to any foreign place. This is not very encouraging. Are any attempts I make to give Ireland a prosperous future and increase the King's Irish revenue to be spurned like this? If so, there is not only no future here for the majority who belong here. There won't be much to make me want to stay either, or invest in the country, or build a home. As I wrote to the Earl of Arundel only yesterday: "Landless I came hither and landless I shall go hence".

Talking of cloth reminds me: I think I've had the wool pulled over my eyes by no less a person than the Irish Lord Chancellor, Lord Adam Loftus. I hear the most alarming rumours that he is corrupt, takes bribes, and takes advantage of his position in the cases he hears to get his hands on any land involved. Some of this is just after- dinner gossip, but more substantial evidence is being gathered by Kit and Radcliffe.

I shall have to tread carefully with this man; he has many influential friends here and in London. Even so, I'm determined to do my utmost to see that here in Ireland, to coin the old adage, justice is not only done, but must be seen to be done.

One of the rumours I've heard is that Loftus used his status as Lord Chancellor to secure the administration of an estate for his son – his favourite son, apparently. This son is Sir Edward Loftus. As the administrator of the estate he could expect to make a lot of money out of the post in fees and costs. What Lord Loftus did to get him this estate was quite illegal, since it preferred Sir Edward to the relative who should have had the administration by law.

Doubtless the son did not have to bribe father to get the estate, but it would hardly be surprising if Sir Edward did not allow his father to pick one or two plums from it. The estate was that of a Mr Metcalf. I shall have to do something about this, but I need more information and evidence.

Thomas. 8th November, 1633. Dublin Castle.

My Dear Coke,

In reply to yours of 24th October, it gives me little pleasure to tell you that I have issued orders to all Irish ports regarding sending wool abroad. I made it a punishable offence to do so, and to export it to England apart from the staple ports. Indeed, two merchants have already been jailed for breaking the order, and even the Governor of County Sligo is to be prosecuted for sending wool to England without a licence.

I shall write to you with further views on this subject in due course.

I am your faithful servant,
Wentworth.

Thomas. 20th November, 1633. Dublin.

My firm if not drastic treatment of Lord Balfour and his Fermanagh rebels for anti-Catholic ferment seems to have worked. I am getting some cooperation from the Catholic nobles and gentry.

Relying to some extent on that, Annesley has been working with me to persuade the Catholics to pay yet another year's subsidy when this one ends in a couple of months time. Lord Chancellor Loftus has been on our side, too, making it hard to pursue him at the moment if he is indeed corrupt. If we could get the Papists to pay, the government would be relatively solvent for 1634. I sensed that Cork might oppose this move, but I knew he wanted the Irish Parliament called, so I suggested to the Council that I call it as soon as possible, and then he harangued us all about how vital a Parliament was.

It is clear to me now, if it wasn't earlier, that Richard, Earl of Cork, is trouble, and I shall have to take care with him. It bothers me that I may have to take care where Annesley is concerned, too. Apart from the fact that I do not like his apparent breaches of the Biblical commandment that a man should not lie with another man as with a woman, I am very worried by his grasp of his role as Treasurer, or should I say lack of grasp? He does not know how much is in the coffers. He does not know how much is outstanding on IOUs drawn against future revenues by previous Treasurers. These damned notes are liable to turn up any time, and seem inevitably to do so when the

Treasury is already financially embarrassed. The men holding these pieces of paper want their money; there is none to give them, so they ask for land, or pensions, or offices. It can be hard to say "No".

This means that when I ask Mountnorris what we owe he cannot give any accurate picture, and mouths platitudes and meaningless phrases as though to assure me all is well. I think this is a method Irish Treasurers have used with the Lord Deputy for longer than I like to contemplate. It's insulting that he thinks I'm so stupid and weak as to be taken in by this just because the others were. I shall have to investigate, but I do not want to alienate him yet; no, not until I have to. I'll get George Radcliffe and brother George to look into it.

Earlier I mentioned the financial state of the Army. How can I do anything about that if I don't know how much money there is to pay the men with? To find out more about the state of the troops I've set up a Commission of Inquiry. I hope it will frighten the officers and bring some relief to the men.

Thomas. 29th January, 1634. Dublin Castle.

To His Grace the Archbishop of Canterbury.

Your Grace,

Your letter of 10th arrived yesterday. I am grateful for all the news of the King, the Privy Council and country. It is somewhat alarming that you think the Queen is the most influential person at the King's side, and aggravating for you and the rest of the Council that she should make so many requests for pensions and Court office for her friends. I experienced this in York as President: I had to decline her demands on a number of occasions. At the moment I am not having that trouble with her here in Ireland, but it may come.

The difficulties I am having mainly come from the strangeness of the ruling elements of society. None of them seem to care anything for the public good, and only go into public service to further their own private ends. They acquire lands by fraud from the King and the Church, and use further frauds to hang on to them.

I had a debate with the Chief Baron of the Irish Law Courts recently. The case concerned the serious undervaluing of an estate to cheat the Crown of the taxes due on it. This estate had already been sold by the fraudster to another man who, it was said, knew nothing of the fraud. The Judge said that in equity the King had no remedy as the new owner was innocent, and the tax could not now be had from the estate.

I argued that the King owned nothing except according to law, and as no man could claim ignorance of the law, even the ignorant purchaser was liable to repay the King. If that were not the case, the King would be worse off than everyone, for having been cheated today he could do nothing if the land is sold to someone else tomorrow. (I say that was my argument but in truth it was laid out for me by Sir George Radcliffe who ties these lawyers in knots for me). A day or so later the Baron came to see me and admitted that the King should be able to recover what was due to him.

Seeing these insolent people stealing from the King and then bending the law to keep their gains is enough to give me another bout of the flux. Thus it grieves me that Your Grace should feel we may be on thin ice if we pursue our 'Thorough' policy too well. If we do not slack the work is possible. I assure you I shall not worry about my own skin until I see the King's authority rise above the Common Law. Sir Edward Coke and his law reports have much to answer for. I was side by side with him when we stood against the Forced Loan and in favour of the Petition of Right, but he goes too far against the Royal Prerogative. The common law must be moderated.

Let me turn to your views about the way to deal with the Catholics. I agree that apart from enforcing the recusancy fines (which I should prefer to do to a more limited extent than you suggest), we should not directly persecute them. Instead I favour bringing to Ireland large numbers of Protestants and settling them in various plantations throughout the country. This will reduce the power and influence of the rich Catholic landowners. This is not a new policy. It has been pursued by my predecessors, but they allowed themselves to be diverted, and did not fight hard enough against those who opposed them. Rest assured: I shall be Thorough. I agree with you that we must strengthen the finances of the Church and recover land for it as well as for the King.

However, I must not move too fast in that direction, since I need the cooperation of the Catholic nobility, at any rate to start with, in putting my policies into effect.

I dare say I shall alienate men on the Protestant and Catholic sides before too long. I do not fear doing that, but it must come once my plans are advancing, and not before, or they will not advance at all. One of the things that makes me sure I shall have trouble with the New English is what has happened to the College of Youghal which is near Cork, and belongs to the Earl, who bought it cheap from the ruination of Sir Walter Raleigh's estates. It was an old Catholic religious institution, and used to have an income, I'm told, of more than a thousand pounds a year. That money was supposed to be used, and was in fact used before Cork got his hands on it, to look after the poor, particularly those who were sick.

Cork has taken the income from nearly all the parishes that used to support the College, and the poor and sick are turned naked and empty away. He has also erected a ridiculous looking edifice in St Patrick's Cathedral in Dublin to the memory of his late wife. What is worse is that he had it put up behind the altar! It's bad enough that the Pope's followers worship the Virgin, without prominent Protestants making it look as though we worship Lady Cork! I foresee big battles between me and the Earl. I wish I were an Earl so that I could deal with him on perfectly equal terms. He doesn't even come from an old family.

I intend to send my brother George to London to the King with a request for permission to call an election, but please keep that to yourself. I fear that I shall be hard put to it to raise any money to keep this government going unless I can put certain measures before an Irish Parliament. Anything you can do to help George secure what I want will be much appreciated by

Your faithful servant,
Wentworth.

Dublin Castle,
31st January, 1634.
To Sir John Coke, Secretary of State.
My Dear Coke,

I am still much concerned by the state of trade in Irish wool. The trade you said I may be permitted to licence with the King's possessions is just not enough to content the sheep-owners and farmers. Ireland must be able to send its wool anywhere, and not just to staple ports. It should go where it is needed. Further, if we can send it abroad, it will render customs duties and licence fees here. If we can send it to England without restriction, it will not only yield revenue here, but when your people have worked it into cloth it will yield another tranche of duty when it is exported.

Not only that, but you will appreciate the risk that if all the Irish wool accumulates here it could fall into the wrong hands through smuggling or piracy, and that would be very disadvantageous to the English cloth trade.

I am against the staple ports system since there is no competition, and the port officials know the wool has to pass through their hands. That means the opportunities for corruption and bribery are legion. Unless palms are crossed with silver, the ships cannot load or unload; the goods are held up in the docks.

If I have the power to grant licences for exports from my ports to any other port I can ensure that with receipts at both ends, the wool has only gone to the intended destination. I beg you to raise this matter once more with the King in Council.

I am your faithful servant,
Wentworth.

George Radcliffe. 23rd February, 1634. Dublin Castle.

For the last few weeks Thomas and I have been working on a dispatch to the King asking for permission to call an Irish Parliament. Most of the ideas and reasons are his, but he likes me to contribute, and tidy up the wording sometimes. He values my legal skills, and contrary to the views of many lawyers, I believe that the simpler you make a proposition, the more chance you stand of getting your point across, and getting your way. Thomas is very good at that too, but occasionally two heads are better than one. He finishes dictating the last parts to his secretary this morning, and he asks me to read it to him, which I do.

Your Majesty,

Greetings from your Irish Kingdom. Having been here for six months I believe I have grasped the essentials of the way Ireland has been governed by your previous Deputies and the Irish Privy Council. I consider some quite drastic changes are called for.

I want to begin by calling a Parliament. I submit that this is vital, as your Government here will soon run short of funds. The Treasury is almost bare, and is reliant on the payment of the subsidies, which were agreed at my instigation before I came here, in return for an extension of the Graces, and they are due to run out soon. There are a number of grievances which clamour for attention - many connected with the Graces and with demands from the Catholics that they should be made into law - but I do not propose to let that prevent the early grant of proper funds for the Government by this Parliament.

With your approval, Sire, I intend to have two sessions of the two Houses. The first will require the replenishment of the Treasury with cash, and if, and only if, they vote the funds, I shall call the second to deal with grievances and those things which concern the people.

I shall make it clear that if the money is given willingly and generously, heavy taxation will not be imposed. The difficult problem is the fact that the Catholics are certain to want the Graces confirmed, and I want to avoid that until we have the money in the coffers. If I can ensure that in both Houses the Protestants and Catholics are fairly evenly represented, it may be easier to deal with them both than if I had to tackle one of these groups on its own when it had a majority.

To secure this I have it in mind to have as many Army Officers elected to the Commons as may hold the balance of power, since as they are your servants they are more likely to do what your Government desires. As for the Lords, the creation of a large number of new titles during the reign of your late Father, and some additional ones granted by you, has made the number of Protestant peers and Church of Ireland Bishops virtually equal to the Catholic Lords; managing the Upper House may be easier than I believe it was in the past. Because many of these new Lords are absentees living in England, I shall appoint as proxies for them men upon whom I can rely to vote the way I demand.

Only my closest advisers know what Bills I propose to put before Parliament. As it is my aim to have more Protestant settlements in Ireland, to make the country more civilised, and to convert the unfortunate natives to your Church, and away from the Pope, I cannot confirm any of the Graces in legislation which would make those settlements impossible. The project for planting new landowners in Connaught would fall at the first hurdle if, for example, the Grace seeking a sixty year title, became law. It could not then be upset by the Crown.

"I think that covers it, George. Do you agree?"

"I do. You can also weight the Commons in your own favour by filling more seats with government servants who are indebted to you for their posts and their pay. I could prepare a list of powerful people and you could ask them to make sure that your candidates are elected."

"Good idea." Thomas smiles. "And I'll tell Cork he cannot have his sons sit in the Lords."

I am a bit shocked. "But they are Lords anyway."

"I know that George, but one is only 12, and the other 16; they are too young, and that's what I shall tell the Earl."

George Wentworth. 26th February, 1634, Chester.

This has to be the most exciting and daunting day of my life. Even more exciting than the day Thomas knighted me. It is exciting because he has sent me to London – yes, London – on the most important mission I've ever had. It is daunting because of the nature of the mission. I have to persuade the King to let Thomas call an election so that he can have an Irish Parliament. It will be the first one for four years.

Of course, I know there's a long letter from Thomas to the King which I have to take, and I know it's a good one, because there's a copy for me, and I've read it. Radcliffe helped him write it, and he doesn't miss a trick, but it'll be down to me really, won't it? I'll have to say the right things, and bow and kneel at the right time, and not bump into the furniture and make a fool of myself. I don't want His Majesty throwing the letter away without reading it because he thinks I'm a clod.

There is something even more frightening than dealing with the King. That will be dealing with Thomas if I don't get his precious permission from Charles, and go back to Dublin empty-handed. I'm sure that the King cannot be as terrifying as Thomas in a bad temper.

My ship crossed to Chester from Dublin today. It was a good voyage, and now I'm in the heart of the city staying at a very good inn. Tomorrow I start for London.

Elizabeth. 18th March, 1634. Dublin Castle.

I am recovering from having been revoltingly sick this morning.

This is not the first time. It has been happening on and off since before Christmas, but it is not every day. I have also missed three of my monthly courses. One of my maids, who has two children of her own, says I must be pregnant. Oh, I do hope so! I love William and Anne and little Arabella, but to have my own baby would be very special.

I know Thomas will be very happy. The fact that I have not conceived before seems to be some sort of blot on his manhood. He never suggests it is my fault, if fault there can be in this sort of problem, but now and again he makes silly jokes about the musket balls he uses being the wrong size, or his powder's damp.

I don't think he suspects anything yet, because we still make love fairly often, and he is usually up and out about his work or hunting before I wake up. So as far I am aware he does not know that I am sick sometimes.

I shall tell him at dinner tonight. We are not expecting any visitors.

****

"Bess, that was an excellent meal. You really do give the cook the most wonderful orders for the things I really like. I'll have to watch out for my paunch or I shall burst out of all my clothes."

"It had to be a good dinner tonight, darling husband; we have cause to celebrate."

"We do?"

"Most certainly." I get up, go round the table, and pour more wine into his glass. "For a toast."

"Will you not take another glass yourself, Beth? I know you are a modest drinker, but if there's to be a toast and a celebration, you ought to have something."

I return to my seat and pour a mouthful into my own glass. "Just a very little then, since wine may not be the thing for me for a while. Thomas, I believe I am expecting your baby. I think I have been carrying him – perhaps her – for two months or so. Should we celebrate?" I hold up my goblet.

Thomas leaps to his feet with a "Thank the Lord!" He rushes round the table with his glass in his hand, kneels at my side, rests his head in my lap, strokes my belly, kisses me hard, stands up, and proposes: "The health of my lovely, loving, clever Elizabeth, and of our tiny person on the way," and downs his wine in a gulp. He runs to the door, and calls a servant, and asks the man to have the nurse get the children up and bring them downstairs. I can see this man look somewhat surprised at the idea of getting the children out of bed at so late an hour, and I try to get Thomas to change his mind, but to no purpose.

He is adamant. "The children should celebrate too. They are going to have a little brother – or sister – and they must – like us – see that it is a very happy thing." He turns back to the servant. "Go on, man, bring them to us."

And the children come down, and Thomas gives them all a tiny, tiny, glass of wine, and tells them the news. They are so happy, and all come and cuddle me and ask me endless questions about it, and how it happened, though I do believe William is getting to understand what nature does.

We both kiss them, and Thomas tells the nurse to put them back to bed. When the door closes he takes me in his arms, and kisses me tenderly, as though I might break. "You have made me feel quite manly with that news, Bess."

I lower my hand to a certain place and stroke it. "So I have, husband. Would you like me to see if I can do anything about it?"

Thomas. 20th March, 1634. Dublin.

Two weeks ago I received the report of the Commission I set up to enquire into the Army. I thought it would be bad. I was wrong. It's far worse than I thought possible. It seems that there are whole squadrons of cavalry and battalions of infantry which have rarely if ever seen their officers; the senior ones at any rate. That is reprehensible, but in a way it is also understandable.

It's the same problem that I complained about in England with the system of buying and selling government appointments, even if I have indulged in it myself to some extent. A man buys a place hoping to make money out of it. In civil life there is always business to do, so the office purchaser only makes money out of his work when he does it. The system is inefficient and corrupt, but at least most of the work gets done.

In the Army it doesn't. There are a few – very few – men of the upper classes who genuinely wish to serve their King and Country, and they buy a commission because, normally, it is the only way to get one. These few are keen, and will drill and train their troops, see that they are properly equipped, fed, and shod. Of course they would like a war, because that gives them, and their men, a chance of glory and booty and loot, as well as Army pay, and on the other side, the prospect of death or ghastly injury.

I've appointed one or two new officers of my own choosing, men I believe have that spirit of desire truly to serve the King. One of these is Harry Percy. He's the brother of Lucy, Countess Carlisle. Her husband the Earl is my friend James Hay. The Percys are Dukes of Northumberland and have been the fiercest sort of soldier for hundreds of years fighting the Scots in the Border Wars. I expect Harry to set an example of dedication to the others. The majority are not there for glory. They are only there for the social cachet of rank, the booty and the Army pay, but if they do not train and equip their soldiers, and learn tactics and how to fight, they have little chance of those. At present there is no war, so they get no booty, and they only get Army pay when the Treasury has funds with which to pay them. Is it any wonder that this type do not turn up, and that their men would not recognise them if they did? Some of these troops do not even have weapons! They are so badly trained that if they do have a lance or pike they are more likely to injure themselves with it than anyone else, let alone the enemy. Many soldiers do not even have food or proper clothing. In some parts of Ireland it is worse than when Buckingham's starving men were robbing farmers of eggs and boots in the English countryside.

The Commission finds that some soldiers barely survive, and do so by 'fetching in every morsel of bread upon their swords' points', which is a quaint way of saying that they beg for meals at farmhouses and cottages, and if refused, draw their swords and frighten the occupants into handing over their dinner, or tomorrow's.

I immediately ordered the senior officers to start training their men at least one day a week, to attend a parade here in Dublin today, and to make sure their regiments have a full complement of men by September. I intended to wake the officers up and I have succeeded. As I arrived at the parade today I overheard one captain say to another – they had never met me so had no idea who I was – "I didn't buy a commission in the Army so that I could play at being a soldier." The other replied: "Neither did I; I did it because Pater said pretty girls like captains in nice uniforms".

The parade is about to start, and as they pass by me, mounted on my beautiful black horse here in the place of honour, they'll know who I am alright.

Elizabeth. 20th March, 1634. Dublin.

My husband sits on his horse so beautifully out there on the parade ground. The horse is black, and so is his armour – black and very shiny. He even has a plume of black feathers atop his helmet. This morning as he rode out I said to him: "You look every inch a warrior; a very good-looking but fearsome warrior, my darling."

He laughed. "I'm not so sure 'darling' is a suitable epithet for a truly fearsome warrior, Bess, but it'll do for me. After all, I've never fought a battle or even a duel. The only thing I know of matters military comes from books, and some very half-hearted fencing lessons!"

Well, that's as may be but he looks just like a general ought to look as far as I'm concerned. I shall have to try to get that painter the King uses, Van Dyck, to paint a portrait of Thomas in armour. The army parading out there is rather impressive, too. Thomas has been so strict and persevering in his attempts to get the soldiers properly dressed and armed. I know little about soldiering but it looks very good to me.

I am in a carriage at the edge of the parade ground. Lots of ladies have come in carriages to watch, and there must be hundreds of ordinary people too. It's quite a spectacle, and it's the first parade the Irish Army has had for years, apparently. There is very little in the way of entertainment in Dublin, for there's only one theatre, so a sight like this is not to be missed for a king's ransom.

Thomas has worked so hard at this army business, and next week he is going to look over the two Georges' report on Mountnorris's accounts, and start trying to reform the Irish navy. "If," he says, "'navy' is not too grand a word for it." He works so hard.

Thomas is quite vain. After this parade he is likely to be quite pleasantly unbearable for a few days.

George Wentworth. 23rd March, 1634, Westminster.

London is wonderful. I've been here since 1st March. There is so much to do and see!! And so many lovely women!! And the theatres!!

So many of them too!! I've seen six plays already. I haven't seen one in Dublin, and I don't suppose there's a decent stage anywhere in Ireland. Mind you, Thomas was talking about licensing one in Dublin before I came here. I wonder if he will?

I've also paid a visit to the Chancellor, Francis, Lord Cottington, and spent a couple of very pleasant hours with him. He's a bit older than Thomas, and very dark, as though he comes from Spain, perhaps. He's certainly very much in favour of Spain, according to my brother, as he's been there as an ambassador twice. I've been told he may be a Catholic; I don't think Thomas knows that. My charge from Thomas was to try to get him to use his influence with the King and the Secretary, Sir John Coke, to make trade and commerce with Ireland easier. I don't think I got very far; pleasant he might be but Lord Cottington was pretty clear that the interests of English industries like the wool and cloth trades come first.

Thomas also told me to see the Treasurer, Richard Weston, Earl of Portland, if I could, about Thomas's plans for increasing trade and collecting the Irish customs and other taxes more efficient. I managed to do that a few days ago. The servants told me the old boy was unwell, but he let me go up to his bedroom anyway. On the way up the stairs I saw a portrait of him with reddish-brown hair, and a parting on the right; hardly anyone has a parting these days. The visit was really a waste of time. Portland was too ill to talk at any length about anything much, apart from the fact that he was only made an Earl last month; he was pretty full of that. To be honest I thought he looked as though he might be on his last legs. His hair and beard were completely grey.

Then I was invited to dinner at Lambeth Palace by the Archbishop. William Laud is a fat little chap, but very pleasant. He is clearly a great admirer of my brother, and I know from what Thomas tells me that the feeling's mutual. His Grace is obsessed, however, with his religious views, and his determination to root out the Puritan element in 'his' Church. He doesn't want dull services which, he told me, reflect the dimness of men's minds. He wants glorious ritual and liturgy that praise the power and majesty of God.

He's very keen on Thomas pursuing these religious aims in Ireland. I reckon they will cause a lot of trouble. There are a lot of people in Ireland amongst the settlers - especially the ones from Scotland - who are strict Presbyterian types, and their view is just the opposite of

Laud's. They think all his gorgeous raiment and theatrical services are the entertainments of the devil, and proper worship of God involves serious prayer and contemplation in a sober and unostentatious fashion. Not that I said anything about it causing trouble. I can do without being crushed between Laud and Thomas like wheat in the mill-stones. Actually, though, that 'proper worship' bit sounds like the sort Thomas prefers; he likes to pray and contemplate and worship privately.

I've also had an audience with the King. He said he had read Thomas's letter about calling an Irish Parliament - had read it carefully more than once - and discussed it with his Council. It looks as though he'll give Thomas everything he wants, but then Thomas usually gets what he wants in the end. Sometimes he does it through the sheer force of his personality, sometimes through what really amounts to bullying, and most of the time through persuasion. It has to be persuasion with Charles. Even Thomas can't bully the King.

I saw the King at Newmarket. It was a pretty unusual interview, I should think. I was taken down there by James, Earl of Carlisle, who is a friend of Thomas's. He took me in to present me to the King, who had been out hunting and was rather muddy, and even sweaty. I knelt before him, and handed over all the documents Thomas had asked me to give him.

Lord Carlisle took me home with him. His wife - Lucy, her name is - must be one of the most beautiful women on Earth. I think Thomas knows them from when he was on the Council of the North, and its President. He doesn't work as President now, even though he still is. He leaves most of that to his Vice-President, a chap called Osborne. Of course, Thomas is kept informed, and keeps in touch, and gives some directions. You'd think he had enough to do, being virtually a king in Ireland, but once my brother gets his finger in a pie, he finds it rather hard to leave it alone. I don't know how he manages it all, with his own business and financial interests to keep an eye on. I think it makes him ill with the flux sometimes.

Thomas. 12th April, 1634. Dublin Castle.

Lord Deputy Lieutenant of Ireland to His Grace, the Archbishop of Canterbury.

Your Grace,

I pray this finds you as well as it leaves me. I am most disturbed by the state of the Church in Ireland. Its finances are deplorable and its ritual and services are not such as to please you.

So far as the spiritual and moral foundations of the Church are concerned, they are rather Presbyterian in tone, which in many ways suits the Protestant population, as they follow Calvin to a considerable extent.

It follows that their Articles differ considerably from the 39 Articles which His Majesty is, with your assistance, anxious to promulgate in England and Scotland. Nevertheless I shall do what I can in pursuit of Thorough to do as the King wishes. I hope that the Church reformed in that style will be attractive to the ordinary people, but I have to say that Archbishop Ussher is not at all happy about it. He says the new Articles and your style of service will make no difference to the Catholics and will upset and anger a great many Puritan people who attend the Irish Church, let alone those who go to more Calvinist places of worship.

I had dinner with him recently. His palace is sumptuously appointed and furnished. The food was superb, and so was the plate on which it was served. In some ways he was quite amusing, whether he meant to be or not. He started off by lecturing me about having granted a licence for a new theatre in Dublin – in fact the only theatre in Dublin. From what he said you'd think a play is the work of the Devil, and that I and the actors are his minions.

I said: "But a play is fun, Your Grace, and many productions are splendid. The King approves of them, and so did his father, King James. As he was such an expert on the occult, he particularly enjoyed the witches in Macbeth. Indeed they say Shakespeare put them in deliberately for the late King's benefit."

Ussher was so gloomy. "It is wrong to put these expensive and magnificent entertainments before the people, My Lord."

"But you live very splendidly, if not magnificently, Your Grace, even if you do not find it fun. Is that a reason why the poorer people should not see some magnificence and fun in a theatre?"

He grew even gloomier. "I may live splendidly now, yet I shall live to want necessities." I laughed, and, looking around at the trappings of extreme wealth, joked: "Then you must go on living for a very long time, for no such thing is in prospect." He laughed not at all. I do not think there are any depths to the gloom from which he suffers, for his retort was: "I shall live to close your eyes!" I just hope he does not have the gifts of Jeremiah.

And so to the finances of the Church. As I say, its finances are deplorable. The problem is that since the Reformation the rectories and livings of far too many parishes have come into the hands of wealthy landowners. If we do not restore the wealth of the Church, your reforms will be impossible. Richard Boyle, Earl of Cork, who has been in Ireland about 40 years or so, has got his hands on about four hundred livings. He keeps all the rents of these places, and from any endowments from which they benefit. He then pays the priests a pittance to run the parish churches, and they have to pay rent for their accommodation instead of occupying their own rectories..

He even rents out the Bishopric of Waterford to one of his relations, and rakes in the cash by renting out the vicarages.

To attempt the reform of this Church and the conversion of Ireland from Papist to good Protestant before the decay of the material parts of the Church is repaired, and before there is money to pay good priests to instruct the people, would be like going to war without ammunition or arms.

Cork must be dealt with. We must get as much Church land and income as we can back into the hands of the Church, and out of the hands of the likes of Cork. At least Ussher is in agreement with us on that question. I shall rely on your support in any wrestling which has to be done with Cork. I shall investigate his doings carefully, and plan how to deal with him.

I am, Your Grace, your servant,
Wentworth.

Elizabeth. 14th April, 1634. Dublin Castle.

"What on earth's the matter, Thomas?" He storms into the room looking like Thor in a bad mood. Thunderbolts are bound to fly. I'm with some of my lady friends sewing clothes for the poor. I send the ladies away.

"King Charles has pissed all over me! Remember how I asked him not to appoint anyone to any posts or commissions here without asking me first, and how he promised – in writing too – not to do so? Well, it didn't take him long to break that promise."

"What has he done?"

"You know I gave Harry Percy the captaincy of a troop of cavalry a few months ago?" I get no chance to reply. "Well, I now have to tell him it isn't his after all, and he's Northumberland's son!"

"But how is that the King's fault, dear?"

"Don't be silly. It isn't the King's fault Harry is the Duke's son."

"You can be aggravating sometimes, Thomas, particularly when you're angry. You know what I mean. How can the King be to blame for your having to tell Harry he can't be a captain?"

"Because he's just written telling me to appoint some relative of Falkland's."

I chance making him angrier still. "Who is Falkland?"

"He was my predecessor – dead now of course. How can I govern this island for the best if I can't even rely on the King's word? As if I haven't enough problems with the people here, without being stabbed in the back from Whitehall."

I have to calm him down, or he will explode. "He is the King, Thomas, and I am sure he did not do it just to ...."

"Whose side are you on, Bess?" He's hurled a few thunderbolts already but that was the first aimed at me.

"You know whose side I'm on! The thing to do is write back to the King, tell him you have complied with his command, and tell him about the embarrassment this will cause with the Percy family, and the Carlisles. He can't afford to upset the Duke of Northumberland, and the Earl of Carlisle is Harry Percy's brother-in-law."

Thomas's expression is full of contrition. He kisses me gently. "I'm so sorry, Bess. You're right. I'll tell the King that if he takes the power of reward and punishment away from me, he can't expect me to be shown any respect or obedience either. I shall be unable to enforce any measures in his name, which is what this is all about in the end."

"And you can remind him that you wrote to tell him you'd given that command to young Harry weeks ago. Or was it months? He must have forgotten."

"Months. It's charitable of you to be so understanding on the King's behalf, my love, but I doubt he forgot either Harry's command or his promise to consult me about appointments here. If he can do this, how can I be sure he won't listen to any rubbish Mountnorris tells him about the embezzlement charges?"

George Wentworth. 27th April, 1634. Dublin Castle.

My ship docked yesterday. I gave the King's letters to Thomas straight away. He was very excited. Even Radcliffe seemed to be, which is pretty unusual for him; he doesn't show his feelings much.

"The King agrees I should call Parliament. He says I should arrange to start in Trinity Term, so I'll make it some time in July. We'll have to get started on organising the elections."

"What did his Majesty say about that?" Radcliffe asks.

"He doesn't like the idea of giving seats in the Commons to Army Officers. He won't agree to it. He says MPs should be picked for their grasp of what motivates others, and their loyalty to the Crown. But he leaves all the rest to my 'courage and dexterity'. And he gives me permission to hear all sorts of cases in the Court of Castle Chamber. That'll make my job easier. I can make sure more people – especially the poorer sort – get justice."

I can barely stand up. "I'm tired after the journey, Thomas. May I go to bed?"

"If you must. But I tell you what. In the morning you can help Radcliffe here write to all the peers and other power brokers with the names of the MPs we want elected. And you can start with the Earl of Cork. Tell him I want six of them for the boroughs in his pocket." He names Philip Mainwaring, Radcliffe, and Christopher, and two others.

Tired I may be, but I can still count. "But that's only five, Thomas."

"That's because I've left the best 'til last. You're number six, George," and suddenly I'm wide awake, but I still go to bed. After all, I've got to help write about a hundred letters tomorrow for Thomas to sign.

George Radcliffe. 29th April, 1634. Dublin Castle.

Thomas marches into the library, whistling and then singing. Since he was told immediately after that wonderful parade a couple of months ago that he is to be a father again he has been marching about singing or whistling nearly all the time.

His brother George takes the urine. Young George seems a lot more confident, if not positively cheeky, since he got back from London a couple of days ago. He takes all the credit for the fact that the King agreed the Irish Parliament should be called. He also claims it was his advocacy of Thomas's plan for exports that caused the King to grant him the warrant to issue licences to send wool to England. "Alright, Thomas. Yes, we know, the parade was a great success, Elizabeth is pregnant, and you are some sort of god."

Even Thomas laughs, and he says: "Don't push your luck, little George. Now the King's given me power to try all sorts of cases in the Court of Castle Chamber I can have you locked up for making a fool of me."

"As you did with that stupid Bellasis boy, brother?"

He laughs. "Well, perhaps not. I don't want to make an enemy of you as well."

I mutter under my breath: "Not on top of all the others."

"What was that, Radcliffe?" That is what he calls me when brother George is about, for obvious reasons. Thomas is suddenly stern.

"Can't jail all your brothers, Thomas."

Thomas sits at the big table we are using, drumming his fingers. Little George and I have spread out Mountnorris's accounts. "What conclusions have we reached, Radcliffe?"

"As you know, most of the Treasurers for ages past anticipated large parts of the Government revenue by selling it to rich people in return for ready cash. They have not kept proper records of how many of these assignments have been granted, and ..."

"So the Treasurer has no idea how much revenue he is entitled to, and how much of it will have to be paid to the men holding the assignments, and no-one knows when or how he will get his money back." Thomas has grasped the problem quickly. Or had he worked this out before?

"Not only that, but these paper IOUs are sold on, and used, in effect, as a sort of black market currency," says George.

"What do you recommend we do, Radcliffe?"

I am ready for this. "I think there's no alternative but to summon Mountnorris before the Council to be questioned about it. We think he has been doing the same thing himself, and also taking 'commissions' to which he is not entitled from the revenue which is collected, and from the money that is paid to the Treasury when he writes out these assignment papers."

Thomas looks at George. "Is that what you think, little brother?"

"Yes, I agree with George – er – Radcliffe. This gets confusing doesn't it? And I wish you'd stop calling me 'little brother'. If you call him Radcliffe you can call me Wentworth."

"Very well, Wentworth and Radcliffe. Thanks for your help. I'll try to get Annesley to resign as Treasurer, but if I fail we ought to arrange for him to be hauled before the Privy Council as soon as possible."

Charles I. 30th April, 1634. Windsor.

My Dear Wentworth,

Your letter of 14th arrived yesterday. I am gratified that you have done as I asked and appointed Viscount Falkland's nephew to the command of the troop of horse. I have also considered very carefully your arguments about why you feel I acted wrongly.

It is not every servant of mine from whom I would tolerate such a rebuke. However, I see much force in what you say, and in your reasoning. I shall assure Northumberland and Carlisle that the mistake was mine, not yours, and I shall assure them, as I now assure you, that such a thing will not occur again.

I regret this slight embarrassment in our conduct towards each other.

I am, as always, your appreciative,
Charles R.

Elizabeth. 10th May, 1634. Dublin Castle.

Thomas has just read me a letter from the King which arrived yesterday when I was out visiting Anne Radcliffe. "It's hardly an apology, but then you could hardly expect one from the King, could you?"

"No, it isn't his style. I don't mind that so much. What worries me is whether I can really rely on him not to let me down over this sort of thing in future. The last thing I need is for Charles to tell me to leave Mountnorris alone with his thefts."

What can I say to that? Thank goodness no servants are present. You cannot be sure whether they report things to members of the Privy Council who don't care for Thomas. I don't believe Charles would have his head chopped off, even if Henry VIII would have done, but I wouldn't want the King to hear that Thomas doubts whether he is trustworthy.

Christopher Wandesford. 12th May, 1634. Dublin Castle.

All of us have been looking into what passes for an Irish navy; that is me, Thomas, and the two Georges. We have had some help from Philip Mainwaring. Apart from Thomas, none of us care for him much – he seems too slimy for my liking – but he has a lot of contacts in England and he's making a lot here now, so he comes up with some very useful information. He's Thomas's secretary now. A double portrait of the two of them together is being done.

He goes round the docks and taverns the sailors use, and comes back with some amazing gossip. He says much of the time the sailors aren't paid – so that's just as it was with the Army before Thomas got here – and half the time the Admiralty doesn't even provide sailors for the ships in Irish waters.

Thomas dictates a letter to me for the Admiralty Board in London. To say he is smouldering is to put it mildly. I'm surprised the paper doesn't catch alight.

You do not need me to tell you that the King's realm of Ireland is theoretically entirely in the hands of the Admiralty so far as naval defence is concerned. In reality it is virtually in the hands of the pirates because you send so few ships here. I have ascertained that sailors serving in Irish waters are hardly ever paid, and that you provide very few sailors for the ships in Irish ports anyway. I am sure you would be delighted if I were to draw this state of affairs to His Majesty's attention.

We have no power, nor the money, to provide our own ships, and the King's protection for Ireland's commerce idles its time away in the docks here. Our merchants either have the goods they are sending to England and abroad stolen on the way out, or they are robbed of those they are bringing back before they reach Dublin or Derry, or any of our other ports.

But that doesn't matter to you, does it? Why should the Lord Deputy in Ireland worry himself, or trouble the Admiralty, about piracy in the Irish Sea? Indeed how dare I even raise such a matter with the exalted Lords of the Admiralty? Our merchant ships are captured and disappear all the time, with their cargos, and more seriously, their sailors. A score of years ago pirates took one ship – yes, just one – which carried cargo bound for Spain. That cargo was valued at 3,000 pounds. And we do not need to go back as far as that for a serious example.

Only two years ago Barbary pirates raided Baltimore, a small town in the far South West of County Cork. I need no reminding that there are similar raids in Cornwall and Devon, but in this raid they carried off no fewer than 107 of the residents of the town, together, naturally, with any valuables they could find. Can you imagine what happened to those people – those subjects of the King? Slaves now, or worse? Where was the protection His Majesty pays you to provide for his people then? You may doubt it, but even the Irish are his people!

Thus I am sorely tried when I think how the prosperity of this Kingdom is reduced by these pirates, and how the revenue we might otherwise send the King is less than it might otherwise be. If I had the means to do something about it I should, but you control the means.

"What do you think, Kit? Will that do it?"

"It won't make them happy, but the idea of your sending anything like that to the King should wake them up. We have to deal with that pirate hide-out on the Isle of Man soon. Mainwaring says the seamen tell him it's not just the shipping and coast which is attacked. They even sail up the rivers to rob settlements on the banks."

"I don't want them to be happy, Kit. I want them to do their duty. When they do, we can stop the pirates."

Thomas. 15th May, 1634. Dublin Castle.

Did I succeed in getting Annesley to resign? Of course not. I really think he cares not a fig for the government of the country, its economy, the people, or whether the King gets a proper share of the Revenue. He is the Treasurer. It is a lucrative post. He has his hands on about 55,000 pounds of the King's money to use for his own purposes, until such time as he chooses to pay it over. Let's be honest here. That is what all officials do. I was no different when I was President of the North, and intend to do the same if I could get my paws on the Irish Treasury, but I always pay the King what is due to him when the due date falls. I take none of it to which I am not legally entitled.

That isn't true of Annesley. He is creaming money off the top as well as his lawful commission. He's been doing it for years. With the assistance of the Georges I formulated some new embezzlement charges against him, and a week ago I sent them to Coke, the Secretary of State, to put before the Privy Council in Whitehall.

When I told Annesley what I had done, he said, by way of a threat: "I shall resign, and take my case up with the King direct." If only he knew how happy he would make me if he did resign, and that the King had given me his written promise not to hear any appeals from here, he would not have been quite so cocky.

Thomas. 16th May, 1634. Dublin Castle.

Today I have taken the first rather big step towards putting Anglican religious standards and a more Anglican form of worship into the Church in Ireland, and, come to that, into Ireland in general. My chaplain, John Bramhall, has been consecrated here in the Castle Chapel today as Bishop of Derry. He's a tall, austere man, a year younger than me, wears his hair short, usually under a black cap covering his ears, and he's completely clean shaven: no beard or moustache. He has one outstanding feature: the longest, sharpest nose I have ever beheld. This is a grand promotion for him, but it won't be a bed of roses. Derry is home to many of the strongly Presbyterian Scots planters. Many of the clergy in Ulster are of a Presbyterian turn of mind, too. John may meet with some resistance.

Still, I chose him because he is firmly in camp with me and Laud. He's a strong character who is unlikely to buckle under pressure to adopt local ways. There will probably be a lot of that, since the outgoing Bishop was George Downham, who was a Puritan, and therefore more acceptable to the Scottish element, and did not annoy them. That is unlikely to be true of Bramhall, but we have discussed that, and he says it won't worry him. It certainly doesn't worry me.

As Head of the Church, and in exercise of his Divine right, Charles is entitled to make these changes. He would get nothing done if everything had to be agreed by Parliament.

Thomas. 20th May, 1634. Dublin Castle.

Coincidence is a curious thing sometimes. Only a few days ago I dictated a letter to the Admiralty Board in London, complaining about the need for better naval protection in the Irish Sea, and all round our coasts. Today I have a letter from Cottington telling me the King has caused writs to be issued to many parts of the country – England, that is – for the payment of Ship Money.

He says if the King does not have more money to build ships, the navy will not have one new vessel this year, or next, or the year after. It doesn't help that much of the cost of a ship lies in the way Charles has all the stately woodwork surrounding the windows aft, where the officers' quarters are, picked out in gold leaf. He might get more ships for his money if he stopped that. You'd think these windows were frames on the priceless paintings he buys to hang on the walls of his palaces.

I wonder whether these writs will cause trouble. They used to call only for Ship Money from the seaside counties, but this new batch calls for contributions from all over the country, coast and inland. Someone is bound to object, I suppose.

Christopher Wandesford. 15th July, 1634. Dublin.

Yesterday was the opening of the new Irish Parliament – Thomas's first Parliament. He's obviously learned a lot from the failure of James and Charles to manage theirs properly. He's done everything he, George Radcliffe and I could think of to make sure he would be in control.

Even the procession down to the House was organised to the last detail. Thomas was splendidly dressed in maroon velvet, with an ermine cape, and had James Butler, the new Earl of Ormonde, bear the Sword of State before him. He was accompanied by all the Irish Peerage, and his government officials. They all had to be placed in order of their rank and importance. That is no easy task, as the nobility are not known for their humility or willingness to accept that someone else should go before them. Several men told me that they could not recall when Ireland had ever seen so impressive an occasion.

After the opening ceremonies, Parliament was adjourned to today, for Thomas to make his opening speech. He is such a polished performer! He could easily have been a Richard Burbage or another of Shakespeare's great actors. He held the assembled peers and MPs enthralled. He had notes, but did not read from them. He knew exactly what he wanted to say, but he spoke in an impromptu fashion, which lends so much more power to true oratory than simply reading from a prepared text.

"My Lords and Members of this Parliament,

We are all honoured to be able to serve our Lord and Master, the King, in this place, and none more so than I, who have received so many blessings and so much advancement at his Royal hands. It is his power which calls us here, and we must be ever mindful of the obligations we owe him. Whether and when he may call for a Parliament is a matter entirely for him to judge, and not for us to enquire into.

But now we are here, and we should rejoice at the opportunities we have to serve the King, and do some good in this place. This government will make every effort to look after the interests of all those who are loyal to Ireland and the King, from rich to poor, from peasant to peer. We shall do all we can to improve the commerce and the industry of this conquered nation, and make it prosperous.

With prosperity we can do more to relieve the burdens of the poor, give them better access to justice, and establish houses of correction for vagabonds and tramps, and people without any means of support, providing them with shelter and some form of work until they are fit to stand on their own feet.

To do any of this it is essential that we make available to the King generous subsidies to enable him to carry his Kingdoms forward, for without the shade of his greatness and goodness we are all diminished. I urge you not to put your own private interests before His Majesty's, since without his protection we are nothing. It is according to the rules of reason and nature that he must come first if he is to care for us. I want you clearly to understand that unless we vote to supply the King with sufficient revenue it will be pointless to put forward any legislation to achieve any of the other objectives the government, or you, may have in mind.

We must also beware of treating the King like a man with a begging bowl, obliged to come here every year to plead with us that he should be given the means with which to carry on the government of the country.

That government is and must be equal for all the people. It makes no difference to the King whether you are English, or Irish, or Papist or Protestant. You are all his good and faithful subjects, and you may rest assured that I shall do my utmost to follow that principle. I shall welcome all who obey the government and the law, and I shall be fearless in the pursuit of those who set themselves up against the King, or seek to divide the people from their lawful Sovereign.

We and those we represent are the body and the King is the head. Neither can live nor function without the other. If the King is prosperous then his people will be too, and both will be happy. If one is rich and the other poor, disaster looms. I pray that you will remember these things, and thus make, and not mar, this Parliament."

When you think about it, a lot of this is pretty vague. The Old English nobility and the Catholics may like to be told they will be treated the same as everyone else, but it is largely to them that Thomas is looking to pay the subsidies and they hope he will pass the Graces into law in return. He has said nothing about that. Meanwhile they are at the mercy of the government, and of having all the laws and fines against recusants enforced against them.

Elizabeth. 21st July, 1634. Dublin Castle.

Thomas is in one of his god-like moods tonight. When he is in one of these, you'd think there was nothing on this Earth he cannot do. Sometimes I wonder whether that is what he thinks, which is a bit frightening. What's so surprising – and I cannot get used to it, even after we've been married for a year – is that he can be so stern and authoritative with other people, and be so determined to get what he wants, yet he is so caring, and gentle, and considerate here at home with me and the children.

But then I suppose he really cares about his work, and trying to do the right thing by the King, and by Ireland, and the people, especially the poorer people. Sometimes I'm not sure that what he tries to do is really the right thing, but he genuinely thinks so, and I'm sure he does what his conscience tells him. For example, he wants to make more work for everybody here, so that everyone will be better off. He is appalled by the lousy – literally – and damp conditions in which the poor live, even if he thinks that's because they don't adopt better methods of farming and other jobs.

Besides, I dare say the real Irish would rather we cleared out altogether, but that's not going to happen. Thomas is realistic enough to know that he has to do whatever it takes to bring Ireland into this modern Seventeenth Century world, whether they, and even he, like it or not.

He likes what happened today, though. He is absolutely cock-a-hoop at the success of getting Parliament to vote the six subsidies he wanted, without any real trouble at all. He says he has not had to promise to make the Graces into law, and he's very proud of that. The consequence is, he tells me, that he can keep the Irish government going for at least another year whilst he puts his other plans into action. I don't understand quite what all that is about; he says it's very complicated. He tried to explain it before but I get a bit bored with this political stuff sometimes, especially about money, so I go off into a dream. It's not that he's boring though, particularly when he's excited like tonight.

We're in bed and he is rabbiting on, and I'm trying to calm him down a bit. At first he didn't even seem to notice that I was softly stroking him, but when it was hard and I stopped he says: "What have you stopped for?"

I make love to him, hoping not just for the pleasure it will give us both, but that it will calm him down a bit.

Has he calmed down? I don't think so, but at least I've taken his mind off Parliament.

George Radcliffe. 2nd August, 1634. Dublin Castle.

Kit Wandesford and I await Thomas in his study. He got back here from Parliament a little while ago, and was delayed getting to his carriage by the press of people wanting to talk to him when the Houses adjourned. The pomp and ceremony with which this first session of Parliament ended was something to behold. It was almost as extravagant in its splendour as the opening was just over two weeks ago.

Thomas managed it so well. He seemed to cast a spell over it. He is very efficient, and a marvellously inspiring speaker, which makes such a difference. On the other hand I suppose it's true to say that his very serious reputation for firmness and discipline may mean that no-one is ready to confront him too early in his Deputyship, and before they have a real opportunity of taking his measure.

There was one potential bit of trouble about the MPs who had been selected by Thomas, and were in fact elected. Some others wanted to have an inquiry whether they had been validly elected. Kit stifled that problem by getting a majority to vote for the inquiry to be put off until the main issues and Bills before the House had been disposed of. Some Protestants thought this inquiry would lead to more Catholics getting into the Commons, so it will come to nothing.

Of course the main business was the matter of the subsidies. Thomas correctly guessed that the Catholics and Old English would vote for them, hoping they would get the Graces passed too, but there was some opposition from Cork and his son, Lord Ranelagh and a few others. What they were worried about, it seemed to me, was that if the subsidies went through, so would the Graces, and they would not want the Catholics to get the benefit of that. They did all they could to make life very awkward for the Pope's followers before Thomas arrived in Ireland, and they would like that policy to continue.

They could have had another reason. I don't think it took Cork long to realise that Thomas is no-one's fool, and will bow down to no-one. He may well have wanted the government to be in financial trouble so that Thomas would be ham-strung right from the start.

Having got his subsidies Thomas put all sorts of minor Bills and debates before the House, releasing huge quantities of hot air but achieving little, which is exactly what he wanted. As a result the question of putting the Graces into an Act of Parliament never truly arose, and had not come anywhere near doing so. One important piece of business was transacted at the end of the session, however, and, surprisingly caused no real stir at all. Thomas placed before the two Houses a Bill to establish the Commission for Defective Titles. Perhaps all sides were hoping that this would, at last give them the secure land titles they yearned for. You might think that some of them, at least, would have foreseen that this Commission could be used to place their titles in doubt, causing them to have to pay fines, higher rents, or even buy the land again.

Thomas came in triumphantly, threw his gloves on the desk, took off his sword, and put it in the stand by the book-cases, and fell into his chair. "Thank the Lord that's over. We got everything we wanted, and gave away nothing they wanted!!"

Kit laughed. “It’s certainly not what we’re used to seeing in the last few Westminster Parliaments. And what is it now – six years – since we had one?”

Thomas laughs too. “I hope you didn’t for one moment think that I’d put up with the sort of attitude the King is presented with at Westminster, did you? I may have to be a bit more generous when we have the next session, but believe me, I intend to remain in full control. And I’m grateful for all the help you two have given me.”

“It was a wise move to tell the Houses that none of the money for the subsidies will go to England,” I say.

Thomas nods sagely. “I’m glad you think so. In fact, didn’t you suggest it when we were talking the other day?”

“Did I?”

“Yes, I’m sure you did. The trouble is, will Treasurer Portland be able to keep his hands off it? I’m worried he’ll ask the King to tell me to send some of it to London. This is just the first bud of spring so far as Ireland goes. We don’t want it nipped off before we have a chance to see it grow.”

Kit joins in. “Why don’t I write to Portland to that effect, and you can sign it? And you could write to Laud, as you usually do, suggesting the line he might take for you with the King and the Privy Council.”

Thomas leaps up, very pleased, and starts to stride about, swinging his arms and making vehement gestures. “Good idea, Kit. Draft a letter to Portland saying just what you said just now. We’ll do another to Laud, telling him that ‘Lord Treasurer Portland promises not to have any of the money sent to him, but I see them on that side of the Irish Channel driven to such straights as, like drowning men, they clutch at any twig that might keep them afloat, and I am in mortal dread of what they may do.’ If Portland gets any of the subsidies sent over, my credit with Parliament and the people here, and their estimation of me, would be completely shipwrecked. If I can’t keep this money in Ireland now, I shall never be able to make Ireland pay its way.”

Thomas. 30th August, 1634. Dublin Castle.

It seems my rather cross and sarcastic letter to the Admiralty in May has had some effect. More sailors turned up and all have received some pay! At least one new ship arrived with a very enterprising captain who sailed out again almost as soon as he came, captured a pirate ship very quickly, and brought it into port yesterday. I called him to the Castle today and knighted him on the spot. I'm hoping he will be able to deal with the Isle of Man gang. I do not understand why my predecessors let this situation go on for so long. Too much trouble, I suppose.

One change I've made which is clearly producing results is to ask the Admiralty to send ships for Ireland's protection at the beginning of spring, and not in the middle of the summer, by which time the pirates and other predators have had three months of good weather to harass or kidnap merchant ships and raid our coastal villages. Bearing in mind that most export goods from Ireland to foreign countries carry customs duties which have to be paid before they can be embarked and shipped out from Irish ports, it would hardly be surprising if merchants were reluctant to risk a lot on foreign trade if, having paid the tax, they then lose all their money to the pirates.

The range of Irish exports is quite amazing. We send abroad live cattle, hides, meat, tallow, and almost anything which can be made from a dead animal. Sheep and pigs go too, and all the products which come from their carcasses. You'd think we could export a lot of wool if we can sell sheep, but the Privy Council in England still protects the English cloth trades, which are so important. This means most of the time Irish wool only goes to English cloth manufacturers, and that spoils the price, as there is usually no competition to buy it.

The fact there is a soap monopoly in England is also unfortunate for the Irish tallow trade. The monopoly is intended to protect England from buying soap from abroad. For England to make its own soap it needs tallow. Accordingly the laws promulgated by England prevent Irish tallow being sent anywhere but to England most of the time. I shall have to give more thought to granting licences for the export of wool and tallow in proper cases. Will the licence fees belong to me for granting them, or to the Crown? In the past, as far as I can make out, previous Deputies such as Chichester and Grandison issued export licences for fees, and kept the money. I ought to share them with the King. I'll have to ask Sir John Coke yet again if it is in order for me to grant export licences.

Farmers sell wheat and rye and barley overseas, but most of it goes to England and Scotland. I recall that it was the delay in getting Irish wheat to England a few years ago that led to my asking Richard Marris to buy it in Yorkshire to send to London.

Irish goods go to France, the Dutch, Spain, parts of Germany, and some, especially live cattle, go across the Atlantic to Virginia. I am not too keen on crossing the Irish Sea. I cannot help wondering what a cow makes of a five or six week journey to America. Do they suffer sea sickness?

Christopher Wandesford. 2nd September, 1634. Limerick.

Tom sent me down here last week to make sure there was no trouble over his latest appointment of a Bishop. A few months ago he put John Bramhall into Derry Cathedral in place of George Downham. Downham was a Puritan, and he had been the choice of the New English Puritans in Ulster. Replacing him with one of Laud's disciples upset many of them. They used to rule the roost here in Ireland over these ecclesiastical matters, and Laud's dogma is too close to Rome for their liking.

Well, they are not going to be too keen on the Bishop of Limerick Thomas has chosen either. The old Bishop died a while ago, and Tom's nominee is George Webb.

He was the King's own chaplain, so it follows as night follows day that he has to be a follower of Laud. As far as the Puritans are concerned they probably think that perpetual night has followed day when someone they see as a virtual Papist is sent to lord it over their worship of God.

Sometimes I do wonder how many people Tom can anger with his devotion to this "Thorough" business he indulges in with the Archbishop. It is very hard to recall Tom compromising over anything with anyone. Maybe that's not quite true. He talks things over with me and George Radcliffe, and sometimes with his brother George as well; he'll adopt some of our ideas, but it doesn't happen often. He's more likely to rely on whatever advice he gets from Laud in his numerous long letters. That's not much help in making deals with people and keeping them on his side, since Laud takes a pretty hard line about everything too.

Anyway, there's been no trouble so far. I think the thought of tangling with Viscount Wentworth this early in his being Deputy

Lieutenant is a test of courage too far, too soon, for most people. Thomas is a mixture. He believes the King should be in control, so he more or less believes in Divine Right. On the other hand he would like Parliaments to be called more often, so that taxes can be levied and grievances addressed, but he'd need a succession of very tame Parliaments, I think. There's an odd play on words in the expression, anyway. It's ambiguous. If the power is Divine because it comes from God, the Right isn't just a possession of the ruler: it ought to mean he has to wield it correctly and fairly. If it is used wickedly or unfairly, it can't be Divine, can it?

Thomas. 17th September, 1634. Dublin Castle.

Can I be happier than I am today? I've been this happy in the past, when William was born to Arabella. Today the feeling is the same. We have another son!! Yes, Elizabeth and I have a son. She is doing well, and came through the delivery with great courage and a lot of noise. I could hear her shouting and screaming through the stone walls, the door of the bedroom, and the door of the library which is some distance away. Yes, I had to wait in the library. Did I read a book? I picked one up, held it upside down for ten minutes without having read a word – hardly surprising really – reading upside down is not an art I've bothered to master. Then I threw it down, and it nearly landed in the fire, which would have been a shame as it was about one hundred years old and pretty valuable.

But then I hardly knew what I was about. You'd think the King's Deputy in a country would be able to give an order that he wanted to be with his wife when she had a baby, wouldn't you? After all, I know that sometimes the poor who live a long way from a village or in the depths of a forest can't always get hold of a woman to help the wife deliver a baby, and if the husband is there he has to do it. Why couldn't I be there? Well, when it comes to giving orders these midwives and nurses give orders that even Caesar and Alexander would have obeyed. They actually pushed me out of the door.

They let me in soon after I had heard the baby utter his first cry, and I went in and there he was on Beth's bosom. He was still a bit bloody, and she was beautiful and rather caked in perspiration. I took them both in my arms, and kissed Beth time and time again. She was already breathless from what she had just been through so she asked me to stop. I told her I was sorry. She said: "No, I'm the one who's sorry. I don't want you to stop, but I have to breathe sometimes."

Then the midwife told me – yes, told me – to leave the room. At times like these it seems that women have all the power and men have no rights at all. But how can I be unhappy? I have a beautiful wife, a healthy looking new son – which means I've got two male heirs now – and I know my baby-making tackle still works well. I can't wait to use it again. Yes, I am a very happy man.

Thomas. 25th September, 1634. Dublin Castle.

I have a letter from Sir John Coke. He must have replied the day he got my letter about export licences. How does the man do it? I know he's got his secretaries or an amanuensis or two, but he still has to read the correspondence, tell them what to write – at least the gist of it – and read and sign the final version. I use a secretary, but Ireland is smaller than England with a smaller population, and far less economic activity, and I get through a few hundred letters a month. Coke must deal with a thousand or more.

This is what the letter says:

Dear Wentworth,

I have considered your letter of 30th August carefully, and discussed it with other Councillors. I regret to say that the state of trade in England, and especially the cloth trade, is so depressed at the moment that it will not be possible for you to issue licences for the export of wool and flax to any place but England, and those exports do not need a licence anyway.

The weavers in the West Country and in Lancashire and Yorkshire are heavily reliant on the supplies of these yarns from Ireland, as there is not enough produced here.

Not only that, but the reason the trade is suffering so much is the competition from the Flemish and other cloth makers in Europe. If they can get your wool and flax, and make their own cloth, they won't buy ours. This is of little consolation to the farmers and weavers of Ireland, who would like to be able to sell their raw wool and yarn everywhere, but the Privy Council has to be realistic. There is, of course, nothing to stop more cloth being woven in Ireland, and sold abroad, but I fancy that even that will meet with protests from manufacturers here who would rather your people did not compete.

I hope that your efforts to revive the Irish economy are progressing well.

With all good wishes.

John Coke.

Secretary to the Privy Council.

The old hypocrite!! How can he think good wishes will do any good when he stops me taking any steps to 'revive the Irish economy', as he puts it? I shall have to find a way to deal with this. I cannot increase the customs for the King if I cannot have more goods going out of Irish ports.

Elizabeth. 1st October, 1634. Dublin Castle.

Most of my servants are Protestants, but one or two are Catholic, and one of the chief cooks is Catholic too. Thomas and I don't seem to have any trouble with the Catholic ones but sometimes there's a real atmosphere between the servants which must be due to religion, I fancy. They don't treat each other ill as far as I can tell, or not directly, but sometimes I hear some whispered comments which sound pretty unpleasant when one side or the other leaves a room. I know there is some ill feeling between the denominations at home but it seems worse here in Ireland. I decide to ask Thomas about it.

"Well, Bess, it goes back to the time King Henry reformed the Church. The Irish and Old English feared that Protestant ways would be forced on them, but nothing much happened until Elizabeth came to the throne. Edward didn't bother much with Ireland, and Mary wasn't likely to do anything to their faith, being a Catholic herself and busy enough persecuting Protestants in England."

"What changed under Elizabeth?"

"Her government saw Ireland as a base where Spain or France could attack England, and the Catholic Irish and the Old English would side with the invader. If she settled lots of Protestants in Ireland, it would be more difficult for anyone to invade as the new settlers would fight to defend their homes."

"Is that why there are quite a few English people round Dublin, and many Scots in Ulster, Thomas?"

"That's it, my love. They were given land, called plantations, and they were - still are - called planters or settlers. Whether they ..."

"Grew any plants was beside the point?"

"Quite." I've made Thomas smile at that. "The trouble was that in Ulster there were powerful Irish chieftains like Hugh O'Neill. These chiefs and their clans were, and almost always had been, opposed to English rule. O'Neill was not just a chieftain. He was Earl of Tyrone, one of the counties of Ulster, and he was the most powerful man in that province. He was known as 'The O'Neill', meaning the leader of the clan, just as in Scotland a man might be known as 'The MacDonald', or 'The Campbell'. His attitude towards English rule hardened against them as time went by. In 1580 the Earl of Desmond, in the Southern province of Munster, rebelled against the English. O'Neill and his men fought on the English side, and Desmond was defeated.

"In 1584 O'Neill fought with the English against an uprising by the Scottish settlers in Ulster, which was successfully put down. He fought against them because, like all the native Irish, O'Neill was a Roman Catholic; the Scots were mainly Presbyterian. Faith made them enemies."

I smile sadly at that. "Jesus didn't want anyone to be enemies, did he? Odd that two different sorts of Christians can hate each other."

"You're right, of course, but it's got a lot to do with power and politics rather than Jesus. Anyway, the object of Queen Elizabeth's plantation of Ulster was to reduce the power of the Irish chiefs, and dilute the strongly Catholic population with pockets of Protestants loyal to the Crown."

I am struggling a bit with what seems to me the unfairness of all this. "But surely this policy was hated by the Ulster Irish? I mean, the English wouldn't put up with it if the French came and took their land away and moved lots of Frenchmen in."

Thomas laughs. "Of course they wouldn't, and that's exactly what happened when William the Conqueror came over. Anyway, about forty years ago O'Neill and a band of fellow chiefs started their own rebellion which lasted nine years. They hoped Philip II of Spain would come to their aid. He sent weapons and munitions, and that was all, but O'Neill lead his army to victory in 1595 at Clontibret and in 1598 at the Yellow Ford on the Blackwater River."

"Still, they couldn't have won the war, or we wouldn't be here."

"No, Bess, the Irish lost. O'Neill even offered Philip the throne of Ireland if he would come and fight, but by then Spain was broke, and what was left of his navy after the Armada had been sunk by the Dutch. However, in 1601 Philip did send an army over. They landed in the South where they weren't much use to O'Neill, who was based in the North. They captured the castle at Kinsale. The English besieged the castle. O'Neill's army marched there in bad conditions, and cut off the English army. The English troops were in bad shape, many suffering with dysentery, but they nevertheless won the Battle of Kinsale and the rebellion was in effect at an end."

I am puzzled. "But if the war went on for nine years, it couldn't have ended then."

"No, it didn't. It rumbled on for another few years, but the Irish did not stand much of a chance after that."

"He must have been a pretty good general, Thomas, if he could march his men all the way down Ireland and still be able to fight."

Thomas nods. "Yes, dear. The fact that he managed to get right to the South of the country with his army before being vanquished shows his rebellion almost succeeded, and what doughty fighters his people were. Still, Ireland became too hot to hold him and his allies, and they fled to Europe."

"But the ordinary people wouldn't be able to escape."

"No, Bess, the peasants always suffer. Ulster was leaderless, and King James's government saw the chance to plant new Protestant settlers all over it; almost all O'Neill's land and property was confiscated and sold to settlers. James was King of Scotland as well as England, so it was easy to get his Scots subjects to emigrate, and many did. Being mainly Presbyterian, their hatred of the Catholic Irish is even greater than the Anglicans, and that's bad enough."

I spend a few moments thinking about all this. "Now I understand this bad feeling between some of the servants. It isn't just praying to the Virgin, or whether the bread and wine really turn into flesh and blood at Communion. It's about loss of land and all the other things, and freedom."

Thomas. 2nd October, 1634. Dublin.

I had a very interesting talk with Bess yesterday. Let's be honest: I did most of the talking, and she mainly asked questions, some of them very astute; it helped straighten my thinking on a lot of the problems of this country and the different people who live here. Bess was right to observe at the end of it that many of the most important difficulties are really about land and power, and freedom. I need to bear that in mind in developing a plantation policy for the province of Connaught, and particularly County Galway. I must discuss it with Kit and Radcliffe, so I call them into my study.

In my usual fashion I do not beat about the bush. "The trouble I'll have with trying to plant or settle Galway will be quite different from the problems King James caused in Ulster, because Connaught is different from Ulster. The O'Neill war hardly touched Connaught, where the most powerful landowner was Richard de Burgh, Earl of Clanricarde."

Kit is quick. "He still is. He's an Old English Catholic, he is loyal to the Crown, and he fought for Queen Elizabeth and King James against O'Neill at the turn of the century. On top of that, there was an Elizabethan settlement, known as the Composition of Connaught, with the local landowners. As a result they believed, as Clanricarde still does, that their properties, including those in Galway, were safe from plantation and other exploitation."

George Radcliffe joins in. "The price of the Composition was the payment of 'rents' to the King, and these were about 3000 pounds a year when you took over as Deputy. Back in James's time, his advisers thought this income could be raised, that Protestants settled on land in Connaught would buy it or pay rent for it. At the same time the title of the Irish to their land could be investigated, and if found inadequate, they could be fined and their rents increased, meaning more cash for the King."

I find that a bit blunt, even for me. "That is what my policy would amount to, when all's said and done. It doesn't make me feel any better about it either."

George continues: "The Jacobean ministers' plans for Connaught caused great alarm in that province, and the Old English sent a petition to England around 1615 seeking more stability for landholders. This would have made planting Protestants there rather hard, since what the Petition asked for was the right to show only a 60 year title to their lands, and not a very old historic one."

I ask: "What happened to that? It sounds like the Graces."

"The Petition came to nought as James did not call Parliament for a very long time. Then in 1623, James sent his Commission to Ireland to reconsider the plantation policy. The Commissioners reported that planting Connaught wasn't worth the effort. First, the other plantations had caused so much trouble that they did not want to stir up any more. Secondly - and this is the really startling point - they said 'that works of that nature had been much perverted by the private aims of many particular persons to get large scopes of land into their hands only for their own profit, without any view to settling them for the strength and safety of the country'."

I cannot help a cynical chortle at that. "Well, that's hardly a surprise in a country where the Lord Chief Justice and Lord Chancellor have to be fired for corruption and worse."

Kit laughs too, and goes on: "Don't think the Commission was all that disturbed by the corruption they revealed; it was rife in all government activities. The 1623 Commission thought it would be a bad time to cause great aggravation to the Irish yet again. They didn't want another war. Oddly though, at the same time some of the Old English Catholics even approved of the plantations."

"One, the Earl of Westmeath, got a huge grant of land in the plantation of County Longford," George adds. "That land belonged to native Irish people, and in Galway and Longford the O'Farrells and the O'Rourkes had old feuds with the Earls of Clanricarde and Westmeath. Taking land from the Irish didn't worry the Earls, even the Catholic ones. It will be different if you touch theirs."

"I'm really grateful for the research you've done on this, George, and you, Kit. I know that in Galway Clanricarde is the biggest landowner, and he will not want his County planted. He expects to lose some of his own property if it happens. He knows what happened to O'Neill. He was lucky; Buckingham took us to war with Spain and France in the 1620s, and the last thing England wanted was hostile Irish and Old English on the West Irish Coast anxious to welcome invading armies from France or Spain."

"That's correct, Tom," Kit says. "Clanricarde's luck changed for the worse when Buckingham was assassinated in 1628 and peace broke out in 1629. Agitation to resume settlement of Protestants in Ireland started again. In April 1631 Boyle, the Earl of Cork, and his friends sent an embassy to England to push their plans forward."

"Yes, gentlemen, and now, two years later, I'm Deputy Lord Lieutenant of Ireland and this idea is being fostered by Boyle, inside the Irish Privy Council, which will put pressure on Charles's government in England. As I am the Deputy they cannot get far without my approval."

George looks puzzled. "Why would Boyle press for the plantation of Connaught, and of Galway in particular?"

"Because he is Johnny-Come-Lately New English Protestant, and Clanricarde is Old English Catholic. Of assistance to Boyle – and to me perhaps – is the fact that some Old English Catholic families side with the New English, hoping to do well out of this plantation policy themselves. I may be able to make considerable use of them in pursuing it."

In May 1632 the King and Privy Council in London gave me the job of implementing the plantations. This was very embarrassing, since I was still in England, and trying to get the Old English to agree to pay the 20,000 pound subsidy for the year. The last thing I needed was for them to be frightened off by threats to plant their land. The Earl of Westmeath, having secured plantations for himself already, came to London to lobby for the new plantations to be stopped. He saw the King, and the Secretaries of State, and he came to see me. That was in January 1633.

He was charming, and persuasive, and we got on well. However, he was not charming enough to get me to abandon the plantation policy when I had no first-hand experience of it, so I let him think that I did not agree with Lord Cork's policy, and that I should probably not follow it. He must have been satisfied with that, because it came back to me that he went about telling people his mission was successful.

I had no intention of doing anything about planting Connaught until I was in Ireland, had learned more about the land to be planted, and had called a successful Parliament. I did not want the Irish Parliament interfering in the policy. I warned the King that that is what could happen, but he nevertheless agreed that I should summon it. I was thinking success with settling the province could be worth 5,000 pounds a year to the King. It depended on the quality of the land and how much could be made available. But the whole thing would be impossible if Parliament confirmed into law the Graces, since one of them, number 25, would give the Catholics the 60 year title they wanted, and hardly any land would then be available for the settlers.

Am I going to involve myself in a great struggle with Clanricarde? Do I need such a struggle at the same time as I have made up my mind that I must rid myself of Mountnorris, and cope with the scheming of Boyle.

Christopher Wandesford. 2nd October, 1634. Dublin.

"You're becoming obsessed with Richard Boyle, Tom."

"That's true, Kit," George Wentworth says. "I'm not sure you should take him on like this, head to head. He's extremely rich, and extremely powerful. His influence reaches almost everywhere in this land."

Tom looks steely. "You think I don't know that, little ..."

George snaps. "Not little brother, Thomas, remember?"

"Sorry. If I can't reduce his power and influence I stand no chance of making any real progress with recovering land for the Church and the Crown – and particularly for the Church – from anyone else. Any sortie I make against lesser folk will be seen as likely to lead to an attack on Boyle and his properties, and he'll ally himself with them to oppose me."

I get information about Boyle all the time. "Tom, I hear that some time ago one of his tenants did away with himself. Now, I don't say that was Boyle's fault, but in view of what followed, it's not impossible that that's in fact the case. The widow of this unfortunate man had no right to take over the tenancy, so Boyle turned her out, took her cattle, and told his friends he was very generous to her because he did not seize her furniture as well."

Tom smacks a hand on the desk. His ink-well bounces. "You see! This is a man who, I'm told on good authority, goes to Church twice at least on Sundays. He lavishes money on his daughters, and gives them dress allowances far larger than the stipends he pays to the clergy in the parishes where he rents out the rectories. He's just a crook."

George laughs. "He may be a noble, but he doesn't know the meaning of the word."

"Right, George," I say. "Here's something else I've found out about him. Boyle has owned the College of Youghal for the last thirty years. He has robbed it of nearly all its properties and income. Somehow – and possibly not legally – this gives him power over the diocese of Lismore. So much power, it seems, that he even lives in the Bishop's palace. I found after some research in Parliamentary records that when in 1613, at the last Irish Parliament, Bishop Lancaster sought an Act to restore to his minute See land Boyle had stolen, Boyle had it thrown out."

Tom is impatient. "So what is happening in Lismore now?"

"Lismore is in far worse shape. The Earl of Cork had his relative Michael Boyle installed as Bishop of Lismore and Waterford a year before you came here as Deputy. And who was running the country then?"

"Cork and Mountnorris were, until the King decided I was to be his Deputy." Tom smiles. What's he got up his sleeve? I go on. "It doesn't stop there, either. Another member of this malign dynasty, rejoicing in the name of Michael Boyle, is Bishop of Cork, Cloyne and Ross. The Earl has misappropriated much of the wealth of all these Bishoprics as well as the College."

Suddenly Tom claps his hands, and stands up, pacing the room in his usual fashion. "Well now, I have to tell you both I have had an amazing stroke of luck. On top of all you tell me, I have a way to deal with Cork, or I should say, a man: that same Bishop, Michael Boyle. William Laud wrote to tell me recently that Michael had asked for help to restore the fortunes of his Diocese. He said the income of his Bishopric was about 900 pounds a year. Cork kept it all and allowed him only 50 pounds a year to live on and perform his Episcopal functions! Not only that, but the Earl was planning to take over the remains of the College of Youghal, and the last bit of its income that he hadn't already purloined."

I realise I've heard something about Michael Boyle before. "Didn't John Bramall tell us Michael was complaining about his poverty and that of his Cathedral and See generally? Laud knew Bishop Michael when they were at college."

"So he did, Kit. I asked John to persuade Michael to write a letter about all of this to Laud. What better way to start an anti-Cork crusade than on behalf of his own relative and to recover Church property for that Bishop? Today Cork was supposed to come before the Court of Castle Chamber on a summons I issued to him a little while ago. He was told he had to prove that he had the consent of the Warden and Fellows of the College of Youghal to take over the collection of their rents and tithes. He didn't turn up so I fined him 6 pounds for court costs. He'll be furious when he gets the order to pay!"

I look at George, then back at Tom. “Why didn’t George and I know about this?”

Tom looks contrite, an unusual attitude for him. “I should have told you, Kit, and I’m surprised Radcliffe didn’t tell you. He’s been dealing with this for me.”

George laughs, and takes the edge off my disappointment. “There’s too much going on for each of us to tell the others everything.”

The door opens, and Elizabeth looks in. “The servants have put lunch on the table. Come along, boys.” We all smile at each other, and as she goes, George says: “Boys, eh? You’d never guess we’re all about twenty years older than Bess, would you?” And we all laugh.

Thomas. 14th October, 1634. Dublin Castle.

This is not the first time Boyle has been hauled before the Court. I’ve had Radcliffe searching out titles to many of Boyle’s Church properties, and persuading the clergy to make representations to the Court; then I can take over. The first time this happened, the Reverend Beresford was induced – perhaps bullied would be a better word – to seek from Castle Chamber an order for some of the land taken from his Parish to be restored to it. The poor man was terrified. His hair was unkempt, as were his clothes, which looked none too clean. Believing that his stipend was less than adequate was not difficult. How a man who appeared so timid in Court could bring himself to preach I have no idea. Maybe his Church was rarely full.

Perhaps when the hearing started I spoke to him a bit too loudly and aggressively, for he passed out in the witness box. When he came round and had had a drink of water he said: “My Lord Deputy, I beg you to let my evidence be taken in private.”

I think he was terrified of what Cork would do to him after the trial. “Mr Beresford, if I hear this matter in private you - and others - may say they have ground to clamour against me for anything done in secret. You will proceed now.”

And he did. Judgment was given for him, just as I had desired. About the same time, I succeeded in getting that awful tomb Boyle had had built behind the altar in the Cathedral removed and re-erected just inside the main doors. I’m told he was furious about that as it had cost him over 1,000 pounds, apart from the slight he felt had been administered to his late wife. But even though she had borne him 14 children, he could hardly expect an altar dedicated to Christ to be rededicated to her.

As for the College, Boyle arranged for two very able Irish Catholic lawyers, Darcy and Martin, to represent him in Court. He tried trickier tactics, too. He wrote to friends in high places in England; he asked them to persuade the King that the case should be heard there, not here in Dublin. I wrote to the King protesting at this request, since, after all, he had promised me that cases about Ireland would not be removed from my Courts, unless there were obvious miscarriages of justice. Clearly there could be no injustice before a case had been heard, and the King refused to gratify Cork or his friends.

Boyle's other trick was to have one of his friends invite me to dinner. When I arrived I found that Boyle was also a guest, and he had brought my old friend Henry, Lord Clifford, too. It became clear during the meal that Boyle hoped Henry's presence would make me withdraw the case about the College. Cork intended it as part of the marriage settlement on his son Lord Dungarvan and Henry's daughter, my niece, Elizabeth. I had a very enjoyable evening apart from that, and let no-one know how I felt about this blatant attempt to use some sort of undue influence upon me.

I was outraged, and if anything, had my resolve to win Youghal back for the Church from Boyle been only an iron one, this event turned it into hardened steel of the finest quality. One might think that when even Old English magnates like the Earl of Clanricarde had more or less voluntarily given back similar lands they had obtained, Cork might have seen the sense of doing likewise, but not he.

I shall now press on with this case with all the vigour I can muster, and get George Radcliffe to prepare every possible answer to every possible argument or question Boyle and Darcy can dream up.

Let's make no bones about it: my job is to turn Ireland into a proper English colony, with English laws for everything including land ownership. I'm not keen on the native Irish because of what I have seen of the way they live and the fact that they are Catholic, but I do not hate them for that. I feel sorry for them. If they learn English ways of farming and working they would be better off and happier, much less superstitious and less likely to bow down to the Priests and Jesuits who, it seems to me, have the power to stop people thinking at all.

It is an important part of my job to have land set aside for plantation of Protestant settlers, and make the rest of the land more secure for all the rest of the inhabitants, whether they're Gaelic Irish, noble Irish, Old English, or New English and Scots.

This means that, while I may have to be pretty harsh in the way I deal with some big landowners such as Cork and Clanricarde over Church and Crown land, I am just as much concerned to give justice to all the small ones. That means letting some of the rich and powerful ones feel the rough edge of justice sometimes. One of these is Lord Balfour. He's an expert at finding loopholes in some poor fellow's title and making a profit out of exploiting it, and making him pay for it, or just taking his land away from him. He's the nasty piece of work I kicked out of the Privy Council almost as soon as I arrived in Dublin. He was fined 200 pounds for the abortive rebellion he'd planned.

I have to take serious action against Mountnorris, too, but I'll deal with him later. The most powerful person I had to rebuke over this sort of thing is no less a man than the Earl Marshall of England, the head of the King's Army, such as it is. He's Thomas Howard, Earl of Arundel. Philip Mainwaring tells me Arundel has two full-time agents in Ireland whose only function is to trawl the countryside looking for dodgy titles so that he can buy and sell, bully and extort, and make a fortune to add to the colossal riches he already has. After all, the Howards are, and have for ages been, one of the richest and most powerful families in England.

I wrote to him pretty severely; "I judge it in no way honourable in your Lordship to hunt at random all over the province of Leinster, searching and prying for extremely obscure legal problems to give you advantage in turning the ancient owners out of their estates, and separating these subjects from the princely protection and grace of His Majesty." This letter had the desired effect, and Arundel caused less trouble on the land front. Arundel had been well-disposed to me on the King's Council in England; now he may be anything but a friend.

Another offender had stolen Crown land, and having done so sold it to small people who knew nothing of his crimes. Through my prerogative Courts I am forcing his victims to give the land back to the King, but I also force the thief to pay back to them the money of which he had fraudulently relieved them.

What of my policy for the plantations? Well, I definitely don't want absentee landlords in England owning large bits of Ireland, taking the rents out, and doing nothing for the country. I want industrious settlers, mainly on smallish plots, who will live and work there, employ local people, help civilise the country, make money, pay taxes, and help run the place. As I see it, the more land you give to one rich man, the less he does with it.

As I say, I intend to make Ireland more English.

Thomas. 30th October, 1634. Dublin Castle.

I've learned what it must be like to be a King. You might think that after ruling Ireland for a year I should know that already. Contrary to popular belief you cannot do exactly as you wish. Nearly all the time you have to do what is expected of you.

Two weeks ago, on the 17th, I'm sitting on my horse on the parade ground watching my troops marching and carrying out manoeuvres I had planned with some of the officers. It is three o'clock in the afternoon, and the parade is to go on for at least another hour. Suddenly I see out of the corner of my eye a colonel riding towards me. He is not exactly cantering, but the horse is going as fast as the dignity of the parade and the circumstances will decently permit. I am annoyed. His advent is not in the schedule for the afternoon. I am about to blast the man, when I realise he must want something pretty important, since everyone knows that I like the parades to go strictly according to the timetable.

He brings his steed parallel to mine and salutes, and takes off his hat. His face is ashen and grave. Is it for fear of me or of what he has to tell me? "Yes, Colonel!"

"My Lord, I hardly know how to begin." He is almost stammering.

""Then just begin, Colonel, as best you can. We don't want to spoil the parade, do we?"

"No, My Lord." He pauses. "My Lord, I have the most dreadful news." He pauses again. I could hit him, but I don't. "Come along man. My sword is still in its scabbard. What are you afraid of?"

"My Lord, I fear to tell you that your son is dead, and the servants say Lady Wentworth is distraught, and has fainted away, and they cannot wake her."

They cannot wake her? Is she dying too? I feel panic rising. I keep it at bay. As calmly as I can I ask: "Which son? William or little Thomas?"

"I believe it is little Thomas, My Lord."

I want to shout. I want to call on God and ask how He could do this. I sit still, keeping my horse still too. If I do not show self-discipline to my soldiers and officers I cannot expect them to display it themselves. I believe order comes from the top. It is my theory of government and the Monarchy, and it is how I try to run my life. Anything else leads to anarchy. I'm sure my face must be as ashen as the colonel's was when he rode up. "How did you find out?"

"Your steward had the sense to come here as fast as he could himself. He sent no-one else as he wanted no chance of any misunderstanding."

I nod. I cannot speak another word. I dare not ride off the field in sight of all the men. For another hour I sit there in a fog of memories of this lost baby, watching men march and manoeuvre, trot, gallop, and wheel about, but I see nothing. I think of his sweet face and cheeks that turned into little apples pretty quickly at Bess's breast, and of her joy at having had him, and mine at having had both of them. I recall, with some guilt now, but with considerable pride ten days ago, how I wrote to the King asking him for an Earldom, confident he would grant it now I have two sons. I ponder the likelihood, now little Thomas is dead, that my hopes of an Earldom are dead likewise. I am ashamed of thinking that.

I tell the colonel to dismiss the men as soon as I depart. I address the men and officers briefly to tell them what a splendid parade it was. I turn my horse and gallop as fast as it will go to the Castle.

That was two weeks ago, a time which I have spent in vigil as much as on official duties and audiences will permit. I have spent so much time by Elizabeth's bed or chair (if she has been compus mentis enough to get up) it reminds me of nursing Margaret before her untimely death.

Today is the first time for a fortnight that I have my lovely Elizabeth back. A doctor comes to tell us that he knows of no reason why little Tom ('my young Irishman', I called him) should have died. I have, of course, had him explain that to me before, but I wanted him to tell Elizabeth, so that she can ask any questions she may have. The most important thing he does is tell her that she was in no way to blame, and that it must have been God's will. That can be a difficult concept to swallow, but Elizabeth's faith is secure, and she understands. She reminds me that there is little point in praying, as Christ instructed us to do, that "Thy will be done," if in fact we want Him to do ours. She is calm, and tells me and the doctor that she knows there is only one cure: we shall have to beget another child as soon as she is recovered from her ordeal.

She is wonderful. Her resolve and serenity put me right, too.

Elizabeth. 30th October, 1634. Dublin Castle.

Last month I had the most painful times of my life so far, in two respects. First, I gave birth to our first child, a little boy whom we called Thomas. Childbirth is no joke. I think he was the consequence of that first really passionate night with Thomas last November. I don't mean I conceived that night, but as that was the first of many such nights I can be pretty sure he started on his way not long after that. Anyway, the screams of passion Thomas says I uttered then were as nothing to those I yelled as little Thomas emerged. They weren't passion, they were just pure pain.

I didn't mind once I held him and the nurse gave him to me to put to my bosom. It all seemed worth it, and he suckled contentedly, and with no difficulty, which the nurse said is not common the first time a baby tries the nipple. He looked healthy, and cried lustily when he felt like it, and Thomas came in and loved him from the start and said he loved me more than ever. The pain was worth all that.

The second painful time, which was not worth it, came about four weeks later. It seems little Thomas was not really healthy at all, because he died. I went in to the nursery to get him from his cradle, and when I picked him up to feed him, he was quite limp and cold. I was so shocked at first I made not a sound. I just stood there. I stared at his sweet small face. I picked him up and held his tiny cheek to mine, but he was clearly not breathing, and then I ran from the room, and screamed even louder than when pushing him into the world.

Servants appeared from everywhere, but I wanted my husband, and he was away on business, inspecting the army or something, which at that moment seemed so terribly trivial. I was led into our bedroom, and made to lie down. Someone tried to take the baby away, but I would not let go, and told them to leave me alone. I do not know what happened then; I think I must have fainted.

Today is the first time I have really known what is going on for what I am told is a fortnight.

Christopher Wandesford. 17th November, 1634. Dublin.

The second session of this Parliament started two weeks ago. Two days later there was an excited atmosphere as Tom was expected to announce his intentions in respect of the Graces. Indications were that the Old English and Irish Catholics were fairly convinced they were going to get the 60 year titles they wanted from the new Commission on Defective Titles. This was a bit strange, since Thomas had been very vague about what he was going to do about them, if anything, and the Commission had power to confirm titles, or reject them if the evidence did not stand up.

Thomas's intent, as he explained it to me, was to make as many owners as possible hold their land direct from the King. This would indeed make them secure, but they would have to pay all the fees and fines such ownership entails. When an owner dies, his estate falls into the hands of the Court of Wards until an application is made to the Court and all fees paid. The revenue from that Court always puts money **into** the Irish Treasury, and if Thomas succeeded it would do better still. And it would be the Old English and the Irish who would have the most trouble with titles and end up paying the most.

After two weeks of getting none of what they wanted, they were very frustrated, and showed it in a rather eccentric fashion. Today a government Bill to outlaw bigamy and do other things to give Ireland a higher moral tone was put before the Commons. It was thrown out by 78 votes to 69. It wouldn't have happened if all MPs who are government supporters had been there to vote, but they were poorly organised. Nevertheless, it was a demonstration by the Catholics that they had some power, and it made manifest their ire at not getting the Graces they wanted. It was, of course, rank hypocrisy on their part, since they are supposed to be firmer believers in Hell and the likelihood of going there than we Protestants, so one might think they would be in favour of wiping out sins like bigamy.

George Radcliffe. 28th November, 1634. Dublin Castle.

Thomas calls “Come in” when I knock at the door of his study.

“I have more information about the Loftuses and the Metcalf estate. I think we have enough evidence to take action against Sir Edward, but although Lord Loftus will be implicated, I doubt that he could be convicted of anything unless Edward gives evidence against him.”

“Seen any flying pigs lately, George?” He gestures for me to sit. “There’s no chance of that happening either. Edward’s not his favourite son for nothing. Anyway, I think it would be dangerous to tackle the Lord Chancellor at the moment. It’s clear we shall have to deal with Mountnorris and Lord Cork severely in due course ...”

“And even you daren’t make too many powerful enemies at once,” I offer.

“Quite right. In any case, Loftus isn’t opposing me in what I’m trying to do yet, but I can’t be sure that’s how he’ll always be towards me. On the other hand, I don’t want to get a reputation for tolerating a corrupt Chancellor at the head of the judiciary in Ireland. We’ll just have to go on looking for evidence and unearthing witnesses.” Thomas thinks for a moment. “Should we move against Sir Edward yet, do you think?”

“His son? I don’t see why not. We have the evidence, and taking action against him might send a warning shot across his father’s bows. He might be a little less greedy if he thinks we might go for him too. Shall I draw up the charges? We can allege Edward obtained the administration by fraud, and helped himself to costs and fees he wasn’t entitled to. I’m pretty sure we can prove that he sold some land for the going price on the market, put only a fraction of the money into the Metcalf accounts, and pocketed the rest.”

“Fine, draw up the indictment. Keep it quiet until you’re quite ready to go ahead.”

“There’s something else, Thomas. I could hardly believe it when I was told. It seems that in at least one case Lord Loftus not only took a lot of bribes from a litigant before giving judgment for him. He also told the man that unless he signed a statement saying that no bribes had been asked for or given, he’d give judgment for the other side!”

Thomas sits back in his chair, puts his quill down, and looks as shocked and incredulous as I did when I heard this tale. “George, this is a man of whom we must be very careful. We cannot afford to attack him until we can be certain of winning. That story ties in with something I heard before we came here. It seems that when Lord Falkland was the Deputy here, he fell out with Loftus, and tried to report his corrupt ways. Loftus went to England, told the King some cock-and-bull story about it all being Falkland's fault, got a lot of help from Mountnorris, and it was Falkland who was recalled, and guess what? The King gave Loftus the job, with Boyle, of running Ireland while he made up his mind who the new Deputy should be."

Thomas. 1st December, 1634. Dublin.

At the meeting of the Irish Privy Councillors today I tore into them about the failure of the government supporters to get all the Protestant MPs into the House to vote on the Graces. I just hope this will have the desired effect and that there will be a substantial majority when the Graces and the government's other Bills come back before Parliament in the next few days.

I can do with a bit of luck with this, because I now have a problem back in Yorkshire, and I can do without fights on two fronts at once. Osborne tells me that my old 'friend' Sir Arthur Ingram has been trying to get his hands on the recusancy fines for the county. How dare he? He knows I am the farmer of these fines, and profit from my commission on the collection of them before they go to the Treasury. We are having the most awful row in letters sailing back and forth across from Dublin to Chester and on to his mansion at Temple Newsome.

I have to do something about the customs farm here, too. It makes not nearly enough money for the King, and Ingram is one of the farmers. Well, we shall see.

Christopher Wandesford. 13th December, 1634. Dublin.

I have had a very successful day to today, and Thomas is very pleased. In fact the last ten days or so of the sitting of the House have gone well. The telling off Thomas gave the Privy Council seems to have worked, and large numbers of government MPs have been turning up regularly. All the government Bills are now Acts of Parliament, including the Bigamy Bill, and above all, the legislation on the Graces. Thomas has, as usual, got what he wants, but how much bitterness may have been stirred up for later is difficult to know. Certainly the fact that the Catholics voted against almost everything, even if unsuccessfully, shows that they are unhappy.

Thomas. 15th December, 1634. Dublin Castle.

There is much rejoicing in the ports of Ireland this week. My intrepid knighted captain and other commanders have finally raided, and raided very successfully, the pirate base on the Isle of Man. There were four naval vessels and they attacked what amounted to a castle on a creek. In turn they were attacked by seven pirate ships, but fortunately the naval ships were in better repair, better armed with heavier cannon, and manned by better trained sailors. One pirate fled but the others were sunk, and the marines overran the castle.

I pardoned many of the more lowly pirates provided they agreed to serve three years in the navy. Those who refused were sent as slaves to colonies in America. I have sent their women there too. The pirate 'captains' and their 'officers' (ranks these criminals do not deserve) numbered about thirty-five. I shall have twenty of them tried in the Court of Castle Chamber, and the rest I've sent to England to enjoy such justice and mercy as the King may afford them.

As for those to be tried here, I cannot conceive that any can mount a successful defence, and sentences of hanging will surely follow. I have taken the liberty of sending a message to the King with his share of the prisoners, urging him to sentence to death all who are found guilty, but confining the actual executions to those of the pirates who are his subjects. Any foreigners amongst them should be released to return to their homelands, to avoid any diplomatic problems with other governments. With luck they will have been so chastened by the threat of an earlier than expected meeting with their Maker that they will consider carefully whether to risk piracy around Ireland again.

I'm sure that the disappearance of pirates from these waters will bring a boost to Irish trade which could not otherwise have been foretold. Exports and imports will be safer. More merchants will take their chances. Customs duties will rise accordingly, and balancing the budget and making more revenue available for the King will be that much easier.

I have adjourned Parliament for Christmas.

Thomas. 14th January, 1635. Dublin Castle.

Have I found a true ally? I believe so. Today he came to the Privy Council of Ireland and was sworn in as a member. He is almost certainly the youngest in this august gathering; he is only twenty-four. He is tall and extremely good-looking – so Elizabeth tells me - but I can in fact see it for myself. He is forthright, well-educated, and literally has all the knightly virtues. I am sure King Arthur would have had him ornament the Round Table.

He is James Butler, Earl of Ormonde. He is unusual, too, because he is Old English, and his family were always Roman Catholic, but his father died when he was young, so he became a ward of the King, and was brought up by Archbishop Abbott in the Protestant Church, which is his faith. He is also a man of considerable courage. I was aware of his existence before I even came to Ireland, because Mountnorris had told me about him, as one of the wealthiest and most powerful of the Old English.

What is unusual is that because of Catholic family on one side and Protestant religion on the other, he has a foot in both the important camps in the country. I first came across him at the opening of Parliament in July. I met him at dinner the evening of my opening speech. He had the temerity to tell me that it was wrong of me to refer to Ireland as a "conquered nation." We discussed this – perhaps argued would be a better word – for a short while but neither of us were prepared to spoil the evening after what had on the whole been a good day.

A day or two later he annoyed me again, though not directly. When Parliament met I gave a direction that no-one was to wear a sword in the House. James Butler turned up wearing his. A Parliamentary servant reminded him of my order and told him to remove his sword. Butler then said, I was told: "I am entitled to wear this sword anywhere at any time, and if you try to take it from me it will end up in your guts!"

A few days later he came before the Privy Council to answer the charge that he had disobeyed my order. He was completely unapologetic, and far from humbled either by me or the rest of the Council. When the charge was put to him he threw a document on the table. "That is the Royal Patent from King Charles making me a Knight of the Sword, an honour which entitles me to wear the weapon anywhere and at any time. I do not take it off at the request or order of any man."

There was no arguing with that! Far from getting any apology from him, he got one from me. That was not an experience to which I was very accustomed. I made the best of it at the time, but I was very angry, and consulted George Radcliffe how I could deal with this young blade. I wanted to humiliate or punish him.

"That won't work, Thomas. Ormonde's too rich, too clever, and too honest. I doubt that we could find anything about him that would bring him low." That was not what I wanted to hear at all.

"I'm not going to leave things as they are, George. The authority of the Deputy is at stake."

"I agree, but you won't assert it by picking the wrong fight with the wrong man. Be his friend; make him your friend. At your side his power and influence will be invaluable; against you he can be more like a spear than a thorn in your side. He's very intelligent, from what I can make out. You need his brains working for you."

"I'll think about it."

"And I'll try to find out more about him. I've heard that he's in favour of the plantation of the country to make it more prosperous. Now you'd find that useful, wouldn't you?"

George was right. He found out nothing to his discredit, and today Ormonde has come to see me with some unpleasant news about the son of the Irish Lord Chancellor. "There's some tittle-tattle going about that Sir Edward Loftus is going to be prosecuted over the maladministration of some estate or other. Is it true?"

"Yes. George Radcliffe has been drawing up the indictment. Sir Edward will probably be arrested soon."

James Butler nods. "That explains it then. There isn't much goes on in any legal office, judicial or professional, that his father doesn't get to know. He must have spies and informants everywhere."

"Sorry; I don't understand. What explains what?"

"Why Sir Edward left the country for England last night. Someone from Radcliffe's office must have talked to someone in the Lord Chancellor's chambers, or maybe someone just helped themselves to a document or two."

I am furious and speechless. I'm often furious; rarely speechless. Eventually I say that this is dreadful, using some expressive adjectives. "How do you know?"

"I happened to be down at the docks, as I was expecting some rather expensive new furniture – splendid oak chairs and a dining table – and I wanted to see them safely unloaded. As I stood there Sir Edward came running down the dock from a carriage, hurried up the gang-plank onto the next ship along the harbour wall, shouted hello and goodbye to me as he went past, and with that the sails were unfurled, the ropes were cast off, and away she went."

"And she was bound for England?"

"That's what the crew of my ship – well, I mean the ship with my furniture on it – told me, yes."

"Well I'm damned. Wait 'til George hears this! He'll be so disappointed after all the work he's done. I'm grateful to you for telling me, Ormonde."

"Can I do anything?"

"You could write to any of your powerful friends in London and ask them to tell him to come back and face the Court."

"Is he likely to?"

That makes me chuckle. "A man of honour would. But then is he one?"

"What will you do?"

"I'll write to Coke, the Secretary of State, and ask him to send him back."

Christopher Wandesford. 26th January, 1635. Dublin.

Parliament meets again today following the Christmas adjournment. It is going to be a busy session, and could be difficult. Tom has a new plan for apportioning the liability to pay the subsidies amongst the counties. There doesn't seem to have been much method in the way it's been done in the past, and certainly no fairness. The rich have usually got away with paying little, but forcing their tenants to pay, and the wealthier areas and counties have used their influence to place much of the burden on the poorer places. Tom will have none of that. His plan is to make the richer areas carry the burden, and for the richer men to find the money, not the poor people. He says that Lord

Cork has only paid about two pounds a year towards the subsidies, leaving his tenants to pay more than their fair share.

I can't see Cork and his ilk being happy about that being changed to their disadvantage. I can see that a lot of the Old English will be hit pretty hard by this, too. On the other hand, I suppose it won't make much difference to men like Tom's new friend Lord Ormonde. If he's as honest and fair as they say, he probably pays his fair share already. But I bet there aren't many like him; the others will be after Tom's blood in due course, even if they don't make much of a stink about it in this Parliament.

Thomas. 30th January, 1635. Dublin.

Sometimes my efforts to reform the Church here seem as problematic as Christ's attempts to reform the scribes and Pharisees and Chief Priests. Not, I hasten to add, that I put myself in His class.

To say that a battle has been going on is to put it mildly, but at least no blood has been shed. It started, I suppose, when I appointed a new Provost to govern Trinity College here in Dublin. William Laud told me that it was a teaching instrument for Puritan points of view. He wanted me to stop it being 'as ill governed as any in Christendom', and turn it into a good seminary for the Church in Ireland. So I got rid of Robert Ussher, a member of Bishop Ussher's family, and put in his place a man called Chappell, a Laudian priest. William himself became the College Chancellor. I suppose that's pretty pointless with him being about three hundred miles away and across the Irish Sea in Canterbury or London, but then a lot of political style appointments look that way.

The next thing that needed tackling was the doctrine of the Church. The Articles of Faith from 1615, on which Bishop Ussher had had a strong Puritan influence, were quite acceptable to the Calvinists. Laud wants me to impose the English 39 Articles, which are a trifle ambiguous so that neither Puritans nor Laudians and Arminians are excluded, but Laud wants his Arminian High Church ways to be paramount.

That's what I have been doing for the last few days. Convocation was summoned to sit at the same time as Parliament, and the main item of business was the introduction of the 39 Articles. I did not make the mistake of leaving the clerics to run the show themselves. Bishop

John Bramhall represents me in the Upper House of Convocation, and my new Chaplain speaks for me in the Lower. I was making sure I got what I wanted in Parliament. I needed strong, reliable men controlling Church deliberations to make sure they went my way too.

On top of the Articles Laud also wants some other items of Canon Law imposed in Ireland which were the work of old Archbishop Bancroft in 1604. These laws leave no-one in any doubt: Puritan worship is not welcome. You could say that putting these in place in the Irish Church really threw down the gauntlet to men like Archbishop Ussher, so some degree of opposition in Convocation was only to be expected. Although I was well-prepared for this, it came as a bit of a surprise that it was the Dean of Limerick, who was its rabble-rouser. You'd have thought that as I had just recently appointed Webb to be his Bishop he'd have seen the way the wind blew, and trimmed his sails to meet it more favourably. He started, as chairman of a committee, to get a debate going on which of the 39 Articles they would accept. If he thought I would compromise over this, he had another think coming. At the same time he proposed that if any of the Church of Ireland priests did not swear to uphold the old 1615 Articles, they should be excommunicated. Did he think he was the Pope?

"You're not fit to be Dean of Limerick," I told him. "As Chairman of that committee you're more like Ananias than a Protestant priest. Where did you think you were? At a Dutch Calvinist Fraternity?"

So today I am at the Convocation myself to make it clear to this assembly that I shall tolerate no nonsense. "There will be no more of this revolutionary Puritan and Calvinist talk here. As you know I have the power, granted by the King, to appoint such Bishops and priests as are acceptable to him. I shall make use of that power to ensure that this Church of Ireland runs in a seemly and Godly fashion. I urge you most strongly not to believe that you can cross me or the King in these matters."

There is no more trouble. Few priests have a saintly urge for martyrdom. I can't see many of them laying down their livings for their beliefs and principles, let alone their lives. They pass the Articles as required, but I let them get away with removing the requirement to bow at the name of Jesus. I insist on retaining kneeling to receive communion as Laud sets so much store by it, but I tell him that "these Puritans have no more joints in their knees for that than an elephant."

I wish things had gone this well in Parliament the last few days. After the trouble with the Bigamy Bill being rejected, the Parliament wanted to take unto itself powers to try an English settler who had written some pretty silly things about almost everyone in Ireland, and had distributed it to all sorts of people. Some rather hot-headed MPs were all for executing him, but there had been enough trouble in England over Parliament's claims to administer justice and hear cases, and I was having none of it, so I told the man off and left it at that.

Then yesterday I pronounced my findings on which of the Graces would be passed into law, and which would not. It was a very unpleasant experience. Once again a lot of government supporters stayed away, and there was a considerable protest. I announced that ten Graces should become law, and binding. The remainder, apart from two, would continue in force but it would be entirely up to me how they operated and how long they would last.

The two Graces which would not be enacted were the ones which would provide secure 60 year titles. When I announced this there was almost uproar, and an MP shouted out: "He's going to put plantations into Connaught. We'll lose our land altogether!"

One of the Graces over which I retain discretion is the one under which I could allow Roman Catholics to hold government jobs, and practise at the Bar, if they took the Oath of Allegiance to the King. However, I have the power to make them take the Oath of Supremacy, agreeing that the King is Head of the Church, and if they're strict Catholics, they would refuse. Then they would lose their jobs or be banned from appearing in Court. There was uproar, and none of the business could be got through.

George Radcliffe. 20th March, 1635. Dublin.

Today the case about the College of Youghal against Richard Boyle, Earl of Cork, is called before the Court of Castle Chamber. I have been doing all the research on this matter, with a lot of help from Kit, and a lot of ideas from Thomas. Boyle is represented by Patrick Darcy and Richard Martin, two very able Irish lawyers, and curiously, both Catholics, which makes them a very strange choice for Boyle, who in the normal course of events, has no time or tolerance for what he calls "spawn of the Pope."

It is their brilliance which recommends them to him. I am, of course their rival, and their opponent in this case, but I should be a fool indeed if I did not acknowledge that they are worthy adversaries. It is a commonplace saying that the Irish are thick, but when you see men with such fine brains and ability, the idiocy of it is patent. Darcy is a few years younger than me. I found out he studied law at the Middle Temple at the same time Thomas was at the Inner Temple. He's in the Irish House of Commons as MP for Navan. He's tall and almost skinny, with dark red hair of the Celts. Richard Martyn is his cousin on his mother's side, but he is shorter, with thick black hair. He looks about the same age.

Thomas is one of the Judges, because this is a prerogative Court, not an ordinary Court of Justice. It takes me a couple of hours to outline the basic facts of the case to the Judges and to draw their attention to the most important documents. I put it to them that the question Cork has to answer is whether he can prove that he had the consent of the authorities of the College to take over their lands, their Churches, their livings, and their income. It is, on the face of it, a simple question, but there are many deeds and documents to be examined that I know of, and Boyle will undoubtedly have many more.

One Judge asks Boyle out of the blue to explain his possession of the College. Quite seriously Boyle answers: "There's nothing unusual about it. I have done nothing that is not a common custom in Ireland." Quite a few people laugh at that, and an Irish voice shouts out: "Stealing is a common custom in Ireland then," and there is more laughter, but Boyle clearly does not see the joke.

Another member of the Court tells him point blank that that was a feeble response, to which Boyle replies arrogantly and almost proudly: "My seizure of Church land is only unlawful if you take into account an Act of State formulated and pronounced by a long dead Deputy which has never been confirmed by Parliament."

If he has any more to say, he doesn't get the chance, for Thomas intervenes immediately in his most magisterial and authoritative fashion. "Great as you are, My Lord, I will make you and all the subjects of Ireland know that any Act of State, made or to be made, shall be as binding on you and the subjects of Ireland during my government as any Act of Parliament."

Darcy then rises to ask the Court for time to prepare Boyle's defence, examine the documents I have produced, find and obtain proofs of evidence from witnesses, estate managers and the like, provide me with copies of their documents, and generally get ready for the trial. After hearing from me, the Court adjourns the case to October, when the Autumn Term starts.

Thomas. 23rd March, 1635. Dublin Castle.

I have just heard that something rather serious has happened in London. The King has been having problems with the Corporation of the City of London. Powerful people are involved. You don't get much more powerful than the Corporation of London. The money made in the city – just a square mile – means that it is one of the richest financial centres. You upset it at your peril.

What was the story behind this problem? When Ulster was being planted in the reigns of Elizabeth and James, a huge area of land there was leased to the Corporation of London. This land was mainly in Derry and Coleraine, and the rent it had to pay was tiny. The lease provided for the Corporation to build fortifications and guard the coast-line, and farm the land. It then let the land to agents who were supposed to carry out these duties for it, but the relevant covenants were ignored, and very little was done to comply with them.

There was, however, an honest man with an interest in all this, and in the plantation of the area. He had made complaints to all the authorities, could not get anyone to take any action, but did not give up. He was Sir Thomas Phillips. About the same time as I was appointed Deputy he managed at last to get the English Privy Council to take his information seriously, and the Council started an inquiry. It has been going on for two or three years, and it came to a head early this month.

I do not seek to hide the fact that I was in favour of the matter being looked into, and pursued, and of action being taken to put matters right. My opinion was that whilst the King and the Council should make the City do its duty under its lease, it would be foolish to be too drastic in seeking remedies, or worse, punishing this body hard. As a Privy Councillor myself what I advised the Council to do was make sure that the Corporation and the tenants paid their rents, that the rents were more profitable, that the land was cultivated to yield more income, and that the ports in the possession of the City produced more customs duties.

When the inquiry finished, the Privy Council found the case proven and ordered the Corporation to pay a fine of 70,000 pounds. That is a huge amount of money, even for the City to find. The Corporation was also told that if it didn't comply with the other duties about forts and guards along the coast, its land grant would be forfeit, and that is what has just happened: the King and his Council have taken away the Corporation's land.

I fear that at some time in the future the City will find a way to take its revenge. They would be a powerful enemy. They might see me as the man in charge here at the time.

Christopher Wandesford. 28th March, 1635. Dublin.

Today Tom calls me and the two Georges in to confer with him about something serious. He says he has just heard that Richard Weston, Lord Portland, the King's Treasurer in England, has died. "Only a few weeks ago somebody wrote and asked me to be the next Treasurer if the chance arose. Now Cottington, Chancellor of the Exchequer, has put it to me as well, and so has the Earl of Newcastle."

Radcliffe is quick off the mark. "It's a great honour and a huge step up, but the choice is the King's."

I refrain from observing that the last bit is otiose. Instead I say: "But is it safe, Tom? You've always said you're not sure you can trust Cottington although he always writes to you in such a friendly way. And you definitely didn't trust Weston. You used to think they suggested to the King that he should send you here to get you out of their way."

"Quite; and I have never seen any reason to think otherwise since. I'm pretty sure Cottington really wants the job himself, and Laud is of the same opinion."

Little George – I really shouldn't call him that - he is 26, after all - contributes. "Well, he - Cottington - was friendly enough when I saw him in London last year."

"That's how he always is, George; it doesn't mean a thing." Tom's smile shows that he is not being dismissive, but George can be a bit naïve sometimes.

I see we have strayed from my point. "But as I put it just now, is it safe? You've got a wonderfully powerful post here, where you're pretty well a King, so how could you be better off in England?"

"You may be right, Kit. It won't be just me and Cottington vying with each other for this Treasurership. Lots of other hats will be thrown in the ring."

Radcliffe says: "Three years ago you wanted to be Treasurer yourself."

"So I did, but that was then. And I wasn't Lord Deputy here then. I don't have to deal with anyone scheming to take this job away from me. I know a lot of men, like Cork and Clanricarde, would love it if I lost it, but as far as anyone can tell no-one else wants it. And I'm enjoying doing it. If I go to England to campaign to be Treasurer, all my work here may be undone. I'll be in a whirlpool of calculating people all trying to do me down or get some benefit out of backing me, and I don't need that."

"It's not an easy job here, though, Thomas."

"No, brother George, it's not, but it is a great challenge, and I enjoy meeting it. Trying to balance the King's books in London would be no fun. So what do you think, Radcliffe?"

"Weighing up what you say, I think you should stay here. That's pretty clearly what you want to do, isn't it?"

"And you, George?"

"I agree with Radcliffe, but I'd do whatever you want anyway, as you know."

"Kit?"

"You've got enemies there, Thomas. Certainly you're finding enemies here, but you seem to be beating those, and you cannot be sure what will happen in England, where the King's in charge. In Ireland there's no-one to over-rule you, and the King does take your advice most of the time. He might not do so if you go over there."

"Well, thank you gentlemen. I have had the advice I hoped to hear, so I shall make it plain that I am not in the running. Two Georges, you can go. Kit, I want you to take a letter down. You can help polish it up later."

Young George and Radcliffe leave the room. I get paper, quill and ink, and take this down to go to the Archbishop:

Your Grace,

You may be aware that there are moves afoot to have me replace the late Lord Portland as Treasurer. I have considered this very carefully, and I acknowledge that it is flattering that I should be thought suitable for the position. Nevertheless I prefer to remain where I am. I have written to Cottington asking him to make sure my appointment is not secured, and I have told Newcastle that I shall not come to England until someone else has been given the job.

You may make it known to all of those who wish to see me in that post that I do not serve the King out of the ordinary ends that the servants of great princes seek. I am far from poor, and great wealth I covet not. Greater powers than those already entrusted to me by His Majesty I do not desire; I should rather have greater ability to discharge those I have than to have more powers still.

Again, I serve not for reward, having received from the King much more than I shall ever be able to deserve.

You may make such use of this letter as you see fit in order to fulfil the duty it asks you to undertake.

I am your friend and obedient servant,

Wentworth.

Later, in my rooms, I reread this epistle. It needs no improvement, but I cannot help a chuckle at the passage about coveting wealth; sometimes Tom can be almost delusional in what he thinks about himself. Even so, I think he is truthful when he says that is not why he serves. He really does want to do good and govern well. Whether that is what he is actually doing is another matter, but at least he's trying to do it. And great wealth just happens to come too.

George Radcliffe. 9th April, 1635. Dublin Castle.

Any hope that Thomas could come to any amicable arrangement with Annesley – Mountnorris – is surely ended now. A couple of weeks ago at one of the Deputy's Army reviews, Annesley's younger brother made a derogatory remark about Thomas to a fellow officer, and followed it up with a rude gesture. When Thomas insisted he apologise, this whelp swore at him, and refused, so Thomas struck him with his cane.

Two weeks ago a cousin of the Annesleys, who was in attendance at a reception for a Dutch emissary, contrived to drop a rather substantial foot-stool on Thomas's foot. Thomas suffers with gout from time to time, and was inconvenienced by it that day.

"Christ Almighty! Save me from this pain," he yelled with all his might, and then swore at this cousin, who apologised for his clumsiness with an extremely contented smile on his face. He then gave the game away by saying, for all to hear: "I trust it is not worse than the pain inflicted on my cousin Annesley at the parade," and turned on his heel and walked out.

To add to that, I have just told Thomas what transpired at a dinner I went to at Chancellor Loftus's house last night. Annesley was dining there too, and at the table one of the guests made a feeble joke about the dropping of the stool. "It would have been less painful if the stool had been a dog's, and not a piece of furniture, but the stink would have been worse."

Then he laughed, and said: "Our cousin may have dropped a stool, but revenge as mild as that would not be enough for my brother for the caning he suffered. When he acts, the Deputy is likely to wish something as mild as another stool being dropped is all that happens to him." There was something of a shocked silence, and then one or two titters of laughter which soon died out. I found it difficult to believe that the man had said so threatening and stupid a thing at such a gathering. I was duty bound to report this to Thomas.

He is in a rage. Ever since little George and I went through Annesley's accounts Thomas has been trying to persuade him to resign the Vice-Treasurership. He is a holder of one-eighth of the Irish customs farm of which Thomas and Sir Arthur Ingram hold bigger shares. The yield of revenue has grown considerably since Thomas has taken charge of the government and made the administration so much more efficient, done so much to encourage trade, and eliminated the pirates. Consequently the bargain he and his partners struck with the King as to the amount they should pay the Crown for the right to collect the customs and other taxes means the King has done very badly out of it. The farmers should have a reasonable amount, the King keeping the rest for himself.

Now Thomas is no altruist, but he doesn't think this is fair to the King and wants to alter the contract so that he and the other farmers do well, but most of the money goes into the Royal coffers. Mountnorris will have none of it. He also refuses to sell his share of the customs farm.

"I'm going to get rid of Mountnorris once and for all. He's an officer in the Army and it is totally unacceptable for such an officer to insult – let alone to threaten – the Commander in Chief, which is what, as Deputy, I am."

"There's your answer, Thomas."

"How?"

"He's an officer. Court Martial him. Write to the King and ask for permission to sentence him in accordance with martial law, and have him arrested and brought before a Court now."

Thomas ponders that. "That's good legal advice, George, but I think we'll continue to look into Annesley's cheating and stealing as Treasurer, and try again to get him to resign over that. If that fails we'll go for the Court Martial. In the meantime draft a letter for me to the King telling him what is alleged against Annesley, and asking, as you suggested, for the power of sentence to be given to me. Then we can use it if we have to."

"There's another thing Thomas. It is clear that he is taking money out of the revenue to which he is not legally entitled, so why don't you ask the King for an Order of the Privy Council to stop him taking these monies. If you get that Order Annesley is unlikely to disobey it, and if he does you can get rid of him on two counts."

"Good idea. Include that in the draft, too, please."

Christopher Wandesford. 18th April, 1635. Dublin.

Tom dissolved Parliament today in another stunningly theatrical ceremony. You could be forgiven for thinking that he was a Jonson or an Inigo Jones producing masques for the Royal entourage's entertainment. There is no doubt that these events help bolster and maintain his prestige, and the showmanship reflects his power in the country.

I've been thinking back over what he – well, I suppose we, with Radcliffe, me, brother George, and Mainwaring, inspired by Tom, to charge on with legislation, reform, and administration - have done. There is no doubt Tom is the driving force. He delegates, but at the same time he cannot leave a project alone. He wants to oversee almost everything everyone is doing. His workload is colossal. He never spares himself, which makes it rather difficult for the rest of us to spare ourselves.

So much of his concern has been for the condition of the poor and neglected. Much of the new legislation has been directed to preventing the poor being exploited and treated unjustly, and to making improvements in their welfare. We have pushed through, and Parliament has passed, Acts outlawing buggery, bigamy, and causing the opening of places for the homeless and beggars to stay. Usurers have been hit hard by laws reducing the interest they can charge; the rich are too powerful, usually, to need to borrow at exorbitant rates, but the poor cannot read the terms they are agreeing to, and have little idea of the ways of business.

Tom was most worried about the way the ignorant get blackmailed by villains who will inform on alleged wrong-doing unless they are paid off; sometimes the allegations are ridiculous, but the ill-educated do not know that, and are terrified. Another evil the poorer tenants suffered was the practice of some landowners making them pay excessive amounts for being able to hand over their property to their heirs on death. We have legislated against that sort of thing, improved the law on murders, and made the kidnapping and marrying of the daughters of the rich to secure big dowries a crime. Offences like that show just how lawless this country was before Tom decided to try to straighten it out.

We have also passed laws to make people build barns to store grain, and stop really stupid ways of using fire to separate the grain from the straw, plucking wool from the sheep instead of shearing them (hardly any shepherds here seem to have suitable knives, let alone shears), and the cruel way they plough by roping their silly little ploughs to the horses' tails.

What bothers me about a lot of this is that if the people have no money, they can't buy shears and other tools, build barns, or do any of the other things these laws provide for. They cannot work hard and get rich if they have nothing to work with in the first place.

Perhaps the best work we have done is in getting Parliament to pass laws tidying up the rights and obligations of landowners, and the titles to land. I have to admit though, that the main object of the exercise has been to give the Crown more control and ownership, and therefore more rent and other income.

There is one category of person who will, however, be rather unhappy with what we have achieved, and that is the lawyers, including the judges. Tom may have qualified as a barrister himself, but he has no sympathy with the way some lawyers charge their clients excessive amounts, nor with the way judges and other Court officials charge too much for issuing writs or hearing a case. Standard charges have been published and displayed in all the law courts.

Thomas. 27th April, 1635. Dublin Castle.

I have become extremely dissatisfied with the new customs arrangements I introduced just before I came here. I did not then particularly want to be involved in the customs farm myself, but I took a moderate share. Those arrangements seemed very good at the time, and worked very well for the farmers, but not so well for the King. I can see, though, that I did not anticipate the changing economic fortunes of this island sufficiently. There has been an enormous increase in trade in the last couple of years. This is partly due to the increase of the customs charges in 1632, but owes more to my efforts to get rid of the pirates, and, if I say so myself, because I've made improvements to the running of the docks and harbours and to the collection of the customs there.

The duty received in the year to March 1633 was about 23,000 pounds and went up to almost 26,000 by 1634. I've just received a report that when last year's figures were done in March, the revenue was over 38,000 pounds! The tax farmers are making a fortune out of it, and the King is not getting a fair share, considering that it is money he needs in order to govern. The farmers – including me - only need it for themselves.

He is not getting enough because the base annual sum is only 8,000 pounds, and the rest is split equally between him and the farmers, so in the last twelve months they got 15,000, and he only received 23,000. They keep theirs; he spends his on the country. I have a plan. I have to get rid of Mountnorris, as he is one of the farmers, and I can buy out Sir Arthur Ingram and others. What I want to do is become a bigger farmer myself, as most of the previous Deputies have been, and bring in George Radcliffe. We'll offer the King a much bigger annual payment and more than half of the profits.

George needs a reward for all he does for me and the King, and I am far from averse to increasing my fortune by helping the King in this way. Having Mountnorris as Vice-Treasurer of Ireland and on the Privy Council here will frustrate all my plans. I have to get rid of him. I wonder whether the King would agree to my appointing Adam Loftus in his place? He's the unloved son of Lord Chancellor Loftus.

Elizabeth. 15th May, 1635. Dublin Castle.

Praise the Lord!! Thomas is much happier with the King today. He has been having such a lot of trouble with that Lord Mountnorris, which is odd when I remember how they seemed to work together so well in England, and at first here in Ireland.

What he says now is that Mountnorris is, for want of a better word, a crook. He steals from the King, and hangs on to the taxes which should go to the King, for far longer than he should. Thomas says: "He's the Treasurer, for God's sake!"

"You know I do not care for that sort of talk, Thomas, and in any case he may be the Treasurer, but it doesn't sound as though it's for God's sake."

"I'm sorry, Bess, but how can I run the country properly when I can't even trust my Treasurer? Governments can't do anything without money."

He's been talking like that for weeks, but today he is all smiles. He has had a letter from Coke, the Secretary of State, sending him an order from the King and Privy Council ordering Mountnorris not to take any more money illegally. That seems a bit odd to me, since if he's taking it illegally, why does he need to be ordered not to? Why can't he just be arrested? I ask Thomas.

"Because he's too powerful. I need to give him more rope and more time."

"And then he'll hang himself?"

"I should be so lucky!" Thomas is striding up and down the room, waving this piece of paper about in triumph. "I'll get George Radcliffe to have this served on Annesley as soon as possible. That'll sort him out one way or the other."

"What is that paper, husband? And what do you mean, one way or the other?"

"It's the King's Order from the Privy Council that he must pay over the money."

"Well surely he'll obey that, won't he?"

"You don't know Annesley, Bess. I don't put anything past him, and if he disobeys and keeps on helping himself to the cash, which is what I expect, I shall be able to get rid of him, and have a Treasurer of my own choosing."

Thomas. 16th May, 1635. Dublin Castle.

Last year I put Bramhall into Derry as its Bishop. Today I've appointed another suitable Bishop to replace the Bishop of Down and Connor. My new man is a Scot, but not, thank the Lord, a Presbyterian. He's a supporter of a bishop-led Church, and not just because he's one now!

Finally, I have also instituted a Court of High Commission for Ireland, resembling the English model. It will help me sort out religious questions, and bring into line recalcitrant priests who do not want, or refuse, to adopt the reforms Laud is forcing through. Naturally, I had a lot of opposition from Archbishop Ussher over this; he was too much of a Puritan to want to see High Church practices introduced.

I wrote to Laud yesterday about all this. I wanted him to know that I would forge ahead with all our policies, and, as I put it in the letter: "And so, Thorough let us go, and spare not."

Elizabeth. 20th May, 1635. Dublin Castle.

Amongst the dispatches received from England this morning is a letter from Lord Henry Clifford and his wife Frances. It informs us that their daughter Elizabeth is to be married on 5th July. When Thomas reads that out we are very happy for her, although I have never met her or the Cliffords. As he reads more he starts to laugh.

"Why is this marriage a laughing matter, Thomas? Is it not a good match?"

"Yes, my dear, a very good match indeed. Can you guess who arranged it?"

"Judging by the expression on your face, I can only surmise that you did. I had no idea your talents extended to brokering weddings."

"Well, limitless as those talents are, they do not normally extend to the betrothal industry, but on this occasion, I was the Eros in the case. Have I not told you how it came about?"

I am intrigued. "No, you haven't, or if you have I don't recall it."

"Maybe I haven't told you because I didn't want to make you think I have women everywhere; in fact apart from you, I have none, and need none. Now we're such an old married couple ..."

"We've only been married three years!!"

Thomas smiles. "After Arabella died, it was well known that I was due to come here as Deputy. Now, as I've said before, the Earl of Cork is a wily old buzzard if ever there was one. Poor Arabella was hardly in the ground when I had a letter from Cork offering me his eldest daughter's hand in marriage."

"Why didn't you take her? Her Father could buy mine up over and over again, and there would have been a much better dowry. Or wasn't she pretty enough?"

"It wouldn't have mattered if she'd been Helen of Troy, or if Boyle had offered to make me as rich as Croesus. The last thing I needed was to be beholden to Boyle in any way at all, let alone tied to him by marriage."

"I know you have a reputation for lack of tact, Thomas, but surely even you didn't just put him off like that?"

"Far from it. I told him I was too upset and still overcome with grief - which was true then - even to think about it, but that it might be a good idea for him to approach Henry Clifford offering his son Richard - you, know, you've heard me talk of him - Lord Dungarvan - as a suitor for his daughter Elizabeth. Well, it's taken some time to arrange, but it has happened at last. And I have you, and I think I have the best of it."

"You old flatterer!"

"I flatter not; I tell only the truth. Boyle is so rich I don't suppose his daughter has ever done anything difficult in her life, let alone bring up three of someone else's children as you are doing."

"From what you tell me, and what I have heard of the Cliffords and the Boyles, I shouldn't have thought it was an obvious match."

"It may look odd, but you have to remember that Henry is pretty poor for the son of an Earl – an Earl who is pretty poor himself, according to him – so the prospect of joining Elizabeth to all the Boyle money was too good to resist."

I'm still puzzled. "But aren't the Cliffords a very old aristocratic family? Why would they want to be related to a really *nouveau riche* bunch like the Boyles?"

"Just the money, Bess. As for Boyle, he doesn't want to be thought of as *nouveau riche*, and an alliance with the old Earls of Cumberland pushes him and his family a couple of rungs up society's ladder. They're doing each other a favour, and in the process doing me one, too."

"You really can be devious, Thomas. What do you get out of it?"

"Henry knows what a struggle I'm having to wrest all those Church and Royal properties back from Boyle for the King. Boyle's such a crook, and does everything he can to frustrate what I'm doing to make Ireland a great asset to the King. He even got a friend to invite me to dinner with himself and Henry in an attempt to ambush me over the College of Youghal, but I wasn't going to let him get away with that. Cork hoped the link with Henry may just make life a bit more difficult for me. He thought I wouldn't want to upset Henry, but I think Henry will side with me if it comes to that"

"Let's hope the youngsters are in love and will be happy, in any event."

"It would be nice to think so."

"But didn't you tell me that Cork was going to give Youghal, or some of its land, to Dungarvan as a marriage settlement? Won't that be awkward?"

"That's a pretty shrewd observation, Bess." He takes both my hands in his and kisses me. "It'll be awkward for me *and* Cork, come to think of it. Henry won't like it if Cork tries to use him against me, but on the other hand he'll be angry with me if what I'm doing to Cork robs Elizabeth of most of her marriage settlement. I doubt that that would restrain Boyle for long. He didn't get where he is today without a lot of scheming. He makes even Arthur Ingram look like a saint. He's forming as many alliances with the English aristocracy as he can. He knows only too well that I am after him. He's got a lot of friends here ...."

"And a lot of enemies, hasn't he? Men he's cheated? And the King is behind you, not him. Cork is hanging on to land that the King should have; you are not." I decide to go off at a tangent. "Are we invited to the wedding?"

Thomas picks up the letter again. "It says: 'We know you are very busy in Ireland, and it may be impossible for you to come over, but we should love to see you at the wedding. Do let us know.'"

This time I take Thomas's hand and say: "There you are then. We can't go as you are so busy, but we can send a generous gift. I mean, even if you are right and this wedding will be used in another of Cork's schemes, Henry and Frances are still your friends, and whatever Cork is up to, he can't be sure Henry will turn against you. So let's just tell them we can't make it, and send all our love and good wishes, and a present for the newly-weds."

Thomas's expression is stern, but gradually he smiles. "You're quite right, Bess. If I offend Henry over this it will make no difference to little Elizabeth and her beau, but it may drive Henry into Cork's camp. It's Henry I must think about, not Cork."

George Radcliffe. 29th May, 1635. Dublin.

The King has rather aggravated Thomas today. We have just been reading a letter of 19th from Sir John Coke telling us that the King wants the Irish Parliament recalled. "Can you credit it, George? Two months ago I wrote to Charles telling him I thought we should keep this Parliament on foot; if a different one were called we might not have an adequate Protestant majority. He replied insisting we should dissolve, and we did so last month."

"Well, you cannot recall it now. Once a Parliament is dissolved it is dissolved for ever. It no longer exists, but it was a successful one for you."

"It was, and I must make sure the next one is equally compliant. The subsidies were voted even though the Graces weren't passed into law. We also got through the Bills to recover Crown and Church lands, and by settling new planters on Crown land in areas which haven't been settled before we've increased government income."

I feel I have to enter a cautious note here. "True, but the laws to take back the old rectories and other church property, and the plans for new plantations are not popular. There'll be a lot of trouble when you try to put them into practice."

Thomas nods. "I'm aware of that George. I've been wondering how to handle it. We have four very powerful prerogative Courts, especially Castle Chamber. Before I got here, Boyle and Loftus used it mainly to pursue their policy of hounding Catholics for recusancy fines and so on. I shall use it against anyone who opposes my policies, Papist or Protestant."

I am doubtful. "That won't be so easy when Boyle, as Lord Treasurer, sits on that Court himself, with Loftus and Mountnorris."

"I've worked that one out too. The King's new patent for the Court gives me power to choose who sits on it. Because of the new allegations by Mountnorris that Boyle has acquired church property illegally – he lives in a Bishop's palace, for goodness sake – he will be one of the first people to appear before it as a defendant. He cannot sit on the Court, that being the case."

"You appointed Christopher Master of the Rolls last year, so he has a seat on the Court. Trouble is already brewing with Mountnorris over his position as Vice-Treasurer and his use of the King's money, so he should be gone soon. I can't imagine any of the other judges will stand in your way."

Thomas grins. "Indeed he should be gone soon. I wrote to Coke last month saying that he was lazy and rude and causes trouble in all the debates, that he should go and Sir Adam Loftus should replace him."

"Mountnorris will be another enemy, Thomas. And if you call another Parliament, how do you propose to manage that if there will be more recusants sitting as MPs?"

"I'm planning to get rid of some of the old rotten boroughs that usually return MPs from the Catholic counties."

That will not be popular. Thomas never seems to care. "And how will you use the Court of Wards?"

"I hardly need to tell a lawyer like you that the most important task of that Court is to hold the title to land whose owner has died."

"Quite right Thomas, you don't need to tell me that, nor that the Court holds on to the land until the heir applies to the Court to prove his title. He has to pay fees to take up the title, and this money goes into the Treasury. He also has to pay fees to get his daughter married, and for permission to sell any of his land."

Thomas laughs. "Well, I suppose I asked for that. Telling you the law is like telling Granny how to suck eggs." He pauses. "When I was appointed Deputy I was told the revenue of that Court was about 7,000 pounds per annum. That was a pretty good slice of total taxes of

50,000, and I could see the way to increase it. The problem was that the vast majority of Catholics were usually too afraid to apply to the Court for their deeds, because they were being hounded for recusancy – for not swearing the Oath of Supremacy. They did not want to acknowledge the King as Head of the Church.”

“They don’t want to go to hell for abandoning the Pope!”

“When the Graces came into force a few years ago, the number of Catholics prepared to apply to the Court shot up. Before that they’d not even been allowed to apply. So there was a big increase in the revenue.”

“So how will you use the Court of Wards?”

“I shall encourage them to apply to the Court by scrapping the Oath of Supremacy. All they have to take is an Oath of Allegiance to the King. Until they do, I shall make sure the properties in our hands are rented out more efficiently and for higher rents.”

I am confused. “But if these owners get their titles confirmed, there will be less rent for the Court to collect, won’t there?”

“Not necessarily. Once their titles are confirmed the ground-rents they pay will go up, so we shall not lose anything, but gain much. I shall impose these new rules on the province of Ulster, as well as the other three.”

“That won’t please the Protestant settlers, and the other measures will upset all the Catholics. Even if it works, will it be worth all the trouble?”

“George, I expect it to yield another 4,000 a year.”

“Very well, but it will do nothing to improve your popularity.”

Thomas. 29th May, 1635. Dublin.

Perhaps George is right and I shall be proved wrong. The Protestant settlers may not like having to pay fees for inheritance and so on, but as they have had their grants of land straight from the Crown in fairly recent times, they won’t have such a hard a job to prove their title, and their legal costs should not be so high, but they will have to pay higher rents. The Old English are in a much worse position, because they have had their land almost since Norman times, and proving that is expensive and very difficult.

If they cannot not prove they are the lawful owners, they will have to pay fines for having bought or sold land illegally, and perhaps buy a pardon, too. Then their rent will go up. I feel that my more tolerant attitude towards the Catholics will work – at least from one point of view: they will get better titles and the government will get more rent.

As I've said, what the Catholics want, and argue for in the Graces, is a law which means that they only have to prove a title to their land going back sixty years. I refuse to agree to that. If I do I cannot get the fees out of them or let the wardship lands for good rents. Where there is no title I couldn't forfeit the land, and the Crown couldn't sell it back to the owners, or to someone else. In the long run I have to follow the King's policy. It's no good worrying about my popularity. I must do my duty.

The Court which investigates whether these people actually have titles or not is the Commission for Defective Titles. I shall make it more efficient, and get its members to work harder, longer hours. I shall use it as a substitute for giving the owners the opportunity to prove a sixty year title. That looks good on paper, but in practice it is a device which will enable me to increase revenue for the King. The Judges won't always find the title the owner says he has. They may find he owns a bit of his land fully, but another part might be on some other sort of ownership, and subject to rents and feudal dues payable to the Crown.

Often the Court may find these men have no title at all, but have taken secret possession of the property, or bought or sold it without paying for a licence. Then the land could be forfeited to the King, or be passed into the hands of the Court of Wards to impose more fines, and other fees.

In many cases the landowners may find they are worse off than they had been before they applied to the Court, but the government will be a lot richer for it. Even so, I hope the Court **will** find for the applicants sometimes; it'll look very dubious if it doesn't!

The fourth of the Courts is that of High Commission. Its job is to seek out those who are not prepared to follow the King's and Archbishop Laud's lead on Church doctrine and ceremony. As these are frequently the same people who need a good title to their land, the High Commission could refer them to one of the other Courts, increasing their business and revenue.

By these means, and the control I intend to exercise over the Irish Parliament, I should be able to achieve all the King and I desire. To tighten my grip even further I shall issue a proclamation preventing anyone from leaving Ireland without my permission, even to go to

England. I know that some go there, or send their servants or agents, to try to appeal to the King against my rule. His Majesty may well have said that he would not entertain such appeals, but I want to ensure that making them is, as far as possible, quite impossible.

Elizabeth. 22nd June, 1635. Dublin Castle.

Thomas reads me a letter come today from William Laud. He is always pleased to get these letters. So often these two men seem to see things through the same eyes, and think the same thoughts. Sometimes I think they're like two big trees which have grown together at a sharp angle; if one were to fall or be chopped down, the other could not stand up on its own.

My Lord,

You will shortly receive a letter from the King giving you permission to proceed with the plantation of Connaught. At the last Privy Council meeting His Majesty expressed some concern about whether the full rigours of title investigation and plantation should be used in County Galway. I doubt that he alludes to it in the letter. He mentioned, but not in an emphatic way, that the Earl of Clanricarde is a very great landowner there, and as he has always been a great supporter of the Monarchy (even if he is a Catholic) it would be as well not to offend him too much.

I interrupt. "Is that advice you will heed, Thomas? If it comes from the King, perhaps it would be wise to do so."

"How can I treat Clanricarde differently from Cork? They both support the King. So far Charles has made no difficulty over my pursuit of Cork and his ill-gotten gains. I shall think about it. Do you want hear the rest? Or am I boring you?"

"Yes, of course."

"I'm boring you?"

"Don't be pedantic, Thomas. I want to hear the rest."

I have been talking to Sir Thomas Roe. Do you know him? He is a very experienced and skilful diplomat – spent some years at the end of Elizabeth's and the start of James's reigns as ambassador at the Court of the Great Mogul of India. He spoke of you, and of having been in Ireland recently. He told me: "Wentworth does great wonders. He has called and managed a Parliament and made a firm understanding and love between the King and his people, besides getting a great deal of money from them. He is severe in public and in the business of government, but he is gentle in private conversation.

"He is relaxed in his friendships, but very firm; a terrifying judge and a strong enemy. He is incredibly zealous in the King's interests, and far from negligent in his own. He will get what he wants, and though he is very rational, sometimes he lets his will over-ride his reason, to make sure he gets it. He will never be content to be moderately successful. He will either be the greatest man in England, or much less than he is now."

"What does he mean by that last bit, dear?"

"I don't know, Bess. He sounds a bit like a 'secret, black and midnight hag' out of Macbeth there. Still, the rest of it is very welcome praise from such a man."

"Certainly most of it sounds like praise, but some makes me wonder whether it isn't tongue in cheek, or even satirical. I mean, that bit about the Mogul? He could mean you're a dictator."

"You just don't want me to be too full of myself."

I laugh. "Could you be more full of yourself, Thomas? Modesty is not one of your faults."

"But then I have little to be modest about, my love." And we both roar with laughter. His vanity is often a joke between us. He continues to read to me.

"It sounds as though you have a fan in Roe. You have another in the Prince of Wales, apparently. His Majesty spent ten minutes at the meeting telling the Council how pleased the Prince is with the present of hawks you sent him on behalf of your son William.

I have no other news of significance for you at this time, and it is strange to be sending you such a personal sort of letter.

I am, as always, your devoted

William + Canterbury.

Thomas. 31st July, 1635. Portumna, Galway.

The Earl of Clanriarde's home here is a rather plain square stone building of no particular merit, but it is comfortable. A letter for me arrives from Cottington. Amongst other things he tells me that Lord

Cork's friends at Court are starting to make representations to the King that the Youghal case should go to England. It is bad enough that Cork has come to Portumna with my friend Lord Clifford, in another attempt to win me over into dropping the case. Henry is understandably concerned that if Cork has to disgorge the College, it will affect his daughter Elizabeth when she marries Cork's son, Lord Dungarvan. If, as Cork claims, the College is to form a large part of the marriage settlement, and he loses it, either the Dungarvans will be rather poorer, or Cork will have to find something else substantial to put into the settlement.

I found an opportunity to take Henry on one side. He is such a good friend. I explained what was going on with the Youghal property, and added: "Neither my friendship with you nor your alliance with Cork, nor anything else, shall ever separate me from my duty to God and the King my master. I cannot take on the burden of someone else's wrongdoing and feel the guilt of it myself when my conscience cries out against it. If I do, I become his partner in crime. I cannot do it; I shall not do it, Henry."

What a gentleman, a moral, upright, gentle soul Henry is. No wonder he's a poet. He put his hand on my arm. "Thomas, I had no idea what was involved here. If you are sworn to the King to recover Church and Crown property, then that is what you must do. Were I in your shoes I should do the same. Say no more about it. You shall hear no more of it from me."

But I may well hear more of it from Cork's friends in London. The letter from Cottington tells me that Cork's main supporters over this case are the Earl of Pembroke, who is Lord Chamberlain, and Lord Salisbury. I write at once to Laud, knowing he will put my arguments faithfully and forcefully before the King and his Council.

If after all this the Earl of Cork, by applying the pressure of his friends on that side of the sea, should stop the proceedings in the Castle Chamber, escape his punishment in this cause, and shake His Majesty from the advice he has had, the consequences would be bad. The Church would not only be dispossessed of Youghal, but those endeavours which have started recently to restore it would be smothered by fear of great and powerful adversaries.

It will be a blemish on the administration of justice in this Kingdom, and raise an overbearing feeling that my authority lies only against the poor and not over the powerful. They are already willing enough to believe something of that sort as, before I came here, fear of the nobility was a tremendous hindrance to the free and steady course of justice.

Making an example of Cork is essential to curb the appetites of these gluttons, and would be a joy and comfort to the people, who are never happier than when they see that right may win against one of these great lords. It is something they have hardly ever seen before.

What makes these efforts of Cork's even more awkward is not just the embarrassment of having him come here with Henry, but that he has done so just when I am here with Kit and Radcliffe to make a start on my policy – the King's policy - for the plantation of Connaught. Of course, Richard de Burgh, the elderly Earl of Clanricarde, is the key to any success those efforts may enjoy. If Cork has any luck in opposing me, de Burgh will feel encouraged to oppose me in turn.

Christopher Wandesford. 31st July, 1635. Portumna.

The Commission for Defective Titles is working well and successfully here in Connaught. The juries called together in the counties of Roscommon, Sligo, and Mayo found the King's title to be proven in much of them, and I hope the same can be said for County Galway, to which we came a few days ago. Everything Tom does is planned and dealt with as one whole, and not in little separate parcels; that is why what he attempts prospers so well. So it should, for I am sure that he intends nothing but justice and honour for the people.

Indeed, so far as allocation of land for the planters goes, he wants much of it to be taken up in separate small parcels, as he believes - rightly in my view - that small landowners will be more industrious than large rich ones who may have no incentive to make their holdings productive as long as the rent is paid to them.

However, I must say I found it strange that local land-owners in the other three counties of Connaught had not arranged any opposition, nor any significant representation. I know that Tom had set me on selecting juries not hostile to the government, but I did not expect them to be quite so malleable in those counties. After all, Tom's plan is that about a third of Connaught will be set aside for new settlers. You'd think that some on the juries would have been against that, but on the other hand the remaining two-thirds will be on secure titles which these people have not enjoyed before. They may have more fees and fines to pay to retain to their land, but that is better than being at risk of having it confiscated altogether.

This lack of opposition, I have discovered, is due to the fact that in Mayo and Sligo juries have been summoned which were very likely to be sympathetic to Tom's plans, and the foreman of the jury for Roscommon was his ally, Sir Lucas Dillon. The Dillons are very keen on getting their hands on plantation land, so it is hardly surprising that the jury had no trouble in upholding the King's title against local 'owners'.

George Radcliffe. 31st July, 1635, Portumna.

I am with Thomas and Christopher in Galway, to help with legal matters. We are staying at Clanricarde's mansion. It is very comfortable, and we have been made most welcome, considering that the Earl ought to be aware that he is more likely to suffer than benefit from the Title investigations. He is not the immediate problem, though.

Back in April Thomas had all that unpleasantness with Mountnorris and his cousin hurting his gouty foot with a stool, and Mountnorris more or less uttering a threat against him on behalf of his insubordinate brother. He asked me to draft a letter to the King asking for permission to investigate the allegations of embezzlement against Mountnorris, and bring him before a Court Martial for the threat he uttered at Loftus's dinner.

However, he decided not to send it immediately, but to wait and try for a little longer to get Mountnorris to cooperate, and resign as Treasurer. He waited in vain. Mountnorris was adamant that he was entitled to the money he took, and he refused to resign his post. Towards the end of June we dispatched the letter.

Today Thomas receives a letter from the King giving him authority to undertake both the investigation and the Court Martial. He calls me into the library Clanricarde has made available to us. Thomas seeks my advice on the Court Martial. I suppose some might think that Thomas is going too far in his attempts to bring Mountnorris to heel; they might say he is being vindictive. I cannot go along with that. The inquiry into embezzlement is founded on several matters, but the basic issue is not merely that the thefts have been going on for a long time, which is not denied. What Mountnorris says is that it is not theft as he is legally entitled to the money. The important point is that three months ago the King made an order forbidding him to take any more than his lawful cut of the revenues. He has refused to obey it. It is a direct order from the King. How can the man think he can disobey and get away with that?

Thomas is quite right to take action against him. If the King is to be disobeyed in this way, it is incumbent upon Thomas, as his deputy, to enforce his commands. The same applies to the Court Martial. For a senior officer in the Army to voice his approval of the insubordination of another officer, and to back that up by what seems to have been a threat, is the kind of behaviour that could start a mutiny. I have researched the law on the point, and the offence, if proved, merits the death penalty.

Thomas says: “I shall convene a Court Martial as soon as I can, George, and get our Privy Council to look into the embezzlement charges.”

I am not sure about this strategy. “I think you should tell Mountnorris what’s likely to happen and give him another chance to see reason. You know that quite a powerful group supports him, and it would be risky to antagonise him and his friends. You have enough trouble in Parliament with the rivalry between Cork and the Catholic nobility, without adding a third bunch of miscreants.”

Thomas flares up at this. “But I am the King’s deputy. It’s not for me – or rather it’s not just for my own sake - that I’m doing this, but for the reputation and authority of the Crown.”

“Of course, but that is not how it may seem to others. Give him a bit more rope, and he will hang himself – literally in this case if the Court accepts your evidence. If you rush into it, your attempt to save the King’s authority may have precisely the opposite result.”

“You are no fool, George. If it weren’t for you my impetuosity would get me into trouble more often that it does. We’ll leave it a while longer.”

Christopher Wandesford. 25th August, 1635. Dublin Castle.

We have returned from Portumna, and Tom is in a furious mood. The jury has dismissed the King’s claims to a title to lands in Galway!! This was inevitable due to the members of it having been pretty well hand-picked by the local sheriff, not by me. Out of the twelve, ten were, one way or another, related to de Burgh, the Earl of Clanricarde. He was represented by Patrick Darcy. I gained the impression that Darcy must have been priming the witnesses on what they should say, and he had, probably, even given the jury some hints.

At the conclusion of the investigation, when the jurymen were asked for their verdict, one of the unrelated men was, it appeared, going to find for the King when with a warning gesture – a raised fist, I'm told, since I did not see it myself - from another member, he was dissuaded from doing so.

The finding against the King was, naturally, of immense benefit to De Burgh, whose land seemed to be protected from being confiscated for planting. It was not to be. I am far from sure of the wisdom or even the legality of what Tom did when we got back to Dublin. He summoned the errant sheriff and the whole jury to the Court of Castle Chamber here, fined the sheriff, and had the jury locked up. He has not prosecuted them yet, though, so it looks like arbitrary imprisonment. However, it turns out this sheriff is Patrick Darcy's brother, so the whole thing looks like a conspracy!

Darcy was made to suffer. He was lucky not to find himself locked up with the jury, but Tom hauled him before the Court, and told him to take the Oath of Supremacy. Showing considerable courage, and the strength of his Catholic faith, Darcy resolutely declined to do that, and Tom then disbarred him from his barrister's practice. He also pronounced a pretty draconian measure against Galway as a whole: it would not be allowed the benefit of the Graces.

This must have been a very heavy blow for the local Catholics, both Irish and Old English. It certainly seemed to be so for the Earl of Clanricarde. What Thomas said was: "It'll teach these people that fighting me is pointless; if they'd found the King's title they'd have had secure titles themselves, and they'd have had the Graces too. Now they've got nothing."

I'm not so sure. You can alienate some of the people all of the time, and all of the people some of the time, but you cannot alienate everybody all the time.

Christopher Wandesford. 20th September, 1635. Dublin.

Tom is a happy man, but I'm not sure he should be. The Earl of

Cork's memorial tomb for his late wife has been removed. It was a hideous thing, and in an entirely unsuitable position, but Cork was very proud of it, was very fond of his wife (after all, she did give him 18 children, they say – or was it 14?), and is going about saying it cost him a thousand pounds. There are rumours it may be re-erected near the entrance to the cathedral. Thomas is content because this is his first victory over Boyle. Was it wise to antagonise so rich and powerful a man over such an issue? We shall see.

A while ago I wrote that Tom succeeds because he works his policies as one whole, but I am beginning to wonder about that. He seems to be annoying too many people, and most of them powerful. He's angered Cork about the tomb and the College of Youghal, and he's done the same with Clanricarde and his clan with his treatment of the sheriff and jury in Galway, and his announcement that the county will not get the benefit of the Graces at all. Getting Darcy disbarred will not have gone down well with a lot of the legal profession, either.

King Charles. 2nd October, 1635. Whitehall.

Me. I'm not sure what to do, my dear. Many people are still urging Wentworth upon me to replace Portland as Treasurer, but I am not at all sure that I want him.

Queen. I'm not sure I want him at all. He is just a nuisance to me and my friends.

Me. But he is extremely useful to me in Ireland, Henrietta.
Queen. Well, keep him there then. I should not be at all happy if he came back.
Me. And why is that?
Queen. I just told you; he's such a nuisance to me and my friends. Look at the soap monopoly.
Me. What about it? It should make me a lot of money. These soap people – the ones I granted the monopoly to – are supposed to pay me four pounds a ton on it, and they said they will make 5,000 tons a year. That's 20,000 pounds a year.
Queen. Yes, Charles. You could buy a lot of paintings with that.
Me. If that was a joke, it was in poor taste. 20,000 would help me govern the country. Anyway, what has Wentworth to do with the soap?

Queen. I'm surprised you don't remember. You wanted to ban the export of tallow from Ireland to stop soap being made from it. That would make it easier for the monopolists to get their soap made out of vegetable oil and sold on the markets. When you told Wentworth about it he refused to allow the ban as it would damage Ireland's exports and its economy.

Me. Of course I remember. He said if the tallow wasn't exported the Irish customs would go down and cancel out the 4 pound a ton on the soap. I couldn't really do much about that as it was a good point. He hates me interfering in Ireland. I still get 4 a ton on soap made from tallow.

Queen. Some of those monopolists are my friends. They say they are losing money because of him. They also tell me that he only fought the ban because he wants the customs to pay well because he is the farmer.

Me. I've heard that too. He has made a lot of enemies, and they will do anything to turn me against him. But they forget, if they ever knew, that I get more out of the customs than he does, so there is little point in my cutting off my nose to spite my face just to please some of your friends. And he is reforming the customs so that I shall get even more revenue.

Queen. Very well, but Wentworth annoys you, too. Look at what he said recently. When you asked him to give 10,000 pounds to Lord Nithsdale, he wrote to you so rudely. "Ten thousand pounds for my Lord of Nithsdale strikes deep into this exchequer"; that's what he said.

Me. Yet he paid it as I asked. But you're right; it did annoy me when he 'humbly supplicated' – it makes me smile, the thought of him doing anything humbly - that no more of this kind of gift be taken from the subsidies he raises until the Irish debts of the Crown are discharged. Whose money is it, if not mine?

Queen. So it sounds as though you won't make him Treasurer, then.

Me. No, my dear. You have helped me make up my mind. In the past he and that rat Cranfield, Lord Middlesex, who was my father's Treasurer, worked together against me and George to ...

Queen. I hate it when you talk about Villiers!

Me. ... try to stop us going to war with Spain. Besides, Wentworth says he doesn't want the job, and I have no intention of trying to change his mind.

Thomas. 13th October, 1635. Dublin Castle.

To Sir John Coke, Secretary of State,

My Dear Sir John,

I am taking action to overcome the ridiculous findings of the Galway jury that the King's title to the land there was not proven. I told you then that Counsel representing Clanricarde and other interests in that County were part of a conspiracy, and this conspiracy was a Catholic one. The jury was led along by these men.

They were Patrick Darcy and another lawyer called Martin. Both of them were in the last Parliament and Martin was a very awkward man indeed, and is, in my view, the ring-leader of the conspiracy. He is a very successful lawyer here, and so is Darcy, but Darcy behaved very well in the Parliament, and I feel was driven into this Galway business by Martin, who is his brother-in-law.

It has come to my notice that Clanricarde has sent these two men to England to act as his agents. They will use all their powers of persuasion to get the King and Council to stop the Title investigation proceeding in Galway. If they succeed, I shall be prevented from increasing the Crown revenue from Galway by way of higher rents and fees for confirming titles, wardship, and other means.

I should esteem it no mean favour if you would make sure that the King and Council are fully informed on these men and their aims.

Everywhere I turn I find Darcy and Martin in the way. They are representing Cork over the Youghal case and in respect of other land he has taken, and I believe they are advising Mountnorris on the action I am taking against him. I fully expect Darcy to try on the latter's behalf to argue before the King that no action should be taken against him either. I hope the King will be persuaded that Mountnorris should be dismissed as Irish Treasurer. He can expect to see a huge increase in his Irish revenue once that man is out of office.

Please keep me informed of what develops.

I am your faithful

Wentworth.

Thomas. 27th October, 1635. Dublin Castle.

Will no-one rid me of these turbulent Earls? Cork and Clanricarde - yes, the new one, who is continuing his late father's struggle against me - are stirring up trouble in London with the King. Cork is still trying to get his case about Youghal dealt with in London, and De Burgh is making a huge fuss there about the Galway jury.

The King has commanded that Cork's case should go back to England. My plans to have new plantations, and to recover land for the King and the Church - plans to which Charles had given his seal of approval - will come to absolutely nothing if this happens. That legal snake Darcy may well have influenced the King.

Cork's case was supposed to be heard this month, but it clearly cannot go ahead under these circumstances. I have to get Laud onto it again. He is bound to be as eloquent as he can since he is even more anxious than I to see property recovered for the Church. I write to Laud today setting the situation out for him to use in the Council and with the King, and I send with it a letter I ask him to hand to Charles.

Your Majesty,

I have received from Secretary Windebanke a letter setting out your desires relating to the case of the Earl of Cork and the College of Youghal. Not long ago Windebank advised me that you wished me to proceed with the case, but now he tells me that you wish the matter to be heard in England after all. I believe that may be because, as I understand it, Cork and his agents have been saying that the case is driven by my personal animosity towards him. I deny that this is so, and so far as the same sort of calumny may be spread by the Earl of Clanricarde, I deny that equally firmly. My only goal has been, and is, to restore to you and to your Church in Ireland all the land and income to which you are rightfully entitled, without which your government and the true faith cannot flourish.

What I cannot deny, and do not, is that I act as vigorously as I am able in pursuit of that objective. In the circumstances, having had two recent indications of your wishes that appear to me to ask contradictory things, I am at a loss to know how to proceed.

I should be most grateful if you would kindly illuminate the darkness in which I am struggling with a full explanation of your pleasure in the case, so that I may proceed to a conclusion which may meet with your approbation. I am fearful that if Cork is not compelled to disgorge the properties he has swallowed so greedily, it will prove impossible to have any effect on other landowners whose seizure of your land and that of the Church should be reversed.

I remain, Your Majesty, Your humble, grateful, and devoted servant,

Wentworth.

Elizabeth. 23rd November, 1635. Dublin Castle.

I have not seen Thomas since early this morning. This is unusual when he is at home. He normally spends a little time with the children or me or both after breakfast, but he ate early and then did not appear for luncheon. I know he spent some time with his brother George and Christopher, because Christopher told me so. I find Thomas in the library, working at his desk. He doesn't even look up when I come in; in fact, he doesn't even seem to have noticed I am there.

I go behind his chair and stroke his hair. "What's wrong, my love? Why didn't you come for lunch?"

"I've been too busy and didn't notice the time."

"But I sent a servant to tell you we were about to eat."

"Did you? I probably ignored him."

"It wasn't a 'him'; it was Kathleen."

"Was it? Well, I still didn't notice. It's all very worrying."

"What is?"

I am still stroking his hair. He takes my hand and kisses the palm, and looks up at me for the first time. "This business with Galway. In the middle of last month Coke wrote to tell me that Darcy and the other agitators Clanricarde sent over to London to stir up trouble with the King about the Title cases and the plantation policy had arrived, and handed the King a Petition against what I have been doing. Now I've had a letter from Lord Danby telling me to lay off the new Earl of Clanricarde. The old one, his father – died at the start of this month."

I pull up a chair and sit beside Thomas and he continues to hold my hand. "Why? What does he say?"

"This is what he writes: 'I have recently returned from Lord St Albans' funeral. He was ....'"

I interrupt. "Who is Lord St Albans?"

"He's Clanricarde, which is the Irish title. In England he - Richard de Burgh, is, or I should say – was, the Earl of St Albans. Danby goes on: 'He was 72, so he had passed his three score years and ten, and was full of honour and days according to King David in the Old Testament. Yet his people report that his worrying about the discourtesy and disrespect you showed him hastened his death. His son Ulick, the new Earl, is very well aware of this.

"'Ulick has many complaints against your government, and I believe he means to seek redress from you personally as soon as the season and the weather allow him to travel to Ireland. I beseech you to remember the extraordinary merits of the deceased nobleman, far above any of his nation in our times.'" Thomas looks at me. "Danby goes on with some other news and views which are not a problem, but I object to his trying to interfere from England with my efforts to govern here."

He looks rather depressed. I kiss him. "Ulick's a strange name. What do you propose to do?"

"I haven't made up my mind. I don't think I can just ignore what Darcy might do. This is the King's policy he's defying, or helping Clanricarde to defy."

"Then why don't you ask the King to send Darcy and the others back here, if it's a policy the King wants you to pursue? You don't have to take any notice of this Danby, do you? He's not the King, is he? It's the King's orders you are supposed to take."

Thomas stands and pulls me up, embraces me closely, and kisses me on the forehead. "That's it, Bess. Sometimes I cannot see the wood for the trees." He kisses me on the lips.

"Well, I don't know all the details, do I? Sometimes too much knowledge is a dangerous thing; it stops you seeing how simple something is. If you've got to pursue this policy to get the King's land and the plantation in Connaught, you can't let this Ulick de Burgh get in your way, if it's the King's way too."

He kisses me again and puts his tongue in my mouth and we kiss passionately like that for some time. "I'll write to the King this evening. But there's another problem I have to deal with first, or rather you do."

"What's that?"

"Those kisses." He pulls me close and hard against him, and I can feel something rather enlarged pressed between us, and getting larger all the time.

"Well, husband, that need not be a problem much longer." We exit the library in a hurry to get to the bedroom. I think we should both be happy doing it there on the floor, but there are too many servants about, as well as a couple of the children.

Christopher Wandesford. 12th December, 1635. Dublin Castle.

Just over two weeks ago the Irish Privy Council started to hear the evidence and look at the records regarding Francis Annesley's - Lord Mountnorris, that is - stealing from the King's revenues. He has told the Council he will take his case up with the King. I am not sure what good that will do him, when the King has promised Tom not to hear any appeals from here save in cases of manifest injustice. I've seen the work the two Georges have done on this. I find their evidence, and the facts as shown by the accounts - Annesley's own slipshod ones for the most part - very convincing. I think the fact that Thomas waited a couple of months before convening the Privy Council is another nail in Annesley's coffin, since he continued arrogantly to refuse to cooperate with Tom or resign.

Today I am in Court with Tom, assisting him and George Radcliffe present the evidence at Annesley's Court Martial. There are some aspects of this that I'm not at all happy about. First, Thomas has appointed the panel of officers which is to conduct the trial, and his choices are, largely, favourable to him. Secondly, although Tom is an able advocate himself, and has George to give evidence – and George is a formidable lawyer – the Court refuses Annesley's request to have any counsel at all. I think that is bad, and may bounce back on Thomas in the future.

On the other hand, this is not an ordinary Court, but a council of war, where different rules apply, and where those rules are in the discretion of the Court. Even so, that does not make me like it. I should not like to be in Annesley's position, even if I believe him guilty. As a lawyer myself I feel all trials should be as fair as possible. How is justice to be done otherwise?

Thomas. My Lords, I appear before you today on my own behalf seeking redress for the offence offered to me, as Commander in Chief of the Army of Ireland, and to the King, whose Deputy I am, by the defendant, Francis Annesley, Lord Mountnorris. Some months ago, a relative of the defendant's brother was insubordinate in a high degree at an Army parade at Dublin. When I reprimanded him, he refused to obey my order, and I struck him with my cane. Shortly after this, a cousin of Annesley's dropped a heavy stool on my foot; I was suffering badly with gout at the time.

Judge. When was the incident on the parade ground?
Thomas. On 24th March, 1635, My Lord.
Judge. And the incident with the dropping of the stool?
Thomas. A week later, my Lord. It was 1st April.
Judge. Neither of these matters can be laid at the defendant's door, My Lord Wentworth.
Thomas. Indeed, My Lord, and I do not suggest that they can, but they are relevant to what happened next, namely the offence, actually a threat, offered to me by the defendant at a dinner at Lord Chancellor Loftus's home at a dinner on 8th April.
Judge. What was the nature of this threat?
Thomas. As to that My lord, I call Sir George Radcliffe to give evidence.
Annesley. May I question Lord Wentworth, My Lord?
Judge. You may.
Annesley. You admit you struck my brother with your cane?
Thomas. I do. He had ...
Annesley. I did not ask you what he had done, if anything. Who dropped the stool on your foot?
Thomas. Your cousin.
Annesley. Wasn't it an accident?
Thomas. Definitely not. I was in agony as I had gout. I told him to apologise, and he did, but with such a smirk on his face he clearly enjoyed...
Annesley. Do you profess to know what he was thinking, Lord Wentworth?
Thomas. I know what he meant when he said he hoped it had hurt as much as the caning had hurt his cousin. That is how I know what he had intended when he dropped the stool.

Judge. Do you have any further questions, Lord Mountnorris?
Annesley. Not for this witness, My Lord.
Judge. Very well. Call Sir George Radcliffe. *(George comes into Court).*
Thomas. Sir George, please tell the Court what happened on the evening of 8th April this year.
George. I attended a dinner at the home of Lord Loftus, the Lord Chancellor of Ireland. During dinner someone made a stupid joke about the time, a week before, when the defendant's cousin dropped a stool on Lord Wentworth's foot. I must confess I do not now recall the joke itself, but I recall clearly the words of the defendant.
Judge. The defendant was at this dinner too, then?
George. Indeed My Lord. The joke barely raised a laugh, and then the defendant said: "My brother would not be content with such a small revenge. When he takes the revenge he has in mind the Lord Deputy may well wish that another stool had been dropped on him instead".
Thomas. Was this said seriously, or in jest?"
Annesley. I object, My Lord. Is this more mind-reading?
George. I did not need to read your mind. The seriousness with which you said it was proved by your tone of voice, and the expression on your face. The way you uttered the words "the Lord Deputy" showed clearly the contempt in which you held him.
Judge. Do you wish to question the witness, Lord Mountnorris?
Annesley. I do, My Lord. Sir George, are you quite clear in your recollection of what I am supposed to have said.
George. I am.
Annesley. Quite sure?
George. Quite sure.
Annesley. Might I not have said: "Our cousin may have dropped a stool, and revenge as mild as that would be enough for my brother for the caning he suffered."
George. I believe you are wrong. You definitely said "would not be enough".
Annesley. It was a jest, was it not, sir?
George. Do you normally sneer and snarl when joking?
Judge. The meaning is a matter for us, Sir George.

Annesley. You are a close friend and associate of the Lord Deputy, are you not, Sir George?

George. I have that honour.

Annesley. You would say anything to help him, tell any lie, wouldn't you?

George. Kindly do not judge me by your own standards, My Lord Mountnorris. As you have admitted the gist of what was said, I have no need to lie.

Annesley. I have no further questions, My Lord.

(Tom calls three more witnesses who were at the dinner. With just enough variation in their evidence to show that they have not colluded in agreeing what they will say, they corroborate George's testimony. Mountnorris makes little headway in casting doubt on any of it).

Judge. Have you anything to say on your own behalf, Lord Mountnorris?

Annesley. I am not responsible for my brother's insubordination, if that is what it was, on the parade ground, nor for my cousin's accidental dropping of a stool. As for that stool, I deny being responsible even if he did it deliberately. I deny with every fibre of my being that I intended the Deputy or the King any harm by what I said in jest at Lord Loftus's dinner on 8th April.

Judge. Have you anything further to add, Lord Wentworth?

Thomas. No, My Lord.

Judge. Then we shall consider our verdict. You will all leave the Court.

Thomas. As the King's representative, and as he is the fount of all justice under God, I shall remain.

Annesley. I object, My Lord. The Lord Deputy's power and reputation are enough to overawe the Court.

Judge. Your objection is disallowed, Lord Mountnorris. We are not overawed by anyone.

So George, Annesley and I leave the Court-room, and Tom remains to hear the deliberations of the Judges.

Tom comes out of the Court after twenty minutes. "They're considering the sentence." It does not take them long. We are summoned back into Court after another twenty minutes. Annesley is told to stand. The Judge tells him that he is found guilty, and that they prefer the evidence of George and the other witnesses to his own on the question of whether the 'revenge' of which he spoke at the dinner was truly meant, or a mere joke. They ask him if he has anything to say before sentence. He is unrepentant and insists on his innocence. The Judge then turns to his colleagues, in turn, and asks if they are still agreed on the penalty, and they all nod.

Annesley is sentenced to death. He is so shocked he falls back into his seat and nearly falls off that. Tom leaps to his feet, and says: "I shall appeal to the King against the sentence. The penalty is too heavy."

I can't tell whether Tom means that he is shocked. He should not have stayed in Court. He knew death could be the punishment. His presence is, in fact, enough to overawe most people, and these Judges would have nothing to gain by upsetting him, whatever they may say about their independence. I do not say they were overawed in making their decision, but this is certainly another aspect of the trial I do not care for. He then says something quite extraordinary to Mountnorris: "Before a hair of your head should perish, I should rather lose my hand."

Thomas. 13th December, 1635. Dublin Castle.

I wish I could have slept properly last night. After all, Mountnorris is now in prison as a traitor. He can't go to England to pursue his case there, and try to prevent me reorganising the customs farm. He can't be the Vice-Treasurer for Ireland when he's a prisoner either. I have exactly what I wanted, even if I didn't want him hanged.

But that achievement did not make me sleep any better than I do normally, which is pretty badly most of the time. Then there's the gout, which is getting more and more frequent, it seems to me; certainly when that fellow dropped the stool on my foot it was not the first time I had had it, by any means.

Just as bad as all that - perhaps worse - are the recurrent bouts of diarrhoea I suffer. It is embarrassing when I have to rush out of important meetings to discharge my bowels at almost no notice at all. I think I am getting old. I worry that I am slowing up, and unable to do as much as I used to do. And I'm only 42!!

Yet I must look on the bright side. The way things are going in Connaught is bringing a change in the attitude in the areas around Dublin. I told Coke in a letter last month that the landowners in the

Pale are beginning to fret that County Meath could be just as ripe for plantation as Connaught. Even the Earl of Arundel is concerned that land he claims in South Leinster may be "ripe for seizure," and he is trying to get it back. As it happens I have no plans to plant these places near Dublin; there are plenty of Old and New English there already.

Another bonus is that as Mountnorris can no longer be Vice-Treasurer, I can have a friend, young Adam Loftus, appointed in his stead. It'll cost me a lot - 6,000 pounds, I dare say - to get Cottington to agree, but it'll be worth it.

Elizabeth. 14th December, 1635. Dublin Castle.

Last night Thomas hardly slept at all. He did not sleep much the night before. In fact he has not slept much for some time. I think he does too much, worries about everything, and cannot leave well alone with governing the country even when he has loyal, clever men like the two Georges and Christopher, to help him. Why can't he delegate things to them and then forget about those while he gets on with the rest?

He worries me, if truth be told. He wasn't like this when we were in England, nor during the first year or so of being in Ireland. He would not admit it but I think being a King in all but name here is a great strain on him. He wasn't born to be a King. His father was a fairly big landowner, and had a couple of manors or so to run, but that's a far cry from a whole country, with a million or more people to govern, and pretty villainous men like Cork and Mountnorris to do battle with, and more honest ones like Clanricarde to bring into line when they oppose the King's policies; and then he worries about the courtiers back in England who help these men and strive to undermine his position.

On top of all that I think his obsession with his work, and the time he spends on it, are ruining his health. Sometimes he goes to the toilet so often and looks so awful when he's been I wonder whether he hasn't got the bloody flux. If he hasn't got it yet, it won't be long before he gets it, at this rate. Having the King's good opinion means such a lot to him, as well. He thinks the King doesn't really trust him, and he's probably right. He does so much, and works so hard, it's almost as though he's a business partner with the King. I know we do well out of it, but I'm sure Thomas is right when he says that it's his duty to the King that drives him on. If it wasn't, he'd spend all his time on his own affairs and lining his pockets at the King's expense, like all the others do.

They get their Earldoms. Why won't the King give Thomas one? And Thomas said something very strange the other day: "I trust God so to humble me as His Majesty shall have no cause to alter his good opinion of me, and then I shall welcome what God sends; I am not too good to die for him." What on earth did he mean? Does he think he has exalted himself too much? Does he expect worse things to come? Does he mean he'd die for God, or for the King? He must mean the King. God forbid that it should come to that!

Charles 1. 23rd January, 1636. Whitehall Palace.

Today I was with Henrietta in the small red drawing room when the Secretary of State, Sir John Coke presented himself. As always, he's small and neat. I chuckle; that's what people say about me. He carries a letter. "Master Secretary, you have news?"

"Indeed, Your Majesty. I have a here a letter from The Lord Deputy in Ireland. He reports on the situation following the trial of Lord Mountnorris. He was convicted and sentenced to death."

"To death? By the Lord, I did not give authority for that. I intended only that Mountnorris should be rebuked and reprimanded. Wentworth has gone too far!"

Henrietta snorts; "Doesn't he always?"

"Unfortunately, Sire, it seems that the wording of the warrant for Mountnorris's arrest and the authority you gave the Deputy to prosecute him does indeed go that far. But Wentworth was not one of the Judges; he was the prosecutor. The prisoner – he's in Dublin Castle jail as a traitor – complains that there should not have been a Court Martial over this when we are at peace and no threat of any kind was on the horizon, let alone close at hand."

"Wentworth is too harsh. He enforces the policies he has adopted too strictly. Lord Wilmot has complained about the treatment he has suffered, being made to give back money to men who bought land from him ..."

"But it was your land Sire, and the policies he enforces are your policies. There has never been a Deputy who was so diligent in your interest as Wentworth is, if I may say so."

"You have already said it, Sir John," Henrietta throws in. To me she adds, "My ladies tell me Lord Cork has bought an estate in England to escape Wentworth, and that Lord Clanricarde died to escape him. He's hounded Darcy out of his profession and rumours say that he has actually had Mountnorris shot dead in the courtyard at Dublin Castle. And he opposes my friends over the soap monopoly, as you know."

"Yes, my dear, I do know. You tell me about it constantly."

"But it is so embarrassing to be moaned at by my friends, and by these people from Ireland coming to moan about your Deputy, and I can do nothing even though I am the Queen."

Sir John is disturbed. "I can assure you there is no truth in the rumour about a shooting, Your Majesty. Mountnorris could hardly pester me and his friends with letters if he were dead, and I have had no report of it."

"I do not believe it anyway, as I have had a letter from Wentworth asking me – appealing to me – to set the sentence of death aside. In any case, I have no intention of letting the man be executed. Of course, there are those who say that this trial and sentence was the Deputy's way of getting Mountnorris out of the Irish Treasury."

Henrietta leaps in again. "I'm told he paid Cottington 6,000 pounds to assist him to get rid of Mountnorris."

Sir John looks apologetic as he says to her: "That is untrue too, Your Grace. The payment was to secure the post of Vice-Treasurer for Sir Adam Loftus, not to secure the dismissal of Mountnorris. Besides, Cottington paid that sum into the Exchequer once these rumours started. I've been told all about it."

I've had enough. "So have I. But to return to this death sentence. We all know that Cardinal Richelieu treats the French King like a subject, not a monarch, and rules him and not the other way round. And we know that the Cardinal tried Count Marillac at his own house, and had him executed there. I cannot afford to have my subjects saying that I dance to Wentworth's tune as Louis dances to Richelieu's, and that my ministers can choose whom they have beheaded."

"Your Majesty".

"Yes, Sir John?"

He waves the letter. "Wentworth writes that he has heard all these rumours, and they are false. He says Mountnorris was sent home after only a couple of weeks in prison, as he said he was ill."

"Was he?"

"The Deputy says if he was it was just his own obstinacy. He could have had your pardon if he apologised, but he refuses to do so, so he stays confined in his own home. Not perhaps a real hardship bearing in mind the size of his estate!"

"Nevertheless, there is a lot about this matter that I don't like, and I fear Wentworth may not be as trustworthy as I had hoped. It is too much of a coincidence, perhaps, that he has put forward this customs reform plan which would give me 15,500 a year plus five-eighths of the profits, and Mountnorris has come up with an offer of 20,000 a year for me and half the profits. Which is the better for me, and for the country? But with Mountnorris imprisoned in his own house and out of office, there is no chance of his plan going ahead. Is that what Wentworth was aiming at?"

"Who can tell, Sire? But Wentworth's offer came in first, and Mountnorris had never before made any attempt to increase your share of the revenue. Perhaps the Deputy was aiming at forcing his adversary out of the race for the customs farm, or maybe it was just a coincidence. Maybe Mountnorris upped his offer hoping to buy you off. There are also the allegations that Mountnorris helps himself to your revenues. Whatever the truth of that, Wentworth is a stickler for authority, and he could not be expected to tolerate that degree of insubordination, that threat of violence, from Mountnorris's brother. In a sense, as he is your Deputy, Your Majesty, and your commander of the Irish Army, the insubordination was directed at you."

"Thank you, Sir John. I shall ponder all this." He goes.

"What will you do now, husband?"

"I shall do as I said; I shall ponder. But it is difficult to see what I can do, since it would be impossible to find another Wentworth to work so hard and diligently. I dare say time will sort it out."

Archbishop Laud. 23rd January, 1636. Lambeth Palace.

A few weeks ago I wrote to Thomas warning him about the things that were being said about him, particularly regarding Lord Mountnorris. I told him that despite all the great services he is rendering in Ireland, there is no lack of those who whisper against him here in England. They speak louder where they think they will get away with it, saying that 'you take a personal delight in persecuting men of rank and property'. I did not need to add that if he hounded little men of no wealth or importance no-one would take any notice.

Now Thomas writes that he wants me to prepare the ground for him coming to England. He wants to counter the rumours that circulate in the court about him and present his own arguments to the King on the new customs farm while Annesley – Mountnorris I should say – is locked up at home in Ireland. Bearing in mind the way Darcy is pleading Mountnorris's case about the customs with anyone and everyone he can corner, Thomas would do well to come here, at least for that.

I shall have to see what I can do.

Thomas. 20th February, 1636. Dublin.

William Chappell comes to see me today. He is the cleric I appointed a couple of years ago at Laud's suggestion to be Provost of Trinity College, to tighten up the teaching there in accordance with the King and the Archbishop's policies. He is shown into my study. After telling me that all is going well at the College, he has some surprising news.

"Ussher has left Dublin Cathedral and gone to his palace in Drogheda."

"Well, he's entitled to take a holiday sometimes, I suppose."

"It's not a holiday, My Lord. He told me that he is no more than a figurehead now, and is no more Primate of the Church in Ireland than the emperor of China."

"What an extraordinary thing for him to say. Of course he's the Primate. Do you mean he won't come back?"

"That seems to be the size of it. I know he is very cast down by the turn that the rituals being forced on his Church has taken. First, as you well know, he is a Puritan at heart and dislikes Archbishop Laud's Arminian views and ostentatious – as he sees them – forms of worship. Secondly, he objected to my appointment as Provost, as he foresaw that the College would expound and teach Laud's views and not his own more Puritan doctrines. And that has, of course, happened. He and I have been virtually at war ever since. Thirdly, he ...."

"Does this list go on forever, William? Ussher is a nice man, though rather weak to be leading the Irish Church."

"There are a few more items. You will recall his firm views on the introduction of the new Articles of Faith into the Irish Church two years since: they needed to take into account the largely Puritan views of so many people, and should not be too High Church."

"I do indeed. He contradicted the wishes of the King and Archbishop Laud who told me that he thinks it would be far from easy to find a man more unfit for government of the Church than James Ussher." I sigh. It is sad. "When did he leave?"

"He went yesterday, My Lord. I must say that he did not give those reasons as his excuse for going. I only know what is really behind his departure because of the things he's told me when we've been arguing in the past. He says he's going because he cannot afford life in Dublin and is going to the country for financial reasons."

I chuckle at that. "He may not be entirely untruthful in saying that, even if his palace is luxurious. My aim with my land policies is to restore to the Church as much as possible of the land and income it used to have. The clergy are under-resourced, and it is hardly surprising that a highly religious and honest priest like Ussher should find himself short of money. Even so, I think you're right; he's going because he cannot tolerate the worship reforms I am putting through for the King and Laud."

"He has another grievance, My Lord."

I am not entirely surprised. "Another? Does he so?"

"He does. He is quite open about it, at any rate to me. He says that while your reforms make life rather hard for Puritans, the Catholics get away with holding their services in private and are not even prosecuted and forced to pay the recusancy fines."

I begin to flare up at this, but manage to keep a lid on my temper. "That just proves Laud is correct to say that Ussher is not fit for government. If these Kingdoms – all of them – England and Wales, Scotland and Ireland – are to be safe, government has to look at a rather larger picture and take many things into account. Who do you imagine would like to see the Catholics hounded and prosecuted – persecuted, even?"

"Well, the ... er ... Puritans, I suppose."

"True, William, which is why Ussher feels as he does. Anyone else?"

"Other protestants, and ..."

"You're missing the point, because you think only in terms of the religious angle. The King of Spain would be delighted if the Catholics in Ireland were persecuted. We are on good terms with them at present and there is no risk of war with them, though many in England would love it to happen. We trade with Spain, and Ireland is not so rich we can afford to throw that trade away."

Chappell sneers. "Ireland isn't rich at all!"

"Now you're beginning to understand. The point is that most of the Old English are Catholics and they're loyal to the King, but that would change if we press them too hard. They are powerful and wealthy and would make very dangerous rebels. The native Irish are Catholic to the tips of their toes, and far from loyal if persecuted, which is understandable. And they have a leader in Owen O'Neill who is in exile in Spain, who would make a perfect focus for a Spanish invasion."

"And if the Catholics are persecuted they may call on Spain to invade, and we would be at war." Chappell has seen the light at last.

"Precisely. A decade ago the Duke of Buckingham proved conclusively that fighting Spain is not easy. Indeed he won nothing. The King does not have a big, well trained Army. I'm doing my best to create one here against just such a threat, but I hope I'm never going to have to put it in the field against Spain. Their Army is huge, well-trained, and hardened by fighting all over Europe and the Americas for decades. Ours hasn't won a battle since before the men in it were born. Between you and me, we might not stand a chance."

"You are probably right, My Lord."

"It's tactful of you to say so, for what chance do you think you'd have of remaining Provost of the College with your Protestant views if this island were another Spanish Catholic colony? And what hope would Ussher have of any Puritan worship being tolerated at all? None. We should have such beheadings and burnings at the stake as would make Queen Mary's reign look positively benign."

"I've never looked at it like that. Now I'll know what to say to those who fear that you are sympathetic to Popery."

"How wrong can they be? I want us all to be brought under one form of Divine Service – the one the King wants – and the Crown will never be safe on this side of the Irish Sea until then. But this isn't the time, and these are not the circumstances. This is not the proper season to disquiet the Catholics by provoking them with persecution and fines. When I have made Ireland more prosperous, and done more to give all classes and creeds and peoples here – yes, even the real Irish – some justice, they will be less likely to want the Spanish Army here. Then we can take other steps to try to bring the Catholics into the Church in Ireland."

I then call for some wine, and some food, but I soon have to dismiss Chappell, as I have a dreadful headache, and I feel so irritable and irritated. I hardly slept last night, and fear I shall not do much better tonight. My bowels are irritable too; last night I had diarrhoea, and there was blood in it. I told Bess. She said I probably have the bloody flux, and she wasn't surprised. She says I work too hard. I said the amount of work is huge and growing, and she said, not unsympathetically, that I try to do too much of it myself, and I ought to leave more to others, as I have good and clever people round me.

She's right about the help I have, and could make more use of, but it's just the way I am. I do not seem to be able to let things go. She says I'll have to let go if God takes me away. Even so, I do not see myself dying in bed of over-work. Bess says I'm hardly ever in bed these days, and I hardly ever make love to her now. I've got to do something about that, but I'm reluctant sometimes as I come so quickly. She says that's worry and anxiety, and in turn it makes me anxious about how I perform.

Elizabeth. 27th February, 1636. Dublin Castle.

Today has been a better day for Thomas. He has hardly done any work at all, and has even been out with his beloved hawks. He complains that there is no real game in this country for his hawks to chase and kill, and that he and the hawks have to be content with catching blackbirds, the poor creatures. Despite the nursery rhyme, I do not fancy 24 of them in a pie. And they sing so beautifully. It's like larks' tongues which are supposed to be a delicacy. How can you hunt those glorious song birds for their tongues and rid the world of song?

Anyway, he comes in this afternoon refreshed and ruddy from the riding and the exercise, and very happy. Well, he seems to be happy. I take him to my drawing room, where I have been doing some embroidery with a couple of my lady friends. There is a log fire burning brightly, and it is cosy and warm, and a couple of candelabra add to the atmosphere of comfort and relaxation.

He greets them lightly and kisses their hands and they tactfully depart.

I take his hands and ask how he has enjoyed his day. He laughs. "It was fun, but bloody cold. Kit and George – Radcliffe, not brother – enjoyed themselves, too. We caught a few birds, but it was the open country and the winter sun that made it so good to be away from the paper-work and the press of business. I wish ...."

"'I could be away from it all for ever'. I know Thomas. You have said it so many times lately, as though you hope to convince yourself. Anyway, enough of that. Let us stay happy and forget about worrying over things, at any rate for this evening. I've told the governess to keep the children in their rooms this evening, and I have arranged for their dinner to be served there. I want you all to myself for once."

He takes me in his arms and kisses me softly on the hair and neck and cheek. He tells me he loves me, and I respond by kissing him on the lips, softly, and then with more meaning and what I hope he takes for a message of desire. Thomas sighs, and kisses me harder, and our tongues touch and touch and seek and linger.

His arms around me pull tighter and tighter, and I hug him back, and caress him passionately, and run my hand down to his breeches. He sighs again, and I stroke him there. I do this for a space as he does not become hard as fast as he was wont to do. This confirms my suspicion that he is worried about his lovemaking, for he has been coming very quickly the last few times we have had sex, and once or twice he has hardly entered me before it is all done.

I do not think his health gives him much confidence either. I shall have to give him that confidence. I go swiftly to the door and lock it. There is a rug before the fire, and I stand on it and unfasten my dress and let it fall to the floor. He starts to remove his doublet, but I tell him to stop. "I want to undress you Thomas. You've undressed me so often. Now it is my turn." And he stops, watching me as I take off my petticoats, and then my bodice and the band around my breasts.

George Radcliffe. 9th March, 1636. Dublin.

Thomas is very buoyant today. The reason for his joy is that he has recently taken another step in the reform of the Irish Church along Laudian lines by appointing John Atherton as the new Bishop of Waterford and Lismore. He replaced Michael Boyle, who died a while ago. Bishop Michael was a relative of Lord Cork's so Thomas is also happy that one of Cork's sources of influence has gone. As I recall it was

Michael Boyle who provided evidence of what Cork had done to get his hands on Youghal; how much influence Cork had with him after that is doubtful. Indeed, he could not have been the cleric's favourite cousin before that, if he was prepared to give damning evidence against him. But then I would not have wanted to be paid only 50 pounds a year either.

The main point is that Atherton follows Laud's ideas, which means he is very acceptable to Thomas. That must explain why he has risen so fast in the hierarchy of the Church since Thomas has been in Ireland. Of course, Cork has also lost the chance of putting one of his nominees in the See. Thomas leaves nothing to chance; where consolidating his own power is involved he is indefatigable.

I overheard him dictating to one of his secretaries earlier on. As far as I could make out he was writing to Archbishop Laud. There was a passage about Atherton, and Thomas was saying: "There is not such a terrier in England or Ireland for the unkennelling of an old fox. Cork will think the devil is let loose upon him".

I have to say Atherton does not sound much like a Bishop to me.

Thomas. 12th March, 1636. Dublin Castle.

Sir John Coke, Secretary of State,

London.

My dear Sir John,

I confess that I am rather angry but shall endeavour to write calmly. On 16th January you wrote that Darcy, Martin, and O'Shagnessy had been ordered to return to Ireland. At the beginning of this month I learned that at last they were on their way back, and yesterday O'Shagnessy and Martin came back, the story being that Martin would not have done so had he not been apprehended in a low dive in Fetter Lane, so he was in the custody of a special messenger!

But Darcy was not with them and I have now been told that he is actually trying in Court circles to interest the King in Mountnorris's new scheme for the customs farm. This is exactly the sort of thing I expected him to do.

Apparently this scheme would increase the farm by 11,000 per annum. I take it that means the share the King receives. My own new scheme will be far more profitable than that for the Crown. If one takes into account that I always pay what is owed to the Treasury, and pay it when it is due, and Mountnorris does neither, it is clear the King will do well to ensure Darcy comes back here and that I can go ahead with my own reform of the farm.

I remain your humble servant and friend,

Wentworth.

Christopher Wandesford. 19th March, 1636. Dublin.

Today is a good news day. Despatches from London arrive here this morning telling Tom that his friend Bishop Juxon, Bishop of London, is the new Treasurer, replacing Lord Portland who died last year.

This is a great relief to Tom, and I have to say, to me too. We've had such a lot of difficulty dealing with the Clanricarde and Mountnorris problems that we feared what would happen if the King chose a Treasurer who was in the anti-Wentworth camp. Tom was never entirely sure of Portland, but his worries on that score never seem to have produced any definite damage to his plans or career. It was just a suspicion.

The worry following Portland's demise was that if an enemy were given the post, that would be another voice being poured into the King's ear against our policies here in Ireland. With Juxon in the job that risk has departed. It makes Tom happy. Why does it make me happy? Because I should be highly unlikely to keep my pleasant, powerful, and remunerative Irish post if Tom were called home. As it is I'm accumulating money and thinking of buying an estate. I have my eye on a large property at a place near Naas, a few miles outside Dublin, with the unbelievable name of Jigginstown. I'm told it's the only place name in Ireland beginning with J.

Thomas. 23rd March, 1636. Dublin Castle.

In early February the King gave me permission to go ahead with the case against Cork over Youghal, and to pursue the Title claims in County Galway. I arranged for the old Galway jury to be brought back to Court.

I cannot believe they will now be inclined to decide the cases against the Crown after what happened to them last time. I am also confident of the outcome because of a letter I received from Ulick, the new Earl of Clanrickarde earlier this month. He wrote: "I have a great a burden of debt to discharge, and my creditors are importunate in calling in their loans. Necessity compels me to make speedy preparation for the sale of some land, or raise some new mortgages, which will just make my position worse in the long run."

I am not sure what reaction he expects from me to that. Does he want sympathy? Well, that he can have, since I have been strapped for cash myself in the past. Does he expect me to forgo the King's plantation policy for him because his father left him some debts? If it's that he will be disappointed. I am finishing off some calculations of the revenue Connaught will yield from the policy when it is fully implemented, and I expect it will be around 20,000 pounds a year. That is much more than I thought this time last year, when Portland estimated 15,000 and I told the King it was only likely to be 6,000. I dare say someone will suggest I am doing that to make my case for going ahead stronger, and weaken the objections of the local landowners. But I've had a lot more information since then.

George Radcliffe. 7th April, 1636. Bishop's Palace, Derry.

Bishop Bramhall is a very happy man. I am not sure his glee is well-founded. I do not think Thomas believes it is either. He has sent me up here from Dublin to find out what Bramhall thinks.

"It is excellent news, George. I have been looking into the records. Complaints have been made to London from Ireland for many years that the City of London has not been fulfilling its obligations here. I've been appointed receiver of the rents and profits to which the City is entitled from this area, and to make sure those obligations are fulfilled. They received a huge grant of plantation land here in Ulster about thirty years ago and they've done virtually nothing."

"You may be right, Your Grace, but ..."

"How many years have we known each other now, George? Four? Five? There's no need to 'Your Grace' me. Call me John. I may be a bishop now, but I hope I'm the same man I was when I was Thomas's chaplain. By the way, how is he?"

"Not as well as he might be, I'm afraid. He works too hard, delegates but can't keep his hand off the tiller, gets headaches, and gout. And he is not sure this business with London is a good idea."

"I'm sorry to hear he is unwell. I shall pray for him. But the City should be forced to make the best use of the land, shouldn't it? Especially when they promised to do so?"

"There's no argument about that, John, but the thought that the rich who dominate the place may become enemies is worrying. Thomas is not afraid to annoy people..." That makes the Bishop grin. ".... but sometimes even he can see that making adversaries out of very powerful wealthy people can be counter-productive. He thinks measures should be taken more gradually to bring them to their senses, and get the same results in the end, by persuasion rather than coercion or force."

Bramhall looks mystified. "But the King agrees with this policy, George. After all, it is the Privy Council in London which appointed me receiver."

"Precisely my point – and Thomas's. Not even the King can afford to have the City against him. Between them those merchant princes have more money than anyone in the Kingdom."

He nods; now he understands. "They can't have been at all happy they were fined 70,000 pounds last year, no matter how much money they have. And that was by the English Privy Council, too." John seems rather more subdued now.

"That's as may be, but Thomas is Deputy in Ireland, and rightly or wrongly they'll see his hand in this. He is, after all, a member of that Council, even if he was here and not there when they made that decision."

Thomas. 20th April, 1636. Dublin Castle.

Richard Boyle, Earl of Cork, one of the richest men, if not the richest, in Ireland, stands before me. We are alone apart from Philip Mainwaring who is to take notes but no part in our discussion. I have not summoned Cork; I wrote and asked him to come, but I was able to say that I was doing so at the King's request. Accordingly he hardly dared refuse. He is arrayed magnificently in what must be his most impressive, and certainly must be the most expensive, of his garments, glittering with gold and precious stones, and soft black leather shoes with diamond buckles. No doubt he wishes to overawe me, but if he is Solomon in all his glory, then I am the Biblical lily who outshines him, for I have not neglected my own raiment today. It is, as usual, rather plain, but to me he looks gaudy.

He is an Earl, and regards me as a mere Viscount, but I am the Deputy Lord Lieutenant, and I represent the King, and he does not. I have to show him who is the mightier.

I invite him to sit, and we both do so. Philip pours red wine for us both, and then sits at a desk with his papers and his quill.

Me. My Lord, as you know, I have invited you here at the request of the King. I am charged with having a talk with you about the possibility of reaching some sort of compromise about the College of Youghal, its land and income.

Cork. And I have come because His Majesty has requested it, and not out of any favour to you, My Lord.

Me. You will realise that if the case goes ahead, in the Court of Castle Chamber, which, as you are well aware, is a prerogative Court of the King's, the chances of your getting away with the land you have taken are remote.

Cork. Let's be clear at the start. I do not accept that I have 'taken' anything. And I shall fight, and fight hard.

Me. But you won't have Darcy to help you; he's in England and cannot appear in these Courts until he takes the Oath, as you well know, and he won't do that just to help you. *(I can see that blow struck home).*

Cork. I shall not give in.

Me. But is the fight worth the risk? The King has nothing to lose. If he does not pursue this matter, he has lost already what you have taken – alright – *(I raise my hands to ward off the protest I can see is coming)* what you are currently possessed of. If he goes ahead, through me and the Court, he can get it back. You can only keep it, but you can gain nothing, and the King's favour will definitely be forfeited for ever. *(Another blow has landed; Cork is still too ambitious to want to be permanently in the Monarch's bad books).*

Cork. But if we proceed to trial and I do lose, I lose it all, and I am not prepared to lie down under that!

Me. I told you at the start that the King wants us to reach a compromise. If you lose in Court you will lose everything to do with the College, as you rightly say. But not only that; you face the likelihood of a fine of 30,000 pounds. Would it not be better, and safer, to make an offer to settle the matter now?

Cork. I'd rather know what the King – and you – have in mind first. I'm not taking a leap in the dark.

Me. The King foresaw that. I've therefore drawn up a list of the College property and some – not by any means all - of its land and parishes which it would be acceptable to the Crown to recover. If you will agree to that, it only remains for you to make an offer in respect of the fine.

Cork. *(He takes the list from me).* I need a while to study this.

Me. Then why don't we take a break for a couple of hours, have some lunch, and have another try this afternoon?

Cork. Very well, but I'll not dine with you!

Me. And I have no desire to be put off my food by the sight of you glowering at me across the table. Your attendants are in the small dining room, and I shall have lunch served to you in there. I shall eat with my family, and I shall see you back here at 2 o'clock. Sir George, would you kindly show the Earl the way?

****

Two hours later we resume, and Philip takes more notes. Cork haggles over some properties; I give ground on the College itself and much of its land, but the Church is to keep all the rectories and parishes Cork had misappropriated. He pleads that his son, Dungarvan, has been in tears at the idea that he would lose all the property in his marriage settlement, and that it is making Lady Dungarvan ill. As she is my niece Elizabeth I cannot be entirely stony hearted about that. Cork also says he has been bullied by Archbishop Ussher to do his duty to the Church, so has decided to effect the compromise the King desires. Ussher can't have retired completely, then!

Having got that far, I ask Cork what he intends to do about the fine. He wants to haggle over that too, and offers 10,000 pounds, which I reject, but to draw the matter to a close, I suggest we call it 15,000, to be paid in three equal instalments, one now, and one for each of the next two years. Reluctantly, very reluctantly, he bows to the inevitable. In return I tell him that when I go to London shortly, I shall ask the King to grant Cork a completely legitimate and secure deed to the College, but I emphasise that I shall not let him have the rectories back.

I'm determined that they will either house Church of Ireland priests or the Church will receive the rents from the tenants. The money will not go into Boyle's coffers.

Having laid this powerful man low, my path is clear with all the others over the matter of recovering land for the Crown and the Church. Next I must finish with the new Earl of Clanricarde.

Thomas. 15th May, 1636. Dublin Castle.

Today I am exhausted. Yesterday I had an attack of the stone. I thought until then that gout was painful, but compared with the stone it is almost a joy. It was the worst and most painful – excruciatingly painful – experience I have ever had and hope ever to have to undergo. It was above anything I have endured since I was a man. Sweat burst from me like a fountain; I said every foul word I could think of, mixed up with calls to God for relief. Even Bess could not stop me swearing. I hardly knew what I was about.

My physician says this happens when a bladder or kidney stone passes through the track from the bladder to the penis. I would have laughed when he said that track – the urethra is what he called it – is not designed for such a purpose if I hadn't been demented by pain at the time. He says I should take a break from my frequent journeys about the country, and that I do too much work. He must have been listening to Bess. When he left me he told her what he had said, so she informed me. When she came in she did not say "I told you so," for she is too kind for that, but clearly it must have been going through her mind.

She is desperate for me to take it easier and spend more time with her and the children, and take some exercise. Even Kit urges me to do so. I should love to, but I cannot let go of the reins at present. There is just too much to be done.

I used to love hawking, but I haven't been for ages. When I have no gout the only fresh air I get is walking in the local lanes and fields, or spending a few days at the hunting lodge, with the family or with some friends.

It's not even as though being home is relaxing all the time. One of the penalties of wealth and success is that you have to maintain appearances. For that you need servants, as well as the family. There are about 300 people in my household. We have many guests.

Obviously I do not run the house; that is what Beth does, with the help of the housekeepers and the steward, but I have a lot to do with the social side. That includes having scions of noble families to stay. Some act as pages or gentlemen-in-waiting for their keep. With some that is no problem, but others can be a real nuisance.

We entertained Secretary Windebanke's son for a while, and Sir Arthur Ingram's. I had to get very stern with both of them and send them home after they had what might be euphemistically termed 'inappropriate relations' with local girls here. I had never envisaged any misconduct from young Windebanke, but I suppose I could not be sure what a son of Sir Arthur might get up to. Arthur didn't get his knighthood for a resemblance to Sir Galahad, though to be fair I have not heard that he was a seducer. He is more of a Shylock.

I have reached the age when my friends and family are dwindling through untimely deaths. Three years ago my friend George Calvert died, though he was not all that young. A few months ago James Hay, Earl of Carlisle, shrugged off this mortal coil. My brother Michael went to fight in Germany on the Protestant side a few years ago and has not been heard of since, and two of the others, Philip and Matthew, died about the same time as Carlisle.

If I did not have George Radcliffe and Christopher Wandesford - and Bess, of course - I should be the most solitary man that ever served such a King in such a place as this.

Christopher Wandesford. 29th May, 1636. Dublin.

The trial of the Galway jury took place over the last two days. They were asked the same questions about the King's title in Galway, to give them a chance to change their minds. The judge – Tom did not try this case himself, thank goodness – said: "The charge against these gentlemen is that, contrary to the evidence, they wilfully refused to find the title of His Majesty to the whole County of Galway. All this Court has to do is decide whether the evidence given to the jury at Portumna was sufficient, in our judgment, to have convinced a rational and unbiased jury."

When this was put to the jury, to my great surprise they gave the same answers they had given at the original hearing. They were fined 4,000 pounds each and sent back to prison. I think you can see the influence of the Old English such as Clanricarde in this matter, since so many of the jury are actually Irish, with names like O'Machermurrough, O'Connor, O'Bryan, and O'Madden. They are clearly men of courage and conviction to make such a stand, though it may be treason to say so.

A rumour has been going the rounds that Tom is off to England and might already be there. That may have helped persuade them he would no longer be the Deputy here, so that they could defy him, but he has not left yet. I cannot think he will not return and continue in office.

The 5th Earl Clanricarde, Ulick, is not at all happy. He and his family blame Thomas for his father's death in November, but when I told him so, he said: "I can hardly be guilty of a crime involving his death when the man had passed his three score years and ten." I'm not happy that the man is dead, but to be honest, I cannot be sorry that his opposition to Tom's plans - well, the King's, if truth be told - has been removed by divine intervention. I hope the 5th Earl will be somewhat more malleable.

Elizabeth. 6th June, 1636. Dublin Castle.

Thomas left for England today. We spent last night in each other's arms, and I am happy about that, sad he is gone, and very tired!! Our love-making has revived a great deal since an afternoon in February when I took charge. His confidence has returned and he seems more relaxed as a result, but I cannot stop him working too hard, he still has headaches sometimes, and gout, and trouble with his bowels. He won't take any notice of the doctor or me despite having an attack of the stone last month.

He spent yesterday with the children, and we took a ride out into the country and had a picnic lunch, and played games. It was a happy time, but he still found a few minutes to write some letters before we went to bed. I hope the crossing to Chester will be smooth and swift. I'm sure he worries about the danger of sea travel, but he keeps it to himself. How do sailors and sea-captains put up with it all the time when they are so familiar with the perils of the deep? Is that it? Does familiarity breed contempt, even for risk of death?

Christopher Wandesford. 10th June, 1636. Dublin Castle.

Tom left for England four days ago. George Radcliffe and

Mainwaring went with him, and a large number of retainers and a huge amount of baggage. He has left me in charge of the Irish Government in his absence. I always knew how hard he worked, or I thought I did. Now the reins are in my hands I can see that he is burdened even more than I had believed. The strain upon him of doing this work for the last three years must have been colossal. In fact it is longer than three years, because he was undertaking some preliminary work on it when we were still in Yorkshire, and then he sent me ahead to organise staff and systems before he arrived.

There is so much correspondence. It comes in from all over England as well as Ireland, and some from abroad. So many wealthy men have fingers in pies here, and they all seek favours and advancement, and they want to know what he thinks about this or that project. He gives some of it to me and Radcliffe and his brother George, but he deals with so much of it himself, probably over half. It would kill me if I had to do it for long, and I do not know that I have the strength of will to keep control as he does, nor the energy to do it. He is a forceful character; I am not. He is a master; I am not. I like to think I am a good servant, and the fact he keeps me by him must support that view. He doesn't tolerate fools gladly and wouldn't have one as close to him as I am. The same must be said of George and Radcliffe.

Already there is a bit of bad news to tell him in my reports. The Sheriff in Galway who summoned the jury which gave the wrong verdict on the King's title has died in prison. He was, apparently, the brother of Patrick Darcy, Cork's lawyer. It is hardly flattering to Tom to say so, but he will barely be upset by it except for the fact that it may embarrass him. I can guess his response: "Rather embarrassing, and I feel sorry for the poor chap, but make sure his executors pay his fine; it's owed to the King. He should not have defied me in the first place."

Having Thomas as a friend is wonderful, but it must be dreadful to have him as an enemy. On the other hand, I can see Darcy being even more antagonistic now.

Thomas. 13th June, 1636. Henrietta Street, London.

I had the fastest possible journey from Dublin to London. The sea crossing was remarkably quick, with a wind behind us. I lost no time in Chester, and stayed only a night or two in a couple of towns on the way south. I went to my new London house here in Covent Garden a couple of days ago, and yesterday I went by river to Hampton Court to an audience with His Majesty. Nothing of moment occurred but the King granted me my own suite of rooms there for the duration of my stay.

I was quite surprised by the reception I received at Court. I don't fool myself that I have ever been popular there, but I was greeted by various courtiers with an unexpected degree of warmth. Maybe it was just what to expect from people who suck up to others who are seen to have money and influence with the King, or to have places to offer, as I do in Ireland and the North.

My house is splendid, built in yellow stone, and set in a new development designed by Inigo Jones, the King's architect. Despite being here for so short a time, I am already besieged by importunate people seeking jobs, grants, land in Ireland, favours in Yorkshire – in fact if you can think of it, they ask for it.

I found time to write a short note to Bess, but I had to ask her to tell Will, Nan, and Arabella that "I am sorry, but in good faith I am so infinitely pestered with company that I have not time to write to them, but God Almighty bless them." I miss her and the children. Society here is better and more lively than in Dublin, but I find little solace in it, such as I find at home.

I hope I can persuade the King to recognise the work I am doing on his behalf, and the importance of fostering Ireland.

Archbishop William Laud. 20th June, 1636. Lambeth Palace.

I stand at the window of my study, overlooking the gate and carriageway into the grounds of my palace. It is a lovely palace, built in Tudor times with Tudor bricks, and has a homely look, even if it is rather large to be a home as such. I shouldn't say 'my palace', as it belongs to the Church of England, which is my Church. I shouldn't say 'my Church', either, as it is God's, but the King made me Archbishop of Canterbury, and the palace is my home and place of business, when I am not in Canterbury, and the Church of England is the business I am in. I suppose the last four sentences show that I'm a vain man, and I cannot deny it, even if I would, since vanity is pride, and pride is a sin. So is denying it.

But my business and the Church of England are not matters of sin. They are a matter of getting England to worship God in a proper and fitting fashion. I go about this campaign of church reform in what I hope to be a thorough manner. Indeed, I call my policy 'Thorough'. It is a policy which has the full backing of the King, and support from the Deputy Lord Lieutenant of Ireland, Thomas, Viscount Wentworth.

I have not seen him since he left to take up this post three years ago. He has not been home since. He has come back now to discuss 'Thorough' with me, and give progress reports to the King on Irish finances, the Irish Army, and the state of the Church in Ireland. He and I shall also discuss the latter point, as much of what he is doing in respect of the Church is to advance my religious reforms there whilst I work on them here. He must want to talk to the King about a new customs farm he has in mind, and persuade Charles to side with him in his dispute with the Earl of Clanricarde and St Albans. The Lord knows how often he has written to ask me to advance these causes with the King privately and in Council.

I may not have seen him but we correspond a great deal; he calls his Irish and political policies 'Thorough', too, and our planning of these policies and our tactics for introducing them form a great part of our letters. Our friendship is fortunate for both of us, since it is useful to be able to bounce our ideas off each other; he can rely on me to present his views reliably to the King and the Privy Council, and my standing with the King benefits from the fact that I can do that.

After all, Charles does not take kindly to criticism, and as he approves of the way we carry out his policies, and as he approves of ours, it makes for a cosy relationship. Thomas writes regularly to the King as well as to me, of course, so the King is familiar with his views, but it helps him no end that I am there to reinforce his ideas as persuasively as I can into the King's ear.

Nevertheless, I am not at all sure that Charles really likes Thomas. He cannot be said to be fond of anyone apart from the Queen, Prince Charles, and his other children, since Buckingham was murdered. There is always a reserve – greater than usual – in what the King says about the Viscount. In my opinion, for what it is worth, it is as though Charles does not trust him, despite having left him in office as President of the North, and, in effect, appointed him the ruler of Ireland, making him largely responsible for running two-thirds of the Kingdom. Perhaps this distrust is due to Thomas's role, all those years ago, in forcing the Petition of Right through Parliament. I don't think it is class prejudice. Charles seems to be impervious to that. After all, he's elevated me from almost nothing, and George Villiers came from exactly nothing to be his bosom friend. Thomas comes from a much higher station than either of us.

These are the thoughts revolving in my mind as I look towards the gate, and then I see Thomas's carriage come through it, and drive up to the door. I see Thomas descend from it. He dresses very soberly, in black, with a little white linen at his neck. I am told he has brought many servants and advisers to London with him. He must be getting very rich.

I remain by the window until a servant knocks, enters, and announces: "Your Grace. My Lord Wentworth, Lord Deputy of Ireland, craves audience.

"Admit him at once. And bring some wine and food. Then leave us."

The servant bows. "Yes, Your Grace." He goes out and comes back almost immediately. "The Lord Deputy of Ireland, Your Grace".

Wentworth enters as the servant goes, closing the door behind him silently. I will not have the cloistered peace of my palace shattered by banging doors, or if I can help it, by any loud noise other than the dinner gong. Thomas seems to fill the room, not because he is fat, unlike me, but because he is tall, well-built, muscular, and has this air of command and authority which is almost spell-binding. It is not vanity for me to say that as Primate of All England I am a pretty important person myself, but Thomas comes from another league altogether. However, I notice that he has put on a little weight since I saw him last. There is a slight glitter of grey in his dark beard and hair, and he seems to limp a little.

We bow to each other in what might be taken for a light-hearted, even mocking fashion, which suits our humour, and we laugh. When I ask him how he is he tells me he is worried about himself and fears he is not long for this world. I cannot stand that kind of talk. I joke with him that busy as he is he cannot afford the time to die. Sometimes I wonder why I indulge this polite custom of asking after people's health. The trouble with doing so is that they invariably tell you. I must try to stop asking. I turn the topic.

Me. My Lord Deputy of Ireland. Why Thomas, how far have we come in - what - six years? I'm Archbishop of Canterbury, and you're

the King's Deputy in Ireland. I am the King's plenipotentiary with his Church ...
Wentworth. And as Lord Deputy in Ireland I stand in his stead in that country. Yes, William, we have come far. We have been thorough.
Me. Yes, Thorough. That is our policy. Thorough order for the Church for me; thorough administration, law, and justice for the people for you. And we are fortunate that his Majesty is our wise and supportive Master.

I invite Thomas to be seated, and sit by him, our chairs facing the windows. We discuss at great length the various matters that we write to each other about. We cover the factions; the Irish, the Old English, the New English, and the Scots, with whom he has to contend.

We rehearse my arguments for reform of the Church in Ireland, and what may be the best policies for dealing with recusants, both Catholic and Puritan. We consider the possibility that persecution of the Pope's followers may drive them into the arms of Spain or France, and Thomas makes it plain that he is against any policy likely to have that effect. We reflect on the fact that the Spanish were able to cause Queen Elizabeth so much trouble in Ireland because of the allegiance of the native Irish to Rome. The resulting wars were a terrible drain on the Exchequer.

We move on from that to the Army, and then back to religious concerns.

Me. You know my views on these matters, Thomas. Faith is the real cause of the trouble. You need more Protestants.
Wentworth. I can assure you I'm trying to put your policies into practice in Ireland. I've recently had quite a triumph over the Earl of Cork, recovering about 400 rectories from him, which, together with their glebe lands will enable many more and much better priests to be the incumbents. Then we may make more progress with conversion of Catholics.
Me. That is excellent.
Wentworth. Indeed. The Church is so poor many parishes are without a competent qualified curate.
Me. I can assure you that's not just a problem in Ireland. The Puritans and I have one thing in common, and that's contempt for priests and vicars who neglect their parish duties. Some rarely hold a service even on holy days, and a parson at Crowland has no discernible

religion at all. He could be anything from a Papist to the rankest Puritan for all that anyone knows; he thinks he's overdoing it if he preaches a sermon four times a year. He's incredibly fat – yes, don't laugh, Thomas, even fatter than I am; they say he owes all his stipend on the slate in the ale-houses, and his arse is falling out of his breeches.

Wentworth. That's the trouble with inadequate revenue. Too much Church land in Ireland has been sold off or simply stolen in the last eighty years or so. If I can recover these lands for the Church, there'll be more rent and there should be more, and better paid, priests. But it breeds resentment amongst the nobility. The Old English are Catholic, and many of them were able to buy up or steal Church land during Henry VIII's reign, and since. And of course the New English have been at it too, and even more greedily.

Me. So the New English will get the dirty end of this stick too.

Wentworth. Precisely: the ones who settled there during Elizabeth and James's reigns acquired enormous estates, often by dubious means. They're mainly Protestants, but they're not above the law, any more than the Catholics are, even if they think they should be. It's a difficult situation, but the King needs the money to keep up the Army, and govern the island efficiently. I'm using the Irish Courts to enquire into the ownership of these lands, and claim a good title for the King. Some owners then buy back what my orders take from them, and if not, the Crown can sell it to others, or enjoy the rents from it.

Me. I've heard the Army is quite formidable.

Wentworth. Quite true. I train them myself when I can spare the time, and I review them regularly. In fact, I shall be conducting a review near Dublin as soon as I get back.

Me. These troops of yours, are they Irish?

Wentworth. Many of them are, and Catholic, and very loyal, which proves my point that the only real threat comes from Spain.

I decide to change the subject. I get up, go to the table and pour some more wine, and sit again. We then discuss the injustice many of the Lords, New and Old English, inflict on their vassals, Thomas's plans to exploit agriculture, build towns and seaports, and turn the pastoral Gaelic way of life into more profitable channels. The Protestants back this policy, but Thomas says it deprives the peasants of their land, and their nomadic way of life. I can't tell if he is sorry for them or not, but it is clear he does not favour their primitive ways. He says it is inevitable they must change if we get many Protestant settlers to come from England, and more important, increase the King's revenue, and take from England's shoulders the burden of maintaining Ireland.

Then we talk about money and taxes.

Me. I've seen from your letters, which incidentally I read to the King and the Council, that, by reducing taxes, increasing trade, and taking control of the collection of customs duties, you've doubled, even trebled, the Crown Revenues of Ireland.

Wentworth. No-one relishes paying tax, but the higher the tax, the greater the effort people will make to avoid paying. Efficient collection of a lower tax produces more money, but leaves everyone better off. That is how I can afford the Army, and try to make the Poor Laws work fairly.

Me. It was your care for the poor and your enforcement of the Poor Laws here in the North that brought you so many enemies, Thomas.

Wentworth. But not amongst the poor!

Me. Perhaps. Have a care you aren't doing the same in Ireland. All your success has come from winning battles with the rich and powerful. They hate you for it.

Wentworth. I do not fear their hate. I shan't let the Earl of Cork and his like oppress the poor, or the Crown, at any rate in Ireland, where I can prevent it.

Me. But it's the wealthy men like Cork who pay the rates and taxes which provide for the poor.

Wentworth. If rich and powerful families didn't oppress the poor, the poor wouldn't become dependent on the Poor Laws, and the rich wouldn't have such heavy taxes to pay.

Me. Thomas, if you continue like this you will be doomed. How many wealthy men have you thwarted?

Wentworth. Few compared with the poor who've been persecuted! The common people who are forced out of their homes become the beggars for whom the poor laws are designed!

Me. Few rich people will thank you for reminding them of it. First, you stop the rich turning the poor off the land. Then you force them to pay rates and taxes to help the poor, to build workhouses and find work for the sturdy beggar. It's just spraying acid in the wound, Thomas. You think you can run the country as a father runs his family?

Wentworth. That is precisely what I believe. A good, loving father governs the home with generosity and firmness, nurtures the small and weak child, fosters the talents of the bright and intelligent son and daughter, and treats all equally.

Me. And you think a wise monarch does the same?

Wentworth. Yes. At least, he should, but on a larger scale. I've striven to get up the ladder only to find myself the equal of those who have not striven at all. Their contempt for me is so obvious I can almost touch it. Making people equal and treating them equally are different things.

Me. Treating them equally in the Law Courts in Ireland is the cause of controversy about you, Thomas.

Wentworth. His Majesty's subjects must all be treated equally in His Majesty's Courts, Your Grace. The Law should apply to and benefit all alike.

Me. Fine words, My Lord, but think how you harm yourself by making enemies of the powerful. Be warned, Thomas; the truth will avail you nothing when all these great men turn against you in unity.

Wentworth. *(Passionately).* I shall not temper my conduct to the likes and dislikes of "Great Men," my friend. Whilst punishment should be used sparingly it should be inescapable and drastic when it is deserved.

Me. But why do the rich and powerful deserve drastic punishment more than others?

Wentworth. I doubt it's more drastic for the rich to pay fines when poor men are hanged for stealing bread! I prefer to punish those who come from the upper ranks of society, since they cannot plead ignorance. They also have the opportunity to do the greater wrong.

Me. And what does punishing them achieve?

Wentworth. It demonstrates at a stroke that they should set the meaner ranks a good example, and that the King is no respecter of persons or wealth.

Me. If these mighty men turn against you, honour will be far from their thoughts. They'll be guided only by vengeance, and then my friendship will be of little help.

Wentworth. Who are they, these people? Is this truth from the mouths of babes and sucklings? No; it comes from those who are jealous of my success with the King. Maybe the inevitable consequence of confronting these men will be to stop my career and fortune in their tracks. Maybe not, but I'm determined to act only in a way which is in the interests of the Crown and Nation - they stand or fall together.

Me. Amen to that! *(One of my servants comes in and informs me that lunch is served in the dining room).* And now, let us eat and talk of other things. How is your wife?

Wentworth. She is well, I hope, and the children.

Me. *(We make our way to the dining room. I change the subject again, since I am not overly interested in family matters)***.** Recently you wrote that you hope to persuade the King to make you an Earl. And gossip reaching the Palace of Lambeth from the Palace of Whitehall says the same. Have a care Thomas; do not annoy the King.

Wentworth. It's the King I'm thinking of. If I can return to Ireland with an earldom, Cork and his cronies will know beyond a shadow of a doubt that I am in the King's favour. Their inclination to oppose my policies - the King's policies - will be that much diminished.

Me. Thomas, the King's favour is his to bestow, not to be importuned by the subject. I beg you, leave this project alone. He will hear no criticism of you in Council, nor elsewhere. Why should you worry?

Wentworth. I welcome your advice, William. I shall think on it, but my inclination is to have one more try. Besides, you've reached the top of the Ecclesiastical Tree, and I'm still working my way up the Secular one.

Me. By the way, do you remember writing to me a couple of years ago about Ship Money, asking whether there would be trouble with people in the Midlands refusing to pay?

Wentworth. Indeed I do. Why?

Me. It seems there is indeed trouble. A gentleman from Buckinghamshire, by the name of Hampden, has refused to pay. He only owes 20 shillings, but he says it's a principle. And he's going to fight it through the Courts.

Thomas. 23rd June, 1636. Whitehall Palace.

Today I am with the King, a couple of days after leaving William Laud. I have much to tell His Majesty. I bring him up to date on how my army (the Irish Army, I correct myself; I cannot afford to let the King think I am setting myself up as King of Ireland) is progressing, on how the campaign to recover Church and Crown lands is going, and how the revenues of the Irish Exchequer are improving. He thanks me for the subsidies which the Irish Parliament and Treasury have been sending to England. He indicates approval of my new version of the customs farm and his increased share of the revenue. He is not happy about antagonising Cork and Clanricarde, but he agrees that if we are to increase Irish revenue and get more land back into the control of the Crown and Church we have no alternative but to proceed.

He tells me how much he approves of Laud's reforms of the Church of England, the order and seemliness of the style of service and Church liturgy Laud has introduced, and how much more pleasing to God this 'beauty of holiness' must be, as well as to him. I find that hardly surprising as Charles is such a formal person. He never seems to lower his guard for a moment.

I try to tell him that, although Laud and I see eye to eye over so much, yet I cannot help but worry that between them they are creating a huge, and hugely resentful, body of worshippers in the country. I say that this body is not solely comprised of non-conformists, but includes a large number of members of the Church of England Communion who are not at all enamoured of High Church ritual, but seek less formality, less of what they see of 'theatrical performances' at the altar, and a more humble service.

The King is not impressed. He is quite content with what the Archbishop is doing and believes that, as God's anointed ruler of the Kingdom, it is up to him to determine, with the assistance of advisers and clerics like Laud, how his people should approach God.

"Sire, I have heard it said that Laud and I are much alike. He has a sharp tongue, and is convinced he is right. I acknowledge that is true of me too. You have Divine Right on your side; we do not. But it behoves all of us to think what the consequences of what we are doing may be, and how others may perceive us."

"You go too far, Thomas, if you presume to tell me what I should think or do. I am the Head of the Church. I think for it."

"If I am presumptuous, Sire, I beg your forgiveness." I pause, being anxious to say what I mean without giving more offence. "The Archbishop told me that the Puritans wish to make the God of all Mercy out to be the fiercest and most unreasonable tyrant in the world, but he does not seem to realise that the non-conformists, inside and outside your Church, think that Laud is doing exactly that himself. Doing it on your behalf may not endear you to your people, Your Majesty."

I get a stony gaze from the King in return for that. "I cannot govern the Kingdom on the basis of what the people think of me and of what I try to do or what my ministers try to do for me. I must govern on the basis of what I believe to be right. Laud tells me the most awful tales of what the Church is like in some parishes. In some villages the upkeep of the church by the parish is so mean, filthy and hopeless that the congregation would certainly not allow such conditions in their own homes. There are homes for some priests which are so stark, poorly maintained and furnished that they are hardly fit for habitation by anyone, let alone the rector or vicar."

I take a deep breath and decide to have another try. "Sire, all that is very distressing, and improper, but as William hauls so many people before the Court of High Commission to enquire into their religious practices and then sends them on to the Star Chamber to be punished, there are many who see yours as the guiding hand behind it all. I am concerned that ..."

"Enough, Thomas. In secular matters you use very similar tactics in Ireland with the men you bring before your Council and your Courts. You may not see the parallel, but I do. As it happens I support both you and William, for you are doing what I want you to do. Let us stick to the religious question." His Majesty pauses. "According to Laud the non-conformists and Puritans are against formal liturgy and ritual because they see it as Roman superstition. This idea has gone so far Laud says that 'it is a display of superstition nowadays if a man goes into Church showing more respect or reverence than a tinker taking his bitch into an ale-house'. Whether the bitch is the tinker's wife or his dog I cannot say."

I am not sure whether that was a royal joke or not so I laugh politely. "We must all show reverence to God, Your Majesty, but many of your subjects mock what they see as the theatrical costumery of many priests. It does no good that priests who do not adhere to the Archbishop's forms of service are kicked out of their parishes, and become itinerant preachers, and poor people who go to hear them speak on village greens are persecuted by Laud's servants. I've heard of some churchwardens, even in my own county, being imprisoned for objecting to the new services, and others being punished for eating meat in Lent. Is this the reason so many families have fled to Massachusetts, Maine, and other New England States?"

The King is now as near to showing anger as I have ever seen him. "If the population of my American colonies is increasing, Thomas, I have no complaints. I cannot tell which of them go to make their fortune, which are running to escape the results of their crimes or debts, and which may, indeed, have some peculiar religious conviction. I thank you for coming, and for your concern and advice, but I shall continue to pursue what I know to be right, with you and with Laud."

He rises, and offers me his hand, which I bow to kiss, and then he surprises me by saying: "Apart from your views on the Puritans and the form of the services, I've found your account of the Irish situation so fascinating that I shall convene a meeting of the full Privy Council. I want you to repeat to them what you have told me. I shall take the chair at the meeting, to show my support for all you do."

The audience is clearly at an end. I rise and bow and back towards the door, and leave. I do not think now is the time to ask for the earldom.

Elizabeth. 28th July, 1636. Dublin Castle.

Today I have a letter from Thomas. I am relieved and happy.

23rd July.

Dearest Bess,

I am so sorry that I have had so little time to write to you. I have simply been too busy. Wherever I go and wherever we stop, people seem to know that I am there and want to see me. Power and riches may be wonderful, but they are also a terrible burden. Often I wonder whether it is all worth it, but I cannot lay down the King's work at this – or perhaps at any – point.

We had a very good and swift crossing, and the captain of the ship told me that there is hardly ever any trouble with pirate attacks in the Irish Sea now. On arrival at the harbour at Chester there was a crowd waiting for me on the dock-side. I had to treat them as if they were just holiday makers or sight-seers or I should have been there for days, but some of them followed me to the home of the Mayor who accommodated me for the night, and I had to give them some time. Some want land in Ireland. Others want favours in Yorkshire (I told them to go and see Osborne; he won't stand for any nonsense). Two wanted me to make representations to the Privy Council and one even handed me a petition to give to the King about a Court case. Nearly all of them offered me bribes, but as you know, I do not play that game.

A week ago I saw the Archbishop, and today I had lunch and a long talk with the King. Laud and I get on so well, despite the fact that we can both be quite prickly, and are perhaps too forthright in expressing our opinions. He asked after you and the children, I'm pleased to say. However, he does not think I should ask the King for the Earldom I want so badly – and need if I am to be able to deal with the likes of Cork and Clanricarde effectively. It would also be gratifying to receive such a mark of Royal favour and put me on an even footing with my late friend James Hay, who was Earl of Carlisle.

Writing of him reminds me that I must visit his widow, Lucy. James was a good friend to me on the Council of the North and a great help to me in the House of Lords. I shall write to her when I have finished this note to you.

The King was kind and is pleased to treat me graciously, so in that regard, which is the most important thing, I stand as favourably as I can desire.

I have been feeling rather lonely in my various beds since I left you; you certainly spiced our love life up again lately.

Please give my love to the children and tell William he must devote himself to his studies, and to being the head of the household while I am away. I long to see you again.

Your loving Thomas.

If only he knew how much I miss him. I must write and tell him.

I'm not sure he is right about the Earldom. He doesn't know the King as well as Laud does, and in any case he gets his own way because of the strength of his personality and his way with words. He frightens a lot of people who do not know his kind side. Hardly anyone dares to stand up to him. He might become quite unbearable if he were an Earl. Mind you, as the wife of a Viscount I'm a Viscountess, which is quite an awkward mouthful. As the wife of an Earl is a Countess, that is much more manageable. Frankly, though, it makes little difference to me. I don't like being in the public eye so it hardly matters what people call me. It's different for him. He's in the public eye all the time, and he loves it, whatever he may say about not wanting so much hard work.

Thomas. 27th July, 1636. London.

I wrote to Lucy Carlisle a couple of days ago, as I told Bess I should. One of her servants brought me a note yesterday inviting me to dinner today, and to dinner I went. She looked stunning in a maroon silk dress, modestly decolettee. She made no pretence of being in mourning although James, her husband, only died in March.

When I arrived a couple of people I did not know were there, but they weren't staying for dinner, and left after a short while. Apart from servants waiting on us at table, we were alone in her pale blue dining room, the walls hung with many beautiful paintings. A portrait of her by Sir Anthony van Dyke looked down at me from the walls, and the dress she wore for that sitting was anything but modest. She is an extraordinarily beautiful woman, and not for nothing was she the most famous beauty of the Courts of King James and King Charles for a decade or more.

Her husband James Hay had been the late King's favourite and came south from Scotland with him when he took the throne in 1603. He was supplanted in James I's affection by Robert Carr, and then by George Villiers. I am repeating myself.

Nevertheless James remained a great friend of the King, and of Charles. The old King knighted him, and then made him a Baron, after finding a rich wife for him. She died in 1614. They had one son, also called James.

I knew all that because I'd become friendly with James when King Charles had made me Baron Wentworth, and I was in the House of Lords. James was often sent abroad on embassies to the Courts of various European Kings, and he was on the Council of the North. He had a terrible reputation for being a spendthrift, but he could be charming, and entertained lavishly.

I also knew, because he had told me, that he had sought to marry Lucy when she was living in the Tower of London. She was very much in love with him, and he with her. They eloped, and married in 1617. Lucy was only just eighteen, but James was about twenty years her senior.

Eloping was a risky thing to do. She was a Percy, a daughter of the Earl of Northumberland, one of the richest and most important men in the Kingdom. James was the son of a Scottish nobody, and only came to England with the King because of his good looks. Lucy was the most beautiful girl at Court. Everyone sought her hand, and James, who was then Viscount Doncaster, won it by running off with her. She had been living in the Tower since the Gunpowder Plot, because her father was caught up in it. He insisted she dwelt there with him. There was no real hardship involved. He had money and they lived in great comfort, but he was not free, and that was a considerable advantage to James and Lucy when they ran away. He was unable to prevent their marriage.

"We were very happy for about three years," she told me rather wistfully as we ate some rather excellent beef, and some of those potatoes Raleigh brought back from America. "And then I became a naughty girl."

I smiled and said nothing. I thought what she was going to tell me was a scandal of which I had heard years ago. I did not want her to think I took much notice of gossip. She spoke between mouthfuls of this excellent meal. "When James and I eloped and married, he often took me to Court. He was still on very good terms with the Royal Family. Do you know, Thomas, I was considered the young beauty of the Court then?"

"Yes, I do. In fact you are still an incredibly beautiful woman, Lucy." I do believe she blushed. She lowered her head in appreciation of the compliment, and then looked up to give me the benefit of her entrancing eyes.

"The trouble started when George Villiers noticed my looks. He was exceptionally handsome and charming. He'd become Earl of Buckingham by then. He was growing rich on the presents the King gave him, and the money and other bribes people gave him in return for favours and using his influence for them with the King. I found him irresistible. I was twenty. Life in the bedroom with James had taught me much, and I wanted to know what this man would be like, and he became my lover."

I couldn't help wondering where this was going. Lucy had a reputation for her own conquests. The only thing I could think of to say was: "Ah! I think I have heard something about that. So it was true."

"Quite true. I was his mistress for three years. It was so exciting. He first made love to me when James had been sent abroad on some diplomatic mission or other. He came to our home in London one evening. He sent the servants away, kissed me passionately on the lips

– I did not resist – and said, somehow with his usual charm – 'I am going to make love to you.'

"I could not speak, Thomas. He took me by the hand and to the bedrooms, and asked me which bed we should go to. At that stage I could not face sleeping with him in our marriage bed, so we went to a guest room. He certainly knew what he was doing. I had thought sex with my husband was good, but this was in a new class altogether."

What was going on here, I wondered. She could not possibly be unaware that I was aroused by this tale. I had never had a woman talk to me so intimately before, unless I was married to her. Even the French girl of my youth had not spoken like this before she took me to bed. At this point a servant came in to ask if we wanted anything more, and Lucy said no, but then summoned him to her and whispered something I could not hear, and he went.

"Then in 1624, I think it was, he took me to France in his entourage when he accompanied Prince Charles to Paris on some marriage negotiations. I was sure he loved me, and I was devastated when, without any attempt to pretend otherwise, he transferred his affections to the French Queen."

I felt I had to say something. "What did you do? Did you return home?"

"I did, but only after I had taken my revenge."

"On Buckingham?"

Lucy laughed. "No; on the Queen. I stole a set of her diamonds."

"What happened with your marriage, Lucy?"

"Well, it became what so many marriages are to start with: a marriage of convenience. We kept up appearances to some extent, but love between us was dead, and we both took other lovers." Now I knew that her reputation was founded on fact.

"So Villiers' influence with Charles and the King didn't harm James or his career."

"Not at all; nor mine. When Charles married Henrietta, I became a Lady of the Bedchamber officially, and unofficially – and I hope I speak without boasting – I became her best friend, and she mine. In fact I think we still are, and James continued to get diplomatic embassies and tasks abroad, and enjoyed the confidence of the late King and of Charles."

"Indeed he did. The King created him Earl of Carlisle four years ago, didn't he?"

"He did, but unlike you, Thomas, he was never capable of turning his luck to good use. He has left me virtually nothing. The lawyers tell me he was 80,000 pounds in debt. Any money he had always went through his hands like grains of sand. He had never had any when he was young in Scotland, and when the King started lavishing gifts on him, he could never stop spending it. He even got through my dowry." She looked at me very earnestly. "If my brother were not so rich and so kind, I don't know what I should do for money."

At last I could add something to the conversation, which up to then had almost been Lucy's soliloquy. "Yes, Harry is a good man. You know I tried to get him a command in the Irish Army a few years ago, but the King gave it to someone else?"

"It's Algie, the Duke, who's the rich one. Harry would be generous, too, but he has little to spare."

By now we had finished eating, and I thought I had moved the conversation away from Lucy's romantic exploits. I thought she might ask me about Ireland and what I was up to there, but she did not. She rose from the table, came round to me, kissed me, took my hand, and said: "I want you to make love to me, Thomas. We have known each other a long time, and I believe it is something we have both wanted equally long."

I had heard that she was supposed to be as bold in asking men for their attentions as men are supposed to be, but this was my first experience of it. I could not have said 'no' even if I wanted to, and I did not want to. "I don't think there can be many men who would not wish to make love to you, Lucy, and I'm certainly not one of them." We put our arms around each other and she walked me out of the dining room.

It started slowly. In her bedroom we undressed each other in gentle candle-light with much kissing and caressing. I was surprised to see that there was a large wooden bath of hot water in the room. When I asked, she said: "I ordered one of the servants to prepare it before we left the table. I normally bathe once a week; I want you to bathe with me."

I had a bed in mind more than a bath, but I was also game for a new experience, having never had a bath with a woman before. Indeed bathing was not something I did at all regularly, but then who does! I'm one of those who wash all over or bath about twice a year, and I wash myself under the pump or in a stream or brook after hunting or using my axe in the woods. I dare say I smell as bad as anyone.

That was a night of tempestuous love-making with entirely new sensations. I was a new man. Gone was the tiredness, the headaches, and the gout.

Thomas. 28th July, 1636. London.

Two days ago the 5th Earl of Clanricarde wrote to me and I have the letter today. He is at his mansion in Hertfordshire. He tells me that his own and his father's debts total something like 25,000 pounds. He adds that on top of that he has to pay his share of the subsidies the Irish Parliament voted for the King last year, and further, he has to sue out his livery to his Irish estate and title in Connaught, "all of which would sink a much better estate than mine."

This is just the same trick he tried in March. It got him nowhere then and it'll get him nowhere now. I have succeeded in keeping the King and the Council on my side over this plantation policy – the money involved is its own recommendation – and I am gaining ground on the new customs farm ideas. I do not think I have much to fear from Earl Ulick now.

Even so, I am really annoyed to hear from Christopher that the Galway jury have gone against me again. A letter I received from Secretary Windebank a couple of days ago has not improved my mood either. He tells me Clanricarde (St Albans, Windebank calls him) asked the King for permission to have one of the Galway jury, John Donnellan, released from prison to come to England to help him with urgent matters regarding his late father's estate. Windebank says it is "His Majesty's pleasure that Mr Donnellan should be given licence" to come here.

Even at the King's request I cannot agree to that for three reasons. First, his release would be interpreted in Connaught as disapproval of my policy, and encourage the jury to hold out against me. Secondly, Clanricarde would be inclined to think that the King is on his side. Thirdly, if Donnellan is so valuable to the Earl, it goes to show that the jury was hand-picked to oppose the plantation policy and the Commission for Defective Titles. No, I cannot let him get away with this.

Christopher Wandesford. 2nd August, 1636. Dublin.

A letter from Tom has arrived today. His mind is constantly seething with all sorts of ideas on a vast variety of subjects. Three years ago, before he even got here, but after he had sent me on ahead, he wrote to the King about his plans to make Ireland more prosperous, not just for the sake of the people, but to increase the income and wealth from which taxes could be extracted. He will never rest until Ireland is financially self-supporting and contributing to government resources in England too.

I know about this letter to the King because Tom sent me a copy. He has normally been meticulous about keeping me, Radcliffe, and his brother George informed about his policies and what he intends to do; that is how I know his brain seethes. He told the King about his plans for Irish wool, encouraging the growth of it, and its export to England to foster the growth of the English cloth trade. He did not want to create a cloth industry in Ireland because he knew that would stunt the industry in the North and West Country. Apart from that Irish merchants who supplied wool to England would have cursed him for undermining their business. He also advocated growing flax and the weaving of linen.

Today's letter is again about these trades and encouraging industry in Ireland. He mentions the good quality flax seed he brought to Ireland, and planted acres of it in order to improve the quality of the product here. He banned the export of finished Irish linen last year as it was not wide enough, and now he is taking measures to ensure that only linen thread of good quality can be used. He doesn't want to harm the weaving of linen here, but he believes we can undercut the prices charged by Holland and France by a substantial margin if we improve its quality.

I hope he is right. The livelihoods of a lot of people, native Irish and settlers in Ulster, will be destroyed if his methods fail. He is having yarn which is said to be below standard confiscated, but I have heard it said that some of this yarn ends up in the looms Thomas has set up in his own work-places. If true, that will be a cause of great discontent amongst those who lose their jobs in the industry should his own manufacturing flourish.

Thomas. 5th August, 1636. Covent Garden.

I am home again after the Privy Council meeting. His Majesty was in the chair, as he had promised, and he told them straight out that what I had told him before was so interesting he wanted them all to hear it, so I said it all again, and the King heard it all for the second time. Afterwards, at dinner, Laud told me quietly that he thinks the King wanted them to know what it sounds like when a part of his dominions is being governed efficiently, and with a minimum of delay and corruption. If that's right, it must have been quite a shock for them.

At the end of the session, I took a chance and reminded them all that they should not ask for money to be sent from Ireland to the English Exchequer yet, and that I wanted a balance of at least 20,000 in hand in Dublin before we send any money to the King on top of the small amounts we can now afford. That was confirmed, so I felt emboldened to take another risk, and stated that there should be no appeals to the King and Council from my decisions in Ireland, and sought assurance of my powers over there. Both requests were upheld.

Having been bold I felt I ought to show a little humility (Bess would laugh at that): "I know that many have reported to you all that I have been too severe in the way I have acted. What I found in Ireland when I got there was little respect for the Crown and the Church, and a population spoilt by being accustomed to getting their own way. I saw no way to redeem them from this lack of direction and leadership with gracious smiles and gentle looks. With the welfare of the Kingdom at the fore, the reforms necessary called for some severity , and so ...."

I got no further. The King held up his hand for silence. "There was no severity, My Lord Wentworth."

That truly humbled me. "If I have done anything inadvisable, I apologise to you, Sire and to the Council. I thank God if it has done nobody any harm but myself."

Charles rose and came to me with outstretched hand and congratulated me with such feeling - unusual for him – that I was so overcome I went on my knees, and kissed his hand. The Councillors clapped. This was a triumph.

I decided to take advantage of the occasion. "Your Majesty, I have a judicial problem in Dublin. Any injustice there reflects on you as the fount of fair dealing in your Kingdoms. It seems a very bad case has occurred with the estate of a man called Metcalf, who died some years ago now. Sir Edward Loftus has ..."

The King holds up a hand to stop me. "I've heard about this. Didn't Sir John Coke tell me you'd written to him to ask that Sir Edward be sent back to Ireland?" I nod. The King continues: "And the Loftuses' friends have badgered me about it from time to time. They say you are acting falsely, and that he dare not go back, as he will be unable to get a fair hearing."

"What can I do but deny it, Sire? We have a good deal of evidence and ..."

"Then write to me with a summary of what this is all about, and with a statement or two from witnesses, and perhaps two or three relevant documents, and I'll raise the matter in Council. If we decide to send him to you, I shall make an order."

Christopher Wandesford. 12th August, 1636. Dublin.

I have a letter from Tom today. It is dated 6th. He must have started writing it as soon as he got home from the Council and then finished it the next day. He is quite excited. Sometimes I get rather tired of his lists of the great things he has done or is doing, but this letter is different since he frequently refers to the help I give him, and the things I have achieved. I can't object to that, now can I? This is what he wrote:

My address to the King and his Council was talked of all over town today, so my servants tell me. Their friends have been telling them what has been over-heard at table in the great houses and in the eating houses, and they tell me. One of the many things I learned from my Father was that you should always be as close to your servants as possible without being too familiar. If there is mutual respect and trust, they will confide in you in a way they would not dare do if they were afraid of you.

It seems that my enemies – or those I take to be so – have lost heart as a result of the way the King greeted and treated me. They have been silenced, though how long that will last is anyone's guess. His Majesty was very keen on all I had to say, and was, I felt, as warm toward me as I could reasonably wish. His devotion to some of his other Councillors appears to be weaker and his interest in me strengthened. He was also very taken with the account I gave him of the valuable assistance I get from you. I did not fail to mention Radcliffe, and brother George, either.

Maybe they took their cue from the King, but Lennox, Hamilton, and Pembroke were kinder to me than I have ever known, and of course it was splendid to be in the Archbishop's company again. I have been received graciously by the Queen, and the Countess of Carlisle, and, quite amazingly, even the Earl of Holland seems to wish to be my friend!! Holland has always been such a thorn in my side, arguing against almost any policy I may suggest. I dare say it is not so much my own merits as have brought about these changes as the fact that anyone in the King's good books (as I now seem to be) is cultivated by all.

How do I feel about all this? The favour I have had from His Majesty and the esteem the others give me for my efforts are better than I deserve, but I shall do nothing to enlighten them!! If I nurture their regard I shall make more progress with our aims, and they will cause me less difficulty, and a quieter life may result.

The tree has already borne fruit to the King's benefit as well as mine. He accepted my plan for the customs farm, and Darcy's advocacy of Mountnorris's version has failed. The King will get the same basic rent of 15,500 per annum I offered before, but he will get five eighths of the rest instead of just half, and he believes my promise that he will be better off than with 20,000 rent from Mountnorris and half the profits.

Despite that, I do not want you to let Mountnorris leave Ireland yet, since if he comes to England himself all may yet be undone.

I brought the case of Metcalf to the King's attention. He knew of it, and wants more detail. Please ask George Radcliffe to put together some evidence and a summary showing why we need to bring Sir Edward before the Court. I'll check it when I get home. There is no hurry. In the meantime I shall keep up the pressure for him to go home voluntarily, so that his contempt for the King's justice will be manifest. He is doing all he can to delay the inevitable, and it will only go worse for him in the end.

I have written to Lady Wentworth about family matters and her family in Yorkshire, but I should be pleased if you would let her read this letter. I like her to know what I am about in government and business.

I am, as always, your devoted
Thomas Wentworth.

I shall, of course, show this to Lady Elizabeth.

Thomas. 12th August, 1636. Covent Garden.

When I get home to Dublin I shall have to be convincing when I tell Bess why we now have a Van Dyck portrait of Lucy Carlisle to hang on our walls. Lucy told me she was having one done for me so I arranged some sittings and had one done of me for her and another for Bess. Lucy and I exchanged the pictures. I shall tell Bess that this was done in memory of my friendships with her late husband James, and her brothers Harry and Algie whom I rarely saw when we were in Ireland all the time. **I'm not sure I convince myself, and I shall feel guilty about telling Bess this,** since she is so trusting, and I love her, even if I find Lucy irresistible.

In the last few days there was an incident about Mountnorris which amused and touched me simultaneously. Lady Mountnorris actually travelled from Dublin to London and called at my home in Covent Garden. She knelt before me and wept, begging me to give her husband his freedom, and let him off the charges of malfeasance in office, but I could not see my way clear to that. I told her that Mountnorris would not be completely free unless and until he acknowledged his crimes and apologised for his conduct towards me.

I raised her up, and did my best to comfort her, which was really rather impossible when I refused to do what she wanted. After ordering some wine and other refreshment for her, I sat with her whilst she partook of it, and asked her whether her husband would have been more merciful to me if the boot had been on the other foot. She almost choked on the wine at that. I think she was trying not to laugh. When she was more tranquil I took her arm and escorted her to her vehicle myself. It was not a job for a servant. It is not her fault her husband is a villain. I felt sorry for her. She is past her best but was undoubtedly a dignified and attractive woman when she married Mountnorris. She is careworn now, and does not deserve what marriage has done to her.

Thomas. 13th August, 1636. Whitehall.

I am with the King again today. I wanted to talk to him about finances in Ireland and the encouragement of work and industry there but it is difficult. My audience was to start at eleven o'clock. I was conducted to a long gallery where I found His Majesty inspecting some – a fraction – of his art collection.

"Before we get down to business, let us spend a little time looking at these pictures. Do you collect, Wentworth?"

"I have a number of paintings, Sire, but not as many as you have just in this one room. I doubt very much that any of them are of as fine a quality, though I have some rather good portraits by Van Dyke."

"Do you, indeed? He is a fine painter. He has done several portraits of me."

He leads me a few paces down the gallery to where a large equestrian portrait hangs above the stone fireplace. "This one, for example, with the horse. And who is the subject of your picture?"

"I am, Your Majesty." I strive to say it modestly, but the King smiles in a knowing way.

"Of course it is. You are a rising star."

"And I have one of Lady Carlisle." I think it better to make that public rather than the subject of gossip. Is it my imagination that His Majesty gives me a knowing look. He says: "How charming." Or was it my guilty conscience?

We continue to wander along the gallery examining the pictures, and discussing them. Well, it's more a case of his discoursing on them to me, as I know little about art, and he is clearly a very knowledgeable connoisseur. We also talk of hunting, about which I can hold my own, but I was surprised to learn that he has already been hunting three times this week. He talks at length of the game killed and the stags and hinds pursued. I marvel that when I work nearly all day every day on his interests in Ireland and pay considerable attention to his affairs in England, he hardly seems to do anything.

He is serious, and so are his pastimes, but he's actually pretty indolent when it comes to the business of government. Before I was dispatched to Ireland, I was in York and the North most of the time and my opportunities for meeting the King were few, even though I was on the Privy Council. I have seen more of him this time as he regards my efforts in Ireland as important, but it has been borne in upon me that he does not seem want to get down to the details of anything. To be fair, though, he does make decisions, but he takes his time, and I cannot say that they are always right, especially if he decides against my advice! But then I would say that, wouldn't I?

I saw him again at the Privy Council yesterday. The best efforts of William Laud and I, and the Secretaries, to get him to listen were frustrated by his desire to talk about his plans for the new Prayer Book and introducing it in Scotland, for Heaven's sake. I wish it were for Heaven's sake! I suspect it will cause nothing but trouble, but it is William's policy too, so I said nothing.

That seems to be the case with many on the Council. It is a strange departure for me, but I told him what I think last month. They know well what interests the King, and they do not tell him much that might disturb him, even if as Ruler, he ought to know.

In the end today we hardly get to talk about Irish industry at all. Within five minutes of my raising the subject he changes it to talk about our sons. Five minutes later I ask him for an Earldom. He says he will think about it. Then he terminates the audience. I shall just have to do as I see fit about industry, and hope it meets with his retrospective approval.

Thomas. 23rd August, 1636. Wentworth Woodhouse.

A letter from the King arrives today. Almost two weeks ago I asked him for a further promotion in the ranks of the nobility. I asked him, not for the first time, to make me an Earl. This letter is his response. I am not pleased. I told him that I needed greater recognition from him in order to put through our policies, since as a mere Viscount I count for less than many of those who oppose me, and of whom, in the King's name, I am supposed to be the Master. I said I feared that I am regarded by some as a kind of dictatorial upstart bully in the service of an Eastern Potentate rather than a loyal servant of a pious and Christian King.

Whitehall Palace.
20th August, 1636.
My dear Wentworth,

I hope that you had a good journey home to Yorkshire, and that all is well there.

I have given serious consideration to your renewed request for a further mark of my favour in the shape of an Earldom. In many ways I can see the virtue of it, but I am reluctant to give such an unqualified indication of approval, not so much of your policies, which are of course to a large extent my own, but of your methods of implementing them.

As you are aware from our talks there are complaints about these matters from many quarters – powerful quarters – and not least from Cork and Clanricarde. I cannot afford entirely to ignore these people. Harsh enforcement of strict policy can have confrontational results, and at a time when I am governing without Parliament here, it would be unwise to risk too much aggravation on the other side of the water.

I am so disappointed I cannot read any more, but throw the letter on the desk. I shall have to try to read it later.

I wish Bess and the children were here. I should like some of the distraction the little ones can provide, and to discuss these things with her.

The letter ends with the King saying he is my friend! I have to say that being told he's my friend comes as something of a surprise; he certainly doesn't act like a bosom pal when we are together, but then I doubt that he has ever been like that with anyone except Buckingham. That is sad; if he only realised how much I want to be his friend as well as his servant, and how unfortunate he is not to have friends like George and Christopher. He must be very lonely, even if the Queen loves him, and he her, devotedly, as people say is now the case.

Thomas. 30th August, 1636. Secretary Coke's house, London.

Today I am with Sir John Coke. We have had lunch, and talk of state and political matters here and in Ireland. It is a pleasant time, and he is a jovial sort of fellow. We get on well.

When a servant knocks at the door of his study, he calls for him to enter. "Sir, the Earl of St Albans and Clanricarde is here, and asks to see you."

Forgetting my manners – after all it is not my house – I say: "What does he want?"

"He did not say, My Lord." He gives me a disapproving look and turns with an apologetic expression to his master. Coke takes it in his stride, and says that he will see the Earl in the library. "Tell him I am coming." The servant goes, and Coke looks at me. "Do you want to come? It might be about this business in Galway."

"I'm damn sure it'll be about Galway. Yes. I'd like to hear what he has to say as long as you've no objection."

Thus we enter the library together, and Ulick rises from his chair. He's a large, burly chap, with a thatch of straw coloured hair and massive shoulders. If it were not for his contemporary clothes he could be a Viking warrior. He advances towards Coke to shake hands, but he stops dead when he sees me.

I smile. "Good afternoon, My Lord."

"What are you doing here, Wentworth? Why is he here, Sir John?"

"The Lord Deputy is my guest. He came to lunch so that we could bring each other up to date on the King's business here and in Ireland. I regret it if you are inconvenienced, but I did not know you were coming."

I smile again. "Neither did I."

Coke is urbane, as befits a holder of the greatest place in England under the King. "Why don't we sit down, and you can tell me why you have come." He pulls out three chairs around a library table, and we sit.

I ask Ulick: "Do you want me to go?"

"I can't say I like it that you are here, but as this is about Galway and the titles to the land, and the jury, I suppose it makes no difference. You'd hear what it's about in due course anyway." He puts a leather satchel on the table and removes some papers. "This is a petition to the King from the gentry of Galway. It submits that these gentlemen have been forced to yield by the might of the Deputy rather than from any regard for the policy, and that there is no justice in what is going on. I want you to present this document to the King on their behalf, Sir John."

Coke takes the papers from him. "Very well, My Lord." He passes them to me after glancing at them.

I am controlled (I hope) but angry, as I glance at them. "I shall lodge my objections to the petition, too. I am accused here of using force, in effect, and that charge has not been put to me before it goes to the King. I cannot accept the validity of the Petition, and shall tell the King so in no uncertain terms."

Ulick is suddenly contrite. "But there is more to the petition than that. There are 170 or more names and signatures on it, of the best men of property in the county. They ask – we all ask – the King to accept that we have completely surrendered to the King's title in Galway, and to the idea of the plantation policy. I for one cannot afford to stand against it any longer. The fact that I cannot have John Donnellan here to help me with his knowledge of my late father's English estate puts enormous pressure on me." "I suppose the fact that the Sheriff who summoned the jury in the first place died in prison in June helped them understand that I am not to be trifled with. I hope he paid the fine beforehand."

"That is uncalled for, Wentworth." Coke is gentle but his displeasure is clear.

Ulick seizes this opening. "It is far from tactful, but I venture to suggest that it is typical of the hard-hearted reputation My Lord Wentworth enjoys – if 'enjoys' is the right word. However, it brings me neatly to the next point." He points to the signatures on the Petition. "These gentlemen and I, hope the King will graciously accept that this surrender to his will and his policies is complete, and free and unanimous. Many are in fear and trembling for their future, and if you, Lord Wentworth, will persuade the King that we have surrendered our estates to His Majesty, and acknowledge that we have been in error all along, then you will gain the gratitude of many people."

Coke is on to the hidden agenda here faster than I am. "You hope that no further action will be taken against them to punish them for their previous recalcitrance, then?"

Ulick's expression is sheepish. "Indeed, that is it exactly, Sir John."

Coke looks at me. He wants me to say this is the end of it. I cannot bring myself to do so. I have won; the King has won. "I shall think about it."

I know already just what I shall do. I shall tell the King that the jury can be released if they submit, and that no-one will be prosecuted or punished. But I shall also advise him that whilst we won't take action against particular persons, we should plant half the forfeited land and not the third or quarter I originally had in mind. And when I have seen the King, I shall go home to Yorkshire for a few days.

Thomas. 14th September, 1636. London.

I spent a fruitful time at home, seeing old friends and neighbours, and spending a great deal of time with Sir Edward Osborne looking into the workings of the Council of the North, and how effective the policies for the care of the poor were faring. I visited as many people on my estates as I could, from the lowest workers to the wealthiest of my tenant farmers. I entertained, and was entertained by, the local notability, except of course, my old enemies such as Savile, and my former friend Sir Arthur Ingram. Amidst all this I had to deal with Privy Council business, both English and Irish, and with reports from and instructions to Christopher, the two Georges, and others.

Today I am with the King again at Whitehall. He shows me some new pictures; a Holbein, a Piero dela Francesca, and another I cannot for the moment recall the name of. He does not tell me, and I do not ask, the cost of these works of art, but I know from what I have spent on those I have that these are expensive collectors' items. The King tries to be as frugal as he can in governing the country, in order to avoid raising those taxes over which he has control, or summoning Parliament. However, he spoils his efforts by devoting so much of his income and resources to his collection. It makes balancing the books impossible.

I also made an alarming discovery during my discussions with Cottington, the Chancellor of the Exchequer, yesterday. He told me that when James came to the throne the Royal lands were so extensive that the income from them in rents and profits, fees and dues, amounted to two-thirds of the government's revenue. Now, after so much of that property has been sold off or given, by James and Charles, to the likes of Somerset, Buckingham, my deceased friend Carlisle, and even to Lord Holland, one of the Queen's favourites, much of it has gone, and the income is reduced to a mere 25,000 pounds a year. That is not much more than twice my personal income. This profligacy with Royal estates is what has made the King's position so perilous financially. Thus his Father was, and he is, either dependent on Parliament, or on taxes of somewhat dubious provenance, to be able to govern at all.

In the light of that Charles's expenditure on art looks even more extraordinary and out of place. Nothing of significance arises from our talks.

There is a ray of sunshine today: I am dining with Lucy again tonight. The only question is whether a four course dinner will precede or be followed by four or five course sex. I do not care; I shall revel in it either way.

Thomas. 19th October, 1636. London.

I have been sleeping with Lucy at every opportunity for the best part of two months now. I do not love her, and as far as I know she does not love me. She is a widow of very strong appetite, and I have been away from home for a long time, and missing Bess, and our sex life.

Lucy is an excellent companion at the dinner table as well as between the sheets. She is also solicitous for my career and political welfare, and does her best to influence the Queen, with whom she is on very good terms, in my favour. Bearing in mind how Henrietta felt about my opposition to her circle's plans to secure Irish tallow just to favour their soap monopoly, I need all the help I can get in pouring some healing balm into her ear. After all, the Queen's ear is also the King's, for she shares everything with him, according to Lucy.

This sexual adventure with Lady Carlisle is the first such affair I have had since I was a very young man, and away from Margaret in Europe. The French ladies whose charms I had then enjoyed were an irresistible temptation for the very simple reason that for years, and especially for the few months before Dad sent me away, I had been enjoying fantastic love-making with Margaret. I was too young and horny to do without.

I felt guilty about that at the time, and I cannot say I do not feel guilty about what I am doing with Lucy if I think about Bess. I cannot make any excuse save to say that being such a famously beautiful and sensuous woman, her charms are such as to inflame the passions of a dying hermit. To take Lucy's breasts alone, if a cross were to hang between them it would be a symbol that Jews would kiss and Mahommedans adore. As a Christian, I have no qualms about such admiration.

Only someone posing as a sodomite could reject Lucy. We shall, I hope, continue to enjoy each other until I return to Ireland and Bess at the end of November.

Thomas. 21st November, 1636. Chester.

I arrived here this morning. I am lodging in a fine inn, and the food is very good. I hope to be on a ship tomorrow or the next day, given a fair wind, and in Ireland the same day. I'm very happy at the idea of seeing Bess and the children. I love her as I do not love Lucy, but Lucy helped me through the difficult times I have been having in London, both with her sense, her knowledge of the Court, and, needless to say, with the magic she weaves in bed, which takes away so many cares.

We had our last rendezvous fourteen nights ago, before I left London for Wentworth, and then came on here. It was fun and fulfilling, and exhausting, as usual. She also asked me to look for and negotiate the acquisition of an Irish estate for her, and I agreed to do so. This might have obvious overtones of lover and mistress were any hint of our affection and lust for each other evidenced in letters, but neither of us has ever been foolish enough to put evidence of it in writing. If what is written is all anyone has to go on they might well think we had a merely platonic relationship.

Elizabeth. 23rd November, 1636. Dublin Castle.

I am ecstatic. Thomas has arrived home from London. A messenger has just come from the harbour to give me these glad tidings. I call my housekeeper, Kathleen. She comes in, seeming quite excited herself. She says she knows His Lordship is on his way, and she is getting everything ready.

Me. What preparations have you made?
Kathleen. My Lady, the children are to dine with their governess and tutor, and you are to dine alone with his Lordship, in the family parlour.
Me. And who is to wait at table?
Kathleen. You said I was to bring in the food, Ma'am, and that you would attend to the Master, and not on any account to be disturbed.
Me. Yes, Kathleen, that is exactly what I want. I'm very pleased with the way you perform your duties, and shall tell His Lordship.
Kathleen. You are kind. When do you want me to serve the dinner, Ma'am?
Me. I cannot be sure, so I shall have to let you know when he comes. He sent a messenger to say his ship was safely berthed, but that he intended to inspect the troops before riding home. He takes this business of the Army very seriously.

Kathleen. His Lordship takes everything a sight too serious, Ma'am, if you ask me. But oh! I am sorry Ma'am, 'cause you didn't ask me and I shouldn't oughter say such things.
Me. No, you shouldn't, but I forgive you, and in any case you're right. Still, at least when he's home for a few days I can get him to relax and put his cares aside.
Kathleen. Oh! so you do. And he do love the children so, don't he Ma'am?
(The door opens; Thomas is there. He looks tired, and windswept, with horse-hair on his hose, and scrapes of mud on his boots).
Thomas. And so I do Kathleen; so I do. Now, off about your business and leave me and the Mistress. *(I make a gesture for Katherine to stay as he takes my hand in both of his, kisses it, and draws me into his arms).* And you, my love, how are you?
Me. Well, my Lord, and so much the happier for your safe return. I don't care for your journeyings all over Ireland, but I like it even less when you go to sea, when I do not see you for weeks, and fear that I may never see you again. There, I sound like a scold, not a loving wife. Let me tell you something happier. I'm truly pleased with Kathleen's work. She is reliable, and makes running this castle and dealing with the other servants easy for me. I should like you to notice her too.
Thomas. So I shall. And so I do. *(He gives Kathleen a small purse; she curtseys and thanks him).* Now, be off with you. *(He whispers to me as Katherine goes).* I forgot: not in front of the servants. *(Thomas and I are still enfolded in each other's arms, and we kiss softly and gradually with more and more passion).* How I have missed you, Elizabeth. *(He kisses me again).*
Me. And I you, Thomas. And the children; they'll be so glad to see you.
Thomas. I know. Sometimes I wonder what all this effort is about. I wonder whether I shouldn't prefer simply to go back to Yorkshire with you and the little ones, but I have so many projects in hand. I can't just leave it all to Kit or George.
Me. Kit seemed to me to deal with everything very well whilst you were in England, dearest, and you should delegate more to him always. Why, even Kathleen was saying that you take everything too seriously, and she's right. The strain you put yourself under is probably what causes all these bowel upsets you suffer.

Thomas. Is this seemly, my darling? Is this delicate?
Me. It is you who will be delicate if you do not take more care, Thomas. Anyone would think Kit and George are not to be trusted. When the King trusts you to govern the whole of his Irish Realm, you should trust your closest friends to take charge of smaller burdens for you.
(Thomas leaves off kissing my face, steps back a little, looks at me searchingly, and then walks to the windows and looks out).
Thomas. You're quite right, Elizabeth, but it's my nature. For the King it is easy. For generations his family have been able to say "Come," and someone comes, and "Go," and someone goes. It hasn't been like that in my family. I am the first, and as I'm answerable to the King, I want it to be right. Besides, I like it.
Me. I know, and I'm so proud of you. And what does the King say? Did you see him?
Thomas. Yes, I saw the King, but I met with the Archbishop first.
Me. And the Earldom. Did you speak of the Earldom?
Thomas. Laud told me not to speak of it. He thinks the King is aggravated by my mentioning it but I just want the King to understand that as an Earl, and backed by the Army, I shall have the authority to deal more effectively with Cork and his gang, and implement Royal policies.
Me. So nothing came of it. You did not talk of it to the King?
(Thomas turns back from the window and paces about the room).
Thomas. The King summoned me to an audience at Newmarket. *(He shrugs).* He said nothing about it when I asked him. I reported the state of things here, and he sought my advice on some English problems.
Me. English problems?
Thomas. Oh! Taxes, Ship money, his new Prayer book; things like that. Something to do with Scotland.
Me. Scotland ? But I didn't think there'd been any real problem with Scotland for a long time. After all, Charles is, in a way, King of Scotland before he's King of England, isn't he?
Thomas. Of course. He was born in Scotland, and his Father was King there first. Anyway, you're right. There isn't a problem with the Scots, yet.
Me. What do you mean by "yet"?

Thomas. It seems the King is determined to start a row. Oh! I don't mean he wants to, but it's this damned Prayer Book. He may be a Scot himself, but he just doesn't seem to realise that where a Scot is concerned, there are two things you don't touch: his money, and his religion.

Me. Why? What is Charles going to do?

Thomas. Once he has introduced the new Prayer book in England, he intends to give it to Scotland. They are Calvinists, for the most part, and a Prayer Book devised by an Anglican King and largely written by our dear Archbishop Laud is likely to drive them into a frenzy.

Me. People say William Laud is a Papist, don't they?

Thomas. They are wrong, but yes, that's what they say. The King should leave well alone. He has no significant trouble in England, nor in Wales. Thanks to me he has none in Ireland. What does he want to stir up the Scots for? They will fight anyone at the drop of a gauntlet, and taking them on over religion is really throwing down a challenge.

Me. Do you think this challenge could lead to war, then? *(I am apprehensive about what this could mean for Thomas. I sit down).*

Thomas. It's what I fear, but I didn't say so.

Me. Why, darling, it's not like you to hold your tongue.

Thomas. Yes. Odd for me to be overcome by tact, but....

Me. But you were thinking of the Earldom.

Thomas. Yes, and in any case, religion is Laud's concern, not mine. As you've heard me say many times, the way a man says his prayers is his business. And God's.

Me. God won't help you to the Earldom if the King doesn't. And you say the King didn't mention it.

Thomas. When I spoke of it, he was, as always, gracious, but only said he would think about it.

Me. Oh! Thomas, was that wise, to ignore the Archbishop's advice? *(He shrugs. I hesitate).* My darling, the King will never welcome you at Court. You may serve him with every muscle and sinew - as you do already - but he will only tolerate you. The King is aesthetic. You are a man of action. He loves fine art and the world of learning for their own sake. For you books are just a means to an end. The King's servant you may be; his friend, never, serve him and love him how you will. Have you heard from him?

Thomas. This is Charles's reply. *(He takes out a letter, and reads from it).* "Certainly I should be much to blame not to admit so good a servant as you are to speak with me, but this desire of yours will hearten rather than discourage your enemies. If they find you are afraid of the storm if I say 'No', they will give you no chance to care about anything but your fears. The marks of my favour which silence malicious tongues are not titles and Earldoms, but the little welcome I give to accusers, and the willing ear I give to my servants. You may rest assured that you have my support, but in both our interests I must have room for manoeuvre should it become necessary to ameliorate these policies. Whilst I listen to what your detractors say, I give little comfort to them, and express my confidence in you at every turn. I am, as always, your inseparable friend, Charles R." *(We are both quiet for a few moments).*

Me. When did you get it?

Thomas. While I was in Yorkshire.

Me. You are hurt.

Thomas. I am hurt. But I am home. I'm with you, and I don't want to think about it anymore. With you there are other things to think about, other things to do, and I haven't seen you for over three months.

Me. *(I put my arms about his neck).* Must I guess what you have in mind, my Lord?

Thomas. You have no need of guessing, my Lady. *(We kiss again passionately for a space).* I want to make love to you so very badly.

Me. So very badly, Thomas, when I should rather you made love to me so very well? Then I shall have to show you how. And I have a mind to do it now, and dine later. You're not the only one who's gone without these last three months.

Thomas. What about the dinner?

Me. I don't think we need to worry about that, do you?"

I take his hand and lead him upstairs to our bedroom. To my surprise, however, he takes me to the large drawing room to show me pictures by Van Dyke of himself and of Countess Carlisle. These portraits stand side by side on a sofa. Thomas tells me to instruct the servants where to hang them. It was so kind of her to give him her picture as a memento of her husband. When we get to the bedroom I'm surprised again; there's a tub filled with hot water standing there.

When I ask, Thomas says: "When I arrived I asked the servants to put it here. I took you to see the pictures to give them a chance."

He takes off my clothes, makes me stand in the bath, and washes me all over, paying particular attention to my breasts, nipples, and a certain place between my legs.

While he is doing this I ask him what made him think of it. He says: "I was talking to a chap I know in London who told me he bathes before sex and gets his women to do so, and I should try it." I don't think we have ever washed like this before sex, and it is very exciting. I come twice before he lets me out of the water, once with his hands, and once with his tongue. Then I do it to him.

I don't think I have ever been so excited. This clean feeling adds to the silky feel of skin and touch, and we keep on touching and feeling and other things until the sun comes up, and Thomas can't.

Thomas. 9th December, 1636. Dublin Castle.

Sir John Coke,

Secretary of State.

My dear Coke,

As I told you a couple of weeks ago, the Counties of Roscommon, Sligo, and Mayo have been surveyed, and now there is more progress for you to report to the King. At last the Galway jury have submitted, and have been told that they will be freed from prison when they admit the King's title to the land. I fully expect that they will soon do that too, and will be released by the end of this month.

I shall then send surveyors to Galway, and set up an inquiry or two to establish exactly the extent of the King's lands. I reckon about thirty surveyors will be needed.

I am disgusted by the Earl of Arundel's claims that he has a title to land in the counties round Dublin. It seems that he and others are frightened that I intend to plant settlers in Meath, Kilkenny, and Carlow, but I have no such intent. These counties are mainly loyal Old English, even if they are Catholic, and nothing would be gained by antagonising them. You would think that Arundel, as Earl Marshall, would have more loyalty to the King than to set up claims to land to which the King might be entitled.

I should be grateful if you would let me know what the King says about this.

I am ever your faithful,
Wentworth.

George Wentworth. 1st March, 1637. Dublin Castle.

Thomas paces up and down the study in front of the windows. He is wound up. George Radcliffe is with us. He says: "Maybe you're right and now is the time to deal with the Lord Chancellor, but I think you should let me handle it. He'll make a fuss anyway, but it will be far worse if you do it."

Thomas stops his march and faces the window. "Why?"

"For a start you've worked with him quite a lot, and he's been very helpful to you in the Defective Titles Commission, getting lots of areas to accept that they need to apply for proper ownership of their land and facilitating the plantation policy."

"Granted. What else?"

"Well, you had Christopher and I write to the Privy Council in England asking that Loftus should get a special grant of 3,000 pounds for the assistance he gave, and when he was complaining that a salary of 300 a year was just not enough for the Chancellor, you agreed with him, and got it increased."

"Nothing extraordinary about that. For years I've always argued that if public officials and judges were properly paid they'd be less likely to be corrupt."

"But it hasn't worked in his case, has it? In any case, I dare say he thinks you did those things because you approved of him and appreciated his help."

"That's as may be. But you're dead right that he hasn't stopped taking bribes and behaving badly."

I feel there's something else going on here. "Why are you bringing Loftus up again? Has something happened?"

Thomas turns back to look at me. "Yes, Wentworth. I've had a petition to the Court of Castle Chamber from Sir John Gifford. He's ..."

"I know who he is Thomas. I'm engaged to his half-sister, Anne Ruish."

Thomas is getting impatient. "I know. That's why I asked you to be here. Sir John says that when his other sister – well, half-sister – married Loftus's eldest son Sir Robert ..."

I interrupt. "I've met him. He's quite a nice chap, but his father doesn't care for him much. Anne's sister Eleanor, she's the one married to Robert."

Thomas looks cross. "I know that, too. As I was saying, when Robert and Eleanor got married Lord Loftus promised to give the newly-weds a house and the estate that went with it. Well, that's what Gifford's petition says, anyway. It's never happened, and they are not such newly-weds now. He's asking the Court to order Loftus to make the gift."

Radcliffe is quick off the mark like the good lawyer he is. "Then all the more reason for you to leave this to me, Thomas."

"Really? What for?"

"Anne's father is dead, and when George and she were betrothed, you spoke to Sir John about their marriage, so there is a clear family connection. In addition, you must have heard people suggest that Eleanor is your mistress."

Thomas stands with arms akimbo, looking furious. "I've heard the rumours. Bloody rubbish."

I say: "But you like her a lot don't you? She's lovely to look at, and ..."

"And highly intelligent, and very entertaining in conversation. I give you all that, and I've made no secret of the fact that I think so; just ask Bess. But I don't sleep with her!"

"Maybe not, and I believe you, but will it look good if you're after him?"

Thomas goes red in the face. "Look here. Sir John is the only man, apart from Robert, who can take action to look after his sisters. Robert can hardly go up against his own father over this. So Gifford has no choice but to come to the Castle Chamber, and that means me."

Radcliffe holds up his palms in a gesture intended to calm Thomas down a bit. "Very well, but at least leave the pursuit of the case to me, even if you sit as a Judge. At least you won't look like Judge, Jury, and Prosecutor."

Thomas nods his head. There is silence for a few moments. "Very well, Radcliffe. You get the evidence together. Keep me informed."

"D'you reckon Lord Loftus thinks you're having your wicked way with Eleanor?" I ask.

"How the hell would I know?" Thomas flares up again. "Just let me hear him say it!"

George Radcliffe. 12th March, 1637. Dublin Castle.

I am with Thomas at his urgent request. I was in the country, hare coursing with my dogs and a couple of friends, when a messenger arrived from the city. I rode to the Castle as fast as I could, and am extremely hot and dirty. Thomas does not notice.

"Do you know about Spain, George?"

I guess he is talking about recent rumours that the King is contemplating war with the Spanish. "These rumours have been floating about for a couple of months now. Is there something new?"

"I've had a letter from Laud. He says that the Elector Palatine – you know, Frederick and Elizabeth's son – is still at Court agitating for Charles to take action against Spain to help France and Richelieu who are already fighting Philip."

"Well, he would, wouldn't he? What's the Elector's ... Oh, Charles Louis, isn't it? Well he seems to have no more political sense than his father. I suppose he thinks Richelieu is fighting Spain for his sake!!"

"He probably does, George. When I was in England last year he was going on and on about it. I tried to tell King Charles that the last thing he needs is war with Spain. Look what happened with the last one. Not one victorious battle, ships lost, and thousands of men. I know the Navy is being built up with Ship Money but ..."

"But a lot of it is wasted on elaborate carving and gold paint."

Thomas shakes his head in resignation, and points to a sheaf of papers on his desk. "I'm writing a memorandum to the Secretaries and the Privy Council."

I pick the memo up. It has a rather cumbrous title: 'Considerations upon the great Question, whether His Majesty should declare a war against the House of Austria'. "Why the House of Austria, Thomas? It's supposed to be war with Spain, isn't it?"

"Of course it is, but what Richelieu is trying to do is stop the Habsburgs – in other words the Austrian and Spanish Empires – swamping the rest of Europe. All Charles Louis can see is that that will help the Protestants in Germany and elsewhere, and he could get his Palatinate back. What I'm trying to point out is what this is really all about, and that French policy has nothing to do with helping him or the

Protestant cause. If we get sucked in, it will be disastrous, especially here in Ireland."

"Yes; it'll be the old threat of what the Catholics will do."

"Precisely. It's already unsettling anyone who was thinking of taking a plantation in Connaught. The men who were originally going to do so are getting cold feet, and the people who might have taken up the farms and smaller acreages are vanishing. Everyone was so enthusiastic for the project, and this war-mongering talk comes along and knocks all our work on the head. That's what I'm putting in this memo." Thomas is very angry.

Perhaps I add fuel to the flames, but I think he needs help here or his emotions will make him miss a few good points. "You could point out that you haven't worked so hard to increase the King's income from here by thirty thousand or more a year to see it cast away by the fools over there on the Privy Council who are working equally hard to get His Majesty to waste it all fighting Spain."

"I haven't overlooked that, George, but there's a more serious matter. If there's war, the Habsburgs will attack us here in Ireland first. They'll think that the Catholic Bishops and priests will urge the people to rise up against the King, and fight for the Pope. That's a much more attractive prospect for a successful invasion than an immediate attack on England. The Armada should have taught them that. Ireland would be a safer stepping-stone than an English beach."

"They may think it, but I'm not so sure anyone but the native Irish would want to be ruled from Spain or Austria. Neither the New or Old English would welcome that, Catholic or not."

Thomas looks up from his papers and smiles. "I hope you're right."

I turn to leave, when he calls me back, and says: "There's something else? Did you prepare the letter and the papers to send to the King about Metcalf and Loftus? I told Kit to ask you?"

"He did, and they're ready for you when you want them, Thomas."

"Excellent. Let me have them tomorrow, and we'll send them off when we've looked at them together. Thanks, George." No matter what Elizabeth says to him, or what advice Kit and I give him, Thomas has to make sure of everything. He trusts us implicitly, I know, but I suppose he's just obsessed. Mind you, I might be the same if the ultimate responsibility rested on my shoulders, and he's not the sort who blames underlings for the things that go wrong on his watch.

William Laud. 19th June, 1637. Canterbury.

Dear Wentworth,

The most useful demonstrations of the folly of opposing my policies have occurred in London this last week. Have you heard of Burton, Bastwicke, and Prynne? In case you have not this is the tale.

They are Puritans who have written about or preached Puritan doctrines (if their views can be dignified with that word). Trouble started in East Anglia a year or so ago. A rag was published called 'News from Ipswich'. It claimed it was printed in Ipswich, but that was a falsehood to put the establishment and the established Church off the scent. Many copies were printed, sold and widely circulated and read. The target of this scandalously libellous document was Bishop Wren's activity in Norwich diocese, seeking and rooting out Puritan priests in the Churches under his jurisdiction.

Wren's views are similar to the King's and my own in upholding the beauty of holiness and orthodox Church of England practice in worship and liturgy. He has been doing no more than his duty in a conscientious manner. In accordance with my wishes he had been looking into the holding of services in their proper and authorised form, whether the clergy were properly dressed when performing their clerical functions, whether there were unauthorised meetings for allegedly religious purposes, and how well or otherwise Churches and graveyards were being maintained. However, he was quite merciful in his pursuit of the malefactors, and did not institute large scale prosecutions, preferring to persuade them to change their ways.

This 'Ipswich' news-sheet did all but call him a criminal. It was seditious nonsense. It was given additional prominence because the Reverend Burton made this garbage the subject of two sermons, calling Wren and other Bishops 'upstarts', and other unpleasant epithets. He was arrested for blasphemy and sedition and with two other men was tried by the Privy Council today.

The second man is William Prynne. He had been a barrister, disbarred some time ago for writing a book alleging that the masques and plays put on at Court were sinful, and making a direct attack on the Queen for taking part in them. He had been successfully prosecuted for that, his ears being cut off whilst standing in the pillory, a fine of 5,000 pounds levied on him, and he was imprisoned in the Tower for life. Now he is found to be the author of this 'Ipswich' paper. Clever and learned he may be but he is an ideological extremist in his Calvinist beliefs.

The third person in this triumvirate is John Bastwicke, a doctor. It is astounding that three educated and intelligent men can give credence to these puritanical dogmas. He had been in trouble earlier this year for writing a pamphlet in Latin maligning Bishops, and had been put in prison for that. He was now before the Council for publishing the same views in English.

All three were convicted, sentenced to the pillory, and Bastwicke and Burton to having their ears shorn from their heads, and fined a huge amount which none of them will ever be able to pay. Having had his ears removed previously, Prynne is to be branded. Finally, all of them are to be banished to far-flung parts of the Kingdom, and incarcerated there for the rest of their lives.

This will teach them and others that the religious policy of the Crown and the Church is not to be trifled with. Their physical punishments are to be inflicted on 30th of this month.

You may wish to let your Irish Council know of this, so that similar measures may be pursued from Dublin.

On another matter, the King in Council considered your submission about Sir Edward Loftus, and he has been ordered to return forthwith to Dublin. He has been arrested, and should be sailing, in custody, for Ireland in the next day or two, if he has not already gone.

I am yours in Christ,
William +

Thomas. 5th July, 1637. Dublin Castle.

I've been giving a great deal of thought to the letter I had from Laud a week or so ago. Is that the kind of religious policy I wish to pursue here? I'm giving the Puritans in the Church of Ireland a fairly hard time as it is, with the appointment of all these supporters of William's taking over all the Sees, without driving them into complete opposition to the Church and the Crown.

Then today I have had this letter from Lucy Carlisle. It's all business, thank God. I do not stop Bess reading my post unless it is 'Secret', from the King, one of the Secretaries of State, or the Royal Spymaster.

30th June.

Dear Wentworth,

I think you should know that there have been the most extraordinary scenes in London today. Three Puritan men of a rather radical kind were subjected to the most horrid punishments for the religious views they express. True, they have expressed them very publicly in print and from the pulpit, so that it may be fitting that they should be publicly punished and humiliated. But these punishments were in my opinion cruel and barbaric for what is, in the end, just saying what they think.

One of these fellows, called Prynne, had been convicted of similar things before and had been pilloried and had his ears cut off. You may know him as he was once a barrister, like you – well, perhaps not like you, but you know what I mean. These three were brought from the Tower to Palace Yard to be put in the pillories. There were only two of these, so it was a ghastly fit for three men!

It was very hot and they had to stand there for at least two hours in the baking sun, but that did not stop them preaching. Prynne's homily was very powerful; so is his voice! I saw a woman – I'm told it was his wife - climb up to Reverend Burton and kiss him. The mob roared its approval, and people started singing hymns and psalms, though some Puritans tried to shout down the hymns.

As you know, normally when these things happen to the ordinary run of criminals, the populace boos them, curses them, and hurls ordure and other filth at them. None of that happened on this occasion. Far from it. The crowd laid posies and other sweet-smelling things about them, and gave them brandy and cups of wine, and fed them gently to keep up their strength.

This time when the guards put Prynne in the stocks he was branded 'S.L' on the forehead, as he had no ears to remove. The torturer shouted out that it stood for 'Seditious Libeller'. Apparently he is so poor he could only afford half-a-crown for the man's fee, so he was deliberately hurt very badly. The other two, a preacher called Burton and a doctor called Bastwicke, were also pilloried, and their ears were cut off. They were very brave, but poor Burton passed out; someone told me he's getting on for sixty-five. Doctor Bastwicke pulled out his own surgeon's knife and told the executioner how to use it.

When they were taken down from the pillories to be carted off to prison many members of the crowd helped and comforted them.

I wasn't the only one wondering whether they would have been treated like this if they had belonged to Rome and the Pope. I've heard from my brother that Archbishop Laud is fearful of the storm he has unleashed if the reaction to the enforcement of his policies is as strong as this.

I expect what I have told you is worrying for you, but if you do not know, you may have difficulty dealing with any problem that may arise in Ireland.

I hope you and your wife and family are well. Have you had any luck looking for a property for me to invest in?

My very best wishes,

Lucy Carlisle

So that is William's outcome. 'Thorough' must be handled very carefully and not pursued regardless of its impact, or nothing will be achieved. I dread to think what volcanic eruption his plans to put his prayer book into Scotland will bring, even if he has the King's support. If William's policy is pursued by the King, fear of using force there must not deter him. Like it or not, I'll have to advise him on that.

His news about Edward Loftus being arrested was welcome, and the miscreant actually arrived a week ago; he's in the Castle prison at the moment awaiting trial. He was notified of the charges when he was arrested, and we've given him another four weeks to prepare his case. I don't want his father, Lord Chancellor Loftus, to have any real grounds for saying his son has been badly treated.

The trial should be on 22nd July in the Court of Castle Chamber.

Christopher Wandesford. 22nd July, 1637. Court of Castle Chamber, Dublin.

Thomas is sitting with two other judges when Sir Edward Loftus is brought in by two guards from the prison. As you'd expect, he looks rather defiant. He's of medium height, with long dark wavy hair, and somewhat over-weight. Two eminent barristers represent him. I'm sitting with Radcliffe to present the prosecution case regarding the Metcalf estate.

After the charges are read, and before Loftus is asked how he pleads, his leading counsel stands and tries yet another delaying tactic; you'd think that after getting this case delayed for two years or more by running away to England he'd give up that strategy. "My Lord Wentworth," he says, "I am instructed by the accused to suggest that you should decline to hear this matter, as you have been instrumental in bringing him before the Court, and whilst a fair trial may indeed take place, justice should ..."

"Not only be done but should be seen to be done, Mr Gilmore. Yes, I know all that, but this is a prerogative Court, those rules do not necessarily apply here, as you will be well aware. Further, whilst I have been active in bringing the case to Court, as befits its senior judge, I have not collected the evidence, I have no relationship with the late Mr Metcalf or his family, and my only interest is in seeing that justice is done in Ireland as between your client and the deceased's family, whatever the outcome may be."

That is the end of that. George and I present the evidence, and Loftus's counsel present theirs. The evidence is overwhelming. As the estate accounts are produced, it is quite clear that a member of Metcalf's family was entitled to be the administrator of the estate, and that, one way or another, Sir Edward has helped himself to more costs than he would have been entitled to even if he had been legally the one appointed to wind up the estate. We also prove that he swindled the family out of a good chunk of the proceeds of sale of the estate property. Loftus is forced to accept the jurisdiction of the Court.

Rather to our surprise the Judges do not send him to prison. They make orders for all the costs to be repaid, the stolen proceeds to be refunded, and they direct the Court officials to secure that these orders are obeyed immediately. They do not want the family to have to wait for Loftus to comply with the orders; they have suffered long enough. Then the Court does something George and I did not expect. They send him back to prison for three months for contempt of Court because he held up the case for so long by fleeing to England.

George and I and our wives dine with Tom and Bess in the evening. During the course of the meal Tom announces that having got Sir Edward out of the way, he wants us, at last, to build a case against Lord Adam Loftus. As far as I know, this will be the first time in history that a Lord Chancellor has been arrested and taken to Court, either here or in England. Exciting times indeed!

That's assuming we can put the case together. Besides, I'm not sure that it will be a wise move. Loftus is very wily, extremely clever, and a brilliant lawyer – you don't get to be Lord Chancellor for nothing - even if he uses his knowledge for the wrong ends. He has a lot of friends in high places. He'll be a bad enemy to have, and he won't be happy with Tom over what has happened to his son.

Thomas. 13th August, 1637. Kilkenny.

To His Grace, the Archbishop of Canterbury.

My Dear William,

I arrived here two days ago. This is a fine city, of which my young friend James Butler, Earl of Ormonde, is the chief magnate. He is entertaining me at his home, and a very fine establishment it is. He is also very fine; a likeable gentleman. In fact you may know him from your early clerical days as he spent many years in Archbishop Abbot's entourage when he was a boy. Unlike the greater part of his family he is a Protestant, not a Catholic.

I had him made a member of the Irish Privy Council two years ago, and he is a great help to me. He has been very cooperative in the work of the Land Titles Commission.

Speaking of titles reminds me to deal with allegations that I have been profiting too much from my office as Deputy, thus enabling me to acquire Irish land for myself. I cannot deny that I have enlarged my estates here. I have laid out almost 13,000 pounds in purchasing property. At present it only produces about 1000 a year in income, but I expect it to do better as time goes by.

The best piece of land I have bought is an estate at a place called Jigginstown near Naas. It is not far from Dublin, and is thus very suitable and convenient for the Residence of the Lord Deputy. This land was Christopher Wandesford's, and he sold it to me as he is looking to buy estates up north, I think in Donegal. I am having a grand mansion erected which will be known as Jigginstown House. The architect tells me it will be about 350 feet long, and very imposing. It is rather different from many edifices going up these days, as it is largely being constructed in brick, but Elizabeth and I find the colour warm and welcoming, and we look forward to living in it.

I make no apology for this grandeur; I think it most important that the King's chief representative in this country should be properly accommodated. It will provide a fitting place for the Monarch to stay should he visit Ireland. In any case, I am paying for the work myself; currently it is estimated to be about 6,000 pounds. On the other hand I have had to borrow about 7,000 for my acquisitions. My debts are now around 20,000.

Besides, I am not the first Deputy to become an Irish landlord; St. John and Falkland did so before me. The lands that they acquired, and which I am acquiring, are as nothing to the property the likes of Boyle of Cork have taken, not bought, though he has had rather longer in which to build his fortune. Most of my property is in County Wicklow. Of that, much is not terribly good land, being somewhat like moorland in England, with a lot of what we might call poor commons in Yorkshire, only just fit for cattle, and some is more or less waste-land.

I hope that one day you may be able to visit me here and see the new house when it is complete, where Lady Wentworth and I shall be pleased to receive you in a manner befitting so eminent a prelate.

I am, as always, your friend,
Wentworth.

James Butler, Earl of Ormonde. 17th August, 1637. Kilkenny.

This month I've had Lord Wentworth to stay. We have been friends for some time, and I admire and support his efforts to make something of Ireland, instead of making Ireland do much for him, which is what my grandfather used to tell me was all that previous Deputies had done.

Fostering the economic well-being of this country is not an easy thing to do, since government policy is largely laid down in England, and the Deputy has to follow it as best he can. Maybe that fact inhibited earlier Deputies, but there is nothing very inhibited about Thomas. He is so energetic, so driven, and so capable. He will rarely take 'no' for an answer to anything he wants to get done. He told me that what he aimed at was making Ireland and the Irish a civil, rich and contented people in a civil, rich and contented land, and he certainly tries.

He doesn't have a free hand because English policy is not to advance Irish trade at the expense of England's. Not that he would want to do that; he wants the two to advance side by side. In the past Ireland has been a drain on English finances, but if Thomas can make Ireland stand on its own two feet with its own Treasury full, it can actually help support the King's government of both countries.

I've been thinking about what Thomas has managed to do since he has been here. A lot of his success is due to the fact that he won't roll over and play dead when London tells him to do something he thinks is stupid, or to abandon something he knows is good for Ireland. He is too tough and independent-minded for that. When I think of how other politicians will agree to anything rather than lose office (and the money that goes with it), it is remarkable that Thomas does not get fired. If it isn't right, or he disagrees with a policy on principle, he stands on that principle.

Take that business of the restriction the Privy Council tried to put on the export of our tallow to anywhere but England – a policy favoured by Lord Holland because of his interests in the new soap project. Thomas opposed that because he thought it was a swindle as well as stupid. He stopped a scheme for England to have the monopoly of selling salt to us; he knew England could not supply enough of it.

He thought the taxes and customs on Irish foreign trade were high enough, so he fought a proposal from London that there should be additional taxes on them. He was quite right to say that they would actually kill off a lot of trade, and then the revenue would be even less; if trade grew, larger amounts of money would come in. He's right about that, too; trade is booming, and our Treasury is brimming.

A potential disaster over coal was averted by what Thomas did. We've hardly any coal in this country, and when the King in Council put taxes on the coal coming here from England, Thomas wrote very eloquently to His Majesty. He warned of the misery that would be caused if no-one had heating in the winter (not that the poor have any at all most of the time), and there would be no fuel for cooking or for industry to make things, and trade would suffer, and the King's revenue with it. This coal tax was cancelled.

Thomas also took action to stop profiteering from coal. Mainwaring – he's Thomas's gossip monitor – heard that the Mayor of Dublin was buying lots of coal cheap, fixing the price much higher here, and then selling in the market he himself had inflated. The Mayor was hauled before the Council, harangued by Thomas in front of a full Court, and fined heavily. Thomas always says that it's the rich and powerful who have to be hit hard if you want the rest of the people to be honest.

Mind you, I've heard a rumour (I think Cork told me of it), that years ago Thomas was said to have done a similar thing in England with wheat in Yorkshire which he then sold dear in London, but I don't credit half the stuff Cork says. He wouldn't give Thomas the time of day, let alone the benefit of the doubt.

Those are all rather negative achievements, but he has had some positive ones as well. Look at horses. We're both interested in horses, and not just for hunting. For quite a long time Irish horses have been very inferior, probably because no-one took much interest in breeding, but also because English horses bought for Ireland were taxed, making them very expensive. Thomas was having none of it. He got the taxes removed, and encouraged importing better breeds, and better breeding in Ireland. As he said, if you don't have a good horse, you can't pull a good plough; then you can't get good crops, trade is no good, and food is insufficient.

That wasn't all: he got the King to cancel a tax on the export of our cattle and sheep to England. That was very good for our farmers, and therefore for the folks who work for them; Thomas encouraged these people to get good breeds of animals and to take more care over breeding them. Apart from that, with the rain and the grass we get in this land, our beef and mutton is really good, so no-one much in England is going to object to getting good food on the table, especially if it's cheaper when the taxes are taken off. In any case, revenue doesn't fall completely, because every ship-full of cows or lambs has to pay fees in the ports here and in England.

His efforts don't stop there, either; he's trying to do more for the wool industry, making it easier for our raw wool to be sold abroad, and he's got this obsession about getting a linen industry going. I suppose, though, that his biggest single success has been getting rid of the pirates; or at least, getting some good captains to do it for him, and badgering the Admiralty to send the ships. I can't understand why none of the previous Deputies did that.

I must raise some of these matters in Council or even in Parliament if I get the chance. It is only right that a Deputy who is really trying to do things for Ireland should get some credit, especially when so many of his efforts succeed.

Thomas. 19th August, 1637. Kilkenny.

Tonight after dinner, James tells me his plans for a speech to our Privy Council or the Lords in Dublin, setting out what he considers to be our achievements in government so far. I say 'our' achievements; he says they are mine.

Well, it's nice to know someone whose judgement counts thinks I'm doing reasonably well. It isn't just politically that I am forging ahead. In the matter of creating wealth I'm doing very well. I now have many sources of income. I have rents from my original family lands and manors, and those from estates and properties I have bought over the last twenty odd years since my Father passed on. These amount to a few thousand pounds a year.

I have acquired some land in Ireland, though the rents from that are modest at this time, and the money I borrowed to buy it means that to some extent I am in debt. I am, however, very fortunate, because in my capacity as a customs farmer, and as receiver for the North of England of knighthood and recusancy fines, I can borrow the money collected until it is time to pay it into the King's Treasury. Sometimes, before paying it over, I can also lend it out to others for short periods, and that can be very profitable, as the interest rate for much of the time has been around 8%.

On the knighthood fines, the customs, and the recusancy fines I am also entitled to my fees, which are deducted before the cash is accounted for. Again, this can be quite lucrative. The fee for being receiver of the fines is sixpence in the pound; at the present time the amount collected is about 12,000 pounds a year, so my profit is nearly 300 pounds, plus the annual fee of 100 pounds. My share of the customs farm, after we bought out the Duchess of Buckingham in 1635, is in the region of 5,000 per annum. If all that is added up, it cannot be disputed that I'm getting to be very rich indeed. That is why I could afford to buy the site at Naas, and build Jigginstown House.

Being me, of course I keep a close eye on all my interests, but I do not have to do all the work myself; I have clerks who do most of it for me, and their salaries are good, but the vast majority of the money is left in my hands.

On top of all that I have secured a large interest in the alum farm in Yorkshire, where alum is dug up at sites near the coast at Whitby and Robin Hood's Bay. It was a vital mineral used for softening wool prior to dyeing it. This alum mining industry is one in which Arthur Ingram was once a big shareholder, but he had, as usual, abused his position, keeping money meant for the King, and he was driven out. However, he knows a great deal about it, and I used him as my agent in negotiating my purchase of my share. I expect to make a good deal of money out of it.

I still receive my salary as Deputy of 2,000 per annum, and I am negotiating the purchase of a monopoly for the import and supply of tobacco in Ireland.

Thomas. 28th August, 1637. Jigginstown House.

My dear Cottington.

I write to you from the site of the new house I am building near Naas. I'm staying in the hunting lodge I had built here a while ago. The estate is just outside the Pale, and to the west of it. Construction is coming along nicely, but I think a year or two will elapse before it is finished. I must come to the point.

As you may recall, I have long considered that Ireland is in a most commodious situation for international trade, since it lies on the edge of Europe and is the gateway or stopping point going to or from the New World. I cannot claim to have been the first to see the country's potential for trade as an entrepot, and must acknowledge the great work Lord Cork has done in that respect with the ports on the South Coast, such as Baltimore, Kinsale, the harbour at Cork, and Dungarvan.

Ships from these ports go to and from the harbours of Devon, Cornwall, and Somerset, Spain, the Low Countries, and France. There is some trade from these and Dublin to the Baltic, which could be expanded. Kinsale should be further developed to enable it to be used by the King of Spain's Navy, and by foreign ships bound for the Americas, for restocking with food and water. This would be a valuable source of revenue, and the port is quite large enough for the purpose. A couple of years ago a huge Danish merchant ship, escorted by a warship the Captain of which was a son of King Christian, docked there for provisions. This young man undertook to drink the locals under the table, and did so with most of them until someone laced his drink with whisky, and he passed out. The real point of the story is that this just shows what income could be produced by encouraging that mercantile supply trade.

There is a little used port inland at Limerick, on the Shannon River. It can take a three-hundred ton vessel, and could take a great deal of the American trade, offering a safe harbour away from the wild Atlantic. The people do nothing to take sensible advantage of it, and I shall have to see if I can inspire them to do so.

This is potentially a fine and prosperous country. Its contribution to the King's income and the wealth of his Kingdoms could be immense. Should you be able to advance a policy in the Privy Council and with His Majesty to pursue these objectives I should be most grateful.

I remain your servant,
Wentworth.

The Gathering Storm.

Thomas. 28th August, 1637. Dublin Castle.

A letter from William Laud arrived this morning.

Lambeth Palace.
21st August, 1637.
My Dear Wentworth,

Have you heard the news from Scotland? In case you have not, here it is. It is extremely alarming. The Scottish Privy Council at the King's request appointed 28th July, a Sunday, naturally, for the introduction of my Prayer Book in Scotland. It was to be used all over the country, but the main celebration of it was to be in St Giles' Cathedral in Edinburgh, and the Councillors were to attend. Curiously two of them did not turn up for what seem to me to have been rather trivial reasons, but the others went.

The service was led by the Dean, a Dr Hannah. He had barely started when what amounted to a riot broke out at the back of the Church, and rapidly spread to the front. There was much shouting, and some started throwing their three legged stools at the clergy. The most accurate was thrown by an elderly lady called Jenny Geddes!!

After a struggle guards evicted the rioters, but they were joined by a mob outside, and this multitude hammered on the doors and threw stones and ordure at the windows throughout the service. Later, those who had attended the Cathedral respectfully were attacked in the streets by ruffians who had been in the mob. Much blood was shed, and the victims were terrified they might be murdered.

Similar scenes have taken place in many other Scottish towns, apparently.

It seems that these riotous doings had been planned for some time, and even the Scots Privy Council knew what was afoot. They were in touch with the zealotry of the people, and expected trouble. They have ordered, now, that the Book should not be used for the time being. They have said that the rioters are traitors and should be executed, but have not arrested anyone.

I have visited the King at his Hunting Lodge at Oatlands, near Weybridge, and he is furious. He has decreed that the Scottish Council reintroduce my Prayer Book at once and the ringleaders be arrested and punished. My understanding from some loyal priests and Bishops there is that the Council simply dare not act on this order. They have inadequate forces to arrest anyone in the face of the hostility of the crowd. The clergy dare not use the Book unless their flocks allow them to do so.

William Annand, a vicar in Glasgow, was severely assaulted by his people for reading from it, and almost torn limb from limb. My colleague the Bishop of Brechin is made of sterner stuff. He pointed loaded pistols at the congregation as he read the liturgy, but he had to run for his life from his Cathedral when the service concluded.

How this will end is hard to foresee. However, there should be more news soon. The King's cousin, the Duke of Lennox, was married by me to the Duke of Buckingham's daughter here very recently, and they went away for their honeymoon, but it did not last long. Lennox's Mother died at their Scottish family seat and he had to go up there to attend to her affairs. He was directed by the King to report in detail what is happening.

I shall advise you when I have further information, since I imagine that use of the Prayer Book in Ireland will attract similar outbursts. Despite that, His Majesty and I are determined to proceed. In Scotland there is no form of religion in practice, no liturgy, nor the least appearance of any beauty of holiness. The Kirk is a disgrace.

I am your faithful friend,
William +.

Why do I not find this entirely surprising? You might think that William would have seen the omen with the crowd supporting Burton, Prynne, and Bastwicke. I recall him telling me years ago that when he spoke to King James about reforming the Kirk, James told him to have a care: "You know not the stomach of the Scots if you hope to make that stubborn Kirk stoop more to the English Church".

It probably hasn't helped Scotland's respect for the Monarchy that having deserted his native land for London in 1603, James only returned once, and that Charles, having taken the crowns of both Kingdoms in 1625, did not go to Scotland for his coronation there until four years ago, and even then his ceremony was so High Church it offended many of his countrymen.

I can see there will probably be more trouble, but the King, having started this, must take steps to enforce his will. All authority will flee if he backs down.

Elizabeth. 30th September, 1637. Dublin.

What a busy summer Thomas has had, but I think he has enjoyed it most of the time. Thomas has been on a progress through much of the South part of the country. He was greeted and entertained right royally wherever he went. It is obviously a very fertile land, but there are not many people living there. Thomas says that if you brought in seven times as many there would still be plenty of room for more, and the country would be much richer and happier.

He loved Limerick, and its river, the Shannon. Thomas says you can't see the bottom, and it could take really big ships, but no-one seems to do anything much to take advantage of it. Mind you, it is an Irish town, and I reckon the local people know how they want to live; not everyone wants to work all the time as Thomas does – making himself ill.

He stayed for a week or two in each place. He had to listen to speeches of welcome from notables in nearly all the towns. Some were very good, but at Clonmel he had to endure two of the longest speeches he thinks can ever have been uttered. Thomas said they were deadly, and he believes he dozed off during one of them. He kept me informed of all that happened by letter. In Limerick he had to listen to three after-dinner lectures – yes, lectures is the word – and they were so boring, and far from brief. When I was younger and rather shy I didn't want to go into society because I was afraid of it. Now I'm not so shy but I'm glad I don't go to these dinners as I do not wish to be talked to death!

Thomas is quite amusing in what he writes. He tells me that: "My Lady Ormonde is not as inclined to be fat as we thought she was when we saw her in Dublin," and that "Lord Castlehaven's sister, if she be not the handsomest in the company, her ladyship is much mistaken." Of another young lady who he thought lovely, he wrote that if he were her adviser, he "would desire her to beware lest she grew fat too soon." I suppose you could say there is a bitchy side to his fun.

More seriously, and modestly for him, he says that the speeches were very complimentary, but "rather taught me what I should be than told me what I am." At least he doesn't take this sort of thing at face value. He's vain enough without believing he's perfect! But then in my view he has quite a lot to be vain about.

Thomas is buoyed up, though. The gentry of Ormonde, Clare, and Limerick have accepted the King's land titles, so that's another victory for my husband. He can do more of his plantations if he wishes.

Elizabeth. 30th October,1637. Dublin Castle.

Thomas has called me into a conference about the Lord Chancellor. He's brought his brother George in, and the other George, and Kit, and added James Butler, Lord Ormonde. None of them are a surprise; I'm the surprise! Thomas talks to me about business, private and public, and once or twice he's had me in on conversations with Radcliffe or Kit, but never like this. Something big must be going on. We all sit down at the table in the family dining room, so that everyone can lay papers out, look at law books if necessary, and have room for a glass of wine or water.

When everyone has their tipple in front of them, Thomas starts. "As you all know, I asked you to come in to discuss what to do about Lord Adam Loftus. I feel we have to do something. His reputation for corruption and incredible injustices tarnishes the King's rule, and will make it impossible for me, in the long run, to make sure that justice is available to all in Ireland."

James asks: "What has brought this to a head?"

"I'm not sure that it has come to a head; it's been simmering away for years."

Radcliffe speaks: "I think we are all agreed that it would have been imprudent to attack him earlier, when there were other men to be got out of the way first."

"You mean Mountnorris and Cork?" says Kit.

Thomas points a finger at him. "That's it exactly, Kit, and some others. I need a clear path, as far as it's possible to get one. We've had more than one battle going on at the same time, and Loftus would have been just too big and influential to handle at the same time as Cork and the others."

Kit nods, but he seems unhappy. "That's true, Tom, but can you afford to make another enemy so soon? Shouldn't we consider what you stand to gain, and what you may lose?"

James is quick. “What Thomas is bound to lose if he does nothing is any real authority where the Lord Chancellor is concerned. If he acts but loses he may be deprived of his Deputyship. If he acts and wins, he’ll have shown that he and the Court of Castle Chamber are above everybody in Ireland, and that even Loftus is under the law.”

I feel compelled to say something. “That may be right gentlemen, but I’m not sure I want Thomas to have too many enemies, or to be sent home to England in disgrace.”

Thomas smiles, reaches across the table, and takes my hand. “I think you know me well enough to believe that I won’t let considerations like that stop me doing what I know to be right. I’m sorry if it worries you, Bess, but I have to do the job the King gave me. I’d rather be honoured than disgraced, but we can’t choose the outcome we want – certainly not by avoiding trying to get a result.”

All the men murmur their assent to that. I smile back at Thomas. He knows I support him, even if I am scared sometimes. Then he adds: “In any case the most important thing – more important than what happens to me, if you can believe I said that – is that His Majesty is, under God, the supreme source of justice, not his judges, however exalted.

“Well, if we’re looking for reasons to go for him, there’s the Fitzgerald case.” That’s the first time brother George has spoken. “Do you know about it?”

Thomas looks round the table. “I know a bit, but in case the others don’t, remind us of the story.”

George settles himself as though in it for the long haul. “It started in September last year, when this chap Fitzgerald was being sued for damages because his sheep had, it was alleged, got into a neighbour’s field and eaten the best part of a whole crop of wheat. The neighbour said they’d broken down the fence and the hedges too. Then it was said that the neighbour’s own sheep had become mixed up with Fitzgerald’s flock, and that he’d taken them all back to his farm.”

Kit leans forward. “Was much money involved?”

“Over 100 pounds – quite a lot between small farmers. There was some good evidence that in fact the neighbour’s own sheep had eaten the crop, broken the fences, and got in with Fitzgerald’s flock on his farm. I’m told the evidence the other way didn’t seem convincing, but the Lord Chancellor said he preferred it, and he wouldn't allow Fitzgerald to call his own witnesses."

James intervenes. "Had the neighbour been bribing Loftus, George?"

George shakes his head. "I don't know for sure. Fitzgerald's friends say they believe so. I've seen no evidence of it. The really terrible thing is that Loftus had the man locked up for hiding his assets so that the neighbour couldn't collect the judgment."

"Why, was he avoiding payment?" Kit asks. "That's serious."

"Far from it, Kit," Tom's brother says, and turns to Radcliffe. "He wasn't, was he, George?"

"Not at all. It was, after all, harvest time. We looked into this quite carefully, Kit. All that he had done was to take his corn stooks out of his fields and put them in his barns. His wife showed them to us. She also told us something very alarming. Fitzgerald tried to send a petition to you, Thomas, but the prison guards took it to Loftus instead of letting it come to you."

Brother George leaps in. "So Loftus hauls him out of prison into Court. He shouts at him: 'Do you, Sir, think you can get away with petitioning the Lord Deputy? You guards, take him back to the prison. And permit no visitors except his wife'".

Thomas says: "But how do you know all this?"

"We've been doing what you asked us to do a year or more ago. We've been looking for evidence against the Chancellor, and when the rumour about Fitzgerald reached us, we decided to look into it. We went to see Mrs Fitzgerald. Honestly, you have to give the man full marks for effort. He'd managed to write another petition to you, and given it to his wife to smuggle out of the jail. She gave it to us, and told us the whole story."

James shakes his head in disbelief. "And a dreadful story it is."

Radcliffe dips into a bag he brought in with him. "Here's the new petition, Thomas. I think we may have the necessary dirt on Loftus now."

"Then we shall call the Privy Council tomorrow and ask for an order that he release Fitzgerald immediately while we hold an inquiry."

"Thomas," I say.

"Yes, my dear?"

"Tread carefully."

"I shall. There's not just this case. Loftus has ignored the order for him to attend Court in the Gifford case, too."

George Radcliffe gets up and starts walking back and forth; perhaps he's aping Thomas without realising it. "Yes, it's rather worrying. Like his son Edward, he's found one excuse after another, applied for every kind of adjournment he can think of. I'm told he's been writing to the King, to the rest of the Privy Council, and his friends in London trying to get you taken off the case, Thomas."

Brother George says: "And he's still sitting as Lord Chancellor, trying cases."

Ormonde joins in. "I heard that he got one adjournment because he was ill, but it wasn't true. He wasn't ill at all. I saw him at the races on the day in question."

Thomas. 15th November, 1637. Jigginstown House.

There is more trouble of a rebellious nature in England. I was only writing to Laud last month about the necessity for the King to act with strength if he cannot make himself and his government popular. That was prompted by the frightful goings-on over Burton, Prynne, and Bastwicke. Clearly the people were not supportive of their prosecution, and even less of their punishment, but now there is an even more serious problem. Ship Money.

I was never in favour of this tax in the first place; at least, not in favour of it being imposed on the whole country, even though I could see the logic of it. My objection was that it would cause problems, and it has. Laud tells me that many people have been refusing to pay it. One is John Hampden. Now these refusals have come to a head, if not a crisis.

The King asked the Judges to say whether, when the country was in peril and danger was close, he might demand, without going to Parliament, money and aid from the people. Most of them decided he could, and even the two, Croke and Hutton, who said he couldn't, signed the decision with the majority. This judgment seems to make the demand for Ship Money lawful.

As a result Hampden is being prosecuted. He is a well-known and respected country gentleman. He has pleaded not guilty and fights the case on the grounds that the tax is illegal. The case started in May, but hasn't finished yet. The King is in a cleft stick. Whatever he does is risky. If he takes no action to recover the tax from Hampden, no-one else will pay. If he prosecutes him to get the Ship Money, Hampden and those like him who refuse to pay get a huge platform from which to shout their case to the nation. There is, of course, a risk that Hampden might be acquitted, and then the King's chances of collecting Ship Money, at any rate from the inland counties, will have vanished.

Hampden has many supporters. According to the Archbishop even the Earl of Warwick has told the King, to his face and at an audience, that he will not pay, and will tell his tenants and family not to pay either.

Nevertheless, on balance I think there's no real alternative but for the King to prosecute. He needs to make an example of people like Hampden. They never want to do what those in authority say they must do, and they need a good whipping to get them to see the error of their ways. They should be grateful to anyone who does this for them. Not only that, but the good citizens who pay the tax would be very unhappy – to put it mildly – to learn that those who don't pay are allowed to get away with it; they'd wonder why they bothered to pay, and very soon no-one would pay. If I compare this with the Forced Loan, do I look like a hypocrite? I doubt it. First, Ship Money is a very old tax; the Forced Loan was an innovation with no real precedent. Secondly, The Courts had not been asked to approve the Loan, as they were with the extension of Ship Money to all counties. Thirdly, Hampden has been brought to trial; Radcliffe, I, and others, were just sent to prison.

Hampden sat in the Commons with me in 1628. He was against the Crown then, and he hasn't changed. He's not the same as me. He's too smooth by half for my liking, though some would say it's charm. He can certainly be pleasant, but unlike me he doesn't usually let everyone know what he thinks; maybe that's diplomatic. For myself I like plain blunt talk, so everyone knows what you mean and stand for.

In any case, Hampden is wasting his own and everyone else's time with this, as he only owes a pound. A pound! He's rich and a pound is nothing to him. He'll say it's a principle, but if his home in Buckinghamshire were threatened by an invasion, wouldn't he want the King to have a navy to send the enemy packing?

I do not agree with Hampden. It is agreed by common consent that in time of danger such a levy may be made. The King must be the sole judge of the danger, the amount to be gathered, how it is to be gathered, and how the liability is apportioned.

Despite all that, I have some reservations about the wisdom of these prosecutions, even if I think they are the only way. If what happened to Prynne and his friends turns some people against the King and his policies, and Ship Money does the same for others, what support will the King be left with in the end?

Christopher Wandesford. 7th December, 1637. Dublin Castle.

"I do not care what my Lord Ancram has written to demand, Kit; I just ..."

"He hasn't demanded anything, Tom. He says he asked the King if he will allow you to grant him a large Irish estate somewhere, and the King told him to ask you."

Radcliffe shakes his head. "So it seems that Ancram has tried to get His Majesty on his side first. This could be awkward."

Tom starts his usual march up and down. He's wagging his finger at us. "I don't see it like that; don't see it at all. If the King wanted him to have the land, he'd have written to me himself, and told me: 'I'll be grateful if you could help Lord Ancram', or something. He hasn't done that, has he? It sounds like a request, but it's really a Royal Command."

I have to agree. "No, he hasn't but what will he think if you don't help him? Do you want to make enemies in Scotland too?"

George says: "That's a good point, Thomas. Perhaps the King would rather have more friends when he has so much trouble brewing in Scotland, trouble with clergy in England, and the Ship Money case not yet over."

"Just because Ancram says he's spoken to the King doesn't mean he has. I don't trust these Scottish Lords at all. The only decent one was James Hay, as far as I'm concerned, and he's dead. Look at Hamilton; he's tried everything to get his hands on as much of the Derry land the City of London forfeited as he can; I'll stop him if it's the last thing I do. We had a request like Ancram's earlier didn't we, Kit?"

"We did, from Lord Mar. We told him he couldn't have a grant of land either."

Tom is in his cross-examination mood. "And why was that?"

"You said you didn't want absentee landlords in Ireland – or rather <u>not</u> in Ireland, but owning huge parcels of land here."

"Exactly. That's always been our policy, hasn't it? We want small landholders who will work the land, or at least live here and take an interest in whether their tenants are doing a good job of farming, or in some other industry."

George tries again. "That's true, Thomas, but we started that policy when there was peace at home in England, and there was no Scottish problem. Hamilton is one of the King's advisers at the moment; he's asking for Irish land too, and upsetting him may be bad news. Standing by your principles was the right thing to do before all this, but now it's ..."

"Now it's different?" Tom stops pacing, and stands, hands on hips, looking most aggressive. He almost shouts, he's so stirred up. "So now it doesn't matter if we abandon our principles? That's a short route to chaos, if ever there was one. We didn't grant any land to Mar, and I'll be damned if we're going to give any to Ancram or Hamilton. Whose side are they on in this Prayer Book tussle? Do we want them having as much influence over what goes on here as they may have in Edinburgh? Or in London? Don't we have enough bother with the Scots settlers in Ulster already? Do you want us to have more?"

I stick my neck out. "But what does the King want?"

"I'll tell you what the King doesn't want, or at any rate what he doesn't need, and that's for me to give land to a Scots leader like Ancram in Ulster. They're Presbyterian to a man, and with a leader from the Scottish aristocracy they'll be a disaster for the King. And for us! Draft a letter to Ancram and tell him what we told Mar – no land!"

Thomas. 20th February, 1638. The Irish Privy Council.

We have Lord Chancellor Loftus in Court at last. To hear him now you'd think he was a really low class criminal type with no respect for anyone. He is rude; he bellows, and he interrupts everyone. He's even used foul language more than once. If anyone did that in his Court he'd imprison them for contempt.

I address him from the Bench. "At the beginning of this month this Court ordered you to transfer to your son Sir Robert, and his wife, Lady Eleanor, the house and land you had promised them in the marriage settlement. There is clear evidence before us from Sir Robert and Lady Loftus that you have not done so, and we have heard from the lawyers for them and Sir John Gifford that their efforts to persuade you to comply have been ignored."

"You should not be hearing this case or having anything to do with it. You're tied up so tight to them that it's a miscarriage of justice."

"You will recall that I am the King's Deputy, this is the King's prerogative Court, and you will kneel in honour of your sovereign."

"You've got to be joking. I'm his Lord Chancellor here. I don't kneel for anyone. You can't make me."

"In addition to everything else you're in danger of being held in custody for contempt of Court."

Loftus actually laughs. "You can't frighten me, Wentworth. This Court is a mockery."

I ignore that. "You were also ordered some time ago to release Mr Fitzgerald from prison, and you have failed to do that as well."

"Why should I? I gave him a fair trial, and ..."

"Didn't allow him to call any witnesses. This Court looked into the matter very carefully, we were satisfied there was a real miscarriage of justice, and that Fitzgerald should be set at liberty."

"Well, I'm going to keep him locked up. I don't recognise you've got any jurisdiction over me at all."

I manage to keep my temper. "Then the Court may have to strip you of your office as Lord Chancellor, and in the meantime you are suspended from it. You will hand over the Great Seal of Ireland immediately and Court officials will be sent round to your residence later today to collect it."

Loftus is unrepentant. "They'll be lucky. It isn't at my home, and I'm damned if I'll tell them or anyone else where to find it."

I confer with my fellow Councillors. They agree with me. "Then you leave us with no alternative but to incarcerate you until such time as you purge your contempt, hand over the Seal, relinquish your office, and comply with the order in the Gifford case. As for Fitzgerald, he will be released on the order of this Court, since, as you are no longer Lord Chancellor, you have no jurisdiction to keep him there."

"You can't lock me up, Wentworth. I've got the King's command to go to London so that this case can be dealt with there and taken out of your dirty grasp."

"We know that. You've been asking for that for a long time. But you are ordered to leave the Great Seal here, are you not? If you don't leave it in this Court, we do not have to let you go to London. Rest assured we won't. Take him down."

As soon as the Court rises I hurry to my study and dictate to my secretary a letter to the King.

Your Majesty,

I seek your assistance to correct the unjust behaviour and conduct of your Irish Lord Chancellor, Lord Adam Loftus. He has disobeyed two orders of the Privy Council here in Dublin, where it is satisfied he has been guilty of substantial injustice, and refuses to hand over the Great Seal. That is despite your having ordered him to leave it here, if he goes to England. We have the copy of your order allowing him to go to London if he hands it over. We know he has been trying to get his case transferred there.

He is so contemptuous of your Council that, in my humble submission, he should not be allowed to travel out of the country. As a result, the Irish Council has imprisoned him for contempt, and has asked me to say that it is very anxious that their decisions should be reinforced from England. The Councillors consider that the administration of justice by the Crown will be severely weakened if you were to support Lord Loftus.

He will not be kept in the Castle Prison long. He will be released in the next day or two to go home under what will amount to house arrest. His position will not be unduly burdensome.

If you agree, Sire, that Lord Loftus should be dismissed from the Chancellorship, consideration must be given to appointing his successor. May I put forward the name of Sir Richard Bolton? He is a judge of impeccable reputation, having sat for some time as Chief Baron of the Exchequer Court in Dublin. He has published a very useful guide for Justices of the Peace on carrying out their functions, and is most conscientious.

I am, Sire, your loyal and obedient servant,
Wentworth.

Thomas. 27th February, 1638. Dublin Castle.

Your Majesty,

I am exceedingly worried about various matters which impinge on your authority and properties here, in addition to the matter of Lord Loftus.

First, a man named Barr is causing a lot of trouble about the collection of customs duties in the ports of Ulster. He has even used violence against your customs officers and employed ruffians to do so. He has been brought before the Court of Castle Chamber for these crimes, but there is some difficulty in dealing with him as harshly as his misconduct deserves, since I have discovered that he is the agent of your friend and adviser Lord Hamilton.

He has used Barr to argue for a large allocation of plantation land in Ulster from the City of London holdings which were confiscated. As you know I am entirely opposed to having large areas of Ireland in the hands of absentee landlords. It is an essential part of my policy that you should get as much revenue as possible from your land here. I cannot achieve that for you if the benefits are conferred on others. The offer from Hamilton and his Scottish partners is not generous, and there is a better one from Sir John Clotworthy of Devon which I prefer, and to which you might give serious consideration.

I await your directions in these matters, Sire,

Your faithful and obedient servant,

Wentworth.

Thomas. 24th February, 1638. Dublin Castle.

The Archbishop has written to me with a report of the Hampden case. I also have a letter about it from Sir John Coke.

What I hear from them is that Hampden's barrister, Oliver St John (there's a rebel if ever there was one), said that Ship Money is only to be levied when there is a war, or likely to be one, or the country is in imminent danger or peril. After all, that is what the judges decided on the King's question last year. St John said all we have at present are thieves, pirates, and robbers at sea. He claimed that Ship Money cannot be taken without new laws from Parliament. This would enable the King to alter the property of the subject for the defence of the realm, but if there is no war, and no imminent danger, there is nothing against which to defend the realm.

Therefore, he argues, there's no necessity for his client, Hampden, or anyone else, to pay Ship Money.

The judges are not issuing their decisions all at once. Three have done so, so far. One of them, Robert Berkely, says that Englishmen are not slaves, their freedom is secured by law, and the law enacts the King's wishes: "*Rex* is *Lex, lex loquens,* a living, a speaking, an acting law." I dare say there will be a big majority for the King, but that

Hutton and Croke will still say Ship Money is illegal when there is no war.

Yet there are excellent reasons for saying that the tax is justified. After all, the King has been able to put more Ships in the water, and a Captain Rainborough was sent to the Mediterranean, raided the Barbary pirates, brought home 300 English people who had been kidnapped and used as slaves, and brought back an emissary from the Sultan to hold talks about putting an end to the pirates.

More good news for Laud is that I shall install his disciple William Chappell as Bishop of Cork and Ross. I am determined that the King's policies will be followed in Ireland.

Thomas. 15th March, 1638. Dublin Castle.

A dreadful crisis is upon us, and I cannot imagine I am going to escape it.

Lambeth Palace.

10th March, 1638.

My Dear Wentworth,

The King presented your letter of 20th February about Lord Loftus to the Privy Council yesterday. He has asked me to tell you the result. It is clear that His Majesty is not at all happy that you have led him into another confrontation with powerful people in Ireland. With the growing trouble over Scotland and the Prayer Book he has enough on his plate.

Frankly he distrusts your account that your Privy Council took action more or less independently to lock Loftus up. Indeed I find it hard to believe myself. On the other hand he accepts that if the injustices of which you write are true – and he doesn't doubt that – no reasonable person could think Loftus is a proper man for such a senior judicial role, or even a minor one.

The King has authorised the Irish Council to continue its efforts to force him to comply with its orders, and his own to hand over the Great Seal. He is not best pleased that another confrontation is going on in Dublin. He has asked that you keep him informed of the progress of this case.

You will be interested in the most recent events in Scotland. The Duke of Lennox returned to London and told the King that Petitions have been delivered to the Scots Council in Edinburgh from all over the Lowlands calling for the new Prayer Book to be removed. He brought some of these to London for the King to see. He found that hundreds of men, if not a thousand or more, who had delivered these Petitions were still in Edinburgh, and the Duke was alarmed.

On hearing this the King was furious. He ordered his Scottish Council to drive the crowds out of town, but when they tried to do so there was an affray which terrified some of the Councillors. Indeed, so frightened were they, that they declined to obey the King further.

As you may imagine, the ordinary people who make up the mobs have not done these things spontaneously. There are some powerful nobles and clergy behind them. It appears that one of the foremost – if not the foremost – is John Leslie, Earl of Rothes. He is a Presbyterian, and that is undoubtedly a major factor in driving him into this conflict with me and the King. However, it would be naïve to think that that is all there is to it.

He, and many of the other lords, possess many estates and great houses which used to form part of the property of the Catholic Church before Henry's reforms. If I succeed in strengthening Bishops in the Scottish Church, these men fear they will have to disgorge their ancestors' ill-gotten gains. That is, of course, exactly what I plan to do, since the Church in Scotland is in the same parlous financial state as the English and Irish ones. I intend to pursue there the same policy you are pursuing in Ireland to enrich the Church, and increase the number and quality of the High Church clergy there.

Rothes has one very able and intelligent ally, James Graham, Earl of Montrose. He is a Calvinist, and with Rothes was one of the main instigators of a Supplication against the use of the Prayer Book. At the head of the clergy opposing the Book is a priest of thirty years standing from Fife, Alexander Henderson. He would almost certainly have been a Bishop by now if he were not diametrically opposed to their existence. I believe he is aided by a strange man, Archibald Johnson, Earl of Warriston. He is not yet thirty but is already a leading light of the Scottish Bar. Despite that, his brilliant brain has not stopped him becoming - indeed, it may even have helped him become - a sort of religious fanatic, who believes he is definitely destined for heaven, and probably for Sainthood, or something equally elevated.

His Majesty and I are convinced that these men, with some members of the Scottish Council are the power behind the riots, and the agitation against the Book.

Three months ago the King sent an envoy to Edinburgh to address the King's commands and wishes to the Council, but I understand he was completely lacking in tact and diplomacy, swore at the Councillors, and advanced the King's case not a jot.

In response the Council sent their Lord Treasurer, Lord Traquair to see the King. I am glad to say that he was unsuccessful in persuading His Majesty to moderate my policy. Traquair said it was the fault of the Scottish Bishops that the situation had arisen, since they had tried to push through reform of the Kirk and the introduction of the new rituals too fast. The King was, predictably, aggravated by this, since the Bishops had been trying to do exactly what the King, through me, had directed them to do. He said that he did not in any way approve the conduct of the Council, because they had been more derogatory to his authority than conducive to the peace and quiet of the country. He could not conceive that there could be tranquillity when Royal rule was infringed.

His Majesty says the appalling Scottish reaction to the Prayer Book will reinforce the opposition of the English Puritans, and we are agreed that stern measures must be used to make our policy successful. He is at present enjoying hunting down at Newmarket. He may have had a happy and relaxing couple of weeks, but if he has received identical news from Edinburgh in the last few days he will be less than content.

The Scottish Council met in Stirling on 20th February. The proclamation the King had given to Lord Traquair was to be read. This said the Prayer Book is to be used and those of the nobility who had agitated against it deserved his highest censure. He would take no action and be merciful if they conformed to his desires and commands, and submitted to his will.

One of the few Bishops who attended tells me that most of his colleagues absented themselves as they feared the mob, some Lords did the same, and others stayed away because they did not agree with the proclamation. Many of the leaders of the opposition group attended with a thousand or more supporters. The scene was explosive, but the Council did not have the forces available to deal with it, so they sent for the Earls of Rothes and Montrose, and asked them to send the people away.

This shows how weak the Council is, and how strong they believe the opposition to the Prayer Book to be.

Two days later this scene repeated itself in Edinburgh at Mercat Cross, except that the crowd was even larger. The proclamation was almost shouted down, and Montrose climbed on a barrel to shout that he was against the Book, too, but urged the people to behave themselves.

The King is not prepared to tolerate this sort of thing, and neither am I. The power of the Crown and the Church must prevail.

The situation is very serious, and got worse on the 28th. The ringleaders of this revolt – there is no other word for it – gathered in Greyfriars Kirk and Warriston and Henderson produced a tract which they are now calling the National Covenant. They are getting as many people as possible to sign it, and those who do are known as Covenanters. Those who don't are, it seems, in danger of a beating or worse. Is this what Christianity is reduced to?

I shall let you know what develops.

I remain your friend,

William +

This has to be one of the most worrying letters I have ever received. How can the King and William insist on enforcing their policy against a people almost all of whom reject it? Such an undertaking would be difficult if the King had a large and effective army to back it up, but he does not. What he does have is neither large nor even very effective. It certainly could not tackle a war-like Scots army with religious fervour in its knapsack, inspiring it to heroic deeds. It surely behoves me to make my Irish Army, which is quite large, as efficient and disciplined as possible. I can see that this situation is going to get much worse. I may have to take my troops to Scotland to help sort things out.

None of the three Kingdoms is so rich that it can afford to fight, and for two of them to do battle with each other will ruin any plans the King and I have for peace and prosperity.

I am not even sure about Laud's remark about Christianity. Neither he nor the King are tolerant of the other point of view, so it can only be the King's belief in the 'Divine Wisdom' which comes to him as King that enables him to override the wishes of Scotland.

Lucy Carlisle. 30th April, 1638. Alnwick Castle.

My Dear Lord Wentworth,

I have just arrived here for a few weeks of this lovely spring, and what I hope will be an equally lovely summer, with my brother. It is a very enjoyable family gathering. I expect to return to London by the end of June.

I received your letter about the Irish estate you have found for me. It was very thoughtful of you to send me a copy of the vendor's solicitor's draft contract. I do so admire the calligraphy skills of these legal clerks; their work is almost a work of art.

My own lawyers say the terms look reasonable, but of course neither they nor I are au fait with Irish land prices, so I must rely on you for that. If, as you say, you think the price is actually on the low side, I am happy to accept, and should be grateful if you would go ahead. I doubt that I shall ever travel to Ireland, so it seems a little odd to become a landowner there, but I find that a lot of the people one knows are doing, or have already done, this sort of thing.

In fact I have heard – how reliably I cannot say – that my friend Lord Holland has a company which owns land on an island in the Carribbean, and that strange MP, Pym, has an interest in it too.

So yes, please go ahead. I shall arrange for the money to be sent to you when you need it. I am sure Harry or Algie will be able to help me with it, and the lawyers will sort it out.

Everyone is well here. I hope that you, Lady Wentworth, and the children, are in robust health.

Algie sends you his best wishes, and says he will write to you soon.

With all friendly good wishes,

Lucy Carlisle.

Post scriptum. Have you heard of John Lilburne? He's another of these Puritan fanatics. He's been handing out religious tracts which are said to be seditious, and had been banned. The Star Chamber ordered him to be whipped and dragged behind a cart from Fleet Street to Westminster, and then pilloried. The crowd which followed him all the way, and then gathered in huge numbers in Palace Yard, was on his side. No-one threw anything at him. When he was put in the pillory, he found the strength to make a speech, and dragged from his pockets more copies of the tract and handed them out. The Privy Council was horrified. I was standing with the Queen in one of the

Palace windows watching all this. That was on the 18th. The next day I set off for Alnwick.

The religious atmosphere is getting worse, and the revolt in Scotland against Archbishop Laud's rituals is not helping. A few days ago copies of a paper called the National Covenant began appearing in the London Streets. I was given a copy. It may be an offence for me to have it but I wanted to tell you what it says. Its author is the Laird of Warriston. He bases it on some Confession of 1580, which was apparently a sort of foundation of the Kirk after the Reformation. The Covenant says that that Confession and what it stands for should not be changed. In other words they say that the true religion is Presbyterian

The words are very strong. 'From the knowledge and conscience of our duty to God, to our King, and to our country, without any worldly respect or inducement, we promise and swear by the great name of the Lord our God to continue in the profession and obedience of the aforesaid religion; that we shall defend the same and resist all those contrary errors and corruptions according to our vocation, and to the utmost of that power that God hath put into our hands, all the days of our life.'

I'm sorry this PS is now longer than the letter, but I felt you should know all this as, somehow or other, you are bound to be involved in something like it here or over there. Can there be a happy outcome?

Thomas. 18th May 1638. Jigginstown House.

I am in my study when George Radcliffe bursts in. "Hampden has been convicted."

"Has he, by God? Well, I can't say I'm surprised. I thought prosecuting him could cause trouble but as you know, I'm never in favour of Royal authority being flouted."

"It may not be what you think, though. It's not just Hutton and Croke who found him innocent. Altogether five out of the twelve judges voted to acquit him."

"That's serious, then."

"It is. Last year, I'm told, Ship Money was pretty well fully paid and the King collected almost all that was demanded, but this year payments have almost dried up. As more and more of the judgments have come out in favour of Hampden the people have been refusing to pay." George shakes his head. "There seems to be an awful lot of defiance in the air these days. The Prayer Book, Scotland, Ship Money ..." He tails off.

"I know. I've just received news of more of it. A man called Lilburne was severely punished for religious sedition, but the crowd reacted just as it did for Prynne and those others. They're on their side. Well, I'm not having any of that sort of thing here. The law will prevail if I have anything to do with it. We must make an example of old Loftus."

Kit comes in. He says: "Did I hear aright? You're going to make an example of the Lord Chancellor?"

Radcliffe turns to him. "Yes, of course. He still refuses to hand over the Seal, or to obey the orders in the Gifford case. He cannot be allowed to get away with it. Loftus has a lot of friends here and in London, but that does not, as you can guess, influence Thomas much."

I get up to stand with them. "Quite. With the attacks on the King's rule in the shape of Lilburne, and the defiance of the Scots and some of the English Bishops and priests over the Prayer Book, a stern lesson is needed throughout the realm that the King is in charge and that what he says goes."

George resumes. "And it's not as though we do not have good cause where Loftus is concerned. He's still delaying doing as he has been told. He's been using Lord Holland to try to persuade the King, through the Queen, to set him free and cancel the orders. He even tried to send that rat of a son of his, Sir Edward, over to London to petition the King, but we got wind of that and stopped him."

"Yes; we must stop Loftus's trickery." I turn to Kit. "Have you had a good journey back from Kilfenora? How did the consecration go?"

"Yes, quite a comfortable ride, thank you, and the ceremony went well. The Reverend Robert Sibthorpe is now Bishop of Kilfenora, as you and Laud wish, so that's another of the Archbishop's High Churchmen with a See here."

"How long have you been on the road?"

"Only three days, which is not bad considering it's due west of here as far as you can go before dropping into the Atlantic."

"You've been away what - three weeks altogether? While you've been gone I had Chappell – you know William Chappell, of course, Kit; he's ..."

"Provost of Trinity College. Yes, I know him well."

"Yes, and he's now Bishop of Cork and Ross. We are getting somewhere with Laud's Church reform policies."

Kit looks serious. "Let's hope they're not as unpopular here as they are in Scotland. Didn't you tell me that when you visited Ussher's Palace at Drogheda a while ago, there was no altar in his chapel? Isn't that a sign of the mood in Ireland against moving from Puritan to Arminian ways?"

I shrug and make no comment. Kit may well be correct. If the Irish Archbishop doesn't want an altar, how likely is it that an ordinary man of Puritan sympathies will tolerate very High Church ritual?

Thomas. 24th May, 1638. Dublin Castle.

The Scottish situation is getting completely out of hand. Algernon, the Earl of Northumberland, has written to me as his sister Lucy said he would. It is another worrying letter.

He starts off by telling me that the King's jester, Archie Armstrong got a bit drunk, and called William Laud a monk, a rogue, and a traitor. He was packed off to prison for it and some talked of a Star Chamber trial, but William spoke against it. He's right, of course. Locking a comedian up is hardly going to teach anyone that England is a free country! Algie goes on:

All sorts of disturbing news reaches me here in Alnwick from Scotland. The antagonism towards the new Prayer Book has reached such a pitch there that I fear war may be inevitable if the King insists on forcing his policy through. These Covenanters are hardly likely to change their minds. How else can they be made to submit other than by force? What worries me is whether His Majesty can raise the necessary troops.

In that respect it is worrying that Alexander Leslie is reported to be in Scotland now. Have you heard of him? He is a general of much experience and formidable reputation. He has been fighting as a mercenary on the Continent ever since Frederick lost the Battle of the White Hill in Bohemia nearly twenty years ago. He's hardly likely to fight for Charles against his own countrymen, and I doubt that the King has anyone of his ability to assist him.

Very few of Laud's Bishops have stayed north of the Border to ride out this storm, and any English clergyman up there at the moment risks life and limb, and robbery with violence. A friend in Edinburgh tells me that children are signing the Covenant in many towns and cities, and that anyone who refuses to sign is likely to be threatened with a drawn sword.

Even here in England the religious mood is fractious. Last month the King denied eight ships bound for American Colonies the right to sail, as he apprehended they were Puritan settlers fleeing the country, but has now given permission. He has, however, ordered that any further emigrant ships may only sail with the Council's permission. The Bishop of Norwich turned a foreign Puritan community out of a chapel they had been using for years, but sympathetic local people let them use a church elsewhere. If that is the general mood in England, how can the King raise a decent Army against a Puritan Scotland?

Your Irish troops may find employment sooner than they expect.

There may at least be some hope for the Navy, even if I should not say so myself. The King has appointed me Lord High Admiral. That fop and dandy, Lord Holland, has been angling for the post himself; he may be a close friend of the Queen, but I doubt that that makes him a fit commander of a fleet. He has been going about the Court claiming that you have been a lunatic – I jest not – since childhood, and this seems to have something to do with a quarrel between you and his friend Sir Piers Crosby. I assume you know what that is about.

I shall write again when more information is to hand.

With my very best wishes,

Northumberland.

I do indeed know what this business with Crosby is about. He is a pal of Mountnorris. He has been scheming and plotting against me ever since I got rid of his friend. They were trying another scheme to get their hands on the customs – and not for the benefit of King and country either. I also had to evict Crosby from the Irish Privy Council some years ago for his misbehaviour and misconduct. What Crosby has been saying is that I beat a man called Esmond to death myself while he was in prison. Absolute rubbish. The man died after he came out of prison from an illness, not a beating, and Mainwaring has uncovered evidence that his widow was bribed by Crosby to make these allegations against me. I think I shall have to sue Crosby for libel in the Star Chamber.

More bad news has come in today in the shape of a letter from Laud. He wrote it a fortnight ago. He says that the King has appointed the Marquis of Hamilton to be his Commissioner to Scotland, and he cannot think of anyone less suitable for the post. Like Holland the would-be admiral, Hamilton thinks he is a great soldier, but he knows hardly anything about that profession and has little fighting experience. He thinks he is a diplomat, but has no real experience of negotiating anything with anyone. Finally, he thinks he is a clever, scheming politician; whilst it is true that he has many weird and wonderful ideas, they amount to no coherent strategy for anything. He schemes for the sake of it, but has no idea what he is trying to achieve.

William says the Marquis was appointed Commissioner on the 8th, and that on the same day Charles wrote to the Scottish Council telling them to meet Hamilton at Dalkeith in early June. Hamilton is going about the Court telling anyone who will listen that he would 'show the Covenanters a thing or two about who was the most powerful', or words to that effect. That may have been his public face. Privately, William writes, Hamilton asked for and got the King's assurance that whatever the outcome in Scotland, the King would not withdraw his favour from him.

Laud's letter goes on:

Apparently the King's instructions to Hamilton are that he can suspend for a while the immediate use of the Prayer Book, and that although he will consider petitions and representations from the people about it, he insists that all copies of the Covenant be destroyed or handed over at once. The Covenanters must also make a full disclaimer of any belief in the document.

Hamilton can sack any members of the Privy Council who are treacherous enough to support the aims of the Covenant, and use force to break up mobs, even if peaceful. The King told him he could bribe different factions of Covenanters to work against each other, arrest people protesting in public, and declare the treachery of any disloyal nobles. He can also tell them that any force required to secure obedience will, if necessary, be reinforced from England, and that the King himself will come to enforce obedience, even at risk to his own life, rather than see royal commands flouted.

I understand Hamilton leaves on this mission in the next two or three days.

This has to be a disastrous enterprise at the present time. If the so-called Trained Bands are called out to train more, they will still be no match for the Scots. The chances of the King finding a Scots Army to fight for him are illusory. This business is going from bad to worse. The King needs someone with real mettle to set things right.

Charles I. 18th June, 1638. Whitehall.

My Dear Wentworth,

I dare say you have considerable knowledge of what goes on in Scotland now. I believe the Archbishop keeps you informed. In fact I often ask him to do so. You may, therefore, be aware that I have given the Marquis of Hamilton my commission to go to Scotland to hold talks with the Covenanters.

I am not sanguine about his chances of success. I expect that nothing but force can reduce that people to obedience, and I have told Hamilton so in a letter I sent him last week. He is to cultivate any hopes they have in any manner he pleases until I am ready to suppress them. As I have told him, and I tell you, I would rather die than yield to these impertinent and damnable demands.

I am having the Royal Armourers make ready at least forty cannon to be sent north, and I have ordered from the Dutch arms and weapons for two thousand cavalry and fourteen thousand infantry. I intend to make a timely end of these traitors the Covenanters. I am preparing orders to the Lords Lieutenant of the six counties nearest the border.

It is reassuring that you are training the Irish Army regularly, but I trust it will not be necessary to bring them to Scotland.

I am told by Chancellor Cottington and Treasurer Juxon that I have 200,000 pounds in hand. I shall be able to afford to go to war. Your recent letter telling me that Irish revenues are up is very welcome, and lends me more confidence. As a result, in two weeks, at the next Privy Council meeting, I intend to announce that there is a Scots rebellion which I shall quell by force.

I shall keep you up to date with developments, or ask Laud or Sir John Coke to do so.

Charles R.

I do not need the benefit of hindsight to tell me that this is a foolishly optimistic letter. I've only just received it and I can see it is unwise as plain as a pikestaff. Laud has written to me to say that, staunch Royalist though he may be, the King's belief that Divine Right and faith in God could alone can take care of these troubles is misguided. He says in one of his letters: *My misgiving soul is deeply apprehensive of no small evils coming on. I can see no cure without a miracle, and I fear that will not happen.*

No doubt he's right. I feel much the same myself.

Thomas. 14th July, 1638. Jigginstown House.

Keeping up with what goes on in Scotland is virtually impossible. The situation in Glasgow and Edinburgh would be confusing if I were in the thick of it. I get some information from contacts there, some second-hand intelligence from Laud and friends in London, and, to make matters more muddled still, a different slant on most of it from Ulster where the Scots immigrants are in close touch with their clans in Scotland.

From these varied sources I gather that Lord Hamilton met the Covenanters in early June. The meeting was in public, and about thirty Scots lords and six hundred ministers of the Kirk were supported by a very large crowd. Hamilton's plan to be backed up by his men and tenants from his estates came to nought. His people were afraid that if they congregated they would be attacked by the followers of all the other lords who had signed the Covenant. Hamilton failed to persuade the leader of the legal profession, Sir Thomas Hope, that the Covenant broke Scots law, so he could not proclaim the Covenanters traitors; he would get no support from the Scottish Courts if he tried.

Rumours are rife. Some say the King has a gunpowder plot to blow up the Covenant leaders. Others say those leaders are buying guns and ammunition abroad. Hamilton's own mother is said to have bought up as much gunpowder as she can to stop the King getting it. If she is a Covenanter, what are the chances that Hamilton is acting solely in the King's interests? He's supposed to have told the leaders privately that as a well-disposed Scot himself, if they went ahead with courage and resolution, they would secure what they wanted, but if they gave ground they would be undone.

Why did he say that? He knows the King will not give in. Was he hoping to make the Scots more determined to dig their heels in so that the King would have more reason to go to war? Or was he giving his fellow countrymen a broad hint that the King was too weak militarily to force them to submit and obey?

Another rumour is aimed at me. I am supposed to be plotting with the Archbishop to send a large contingent of my Irish soldiery to Scotland to crush the Covenant. That is plain daft. I need the Army here because the Scots in Ulster are likely to rise up in support of the Kirk. Bishop Henry Leslie of Down tells me that many of these Scots fail to attend the Eucharist, that this has been going on since at least Easter, and is getting worse. They are being egged on by the arrival in the country of copies of the Covenant which are being signed by them in the hundreds, despite my efforts to have it stamped out and destroyed.

I am also being asked to take part in a violent quarrel between the Irish Macdonnells and the Scots Archibald Campbell, Earl of Argyle. The Macdonnells are led by the Earl of Antrim. Antrim has no money; he had Kintyre taken off him by Argyle in a clan war some years ago. He is a very handsome, feckless charmer. He's hopelessly in debt, lives most of the time at the Royal court in England, and he's a great favourite with the King and Queen. Antrim has, apparently, told the King that he can land a huge force on the Mull of Kintyre, and defeat Argyle's forces. The King would undoubtedly like to believe that that is possible, because Argyle is one of the richest and most powerful men in Scotland, and one of the leading Covenanters. He also has one of the largest private armies north of the Border.

Antrim has asked me to supply him with men to pursue this day-dream, and he's asked the King to tell me to do so. I've had more than enough trouble with the Macdonnells, who are just a band of smugglers, pirates, and thieves. I'd rather put them down than help them fight. Antrim is as capable of taking an army to Scotland as I am of raising the dead.

The King is wrong to support Antrim against Argyle; he should do all he can to recruit Argyle to his own cause. The last thing we need is to encourage defiance from the Irish Catholics (and that is what the Macdonnells are), and make the Ulster Protestants fear we are trying to get military help from Spain.

I have no intention of sending my men to Scotland under My Lord Antrim.

Thomas. 27th July, 1638. Jigginstown House, County Wicklow.

My Dear Archbishop,

There are very unpleasant developments in Ulster. Our 'Thorough' Church reforms are resulting in violence and threats being made by the Scots settlers to the new Bishops we have appointed, and those of the clergy who support them. My chaplain has told me a horrifying tale of what happened to him not long ago. He was walking in the street in Belfast when he was set upon by some of the Calvinist ruffians. They started by taunting him for wearing his cassock and his clerical sash, and insulting him for being, as they put it, 'the Bishop's prick in the Bishopric."

He told me he offered them no riposte, but tried peacefully to go on his way. This seemed to make them angrier than if he had remonstrated with them, and they assaulted him atrociously. They knocked him down, kicked him and hit him, stripped off his clothes, and robbed him of all he carried. He made it sound almost as bad as the unfortunate Jew in the parable of the Good Samaritan. Fortunately they did not leave him for dead, as the thieves outside Jericho did, but he says that if they had known he was my chaplain, he is certain they would have taken his life, and in no pleasant fashion.

The Catholic Irish are not quiet, either. There have been uprisings in Donegal, Antrim, and Down among all the clans of O'this and Mac-that. It maybe that these riotous goings-on are fomented by the attitude of the Scots planters to their Catholic neighbours. It is an aggravation, but not too serious, and I can deal with both Scots and Irish with the Army.

Your 'Thorough' ally,
Wentworth.

Thomas. 7th August, 1638. Dublin Castle.

It is some time since I had a letter from Algie about political matters. He must be worried.

Alnwick Castle,
Northumberland.
27th July, 1638.
My Dear Thomas,

I hope that you and the family are well. Lucy is with us for the summer and sends you her regards. All is well here on a personal front. I wish I could say the same about the situation with Scotland. War now looks inevitable, and England is in no state to fight.

The Treasury is just about empty, Juxon tells me. Cottington says he doubts he will collect more than 100,000 in taxes this year. This means we cannot afford to buy any more armaments, and will be fortunate to find the cash to pay for those we have received from abroad. As a consequence, the King's magazines are totally bereft of arms and all sorts of ammunition, and of commanders we have none, either for advice or execution of tactics.

The people throughout England are generally so discontented because of the multitude of projects daily imposed upon them, as I think there is reason to fear that a great part of them will be readier to join with the Scots than to draw their swords in the King's service.

They might feel differently if it were not for the trouble over the Prayer Book here, and above all, the Ship Money farce which has resulted in the Sheriff of Northampton going about saying the people should revolt properly against it, like the Scots. The Archbishop has prohibited the academics at Oxford from debating whether Ship Money is legal. That shows just how hollow the King's 'victory' over Hampden really is.

I should be pleased to receive your observations on this crisis, for that is what I think it is.

As always, your affectionate
Algie.

So that's what Northumberland, the Lord High Admiral, thinks! Well, I knew things were dire, and this confirms it. He asks for my views. I'll have to put pen to paper fairly soon. This needs thought.

Yet I must get a letter off to Laud first. I have to tell him how badly the situation between Antrim and Argyle is affecting the running of Ireland, and will do no good in Scotland either. Lord Antrim is here telling all and sundry that he has the King's permission to go to war – that is what he calls it – with Argyle. In some ways I could wish he would, because Antrim's people run what amounts to a small pirate navy on Scotland's West Coast. I just do not have enough navy ships here to do much about that, and these raiders go wherever they like. I resent very much their raiding my ports and harbours and sea-side villages. Hamilton has the navy out in the North Sea trying to blockade Scotland and keep the Dutch and the arms they are selling the Covenanters out, so he's no help.

If Antrim tries to fight Argyle, however, the Scots planters here will rebel, and if I let him take a goodly part of my army across the water, I may be unable to put such a rebellion down. In effect I'd be handing him all the fortifications in Ulster. It would be folly on a grand scale.

Having started my letter to the Archbishop thus, I go on:

I have instituted an oath which the Scots here must take, commanding their loyalty to the King and their opposition to the Covenanters. I shall give Antrim no help to fight Argyle. If I supply him with men and arms we shall not only risk uprisings in Scotland, at the sight of an Irish chieftain made powerful, but also by the settlers in Ulster should Antrim decide to make use of his forces here instead of in the West of Scotland.

I'm told that he says he can fight the Scots and it won't cost the King a penny, but he doesn't fool me. Antrim says he 'will beat and bang and conquer the Scots', but details of how he will make good his word have not been provided to me or my government.

He has asked me for weapons, ammunition, horses, cash for the soldiers and their food, plus 10,000 cattle to take with them for their dinners. He also wants me to provide ships to take them there.

I shall not be at all surprised if, in the end, Antrim shuffles the pack so dextrously, that while pretending he is fighting at his own cost, he can presently shift off the cost upon the King, make himself an admiral at sea and a general on land, and command his own army, his own artillery, his own navy, and appoint his friends and family as the officers.

I am totally against this way of running the army and navy. Only worthy officers should be given commands. My life shall be as freely laid down for my gracious master as any that lives; yet I am not weary of it either, and should be very unwilling to die like a fool, or, to put it plainly, desirous of fighting but in the company of those who understand their profession.

I take the liberty of troubling you with all this, in the hope that in Council, or privately, you may tactfully inform the King of the difficulties that too much reliance on Antrim may cause.

I remain your sincere friend,

Wentworth.

Thomas. 10th August, 1638. Dublin.

Philip Mainwaring comes into my study carrying an account book. He looks very happy. I'm sitting at my desk and wave him to a chair opposite. He opens the accounts, puts them before me, and sits.

"My Lord, you have done it three years in a row."

"Done what?"

"The revenue has increased again. All those reforms you put through for taxes and the customs five or six years ago, and the new customs farm agreement with the King, have paid off."

I laugh and slap the desk with both hands. "Thank the Lord for that. I remember the customs farm yielded 38,000 pounds the year after I got to Ireland. What's the result this year then?"

Philip rises and comes to my side of the desk. He leans across and points to the page at which the accounts lie open. "There it is, My Lord. These accounts have just been completed at the Treasury for the last twelve months. 58,000 pounds!! And that's just the customs, without other revenue."

"This calls for a celebration, Philip," and I go to the bookshelf and pour us both a goblet of wine. "At least I've been doing better that Mountnorris ever did."

Now Philip laughs. "It would have been hard to do worse, no matter how you might try."

We drain our goblets and I pour another. "If I can stay at the helm of this Irish Ship of State with you, the Georges, and Christopher at my side, I think we can make this a truly great Kingdom."

Thomas, 13th August, 1638. Jigginstown House.

My Dear Lady Carlisle,

I write in haste as there is much to do, but I know you will be pleased to learn that the purchase of your Irish estate was completed two days ago. I expect to receive an account from the solicitors in the next week or so, and shall forward all the details to you when they are to hand.

The family and I are well, and I trust you are too.

Let us pray that the King's business in Scotland will have a happy outcome. It must be a worry to you and all the Percys to think that war with Scotland may yet occur. Your family has hundreds of years of experience of defending England's Northern Border against the Scots, but the prospect of more fighting can never be a pleasant one.

I am your faithful

Wentworth.

Thomas. 28th August, 1638. Dublin Castle.

I am in my study dictating to Kit.

My Dear Algie,

Your letter of 27th July arrived three weeks ago. I am very busy but have given much thought to what you wrote. I think that war must follow, and we have to be ready. Your responsibilities are awesome, and I trust you will not take too strong an objection to my offering you some suggestions. It might be taken as a liberty on my part, when your forefathers have been at war for generations with the Scots, and I and mine have not.

However, if the King's forces are in the weak state you describe, the situation may be different from any which England has previously encountered.

First, Scotland must be cut off, as far as possible, from being supplied from abroad. As the sea is the only route into Scotland apart from England, this means the main Scottish ports must be garrisoned strongly as soon as possible. The Edinburgh docks at Leith must be seized, as well as Dumbarton and Arran.

When the rebels have been defeated, the country must be governed by an English Deputy, even if not under English Law. He may be a curb on the unruly notions of that people against the Crown, by foreseeing early and preventing in a timely manner their tumults, by settling the revenue of the Crown in that country, and turning it into the right channels.

In my view Scottish taxes are supped up for private benefit, but ought to flow into the Royal Exchequer. Their customs duties should be farmed out to someone who can make a proper job of collecting them, as is happening here in Ireland.

With these resources the King can, after triumphing over them, man Leith and Dumbarton at the expense of the Scots with strong forces, to ensure the reforms go through, and to secure peace in future. When that occurs, the King will be King of Great Britain indeed, and that nation a strength which has now become an offence.

Kit looks up. “You don’t hide your contempt for the Scottish, do you, Tom?”

“Why on earth should I? They are the most troublesome people I can think of.”

“You used to say that about the Irish?”

“Perhaps I did, but they are hardly in the same league.”

“Or is it the way you manage them, Tom?” Kit asks with a smile. “The way this letter is going it doesn’t take a genius to work out that you think you should be governor of Scotland, and Ireland, and President of the North.” He laughs. “Soon you’ll rule more of the Kingdom that the King!!”

“Is it that obvious? I don’t trust the Scots, you know that.”

“We all know that, Tom. I don’t think the King would ever make you his Deputy in Scotland though. Don’t forget he was born there. He’s a Scot first, and only a bit English after that. He wants a Scotsman to run Scotland for him.”

“You’re right Kit. I must bear in mind who Charles’s father was.”

“Yes, you should try to remember that.” He smiles again. “It’s hardly surprising that the Covenanters say you are the most evil enemy they could possibly have. The last thing they would want is a strong man to govern them. They prefer to be out of control – except where their faith and religion are concerned.”

“All the more reason why the King should get me to do the governing!” I cannot help laughing. “And I say that in all modesty.”

“Some would say you have much to be modest about, Tom, but not me; definitely not me!” We both laugh.

“Well, let’s finish the letter. Then I’m off to Cosha for a holiday.”

“Going hunting, then? Are you pleased with the new hunting lodge?”

“I shall be when it’s finished. You must come down and join in a chase or two yourself. I’m having the place landscaped a little, to make it more picturesque, but without spoiling the hunting. I hope it will be the park of parks, to rival anything in England.”

"George was telling me you're starting a breed of horses there, and a small ironworks. Haven't you got enough to do? It won't be much of a holiday if you're working on so many projects all the time, will it?"

"Oh, I don't know about that, Kit. The King's affairs, God be praised, go on quietly and prosperously in this land, and are likely so to continue."

Thomas. 20th September, 1638. Jigginstown House.

My Dear William,

Perhaps I should leave out the 'My Dear', or address you as 'Savile', as if I do not care for you, since I have reason to be just a little cross with you.

My Vice-President of the North, Sir Edward Osborne, who is very loyal, and keeps in regular touch, wrote last November to tell me that some people, whom one would suppose to be loyal, have been showing rather unhelpful tendencies. As my beloved nephew, and the son of my equally beloved sister Anne, I would not have supposed that you would be among them. He told me that you are part of a movement to have me dismissed from the Lord Lieutenancy of Yorkshire.

The reasons for this are not entirely clear, but one may guess that it has something to do with the fact that I am not in Yorkshire now, and apart from some visits two years ago, have not been there for five years. That ignores the fact that Sir Edward knows exactly what he is doing, writes to me regularly about all the important local developments, asks my advice, and acts on it. Mayhap the North and the King would be well served should Sir Edward become Lord Lieutenant himself, but it is more likely that the role would be taken by someone closer to the King, such as Lord Holland, or some other fop who knows nothing, and could do less, unless it were to do harm.

Or perhaps it would be Sir Arthur Ingram, in which case not a penny of the Northern Army's revenue would be safe. Or worse, Sir John Savile, from the distaff side of your father's family tree, from whose scheming and cheating no-one would be safe. Is that what you would wish upon the North of England?

Is there not trouble enough up there, with the Scots on the verge of war, and perhaps invasion? Osborne tells me the local Lords and Squires are not doing their duty by raising troops to fight for the King, and that you disobeyed the orders you had been given to bring a troop of cavalry to York.

But I cannot be that angry with you. You are playing the part of a very young man, and showing your independence of spirit much as I did at your age; I can hardly criticise you for being like me. Thus, I should be grateful if you would do your duty, and set a good example by leading your men as you are commanded, and helping Osborne and his servants and agents collect Ship Money instead of siding with those who refuse to pay. If there is to be a Scottish war it is vital that we have a strong navy to blockade Scotland, and keep the Dutch and others from landing cannon and other weapons the rebels may use to slaughter your men. Or you.

Too many of your neighbours are turning traitor. I hear families have fled to Holland rather than face the new Prayer Book, unless it is merely that they are scared to fight the Scots. The Bellasis and some other families, with whom I had much trouble, are completely untrustworthy, and I have written to tell Sir Edward that he must not retain them in any important position. It is vital that you do all you can to assist him in the crisis.

I care little or nothing for the fact that some of these Northern nobles whisper that I have become a stranger to them. This is not a time to let go my control of all those who may oppose the King.

Please write as soon as possible to let me know that you will do as I ask in all these matters.

My love to you and your family and especially to your dear Mother.

Your very affectionate Uncle,
Thomas.

Elizabeth. 24th September, 1638. Jigginstown House.

I am playing my harpsichord, one of the most beautiful gifts I have ever had from Thomas. It is a lovely instrument. Its rather plain shape, which, contrarily, often makes me think of a coffin, is painted a delicate pale green decorated with vines and flowers in subtle colours. The music, Byrd's *'Parthenia'*, is suddenly interrupted as the door flies open.

"The Bastard!! The ..."

"Thomas! How dare you! You know I hate it when you swear."

"Yes, damn it, I know. But anyway, he's a bast..."

"Thomas! Enough! I understand the message, alright? You're annoyed, furious, upset, angry. But just tell me what the problem is, and stop swearing! Just calm down!"

He flings himself into a chair so hard it nearly overbalances, and thankfully that makes us both laugh. He's calmer but I can see, still seething. "It's Loftus."

"I might have guessed. Don't tell me. He didn't turn up again."

"That's three times since he was before the Council last time. I think it's almost once a month."

"What was his excuse this time?"

"Hah! He's gone beyond that now. He didn't even bother to send one. He's in contempt, and if he were anyone else I'd have him put back in prison and throw away the key."

"Well, Thomas, you can't do that. The King doesn't want him in prison with everything else that's going on, does he?"

"No, Bess, he doesn't, but he doesn't want his commands and decrees disobeyed either. I'll have to ask the King for permission to jail him."

I put my hand on his arm. "Yes, that's best. But why don't you summon the old villain to Court once more, and then tell the King if he stays away again? You could even tell Loftus that's what you'll do."

Thomas takes my face in both hands and kisses me. "That's it Bess. That's exactly it. We'll send him a summons and a letter saying that is what will happen. Mind you, if the King says 'No' I'll look damn silly."

"I don't think you need worry about that. His Majesty will be bound to see that it's really *his* authority that's being flouted. After all, you only do all this for him."

He kisses me long and hard. I know where this is headed. Thank goodness!

Elizabeth. 25th November, 1638. Dublin Castle.

"My darling, you look so ... so ..."

"Distressed? Well, that's so, Bess. The most tragic news has just arrived from York." Thomas slumps into a chair. He has just come into our sitting room from the Parliament Building. Am I mistaken, or has he tears in his eyes? He drags his hand across them, and I was right; the back of his hand is wet with his tears.

I go to him and kneel by his side and take his hands in mine. "What is it, then? Has someone died?"

"Not just died Bess; been killed. You remember Sir Edward?"

"Sir Edward?"

"Yes, Osborne. Didn't you meet him?"

"I did, but with my father years ago, not with you. My father and he were well acquainted. He's been killed?"

"For my sake, fortunately not, but his eldest son was killed in a storm. He was playing with his little brother, and as they ran into a room in the course of their game, lightning struck the chimney. The smaller boy dived under a table to catch his pet cat, and was saved by it, but the chimney crashed through the roof and hit the bigger boy full on. He died instantly." Thomas waves a letter. "That's what Osborne says in this letter."

I am downcast. "How sad he must be. How sad we were when we lost our little Thomas, and he was so young we had hardly got to know him." I start to cry, and Thomas puts his arms around me as tears drift down the side of his nose, too.

"Edward is such a good man, and a good friend to me. And such a loving father. He must be devastated. Well, he is; he says so in this." He holds the letter up again, and I take it from him to read. We sit in silence as I do so.

"Thomas, he says here that some of the Councillors are being urged by others to have him removed from office. That's appalling at such a time."

"Yes, I was coming to that. It's unforgiveable when he is stricken with grief, but some of these political people are more like vultures than men. I'll frighten them away from their prey, don't you fret. I cannot think of a man who is likely to make a better Vice-President than he, and I'm damned – sorry Bess – I'll be blowed if I'll let them get away with it."

"What will you do?"

"I'll rally my friends. Harry Percy and his brother, the Earl, have a lot of influence, and so does Margaret's family, the Cliffords. Between them they are the North – well, the Border, anyway – and there are many others who will support Osborne if I ask them."

"But you had a lot of opposition from other people in Yorkshire and the rest of the North before we came here, didn't you, Thomas?"

"True enough, my love, but I'm sure the King will side with me over this, and with the friends I've mentioned, Osborne's job is safe enough. I just hope he's soon feeling strong enough to do his work. He must sorely need some time off."

Charles I. 10th January, 1639. My Audience Chamber. Whitehall Palace.

A servant knocks and enters. I am looking at the pictures which are hanging in this room. The Queen is seated on her throne watching me and listening to what I have to say about the artists and the paintings, while we await Archbishop Laud. We have to talk about the situation in Scotland.

Me. Yes, what is it?

Servant. The Archbishop, Your Majesty.

Me. Show him in immediately.

Servant. *(As he goes).* At once, Your Majesty. *(Re-entering).* The Archbishop, Sire.

Laud enters, as the Servant goes.

Laud. I came at once, Your Majesty. *(To the Queen).* Good afternoon, Ma'am. I trust I find you well.

Queen. I shall be well when I know what is going on and what you will tell His Majesty to do about it. But first, what has caused this terrible news? Why should the Scots send an Army against their own King?

Me. It is the new Prayer Book, my dear. They do not like it.

Laud. If you will forgive my saying so, Your Majesty, that is something of an understatement. When the clergy started to use it in St. Giles Cathedral an old woman stood up and flung a stool at the pulpit. The Service turned into a riot. The most worrying thing about the situation is that the Scottish Calvinists and Catholics are united over this matter.

Me. That is what I hear, too. They have met in huge gatherings, and entered into what they are calling a Covenant. Anyone of any importance at all is required to sign this Covenant, and I am told that hardly anyone of importance has refused. There are some exceptions, I'm glad to say. Lord Huntly in Aberdeen went to the Eucharist Service to take Communion from the Archbishop – the very one who'd been excommunicated by the Kirk Assembly in Glasgow. That Assembly has, in effect, torn up my religious policy and has disobeyed Hamilton, my Commissioner to Scotland.

Queen. That is treason.

Laud. It amounts, more or less, to a declaration of war, Your Majesty.

Me. Indeed it does. I was, but a moment ago, telling the Queen that I shall have to raise an Army. The Counties will have to call out the men, and the Lords will have to put their forces at my disposal.

Laud. With some trepidation I must remind you, Sire, that without Parliament it will be impossible to pay them, or provide them with food, let alone weapons. Will your Majesty call Parliament?

Queen. Why should the King have to call Parliament? Is it not his right to decide to go to war? Especially if the enemy invades us? And what about Lord Wentworth? Doesn't he keep a large Army in Ireland? How does he have an Army when the King does not?

Me. He has an Army because he has the Irish Parliament eating out of his hand. When he wants money they grant him subsidies - large subsidies. When he wants to raise taxes or change the way the Customs are collected, they pass the laws he needs. He manages the Irish Parliament - manipulates it would be a better word - in a way which is almost magical. I have no-one in England to manage the House of Commons, and there I am faced with Mr. Pym.

Queen. Pym?

Laud. He was the Member of Parliament for Tavistock, Ma'am. It is a town in Devon. Somehow he has the same knack of managing - or rather manipulating - the Commons here as Wentworth does in Ireland. At least, he would manage them if Parliament were called, and he would strive to ensure that no taxes would be voted to fight the Scots.

Queen. Is he not an Englishman? Are the Scots not his enemy if they invade his country? Why should he oppose the King?

Me. Because he's a Puritan, and because he would rather side with them than see them forced to use our new Prayer Book.

Laud. That is how things stand, Ma'am, as the King says. The Scots have other grievances, but effectively we are likely to be at war with them over the Prayer Book.

Queen. Then you are much to blame, are you not, Your Grace? After all, you wrote this Prayer Book, didn't you?

Me. He wrote it at my command, my dear. It was my idea to introduce it in Scotland. I didn't expect to need an Army to get my subjects to read a book

Queen. And when you have an Army, who will lead it? No Englishmen have fought a proper battle since before the Duke of Buckingham was murdered, and when they did they lost. Who is there to help you? Will you send for the Lord Deputy, for Wentworth?

Me. I shall consult with him, but his proper place is in Ireland at present. No, I shall lead the Army myself, and shall see its numbers swell as men flock to the Royal Standard.

Laud. If I may be so bold, Sire, I have here a letter from the Deputy, which I should like to read to you. *(I nod and Laud reads).* "I must advise the King against a rash and sudden declaring of war, although I am not fearful of sacrificing my life and honour to the Scots mutiny. The answer most becoming His Majesty is to tell them it is not the custom of the best and mildest of Kings to be threatened into calling Parliaments. I am confident this will not provoke them into an early offensive war on England. The King should resolve not to fight with them hastily, first because the King could give them time to come to their senses, and because he has much to lose, and they little. By gaining time the King can strengthen his position, and garrison Berwick and Carlisle. I can muster the Irish Army for him on the Ulster Coast, only a day's shipping from Scotland, and the King can make ready to seize the Leith ports in the spring."

Me. My Lord Wentworth is very ready with his advice. He has even broadcast his opinion on Naval strategy to the Lord Admiral, who tells me that the Deputy has told him to occupy Leith, Dumbarton, and the Isle of Arran. The ports of Scotland can then be blockaded, and the rebels more easily brought under control. He even goes so far as to suggest that I should appoint an English Deputy for Scotland, and bring in English law! Now who do you suppose he has in mind for Deputy?

Queen. Hah! He will never be happy until he is first in the land. Yorkshiremen hate the Scots, and Wentworth is no exception. And he causes such trouble with your supporters in Scotland, like the Marquess of Hamilton.

Me. Certainly the Scots have no liking for my Lord Deputy. In Glasgow the Assembly of the Scottish Church denounced him as an "enemy of God." And it is not just in Scotland that he makes enemies.

The names of those who claim to be his victims read like a roll-call of the Irish Peerage - Cork, Clanricarde, Mountnorris - why, he would even have the Irish Lord Chancellor in prison.

Laud. But all these men, including Lord Chancellor Loftus, have behaved in a manner that merited punishment, Sire, whilst the Deputy's advice is invariably of the best.

Me. So it is, so it is. And I accept that these men are only victims in their own eyes - not in the eyes of the law, but Wentworth's obsession with Justice for all and acting according to his conscience is politically impossible. I need money for war with Scotland. I hope to have some from Clanricarde - he is now a wealthy man in Ireland, and Earl of St. Albans here - but how am I to borrow from him when my Deputy stands between us?

Laud. He does so because he considers men like Clanricarde should be made an example of, Sire.

Me. I am well aware of that! The Earl's father misappropriated land in Western Ireland, and Wentworth has recovered it for me. True. But Clanricarde will lend me the money if I restore the land to him. It is politic to do so, Your Grace, but Wentworth sees only what he believes to be right, and to hell with the politics.

Queen. One day he will regret having made all these enemies, Charles......

Laud. I have warned him of it repeatedly, Ma'am.

Queen. ....and he may give you cause to regret it too.

Me. He may, but nevertheless I wish - oh! how I wish - I had a Deputy like him in Scotland.

Queen. He wants to be Lord Deputy in Ireland and Scotland.

Laud. Though I am his friend, I fancy he has an opinion of himself and his abilities high enough to let him believe he could rule both Scotland and Ireland for you, Sire. Yet at the same time he thinks he is humble and modest. *(He pauses).* He is a paradox.

Queen. He is a hypocrite. He thinks he has nothing to be modest about.

Me. You may be right. I am not ignorant of his faults. He's overconfident, impatient, and proud; and I tell him so. He is still Lord President of the North. I've heard it said that if I give him Scotland as well as Ireland and the North he will rule more of the Kingdom than I do!! But this is no subject for jest. His loyalty is unquestioned.

Laud. But the loyalty of others may not be, Sire. It seems the aristocracy in Yorkshire and other parts of the North are slow to raise troops to march on Scotland.
Me. We shall see. I'm confident the people will clamour to join me when I journey north. I hope to be in York with my army by Easter.
Laud. Sire, there is an aspect of this affair which may have escaped you. However, I am rather reluctant to speak of it before Her Majesty.
Me. Whatever you may wish to say to me may be said in front of the Queen, Your Grace.
Laud. Then I trust you will forgive my speaking frankly, Ma'am, since I think this crisis requires the truth.
Queen. Speak. You will not upset or offend me!
Laud. Then, Sire, you should be aware that the fact that Her Majesty's Catholic mother lives here at English expense whilst your ...
Queen. How dare you!! How do you expect my mother to live? She is of the Royal House of ...
Me. Henrietta! Please!! I need to hear what the Archbishop has to say. You said you would not be upset. If you are, then may I suggest you withdraw. *(It is a statement, not a question).*
Queen. Huh! Huh!! Very well. I stay.
Me. *(To Laud).* Pray go on, Your Grace.
Laud. Thank you Sire, and I apologise in advance for any distress I may cause you, Ma'am. Your mother, Ma'am, like you, is a Catholic, as I was saying, and is maintained at Court by His Majesty.
Queen. Quite right, too!
Me. Henrietta! *(I take her hand to show that I am not too angry, but I look at her sternly).* Go, on, Archbishop.
Laud. At the same time, whilst you send your sister, Elizabeth, such sums as you can afford, we do nothing to help her, a loyal Protestant, to regain her Kingdom of Bohemia or the Palatinate from other Popish powers. I hear from clergymen all over the country that their parishioners resent our helping the faithful of the Pope but not those who follow our faith.
Me. They resent it because they do not understand. They are, for the most part, completely ignorant of what goes on across the Channel. Foreign policy is my responsibility, and mine alone. It is not for the people to Dictate policy to me.
Queen. *Exactement!!*

Laud. I do not question that, Sire. I merely mention it because I think it may contribute to the difficulties of recruiting an Army.

Charles I. 2nd March, 1639. Windsor, Castle.

My Dear Wentworth,

I received your recent letter about my Irish Lord Chancellor, Loftus. I note that you warned him that if he did not attend the Council when required to do so you would inform me, and ask for permission to have him properly incarcerated until he submits to the jurisdiction of the Privy Council and obeys my command to hand over the Great Seal of Office.

I further note that he has not attended hearings on two further occasions, and I have seen the certificates from the Clerk to the Council that that is so. I cannot say that I am at all happy to give you authority to proceed in this matter in the way you suggest, since there are troubles enough besetting the three Kingdoms without this aggravation. However, the challenge to your authority, and therefore mine, by Lord Loftus has reached such a pitch that there is now no alternative.

I am not at all sure I agree with you that a demonstration of firmness in this case will send a wider lesson to others inclined to be defiant, since this is a problem involving, in essence, one difficult old man, and not a defiant nation north of the border, nor what amounts to a revolt amongst some members of the Anglican clergy here in England.

Nevertheless, I hereby give you my permission to have Loftus brought before the Council, and if he fails to comply with any of the orders which have been made, to imprison him securely, and remove those liberties which he currently enjoys.

Please report the outcome to me.

I am your appreciative Charles R.

George Radcliffe. 29th March, 1639. Jigginstown House.

Striding up and down as Thomas usually does when in a rage, Christopher and I follow along behind him, dragging in his wake, and trying to keep up. No sign of gout hampers him today. We reach one end of the terrace at the back of this magnificent brick edifice he is building, and he turns smartly as if we were on parade, and starts marching back the way we came.

As we pass an open garden door into a drawing room he yells to a servant to bring us some ale, but he always says 'please' to his staff. No-one would think a request from Thomas anything but an order to be obeyed with alacrity, however.

"Why don't I want to wait for arms and ammunition from England, George? You know why. I've said it often enough. I simply do not trust that sufficient supplies of good quality weapons can come from the King in time for the war that is surely almost upon us. Northumberland tells me that the Treasury in England is empty. Is it likely that the Dutch will supply arms on credit? They are Puritans and Calvinists for the most part themselves. Will they have sympathy for a King trying to impose a High Church Prayer Book and rituals to match on the Calvinist Scots?"

Christopher volunteers: "I thought the Dutch would do anything for money."

Thomas stops and faces him. "They won't sell their souls. If they would, they'd hardly have fought the Spanish efforts to keep them in the Church of Rome for the last hundred years or so. And it's not just arms. Look at what's happened to Lord Clifford." Then he's off again along the terrace.

Christopher manages to catch him. "You mean Henry? He's your brother-in-law, isn't he? What's happened to him?"

"You remember he was Governor of Carlisle? Meaning he was responsible for defending Westmoreland and Cumberland. Well, he's no longer Governor."

I am amazed. "But Henry's father is the Earl of Cumberland, and Henry exercises all his responsibilities for him, doesn't he? They're like the Percys in Northumberland. They've been fighting the Scots and keeping the North free of them for centuries. What they don't know about fighting in the Border terrain and the way to make war on Scotland is hardly worth knowing. Why would anyone replace him?"

"God knows, George, but that is what the King has done. He's relieved Henry of the job, and put in his place one of the Earl of Arundel's boys. What do they know down in Sussex of fighting the Clans? Maybe this young man is a warrior, but if so, I haven't heard much of his bold deeds or victories over enemies. As far as I know he's just another socialite, like Holland. What really galls me is that Arundel now has command of the 500 soldiers we sent over to garrison the city!'

We're still marching, going back the other way again. Kit breathlessly asks: "Hasn't Lord Holland been appointed commander of the King's cavalry?"

"Yes he has. He's more used to having his legs between a woman's thighs than having a horse between his own. If you don't need military training and experience to command the King's forces, then the Scots will win. The King is surrounded by idiots. I'll wager Hamilton put Holland's name forward, so the King has Hamilton as an incompetent ruler of his Navy; Holland, who may be worse, in charge of the cavalry; a nincompoop to govern Carlisle, and above all that, he now has the Earl of Arundel himself as Commander in Chief."

I feel as though a ray of light has suddenly shone upon me. "That explains it then. I wondered how on earth the rebels could have captured Dumbarton, when you had advised the King and Northumberland that he should put a strong garrison in it last year."

Thomas shrugs. "How can that coterie of tumblers and jesters understand how serious all this is? They've barely got a complete brain between them. If the ports and forts are in the hands of the Covenanters, the King's cause is as good as lost."

"But you write to the King and to Laud offering advice often enough. Don't your letters have any effect?"

"I wish they did, George, but it seems they do not. I even offered to send some of our Irish troops to garrison Dumbarton, but my offer was not taken up. I planned to put one of my good, loyal officers in command. Catholic troops have no qualms about fighting Scots Presbyterians, and the port would have been safe. As it was, the Scottish officer commanding took the Governor prisoner six days ago, and just let the Covenanters in without a shot being fired."

The servant emerges from the end of the terrace bearing a tray loaded with three silver mugs and a large jug of ale. He puts it on a marble table, and we all stop at it, pour ourselves a drink, and sit on the balustrade. Christopher speaks. "The letter from Laud this morning doesn't make happy reading either."

Thomas looks as though that's the last thing he wants to hear. "Doesn't it? I didn't get to see all the post this morning. I decided to play with the children for a while and took a walk with my son William. So what's this unhappy letter about?"

"It's about Lord Antrim, and Lord Holland. Antrim's been complaining to the King that you won't help him get his army across to fight in Scotland. He says it's all your fault."

Thomas crashes his mug on the table and most of his beer flies out. I pour some more into it. "What a bloody cheek. Do I have a navy? No. Can I get this army to Scotland without ships? No. Who's got the ships?"

"Hamilton!" Christopher replies very quickly. "And he's got them on the other side of Scotland."

"A fat lot of use they are there, sailing up and down and not even managing to stop the Dutch sending arms to the Covenanters, or stopping their General Leslie sailing in and out as he pleases. In any case I don't want Antrim to have an army, nor any of the money out of the Irish Treasury, nor any of my soldiers. He tells the King he can raise an army at his own expense, but Philip Mainwaring tells me Antrim couldn't even borrow as little as 300 pounds from anyone in Ireland."

"Perhaps you should go to London to tell the King how things are here," I suggest.

Thomas nods in appreciation. "I think I'll have to. I've been thinking about it. When we go in we'll do a letter to the King and one to Laud saying that's what I want to do. It's not just that I want him to know what I think."

Christopher laughs. "Well, no-one could say you're backward in coming forward with your advice. Last week you wrote asking him to shelve any plans to invade Scotland for at least a year."

Thomas pretty well ignores that, and certainly doesn't laugh. "I don't just want to tell him what to do. I want to find out what's really going on. The King tells me little, Laud tells me as much as he can, and so does Algie Percy, but I still don't get the whole picture. A servant who is untaught and unguided by his master's word and directions yet can serve according to his masters wishes is a wise and fortunate man indeed!"

I say: "More of a magician than a servant." I look at Christopher. "Didn't you say Laud's letter mentions Lord Holland?"

"Yes, it does. It ties in with what Tom said about Holland and the ladies. You heard that the Queen's French friend is with her in London?"

"You mean the Duchess of Chevreuse?" Thomas asks.

"Exactly. Well, she'd hardly got off the boat when Holland was flirting with her outrageously and publicly, and it is no secret that they're in and out of each others' bedrooms as often as they can manage."

Thomas laughs for the first time this afternoon. "Holland can manage it pretty frequently, so they say. Seriously, though, with a war looming, you'd think he'd be thinking with his head and not his prick if he's got to lead some cavalry charges soon. How is a man like that one of the King's bosom pals? Charles is such a moral person."

Thomas. 17th April, 1639. Jigginstown House.

Another of Laud's High Church placemen is to be installed as a Bishop this week. This time it is Henry Tilson, who is now Bishop of Elphin. It's a long, fairly narrow Bishopric, stretching south from the sea coast just below Donegal, down through Sligo and Roscommon, and parts of Galway. There are many Catholics in these counties.

On the Scottish front things go from bad to worse. A couple of days ago I wrote to the Secretary of the Privy Council in London asking him to tell the King again that in my view he should abandon any hope of marching on Scotland until next year. In the meanwhile he should build up his forces and his armaments and send scouts to examine the lie of the land carefully on both sides of the Border so that he can, when battle comes, pick the most favourable terrain. That is what Algie or Henry would do.

I even told the King, albeit with some trepidation: "You will, after all, be at war with Your Majesty's own subjects, even if they are rebellious. It would be a tender point to draw blood first. I would not act so as to give them any cause to say that you have pushed everything to the extremity, until their acts as well as their words force you to it. In your place, if I may be so bold as to say so (without for a moment suggesting I should be in your exalted place), I should carry on talks and enter into treaties with them, and miss no opportunity to strengthen Your Majesty's forces, and prepare to fight in a twelvemonth."

I hear from Northumberland that recruiting is going badly. Arabella's father, Lord Clare, who is very wealthy, says he's too old to fight or raise any men, which may be true, but he also says he can't afford to do it because he's got seven young daughters to marry off with dowries! Will he be richer if the Scots invade England? According to Laud many people are unhappy because Catholic Lords like Worcester and Winchester are giving the King large amounts for the war effort, and that just shows that the King is really a Catholic too. Pretty preposterous, if you ask me. The last thing English Catholics want is for Scottish Calvinists to rule the religious roost, so they provide the finances so the King can fight.

I'm told a London jeweller and Turkey merchant has given the King 100,000 pounds for the war. He doesn't trade in turkeys, that exotic species of poultry from the Americas. He trades with Turkey, importing luxury carpets, rugs, silks, and other luxurious goods coming usually by camel train, across from the Middle and Far East, and exporting English wool.

The Inns of Court and the City itself have refused to give anything. That won't help much if Hamilton, Arundel, and Holland keep helping themselves to dollops of cash out of the Treasury. Algie Percy writes that his generals, Astley and Jacob, who were advising the cities of Hull and Newcastle on reinforcing their fortifications and defences, have been reduced to telling the Aldermen that they'll have to pay for the work themselves. I cannot imagine that will endear the King's cause to the people up the North-East Coast.

Astley also complains that Lord Arundel has supplied such troops as there are on the Borders with bows and arrows!! How ridiculous is that? This is the 17th Century, not the 14th!!

There have been some nasty happenings here, too. My intelligence service discovered a plot to open up the port of Carrickfergus to the Scottish Covenanters, which would have been a disaster, as the Ulster Covenanters would immediately be able to join with them against my Government. Sending any of my troops to Scotland would then have proved impossible. I must write and tell Laud about that. As it is, I have moved 2,000 soldiers into the town with 1000 cavalry to prevent an uprising.

The more I think about, it, I'm not at all sure that all this trouble in Scotland is really about the right brand of Christianity. It's more likely to be political, to get more power and independence for Scotland, or something of the sort. If I'm wrong about that, it just shows the folly of trying to control men's consciences and the way they wish to relate to God. Even so, I think the King has no alternative but to try to enforce his will. If he loses the war – if war comes – he's lost his authority. If he gives in over his Prayer Book, then his authority as Head of the Church is lost, and it amounts to the same thing. I have to help him win.

Charles I. 20th April, 1639. The King's House, York.

My Dear Wentworth,

I am greatly impressed by the commodious accommodation this house provides, and am grateful to you for undertaking the excellent improvements.

I arrived here three weeks ago with the Duke of Lennox and Lord Holland. The same day it seems Lord Huntly was obliged to leave his stronghold of Aberdeen in the hands of the Covenanters; I have not had such awful news since I left London.

As you will be well aware, there is much discontent here and in Scotland over the introduction of the Prayer Book, and the refusal of many to pay Ship Money following the outcome of the Hampden case. Many people seem to think that as only seven out of twelve judges convicted him, they need not pay, and they do not.

In these circumstances I simply cannot afford to run the risk of alienating such a powerful man in Ireland as the Earl of St Albans and Clanricarde. I must therefore insist that you re-convey to the Earl all the land taken from him in Galway as a result of the inquiry by the Commission for Defective Titles.

I apprehend that you will be unhappy with this instruction, but there is no alternative. The Earl's loyalty – never previously in doubt – has been severely tested, and the danger that it may pass its breaking point is now a vital consideration. Kindly obey as soon as possible and report to me that this has been done.

What is the situation with Lord Loftus? I do not seem to have had a report from you since I gave you leave to have him imprisoned.

I have received, and considered your request to come to England, and I shall be glad if you do so, as your counsel will be welcome. However, I have no intention of acting on your advice to put off this war for a year or so. Further, you may take this letter as my command to you to assist the Earl of Antrim in attacking Lord Argyle in Scotland by leading the Irish Army there yourself before coming here.

I am, as always, your grateful
Charles R.

This letter is like the curate's egg. I am, of course, delighted to get that bit of it about going to York, but I'm really annoyed about the King's attitude to the plantation policy. I am very keen –anxious, even – to help the King as best I can. On the other hand I'm concerned that Ireland is in a state in which it could explode like a keg of gun-powder touched by the slow match. Can I afford to leave? I suppose I have to, and must make preparations to sail away, but not to Scotland with Antrim, and certainly not with my army.

I need many ships to put to sea with an army, I have no ships, and the navy is in the North Sea. Not only that, but as Dumbarton is now held by the enemy, there is nowhere I could land the troops near enough to help Antrim even if I desired to do so. The King doesn't seem to have thought about logistics at all.

I shall confer with the Georges and Kit, for I feel that I can rely on them to act with sense and keep control in my absence.

Elizabeth. 14th May, 1639. Dublin Castle.

I'd been supervising the packing of my dear husband's travelling chests, and within two weeks of the King's letter arriving, all was nearly ready for his departure. Then Thomas received another missive from him telling him to stay in Ireland for the time being. His Majesty's reason for this change of heart, which Thomas found frustrating (and made me cross because the servants and I had to unpack), was that he felt he would be of more use here in Ireland for the time being.

Thomas. 14th May, 1639. Dublin Castle.

So now I have to stay here after all! Two weeks ago I'm told to report to His Majesty in England. Two days ago I'm ordered to remain here, after we rushed back from Jigginstown, and Bess has been getting all my clothes, papers, and equipment ready for the journey, and my armourer has been readying me for war.

I wrote back to the King and told him I would stay put, but would come at once if needed.

By the same post I received a letter from the Archbishop telling me of a speech he had made in the Star Chamber a week or so ago. "The State," as he reported his address to the Court, "owes not a little to my Lord Deputy that the Kingdom of Ireland is kept in great peace and security; for at this day (God be thanked) that Kingdom is at peace, notwithstanding the multitude of Scots in that country, and those rebels who are within an hour-and-a-half's passage of Ireland. No part of England is more secure than the Irish are at this time, and under God and the King I can attribute it to nothing but the wisdom, courage, and care of my Lord Deputy. Therefore God forbid offenders against his reputation should get away without exemplary punishment."

Who is this offender, this libeller? Why, none other than Sir Piers Crosby, who has had a quarrel with me ever since the Titles Commission interfered with land he claimed to own. He has been spreading false and evil rumours about my lands and plantation policy, and siding with Lord Cork in my battle with him. He's also the MP I had to turn out of the Irish Commons during my first Parliament for the trouble he caused. Only last autumn he was doing all he could to impede the recruitment of soldiers for the Irish Army.

The awful things he said and wrote about me caused him to be prosecuted in Star Chamber, and he had to go to England for the trial. Naturally I appreciate the rather fulsome way in which my friend William spoke about me in order to have Crosby severely punished, but I can see that seeds of trouble can be sown in Ireland whether action is taken against men like Crosby or not. If they are punished, resentment follows. If they are left alone, they feel they can do as they like, and others copy the example they set. Indeed the Carrickfergus plot proved it.

Christopher Wandesford. 15th May, 1639. Dublin.

It seems to me that underneath a seemingly quiet exterior a cauldron of opposition to Tom is beginning to bubble. He has annoyed, with one policy or another, each of the elements of Irish society: the real Irish; the Old English (apart from Protestants like Ormonde and a few Catholics); the New English; and the Scots planters. Why is there no rebellion? I think his overpowering personality, and the fact that he has a strong Army, may be enough to keep all of them quiet through fear. Fortunately none of them appears to have the sense to try and combine with the others at this time.

Of course, there's talk. Tom must be aware of it, but he will not trouble himself with it. "My path is clear, my conduct correct, and my principles are to be adhered to." That is his attitude.

Charles I. 16th May, 1639. Newcastle.

I am in Newcastle, and staying with the Earl, William Cavendish. He is most hospitable. It is evening now. My entry into the city ten days ago, at the head of my army (even if, between me and this sheet of paper, it is by no means the magnificent force I wish I were leading), was splendid, with 21 gun salutes fired and church and cathedral bells rung everywhere.

General circumstances here, however, are not so splendid. Reports from the patrols come in to the effect that Scotsmen are still welcomed in the town and drink and stay in the inns, and talk to the soldiers of mutinying against my command. Seditious talk.

I had Lord Roxburgh, one of my Scots supporters, arrested, when his son defected to the Covenanters, and I was afraid the father might follow suit. It was a mistake, for another loyal Scot, Lord Southesk, deserted at once for fear that, as his daughters are married to two very prominent Covenanting Lords, I might incarcerate him, too.

On the credit side, Lord Aboyne crept into Newcastle a few days ago. He is the younger son of Lord Huntly, Laird of the Aberdeen region and Chief of the Clan Gordon, which is loyal to me. Huntly, with his sons had gone into Aberdeen, which had been occupied by Montrose and his Covenant forces. They believed they were not threatened by Montrose, but they were wrong, and were seized and taken, more or less by force, to Edinburgh. Huntly told the younger boy to escape.

Aboyne, having been betrayed by Montrose, saw no harm in lying that he needed to go home for clothes, cash, and other things, was granted parole, and immediately made his way to me. He assures me that the Gordons are as loyal as ever, and would rise against Montrose because of the capture of Lord Huntly. Indeed, a couple of days ago a message arrived from his Clan that they had recaptured Aberdeen for a short while, and had in turn been driven out two or three days later, but were determined to try again.

Consequently I gave him a letter of recommendation to Hamilton to provide him with men and transport by sea so that, as the Clan attacked Aberdeen from the landward, Aboyne could come at the occupiers from the beaches.

This was all encouraging news. I must let Wentworth know of it. I'll get a scribe in to take a dispatch.

Christopher Wandesford. 26th May, 1639. Jigginstown House.

Tom and I are walking with his brother George in the grounds – the magnificent park-like grounds – of this new palace of Tom's. It is enormous, or will be when finished. It is drawing near to completion. George has come back from a tour of much of the country, particularly in the Catholic Irish areas. He's been trying to drum up larger numbers of men willing to join the army.

He seems somewhat depressed as a result of his labours. "There is no doubt about it, Thomas; the recruiting officers are having a hard time of it."

"Surely it can't be that old trouble with Crosby interfering, can it?" I say.

"No, of course it can't, Kit. He's in England before the Star Chamber. I'm sure we'd put a stop to that problem before he left for London. There must be something new. Have you any idea what it is, George?"

"I'm sorry to say I have. Would you believe it Thomas, if I tell you that Cardinal Richelieu has been sending agents here to recruit Irish men for the French Army?"

"I can believe it, alright." Thomas stops, staring at the ground for a moment. "Scots and Irish regiments have been fighting as mercenaries for one side or another ever since this European War began, so maybe King Louis really wants more of them. But there could be another explanation."

I'm puzzled. "Could there?"

Tom looks up, and nods. "Yes. Richelieu hates the idea of our King doing any sort of business with Spain, especially if it involves helping the Spanish Army or Navy. France may be as Catholic as Spain, but doesn't want Spain taking over Europe, so Richelieu and his King side with the Protestant powers in fighting the Habsburg Empire."

"But what has that to do with us?" I ask.

"Richelieu knows that Charles is likely to be at war with Scotland soon. He knows we need all the men we can get for that. If he can make it difficult for us to build up the Army by denying us men, he hopes he'll make the King think twice about helping Spain."

I'm beginning to feel out of my depth. "What I don't understand is why the Irish would rather fight for France than for us. The Irish don't love the Puritanical Scots."

George has the answer. "It's simple, Kit. The Irish and the French are Catholic, for one thing. But the most important point is that Richelieu's agents are offering far higher pay than we can afford. Mercenaries don't enlist for glory. They enlist for cash. That's what I've been finding everywhere I've been."

Thomas is very attentive now. "Did you see Ormonde? How is he getting on?"

"Not too badly. I saw Sir William St Ledger too. They say numbers are growing, but not as fast as they'd like. They say Richelieu's agents are having some impact, but it will be possible to raise the army you want and ..."

"8,000 infantry and 1,000 horsemen, George."

"Exactly, Thomas. Sir William's as trustworthy an old campaigner as you could wish to meet in a long day's march, and you know Ormonde always does all he can. However, it will be a close race to get the Army up to full strength if the King wants to fight soon."

Tom is frustrated and angry, but not with George. "You don't need to tell me! And the King is already on his way to Scotland. He hopes to raise an Army on the way! How can anyone hope to go to war and win if they do not even know whether they'll have an army?"

George smiles in a curious way. "That's the trouble, isn't it, Tom? None of us knows enough about what is going on. I've found out what I can here, but what about England, let alone Scotland? The information you get is always at least a few days old before you get it, and as much of it comes from Laud, it is only second-hand."

"Dead right! The King gives me no information, keeps me in the dark, so I'm disabled either to counsel him or execute anything for the service of His Majesty or the public."

George and I speak at once: "You need someone over there".

"Correct. Do either of you want the job?"

Another duet from us. "I don't!" I say: "I'm not forceful enough." George adds: "I'm not sure I'm sufficiently diplomatic."

Tom laughs. "Just as well then. I've been thinking I need my own eyes and ears with the King, but also someone who can advise him, and put my point of view. Do either of you know John Lesley, Bishop of Raphoe?"

I tell him I do not know the man, but have heard of him. George says he has met him once, and adds: "Didn't we go to hear him preach in Dublin Cathedral a while ago? Wasn't Bess with us?"

Tom nods: "I think you're right. Well, I've seen a lot of him lately. He seems very wise, very diplomatic, but not at all afraid to say what he thinks, and he and I see eye to eye on this Scottish crisis."

George looks surprised. "But he's Scottish himself, isn't he?"

"True, but he's right behind the King, believes in the supremacy of the Monarch, even if not quite in Divine Right, and he is far from being a Calvinist. He espouses Laud's reforms."

Thomas. 12th June, 1639. Jigginstown House.

About three weeks ago a letter came from His Majesty. He was concerned about the state of his army, but still rather confident about the eventual outcome of this struggle with Scotland. News about Lord Huntly's Clan, and the fact that he has sent Lord Aboyne to see Hamilton, appear to account for this continuing optimism.

I am beginning to fancy it may misplaced. News has reached me from Algie Percy, and in a more hearsay fashion from Laud, that Hamilton is not of much assistance to anyone. His fleet cannot land in Scotland because all the coastal people keep watch, and the beaches and ports are constantly manned against him. He cannot even get water without sailing back and forth between Holy Island, and the Firth of Forth, achieving nothing.

Hamilton grudgingly let Aboyne have a warship – he'd asked for two - and some men, but that proved to be enough. Aboyne is only eighteen, but he bravely took his ship close to shore, and Montrose evacuated the city. I'm told he feared that he could not fight a two pronged attack, from land and sea, and believed that the townsfolk, loyal Gordons to a man (and woman) would rise up, making the defence of the place impossible.

Although General Alexander Leslie is still in Scotland, with many of the Covenanters and their artillery under his command, fortunately for the Gordons, he had taken them all South towards the King. Whilst that may be fortunate for Aberdeen, it will be a menace for the King if he is faced with a man of such experience.

My doubts arise, despite Aboyne's success, first, because this victory is not of the King's making, and secondly, because I fail to see how I am to get my troops to Scotland when the time comes, if Hamilton keeps his ships in the North Sea, and whilst the north part of the Irish Sea is full of Lord Argyle's hostile boats and equally hostile sailors and fighting men.

Algie's letters inform me that the King left Newcastle towards the end of May. The army was caught in the most fearsome heat on the march, and no provision had made for meals or water for it. There was nowhere proper for the men to sleep, and the officers almost fought over who got to lie on the floor of an alehouse, let alone in a bed. Algie could not even provide the King with a proper billet as Alnwick Castle has, apparently, not been well maintained for some years, so he had to find a bed in an Abbey close by. If this is war planning, one can only despair.

His Majesty and his army moved from Alnwick to Berwick, and found that the inhabitants had more in common with the enemy than with their Monarch, and there was insufficient room for the army anyway, so they camped, and the King did too.

By then the hot weather had given way to the wet, and the men were fed up, famished, and dismally damp. The King bucked them up by inspecting everyone and everything industriously, but that did not, according to Algie last long. All the best intelligence, and the worst, suggested the Scots were much stronger than the English, and the men lost heart. If they had ever had any.

The atmosphere was hardly helped when, on 1st June, Arundel, Earl Marshal of England, dressed with all the pomp he thought appropriate, and surrounded by equally impressively out-fitted troops, rode across the River Tweed, to read a proclamation from the King. This said that anyone who gave up supporting the Covenant and swore their allegiance to Charles would not be punished as a traitor, but pardoned.

This had no noticeable effect at all. No men were there, and the women stood about patiently waiting for a chance to sell food to the soldiers, who bought it.

On the 2nd, while the King was in camp, scouts reported that General Leslie and his army were now in Kelso, and the next morning, at dawn, Lord Holland set off with 1,000 horsemen and 3,000 infantry to confront him. Holland's incompetence was laid bare when he rode the cavalry forward faster than anyone could march and arrived at the scene of potential battle with no-one to support his horsemen. He arrived before Kelso to find his 1,000 men faced by, in his view, not less than 8,000 Scottish foot-soldiers and a few cavalry-men. Leslie would not withdraw, and so Holland was obliged to turn tail and run.

How can the King continue like this? His so-called helpers are worse than the enemy. I have to get him to listen to me.

Thomas. 20th June, 1639. Dublin Castle.

A week ago I called Bishop Lesley to see me. He's a tall, spare, quite athletic looking man. He's about 65, maybe a bit more, but very lively, and extremely bright. He was born near Aberdeen, and went to the University there before going to France, and much of Europe. He speaks much better French, Spanish, and Italian than I do, and he can converse easily in Latin. His facility with languages must owe something to his having lived in Europe for about twenty years.

I find him a most entertaining companion. He was chaplain to several noble houses before he became King James's chaplain. He says that was in 1621. As well as all his University and foreign education he was ordained a priest, and after becoming a Royal Chaplain he became a Doctor of Divinity at Cambridge. He is one of the Archbishop's staunch supporters. He knows this King, too, from having been in the Royal Household as Chaplain.

He tells me he even has some war experience, as he accompanied the Buckingham expeditions to France. They may have been disasters, but as it looks as though Charles is heading for one at the moment, Lesley will be in a strong position to advise him against going ahead for the time being, and advise me on the prospects. He knows what a military disaster looks like!

He first became a Bishop in 1628, under the patronage of the Duke; he was appointed to the See of the Isles, and soon after that became a member of the Scottish Privy Council. That made him one of the few Scots Councillors upon whose advice Charles could rely!

He served in the Isles for five years and was then given the Bishopric of Raphoe in northern Ireland. He soon became a friend of mine and of John Bramhall, my Bishop of Derry. Lesley's See benefited a great deal from the Titles Commission decisions, recovering land and granting leases of it so that his rents almost doubled. He's a married man now, having only wed his Katherine last year when she was eighteen to his sixty-five or thereabouts. (I thought I was a bit of a cradle snatcher when I married Bess!)

In his bishopric of the Isles he did much to enforce conformity with the rituals of the Anglican Church, and he's been doing the same here at Raphoe. He prosecuted a man and wife who preached that bishops were unlawful, and that the congregation should sign the Scottish Covenant. There cannot be any doubt where his loyalties lie: he is the King's man. He is just the man for the mission I have sent him on. He left for Scotland this morning, and I saw him off from the harbour.

During our conversation last week I thought to brief him on what he might say to the King, but when he told me his own thinking on the situation in Scotland, I found there was little I needed to say.

"You see, Thomas, being a Scot myself, I know pretty well how their minds work. From what I hear from home, they are very happy with the situation. They feel they have a cause, and a good one. They think the King's cause is bad, and that vast numbers of English people have little faith in it. They know that many of their men have been much in battle in Europe over the last two decades, and the only experience of war some of the King's men have was with Buckingham, and they won't have learnt much from that."

I am impressed with his knowledge. "On top of that, John, from what I hear, while I get hardly any information from the King or his Council, the Covenanters receive all sorts of leaked intelligence all the time."

John agrees. "That's what my friends in Scotland tell me, too. The Covenanters are also well armed, and getting more supplies from abroad regularly."

"I'm so fed up with what I hear about the King's supplies I've ordered my own arms from London and the Dutch. I will not have my army poorly equipped."

John nods. "For all these reasons my countrymen are very confident indeed. It is easier to fight for a cause you believe in and believe to be right, when you are well armed, experienced, and especially if you believe your enemy is weaker. For what it's worth, my advice to the King – if I get a chance to offer it – will be to run no risk of being defeated, and damaging his authority, but to negotiate, cause as much delay as possible, secure a truce, and only go to war when he knows he is strong enough to win."

"I couldn't put it better myself, John. I want you to join the King as soon as possible, and send me as much information as you can."

When his ship had sailed today, as I turned away from the harbour side, I caught myself thinking that for me to be so friendly with and trusting of a Scot was a new departure indeed for Thomas Wentworth.

John Lesley. 1st July, 1639. Berwick.

My Dear Thomas,

My journey here was relatively uneventful, and I arrived two days ago. All the talk in the army camp is of the Pacification of Berwick. It was signed the day before I left you. Its purpose is to effect a truce between the King and the Scots.

My information is that several Lords told the King that he should not go ahead with his Prayer Book and Ritual policy in Scotland without calling Parliament. I'm told Lord Bristol spent two hours with His Majesty trying to persuade him to this point of view, which was pretty brave considering that Bristol was not in the King's good books to start with.

The King has received me graciously, and told me privately, and for your information only, that as he had been unable to get a loan from the City of London, and in the light of the peers' opposition, he decided to put off any idea of attacking Scotland until next year, but he insists he will go ahead with his religious policy, and will not abandon it.

In effect, therefore, he has acted on the advice you had offered him.

As I understand it, negotiations were carried on in a civilized fashion, the vast majority of the Scots nobles according the King due respect, but a lawyer called Johnston of Warriston was offensive, telling him that he did not trust him. He made things worse by what he said when the King offered to call another Church Assembly and a Scottish Parliament to discuss the reform of the Kirk. He accused the King of deliberately using delaying tactics so that he could build up the strength to get his own way by battle.

The King was furious and said, I am told: "The Devil himself could not make a more uncharitable construction." Of course, that is, in reality, exactly what His Majesty had in mind. He was probably angry at being found out.

Be that as it may, this Treaty, or Pacification as it is called, was signed on 19th June. Both armies are to disband, and the King will attend the Parliament, and call an Assembly in the autumn.

Getting here when I did I missed a good dinner, because on the day after the Treaty, General Leslie (who, by the way is quite old, rather small, and looks almost deformed) invited a number of English Lords to dine with him and some Scots lairds in their camp, and took them on a tour of it. These peers told me the Scottish soldiers were in great spirits, made it plain what their opinion was by shouting "God bless His Majesty, and the Devil confound the Bishops."

They also remarked on how well Leslie gets on with his men and his officers, and that while his discipline is evident, the camp is clearly very friendly, and very well provisioned. That is a strong contrast with the atmosphere I've found in the English camp. Nothing could illustrate that more clearly than the tale circulating in our camp that my Lords Holland and Newcastle are to have a duel, apparently due to the former having ordered the latter to lead his troops at the back of a column, a position Newcastle considered beneath him as his men were the bearers of the Prince of Wales' flag.

My final item of news for you is that on the same day as the Treaty, Lord Montrose, on the Covenant side, attacked Aberdeen, and after two days fighting, drove the Gordons out once more, so that is a loss for the King. However, Hamilton read the proclamation of the Pacification in Edinburgh on 24th, and was given the keys of the Castle in his role as the King's Commissioner.

Conditions here are anything but good, and it is a mercy the King has acted on your advice, wittingly or otherwise, to postpone fighting the Scots.

I shall report again as soon as there is anything significant to tell you.

Your friend,
John + Raphoe.

Thomas. 9th July, 1639. Dublin Castle.

Your Majesty,

I thank you for your most recent letter. Let me commence by apologising for failing to respond to your letter of 20th April about Lord Loftus. I acted swiftly on the authority you gave me to have him imprisoned, but I regret to say that that is all there is to tell you, which is the reason (not, I hasten to add, an excuse) for my failure to report on that before.

He was told by your Irish Council that if he handed over the Great Seal and complied with various other orders, he would be set free immediately. He was abusive and contemptuous, and showed none of the respect due to me as, and only as, Your Majesty's Deputy. He point blank refused to comply.

He is, of course, an old man, but his wits are not addled. Even so, I fancy that he simply does not take heed of the fact that his defiance is, in reality, aimed at your own Royal authority. I cannot see any alternative but to keep him securely locked up until he comes to his senses.

I now turn to the question of the Earl of Clanricarde's title to land in Galway. I have at once obeyed your command and restored to him all his titles set aside by the Titles Commission. As you anticipated, I am not happy about it. I fear that the plantation of Connaught, of which Galway is a part, will now be virtually impossible. Five of the most valuable baronial estates in the county will be lost to the Crown. Perversely, whilst many who did not oppose your plantation and titles policy have lost much, and will get nothing back, the Earl not only loses nothing for his opposition, but is now put into a much better position that those who have done Your Majesty most effectual service. I anticipate that all the rest of the nobility of Connaught will petition you, Sire, for the same relief as Clanricarde has been granted.

As you know by now, I sent my trusted friend Bishop John Lesley of Raphoe to join your camp. You will, I am sure, find that he is not only an excellent military chaplain, but may be of great assistance to you in many other ways in dealing with his fellow Scots.

I am Your Majesty's loyal, obedient, and grateful servant,

Wentworth.

Thomas. 5th August, 1639. Jigginstown House. County Wicklow.

John Lesley is with me in my study. He has returned from Scotland. He has been reporting to me on the state of readiness of the English Army, and how the likely war is developing, in regular letters. Now he is here with his final report. As usual when discussing serious matters I have been walking up and down, but I am in dreadful pain from gout, and I soon have to sit.

Me. And what did the King say to that?

Lesley. He said he'd been so confident that the people would clamour to join him as he marched north.

Me. But they didn't. Did the gentry join forces with the King?

Lesley. In some parts of the country there was good support for the war, but mostly, and especially in the North, the turnout was very poor. His Majesty was very disappointed with the number of troops he had been able to recruit as he marched towards Scotland.

Me. I warned the King against this. Could I have been plainer? I told him to bide his time, gather adequate forces, make sure of the money, and garrison the strong points - the main ports and towns - before risking a fight. So, what happened? Apart from your letters I have had no reliable intelligence from England since I sent you as my eyes and ears, John. What happened?

Lesley. When I reached the North I found the two armies drawn up on opposite banks of the Tweed. The King had slightly the larger force, but discipline was poor, and - well - with the Earl of Arundel as Commander in Chief and.......

Me. I can imagine! May God save the King now. What was he thinking?

Lesley. I know not My Lord, but there is worse yet. That dandy Holland was in charge of the Cavalry.

Me . That is almost beyond imagining. Why, he's nothing but a ladies man, a lecher.

Lesley. After facing the Scots for a few days the King offered to negotiate, and a Treaty was drawn up - the Pacification of Berwick; I wrote to you about it. The King's been let down by everyone he trusted, though he was much to blame for embarking on this venture without acting on your advice first.

Me. Who let him down?

Lesley. The City of London voted a mere £5000 for the war, I'm told, and although Holland had advanced boldly enough at the start, he turned tail and fled the first time the Scots came in sight. Their bagpipes – the Great Highland War Pipe, it's called – seemed to strike terror in the cavalry.

Me. And now? What happens now?

Lesley. The King asked me to tell you that he wants you to join him, and take charge of his government. And he asked me to deliver this. *(He hands me a letter which I read; it takes but a moment, it is so brief).*

Me. And so, it has come at last.

(At this moment Elizabeth enters, speaking as she does so; she closes the door. She obviously does not realise someone is with me).

Elizabeth. I've just put the baby to bed, Thomas. *(Then she sees Lesley).* I'm so sorry, I didn't know you had anyone with you.

Me. Not just anyone, my dear. I think you know John Lesley, Bishop of Raphoe?

Elizabeth. No, I do not; but I have seen you before, at the Cathedral, and I have heard you preach there, Your Grace.

Lesley. *(He laughs).* Now should I be worried or flattered, My Lady? I fear you recall my preaching because my sermon was boring.

Elizabeth. Far from it, Your Grace. It was stimulating and your style most engaging. I even remember the text was from the parable about the sheep and the goats. To be frank, I cannot imagine his Lordship choosing anyone boring as his emissary to the King. You've just returned from Scotland, haven't you?

Me. He has, and with most welcome yet most burdensome news, Elizabeth. But let us cease this formality. John Lesley and I are old friends, and you must become friends too. John, my wife Elizabeth; Elizabeth - John Lesley. *(John bows and Beth curtseys to him).*

Elizabeth. And what is this 'welcome yet burdensome' news you have brought us, John?

Lesley. Happily as yet there is no war, no fighting, but an uneasy truce. War will come, I have no doubt, but not yet. The King made it quite plain to me that he has no intention of giving in to the Scots Army. What he is doing at the moment is to play for time while he builds up his strength.

Me. John learned that the King took little heed of my advice, apart from delaying the war for a year. You remember I said he should occupy Leith, Dumbarton, and other ports and towns before embarking on fighting? Well, he confirms that Charles let the Scots seize the initiative, and they garrisoned Dumbarton first. I could so easily have held these places for him with my Irish soldiers.

Lesley. Yes, the King allowed his position to be much weakened, and those fools Arundel and Holland were worse than useless. Arundel is so ponderous it takes him an age to make any decision at all, and, as I told Thomas, Holland ran away as soon as he saw the Scottish troops.

Elizabeth. I thought you said there was welcome news. This sounds like nothing but doom and gloom.

Me. John brought this letter from the King. It is brief. Most of what he had to say he would only entrust to John by word of mouth.

Elizabeth. What does the letter say?

Me. *(I read aloud).* 'Come when you will, you shall be welcome to your assured friend, Charles R'. It's dated 27th July.

Lesley. I hadn't finished telling Thomas the rest.

Me. His Majesty wants me to go immediately to England to take control of his Government.

Lesley. His Majesty hinted that he realised that he had been unwise to accept the Queen's party as his advisers, and that he should have taken counsel with Thomas long ago.

Elizabeth. Is this the welcome news?

Me. The welcome news is that at last the King is to grant me the greatest opportunity to serve him, and the greatest powers with which to do so. I shall be the greatest in the land. It is welcome, yes, but even more awe-inspiring.

Elizabeth. And the bad news?

Me. Why, to have to take charge when the King's matters have fallen to such a low ebb, and to have to leave you and the children, and our new darling daughter, at such a time. My pride may be sinfully exalted, but there is much heaviness in my heart. I may have to fight.

Elizabeth. Are you afraid, Thomas? You're not a soldier, after all.

Me. That's why I'm so glad that Holland and Arundel have been stripped of their commands, and that Northumberland is now Commander in Chief.

Elizabeth. The Duke of Northumberland? How do you know that?

Me. John told me as I was showing him round our new building works.

Lesley. Yes, My Lady. Jigginstown is going to be quite the most important house in Ireland - more a palace than a house. And being built of brick, too - not stone. Most unusual.

Me. Hampton Court is a superb brick-built precedent, John. I like Tudor architecture.

Elizabeth. Take care then Thomas. Wolsey built Hampton, and look what happened to him. *(She turns to Lesley, speaking very jocularly)*. If I am not to call you "Your Grace," My Lord Bishop, you are not to address me as "My Lady." I prefer Elizabeth, and I should prefer it if you did not divert me from my concern for my husband and family by talking about bricks and buildings. *(She turns back to me)*. My love, you may not be afraid, but you cannot stop me being afraid for you. And you're not well. Your gout has crippled you these last weeks, and in Army Camp your - forgive me John - your bowels will let you down again.

Me. Dysentry is endemic in a fighting force - so many men herded together - but it will – er - pass. *(Lesley laughs)*. Seriously though, my gout is bad, but it will improve, and by the time I sail for England I shall be well. It's August 5th now. In four or five weeks I shall be in England.

Lesley. What preparations will you make? You have much to do, both in government and in your own business affairs.

Elizabeth. He takes too much upon himself. Now His Majesty has piled on this final load, as if Thomas were a beast of burden.

Me. That is unfair, Elizabeth. The King is merely taking me up at last on what I have long asked him - nay, begged him - to let me do. What is hard is that he has taken such a confoundedly long time to do so. The situation now is so much more dangerous than it was when I offered my help two years ago, and the Scots are that much stronger.

Lesley. What will you do here?

Me. Christopher Wandesford and Lord Dillon will rule as regents in my stead. Finance I shall entrust to Radcliffe, as well as my private business.
Elizabeth. Have you decided about the Army? Who will command the Army for you?
Me. James will.
Elizabeth. The Earl of Ormonde?
Lesley. He's an admirable choice, and very loyal to you and the King.
Me. Yes, he is admirable, in every way, and very popular generally. *(I pause for a few seconds, contemplating the wrench that leaving Bess and the children means).* My wife and children I put in your care, John, to pray for and protect whilst I am gone.
Lesley. Won't you at least take your son Will? He would learn so much from such a venture. But perhaps he is too young. *(He turns to Bess).* And what about the girls?
Elizabeth. There's not enough time for all of us to get ready. Anyway, you will feel happier, Thomas, I'm sure, if you know we are safe here. We have discussed sending the girls to stay with Arabella's mother, Lady Clare, to complete their education, but now may not be a good time.
Lesley. How old are they?
Me. Ten and twelve, and picking up Irish ways, and a strange accent from their maid, who comes from Guernsey. If they are to grow up as English ladies they must start soon.
Elizabeth. We can talk about it again, Thomas. Will is very happy at the College in Dublin. He will miss you but perhaps he should stay here.
Me. As you say, we must speak further about these things. And about what we say to Lady Clare. There's no love lost between us, but if I get time off from the fray, at least I shall be able to visit them more easily than if they were in Dublin.
Elizabeth. She was your Mother-in-law, Thomas, and her daughter died. Arabella died, and she cannot forgive you for that, whether it was you or the wasp who killed her.
Lesley. *(There is a pause; then Lesley speaks again).* The King doesn't want to admit, publicly, that his affairs in Scotland go so poorly, Thomas. He asked me to tell you that he wishes you to find some other excuse for going to England.

Elizabeth. Then if you take the girls with you, my darling, that will provide the excuse. *(She turns to John.)* I hope this is not a silly question, John, but does it strike you as strange that the Scottish people should have been so ready to fall out with their King? After all, he is a Scot himself.

Me. Heavens! What a question.

Lesley. Well, perhaps it should – um - strike me as strange, Elizabeth, but in fact it does not, or not entirely. You see, King James was against Bishops when young, but as he got older he saw the value of them to a Monarch who believed in his Divine Right to rule. That did not please the Presbyterians at all, and that is what the vast majority of Scotsmen are. Charles is intensifying that policy. There's another thing. When Charles became King, an Act of the Scottish Parliament ordered the handing over of all land and estates taken from the Crown and the Church during James's reign to be handed back. A large number of Scots nobles knew this would hit them very hard.

Me. So there *is* a political motive mixed up in all this, too. Well, well! Laud and I have always thought as much.

Elizabeth. Was this Charles's own Act? He couldn't have done it all on his own, could he?

Lesley. *(Laughing).* No, Elizabeth, he could not. It had to be passed by the four sections of the Parliament. All he had to do was assent to it, or get his Deputy to do so. And it had been done in the reign of many other Kings before him. It was not a novel idea.

Elizabeth. Then it's a mystery that the nobles have objected this time.

Me. It's no mystery. It's an excuse to get what they want.

Thomas. 6th August, 1639. Jigginstown House.

Your Majesty,

Your letter and the messages brought to me by Bishop Lesley excited me so much I hardly slept last night for thinking of the honour you do me, the opportunity I shall have to exercise enormous responsibility on your behalf, and less happily, the pain I am suffering from being struck by the most awful gout I have yet experienced. Yesterday I could hardly walk. Today I cannot even stand for more than a few moments.

I trust in God that He has not given Your Majesty so just a cause, nor me so good a heart, to take my legs from me in such a juncture of your affairs.

I shall be unable to travel until the gout diminishes, but shall make use of the time to settle the business of your Kingdom here before leaving to join you. I shall leave Ireland in good hands.

I am, Sire, your obedient servant, Wentworth.

Algernon Percy, Earl of Northumberland. 13th August, 1639. Alnwick.

My Dear Thomas,

First, I must congratulate you that the King has at last recognised you are needed here, and secondly, I want you to know that I look forward to welcoming you with all the warmth that old friendship and my county can bestow. As you know, I have been disgusted with the King's poor choice of commanders and advisers in the shape of men like Holland and Hamilton, but I hope your selection indicates a new beginning.

You will require a strong team on your Privy Council in Dublin when you are here. At least you've got rid of Loftus, I hear, but you still have too much clutter and corruption in the shape of Cork and his ilk. Wandesford, Radcliffe, and Mainwaring should be able to hold the fort while you are away. I met Bishop Lesley when he was with the King last month, and found him very wise and practical, so they will get good value from him, I dare say.

I was pleased to read in your last letter that young Ormonde will lead your army in your absence. I know him fairly well, he was more or less brought up by old Archbishop Abbott, and was often around the Court then, and has been here since. He seemed to have all the sense and self-discipline necessary to make a good commander.

On the other hand I was a bit taken aback, to put it mildly, at your telling me that you have had many Scottish planters who signed the Covenant in Ireland charged with treason before your Castle Chamber court, and above all, that forfeiture of their estates was ordered. Although that may send out a strong message now, it troubles me that it may lead to more trouble than it is worth in the long run.

I have one or two loyal Scots in my household, and one of them has just returned from Edinburgh with news that the Kirk Assembly met yesterday. Lord Huntly was there, but my man says most people knew he was the Covenanters' prisoner, so his appearance did little for the King, loyal as he may be. What was worse for the Royal policy was that the Bishop of Orkney made a speech to the whole gathering saying he no longer believed in Bishops, and no longer regarded himself as one.

I cannot see that this Assembly will do anything but strengthen the will of the Kirk to fight the King over his reforms. Lord Traquair is nominally the chairman of the Assembly, but he is too weak. The head men in this struggle, Montrose, Warriston, and others, will run rings round him and Traquair will have the job of opening Parliament for the King when it meets on 31st August. May God help His Majesty then, for it is certain Traquair will not have the wit or the strength.

As always, Thomas, I remain your true friend,

Algie.

James VI of Scotland and I of England was a learned and clever man, but was called 'The Wisest Fool in Christendom' by many. That may have been partly due to his penchant for handsome young men whose skill and willingness as favourites was not matched by any similar attributes in the high political positions to which he raised them. It may owe more to his ability to see a problem and what needed to be done about it, and an almost complete inability to act accordingly.

However, there's one area in which he acted very sensibly in his own interests, and, as he saw it, in the interests of Scottish government. In England, the Reformation took the form, with the Established Church, of an organization not very different from the Roman one, save that it had a King at its head instead of a Pope, and no cardinals. But it kept its Bishops, and because the Bishops were appointed by the Monarch, they tended to side with their ruler on matters of Church policy, and much else.

Not so in Scotland. There, the strong Calvinist influence, which recognised no Bishops, emasculated them. James had, as a very young King of Scotland, hated his upbringing, and when he became King of England he fought valiantly against any diminution of the role of Bishops in his new Kingdom. His battle-cry was "No Bishop, No King." He saw clearly that if he had no English Bishops, or a castrated set of them, his own power would be weakened. He also aimed to strengthen the power of his Scottish Bishops, if possible.

This policy has not merely been adopted by King Charles and William Laud, but vigorously fostered by their reforms of the Prayer Book and Church ritual, and that is the cause of the struggle with Scotland in this year of 1639. I endorse that policy too, for I am convinced of the correctness of the King being the Head of the Government, and if Bishops strengthen the King's hand, I'm all for it. Whether for a man like me, whose faith is expressed more in terms of contemplation, meditation, and private prayer than public ritual, it is as important from a religious perspective, is a different matter.

The Earl of Northumberland is right to say that Lord Traquair does not have the wit or strength to help the King much in a Scots Parliament. Indeed, I'm told that he advised the King to weaken the Parliament by not having the Scots Bishops at it, giving grounds for legal repudiation of anything it might decide. Surely that will turn out to have been a dreadful mistake? The leaders of the Covenanters will be handed the chance to take over the Scots government on a plate, since without the Bishops, there will be no restraining influence on the powerful Lords who lead the movement.

Thomas. 25th August, 1639. Dublin Castle.

Four weeks ago the Lord blest me and Elizabeth with a baby girl. This is the second of our babies to survive this long with what appears to be a chance of going on to live a healthy life. Little Thomas died after a few weeks and the others have been sickly and died in earliest infancy. Elizabeth is so kind and thoughtful; she suggested the child should be christened Margaret, after my first wife, as we already have an Arabella. I wanted her to be called Elizabeth, but my dear Bess was insistent, and persuasive.

Thomas. 4th September, 1639. Dublin Castle.

"Lord Loftus, You have been brought into the Council today to give you another chance to purge your contempt, to hand over the Great Seal, and to obey the Council's orders in the Fitzgerald and Gifford cases."

"My Lord Wentworth, I have been in virtual solitary confinement for six months. I have been humbled, and seek to set matters right. I am an old man, and ask to be treated with leniency, and with the respect due to my office. As you know, the farmer, the man Fitzgerald, was released about a year ago, since you and the Council ordered it." Loftus is old, and stooped, but looks as though he was tall when young. He has a grasping demeanour, and is very sure of himself, even as he tries to appear humble.

I am quite unmoved by this sham show of contrition. "Then you can hardly claim that it is today's alleged humility that brought that about. What is now required is that you should compensate him for the imprisonment you inflicted on him, quite unjustly and without, as this Court found, any evidence on which to do so. What about the other matters?"

"I was allowed to see my lawyers ..."

"Unlike Mr Fitzgerald," I cannot help adding.

"And I instructed them to transfer the house and land to Sir Robert and Lady Eleanor Loftus." Perhaps he has learned a bit of a lesson. He is not being as rude and truculent as he has been in the past.

"Then that is some progress. When will the deeds be ready?"

Loftus's barrister rises and bows. "My Lord, my instructing solicitor," and he gestures to indicate a black-clad gentleman sitting behind him, "tells me that he has the documents with him and hopes that you will allow Lord Loftus the opportunity to sign them today."

"Most certainly, Mr Johnson, and the Council clerk here, and you, can be the witnesses. There can then be no suggestion that his Lordship's acceptance of the jurisdiction of the Council, his submission to it, and his signature on the documents are anything but his own, and genuine, and freely given."

"If it please you, My Lord."

I lean forward from the Bench. "And what of the Great Seal, Mr Johnson?"

Johnson turns to confer with the solicitor and his client, but Lord Loftus stands, bows, and addresses me. "My Lord, I had my solicitor collect the Seal from my home, and he has it here. I apologise to the Council and above all to His Majesty for all the trouble this matter has caused. I am an old man and ..."

I cannot abide this cringing attitude he now adopts any longer. "My Lord Loftus, you were an old man when you started the trouble in 'this matter'. Your sudden conversion to humility does not ring true, but you have apologised and the Council will take that apology at its face value, which is not much." Meanwhile the man in black has left his seat and handed the Seal to the Clerk to the Council.

"You are free, but you are no longer Lord Chancellor. His Majesty has written to me recently to approve the appointment of Sir Richard Bolton in your stead." I turn to the Guards. "You will make sure that the prisoner – well, not now the prisoner, perhaps – rather Lord Loftus, does not leave the precincts of the Court until he has signed the deeds. And," I look down at the Clerk, "you will accompany His Lordship and Mr Johnson to be a witness to the signatures, as I directed a minute ago. When that has been done, you may direct the Guards to set Lord Loftus free. The Council session is now concluded." My colleagues and I rise, and all those present bow to us, and we file out.

I thank God that that episode is over and behind us. There are much more serious events to worry about and deal with. I have to go to England for that.

Thomas. 22nd September, 1639. Covent Garden,

I am at my desk in my study at home in Covent Garden. My secretary, Mainwaring, is with me, taking dictation. It is quite hot and London is rather smelly. I'm looking out of the window, thinking how incredibly busy the streets of London are compared with those of Dublin. Yet I was busy enough there in the weeks before I left. So much to do; so many important posts to be entrusted to reliable and loyal men in my absence. Sir Adam Loftus at the Treasury is so much better than that rogue Mountnorris; odd that the son of Lord Adam Loftus can be so upright and honest; but that may be why his Father had no time for him, but preferred the roguish Sir Edward. Ormonde will do well with the army. Kit and the two Georges I know I can have faith in.

I realise I've forgotten what I am supposed to be doing.

Me. Where was I?

Mainwaring. You were about to dictate a letter to Sir George Radcliffe, My Lord.

Me. So I was. Proceed. Usual greeting. *We eventually sailed on a favourable tide and wind from Dublin on 12th September and landed at Chester the next day. After resting there for a day it took only a week by carriage and horse to get here to London. Thank the Lord my gout has abated, or such a journey would have been nigh on impossible. All is well. I settled Nan and Arabella, with their grandmother, though I fancy they may find her stricter than My Lady Elizabeth, who is so loving to them. Sometimes I almost have to remind myself that she is their step-mother.*

I am well received here. Even the Queen has written to me in the kindest terms, to say that my nominee for Bishop of Elphin shall, after all, be preferred to the King's, a man named Maxwell, who is anything but popular. He is to be Bishop of Killaloe instead. She says that she is my "tres bonne amie."

Others are not so kind. Lord Holland has gone back to his old ways and told me to my face that he hoped I would save the reputations of the Queen's friends by failing as miserably as they did in handling this Scottish crisis. The nearer I come to it the more my heart fails me; nor can I promise myself any good by this journey, but God's will be done. What weighs me down is the thought that this situation is not of my making. I was never wholly in favour of the enforcement of Ship-money - it reminds me too much of the forced loans for which I went to prison in the Twenties - and had I been consulted on the Church and Prayer Book policy for Scotland, I should have stood against it. But the King's obedient servant I am, and if it is his wish to force these policies home, force them home I shall.

Mainwaring. If I may say so, My Lord, the King would have done well to call upon you a year or more ago, when there was some scope for you to organise the government and raise the money.

Me. That is how I see it too. But these doubts will pass; they always do. Whilst it's depressing to estimate the problems ahead, it is essential if I am to deal with them.

(A servant enters and announces the Archbishop. I call to William to come straight in).

Laud. *(Entering).* My Lord, forgive this intrusion but I come in haste from an audience with the King, and felt sure you would want the news at once.

Me. Certainly, Your Grace. *(To the Secretary).* You may go, Philip, thank you. We shall finish the correspondence later. I shall send for you.
Mainwaring. I await your command, My Lord. *(He exits).*
Me. And now William, what is this news?
Laud. The King is much heartened by your arrival, Thomas. He says what is needed to deal with the Scots and get the funds for war from Parliament are your ruthlessness, your arrogance and self assurance, and your formidable will-power.
Me. That makes me look a very pleasant fellow, doesn't it? Nevertheless, they are the qualities needed now, I suppose. I just hope I have them in good measure, and they will be enough. The King is resolved on a Parliament then? He has accepted my view on that?
Laud. I believe he has. I am worried, however, Thomas, that you are not subtle enough in this situation. I fear you underestimate the feelings of the people. Many of them take sides with the Scots over these religious matters.
Me. The Scots and the English are traditional enemies, William. If the people think an invasion from Scotland is likely, they'll unite behind the King, and Parliament will find the money.
Laud. I hope you're right, My Lord. Parliament is an unruly horse at the best of times, and this one is likely to have the bit between its teeth. I hear John Pym will stand for Tavistock, and is likely to be returned.
Me. I can handle Parliament, with or without Master Pym, though he will make it more difficult. I shall recommend to the King that Parliament is called in Ireland first, in March, at which I shall secure subsidies and the use of the Army. I shall return to Westminster for another here in April. I shall get what I want in Dublin, and then the Commons here will not have the stomach to refuse the King what he needs in England.
Laud. I'm afraid you may have all your eggs in one basket, Thomas.
Me. By no means. I think Lord Mayor Garraway will persuade the City of London to make a loan of £100,000 to put down the Scots, and that is not all. The Spanish Ambassador has let it be known that if we provide Naval escorts for their troop ships and bullion cargoes they would be prepared to pay.
Laud. For their war with the Dutch? How much?

Me. We are negotiating with them. At the moment I don't know the amount, but money is not their problem. Gold and silver still pour out of their South American colonies. The Dutch fleet is too strong for them, so they cannot get troops to the war, and when they do, they can't get the gold there to pay them. They lose battle after battle, and strongholds and cities one after the other. I am sure that if we help them, they will pay handsomely, and then the money to fight the Scots would be assured.
Laud. You may think so, and the King may agree with you, but I'm not at all sure that Parliament will want to see a stronger Catholic Spain beating the Dutch.
Me. Maybe you're right, though I hope the two Houses will recall that they owe their loyalty to the King, and need to keep the Scots out of England. But tell me now, is there any other news from Whitehall Palace?
Laud. Oh yes. You will be delighted to know that Lord Chancellor Loftus - or should I say Ex-Chancellor Loftus - appeared before the Council. His attempt to put the blame on you for everything failed. It was all angry bluster. He was unanimously condemned, and your actions in removing him from office vindicated.
Me. Excellent news.

When William departs, Mainwaring returns with a letter from Algie. He tells me that he was quite right to say, in his last letter, that Traquair's advice to the King would be weak. Traquair's idea of excluding the Bishops from the Scots Parliament was the disaster I foresaw.

Led by Lord Argyle, the Lords seized their chance enthusiastically and skilfully. Their Parliament (which in reality it had become, since it had no intention of serving the King), turned the decisions of the Kirk Assembly into Acts of Parliament, abolished the Bishops, made it illegal for any cleric to hold any civil government position, and gave themselves all the plum and powerful jobs that had been occupied by Churchmen.

The King's position is going from bad to worse.

Charles I. 25th September, 1639. Whitehall.

Wentworth is with me. He is so positive. He never seems to entertain doubts about anything. He makes up his mind with bewildering speed over matters which would keep me awake night after night debating with myself what I should do. Even so, I cannot help wondering whether I have done the right thing in calling him to me. When he was in Yorkshire, and actually performing the functions of President of the Council of the North, he made enemies there by his arrogant behaviour. Sir John Savile is one; the Bellasis family is another. He fell out with his old colleague Ingram.

Then in Ireland he has done the same with Loftus, Mountnorris, Cork, and Clanricarde, and others. Yet how can I fairly complain? In every instance he has been pursuing my policies, or policies which are of benefit to me, to England, to Ireland, and to the Church. Although he has this knack of upsetting people, he also strides over the opposition and succeeds with almost everything he sets out to do, or which I have laid down for him to do. I cannot let it be known that he is the only person who can take control and master this Scottish nightmare. I shall have to take his advice, and act on it, or allow him to do so, somewhat secretively.

"The trouble is, Sire, that Lord Traquair is too weak to manage the Scots Parliament."

"Or the Parliament is too strong, which is much the same thing."

"You must – I apologise for that 'must', Your Majesty, but it is no use beating about the bush – you must give Traquair very definite instructions. He has to make it clear to them that they cannot abolish the Bishops because they think they are 'unlawful'. This is a religious dispute, not a political one, and if you accept the illegality of the Bishops, you allow Parliament to score a political victory. Nothing will indicate more clearly that they are usurping your powers, and doing so successfully."

"Then what should I do?"

"You must order Traquair to forbid the use of the word 'unlawful'. Tell him to let them know you will not tolerate the use of that word, and that no law saying Bishops are unlawful will receive your assent. Make it clear to Parliament in Edinburgh that you will fight them on political but not on religious grounds. You are Head of the Church, and they are not there to govern men's consciences. They are there for political purposes only, to advise you on the state of their nation and on such laws as they see fit should apply there."

"Then you had better have suitable instructions drafted for me to sign and send to Lord Traquair. Wentworth, I am grateful to you for your assistance, and very glad indeed that you are here."

John Pym. 30th September, 1639. Westminster.

I am talking with Sir Harry Vane in a corridor of the Parliament Buildings when Wentworth comes limping along. Much as I dislike the man even I can see, or perhaps feel, his power and authority.

Me. Why, Wentworth!! Back in England then? The gout no better then? *(Wentworth walks straight past me).* Still peddling poor advice to the King, are we?

Wentworth. *(He turns and advances on me, and I have to admit I back off a little).* If you wish to talk to me I'd be obliged if you would address me as "My Lord." You don't like me, and I can't say I particularly care for you, Master Pym, but being civil to each other helps keep the peace.

Me. *(He sounds so pompous. Hardly surprising really; he can be very pompous. I cannot resist replying contemptuously with a mockery of a bow).* Very well, My Lord. I repeat, still peddling poor advice to the King? What about that disastrous battle with the Scots, then? The King's forces were inferior and out-manoeuvered. The Scots are in control.

Wentworth. It may have escaped your notice, Master Pym, that I was in Ireland at the time. And as for the advice I give the King, it would be treason to tell you.

Me. The King was so confident that the people would clamour to join him as he marched north! But they didn't, did they?

Wentworth. Wouldn't you have been alarmed if they had? You and your friends have done everything you could to befriend the Scots, and spread disaffection amongst the people.

Me. Not even the gentry joined forces with the King.

Wentworth. Most of the 'gentry' did what they always do. They consult their own interests first!

Me. So why didn't you warn the King? Why didn't you tell him to bide his time, gather adequate forces, garrison the main ports and towns, and make sure of the money before risking a fight?

Wentworth. Make sure of the money? You hypocrite! *(And he walks off).* I shall not discuss my advice to the King with you.

Me. *(That makes me really angry. Hypocrite is what Christ called the Pharisees. Does he think I'm a Pharisee? I shout after him).* Why? What have you got to hide?

Vane. He has nothing to hide. He did exactly what you just suggested – told the King to raise the money, build up the Army, and take over all the important ports and towns. The King had slightly the larger force, but - well - with the Earl of Arundel as Commander in Chief and that dandy Holland still in charge of the Cavalry ....

Me. Arundel Commander in Chief! Was the King trying to lose?

Vane. I don't know, but the Scots took the initiative, and they seized the towns. Wentworth wanted to hold these places for the King with his Irish soldiers.

Me. *(Triumphantly).* So the King has been let down by everyone he trusted.

Vane. Everyone the Queen told him to trust! Everyone except Wentworth.

Me. Thank God the King doesn't always listen to him. What happens now?

Vane. The King asked Wentworth to join him in London, and take charge of the government. He's even hinted to the Council that he should have taken his Counsel earlier.

Me. So, finally it's happened. Finally the King has given our enemy unlimited power. He'll be king of the castle.

Vane. More like a dirty rascal. We'll have to fight even harder to get rid of him now - ruthless, arrogant, self-assured bastard.

Me. *(I speak more thoughtfully).* But Wentworth may have been handed the poisoned chalice. *(We start to walk away down the corridor).*

Vane. *(He uses his ear-trumpet).* Poisoned chalice?

Me. Why, to have to take charge when the King's position is so weak.

Thomas. 18th October, 1639. Westminster.

There is a problem about the Spanish paying us to escort their troop and supply ships bound for Flanders. Some time before I reached London, a large Spanish fleet – almost a new Armada, some said – sailed up the Channel bound for the Low Countries, and was intercepted by the Dutch warships. Rumour ran riot that this fleet was intended for another invasion of England, a repeat of 1588. The

Spanish took refuge off the Kentish coast, and some of the King's navy were nearby, supposedly to protect them.

Some Spanish soldiers had landed in the West Country with the King's permission, and marched across Southern England to the Kent ports, being billeted on the inhabitants on the way. This caused immense bad feeling. Many people were still seething that the King did little to help his nephew, Charles Louis, the Elector Palatine, in his war with the Habsburg Empire, yet allowed the armies of the Pope to walk across England to avoid being attacked by Dutch ships. The Elector is, at this time, a prisoner of Cardinal Richelieu in France, and Prince Rupert is held by the House of Austria

The King is doing all he reasonably can to get them released, but none of it is enough to satisfy the public. Matters came to a head when the Dutch Admiral, Van Tromp, decided he could wait no longer for the Spanish fleet to leave the protection of English waters. He sent fire ships in amongst them, and fired on the rest. Fire destroyed a number, fourteen lowered their flags, and twenty, trying to escape, ran aground near Deal, where the locals rejoiced and plundered the wrecks.

Instead of coming to the rescue of Spain, our Admiral, knowing that his crews would mutiny if ordered to fire on the Protestant Dutch ships, ignored his orders to help them. He said the fog and the wind made it impossible for him to render any assistance.

I had arrived in London in the middle of this ferment. The King believes that this public discontent is not serious, and I hope so, too.

Charles I. 7th November, 1639. Whitehall.

My Lord Wentworth is with me again. He is always here at present, it seems. Henrietta is with us, too. She seems to like him rather more than she did, and is certainly more polite to him, even if it is clear that she does not think him sufficiently noble to mix with Kings and Queens regularly.

Wentworth is plainly free of gout for the time being, for he is striding back and forth, expounding his views on the Scottish problem. "I'm told that the Scots Parliament has been adjourned, Sire."

"That is so. I had a letter from Traquair a few days ago telling me he brought the session to an end so that the laws making Bishops 'unlawful' could not be passed."

Henrietta laughs. “How can you possibly have a Church without Bishops? The idea is ludicrous.”

I turn to her with a smile. “I agree my dear, but these things are tricky. Once no-one could envisage a Church without a Pope, but we have one, and I am its head. My Scots subjects think that gives them the right to get rid of Bishops, too, just as they have in most of Germany.” I turn to Wentworth again. “Traquair wrote that the Covenanters have sent some nobles to see me. They must be here soon, if not already. He refused them liberty to come out of Scotland. They came anyway.”

There is a knock at the door, and a servant comes in apologetically. “Your Majesty.” He bows.

“Yes, Benson.”

“Two Scottish gentlemen – well, they say they are lords – are here seeking audience with you.”

“From whom have they come?”

“From the Covenanters, Sire.”

Wentworth is positive, as usual. “You should not see them, Sire. Send them away. If you are taking a firm line in Edinburgh it will be taken as a sign of weakness if you see them here.”

“Very well. Benson, kindly tell these lords that they are not welcome here, and must make haste to be gone from London in six hours, or they will not be allowed to leave for Scotland at all.”

Benson nods, bows and departs. Wentworth is ready with another move. “With your permission, Sire, I shall draft a letter for you to Lord Traquair. It will be in the form of a command to prorogue this Parliament for six months or more. That should buy you more time to prepare your army and its supplies.”

“That would be useful if it works, Wentworth, but I fear the Lords of the Articles – that’s a small body elected from each of the Estates making up the Parliament ....”

Henrietta leans forward. “Estates, Charles? Are they the same as in France?”

“Not quite, Henrietta; they are the Nobility, the Bishops, the gentry, and the commoners, so there are four estates. France has only three.”

She smiles. “And they do not meet at all. If only you could govern without all these elections, parliaments, and people trying to tell you what you must do.”

"If only, my dear. I have been trying it for ten years, but I'm beginning to think it doesn't work in this country. The Kings of England have been calling parliaments for about 600 years. Even I can't stop it, it seems."

Wentworth intervenes, politely for him. "You were saying something about the Lords of the Articles, Your Majesty."

"So I was. It will be interesting to see if they will accept Parliament being prorogued."

"Then Sire, if they disobey, it is a clear sign of rebellion."

Lucy Carlisle. 11th November, 1639. My London House.

"My Lady," a manservant says, coming into the room where I am playing the virginals, "the Viscount Wentworth is here, and asks to see you."

I just manage to restrain my excitement and stop myself leaping up. I have no objection to showing my joy to Thomas, but doing so in front of a servant would be unwise. Rumours of our relationship would be bad enough, but I do not want to provide evidence to support them. I play a few more phrases, and then say: "You may admit him".

We have seen each other several times since he arrived in London a couple of months ago. Some of the time we have met at friends houses, but mostly he has been here, or I have been to him in Covent Garden, and on some of those occasions we have invited others. As often as not, though, we are alone in our homes together, and have resumed our sexual adventures with enthusiasm. The first meeting he came here. When he came in I started to run across the room towards him, but as I got a good look at him I was reduced by surprise to a walking pace. He was slightly stooped instead of so upright. His hair has more than a touch of grey, his eyes looked tired, and his face was lined rather more than I remembered. I knew he had been unwell, and suffers with gout, but I had not expected to see quite such a change in him in three years.

He did not seem to notice my reaction. "Lucy, how glad I am to see you," and he came to me as I walked to him and we embraced closely, and kissed longingly. He seemed still as energetic as ever.

"And I am glad to see you, Thomas. How long it seems! Will you stay to dinner? I do not expect anyone else."

"I should like nothing better."

We dined happily, talking all the while of our interests, his family, my estate in Ireland, and particularly of his role in the politics of England and Ireland. After dinner we went to bed. I usually get a servant to show him to a guest room, but one that is very near to my own, and shortly he came to my room. We were both excited, and considering how keen we were to get to the main course, enjoyed some fairly prolonged hors d'oeuvres. Unfortunately when we eventually got down to the real business, Thomas came as quickly as if it were his first time ever and he were only sixteen.

He was ashamed, and I thought it a sign of his continued weakness from his gout and the flux, and the anxiety he must feel with all his work for the King, his responsibilities, the machinations of his enemies, and, of course, his family and his own multitudinous financial interests.

He slept for a while, and then we tried again, with rather more satisfaction on both sides. He needs more fun and relaxation, I thought, and I was determined to provide some for both of us. I succeeded, for our subsequent encounters have been most fulfilling, and we enjoy each other's company out of as well as in bed.

But to return to the present, I play some more until the man announces Thomas, and shuts the door behind him as he enters.

"You look tired, Thomas."

"No doubt. The King's business is hard work, and there's so much to do and think about. This Scottish row is likely to lead to war, and we are not ready." He sighs, then laughs. "Never mind that now. Anyway, it livens me up, and I thrive on it, even if it might exhaust me some of the time."

"My brother Algie tells me in his letters that he's not happy with the King's choice of commanders, and that there are not enough weapons or gunpowder."

"Well, he should know, Lucy. He'll be in the thick of it up in Northumberland. I haven't been up North to see for myself yet. Of course, you must keep all that to yourself."

"You've got a nerve, Thomas. I'm a Percy, aren't I? Do you think I'd betray my brother? Or put him in danger from the Scots?"

"Sorry, just political caution. It's the sort of thing we always say. You know, like: 'just between you and me', or 'just between you, me and the gatepost'. Half the time no-one takes any notice, and some of the time we don't even expect them to."

That makes me laugh. "Let's face it, Thomas, politicians often say 'Keep it to yourself', knowing full well, or even hoping, that the gossip will soon be out to their advantage or someone else's disadvantage."

"Yes, and I dare say the Percy family have been playing the game as well as anyone else for a very long time."

"Of course they have. Look at all the intrigues and rebellions and wars we've been involved in. Look at Harry Hotspur. When he rebelled against the King 200 years ago it's a wonder we weren't all wiped out with beheadings, poison, and all the rest of it." I almost change the subject. "Talking of that sort of thing, I hear the proceedings against Lord Loftus have gone entirely in your favour. Apparently he was very rude, and shouted and behaved very unlike a senior lawyer, let alone a Lord Chancellor, even if only of Ireland."

"You're right, Lucy. He behaved very badly. The Privy Council upheld every allegation against him, confirmed he should lose his post, and found that all I had done to get rid of him and bring him to justice was fully justified."

"That won't have done you any harm at Court, will it? He's been saying dreadful things about you, and many of his friends, like Lord Holland, have been glad to repeat them. Let's hope it will shut them up."

"Let's hope so, but Holland is not an easy man to gag."

"Well, enough of all that. Dinner should be ready soon. I expect to be told it'll be served any moment now. Will you join me?"

"Is water welcome in the desert? I should be delighted."

"And will you stay afterwards?"

"Do you need to ask, Lucy?"

Laud. 22nd November, 1639. Lambeth Palace.

"Hey there! You! Bring me some wine, and put some more coal on the fire in my study when you've done so. Thank you." I have just returned home from a most exhausting afternoon at Whitehall with the King and Wentworth. Lord Hamilton was there too. We had been notified that Lord Traquair was travelling to London from Edinburgh as fast as he could, and was likely to arrive today. In fact we arrived at the Palace together, and were shown straight into the King's presence.

Traquair was in a dreadful state, not just through such a long journey undertaken in so short a time – and the King's highways are never of the best in November – but, it seemed to me, because he feared what reaction he might get from the King to the news he had to impart, making him look paler and more like an unsuccessful student than usual. He said the King had sent him orders to prorogue the Scots Parliament, and he had done this the week before.

"There was uproar. I was called a traitor and worse. They told me I was Your Majesty's lick-spittle. Worse, they said you, Sire, had spat on them and that that was the spittle I was licking! Several times I stood to carry out your order. I was howled down. Someone threw an apple at me, but it missed and hit the man behind me."

"Shame on them!"

"Oh, I didn't mind the apple, Wentworth. The man it struck had been saying some of the nastiest things!"

"You are my representative there, Traquair. They cannot ignore my command to prorogue a session of Parliament."

"Indeed they cannot, Sire, but there was such a row it was some time before I could make myself heard. I made it absolutely clear that that is what was to happen. Apart from the insults, one of the things said most often was that the session should not be terminated so abruptly before any new laws could be enacted."

I spoke at last. "But surely, that was just the very reason it had to be prorogued: to stop them passing any of their ludicrous laws to reform the Kirk."

The King nodded. "Precisely. Wentworth suggested it, and I concurred."

Wentworth stood and started one of his marches. "What else did they say?"

"That even if His Majesty ended the Parliament, he could not stop the Lords of the Articles continuing to sit."

"That is almost, but not quite, what you thought might happen, Sire. But it's not quite as bad a rebellion as if they had pretended they could keep Parliament open against your will." Wentworth looked very serious indeed.

"No, it is not, but it is, nevertheless, another rebellion."

Traquair rubbed his hands one over the other like an actor at the Globe playing the part of a worried man, the difference being that he really was worried. "The Covenanters, Sire, are in league with the Devil.

You have no choice but to undertake another campaign against them next year."

The King was, for him, quite angry and passionate, and as his mood advanced his Scots accent strengthened with a vengeance, the Rs rolling ferociously and the vowel sounds changing. His next sentence sounded to me much like: "Do no' trouble your heed aboot tha', Traquair. Much has been doen a'ready. Tell him, Wentworth."

"Certainly, Sire. Strengthening of the defences of Hull and the Border towns is well under way. Demands for Ship money have been dispatched; the workshops manufacturing weapons and cannon are going at full tilt. More armaments have been purchased from Europe. Fund raising should go well. We have a loyal Royalist Lord Mayor of London, and hope for a loan from the City of 100,000 pounds. I am also urging men of property to contribute generously to the war chest, and have myself donated – and I do not say this boastfully, but to show the sort of sum which should be given – I have given 20,000 pounds. Have you anything else in mind Sire?"

"We must not overlook your Irish Army, My Lord. Hamilton, you must make sure Wentworth has ships enough to take his men to Scotland."

Hamilton nodded his head of sandy hair and spoke, I think for the first time. "Indeed I shall, Sire. He and I have been discussing another matter which we are agreed it may be politic for you to do."

The King smiled. "I like the 'may', Hamilton. Wentworth here usually tells me what I 'must' do." We all laugh, even Thomas. "What is this thing I should do?"

"We believe you should call an English Parliament. Your war effort will be the more effective if you have the representatives of the people behind you."

Wentworth sat again, at last. "That is my view, Your Majesty. You stand more chance, too, of getting the money you need if Parliament can be persuaded to raise it."

"Well, gentlemen, we haven't had much luck with the Parliament in Edinburgh." The King turned to me. What do you think, Your Grace?"

"I am of the same mind, Sire. And if Thom – er, Wentworth - is able to manage this Parliament as well as he has been dealing with those in Dublin, and assist with the war in the same brilliant fashion, the outcome should be all you could desire."

The King smiles. “Indeed. And in 1628 he was virtually running the last Parliament here, and running it against me, too!”

Wentworth rises to the bait. “Not so much against you, Sire, as against some of your policies, but I was trying to ...”

“Get some measure of agreement between me and Parliament, My Lord. Yes, I know and remember all that. After all, it was why I brought you into the government in the first place, as I told you at the time. Even so, I am not convinced of the case for calling Parliament just yet. We shall consider it further.

Thomas. 8th January, 1640. Covent Garden.

It is bitterly cold out. It is dark, and snowing, and I am expecting Lady Carlisle to dinner. She will be my only guest. We have not been together since before Christmas. I have so much news to tell her, news which I have already imparted to Elizabeth by a letter I wrote this morning. I am in the drawing room, which is at the front of the house, but even there I cannot hear the rumble of carriage wheels, for the snow lies too thick on the ground. The fire is banked up with logs and some coal, and roars gently. The thick curtains are drawn against the cold but I hold the corner of one aside to look for her arrival.

Dinner will be served in the small dining room, and the bedroom she usually sleeps in is prepared. I fancy sleep may be in short supply tonight. And then I see the carriage approaching, quite silently. I step into the hall and tell a footman to be ready to open the door in a few seconds. I return to the room and stand with my back to the fire.

The footman knocks, opens the door, and announces the Countess of Carlisle. As she comes in I see that she still wears her cloak, and start to reprimand the servant for his laxity, but she stops me short. “I told him I wished to keep it on as I am quite chilled to the bone.”

“Very well, Jordan, you may go. Please shut the door, so we can keep the warmth in here. And make sure the fire is going well in the small dining room, and that you are all warm in the servants hall.” He bows and goes.

Lucy drops me a full curtsey, and rises with a devastating smile. “Well, My Lord, Earl of Strafford, I am honoured to be here.”

I cross the room and make her the deepest of bows. “And I, My Lady, am even more honoured to have you as my guest. You, after all, are from an old and famous noble family, and I am a newcomer to this rank."

"We all have to start somewhere, Thomas, even that 'old and noble family' had to do something to earn its place. You have certainly earned yours. You're still doing so. Where would the King be without you?"

"Possibly not on the verge of going to war with the Scots if I had been with him earlier. But how are you? Come and kiss me." And she does, and then moves away to stand by the fire, clutching her cloak to her all the while.

"So, on New Year's Day the King raised you from a Viscount to an Earl; the Earl of Strafford." Lucy curtseys again, but in a more humorous fashion this time. "How did you feel?"

"Absolutely delighted. I have wanted it for so long. I've found it difficult dealing with some of the aristocrats in Ireland who have been Earls for longer, feeling they looked down on me, a mere Viscount."

"Then many of them have a damn cheek, Thomas. Look at Cork; his title is so new my brother would barely give him the time of day. And it's based on money-making and his ability to pay for promotion, or hopes that he would part with some gold for Royal coffers. It is not based on valour, like the Percys, or loyal service to the Crown, as yours has been."

"I don't need reminding that James sold titles. That was how my Father became a baronet. I believe 1000 pounds was the going rate, but he paid more."

"Your father wasn't alone. Anyway, these Irish Lords whose opinion you think about so much haven't been able to hold out against you, have they? You've triumphed in every field where you've had to challenge them, haven't you? Their opinion matters little. It's the King's that counts. Word around the Court is that the King approves of what you do, so why should you worry?"

"Perhaps in private with you I am not as sure of myself as I have to pretend to be to others, Lucy."

"Look at me, Thomas. When these antagonists of yours come to Court and talk, they all say you always get the better of everyone. Why would they say that if they didn't believe it? And, most important, why would the King make you Lord Lieutenant of Ireland instead of keeping you as the Deputy if he didn't have complete faith in you?"

That makes me laugh. "Complete faith. I wish it were so. I doubt the King has complete faith in anyone, let alone me. He has at last given me what I wanted because he knows, I think, that I have an almost impossible task ahead of me, and need every advantage in title and authority if I am ..... I should say 'if he', really, as it is his battle I am fighting." I pause, shaking my head and looking at the carpet as I think of this. "It is hard work, Lucy, especially trying to persuade His Majesty that he needs to call a Parliament to raise money. Even then I enjoy it, though. And I do enjoy it, there's no doubt about that."

"It's kept you away from me for three weeks," she says in mock rebuke.

"Now that is one of the hard parts!! Seriously though, the Council of War has been meeting three times a week, raising money, or trying to, ordering weapons, cannon, ships, repairs to ships, and castles."

Lucy smiles. "I know about that, Thomas. My brother Algie is on that Council."

"Thank God he is, Lucy. He's replaced Arundel as Commander in Chief under the King. All we need now," and I laugh without mirth, "is an Army for him to command. We want an army of at least 35, 000 infantry and 3000 cavalry. They need swords, muskets, cannon, powder, shot, food, and more besides. We hope to get much of this made here, but the rest we have to buy abroad." A memory makes me laugh. "But there are some lighter moments. People come up with some crackpot ideas which we have to look at in case there's anything in them. One fellow sent us a design for a gadget which he says would fire two hundred guns at once. Ludicrous. How could you line them up and be sure the enemy would still be there when you'd finished? And how long would it take to load them? You'd need two hundred men to do it if it weren't to take a couple of hours."

"Talking of weapons, Thomas, as an Earl you need a new scabbard for your sword. I'm sure the old sword is just as good, but I thought you could sheath it here." And she whips open her cloak, and stands before me stark naked. Her nipples stand out hard, and she places her feet apart. I can see where this weapon of mine is to find its home. The steel is getting harder by the second.

I turn and lock the door.

Elizabeth. 15th January, 1640. Dublin Castle.

It is a filthy day outside. Rain is crashing - yes, crashing - against the windows. This has been going on for a few days. I have not been able to go out. I am sewing in my sitting room, before a very cosy fire. The two girls went to England when Thomas sailed. We decided it would be better if they went to stay with Arabella's mother, and William is with Thomas. I have only little Margaret at home..

Suddenly there is a knock at the door, and before I can call out, Kathleen bursts into the room. She is very excited. "A special messenger has just come with this for you, My Lady." She hands me a letter, which is wrapped in a greased leather pouch, thankfully, or it would be ruined by the rain. "He says it's from his Lordship."

Elizabeth. Yes. Oh Yes! This is his seal on the opening. Stay, Kathleen. Let us share his news. *(I rip open the letter).* "My dearest, the King has decorated me with an Earldom, and I have chosen the title of Earl of Strafford, and you are now a Countess! Strafford is that part of Yorkshire where our home is, whence I started this long political journey, and I have arrived at last. And I am no longer the Deputy in Ireland."

Kathleen. No longer the Deputy, Madam? What has gone wrong?

Elizabeth. Patience, Kathleen. Nothing is wrong. Listen. "I am now no Deputy but Lord Lieutenant of Ireland, and I have the right to choose my own Deputy! Isn't it wonderful?"

Kathleen. It is wonderful, Madam, so it is.

Elizabeth. So it is. "I have also obtained from the King the title of Baron Raby to pass on to our son Will at a time of my choosing, and I am pleased that the King agreed to this although Sir Harry Vane wanted the title for himself. I am hard pressed on the King's business here in London, so I must be brief. The King has consented to the calling of Parliaments here and in Dublin, and I plan to be with you in March to manage the Irish Houses, and then return to London for the Westminster sittings. I hope to persuade the Irish Houses to grant four subsidies of Forty-five thousand pounds each, and the English to give much more. I am doing all I can to induce the powerful and rich to make substantial loans and have myself put up 20,000 pounds on top of what I have already given. I miss you and long to be with you again. Greet Will for me, and tell him I have work for him to do when I return. Give my kisses to baby Margaret. I wish I were with you to ..." Well, I do not think I need read that bit just now, Kathleen. By the way, did you send the messenger to the kitchen for food and drink?

Kathleen. That I did, ma'am, and told the steward to get him some dry clothes. He was as wet as a bog, sailing and riding in this weather.

(The door opens again and John Lesley walks in, looking every inch a Bishop).

Elizabeth. Why John, what a happy chance brings you now. A letter has just come from Thomas. I was reading it with Kathleen. There is good news. Thomas has his Earldom, and the Barony of Raby for Will. You may go, Kathleen.

Kathleen. Yes, My Lady. *(She curtsies to both of us and goes).*

Lesley. I have had a letter from Thomas too, Elizabeth. I've already written to congratulate him on the Earldom, and on being able to make Will Baron Raby, but I'm not certain that stealing the Barony from under Sir Harry Vane's nose was wise. His home is Castle Raby near Durham. The King stayed there with him on his way to Newcastle. I've learned that Vane is in the running to be made joint Secretary of State with Windebanke. He'll be a powerful enemy if he resents losing the title, and the Secretary is in constant attendance on the King, as well as the Privy Council. Besides, he is elderly, and I am not at all sure that he is up to the job. I've met him, and thought he seemed rather deaf. Will he be quick enough to hear what is said in Council and take proper notes? I doubt it. I'm told he's said as much himself.

Elizabeth. At least Vane won't be here in Dublin to tangle Thomas's efforts. Has Thomas told you that he is coming home soon to seek subsidies from the Irish Parliament?

Lesley. He has, and is likely to get them. On top of that, my fellow Bishops have resolved that the Church will also grant large subsidies.

Elizabeth. He seems very confident he'll get what he wants from Ireland, and that he'll have similar success at Westminster on his return.

Lesley. He does, but I'm not so sure. When Parliament is called he'll still have John Pym to contend with, and I foresee other problems.

Elizabeth. What are they? Thomas is very pleased that the Duke of Northumberland is Commander in Chief, and says he is very able.

Lesley. Northumberland's ability is not in question. What bothers me is that he may have no enthusiasm for fighting the Scots. A war with them is likely to be as much on his land as on theirs, and he will lose heavily in money terms, even if he beats them. What bothers me more is that he is also in charge of the Navy. Northumberland will be fighting in the North of England or in Scotland. He can't be an Admiral in the Irish Sea at the same time. If Thomas intends to send his Irish Army to fight in Scotland, he must be sure that Northumberland makes Hamilton provide the ships.

Elizabeth. Can he - can the King - beat the Scots if this doesn't happen?

Thomas. 31st January, 1640. Covent Garden.

Dear Kit,

I hope to be on my way back to Ireland in little more than a month. I have been working with the King and Northumberland, and Secretary Windebanke, on a plan to raise an Irish Army to cross over to Scotland in the late spring or early summer. I need hardly tell you that you must not, under any circumstances, mention this to anyone but Radcliffe. I shall, in any event be writing to them about this myself.

It is essential that they keep the officers on their toes and training the existing soldiers even more regularly than has been the case since I took command. Most of the new troops will be Catholic Irish, and they will be leavened by the Protestants already enlisted, by the addition of more Protestant officers, and some Old English officers.

I am exultant that His Majesty has appointed Lord Conway to be general of the cavalry. With Northumberland as Commander in Chief, Conway leading the cavalry, and some very experienced soldiers the King has persuaded (with money and prospects of promotion, of course) to return from Germany, the upper echelons of the Army are beginning to look very competent and warlike.

This force will be 8,000 strong. The King expects to find 500 cavalry but only 2,000 foot. I pray to God that we shall be strong enough. We were talking of 35,000 foot and 3000 horse. Perhaps we shall get that from the rest of England if the Lords Lieutenant do their duty eventually.

Please keep me informed of events in Dublin,

Your friend,

Thomas.

My Dearest Bess,

I have time for a short note only as much is going on here. My thanks for your recent letter. I am glad that you are well, and that little Margaret thrives. I am looking forward to seeing you and holding you again so very much. I hear from Anne and Arabella that they are in good health, and as happy with their grandmother, Lady Clare, as her regime – rather more strict than yours, apparently – will permit.

I have some gossip. First, over Christmas there was a marvellous masque. It was designed by Inigo Jones, who seems to do so much of this sort of thing, as well as designing buildings and goodness knows what else. The Queen often takes a part in these dramas, but this time the King did so. Everyone says he was very good, but who would care to say he wasn't? For myself I thought he did well. The dialogue was written by a chap called Davenant, and the theme was a King who loved his people.

There was something even more entertaining, though it was not intended to be entertaining at all. Three of the Earl of Cork's sons were old enough to be married, and naturally their greedy father wanted wealthy young ladies for them. His Majesty acted, would you believe it, as match-maker, and found these young men three very rich and aristocratic maidens indeed. The first wedding went off well, but the second caused the third to be aborted! Bride number 2 was so frustrated with her new groom's performance (or lack of it) on the nuptial night that she told intended bride number 3 all about it. Bride number 3 then jilted her husband to be!! She then revived her courtship with an old flame, who was then challenged to a duel by non-bridegroom 3.

I'm told that Charles negotiated these marriages because he believed Cork would then lend or give him a suitably large amount of money. He was out of luck. As you know, Cork is not only greedy; he is also incredibly mean. He bought one pair of wedding shoes, and got each of the boys to wear them one after the other. I happened to be at Court when he drove the new brides to meet the King and told him that he could not afford to help him as he now had so many more mouths to feed!!

Waiting until March before I see you is very hard. You are my sweetheart.

Your loving Thomas.

William Laud. 3rd February 1640. Lambeth Palace.

I've just come home from the Privy Council. I need some strong wine. Harry Vane has just been installed as the additional Secretary of State. He's been Comptroller of the Royal Household for some years. You cannot fault him for ambition, but even he wonders whether he is up to this particular post, as he'll have to be Secretary to the Privy Council, too. He knows he writes ponderously, and talk at the Council table tends to be rapid.

I noticed that he uses an ear trumpet quite frequently. There is bound to be trouble arising from his notes and minutes of meetings. On top of that Thomas asked the King to make his son William Viscount Raby. Vane's home is Raby Castle; he thought he deserved that title. He is moaning about it to everyone he meets at every opportunity. I'm sick of it, but Thomas should have taken more care.

Neither of us got what we wanted with the appointment of Vane. Thomas wanted the Earl of Leicester to be the new Secretary. I did not care for that, doubting his ability. My choice was Sir Thomas Roe, the diplomat, and, as it happens, a great admirer of Thomas's rule in Ireland.

One good thing that has occurred is that Northumberland is not just Commander in Chief, but also President of the Council of War; Thomas and I see eye to eye on that, but I cannot help wondering whether even Algie Percy can combine these two posts with being Lord High Admiral at the same time. It also remains to be seen whether he can work with that clot Hamilton in charge of the fleet off Scotland as well as the army when it gets to Scotland.

Thomas. 21st February, 1640. Whitehall.

Yesterday a party of Scotsmen arrived in London. They were headed by Lord Loudoun, dressed in full Scottish regalia. He's a cousin of the Earl of Argyle, so he's really a traitor, too. Argyle is firmly behind the Covenant, and the foremost of its leaders, and Loudoun will do whatever he tells him to do. I advised the King to send them away again, but he agreed to see them. It plays for more time, after all.

Today they have come to see him at St James's. The King sits on a throne; I sit at his side. Other Councillors are there when the Scots are ushered in.

They express themselves strangely. After the formal greetings and other niceties they come straight to the point. "On the knees of our hearts we ask Your Majesty to accept the reform of the Church in Scotland for which our Parliament has legislated, and the new method of appointing the Lords of the Articles from all the Scottish Estates."

The King gives them what is, for so civilised a man, the rough edge of his tongue. He hands me a sheet of paper, and gets the usher to hand one to each of the Scotsmen. "Do you recognise this, gentlemen?"

Loudoun blushes. "This is our account of the Pacification of Berwick, Sire."

"And I say it is a very one-sided and false account. I'm told that as you handed it out, you told people I had, like a naughty boy, promised your people anything and everything they wanted while I was in Berwick, but that when I was back in London and in charge of Headmaster Laud, I took it all away again."

Loudoun is unable to deny it. He also admits that he had supplied Lords Salisbury and Pembroke with Covenanters' literature to hand around. The King then produces a letter which had come into his hands asking Pembroke to intercede on the Covenanters' behalf with the King. It is Pembroke's turn to blush until his cheeks match his maroon doublet, and he becomes angry, rejecting the allegation and the letter vehemently. I am not convinced by his outburst, but can see that he dare not admit his sympathy for the Scots and their religion before his King.

It becomes clear that His Majesty has no intention of giving way over anything. These mighty Scots are put down from their seats, and there are none of the humble and meek there to be exalted on this occasion.

Three years ago I was very worried that there might be war with Spain or Austria. I wrote to Coke and Cottington several times from May to August expressing my concerns in rather strong and undiplomatic terms. It was very frustrating. By the end of that August the King's title to the land had been found in Ormonde and Clare, and I had achieved almost all I had set out to do in setting up a regime for a huge amount of planting and the introduction of a large number of settlers. However, the rumour of a Spanish war at that time brought most of it to nought. What a difference it would have made to the Royal finances if I could have got on with it there and in Connaught! What success might the King have now if he had those extra resources at his command! Still, the 'what if' game is not a very useful exercise, no matter how often we politicians might play it.

But I can't help it! It looks as though we are to be at war with Scotland again. Will this kill off my – the King's - plantation policy for Connaught? What will happen to the extra revenue I have raised for the Crown with increased customs duties, and increased Irish trade?

Elizabeth. 28th February, 1640. Jigginstown House.

Henrietta Street,
Covent Garden.
21st February, 1640.
Dearest Bess,

How are you? I am well, and so are the girls, Lady Clare tells me. How is little Margaret? William is well, and a great help to me, and learning to be a courtier. I enjoy his company very much, as a lucky father should.

Today I was with the King when he saw a deputation of Scotsmen. They still seem to think they can change his mind over the Prayer Book and Laud's other reforms. They do not know him. When he has set his mind on an objective he is immovable. He gave them a very hard time, but he has not sent them packing. He has commanded them to stay in London for the time being. Partly I think it a device to gain more time to prepare for battle, but he also intends to have them at the Palace as often as he wishes, to get as much information out of them as he can.

A letter has come into his hands – actually Lord Traquair gave it to him when he came here from Edinburgh last year – which was written by the Covenanters to the King of France asking him to help them negotiate with us. It is a curious effort. They rely on the fact that France has always been their ally against England, but it seems to me they forget that Louis is a devout Catholic, and hardly likely to fall over himself to assist a bunch of Puritanical Calvinists.

Be that as it may, the letter is real evidence of treachery to the King and to England. We have discussed how to use this document, and agree that as soon as Parliament opens it should be presented to both Houses. Surely they will see that this is a real threat to their own country! Surely Parliament will not think that inviting the French in the back door via Scotland will allow them to go on practising their own versions of Christianity if the French King is in charge and their conquerors are the Scots?

His Majesty and I are very optimistic that Parliament will be loyal, and I am looking forward to managing it in his interests, which are the country's too.

There are some local disturbances, but they do not mean much, of that I am sure. For example, some people are copying Puritans, and refusing to kneel and take communion at the altar rails. One rector has written to the Council about it. He says that in his parish two Puritans have persuaded the rest of his congregation to behave in this disrespectful way. But it is only two who are responsible for this disobedience. Neither the King nor I attach much significance to this.

I am very hard pressed with all the King's business, and on the correspondence from Kit and the Georges, as well as keeping in touch with Osborne and Peter Man up in York, both on the county and the business fronts, but I get out to the theatre and to dinner with friends now and again. None of that makes up for your not being by my side. I miss you, Bess, but I should be home soon. I leave here in three days to come home to you, and deal with the Irish Parliament. I shall then have to hurry back here for the London Parliament in April.

A quite remarkable thing has happened. To get me to Chester and my ship, the Queen has offered me her own coach! She says she knows I am not as well as I could be, and that her coach is most comfortable and will make my journey much easier to bear. The gout is troublesome at present, and I need all the ease I can get. I shall collect Nan and Arabella from Lady Clare, and bring them and William with me to Dublin, so we shall all be together again, if only for a while.

Kiss Margaret for me and tell her that her Daddy loves her. I wish I were there to kiss you and show you my love myself.

Your loving husband,
Thomas.

I do love to get letters from Thomas. I am sure I miss him at least as much as he says he misses me, and I have more time in which to think about it! I hope he is right to be so confident. Some of the things in his letter look to me different from how they seem to appear to him.

Have he and the King thought this business of the Communion through properly? Perhaps Thomas has forgotten that I come from a fairly Puritan family myself. Perhaps I see things through a more Puritan pair of eyes than he does, and certainly more than the King does. Charles seems to have no Puritan sympathies at all. If two people stay away from the Eucharist, or fail to kneel at the altar rail, that is one thing, and not very important. But when the rest of the congregation agree with them and defy their own priest to do so, isn't that a sign of a more serious problem?

Bishop Lesley still has many contacts in England and tells me that there are many scenes of discontent with Laud's policies, and the King's attempts to enforce them. There are riots and affrays in many parts of the country. A civil servant was stoned to death in Suffolk; a clerk to a Bishop was murdered by a mob of peasants when he tried to take their common land for the Church; in some places Laud's alterations to Church buildings are objected to, not just by the people but by the Justices of the Peace – and they are supposed to be the King's men! The worst thing, John says, is that in some parts of the North the people give bed and board to Scotsmen, and the Mayor of Newcastle even allowed some to wander all over the town's defences. If all this is true – and why should I doubt it if John does not? – the King is wrong to think all goes his way. Thomas would be wrong to encourage that line of thought.

I must talk to Thomas about that when he arrives home. I'd write to him today, but I have no idea where he'll be on the road, nor how soon he'll be here. I'd better get back to Dublin. I only came here to see how the house is coming on. It's still not finished. We always have to stay in the hunting lodge when we come here, but Margaret seems to like it better than the Castle; it is so much brighter than that gloomy stone stronghold; not a place for a baby at all. I'll find out more about how the elections for the new Parliament are going in Dublin, too. I don't hear much in this rural paradise. Perhaps that is why it is a rural paradise.

Christopher Wandesford. 18th March, 1640. Dublin Castle.

Tom arrived home today with his son. He looks exhausted. He says he had a terrible attack of the gout at the end of the month, had hoped to leave London on the 1st, and didn't feel fit enough to travel until the 5th. He then decided to sail from Anglesea, not Chester. The Queen's coach then bumped and banged him all the way there, which took until the 16th because he could not travel very far each day as he was still in some pain. He stayed the night at Beaumaris and sailed the next day.

I tell him that as Lord Deputy I opened the Irish Parliament two days ago. He seems to have recovered all his old confidence. "We'll have no trouble there. I'm sure I can manage the Parliaments. I'm not afraid of Pym, and I'd manage the London one even if Sir John Eliot were still there." He laughs. "If I'm this brave with no legs, how will I be when they are better?"

"I'm sure of that, Tom. The Commons here are controlled by some MPs who are loyal to you, and you'll run the Lords yourself. The Council is yours, with Ormonde in charge, and Loftus, Mountnorris and Cork away in London."

"Yes, Kit. All should be well. I think I'll rest tomorrow, as I'm worn out. I'll come to the House in a couple of days."

Elizabeth. 3rd April, 1640. Dublin Castle.

Me. You are not well enough to go, Thomas. The weather is bad and will be worse at sea. Even the ship's captain has told you not to sail into these storms. What will you do if the flux returns? You've had it very badly for a while now.

Lesley. Elizabeth is right, My Lord. You are unwell, and you've been working too hard. You have only been here three weeks, and look what you have accomplished? Four subsidies - £180,000 - obtained from Parliament, the promise of Eight thousand soldiers and one thousand cavalry, more money from the Church, all the arrangements made for running the country in your absence again? It is too much. You are killing yourself.

Thomas. There's too much to be done to worry about that. I shall make shift and put myself to all the pain I can endure before I am found wanting to the King in this affair. Sound or lame I intend to be at the opening of the English Parliament, loyal to my gracious master. And I have not done it all myself, Elizabeth. I have your support, Kit's and

Radcliffe's, and Will's. Look how he helped me when I attended Parliament.

Me. All he did was carry your train. *(We all laugh).*

Thomas. Besides, Radcliffe and Kit do all I ask of them, and I can rely utterly on the Earl of Ormonde to command my Army, and get them to the Ulster coast to sail to Scotland.

Me. *(I mutter).* Provided there are some ships to take them.

Thomas. *(He indicates Lesley).* John's contribution mustn't be forgotten, either. I am well served by my friends. I can ask no more.

Lesley. Elizabeth, don't you think Thomas in modest mood a strange sight? Has he told you what the Dublin Parliament said? Having promised him all that money and all those soldiers to present to the King, they issued a Proclamation.

Me. A Proclamation? What did it say?

Lesley. As near as I can remember, it was something like; "Welcome, most worthy Lord, this is the voice of the House of Commons. We see your Lordship like an Ancient Greek sage, studying the needs of this your country; your country, let us call it now." The Speaker of the House went on to praise everything Thomas has done for the justice, order, and prosperity "which a grateful Ireland owes to the best of Governors." They even thanked the King for his tender care in sending them so good a man to rule them.

Thomas. Enough, Your Grace, enough. You know sufficient of politics to realise these praises are not spontaneous. Kit will have been working hard to arrange them.

Me. But there are many men in Parliament, Thomas, and if the majority did not agree, it would not come about. You are the uncrowned King of Ireland. *(I say that with a gay smile, but then become thoughtful, and hesitant).* What concerns me is what they will say if you do not have similar success in England, or if the war against the Scots goes badly.

Wentworth. I need no reminding of the difficulties I face, Elizabeth. I must go and face them, but Parliament was prorogued four days ago so it can't cause much trouble now. Could you ask Kathleen to organize the packing of my trunks? I shall find Will and get him to help me sort out the papers I'll need.

Me. Are you taking Will back with you?

Thomas. Yes, my love, but I think I shall soon send him back here to look after you and the girls and little Margaret. It'll do him no harm to be the head of the household for a while.

Henry Clifford. 5th April, 1640. London.

I believe Thomas must be on his way back to England by now. I must see him as soon as he arrives, or get a letter to him at any rate. He needs to be aware of new developments here. Ship Money is still causing dreadful problems, and I understand the money is hardly coming in at all. Some Sheriffs tell their men, and even the Magistrates, not to collect it, and others are say that the tax isn't even legal, despite what the Courts have said.

The King gave the Duke of Lennox a monopoly on the collection of customs on the export of raw wool. He wants to stop it being sold abroad, and wants it kept here for the English spinners and weavers to work, as so many are unemployed in the villages. It doesn't work. The Duke's men collect small amounts to line the Duke's purse, and some for themselves. That doesn't stop the merchants sending it abroad. It's just set the Merchant Adventurers at logger-heads with the King, and not helped anyone in the countryside. I can't see Lord Mayor Garraway getting much cash from the City if these merchants are against it.

The worst thing is that the King has released the two MPs who were still in prison for holding the Speaker in his chair all those years ago. Maybe he thought it would look like mercy, since they have been there more than a decade. All I think it will do is put two very able and resentful opponents of the King back into the Commons. Life may be more difficult than Thomas expects with William Strode and Benjamin Valentine back in the House.

Thomas. 18th April, 1640. Leicester Place.

Sweetheart,

I am sorry that I have not been able to write to you before, but had an appalling voyage from Dublin to Chester on the 3rd, not getting ashore until 6 o'clock the next day, and I have had the most awful journey since. I thank God I had William with me for company and comfort. When we landed my gout returned with a vengeance. I had to spend four days in bed at the best inn I could find in Chester before I could move, and it was another two days before I was well enough to leave. Then we had to make frequent stops on the way South as my legs would not take the jolting. That meant we had to stay overnight in more towns than I had expected, and I only arrived here today.

Whilst on the road I heard that the King's forces had recaptured Dumbarton. I am trying to find out from Northumberland how to get the troops there from Ireland. The weather is too treacherous for the ships in port at Chester to cross to Ireland, and the Earl of Argyle has a warship with eighteen cannon stationed in the Clyde Estuary waiting to attack any vessel coming its way.

Secretary Windebanke wrote to me with news, and it is nearly all bad. I wrote back telling him in no uncertain terms that he has to give no quarter to Lords Lieutenant and country gentlemen who do not do their duty in raising men for the King. In our own Yorkshire they have told the King they will not send the men unless their uniforms and pay and travel are paid for. Do they not recall their obligation to help defend the country?

Fortunately I was invited to stay at the home of the Earl of Leicester, which is nearer to Whitehall than our own house.

The pain finally went yesterday, but I am not much recovered today. I am not well enough to attend Parliament yet. Luckily Henry called to see me soon after we got here, and stayed for dinner. Had I been here three days ago I should have been at the opening of Parliament, but Henry was able to tell me something of what had occurred. After His Majesty opened the sitting, Lord Keeper Finch praised the King and told the Members to vote generous supplies to pay for war against Scotland. He produced the letter from the rebels to Richelieu asking for help from France, which the King had thought would stir everyone to regard the Scots as traitors, but Henry said it had no effect at all.

On the 16th Pym spoke. He made it clear that there is virtually no support for the King's religious policy in the Commons, and the Members feel even more strongly about Ship Money and the other taxes the King has collected without Parliament. Pym and his supporters want these and other complaints resolved before there can be any question of money for the King.

I hope you and Margaret, Nan and Arabella are well and happy. For myself I am not at all content being away from you and finding myself in the midst of this political nightmare . I just hope that with brother George sitting for Pontefract, and the other friends for whom I and Algie have found seats, I can regain control.

William sends his love. Many say he is a charming, handsome fellow.

With all my love, Bess,
Thomas.

Thomas. 23rd April, 1640. Westminster.

I'm still rather weak, but at last I have been able to come to the House of Lords. It is the first time I have sat in this august place as a peer of the realm. Curiously my sponsors were both brothers of my late wives. Margaret's brother Henry, Earl of Cleveland, was on my left, and Arabella's brother, who is now Earl of Clare, was on my right. They almost have to hold me up!

I learn that yesterday the Church in Convocation voted the King six subsidies, but that made no impression on the Commons, and Pym has asked for a meeting with the Lords. He says that the two Houses together must decide whether they have any money for the King, and then only after their grievances have been dealt with.

I shall see the King tonight. He must get to the Lords first thing tomorrow, before Pym can.

William Wentworth, Lord Raby. 24th April, 1640. Westminster.

I went to the House of Lords with my Father this morning. The King came, and told the peers that he would hold a second session of Parliament if they granted money in this one. Then Father spoke in favour of the King's proposal.

He is such a powerful orator. I should like to be able to speak like that when I am full grown. He was so eloquent he made – and I mean made – the majority agree to what the King said. I am so proud to be with him.

John Pym. 4th May, 1640. St. Stephen's Hall.

I am with two Harry Vanes. One is Sir Harry, and the other his son, a very enthusiastic young man, totally opposed to the King's policies, and to our new Earl of Strafford. Young Harry is very like his father, florid of face, and large, but slimmer. We stroll up and down near the Thames, talking as quietly as Sir Harry's deafness will permit. It is a glorious spring day. We discuss our tactics to retain control of this Parliament.

Vane. It was a master-stroke, Master Pym. Your strategy is second to none.

Me. I'm not so sure. With Strafford as an opponent you have to be up very early in the morning.

Sir Harry. Why have we got to be up early in the morning?

Vane. No, Father. We haven't got to be up early in the morning. John said you have to get up early to keep up with Strafford. *(To me).* You're right not to under-rate him.

Me. I should never do that. When he got back from Ireland he was so ill I'm told he couldn't even walk round his bedroom. Yet he continued to send advice to the King, and was back in the thick of it as soon as he could get up. I had a plan to oppose the subsidy vote and Strafford even managed to thwart that.

Vane. How?

Me. I proposed a joint conference of Commons and Lords to persuade them that until the King redressed our grievances we could not vote money for the war, but Strafford got there first.

Sir Harry. It was my fault. Being an MP and Secretary to the Council makes life complex. The Secretary obviously has to tell the Council all he knows. As an MP I knew Master Pym had proposed a parley with the Lords. When I went to the Privy Council meeting I had to tell the King. No-one would have believed it if I'd said I didn't know.

Vane. So what did Strafford do?

Me. Don't forget he was an MP himself, and a great one, before he went over to the King's party.

(We reach a Tavern by the river. We sit in the spring sunshine, and I order wine for Sir Harry and me, and a mug of ale for young Vane).

Sir Harry. He told the King to appeal to the House of Lords in person. The King went there the next morning, and promised that he would redress grievances at the next session if Parliament voted the money now, and the Peers went along with it.

Me. Only after a very powerful and persuasive dose of Strafford's oratory. *(I address myself to young Vane).* It was only because Sir Harry told me of Strafford's tactics over the subsidy vote that I hit on my own plan.
Sir Harry. The King proposed in Council that the Commons should be asked to vote twelve subsidies. £840,000! Wentworth was against it. He said it was too much, and suggested six subsidies would be more easily approved. He pointed out that the English Convocation of Bishops had already given six, but the King wanted more. He even said he would withdraw his right to Ship Money if he got more, but in the end Wentworth - I cannot get used to calling him Strafford - persuaded the King to ask for eight.
Me. When your Father told me the King wanted to ask for twelve subsidies but had been persuaded to ask for eight, I realised it could be our truly great opportunity. I got the Lords to be more cooperative by accusing them of breach of privilege. I asked Sir Harry to tell the Commons the King wanted twelve, and that only the withdrawal of Ship Money was on offer, not the general redress of grievances that had been offered to the Lords.
Sir Harry. I blamed my deafness for not understanding what had happened at the Privy Council. Strafford was beside himself with fury, but I was glad. I have never forgiven him for taking the Raby Baronetcy, my son. It should have been ours.
Vane. What is our next move, Master Pym?
Me. Strafford's already threatened the Lords that if the King doesn't get the money for the war, Parliament will be dissolved. We have to provoke a dissolution. Then the King will not get the money, at any rate from us, and he won't be able to afford to fight the Scots.
Vane. What sort of provocation do you have in mind?
Sir Harry. Convocation? What have they to do with it?
Me. Not convocation, Sir Harry. Provocation. I intend to tell the House that its consider that the religious grievances of Scotland, in particular in regard to the Prayer Book, are the same as our own. When he hears that, the King will dissolve Parliament.
Vane. Then the King could not go on with the war.
Me. Exactly. Even if he goes ahead - and I think he is obstinate enough - he will be in an impossible position. The war will go badly, and he will be forced to call another Parliament.

Vane. And when he does so, we shall have him in our grasp.

Charles I. 5th May, 1640. My Audience Chamber, Whitehall.

The Queen and I are seated. Wentworth and Laud stand before us. Sir Harry Vane sits at a table to take notes. Northumberland and Cottington also stand. Northumberland looks every inch a fighting man and a leader.

Wentworth. Your Majesty, the possibility that the Commons might make common cause with the Scots is not to be tolerated, but I would not have dissolved Parliament on that account.

Laud. But at the meeting this morning you agreed to it.

Wentworth. If you had not arrived late, Your Grace, you would have heard me arguing for at least an hour against the dissolution. How are we to find the money for war if we have no Parliament? That is why I advised that it should be called in the first place, but as I was virtually alone in arguing against dissolution, I went along with the majority. Perhaps I should not have done.

Me. And I dissolved Parliament at noon. There is no point in going over all that again. We have to find the money another way. What happened to the idea of the Navy providing escorts for the Spanish fleets? *(Wentworth appears to be swaying in pain, and finding it difficult to stand. I raise a hand and make a sign. A servant steps out of the shadows).* Bring a chair for My Lord Strafford. In fact, bring chairs for everyone. *(The servant retires).*

Wentworth. You are gracious, Sire. I am still unwell, I fear.

Queen. I have heard of your journey from Ireland last month. They say you were ill when you left Dublin, and your ship was caught in a storm.

Wentworth. Yes Ma'am, it was.

Laud. And when he reached Chester he was so ill he was kept in bed by the doctors. At least, that is what Thomas says. Other, possibly more accurate, reports say that he was so ill he couldn't get out of bed.

Wentworth. My physicians hadn't wanted me to sail in the first place. Nor did my wife.

Queen. Wives have their uses, and so do husbands, and a wife knows that a live one is more use than a dead one.

Me. I fancy not all wives would agree with you, my dear.

(Four servants enter with chairs).

Servant. The chairs, Sire.
Me. Thank you. Put them here. Leave us. *(I gesture for the men to sit).* Now then, this Council of War resumes. I should welcome your suggestions. I shall not back down or give in. The war in Scotland must go on. There has already been fighting in Edinburgh; my garrison was fired on.
Algie. Who fired first is difficult to tell. It depends who is telling the tale.
Queen. It matters little. If the Covenanters fired first you cannot let it go unpunished. And if the soldiers fired first it is because the Scots are defying their King, so you have to fight on.
Wentworth. That is true, Your Majesty. *(He turns to me).* As for Parliament, you asked them and they refused. You are acquitted before God and man. If Parliament will do nothing to defend the country against the Scots you are free to use the Royal Prerogative to raise an army and money for the war. We can only fight on with money and an Army, Sire. You asked about the Spanish business. It is going well. After the Council has met I have a meeting with the King of Spain's representatives. I'm told that this evening they are likely to say that for our escorts in the Channel Spain will pay four million ducats.
Laud. Four Million?
Wentworth. Golden ducats! And the Earl of Ormonde will have your Majesty's Irish Army in the Ulster ports in the next two weeks, ready to be shipped to Scotland. If your Majesty brings an Army from England to the Border, the Scots will be caught in a pincer movement by my Irish troops - eight thousand foot and one thousand cavalry. Victory should be yours, Sire. There is an army in Ireland you may employ here to reduce the Scottish Kingdom.
Cottington. I dislike the idea of money from Spain. It pains me to say so, Your Majesty, but the people seem to me to be wary of both you and the Church.
Wentworth. *(Despite his weakness he stands rather vigorously and speaks in the same manner).* We must stand firm, Sire. You must show any who disapprove of the dissolution who is master here. Your offer to withdraw Ship Money has not been implemented; why should it be when Parliament gave you no money? Give orders for its collection immediately. Let us issue directions – to be enforced – for regiments to be raised and marched to Scotland at once.

He is very forceful as usual, and therefore, as usual, very persuasive. Laud agrees with him enthusiastically, Cottington says, “Oh! Very well,” or something similar, and Northumberland comes aboard, too, but, as it seems to me, somewhat reluctantly.

In the evening Wentworth returns to give me an account of his meeting with the Spaniards. The outcome is extraordinary. The King of Spain has indeed instructed them to offer four million ducats to have my navy escort his supply and troop convoys past the Dutch warships. This money would change my position completely. I should no longer be dependent on Parliament. I could make war on the Scots, as they deserved, and I could afford it. I could also take action at once to enforce my will in London too.

My confidence is also boosted by Wentworth – I must learn to call him Strafford now – telling me that King Philip is prepared to consider marrying his son – heir to his throne – to my daughter Princess Mary. She is only eight, but that is how these dynastic unions work; it may be years before I have to part with her.

Once Strafford leaves I send at once for the commander of my guards and give him his orders.

William Laud. 11th May, 1640. Canterbury.

I have been at my Palace here for four days. The day after the Council of War, His Majesty sent his guards to the homes of Pym, Hampden, another MP, and the Earl of Warwick and two other peers. Their homes were searched, the guards looking for letters proving contact with the Scottish rebels. The day after that another four MPs were arrested. All ten were hauled before the Privy Council, together with another MP who had chaired the Commons Committee taking complaints about religious matters. The seven MPs were all sent to the Tower. The lords were not.

Today I have received a message from London that four Aldermen from the City have been sent to prison, too, for refusing to tell the Council which merchants are rich enough to make loans to the King for the war. The King told the Lord Mayor that the original 100,000 pounds was not enough, and if they did not come up straight away with 200,000, he’d send out the troops to collect 300,000. London is in the grip of madness. That is why I am here.

The day after the War Council, news of the arrest of the MPs, and Pym especially, reached the streets. I suspect that the offer of money from Spain for the escort of Spanish troop-ships must have leaked out, too. The apprentices went berserk. They were joined by dockers - big, strong violent people - sailors, and others, and all rioted through the streets. An enormous crowd besieged my palace at Lambeth. Luckily they only did so from the land, and I was able to escape in my barge from the wharf outside the palace. It was terrifying. I'm told that many were arrested and put in prison, but not for long, as the rest of the mob stormed the jail and released them, fighting off the Watch who tried to arrest them again.

The Trained Bands were to be used to deal with the rioters, but a dreadful storm drove them away before the militia arrived. A nineteen year-old, Thomas Bensted, was arrested for trying to break down the door at Lambeth. He is to be charged with treason.

I cannot believe that Government policies have reduced the people to this criminal condition. It must be the work of that villainous Pym and his friends. I must act. I shall get Convocation to reinforce my reforms of Church and worship. We shall insist on an oath upholding the Church of England. All priests and all other professional people must swear it.

William, Lord Raby. 5th July, 1640. Covent Garden.

The Lord be praised, for today is a good day. Such days have been in short measure these last seven weeks, and it seems longer. Father has been so ill. He has not really recovered his strength since we left Dublin, but I think the strain of the Parliament and the Council of War, and the rioting in the streets took a dreadful toll on him. It did not scare him, but it did not cheer me to see posters put up and words painted or chalked on walls calling for his head and that of the Archbishop.

Father was talking of the need for the King to get a strong message across to the people that the nation is in real danger from a Scottish invasion. Only then will it be possible to collect money and supplies for the army. His Majesty must explain that he is only acting as he is because Parliament has abandoned the country to its fate. He must tell everyone that this state of affairs is only to last until the threat from Scotland has been overcome.

For my own part, I'm not sure how well such a message will succeed. After all, with the mob in the mood it's in, won't it think that 'temporary' is a strange word to use when the King has ruled without Parliament for ten years, has had one for less than a month, and now wants to rule without it again? I'm also not too sure about the money from Spain either. Last year our Navy let the Dutch sink a lot of that Spanish Fleet just off the coast here, without doing a thing to help them. How can their King – come to that how can our King – be sure the same thing won't happen again? Let's face it, if it is true that a lot of sailors were amongst the rioters, how can anyone be sure they will be willing to help Spain fight the Dutch? Which is what it would amount to.

Back to my Father, though. The week after Parliament was dissolved he collapsed. He'd had really bad flux, and the doctors were letting his blood so often it was a wonder he had any left. Then he got some sort of chest infection. He was so ill even the King came here to see him, which was a real honour for us. I thought Dad was going to die. I think he did too, for he wrote and asked Uncle George and Sir George Radcliffe to come to London.

Father was in bed for ages. Early last month he was able to do some work, getting his secretary into his bedroom to take dictation, and a couple of weeks later he got up.

Even in bed, though, his worries did not cease. He had letters from Sir Edward Osborne, his Deputy on the Council of the North, telling him that the gentry were mostly totally uncooperative about raising troops or money. Many of those who might have helped had been sent to Westminster as MPs, which gave the Puritan Lords and Squires a free rein to hamper all recruitment efforts. He says the only real support he gets comes from the Catholics. They are willing to be army officers, but the sons of Protestant gentry refuse. This makes the soldiers, who are mainly Protestant – and many are Puritans at that – unhappy; they say they won't fight for Papists against good Scots Calvinists. Similar news came in from most parts of the country.

He had letters from Sir Christopher, who had been left in charge of the Irish Government, saying that Parliament had met on 1st June, and that it was in rebellious mood. It resulted in Father's plans for an Act for the plantation of Connaught being abandoned. The Houses also made huge changes to his scheme for dividing payment of the subsidies more fairly between the rich and poor counties.

Kit is losing his grip over Parliament. That is, if he ever had a grip. After all, he's not a forceful, persuasive man like Father. He's more gentle, and likely to give way unless he's got Dad right behind him. With Dad sick in bed in England Kit just isn't strong enough, I suppose. He upset Dad by telling him that as the Navy is patrolling Scotland, especially in the North Sea, the pirates are back on the Irish beaches and in the rivers. Things became so bad with the MPs Kit dissolved the Parliament in its third week!

There's also been more trouble here. The Archbishop's new Canon Laws about oaths have upset a lot of people, even Anglicans. One Bishop says he can't go along with them because they offer no chance that England can be part of one Holy Catholic Church with Rome, a lot of the clergy are unhappy, and of course the Puritans are furious because Convocation passed these laws when Parliament has been dissolved. They say the laws are illegal.

I've heard Laud talking to Father about these things. I've heard other people wondering how the public will support a war against Protestant Scotland if they still have to pay illegal taxes, and cannot go to the sort of Churches they want. When I told Dad and Laud this, they said that the King has to be obeyed. Even so, I think Father is feeling less confident about what will happen. In one of his letters Kit said that his Parliament wants to keep the Irish Army at home as it fears trouble with all the Scottish settlers in Ulster.

Why is today a good day, then? Father was well enough to go to the Council meeting again. Further, we were all celebrating because Queen Henrietta Maria gave birth to another boy, Prince Henry, Duke of Gloucester. That means there are three male heirs to the throne in line now. The King's got eight children now.

John Pym. 15th July, 1640. St. Stephen's Hall, Westminster.

Sir Harry, his son, and I are conversing in a corner out of earshot of anyone – I hope! We always seem to be lurking somewhere these days, like conspirators. Hardly surprising really; conspiring to bring down Strafford and wrest power from the King is just about all we think of.

Sir Harry. In Council the talk is that the Scottish Covenanters are ready to march into England. As a Member of Parliament I'm delighted at the trouble befalling the King's plans for war. As one of the Secretaries of State, I ought to be crestfallen for the same reason.

Vane. God is on our side. Let's review our position. Then we can decide whether to take the initiative or await events.

Me. At present the initiative probably rests with Scotland, but you're right, Master Vane; we must see where we stand before deciding where we go next. What reports do we have?

Sir Harry. Wentworth has told the Council the Spanish deal is dead. Apparently the King of Spain was prepared to pay Four Million ducats for Royal Navy escorts in the Channel, to protect Spanish transports from the Dutch. The Dutch rulers let it be known that if England helped Spain they would regard it as an act of war. The King and Council decided they could not afford to be at war with Holland and Scotland at the same time. In any case, the Spanish have chartered a lot of merchant ships from England to transport their soldiers, cannon and horses in the past, but the merchants don't want to do that now if there is more war with Holland. They see the Dutch as fellow Protestants.

Vane. They may also be worried about losing their ships, because the Dutch Navy is very strong. Look what they did to that Spanish fleet last autumn. The City of London won't want its trading vessels sunk.

Sir Harry. What I don't understand is how the Dutch found out about the Spanish offer.

Me. You told me; I told the Dutch Ambassador. *(There is a pause).*

Vane. No money from Spain, and none from Parliament! The King can't afford to be at war with anyone. And the mood of the people tends in our favour too. Mobs of seamen who don't want to fight, and of apprentices who don't want to join the army, have been rioting. They stormed Lambeth Palace, and Archbishop Laud had to escape by boat on the Thames. There've been more riots in Whitehall, and in other parts of the country. Complaints come in daily about the expense of the troop levies, and some officers have been murdered.

Sir Harry. The King's answer, which he gets from Strafford, is that this is all Parliament's fault. The nation is in danger from the Scots; Parliament refuses to provide the money or the Army, and the King must put the safety of his people first.

Me. But nobody is listening. The King is fighting the Scots because of his Prayer Book, which most of the English don't care for either. I don’t suppose Strafford cares one way or the other about that, but he believes the Monarch should be obeyed, and that means enforcing his own authority.

Vane. He certainly does that! He is fearless and won't be attended by a guard. He goes out amongst the people even in their violent mood. Black Tom they call him, and say “Black Tom has enough terror in his eyebrows to frighten the apprentices away”.

Sir Harry. When he’s well enough to go out. He was ill when he came back from Ireland. He was worse after Parliament was dissolved in May. He was so ill that the King himself visited him at his London house. How often does the King do that for anyone? But now he’s well again.

Me. And causing us more trouble. Why can’t he be ill again? The worse he gets the better I shall like it, though I’d prefer to see him die on the block. Well or ill, his situation is getting worse in Ireland. The Irish Commons has retreated on the subsidies it granted in March. They won't send money and an Army to help a King who can’t get a penny out of us.

Vane. Some say they only voted the subsidies because it was dangerous to defy Strafford. They won't pay if they no longer have any reason to be afraid of him.

Me. We’re are bringing him down, and the King with him. Thank the Lord the King did not call upon him sooner. If he’d had Strafford at his side in England in '37 when these Scottish troubles started, we’d all have been doomed.

Thomas. 25th July, 1640. Northumberland Place.

“You know the King is hunting down at Oatlands, Thomas?” Algie says. I am dining at his London house. He’s far from being a happy man.

“Yes, I’ve been summoned to see him when he rides into town.”

“You’d think he’d spend more time here consulting us and making plans. The quarrel with Scotland is going from bad to worse, as far as I can see.”

That makes me chuckle. “Well, if you don’t know, Algie, Commander of all the King’s Horses and all the King’s Men, I don’t know who does.”

"Trouble is, the way it's going I doubt the horses and men will be able to put the Kingdom together again. The news is dreadful. Recruitment for the army is going very slowly, and the men we get are not much use. Hardly any of them have used a weapon in anger before, and even fewer have any experience of battle or war. They won't have learned much from Buckingham back in the '20s."

If the Commander feels like that, how can he inspire the soldiers with loyalty and fighting spirit? "Are the Covenanters doing any better?"

Algie shakes his head in what appears to me to be something very like despair. "That's the trouble. All the intelligence I receive tells me that they are gathering huge forces, and many are highly experienced."

I smile. "Well, they've never stopped fighting amongst themselves, for one thing, have they? They get plenty of fighting practice."

"There's that, of course. But the serious point is, so many of them, and their officers, have come back from Germany and the Low Countries after fighting as mercenaries for the Dutch, the French, or the German princes against Spain and Austria. We have hardly anyone like that."

I am taken aback. "But surely they can't have that many men. England is much more heavily populated, isn't it?"

"True, but that doesn't mean thousands of Englishmen want to take up the sword against Scotland. Not over what they see as a Prayer Book and ritual many of them don't much care for themselves. In Scotland, I'm told, it's quite different. For them it's a matter of religious principle, and they believe in it. To win a war you need faith in what you're doing. As far as I can see our men do not have that driving need."

"I suppose they say; 'Why should I worry. Why should I die for the Prayer Book? Why should I care what happens in Scotland? It's not my homeland'. But we have to make this work, Algie. The King's authority will be lost if we lose, and then ours will be at risk too."

"You may be right, Thomas, but if we lose the war, we may lose it all anyway. As every Scots village - except the ones round Aberdeen, the Gordons - sends all the men and arms they can, and as the Dutch send them weapons, their army may be three times as large as ours, and better equipped. And with all these officers and soldiers back from Europe they have more skilled people to train them."

"What the devil have I come back to, my dear Algie?"

"You may well ask; you may well ask. If I knew, I'd tell you, but I don't."

I feel almost as depressed as Algie seemed when we started this conversation. "My friend Osborne in York tells me the squires and lords there are not raising the troops they are supposed to muster."

"And that's another thing, Thomas. What a difference in Edinburgh! My spies tell me the ladies – and I mean ladies – are side by side with working men and women carrying buckets of earth and stones to build up the city defences, and have used hundreds of sheets off their beds to make tents for the troops. Now I call that dedication, don't you?"

"Yes, but the King told me he's had a letter from the Earl of Montrose, who's fallen out with Argyle. When the Scottish Parliament met last month, and ignored Charles's Commissioner when he prorogued it, Montrose said it was unconstitutional for it to continue sitting. Argyle then arrested a lot of important Stewart leaders, and took action against the Ogilvys too, because they were supposed to be on the King's side. He burned Airlie Castle when Lady Ogilvy was there, but Lord Ogilvy and her son were with the King. She was heavily pregnant, and was driven out by Argyle's men, who looted the castle before torching it. Montrose is Ogilvy's cousin; he was beside himself with fury. That's what the King told me, Algie. His Majesty hopes the Covenanters are falling apart, and Montrose will join him."

"It would be nice to think so, wouldn't it? But I believe Argyle is just too strong. He's rounding up the small opposition, and has many more clans behind him, unto the death."

Algie Percy. 16th August, 1640. London.

The Council of War has to go North. It has to. On 1st August the Scots Army massed on the Border at Coldstream, not many miles from my home in Alnwick. Being an Earl on the Border may be very fine in times of peace, but it's the very devil when the Scots are on the war-path. It would be different if I had any confidence we could beat them, but I don't.

How often does someone like me say he's sorry he was right? And I was right about our army. It is in a dreadful state. I'm even sorrier that Thomas and the King were wrong. And Charles was wrong about the quarrel between Montrose and Argyle. Serious it may have been, but it did not stop Montrose and his men marching to join the Army on the Border. They are very strong. Then this morning a report came in to the Council from Lord Conway that the Scots are about to cross the Border and invade. Yet only a week ago Conway told us that they weren't strong enough to do so!

He says he won't be able to keep the Scots out of Newcastle, so I suppose he'll just abandon the place. What a tremendous start to the war that would be!! Thomas used to think Conway was a good commander. Well, he must be changing his mind now. I wondered what the King will do. He takes the devil of a lot of time to make up his mind about things sometimes. Some of the Councillors tried to talk him out of going there himself. They hardly dared say they don't know what good that will do, but that was the implication.

Charles isn't stupid, and he realised what they were hinting at. I have never seen him make a decision so quickly. He showed just a trace of anger – how he controls himself so well I do not know – and said he would join his army as soon as possible, and would leave in the next few days. He silenced the voices which wanted him to stay here. He can't be criticised for lack of bravery.

As for Thomas, he looks at every challenge as an opportunity. This challenge just looks like an invitation to a disaster to me.

Thomas. 24th August, 1640. Covent Garden.

I am packing – or at least, my housekeeper and manservant are packing for me. I'm leaving for York today. I'll take only two men; the smaller my party and the less baggage there is to move the faster we should be able to travel. At least the roads are dry at this time of year. The King left five days ago. He has been far from happy for some time with his problems with the Scots going from bad to worse, but Conway's news that they might be about to invade seemed to stiffen his resolve, and fill him with determination. He shocked a number of my fellow Councillors with his sudden announcement that he would travel North.

I should have gone with him if I could, but something unforeseen changed my plans since that Council meeting. I had intended to go over to Ireland so that I could muster ships to sail my army to Scotland.

Why do I have to muster ships? Because that idiot Hamilton hasn't sent me any. He's still messing about in the North Sea, but can't stop arms and ammunition coming across from Holland to the Scots, so he's wasting his time there, and doing nothing to help me. Sometimes I can't help wondering whether he isn't really on the Covenant side himself. That would explain why he seems so incompetent. With fellow commanders like him and Conway, it's hard to keep any optimism alive, but I shan't give up. I wrote to Conway giving him a roasting for his lack of back-bone.

Then, to put the lid on it, a few days ago, just before the King left, Northumberland stopped coming to the War Council saying he was ill. I wonder. He's been so despondent lately, perhaps the strain has made him ill. If he's really ill, he cannot lead the army, and if he's too depressed about it all, and can't face it when duty calls, he'd be no use anyway. I've been trying to buck him up for months, but it was no good.

So what happened? The King told me I have to go to York too. That means I can't go to Ireland, which means I cannot get my army to Scotland. We shall be weaker than I hoped. Today bad news and good news arrives. The Scots have crossed the River Tweed. It's bad because no-one wants their country invaded, but it is good news, too, because surely my countrymen will now rise up to expel the enemy, as they always have done for hundreds of years.

Yes, the enemy left Coldstream and crossed the Tweed. They are in England! I'm told young Montrose, at the head of the Scots army, showed his mettle. He got off his horse, plunged into the river, which had burst its banks after a lot of rain, and waded across calling his men to follow. And they did.

Can I be a hero like that? How I wish I could, but I doubt it. Montrose is what, twenty now? And fit as a flea, no doubt. I was born getting on for fifty years ago, I have had more torture from attacks of the stone, and I get gout at all the wrong times. Is there a right time to have it? If it's not that it's the flux, or both.

But I can't let that stop me. As I said, I won't give up. I had to stay here to write to George and Kit and tell them what has happened. Will they be able to send my army over? They don't have my strength; they may not be able to find boats and sailors, and bully people into doing the right thing. Of course, I had to attend to all sorts of business, personal and government, and let Elizabeth know that I cannot get home after all, before I could leave. Bess can never have guessed what a life she would end up living when she married me. How could she? I had no idea myself that I'd end up helping the King lead his army as well as being his chief councillor. And I'm not even a soldier, for all that I've tried to train my army.

Two nights ago I had dinner with Lucy. She was very kind. After we'd eaten she said I looked too tired for any 'games', and that as I was so busy, I should go home to bed. I wasn't all that sorry, either. I was debilitated, and felt impotent, and probably was. I cannot help wondering when I shall see her again.

Thomas. 26th August, 1640. York.

If I thought I was tired in London I must be almost inert now! I travel as far as Huntingdon on the 24th. I suffer another attack of the flux, and it even hurts me to breathe. The doctors wanted to take more of my blood, but I refused; I was weak enough already.

Today I arrive late in York and join the King. Almost before anyone says as much as "Hello" I'm told that the Scots have now marched from the Tweed to the Tyne. The King tells me he had a long meeting with a fair number of the local gentry yesterday, and they have now agreed to raise more troops and send them to prevent the Scots crossing the River Tees. That, of course, is a second line of defence. The first must be Newcastle and the Tyne. Anyway, winning the gentry over to that extent must count as a success, since only a week ago, in Council, the King was reading a Petition from them and other big landowners complaining about the cost of raising armed men, and demanding a new Parliament.

"I agreed to command the troops at the Tees, Strafford. I won them over by telling them that."

"What are your plans, Your Majesty?"

"Newcastle has to be held; we simply cannot afford to lose it. And we must stop the enemy crossing the Tyne, if they reach it."

"'Enemy' is a new view, Your Majesty. The Scots are your subjects too." That seems a bit blunt, even for me, but I smile as I say it.

"It is a rebel army. I do not believe it represents all my Scottish subjects, and if a rebel army is what it is, they are the enemy."

"If we can persuade the people of that, Sire, our hand will be much strengthened. I shall send out messengers tonight to summon the gentry who are in and around York to ask them to give you more assistance."

The King shakes his head rather despondently. "I can only wish you luck, then. I am not too hopeful about that. I have discovered there is a lot of local bad feeling because two of their MPs were arrested three months ago in all that trouble with Parliament. I also thought it pretty offensive to you that they sent their Petitions straight to me telling me they should not have to pay so much to send men to the army. They should have written to you; you're the Lord Lieutenant for Yorkshire, after all."

"I cannot afford to let that bother me. I have to try to persuade them to cooperate, but I may also resort to a bit of bullying. I think I can do it."

Thomas. 27th August, 1640. York.

I'm in the large hall at the King's residence. About forty local nobles, squires, and other landowners are before me. Someone starts off by telling me they hardly know me now, as I have been away from Yorkshire for so long. I tell them that I keep a close eye on the county through Sir Edward Osborne, and as they do not doubt that, I can go on to the main business of this gathering. I find I'm slipping back a little into the way I used to speak when I lived here, before I went to University and London.

"Like most of you, I'm a Yorkshireman, so you don't expect a lot of nice ambiguous talk from me, saying a lot and meaning nowt. I'll tell it straight, just as you do." If I talk to them in their own language they may take me more seriously than if I talk like what they would call "one o' them Southern nincompoops," with an emphasis on the last syllable.

"Now is not the time for disputes with your King. Now is the time for preparation and action. I'm not afraid to say that it is treason for anyone to refuse to help the King at this time. Such a refusal is, in truth, a betrayal of England. If the Scots defeat us, what happens to your land, your homes, your families? Loyal men - and that, I'm sure, is what you are - will strain every sinew to give His Majesty any and everything he may need, anything he may demand. That kind of disciplined attitude is what is needed now.

"We are bound to do this by the Common Law of England, and nature, and reason itself, to do all we can to defend England from its invaders – and that is what they are. If any one of you fails in this, then he is no better than a beast. Bear in mind that His Majesty offers in person to lead you. If he will do that, will you do less for yourselves, for your families, your land, and your motherland?

"In the name of the King, who has instructed me to promise – he has promised – that when this war is over, the law will be changed to relieve you of the burdens of providing military service, but there, is, as you must realise, no time for that now."

Thank the Lord they are persuaded. They will help.

I shall return to the King and tell him that we must hold Newcastle at all costs, and that we should set off with what forces we have here at once.

* * * *

The King is on the road, and I am in bed. When I left the meeting I had another severe attack of the flux. I wanted to ride to join Conway and help him to protect Newcastle and prevent the Scots crossing the Tyne. The King forbade it. He said: "I fear for you, Strafford. I fancy you are near death, and to be as blunt as you normally are, I cannot afford to lose you. That is just the selfish view. You have a young wife and a younger family. To lose you is something they can afford even less than I can."

"But your Majesty, I can do it. I want to do it. I want to be with you. I want to help Conway build up his defences. He has to stop them crossing the river whatever happens. If they cross, our army may not be able to resist retreating - fleeing, even. So many of them have only just joined. They have no battle-hardened spirits to toughen them. If I am there – if we are there together, we can inspire them."

"I am your King and this is my command, and you will obey. You will - yes, will - take to your bed for at least two days. You will look after yourself for a minimum of two days, you will rest, and then, and only then, you can follow me and we shall confront the enemy, and inspire the troops together. Is my order clear?"

"Only too clear, Sire, but ..."

"But me no buts, Wentworth. I must go, and cannot stay to debate this with you. Think what our plight would be if you make an effort which kills you. What help could you be to Conway then? You are my rod, my staff, here on earth. I need you with me, not in your coffin." The King turns on his heel and is gone.

I obey. I go straight to bed, and call my secretary. I dictate a letter to Conway reiterating what I had told him earlier, that he must fight the Scots, prevent them crossing the river, and defend Newcastle come what may. I also tell him to "take the advice of the best men and do something worthy of yourself. The King is on his way, and I shall join you as soon as I shake off this bout of sickness."

I'd like to tell him not to hesitate or procrastinate, but offending him is not what I'm about. I just want him to be courageous. If he is not, how can we hope his men will be brave? The letter is dispatched at once by a messenger.

Thomas. 29th August, 1640. York.

It is early morning. I am woken by the shouting of many men and the clatter of horses hooves. Thank God I feel better than I did two days ago. I rise from my bed to dress as rapidly as I can. I cannot do it. I cannot make my way downstairs, but have to go back to bed. A servant tells me the house is full of dirty, mud-spattered men soaked in perspiration. It is impossible for him to sort out from the many who are talking and yelling all at the same time what has happened, but I am able to gather at last that there has been some sort of fighting. The detail escapes me until in mid-morning one of the commanders, Sir Jacob Astley, gallops into the court-yard.

I have him shown straight in to me. He sits on the edge of my bed; I tell a servant to bring him a drink, and some food. He is tiny, and as filthy, hot and sweaty as all the men are, but he exudes authority. He says he's famished and thirsty and asks for ale. He has a terrible tale to tell.

"We were camped on the river at Newburn, which is the only crossing point, a ford, near to Newcastle on the west side. Conway was there, too, some defences constructed, but they weren't finished."

"Why hadn't he done that before?"

"We got your letter. He read it out, but it had come too late. Meant nothing in the circumstances, for as Conway read it to us, a soldier came in and told us that the Scots were crossing the ford. One brave but foolhardy young officer led his men forward to attack, but was driven off quickly. Conway ordered the men to fire, but that didn't stop them coming at us. Their General Leslie had a cannon taken up into the Tower of the Church in Newburn village, and firing from there drove us back from the ford so his men could get across. Conway decided we should retreat. Gave the order. Sent a some cavalry into the attack, but their charge was defeated, and their Captain was taken prisoner. When the Scots pursued in good formation, the troops abandoned their earthwork and fled."

I'm not surprised to hear that. "Exhausted men have been riding into York all night, Sir Jacob. Now I understand why."

"A number of officers and men were captured. The hills and valleys are full of infantry-men running as fast as their legs will carry them."

"What about Newcastle. Can it be defended? Why weren't the defences fully reinforced?"

"There just wasn't enough money."

There's a knock at the door and Hamilton comes in. I don't know what he wants so I send Astley away. "I was asking him about Conway's defences for Newcastle. He looked quite angry."

"He's a friend of Conway's, Strafford, so if he thinks you're attacking his friend he'll resent it. Anyway, I'm not here to talk about that, but what's going on with the navy." And he does, for about twenty minutes. I express little interest, since he can't help me bring the Irish army over at the moment, I really want to talk about Newcastle, and I need Astley back in here. Eventually Hamilton leaves, and I send for Astley again. I'm in quite a temper, what with Astley defending Conway and Hamilton wasting my time.

I invite him to sit. "Finish telling me about the battle."

He takes a huge swig from his beer mug, wipes the back of his hand over his lips and says: "Not much more to tell. Not that I know of, anyway."

"Let's go back to the defence of Newcastle. Surely something could have been done?"

"Look, Wentworth, no-one foresaw that the Scots would go to Coldstream and march round Berwick. What money there was had been spent on fortifying Berwick."

"No point in going into that, then; the milk's spilt. Can Conway defend the Tyne at Newcastle?"

"Not a chance. Leslie's an excellent commander – we've fought together. Will have his army there before we can put artillery in place. No time to build any earthworks there now. Newcastle is as good as lost."

"Then there's only one question, Astley, isn't there. Should we take this army and head for Newcastle to reinforce Conway's, or go to fight the Scots somewhere else without him?"

That is a tough question even for a truly experienced soldier like him, but he hardly takes any time to consider it. "We must go and join up with Conway."

I don't know what it is, the excitement, the possibility of glory, or the fear of death on the battlefield, or all three, but my illness seems to have vanished. I shout for a servant to get my horse, and I get up, and dress. After a very quick and early lunch we are in the saddle.

* * * *

We have travelled about forty-five miles since noon, and are camped at Darlington. The King is here already with his army. My forces are on their way from York, but they are marching, not riding. By tomorrow evening I hope that, between us, we shall have about 12,500 men, including cavalry, in this small town.

Thomas. 31st August, 1640. Northallerton.

Today we have retraced our steps to Northallerton. It's a small town about thirteen or so miles south of Darlington. Why did we do that? Because yesterday the most appalling news came from Lord Conway. He brought the news himself. He had decided that as he could not defend Newcastle he would vacate it, and that is what he did. He loaded the town's store of gunpowder onto ships, together with as many of his troops as could get aboard, sailed down the Tyne, out to sea, and came ashore down the coast to join us. The majority of his soldiery had to march by road with their artillery to Durham, avoiding being trapped and ambushed by Leslie's Scots advancing through Gateshead, on the South side of Newcastle.

Later that day, Conway's spies had reported, Leslie's army entered Newcastle without a blow being struck, and were welcomed by the townsfolk. Leslie was apparently amazed that he had encountered no resistance. That was yesterday. Today, with Conway's men added to our own, the King now has around 17,000 men under his command. Nevertheless, he seems to be leaving a lot to me.

I have the army parade before me and the King and I address them in as inspirational a fashion as I can muster. I urge them to stand by their King, and their country, and their families, and above all their own honour and valour. It's no use to tell them that running away from Newburn and Newcastle was not the thing to do. In any case, I hint that they had no choice but to leave Newcastle as that's what they were ordered to do, but with the King at their head, they would be capable of better things now. I felt that there was a positive response, but that may be wishful thinking.

I then call all the senior officers to me. I lecture them on the state of the armies that have gathered, and on the lack of training, which is their responsibility. I order them to conduct strict training schedules at once. Then I issue orders that patrols are to be sent from here to the coast, and from here another thirty miles to the West, to seek out every mill they can find, and have the grinding stones destroyed. I explain that we have to deprive the Scots of any means of feeding themselves. That seems like a strange order, taking into account that if we drive the enemy back to Scotland we shall have no method of grinding our own corn, but I rely on the fact that supplies will come up from the South by road and ship.

After all this I feel unwell again and retire to bed to write to Bess, and to sleep.

Thomas. 2nd September, 1640. Northallerton.

"To sleep, perchance to dream"? Not a hope. I hardly slept, although my quarters are very comfortable. The King's distant cousin Richard Metcalfe is our host in his large thatched house, where I am also staying. It is an interesting and typically Tudor place, being of timber and lath and plaster. The oak is grey and the plaster whitewashed. On one beam in the main hall is carved the legend "RM & MM 1584," for Richard and his wife Margaret; curiously the R is back-to-front.

I've waited all day for news that my Irish soldiers have been brought over, but there is no such news. Hamilton has failed as usual. If the Irish could come at the Scots from behind we could trounce them. Without that the outlook is bleak.

I hear the sounds of soldiers drilling, firing at targets, and being put through their paces in training. I hope it makes a difference. I have ordered the generals and officers that their main task is to defend and hold the Yorkshire county boundary against the Scots. I hear that they are now advancing South without any opposition.

I am cast down. After dinner I go to my room to write to Sir George.

Dear Cousin Radcliffe,

Pity me, for never came any man to so mightily lost a business. The army altogether unexercised and unprovided for. The troops newly arrived from Durham with Lord Conway are the worst I ever saw. Our cavalry are all cowardly, the country from Berwick to the Yorkshire Border in the power of the Scots, universal fright in all the men, a general disaffection with serving the King, and no-one concerned for his dishonour. In one word, I'm here alone with none to help.

Most of the officers are slothful, reluctant, or dimwitted, and sometimes all three. Hamilton's conduct I fail to understand. I begin to think that he does not want me to get our Irish Army into this fight. There are rumours that he may in truth be on the Covenant side.

I have given offence to a few veteran commanders by demanding that a gallows be constructed in front of every regimental HQ in the camps to warn the men that disobedience will be harshly punished. If these officers had done their work efficiently there would be no need for this. I have to make it clear that my control over the army really counts. If they had instilled discipline I should not have to do it, but at least in that I seem to be succeeding.

God of his goodness deliver me out of this, the greatest evil of my life.

Fare you well,
Thomas.

And then before I can get to bed, the pain begins. I have another attack of the stone. I pass out from the pain, and when I come to my senses, I am writhing in agony on the floor. I cry out; I scream. My manservant comes running. He fetches my physician. Neither can do a thing to relieve my suffering. It lasts an hour or two, but seems to last a life-time.

Charles I. 3rd September, 1640. Northallerton.

Yesterday I received a Remonstrance from that unholy alliance of

Pym and Oliver St. John, but signed by a gaggle of Earls – including Warwick - and other peers, blast them. It raises the same complaints which Pym spoke about in the Parliament earlier in the year. It goes on yet again about objections to changes in worship; the allegation that I show preferences to Catholics; objections to my selling monopolies; and of course, Ship Money. But they have added something new: they beg me not to allow Irish troops to be brought over from Ireland.

How shall I deal with this? I must see Wentworth. He was very ill last night, or I should have seen him then, but I shall call on him now. I hope he is well enough to deal with it. I need the Lords on my side; at least, those who are not already lending moral support to the Scots! Only twelve of them signed the Remonstrance; that's a tiny proportion of the House of Lords.

I find Strafford – I must get used to calling him that – he's been the Earl for nine months. I find Strafford up, but looking very pale and tired out. We sit in his room. He is dressed but looks as though he should be back in bed. He tells me he had another bout of the stone, and says he would not wish it on his worst enemy, not even on Cork or Pym! Even I can laugh at that.

I hand him the Remonstrance. He reads it quickly, and then again. The speed at which he works astounds me, and he makes his decisions just as rapidly. "This is rather strong stuff, Your Majesty. Look at how it starts: 'Your whole Kingdom is become full of fear and discontent'. Pym is trying to separate you from your peers. It's what he tried to do, I thwarted and he then did again in May. What they are aiming at is to get you to call another Parliament."

"We know what will happen then; just what happened last time. Pym and his friends will get the apprentices and other London mobs out to terrify everyone into doing what Pym wants, and hardly any MP or peer who thinks as we do will dare show his face, let alone vote against Pym."

"Then don't have a Parliament in London, Sire. Call a Council of Peers to meet in York. Let us return to York, and send out summonses to the Lords to attend you in a Council in York. Give the summonses a week to reach them, and give them two weeks to prepare and make the journey."

"But why, Strafford? What's the advantage?"

"In York you do not get London mobs frightening anyone, and you keep the Lords apart from the MPs, because you don't ask the Commons to come. We should – you and I – be able to keep, or at any rate get, most of them on our side."

I ponder that for a moment or two. "Well, calling the Council is an idea the Privy Council in London has put to me. It would certainly be a useful move, wouldn't it? After all, the peers are the richest men in the land, and can help financially ..."

"If they want to, Sire." Strafford mutters. "They haven't been too willing to hand over much cash so far, but they should see that if you lose your power, theirs will go with it. And if enough of them are with you, they may be able to control the Commons at the next Parliament, and not the other way round."

"They are a huge influence on the way the counties and the Justices are run, too. Yes, let us return to York quickly, and send out writs to the peers to attend there, let's say on the 24th. That should be plenty of time."

"I'll go now and give the order to break camp and march tomorrow, Sire," Strafford says, as he rises from his chair.

I get up faster. I put my hand on his shoulder and push him back into his seat. "There's something else. This business about the Irish army. I had a message from the Queen a few days ago. She knew the Remonstrance was on its way to me, and she knew it referred to the Irish troops. She says the Londoners are infected with the idea that we shall turn the Irish – the barbaric Irish, they say, onto them and other Englishmen."

"That is pure fantasy, Sire. I've said all along that I want them in Scotland to fight the Scots. I've said all along that I want Hamilton to provide ships to get them there, and he is doing nothing. My soldiers are still Ireland, and there's precious little hope of getting them to Scotland in the near future, if at all. In any case, can you see English tars landing Irish Catholic troops in English ports? They'd rather scuttle the ships with the Irish on board and watch them drown." He starts to get up again. "I must go and give the orders."

"No you will not. You will stay here and rest. You need your strength to ride back to York, and I can call the officers and have them give the orders." It looks as though he's going to get up again and protest. I hold up my hand to stop him. "You will do as you are told, man. I told you before that you are more use to me alive than dead. I want you with me in York as soon as possible." He subsides, and I go to give the orders.

I stop at the door. "By the way, there's some good news. Apparently a large store of gunpowder and other military equipment at Dunglass blew up, and at least one senior enemy commander – Haddington – was killed. This has halted the Scottish advance for a while, but I dare say they'll recover and be on the move again soon. As well as that, I'm told the people of Newcastle have already had enough of their Scots guests. The invaders have been so cock-a-hoop about their victory and the cowardice of the English that they have offended almost everyone. Nobody really wants an occupation force in their city, do they? It means that Englishmen generally are about to rally to the flag. I always knew they would."

Thomas. 24th September, 1640. York.

It's been a busy three weeks. I felt a good bit better the day after the King's visit. We left for York that day. The next few days were spent organizing the writs to the Peers summoning them to the Council, and in extra training for the army, ensuring stores and weapons were coming in, and getting reports on General Leslie's manoeuvres. Not only that, but we have had a lot of messages and visitors from Durham and Northumberland saying that the invaders have been looting and stirring up a lot of animosity in the people, which can only serve our interests.

The King signed the writs on the 7th. Three days later he reviewed the army in a huge parade of 2,000 cavalry and 16,000 infantry. They certainly look a lot better than they were wont to do, thanks to the work Sir Jacob Astley and I have been doing with them, but I do not think they deceive me, and certainly not the real professionals, that they are a potentially victorious fighting army. However, the King played his part well, riding up and down the lines, talking to individuals, and exhorting them all to do their very best. They appeared to enjoy that.

Then a few days later I was called to a meeting with about two hundred of the gentry of the county. They handed me a Petition. It said that as they had been asked to find another month's money for the soldiers they had provided, they would only pay if the King called another Parliament. I spoke to them with some anger.

I called on their loyalty. I told them that I could not hand the Petition to the King if it asked for a Parliament. I said that the King was calling a Parliament, but I did not tell them that in fact it was only the Lords as a Council. I said they could not demand an election as summoning Parliament was exclusively a matter for the King.

I told them all I was doing and sacrificing for King and Country, and someone shouted out "You're just telling us you're better than we are," which I'm sorry to say got a laugh. Despite that, whilst a few continued to argue that the request for Parliament should stand, most of them agreed to drop it, so I took them in to see the King. The King told them that if they paid up for the next few weeks he would have the law changed when Parliament met. He'd cut the military demands on Yorkshire in half, and then he made an offer they - and I - did not expect. He said that if any of them should be killed in the war, the Crown would not claim the wardship of their children. That was an amazingly generous offer, as the right to administer wardships or sell them to others was a huge source of Crown income and a huge cause of annoyance and expense to these people.

There was one event of enormous importance to me. On the 13th of this month I was called to a Chapter of the Knights of the Garter, where the King had me elected a member, and installed me there and then. I cannot say how overjoyed I was. As far as I know it is the oldest order of chivalry in the world, and a very select band of the people the King values most. I cannot think of a greater honour.

I have to say, though, that the edge was slightly taken off my pleasure by being brought before the King by the Earl of Holland and the Marquis of Hamilton, who are far from being my supporters of choice, but my resentment vanished when I received the blue garter from the King. As soon as I got to my accommodation I wrote to tell Bess of my good fortune.

There was some celebrating in camp by a few professional soldiers a few days after that when a young officer, Captain Smith, rode into York with a small number of Scottish prisoners. He and his troop had ambushed some of the invaders who had ventured on a raid not far away, having crossed the River Tees, and had defeated them. I joined in the celebrations, and noted that the King was very buoyed up by this, as he had been by the news of the discontent in the Northern counties at the conduct of the Scots army. Nevertheless, I am beginning to despair.

I look at the state of our men, still badly in need of training; I look at the snail's pace at which money comes into the King's coffers. I worry that the discontented people may be unhappier with the King's Prayer Book policies than with the Scots. I hear that country-folk are saying that Smith is a Catholic, and he's no business fighting the Scots. I cannot tell anyone how I feel. I went far enough with my letter to Radcliffe. I put on a brave face and try to give the men confidence and courage. They care nothing for Smith's victory. I know that the King will not contemplate abandoning his religious plans, and will not give way over anything much other than temporarily to gain time. He was told that a Petition is coming up from London asking for a new Parliament. He said he'd have the men who bring it thrown in prison, and there would be no Parliament.

Then he changed his mind. News came in that a week ago Edinburgh Castle had been surrendered with only one shot being fired. Mind you, it was a lucky shot over two months ago, and it hit the castle water supply. Just like a ship at sea with no decent water or fresh food, men suffered with scurvy. Men died; men were ill; men lost their teeth, including the governor, Lord Ruthven, and he lost all of his. The castle could not hold out any longer, and if all the men died, the castle would fall anyway. I thought Ruthven showed remarkable leadership that he suffered precisely the same degree of discomfort that his men had to endure. The Scots captured Carlaverock Castle, too.

These blows have a heavy effect on the King, and when the Petitioners from London turned up two days ago, he agreed to see them. He even let them infer from what he said, that he would call Parliament.

Today the Council of Peers assembles in the hall of the Deanery. That must be a shock to the Petitioners from London. The hall is gloriously hung with some of the most exquisite arrases I have ever seen.

Thomas. 12th October, 1640. York.

The King announced early on to the Peers that he had called a new Parliament which he would open on 2nd November. In spite of that the Council got off to a rather bad start, and never really got any better, at least from my point of view. I had not been in favour of this war from the outset, as my letters to Windebanke and others showed over the last few months. The King's army was ill prepared, and there was no chance that the Irish army could be brought in without ships. I was not keen on a formal treaty with the enemy, but I thought the King would be right to play for time. A truce so that talks could be held would be the way forward for the time being.

The King opened the proceedings last month by asking the Lords how to deal with the Scots' request for redress of grievances, and how to find the money to pay his army until Parliament met in six weeks time. Their answer to the first question was that the two sides would have to negotiate and the King would have to act on the advice he received after the talks. Their answer to the second was that they would put up some money, but it was clear they were reluctant. It seemed to me they would rather the King did not have an army at all.

The Council was led by a group of Lords who wielded a lot of influence, and they wanted another peace treaty. One of them was Lord Bristol, who was on such good terms with the Covenanters that he seemed to be their personal messenger. He played that role to such an extent that I referred to him as "their Mercury." A god with winged feet he was not, but the pro-treaty men got their way.

A truce was agreed upon so that negotiations could occur. The next task of the Council was to choose a team of negotiators. This went badly for me and the King. The Council chose men who were almost all in favour of getting a treaty, so there was little chance of a hard line being taken to ensure that its terms were in England's interests, let alone the King's. Selecting these people took up two or three days at the start of the Council. This process was held up when it was discovered that a letter had been sent to the Covenanters apparently signed by several Lords who were, for the most part, amongst those desirous of a treaty. When the meeting was told of this letter, many of the Lords whose names were on it were rather shocked, and denied they had signed any such message.

It turned out that this document was the work (as I might well have imagined it would be) of young Savile, now a Lord, the son of my old adversary Sir John Savile, and certainly not the son of my sister Anne. Of course, it created the impression amongst the Scots that the English were much readier to treat for peace than was in fact the case with the King. He wanted to maintain the pretence, as realistically as possible, that he was ready to fight there and then.

Our negotiators, or Commissioners, as we called them, were mainly men who argued against the King's Prayer Book policy for Scotland, largely because they did not care for the Church reforms being imposed in England, so they saw the Scots as religious allies. Most of these men were also my personal enemies for various reasons, many of which I have indicated already.

The Council agreed to ask the Scots to send their representatives to York to hold the talks. They refused. They said the men they had sent to London were threatened with arrest, and that a rumour had reached them that in early in September the King had talked of arresting the Londoners who had come to York to ask for a Parliament. In view of that, they believed the King might have them arrested when they set foot in York. They added that as "we know that the Earl of Strafford is with the King, is ill-disposed towards our nation, and has had our Covenant supporters in Ireland arrested as traitors, we apprehend that he will deal with us in similar fashion".

Even I could see that this was not an entirely unreasonable point of view, especially as our whole army was billeted and bivouacked around the city, whereas they could only send in a number of their own negotiators with a small escort, and their army was on the other side of the Yorkshire border at the far end of the county.

The Scots took so long to reach agreement about this one opening point that many of us began to doubt whether they really wanted to hold talks at all. If they could take days to agree on a meeting place, how long would they take over the important terms, let alone the fine detail? Would they lull us into a false sense of security, and then attack us?

Subtly I did all I could to encourage these ideas, but I was not subtle enough. Four days after the Council opened Lord Bristol attacked me. "It seems to me, My Lord Strafford, that you are doing your best to drive a wedge between us and the Scots, to abort any talks. Kindly be plain with us. If the Scots insist they will not come to York, are you for ending all talks with them?"

Now that was a hard question, and needed some thought, so I did not reply immediately. He tried a different approach. "If the truce and the talks end, can the army fight?" That was not only a hard question; it was ambiguous into the bargain. Did he mean "Will you or the King order them to fight?" Or did he mean "If they fight will they win?"

Again I had to think about an appropriate reply. I could hardly say that I would order them to fight, when I had for months been arguing that we needed to play for time. Nor could I say, "The army is in no condition to fight"; or "I'd order them to fight but they would probably lose." At this point the King interrupted to ask Bristol to clarify his questions, and while he was doing that I indicated that I was able to answer. "My Lord Bristol, I am as ready to negotiate as any man, provided honourable terms are what is in question, but if no such terms are offered or can be agreed, the King must stand upon his honour, and if that means battle so be it, though the decision is his. We have an army of 16,000 foot and 2,000 cavalry, and they are being trained hard, and are well equipped, and supplies are getting more plentiful. On the other hand, we believe that Leslie's Scots are 20,000 strong, and he has 60 cannon. As for the army's chances of winning, I have the honour to be a member of His Majesty's Privy Council but I am not the Almighty, to be able to foretell the outcome of war in advance."

I had no intention of giving any hostages to fortune by provoking a fight I did not believe we could win at that stage. On the other hand I thought it vital that the King's position as against the Scots should not be undermined by making it look as though neither he nor I had any intention of fighting if we had to. As I sat down Bristol turned to the gallery and said: "He explains all" with such sarcasm as is hard to imagine if you were not there.

In the end a compromise was reached. The King's army would stay in York; the treaty would be dealt with in Ripon, a lovely small city with its own beautiful cathedral, in the North of the County, and therefore closer to the Scots' own camp.

George Radcliffe. 14th October, 1640. Dublin.

The Irish Parliament met here on 1st October. I wish Christopher had not had to call it. Since Thomas left for England evidence of discontent has emerged from so many sources it hardly seems like the same country. Thomas held it all in his hand, but once his hand was taken away, all sorts of people began to voice their complaints.

The main reason it was necessary to recall Parliament was the cost of keeping the Army on foot. It is not popular, partly because it has so many Catholics in it, but mainly because of the cost. Christopher cannot afford to disband or reduce it. The Ulster Scots have always been a problem, but since they heard from their cousins that they won the Battle of Newburn and have forced the King into an armistice, they have become insufferable. If we had no army, we should be likely to perish. If Thomas had the ships to take them to Scotland, as he had planned, I cannot think how we should manage. Christopher does not have his strength, his ability to subdue anyone and everyone. Neither do I.

I have called to see Christopher. I say: "I have to say I'm worried about Thomas's state of mind. I've had the most peculiar letter from him."

"I've had a letter from him, too, George. He says: '*At the Council meetings in York the King told the assembly he had called for an election for Parliament to meet on 2nd November. The peers had demanded that he do so. His Majesty also asked the City of London for a loan; they replied that they would put up 200,000 pounds. I have told the King with that money we should be able to take some action against the Scots if necessary, though I am still reluctant to fight until the army is in a readier state*'."

"Yes, he told me all that too, but this is the worrying bit:

'I am worried about the possibility that if we act against the Scots, their countrymen in Ireland will take the opportunity while we are engaged here in the North to inflict damage upon us in Ulster. They could stage an uprising which it would take the Irish troops to control, thus taking them out of the equation for coming over to Scotland to catch the rebels in a pincer movement as the King advances from the South. Without them the King's force is slightly outnumbered, and as our men are less experienced than the rebels, we need all the strength we can muster.

'What to do? I have given it a lot of thought. I want you to take immediate action to drive the Scots out of Ulster. Use small contingents of troops to seize their farms and lands, make it hard for them to trade. Find reasons to arrest and prosecute them, and keep their leaders locked up as long as possible, or deport them.'

What do you think, Christopher?"

"I think he must be under terrible strain. He told me that everyone seems to be against him, and the King does hardly anything to support him. I think it's a crazy idea."

"Exactly. It is crazy. If we do this, the uprising he fears will happen for certain. It won't be just a possibility; it'll be guaranteed. And even if it succeeded, what would happen then? Where are all these Scots going to go? A few might head for New England, I suppose, but most would just go to Scotland and reinforce the rebels. Then if the Scots win, they'll come back here, and we'd have hell on earth. As the Irish Army is mainly Catholic, the hatred between the settlers and the Irish would get even worse."

Christopher nods, and says: "Quite. We need more harmony here, not less."

"Very well. If we're agreed I shall write to Thomas and tell him we shall not act on this at all."

Christopher looks worried. "Yes, you must write to him. Such a letter won't help his state of mind, though, will it? I wrote to him only yesterday to tell him that I seem to have lost control of the House of Commons here. Sir John Clotworthy has stirred up a great deal of bad feeling, saying his wife was imprisoned by Tom when there was trouble in Ulster with the Presbyterians. I don't think I can even rely on the Old English to provide enough support to keep Tom's policies alive."

Charles I. 20th October, 1640. York,

The Council of Peers ended on 18th October. Today I leave for London, to open Parliament on 2nd November. These last two or three weeks have been tumultuous here in the Council of Peers. My Lord Strafford has been under almost constant attack, and I can do little to defend him. If I do not do so, it looks as though I do not support him, and that he and I do not agree on the Scottish policy. If I defend him, then the extremely unpopular phase through which he is passing will just attach itself to me. I have seen since leaving London two months ago that this war and I are not popular anyway. I cannot afford to make it worse.

I think Strafford understands that. He advocated taking action against the Scots, though he stopped short of making it clear what he had in mind. His ideas strike a sympathetic chord with some of their lordships. Lord Herbert, for example, beseeched me to strengthen the defences here at York, call off the negotiations for a treaty, and re-launch the war. In many ways that was attractive to me, since I cannot bear the way in which my Royal authority is being flouted, but I cannot ignore the fact that for months Strafford advised me to avoid fighting until I was in a position of strength. His aggressive posturing was not for my benefit, but to keep the flame of resistance burning, and stop the Scots thinking we are in a weak state.

His attitude was undermined by Lord Bristol. "You rely, My Lord Strafford, on the 200,000 pound loan from the City; it was not furnished for the war, but to fund peace talks, and to induce His Majesty to call Parliament, which he has done. Specifically, the City money is to be advanced on the basis it will pay the Scots during the armistice, and for no other purpose. If you try to use it for battle, the City will not pay it."

As a result, negotiations with the enemy (my own countrymen, for God's sake!) went on, and a few days ago I asked for Scots Commissioners to go to London to ratify the treaty when it has been before Parliament. I was forced to agree that the Scottish Army could remain in occupation of the Northern counties, namely Northumberland, Durham, Cumberland, Westmoreland, and Lancashire. They are living off the land and the local people. It is humiliating.

I had to risk further humiliation for Strafford by doing something to strengthen my hand in Ireland. I felt I could not continue to oppress loyal landowners whose support I might need, so I called in Ulick de Burgh, Earl of Clanricarde and St Albans, to meet me and Strafford. It was a long meeting, and rather acrimonious. Burke wanted his land returned; Strafford wanted to pursue the plantation policy in Galway. They were irreconcilable positions. After about two hours of their verbal fisticuffs, I told them both that Clanricarde's estates in Galway were safe from being taken away from him to be planted with settlers. He was relieved. Strafford was downcast. I was not without sympathy for him; he had worked very hard on this, and it was, after all is said and done, my policy. In truth, he was only my agent.

There was another side to this, which I did not mention to either of these men, though Clanricarde may well have been aware that it would influence me. That was his half brother, the Earl of Essex. Essex was one of the most outspoken of my critics and opponents. If I continued to let Strafford hound Clanricarde, Essex might have been even more implacable that he already was.

During the meeting of the Council a day or so after that, Strafford was again savaged by Lord Bristol. "You are the man who has done more than any other to orchestrate this war, and bring it about," he said. I suppose I should have intervened and pointed out that Strafford was in Ireland until recently, and had no part in promoting my Prayer Book and Laud's rituals in England or Scotland. For the reasons I gave earlier, I said nothing. Strafford made a reply in much those terms, but if I had done so it would have been more effective.

Bristol then said: "You have boasted of your Irish Army. You have boasted that it would trounce the Scots. Where is it? Why have you not brought it?"

Strafford was angry. "My Lord Bristol, the army is ready and waiting in Ireland for the Admiral of the Fleet, the Earl of Hamilton, to send ships into the Irish Sea to collect those troops and sail them over to Scotland. Do you expect them to swim? Do I have a navy? Do I have ships sufficient? No, no, and no."

I interrupted at this point. I could not let one of my commanders openly criticise another in such a public forum. It looked as though I was siding with the attack on Strafford, but that was not my intent. On the other hand I had appointed Strafford as Commander of my Army, and he was left to bear Bristol's accusations without my support. This dreadful scene was brought to an end by some gentlemen from two of the occupied counties arriving with their share of the money – 850 pounds a day – the Council of Peers had agreed to pay the Scots,hoping this would stop Scots marauders robbing and pillaging farms for food and other supplies.

By that stage the writs had gone out for an election, and I was preparing to leave York for London. The day the Council met for the last time the most ludicrous allegations were made against Strafford. I did not defend him this time either. Some derided him for being the author of the Treaty with the Scots from which they got all they wanted, and England got nothing – except to halt the enemy advancing further into the country. Without realising that they were then accusing him of completely opposite wrongs, others said he had been the one who had advised me to go to war, and then had been so hopeless as a general, that he had engineered victory for the Scots.

He kept his temper. "When I arrived in York, and went North to join the fighting, the battle was already lost. I was not in charge at Berwick, or Newburn, or Newcastle. I would to God I had been, for then the result might have been a success, but if it had been a failure under my command, then at least your current criticism would have some justification. As it is, it is just the carping of cowards who have done nothing to help the King or the country in the hour of need. As for the Treaty, it may have escaped your notice that I was not one of the Commissioners. You selected them, and His Majesty appointed the men you had chosen. If they let you down, you have only yourselves to blame. It is no use pointing the finger at me."

He was quite right, of course, but that made him no friends. They have decided that he is the enemy.

Damocles' Sword?

Thomas. 20th October, 1640. York.

I am seated with the King in a chamber in the King's House.

Me. *(Determined).* It would be crazy for me to stay here in York and then accompany you to London. I'm needed in Ireland.

King. *(Equally determined).* Not as much as I need you here.

Me. The Irish Parliament has gone mad, Sire. I must go back to restore order. And what about the Army? They were assembled to go to Scotland, but Hamilton did nothing to get the ships to Ulster to ferry them across. The Army may rebel too unless I'm there to prevent it.

King. For the time being the Scots are the victors, Thomas. The real seat of power is not here in York, nor in Ireland, but in London. Unless we are there we can do nothing worthwhile.

Me. Sire, forgive my being blunt, but –

King. *(Wryly, with a smile).* Aren't you always? My Army has lost every skirmish but one, or run away! They couldn't hold Newcastle, and then ran away before your reinforcements could reach them.

Me. *(With resignation and a sigh).* I should have been there sooner.

King. You were ill with the Flux!! You still rode to Newcastle as soon as you were sent for. It was hardly your fault the Army had become a rabble, fleeing in all directions.

Me. I am Your Majesty's servant, and I should have been there, but at present I can serve you best by returning to Ireland.

King. I shall not yield on this, Thomas. Your place is with me in London, not Dublin. The war is lost. We must deflect the people's wrath away from me –

Me. *(Cynically)* - and on to me!!

King. If we don't do that, my position will be impossible, and yours will be worse.

Me. Sire, if I come to London I shall be impeached. You know this. I know this. And if impeachment succeeds the penalty ....

King. *(Nodding).* May be death.

Me. I do not fear death, Sire, but I have a young family, and I'm reluctant to think I may never see them again. *(Pause).* The Duke of Hamilton says I ought to leave the country.

King. He thinks that if you stay, you will take the blame for his mistakes,

Me. Oh, I think not! He may *say* that's what he thinks, but people will ask why I fled. They'll conclude that all the guilt attaches to me, and I won't be here to argue about it. Hamilton will look blameless.

King. He is too honourable to want that. After all, it was his failure to sail to Ulster to fetch your Irish troops which made your efforts here useless. I could not say that to the Peers and undermine him, but it is true nevertheless.

Me. But if no-one says so, and if I flee, who will know that?

King. *(With finality).* Hamilton is one of my oldest friends as well as one of my Councillors. I cannot believe he thinks like that, and I don't want to hear it.

Me. *(Resignedly).* Very well. *(Pause).* I am overwrought. I do not want to go into exile, even for the sake of my family, but I have to return to Ireland to restore order. My family and I will be safe there.

King. Thomas, I have already promised you my protection; I shall never let them execute you, or rob you of your fortune, and I want and need you in London. I shall not let you return to Ireland. If necessary I shall command you to attend upon me in London.

Me. Then, Sire, I shall obey. But first I crave a favour, that I may go to my home in Wentworth to set my affairs in order. If Parliament decides to impeach me, the Lord alone knows when, or if, I may be free to go there again.

King. I shall never let them kill you, Thomas. You have my oath as a King.

Thomas. 1st November, 1640. Wentworth Woodhouse.

Dearest Bess,

I am at home, and it is lovely to be here, but it would be so much better if you were with me. The Council of Peers ended two weeks ago. It was a far from happy time for me, but I shall not trouble you with all that. The King left for London a couple of days later, but before he went, we had a long talk.

I thought he would leave me in York in command of the army, or let me go back to Ireland and to you; he asked me to go to London with him instead. It was a shock. You will know from Kit and Radcliffe that the Irish Parliament is trying to undo a lot of my work. The MPs

in Dublin feel they can get away with this sort of thing because I am not there, and also because they must have heard that the Scots have the upper hand over the King at the moment. In addition, they probably had news from the Council of Peers that I was under attack, so they may think that they do not have to worry about me any longer.

I do not want to go to London. If I go, I am sure the new Parliament in Westminster will be after me like hounds after a stag. I expect to be impeached. It is a very old legal process which had not been used for a hundred years or more, but Parliament revived it twenty years ago, to get rid of the Treasurer, Cranfield, who was a friend of mine; then they used it against the Duke of Buckingham, but that failed.

If they impeach me I think they will have trouble proving their charges against me, and I am confident that I can mount a solid defence, for I am innocent. Even so, I could do without it. I am not strong, and have had many bouts of the flux, and gout, and the worry of the war and the King's problems rob me of sleep. I have prejudiced our finances somewhat by doing all I could to help the King pay the Army. I borrowed 4,000 against my interest in the alum farm here in Yorkshire, and another 6,000 against our tobacco store over there. That is on top of the 20,000 I lent him at the outset. I have laid out all the ready money I had with me to the same end. I even asked Radcliffe to send over money from the Dublin Treasury, but it has not come.

My repute is at a low ebb now, but I shall confront the allegations against me and set them at nought; when I do, my current infamy will become true fame. In the meantime I could well do with the comfort of your arms about me, and it hurts that I have no idea when I may see you again.

William is well. Please kiss our three girls for me, and remember that I love you next to God above all things.

Your Thomas.

William Laud. 3rd November, 1640 Lambeth Palace.

Parliament meets today for the King's Speech, and Lord Keeper Finch will propose the loyal address. Is that wise? The man is so unpopular. He is known as a royalist toady, and has never recovered any sort of good name after being held in his chair as Speaker in 1629.

I am up relatively early to go to the Upper House, and when I walk into my study I find the worst of auguries, or that is how it seems to me. There, on the floor, face down, is my portrait. When I went to bed it was in its place on the wall. It must have fallen down in the night. Is this an indication of what will happen to me and Thomas? I pray to Jesus that it may not be true.

John Pym. 3rd November, 1640. St Stephen's Hall. Westminster.

Sir Harry Vane and I stroll about in one of the corridors of this Palace. We talk quietly – at least, as quietly as Harry's poor hearing will permit.

Me. Strafford is on his way back to London.

Vane. Then we must lay the charges against him before Parliament without delay.

Me. *(I am petulant, as though instructing a child).* No. No. No. If he hears that, he may disappear. He may go to Spain, or back to Ireland. If he escapes us now, we may never have a chance at him again. We'll end up in prison instead! And he will have the King on his side; we won't!

Vane. The King and Strafford are not without supporters, even in the Commons. We must make sure of our own backing.

(The idea of scheming Strafford's doom excites us both. It is almost impossible to keep calm, but we must; our plans must be laid with care).

Me. Then this is our strategy. As soon as Strafford's in London, we lay the Charges before the Commons and ask the House to impeach him.

Vane. I suppose we have enough support to be sure that the impeachment will go ahead?

Me. We must pray that we have. Next we must arrest him and put him in the Tower. With Strafford a prisoner we can set about controlling Parliament to secure his conviction.

Vane. We've made a good start! Strafford managed to get his brother George and a cousin of the same name elected for Pontefract. He had a friend returned for Richmond, but most of his other friends were defeated in the elections, and the King's candidates did little better.

Me. Any Member who has interests in Ireland will vote against Strafford. The Commons will hear as many of these Irish complaints as possible.
Vane. They allege he abused his powers for his own ends.
Me. Next, we'll call for a vote to exclude from the House anyone who'd be likely to side with the King, and therefore with Strafford.
Vane. That will see off another dozen of our opponents. What else?
Me. My master-stroke: an inquiry into anyone who's had any part in collecting Ship Money.
Vane. Brilliant! They'll be terrified of what we'll do to them if they side with Strafford.
Me. Precisely. *(I pause).* I've a further refinement. We shall make it clear that the inquiry will not start until after Strafford has been dealt with. We shan't proceed against them if they vote against him, and those who do vote for him.....
Vane. Will be persecuted over Ship Money! Quite brilliant.
Me. Flattery won't help: success will! The risks of failure are huge, but we have to take them because Strafford is the only able minister the King has. If we give him the least advantage he will defeat us.
Vane. You and he are well matched, Master Pym.
Me. As long as Strafford is alive he's dangerous, and if we fail, we are dead men. *(I pause).* You know, I'll never forget how brilliantly he spoke up for the Petition of Right. Then he changed sides and used all that power against us!! By God, I hate him!! *(I take a deep breath and endeavour to regain my self-control).* We intend to impeach him for treason, but the charges are hard to frame. Treason is, in the end, treachery to the King. We have to get the London mob to riot and frighten Parliament into our way of thinking.
Vane. The London mob would frighten anyone - except Black Tom, perhaps. He has only to arch an eye-brow to quell the passions of a riot. *(We are both silent for a moment).* I have something for you which may strengthen our hand. *(He produces a paper).*
Me. *(I take the paper from Vane).* What is this?
Vane. *(He glances around to check no-one is in ear-shot).* Notes of what Strafford said to the King about the Irish Army. His head is ours!!
Me. Time to stir up the Commons, then! Let's get in there.

Christopher Wandesford. 7th November, 1640. Dublin.

Three weeks ago the Irish Commons tried to change Tom's scheme for collection of the subsidies. I could not tolerate that, and cancelled the resolution. I hear it said that I have been stupid, and that this, in Pym's hands, will merely make matters worse for Tom at Westminster.

Today a Petition of Remonstrance has been presented to me and the House. I find something odd about it. There are, of course, many complaints from the planters about Tom's conduct. These are about a slow-down in trade, and the conduct of cases in the Courts. The oddity is that there are almost as many complaints from the Old English, about the failure to implement or legislate for the Graces. I cannot see that Pym will make much use of those. After all, the majority of the Old English are Catholics. If Pym intends to make Tom appear to be an agent of the Pope and in league with Rome, it would be ridiculous to use Catholic complaints that he has been ill-treating them too.

Many squeal about monopolies and excessive sums payable to the Church and the judges and Courts. One objection is to the power of some ministers of state. No name is given, but that is almost certainly an attack on Tom, primarily, but also on me and Radcliffe.

Beware of this Remonstrance, Tom!

Thomas. 8th November, 1641. Huntingdon.

I left my home at Wentworth on the anniversary of the Gun-Powder Plot. I am still rather poorly with gout and flux, so I am taking the journey in very short stages to give myself time to rest. As I wrote to George Radcliffe just before I left: "I am tomorrow off to London beset by more danger than ever a man went out of Yorkshire," but I was not without hope. I am staying in Huntingdon tonight. A messenger brought me bulletins about what was happening at Westminster. Many letters and petitions from Ireland have come in moaning about my 'tyranny'. Pym proposes that a Committee of the whole House of Commons should look into Irish affairs. He had a bit of a struggle, for he got his way with only 165 votes to 152. A majority of only thirteen was a healthy sign that the margin against me was fairly narrow.

This evening I pen a letter to Radcliffe. Having given him some account of the Council of Peers and my interview with the King, I write:

To the best of my judgment we gain much rather than lose. I trust God will preserve us; and as of all other passions I am free of fear, the allegations that are coming I apprehend not. The Irish business is past, and better than I expected, their proofs being very scant. God's hand is with us, for what might we not have expected them to swear in Ireland? All will be well, and every hour gives more hope than the one before. God Almighty protect and guide us.

Thomas. 10th November, 1641. Henrietta Street, London.

I am in London. I'm exhausted from travelling and from my illness. Tomorrow I may not be well enough to go to Parliament, but I have heard that Pym has again taken charge of the Lower House. The mood of the Commons is very much against the King because he dissolved the May sittings peremptorily, as they saw it. It is not difficult to see that the 'dust and cobwebs' which Pym spoke of sweeping out include me, and perhaps even the King.

He has a lot of power at his disposal. Many of my enemies from Ireland have been elected as Westminster MPs, including Clotworthy, and even Lord Cork's eldest son and two of his daughters' husbands. On the other hand my friend Sir Edward Osborne from the Council of the North, and my nephew William (now Lord) Savile have found seats, even though they were unable to do so in my own County. My brother George, and a cousin, Peter Wentworth, have also been elected, but for the borough of Pontefract.

George came almost as soon as I got here. He said that Clotworthy attacked me in a Commons Committee set up to consider Irish affairs – meaning, naturally, the way I had dealt with them. He alleged I had hounded honest Protestants for standing out against Bishops, and left the Catholics alone. This Committee also heard evidence from Mountnorris and Lord Loftus. The fact that I was not there, so that they could say what they liked without fear of correction, gives some indication of how the rule of law as to independent minded tribunals, fair trials, and the right of an accused person to be heard, will be likely to operate in my case!

Today, the very day I arrive in London, I am betrayed by Yorkshire. My fellow gentry present the complaints of the County about the Archbishop's reforms and rituals, and the cost to them of the war.

John Pym. 11th November, 1640. The House of Commons.

I am on my feet, addressing the House. The place is packed. Hardly any MP is absent today. The atmosphere vibrates with energy and tension. I wish I could claim that it is my oratory that provides this spark, but in truth it is the fact that Wentworth is now in London, and we have a chance to bring him down.

Me. Honourable Members, petitions have come in from all over the country against the Scots war.

Members. Hear, hear.

Me. Formidable complaints have also come in from Ireland.....

A Member. Black Tom Tyrant's Kingdom!

Me. Indeed, complaints from Black Tom's own Kingdom. He governs Ireland in a fiery and violent way. He will govern us in the same fashion. The Irish Army raised by Strafford will be used to conquer England! We should take these matters to their Lordships House at once. *(Uproar).*

Speaker. *(Shouting).* Order! Order!! I call upon Sir John Clotworthy.

Clotworthy. Our Honourable friend, Master Pym, is right. True Protestants in Ulster have been persecuted and prosecuted for opposing the Bishops and having sympathy with the Scots. Yet Irish Papists continue to lie down with the Whore of Rome and nothing is done.

A Member. The Queen is a Papist!

A Member. A Roman Whore!

Speaker. *(Shouting).* Order. Order.

Clotworthy. The Irish Army are all Papists. They are regularly paid. The true Army, the Protestant force, is neglected and goes unpaid.

Members. Shame! Where is the evidence for this? Is there any evidence?

A Member. That is the vital point. This House should consider the evidence, if there is any, before we refer these charges to the Upper House.

Me. What need have we of evidence? Does the House doubt the Honourable Gentleman's word?

Clotworthy. That isn't all. Only five months ago George Radcliffe.....

A Member. Strafford's creature!

Clotworthy. Indeed, Radcliffe, Strafford's creature, reported that the King can do what he pleases in England by using the Irish Army.

Me. Why ask what Strafford thinks, if that is what his minion says? He is a tool of the Jesuits. Do we not hear of Popish plots? Have you, Mr. Speaker, not caused the doors of this House to be locked for fear of interruption, or worse?

Speaker. The Upper House asks us to join them in discussing the treaty with the Scots.

Me. It is a trick. Strafford will be there. We are resolved to impeach him for high treason. If we go up to the Lords, that is the reason we go.

Members. Hear, hear.

A Member. Should we not consider the evidence first? This is a very grave step.

Me. Before we consider the evidence, Members should know that there is to be an inquiry into those who have helped the King collect Ship Money.

A Member. How can the King build ships for the Navy without Ship Money?

Vane. When we consider the evidence Strafford will go to his grave. The question is not the Scots, but the impeachment of the Lord Lieutenant of Ireland for high treason!

(Chaos erupts as there are loud shouts by many Members of: Hear, hear. Treason, High Treason. Impeach him. Strafford to the block, etc.**).**

Me. We must have him arrested, and prohibit him from attending Parliament.

Steward. The House is adjourned. *(Harry Vane and I move to the side of the house. We speak in whispered, conspiratorial tones).*

Me. I shall copy out the notes you gave me. By the time I've finished with them, the noose will be round Strafford's neck.

Vane. What about my real notes?

Me. *(With a laugh).* I expect they'll get lost, don't you?

Thomas. 11th November, 1640. House of Lords.

I have been here in the House since morning. I have done nothing to draw attention to myself, but I cannot imagine that no-one noticed my arrival. After a couple of hours or so I observe some messengers come to the Lord Chancellor's woolsack. His Lordship announces that the Commons want a meeting this afternoon. If this means the onslaught on me is about to start, I must see the King. I leave my seat as quietly as I arrived and make my way to Whitehall Palace.

The King receives me graciously. He tells me that in the City the royalist candidate for Lord Mayor was defeated in the election, an opponent selected, and immediately the City Council cancelled payment of the 200,000 pound loan. He also says that he had hoped the Recorder of London, a man called Gardiner, would be chosen as MP for the City, but he was defeated.

I tell him that something definitely seems to be afoot in the Commons, and whatever it is, it is almost certainly directed at me. His Majesty reassures me that he will not let me suffer, come what may, apart from perhaps being banned from politics and high office for the rest of my life. Well, after what I have been through lately, and with what is happening to me currently, I can look forward to that. A little peace would be very welcome.

However, I have no intention of giving in, or succumbing to the pressure upon me. I shall fight to the uttermost of my strength, sure I shall triumph. Then I can retire to my family and my estates with a clear conscience, knowing I have done my best.

One thing niggles at the back of my mind, and it is disloyal to my Royal Master to think it. I am not entirely sure of his promise of protection. I cannot put my finger on it. I have said before that a plan to lay all the allegations of wrong-doing at my door may provide him with an escape route, and indeed we have discussed that. I am confident I can convince the Lords – which is where I should be tried, amongst my peers – of my innocence, but if I should fail, can I be sure the King will look after me and my family and fortune? Can I ask him about this? Of course not! If he is not to be trusted, he would just lie and say my fears are groundless. If he is to be relied upon, he would be mortally offended by my mentioning it.

So, we skirt round these thoughts, and talk for an hour about what is likely to happen, and whether the Commons will in fact try to impeach me, and whether the Lords will go along with it, when suddenly a footman knocks at the door and announces Lord Harry Percy. He is flushed, and almost out of breath.

"Your Majesty, My Lord Strafford, forgive my intrusion and my hurried appearance, but I bring important news."

The King calls for some ale for him, and invites him to sit. "Is your news for me or for Lord Strafford, Percy?"

"Sire, it is mainly for Thomas – forgive me – Lord Strafford, but it concerns you as well."

"You are old friends, I know, so call him Thomas if you wish, and you, Strafford, may call him Harry. Now,you had better tell us what brings you here."

"Sire, Thomas, I've run across from Parliament. A minute or two before I left a messenger from the Other Place came to the House saying that the MPs have selected a Committee for your Impeachment, Thomas, and that they wanted to meet with the Lords to proceed with it." Harry is clearly distressed, and the King looks worried. Perhaps I was wrong to suspect him of chicanery.

"I shall go and look my accusers in the face." I rise and bow to the King. "With your leave, Sire, I shall go at once to the House. I hope to get there before Pym and his gang of conspirators."

The King rises, too, and gives me his hand. "Of course you must go at once, and I wish you all good fortune in this evil time."

I thank him, I thank Harry for his concern and his trouble in bringing his news, and I stride from the Palace to my carriage as fast as my gouty legs will carry me. I am too late. I find the lobby and doors crowded with MPs listening to what goes on in the Lords, and I hear Pym telling my peers that "The Commons of England charge Thomas Wentworth, Earl of Strafford and Lord Lieutenant of Ireland, with High Treason." The Lord Keeper tells him he must withdraw while their Lordships talk about it, and it looks to me as if the Lords expected these developments as much as I did. What I don't expect is what happens next.

Thinking I might have a chance to say something in my defence, I push my way through the crowd towards my seat. I am greeted by many of my peers shouting to me to "Withdraw," but I plough on, until my path is blocked by two or three Lords. I halt before them, and there is silence. I address the Lord Keeper. "What is the meaning of this? Why should I not resume my seat?"

Finch looks even more inadequate for his task than usual. He reads out to me and the whole assembly the accusation Pym brought from the Commons. "My Lord Strafford, you must withdraw whilst this House considers whether to take action on the request from the Other Place."

I turn, and with as much dignity as I can muster, and my head held high, I walk back the way I came.

George Wentworth. 11th November, 1640. Houses of Parliament.

I am in a crowd of MPs in the lobby outside the door to the House of Lords. I cannot believe what is going on. Not long since we were all in the Commons, Pym was arguing for a meeting with the House of Lords, and we came here to watch what happened. I cannot get very near the door, so I do not hear what Pym is telling the Peers, but someone at the front is sending back the gist of what he can hear. Pym is accusing my brother, Thomas, of High Treason, and asking the Lords to try him for it.

I knew from what was said in the Commons earlier that this is what he intended, but it is still a real shock to me. My brother is one of the greatest in the land after the King and the Earl of Northumberland; how can this be happening to him? Then there is a rustle of movement in the press of men behind me, and I turn to see Thomas pushing his way through the crowd towards the door into the Lords. I cannot get near him, but the whispers that he is here clear a path for him. As he reaches the door I manage to struggle forward to the door, and find myself by chance next to his friend Sir Edward Osborne.

"This is a pretty kettle of fish, Sir George. I cannot believe it."

"Neither can I Sir Edward. But look, they're shouting for him to withdraw!"

We stand still trying to hear what is being said but there is a lot of talking going on out here in the lobby, and we see him turn round and walk back out. Once men would have uncovered in his presence but many keep their hats on. To be fair to them, however, some of them would not recognise him as they are as new to Parliament as I am. If they haven't heard anyone say who he is, how could they know? But the word soon spreads.

Thomas stands alone, and still I cannot get to him. Frankly, I'm not sure I dare to. Then Black Rod, a man called Maxwell, summons him back into the Lords. There is a profound silence now. I hear Thomas ordered to kneel, and he does so. The Earl of Manchester tells him what the Commons proposes, and that he must be placed under arrest, and prohibited from coming to the Lords until the case is heard. I hear

Thomas say: "I do not understand these strict steps for which there is no precedent. May I address the House on this?"

The Earl tells him he may not, but can send petitions to the Lords which will be considered. Thomas is told to leave, and he walks ponderously back towards the lobby. As he passes the Lords I can see Lord Cork in the front row, grinning like a gargoyle at Thomas. He is gloating, for he has never been able to get the better of my brother before. Thomas's shoulders are bowed down, and he looks at the ground. As he passes me I call to him but he does hear. Then Maxwell commands him to surrender his sword, and silently Thomas gives it to him.

The tongues of the MPs are now unlocked and begin to make fun of him. Someone shouts: "What is the matter?" and Thomas replies: "A small matter, I promise you!"

Back comes another shout: "Yes, indeed! High Treason is a small business!" and others take up that cry. Thomas reaches the outer door, but Maxwell takes his arm, and I hear him say: "Your coach is not here, My Lord. I have sent it away. You are my prisoner, and must come home with me." Thomas makes no protest. He goes with Maxwell, and still no-one takes off their hat, apart from me and Sir Edward, and one or two others I know to be Thomas's friends or supporters.

I manage to get outside, and watch them drive away. I feel like weeping. When will I see my dear brother again?

Thomas. 11th November, 1640. Westminster.

As I left the Lords this afternoon I was arrested by Black Rod. I have to admit I was downcast by the turn of events, and having to hand over my sword brought back painful memories of my encounter with young Ormonde over the wearing of his sword in the House in Dublin.

But Maxwell is civil enough, and is performing the duty he is bound to carry out. I cannot blame him for that. He took me to his house, which is not far from the Palace of Westminster. He fed me well; it was a pity I had little appetite for food. I have a comfortable room, and I am not actually imprisoned, even if I am his prisoner. I have writing paper, quills, ink, and a desk, and I sit down at it to write to Bess.

Sweetheart,
You have heard before this what has befallen me since I left you,

but be confident that if fortune is to be blamed, yet I shall not, with God's help, be shamed. I advise you to be calm in the way you carry yourself in this misfortune, not neglecting the trouble in which I stand, yet so that you may not appear to be dejected. Continue to look after the family as you always do, and make much of our children. Please tell Will, Nan, and Arabella I will write to them by the next mail. In the meantime I shall pray to God that He may bless them, and for their sakes deliver me out of the furious malice of my enemies, which yet I trust, through the goodness of God, shall do me no hurt. God have us all in his blessed keeping. Your very loving husband, Strafford.

Thank Heaven I thought to send William back to Dublin when we Left Wentworth Woodhouse.

I call a servant and give him the letter to take to the mail. It is not until after I have done so that I realise I have signed it with my title, and not my name, as if it were a business letter. I must be distracted. I must pull myself together if I am to defeat Pym and acquit myself before the Lords.

George Wentworth. 12th November, 1640. Maxwell's House, Westminster.

When I knock at Black Rod's door he answers it himself. He is a tall, broad-shouldered, athletic looking man, with a large brown moustache. I tell him I have come to visit Thomas. He greets me kindly, admits me, and shows me to Thomas's room, which is large and quite light, and airy, but with a good fire, for it is evening, and chilly out in the street.

Thomas greets me heartily, but I'm surprised how he seems to have aged. Perhaps I did not notice that yesterday, in all the drama and sickening excitement. He doesn't like to talk about his health, so I leave the subject alone. He gets straight down to business.

"Have you been in the Commons today, George? Tell me what's been happening."

"Yes, I've been there. Where do I start?"

"How about at the beginning?"

"Well, the first thing is that Denzil Holles has resigned from the Impeachment Committee. I'm not on it, so I didn't hear what he said, but I met him when he came out, and he told me why. He said he realized that Pym will be satisfied with nothing less than your head on a platter."

Thomas chuckles. "That's odd. I'm no angel, and John the Baptist was a saint. Such a death might be too good for me!"

"That's not the point. Denzil said what Pym is after is judicial murder. He admits he hates the policies you've been pursuing for the King, but he doesn't hate you personally. He doesn't want the Father of his dead sister's children to suffer death because of some trumped up charges supported by manufactured evidence. He says he's put that silly rumour about you killing Arabella behind him. He knows you loved her."

"He's right there, George. I loved Margaret, I loved Arabella, and I love Bess. I've been blessed in the marriage department, because they all loved me too. Did Denzil say anything else?"

"Unfortunately he did. He told me that Hampden and another man on Pym's side have replaced him on the Committee. So the Committee is now more strongly against you than it was before."

Thomas shakes his head, and looks glum. "Then it's a shame Denzil left, for at least he would have been one person able to argue for me to be treated fairly." But then Thomas looks up and smiles. "Maybe it's not such bad news after all. The more extreme the Committee is, the more mistakes they will make in framing charges against me, and if God's on my side, I shall be able to make the Lords see how silly they've been, and how ridiculous the charges are."

"I hope you're right, Thomas. Next, I must tell you that your order that no-one could come over from Ireland without your permission has been rescinded. That means all those who want to give evidence against you can turn up in Court."

"But it also means that all the witnesses I want to come over can also come!"

"No such luck Thomas. Pym's too clever for that. He hasn't said they can't come, but tomorrow he's sending a warrant to Dublin for George Radcliffe to be arrested and charged with treason, and kept in Ireland, and I'm told that some of your other friends and supporters will be treated the same way. You'll be lucky to get anyone from Ireland over here to say you're a good chap."

Thomas leaves the room and asks a servant if we can have some wine, and quite graciously, and surprisingly, Maxwell brings it himself.

Perhaps I'm getting cynical now I'm in politics, but perhaps he fears the servants may give Thomas secret messages, or even poison.

We sit and drink a glass or two, and Maxwell even drinks with us for a short space. When he goes, I notice that Thomas looks more tired and grey than when I arrived, and I wonder whether I have done that to him with the news I brought. There is not much joy on the Wentworth horizon at present.

Thomas. 20th November, 1640. Maxwell's House.

The day before yesterday I was in my room writing to Bess. I have much time on my hands, and have not yet been told in any detail what the allegations against me are, so I cannot even get to work on that. I write to Bess and the children as often as I can. I read and read again and again any letters which come from them. Prayer and those letters are my only comfort, besides some visits from peers and MPs who are sympathetic to me.

The former include Harry Percy, and Margaret's brother Henry, who is now Earl of Cumberland after his Father's demise. The latter include brother George, my cousin Peter Wentworth, Sir Edward Osborne, Denzil, and one or two others. I was about half-way through my letter to my wife when there was a knock at the door. I find that Maxwell and his servants - my warders, in effect – are invariably polite and treat me as well as can be expected, so they never just charge into the room. They knock, and wait to be summoned. Is this because that is how they would treat anyone under any circumstances? Or is it because they fear that if they do otherwise, and I am acquitted, and regain my rightful place, I should take my revenge? I do not know, and I do not really care. I should rather be treated well than badly, and Maxwell is, when all is said and done, a gentleman.

The knock was just repeated as I called out simultaneously "Come in!" It was Maxwell himself. He gave a slight bow, and said: "My Lord, I've come from the Commons with a message for you. I have been instructed to inform you that from today no MP is to visit you here without the permission of the Lower House, and no MP is to tell you what occurs there."

"What? Not even my brother? Not even my brother-in-law Holles? Not any of them?"

"Those are my orders, My Lord. As those you have mentioned are MPs, that is how it must be. I am not proud to have to obey such an order, but obey it I must."

It was a heavy blow. Yesterday I suffered another. I applied to the House of Lords for bail. Having been told that I could only approach the Lords by petition, that is how I applied. Normally a common criminal, or someone awaiting trial is entitled to appear in Court to make his application or hear his Counsel do so. I do not have Counsel, I do not know if I shall be allowed Counsel, and I am not even allowed to make my own application. I did not treat Lord Loftus like this. I am being treated more like Bushin was treated by Lord Chief Justice Killmallock in Dublin. The more I think about it, the more I begin to believe that Pym is absolutely terrified that I may be found not guilty, and if that happens, it will be his head on a platter.

I must not get excited about that. I don't want his head; I just want my freedom, and as the King said, it doesn't matter much if I lose all public office and standing. I must keep calm and, when I know what the case against me is, prepare my defence with as much skill and logic as I can summon.

I suppose the nearest I could ever be said to have come to doing this to anyone was when Mountjoy had no Counsel, and was sentenced to death, but that was a Court-Martial, where the rules are different, and I was the prosecutor, not the judge, and it was not my decision that Defence Counsel was denied.

Then today I've had another foul punch. Thankfully the Lords have not allowed Pym to bully them into agreeing that no-one should visit me, and Lucy's brother Algie, the Earl of Northumberland, comes to see me with bad news – more bad news. He and I are not the friends we were. He was offended by the King's giving me command of the Army, and probably by my trying to advise him before that, on how to fight the war and use the army. Even so, he is a fair minded man, and is not happy with the news he brings.

"Thomas, I have come straight from the House. That chap Pym turned up again today. He demanded that we should allow him to interrogate all the Privy Councillors."

"God in Heaven! Is there no depth to which that man will not sink? The Council is called 'Privy' because the advice given to the King is private."

"Of course, Thomas, and some of our fellows raised that argument. One pointed out that if Councillors are to be taken to task for the advice they give, no-one will be prepared to give any advice."

"Be honest with me, Algie. Did you vote for or against?"

"I voted against, but many voted for what Pym wanted. You must know you've made a lot of enemies, Thomas. You've upset me in the last few months, but I am a Councillor, and I have no desire to be a whipping boy for Pym, so I voted against. Cork was there, and Mountjoy, and St. Albans, bleating on about his land in Galway. Newport and Holland despise you, as you are only too well aware, and the Earl of Leicester is not in your camp any longer. How do you think they voted? With Pym's band, of course, opposing all the King's policies."

Thomas. 21st November, 1640. Maxwell's House.

Today Maxwell comes to see me. He brings a letter from Kit, and news from the Commons. He is Black Rod, not an MP, so he feels free to tell me of some events. Today, he says, an Irish MP turned up from Dublin, and presented to the Lower House a Remonstrance from Ireland of all the grievances they claim to have suffered at my hands. Apparently I managed to convert that previously happy and wealthy Isle during my rule into the most extreme and universal poverty she had ever had the misfortune to experience since time began.

I actually laugh, and say to Maxwell: "There must be another Ireland somewhere on Earth, for the one described is not the one I left a few months ago."

Maxwell makes no comment, and withdraws. I open the letter.

Dublin Castle, 15th November.

My Dear Thomas,

I have the most dreadful news for you, and I could not be sorrier to have to impart it. I write with a sense of guilt, for I simply do not have your Parliamentary skills. I have been out-manoeuvred by Clotworthy's friends, and he is not even here, but helping to torment you over there. His party produced a Remonstrance of all the ills they say you have inflicted on Ireland. It came before the Commons, and before I could prorogue Parliament to put a stop to it, the MPs voted in favour of it being taken to London. George Radcliffe was in the

House and tried to defeat it, but he was howled out and could not be heard. There was uproar and this fearsome document was not debated at all. None of us on the government side knew anything about it beforehand. I understand an MP called Mervyn is sailing for Holyhead tomorrow, wind and weather permitting.

Your faithful but regretful friend,

Christopher Wandesford.

Well, Kit, I say to myself, I have little to laugh at now. When shall I see this monstrous Remonstrance?

William Laud. 23rd November, 1640. Maxwell's House.

Today is one of the saddest days of my life so far. This morning the King called together as many of the Privy Council as were available, and asked us to visit the Earl of Strafford in his place of custody. His Majesty handed us an Irish Remonstrance which he had received from the Commons the day before. Hamilton came, and Northumberland, one or two others, and the Earl of Cork, who looked like a bear who had just found the most enormous store of honeycomb. Christian as I am, or try to be, I cannot stand the man.

I handed this Remonstrance to Thomas, and told him the King would like his answer to these allegations as soon as possible. Cork looked as though he were about to drool with the joy of it all, but Thomas was calm, which seemed to anger Cork, who began to scowl instead of grin, with a rictus like death.

"My Lords, the essence of this charge is that I bankrupted Ireland all on my own. It is false. Ireland was not a happy place when I arrived seven years ago. It was not a prosperous island. I have turned its fortunes round so that it now contributes to the King's coffers instead of depleting them, and is not in debt. I have done much to create jobs, and encourage agriculture and trade. I drove the pirates out of the Irish sea, and I righted many injustices, such as those inflicted on the poor by judges like Killmallock and Lord Loftus. I shall study this paper in detail and answer it in the same manner. But I ask that there should be an inquiry into the truth of these charges before they go much further. Is that to be done?"

Cork exploded. "How dare you, Strafford! The Commons in Ireland are entitled to be trusted with their veracity. They say it is completely unlawful for the Parliament here to question the charges they have put forward."

Thomas remained under control, but he was scathing. "Perhaps you have forgotten that that same House of Commons told me in March just gone that I was as wise as Solon, and that they were very lucky to have so good a King as to send them the best Governor they had ever had. If that was true this must be a lie, or vice versa. Either way, no-one should rely on their 'veracity'. I doubt they can spell the word. They wrote that tribute into the subsidy bill, and they then voted on and passed it."

Cork spat back. "They say you had that put in and they knew nothing about it."

Thomas laughed. "If you believe that, you'll believe anything! When you're in a pit, Cork, you should stop digging. If they didn't read the Bill, that is hardly my fault, and in any case, the drafting of the Bill was not my task. You are simply making their position look worse and worse. Your Grace," Thomas addressed me, "I thank you for your attendance upon me." He gestures with the Remonstrance. "My Lords, I should be grateful if you would now kindly withdraw so that I may read this, and prepare my reply for the King."

I had had enough. I saw that Cork was about to speak and I could tell he wanted to be offensive. I told him to hold his peace, and to my surprise others said "Hear Hear," and Cork kept his mouth shut. We all left, and Strafford bowed to us as we departed.

Yes, it is a rotten day. I have never felt so tired and so old. I dread to think how Thomas must be feeling with all he is going through. I must pray for him. Come to think of it, as his policies, which have brought him to this pass, are my policies too, I'd better pray for both of us. Will it be long before Pym comes for me?

Thomas. 25th November, 1640. The House of Lords.

This morning, just before lunch, a messenger came to Maxwell's home to tell me that I must go to the Upper House in the afternoon. Maxwell himself comes to escort me to Westminster Palace, and we go in his closed coach.

Guards lead me into the chamber as a prisoner might be lead into any ordinary Court of Law, but this is no ordinary court. It is full of peers of the realm, and the Earl of Manchester acts, again, as the presiding judge. At least I am not told to kneel this time. It did my gouty legs no good last time, and they are no better now. I stand at the bar of the House, and a chair is brought for me to sit. I say that I am grateful. Despite candles and oil lamps, the light is dull as the evening approaches.

Manchester, rather fat and self-important, tells me that this morning Pym brought the Articles of Charges against me to this House, which has read and considered them, and I have been brought here to hear them read. One of the Clerks of the House reads them aloud. There are nine general articles which carry little in the way of particulars, so they are difficult to answer other than in a general fashion; they seem calculated to create an atmosphere of pure prejudice and fear. Then follow twenty-eight specific articles which I can rebut. Some seem to me so ludicrous I can only just stop myself smiling, since giving the impression I take all this lightly would be a mistake. When that scene of the drama is over I stand and address this, the highest tribunal in the land.

"My Lords, My Lord Manchester, I have paid very close attention to the allegations against me. They are long and complex, and I should like to be granted time to consider them and draft my response."

Manchester confers with some colleagues; "My Lord Strafford, you must make requests by petition, as you have been told before. Is there anything else?"

"Yes, My Lord. In the preamble to the accusations the Commons asks that I may be called to answer the Articles, and that they may be made acquainted with my answers. If it please the House, may I be permitted to appoint Counsel, and summon witnesses? May I be told the names of the witnesses for the prosecution?"

"The answer is the same, My Lord. You may make all those requests by petition, and we shall let you know our decision. That is all. You may not again take your seat in this House, and all your offices and appointments under the Crown are forfeit immediately."

"Then I am being penalised before trial."

Manchester ignores that. "You are now to be taken to the Tower of London where you shall remain until your trial." Manchester then calls to my guards to take me there.

I am again shown into Maxwell's closed coach, and driven to the Tower. I am received by Sir William Balfour, Lieutenant of this huge

Norman castle, from where so many men and women have gone to their death on the block or scaffold. Even so, I am not cast down, for I know for definite now that I can defeat them, given a reasonably fair trial.

I am given a comfortable suite of rooms, and servants to attend to my needs. After I have dined I have a visitor, no less a person than Lord Keeper Finch. Like Manchester, he is overweight, but taller, and far from self-important. In fact he would be better suited to the position he holds were he more imposing. "Parliament will allow me to act as a go-between for you and the King. He stands in urgent need of your counsel on many matters of State, and hardly has anyone of real ability left on the Privy Council. The Archbishop is just a tired and frightened old man now. He hopes he can continue to rely on you."

I have little to say to the man. I thank him for coming. I tell him to inform the King that I am still his loyal and humble servant and will do whatever I can and whatever my imprisonment will allow. Finch tells me that MPs, and now the Lords too, need the licence of Parliament before they can visit me. He departs.

Is it my imagination, or do people keep saying odd things which almost make me laugh, when I am in a pretty desperate situation myself? Am I not going to be busy enough, working on answers to the charges, and drafting petitions to the Lords to grant me what really are only the basic rights of any defendant to ensure a trial is fair?

Am I really the only person to whom the King can turn? Well, he can hardly expect good advice from Hamilton, or the likes of Holland, much as he may be the Queen's favourite. He knows well enough that Northumberland may be capable, but he does not agree with the policies that have brought war with Scotland, nor with the necessity of a war to enforce those policies. If Laud is worried, frightened, tired, and too old, he can be of little help. It follows that I am the one and only person His Majesty can call upon, even if I am a prisoner, and I can see he needs someone. He's never been swift at making up his mind, and events are moving faster and faster now.

In fact, Charles may not be in very good shape himself. He's been defeated twice by the Scots, even if there have been no really serious battles; the Council of Peers forced him into negotiations he did not really want; and Pym and his gang of Parliamentary thugs have him pinned in an alley like footpads. Could he have done anything to keep me from this incarceration? I doubt it; anyway, he didn't even try, and I do not think Parliament would have agreed. The Lords seem to be lying supine before the Commons.

Elizabeth. 25th November, 1640. Dublin Castle.

I sit in my chair before the fire in my sitting room. Kathleen stands by me. I put down my embroidery, and pick up Thomas's letter dated two weeks ago. I am desperate to share it with someone, and I need a woman I can trust. I do trust Kathleen. She's a true Colleen, about 30, with thick black hair, white skin, and piercing blue eyes. George Radcliffe and Kit would not be as sympathetic. I read the letter to her, but omit the endearment with which it opens. Tears run down my face, and I see Kathleen wiping her eyes. "He is in so much trouble but he worries more about me and the children, and he believes God will look after him. That hasn't stopped them sending him to the Tower, though, has it?"

Kathleen says: "I fear nothing will be after stopping them, My Lady." She becomes distressed but controls herself. "Holy Mary Mother of God, how does he keep up his courage? Everyone is against him - the Lords, the Commons, the Scots ..."

"They all bay for his blood, yet he remains cheerful. He's pleased that the King's letters come and go freely. He's also very cast down about the new Constable of the Tower. He told me the old one, who was quite kind and considerate to him, has been replaced by a man called Mountjoy Blount. This Blount is Earl of Newport. He is no friend of my husband's. They have been at loggerheads ever since he told Blount what to do about some disobedience in the Irish Army; something about putting up gallows outside barracks to frighten the troops, and to hang them if they mutiny."

"I've heard of this Blount, My Lady. His father was a famous general for Queen Elizabeth in the Irish war fifty years ago. It's as maybe he didn't like getting told what to do. He's quite a soldier himself."

I mutter to myself, very quietly: "And Thomas isn't!" More loudly I say: "He has a great deal to do - advising the King, dealing with these awful charges, and preparing his case, but he still finds time to write to me and the children. The letter ends: "God have us all in his blessed keeping. Your very loving husband." And then he signs it "Strafford" instead of "Thomas." I laugh hysterically, and begin to cry again.

Kathleen kneels at my side, takes me in her arms, and pulls my head to her shoulder. "His faith is an example to us all, so it is."

"Yes. His kindness is such a contrast with Pym's vitriolic conduct."

"The poor Master. He was always kind to me. I don't know how he supports it all. Oh! Ma'am, and so near Christmas too!!"

I break down again, and Kathleen comforts me. "Come Ma'am. The children are in bed. Will you be after wishing them Goodnight?"

John Pym. 30th November, 1640. House of Commons.

Today a Committee of sixty MPs is appointed to have a conference with the Lords to agree concerning the Impeachment of the Earl of Strafford. Our sixty include me, naturally, St.John, Lord George Digby, Clotworthy, Sir Walter Earle, Hampden, Glynn, Selden, Bellasis, Sir Arthur Ingram, and Bulstrode Whitlock. They are all staunchly anti-Strafford, and Bellasis and Clotworthy positively hate him. An exception may be Sir Thomas Roe, a former diplomat, who is said to have been an admirer of Strafford's at one time. All the other forty-eight are known to be in favour of getting rid of the Lord Lieutenant once and for all.

George Digby is an MP because he is the son of the Earl of Bristol, and is, therefore, not a member of the House of Lords. The aristocracy can be represented in both Houses. I'll have to try to do something about that one day.

Thomas. 10th December, 1640. The Tower.

Today I have received the most grievous news by letter from Bess. When I say grievous that is precisely the word. She tells me that on the 3rd our dear friend Christopher passed away, and if anyone deserves to go to his Maker rather than the other place, it is Kit, the friend of my boyhood, the best, most gentle, the kindest friend a man could wish for.

Bess says that Kit had been having a terrible time with the Irish Parliament, and knew that his attempts to govern Ireland in my absence were a dismal failure; it made him ill. He failed to get my subsidies confirmed at 45,000 pounds each; he failed to stop the approval of the Irish Remonstrance; and it seems that the news of my impeachment utterly broke what was left of his spirit. He even seemed to blame himself for his failure to get the laws passed for the plantation in Connaught, but as the King himself had said Clanricarde was to keep his land, how could it have been Kit's fault?

Yet curiously the native Irish actually mourned him, she writes, and the keening, as they call it, could be heard for miles around. Why was that? I do not know, and can only guess. People say I am a bully, and aggressive, but even though he was trying to pursue my policies, no-one could say those things about Kit. His was a charming personality. Only last month I wrote to George Radcliffe asking him to tell Kit that his method of moderate counsel would not serve his turn in the extremities he was facing with the Irish Parliament, for to be a fine, well-natured gentleman would not do it. And that is exactly what Kit was: a fine old-fashioned gentleman.

I feel guilty for his death. I should have recognised that he had not the ruthless streak necessary to be my Deputy.

Bess! This news will be so sad for Bess, and for Kit's Alice. I must write to Bess and tell her I'll be sure to be home soon, and we can help each other find some joy. She must feel so cut off, so lonely. She was as fond of Kit as I was; who could not be?

Radcliffe is in not much better case. He was ordered to come to London recently, and now I hear he was imprisoned yesterday in the Gatehouse at the Palace of Westminster. At least he is here now. We may be able to help each other.

Thomas. 22nd December, 1640. The Tower.

I am at my desk, working on the answers to the charges, when to my surprise the King enters. I put down my quill and stand to bow, in some discomfort.

Me. This is a great honour, Sire. I trust you are well?

King. Well enough, Thomas. And you? Sit down, man.

Me. How would anyone be in this damp, cold place? *(I go to the door).* Jailer? Jailer! A chair for the King.

King. You still have the flux?

Me. I do occasionally, and now I keep on ....

(The Jailer, who is a cockney I now know very well indeed, a rough, tough, but kindly man, dressed entirely in brown, with a hair-cut the shape of a pudding bowl, enters with a chair, puts it down, bows low

to the King, and places it in accordance with a gesture from me. I smile and thank him).

Jailer. My Lord, I'm commanded ter tell yer tha' fr'm nah on you're confined to these 'ere three rooms. There'll be two guards on the ou'er door, which'll be locked a' nigh', and then them guards'll sit in the ou'er room 'til mornin'.

Me. Am I allowed no exercise and fresh air?

Jailer. Only wiv me, Me Lord.

King. This is iniquitous!

Jailer. Orders is orders, Yer Majesty. An' his visi'ors can only come afore dark from now on.

King. Pym's orders, no doubt!! *(He sits, and I do so immediately afterwards).*

Jailer. No, Yer Majesty, it weren'. It's the 'ouse a' Lords what done it. *(He bows to both of us, and leaves).*

King. They are all mightily afraid of you, Thomas.

Me. *(I smile at that).* Perhaps, but not that cockney. And Parliament is not nearly afraid enough! If they were they would not be doing this. They must have been really annoyed that I had so many visitors. None of them were supposed to tell me what was going on in Parliament, but most of them did.

King. Perhaps you are right, but equally, perhaps they are taking all these extreme measures because they're afraid of what you will do if you are at liberty when this is all over.

Me. You mean if I get a "Not Guilty" verdict?

King. Exactly. They had the Archbishop arrested four days ago, and he's locked up with Black Rod, just as you were. Others are to be charged including the judges. Few have your courage, Thomas. Many are fleeing the country. Lord Keeper Finch was impeached yesterday and I'm told he fled and took a boat to France last night. Windebanke asked me if he could leave the country about two weeks ago, and he left straight away. *(He pauses).* Do you have a lawyer?

Me. *(This time I laugh rather cynically).* The bad news is that the Lords refuse to let me have Counsel to deal with the evidence, so I have to present my case and cross-examine the prosecution witnesses myself. The good news is I'm allowed barristers to help me with the law.

King. Whom did you brief?

Me. Hah! I was not exactly free to choose, for Pym's gang chose seven Barristers I could ask to help me. *(I grimace and shift my gouty legs).* I am Black Tom Tyrant! Even I never told a defendant who his lawyer was to be. Being chosen as my Counsel may be a sentence of death; the London mob hounds anyone who may be on my side.
King. The Queen is terrified of the mob. *(He gives a wry smile).* I'm not so keen on it myself. I'd be surprised if any lawyer had the courage to face them.
Me. Then you'd be wrong, Sire. Not one of those lawyers let me down. Not one found an excuse, or said he's too busy. My leading Counsel is Richard Lane, and right glad am I to have him by me. His advice is invaluable.
King. Just as well. Masses of complaints and evidence against you pour in from Ireland. None of it is carefully scrutinised.
Me. Then Pym does his case more damage than he knows. These complaints are not about treason, and I shall prove it. Is there anything .... *(I am suddenly gripped by excruciating pain in the lower abdomen, and rise, clutching my groin, and gasp)* .....more?
King. *(He rises in alarm).* Thomas, what is it?
Me. Aaaagh! *(I rush to the corner, undoing my breeches as I go, and pick up a chamber pot).* I have to piss!! Aaaaaagh! *(I double over in pain, drop the pot, straighten up, and the world fades away).*

Charles I. 22nd December, 1640. The Tower of London.

I have been talking with Strafford in his prison quarters for half an hour or so, when he is suddenly in great pain, and then falls senseless to the floor.
Me. *(I rush to him and kneel by him).* Thomas! Jailer! *(I run to the door).* Jailer!! Quickly, damn you!!
Jailer. *(Running in).* Yer Majesty, what is.... *(He sees Thomas).* Oh shit! Not again.
Me. Not again what?
Jailer. Not again, Yer Majesty.
Me. Don't be an idiot. I mean has this happened before?
Jailer. Too bloody righ'! 'e's got the stone.
Me. The stone?

Jailer. 'e keeps passin' bladder stones. The flux was bad enough wiv all the shit I 'ave to clear up for 'im, and now I get to wipe up the piss an' all.

(Strafford begins to stir).

Me. *(I kneel again).* Thomas? When on earth ...

Strafford. *(He endeavours to rise but I gently push him back***).** Sire, I am sorry.

Me. Don't be daft, Thomas. You're ill. *(To the Jailer).* Well, go on man, get your mop and bucket, why don't you? *(The Jailer exits).* The Jailer says you have the stone.

Strafford. It's torture. Literally. Like having a red hot poker pushed up your cock. I beg your..... *(I wave away the apology).* The sweat just drips off me. If Pym has put a curse on me, this is it. *(He raises himself onto an elbow).* I must get up. It hurts less if I'm sitting. *(I help him to his chair).* You didn't come here to talk about my health.

Me. No, but ......

Strafford. There is little time, Sire.

Me. Very well. The Secretary to the Council –

Wentworth. *(Contemptuously).* Sir Harry Vane!

Me. - has been examined as to the evidence he will give. His memory seems very vague until he has worked out what Pym wants him to say, and then he suddenly remembers exactly.

Strafford. What is Pym up to?

Me. His usual tricks. He renews the threat to investigate the Sheriffs and Justices over Ship money, then says this won't happen until after your trial. My people will either be frightened off, or will co-operate with Pym. Any support you and I have is vanishing fast! He has already persuaded the Commons to drive out all the monopolist MPs in case they side with you.

Starfford. Pym will only be safe if he can destroy me.

Me. Quite! Apparently there's some funny business going on between Vane and Pym over some documents.

Strafford. *(Angrily).* Well, I wouldn't put anything past them. Pym will stop at nothing to have me executed.

I then ask Strafford about other matters, including the Scots, the Army, and the Irish troops, he advises me, and I depart. He looks so ill. I am amazed at his courage.

John Pym. 29th December, 1640. House of Commons.

Well, today we have succeeded in preventing Strafford making much use of his friend Radcliffe. He was dispatched here from Ireland on the orders of the Irish Parliament a little while ago when they resolved to impeach him, but he is to be tried here. He is now lodged in the Gatehouse of the Palace. We pass Articles of his Impeachment for Treason before the House, and I am ordered to take them to the Lords.

Thomas. 16th January, 1641. The Tower.

As I told the King, my leading Counsel is Richard Lane. He is a formidable barrister of good repute, with a very formidable brain, and considerable courage to be representing me in this crisis. I believe he's about 55, and tells me he's been an advocate for 30 years, so I have every confidence he knows what he is about. He has served as a judge in Northampton, and for seven years he's been the Prince of Wales' Attorney General. He's a little shorter than me, with dark hair going grey and a little thin on top, and is always soberly dressed in black. He comes to confer with me today. We have rapidly become friends.

Lane. The Lords finished examining the witnesses yesterday. *(He is exasperated)*. Even I wasn't allowed to be there, let alone you, Thomas. It may be that Lords and Commons are falling out a little. Pym wanted to have MPs listen to the witnesses being questioned. The Lords said: "No, you can't. This House has its privileges too, and Strafford is a member of it." But then they let Pym have his way. I think they are afraid of him. You are allowed to answer the new allegations –

Me. What new allegations? I haven't even seen the detailed ones yet!

Lane. A lot of new information came out of what the witnesses told the Lords. They gave it to Pym and his friends and they are incorporating it into the indictment.

Me. You must help draft my answers when I know the charges.

Lane. Delighted, Thomas. By the way, I had your petition to be allowed to read the evidence handed in to the Upper House, but it was rejected.

Me. I wanted to see what was said so that I could let them know what was wrong with it.

Lane. I know, but the Lords gave it to the Commons as it was.

Me. They may have made a mistake. If they do not know what my comments are, I can expose any errors, and there will be nothing Pym can do about it.

Lane. Let us hope so! One more thing before I go. Obviously you will be giving a lot of thought to the preparation of your case, based on what you heard in November, but we cannot get to work together until we hear the final version of the indictment, which, let us pray, will not be long delayed. What I want you to bear in mind in your deliberations is that it would not be sensible to conduct your defence on the basis of attacking the Prosecutors and all the witnesses.

Me. I shall find it hard not to attack the likes of Cork and Mountjoy if they lie.

Lane. Show them up as liars by all means, but don't start off by attacking them. Remember, this case has been brought by your enemies, but they are conducting it on the basis that they are protecting King and Country, and that you are the enemy. If you appear to be waging war on them, it will seem to confirm what they say about you. You must – we must – pitch your case on the grounds that they are honourable men – except when they lie – that the facts are otherwise than they allege, and your part has been misunderstood.

Me. In other words, let them rant and rave at me, but I must not do the same to them. Yes, I agree. Thanks for your advice. I'm impressed.

John Pym. 23rd January, 1641. House of Commons.

A strong team has been appointed today to prepare the final draft of the Articles against Strafford which should be laid before him and the Lords soon. Selden is on this group with Geoffrey Palmer, Whitlock, and Maynard.

My Committee has been working frantically on the Impeachment this month. We have been active with it, almost daily, and there has been much coming and going between the two Houses. For the most part we have been sending messages to the Lords asking for this or that to be done, trying to ensure, as far as we possibly can, that the whole trial is skewed in our favour.

Of course, Strafford is never consulted about any of this. He will have to take his chances with whatever procedures the Lords lay down.

Thomas. 30th January, 1641. The House of Lords.

It is hard to believe, but I have only just been brought to the House to hear the amended charges against me. They are, indeed, somewhat different from those which were read to me in November. There are the original nine general charges, plus twenty-eight specific articles which I can rebut. Some seem so ludicrous I can hardly stop myself smiling. Giving the impression I am amused would be a mistake.

My agent here in London, Railton, told me he saw huge threatening crowds outside the Tower and Westminster yesterday, and managed to ask the Upper House if I could come here at night and be held at Maxwell's home. He was worried for my safety. Clearly my safety is the last thing on anyone else's mind; they'd probably have preferred it if I were assassinated, so saving them a lot of bother, and the risk I might 'get away with it'.

As it happens he need not have worried. Nothing happens.

The reading of the indictment against me takes a very long time, and then Mr Lane asks the House to allow the two of us time to write out our answers to the charges. He tells the Lords that the Other Place has taken two months to get their allegations ready and written out. I think he hopes the Lords will give me the same amount of time. They do not. They give me two weeks!

Then I am escorted back to my prison, but I am far from unhappy. In fact I am almost gleeful, for I cannot see that any of the individual counts on the indictment amounts to treason, and the law does not allow a collection of non-treasonable acts to be added up to make a treason. I can now get to work with Richard Lane and his colleaugues.

I write at once to dearest Bess.

Sweetheart,

The charge is now come in, and I am able, I praise God, to tell you that I conceive there is no capital offence in it. For the rest, I know at the worst, His Majesty will pardon all if I am condemned, without allowing my fortune to be hurt, and then we shall be happy by God's grace. Therefore comfort yourself, for I trust these clouds will pass away and that we shall have fair weather afterwards. You have all my love. I long to be with you, and shall be soon. Thomas.

Lucy Carlisle. 30th January, 1641. Westminster.

I saw Thomas once in the Tower. It was cold and damp there, but what else would it be in December? There was a fire, and we were able to dine together, but nothing else. He looked so ill, I do not think he could have managed anything else, and frankly, I am glad. It would have been like making love to an invalid; a very poorly one at that.

Today I sit in the gallery of the Lords. I watch Thomas brought in. A clerk says the charges of treason against him are to be read out, and he will be given a copy.

Thomas looks so frail, even worse than he did before Christmas. He is bent at the shoulders, as if bearing a load of enormous weight, and I suppose he is. A gentleman comes to the bar of the House and begs Lord Arundel to let the prisoner have a chair to sit on. He is a friend of Thomas's, named Railton. I breathe a sigh of relief when one is brought to him, and he sinks onto it in pain.

The reading of the allegations against him takes an age, and then soldiers take him away, back to the Tower, I suppose. The Lords then have a debate about how the trial should be organised. First, they decide that it should not take place in their Lordships House, as the Lower House wanted to be there, and there would not be room for everyone, nor for members of the public to attend. Seating will be constructed in Westminster Hall, with a box for the Royal Family, and places for the prosecutors and the Defendant and his lawyers.

Unbelievably they discuss whether the MPs should be allowed to sit in the presence of the Lords with their hats on!! The Commons agree that they will go bareheaded. The Lords agree Pym and his Impeachment Committee can present the prosecution evidence.

Bishop Williams then addresses the House on whether Bishops can take part in the trial as judges. He's a slender, tall, ascetic looking man, unctuous in manner; there's something slimy about him which makes me shudder. He says that as clergy should not, by some old canon law, take decisions which might mean they would have blood on their hands, the Bishops should stay away. Amazingly, the Bishops agree. I am sure this is a terrible blow to the chances of Thomas getting justice, for the higher clergy usually support the King on policy matters, and Thomas was just following the King's policy, as I understand it. With the Bishops absolving themselves of any responsibility in the case, there are fewer people to find him 'Not Guilty'.

Am I surprised Williams should speak as he did? Not really. It is well-known that he has hated Thomas and Laud ever since he was convicted of perjury all those years ago, and stripped of some of his offices. Perhaps I shouldn't be amazed at the way the Bishops voted, either. They know that Archbishop Laud has been impeached too, so they will do anything to save their necks. Christian martyrs are a rarity these days. Joining Jesus in paradise is the last thing on their minds.

The Peers decide that no-one who was elevated to the peerage since the charges were first laid before the House back in November could be a member of the House sitting as the trial Court, in case they were friendly to Thomas; one peer immediately left for that reason, but some refused to stand aside.

I began to get the feeling that everything was being stacked against Thomas when the House refused his request to be able to subpoena witnesses, including MPs. They said he could call witnesses, but it was up to them whether they came or not. This dreadful feeling was hammered home when the Lords chose as President of the Court the Earl of Arundel. He is notoriously one of Thomas's greatest enemies. Thomas tells me it is to do with land in Ireland Arundel wanted, which Thomas refused to let him have, as it was the King's, and because he had tried to give Arundel advice about how to fight the Scots. I know that this is true because I have dined with Arundel and his family many times, and he never misses an opportunity of running Thomas down to all and sundry in the most violent language.

It seems that the Trial is now fixed for 22nd March. I suppose Thomas will have to let Pym have his Answers well before then, giving Pym plenty of time to try to beat him. I must try to attend the hearing as often as I can.

John Pym. 24th February, 1641. House of Commons.

Another month of frenetic activity on our part, with many conferences with the Lords. Three days ago the Lower House, on my suggestion, instructed the Strafford Impeachment Committee to open all letters going to Sir George Radcliffe. If they see anything useful to us, they are to report it to us and to the House. This will be another nail in Strafford's coffin should anyone – including the Earl – write anything incriminating to Radcliffe.

Today Strafford's Answers to the Articles are delivered to the House of Commons from the Lords, who received them yesterday. It took more than three hours to read them aloud. There are over two hundred pages of them.

I am sure we shall be just as busy in March manipulating the procedure and the way the evidence may be taken as we were in January and have been this month. The only brake on this is whether the Lords will agree to all we want.

I shall leave no stone unturned, and no mud unthrown to secure Strafford's death. If he is acquitted he will do the same for me, I have no doubt.

Bishop Juxon. 11th March, 1641. The Tower.

Today I visit Thomas. He looks awfully tired and ill. I am the harbinger of bad news. I tell him that, inspired by Bishop Williams, the Bishops have decided to tell the Commons that they will be absent from the trial because they do not believe it is right for them to sit in judgment in cases where the life of the prisoner is at stake. The excuse offered to the Commons is that their seats at the trial will be needed for all the Earls and other peers.

I tell Thomas that I am ashamed. He says he expects nothing else from Williams who has borne a grudge against him for years. Despite this blow he remains cheerful and confident, as far as I can tell. He seems to be working very hard at his defence, and is constantly sending his servants here and there with letters and requests for information or documents to support his arguments. He is tireless in his efforts, which must be why he looks so poorly.

Thomas. 12th March, 1641. The Tower.

Yesterday was frightful. It has taken most of a wakeful night to sort out in my head what has happened. I think my fate may have been sealed, not because Pym's case is unanswerable – I can answer it well, I have no doubt - but because a most important source of support I thought I could count on has been swept from under me. The culprit is Bishop Williams. Why would he do something so deadly to hurt me? Why should he tell his fellow Bishops not to take part in my trial, when most of them support the King, and therefore can be expected to support me?

The answer lies in several things which have happened over the years which have made him something of an enemy to the King, and therefore to me, because I serve him. These events occurred in England when I was ruling Ireland, so I had little if anything to do with them. That does not stop them having a dramatic effect on my fate.

John Williams is the Bishop of Lincoln and an extremely intelligent and learned cleric. He was also Dean of Westminster. He had been King James's Lord Chancellor of England, but he annoyed Charles, who was then still Prince of Wales, and George Villiers, the Duke of Buckingham, by opposing their seduction trip to Madrid, so when James died, Charles got rid of him. He thought at one time that he could be Archbishop of Canterbury, but Laud got the top job instead, and that's when Williams became Bishop of Lincoln, as well as being Dean of Westminster. Jesus may have told the rich young man to sell all he had and give it to the poor 'and follow me', but Bishop Williams had no problem being a pluralist holding two exceedingly well-paid Church offices at once. Perhaps I shouldn't say that bearing in mind that once I was doing all I could to get rich myself, but I hadn't taken Holy Orders.

We were often in touch by letter, particularly once I had been posted to Ireland. We used a code which was also employed in letters to and from Laud. We didn't use weird alphabets or anything like that, but we referred to people by numbers so that no-one would know who we were writing about. For example, Cottington, the Chancellor of the Exchequer, was 110. Even Laud and Williams and I had numbers, so that in a letter to one of them I referred to myself by my number and them by their numbers, so strangers would not even know we were referring to ourselves, should our letters be intercepted.

Williams wrote to me about all sorts of subjects, such as Cork's wife's tomb, and Prynne, Burton and Bastwicke. He asked me to help a Norfolk Squire acquire land in Ireland, and he subjected me to constant pressure to grant land to Lord Antrim. He wrote, quite misguidedly, "I am confident of your favour to this young Lord," favour I had very little intention of showing; Antrim was such a nuisance. Perhaps Williams was offered money to seek these favours, since I know not why else he would importune me.

But greed wasn't Williams only sin. He also broke the 9th Commandment, and perjured himself. I do not understand the background to this case fully, but it isn't strictly relevant to this story. What I can say is that he was originally accused of some treason, perhaps involving selling state secrets, but it was very complicated and the case against him failed.

However, it was discovered that in order to make sure it failed, he told lies, and bribed others to lie for him. He even sought the help of one of his cleric friends to have his records nailed up in a secret room so that the prosecution could not find them. This friend was no less a person than the Dean of Canterbury, so this was done right under Laud's nose. When these facts came out Williams could not successfully deny his crimes. On 15th July of 1637 he was sentenced for perjury, and the related bribery and suborning of witnesses. My friend Laud was delighted by this, for Williams was opposed to his reforms, and it was common knowledge that he was doing all he could to bring the two sides of the Church – those who were opposed to reform and those who supported Laud – together. Such a reconciliation could only work if there were concessions, and Laud's 'Thorough' policy would permit none.

Williams had been tried, in effect, by a combination of the Star Chamber and the High Commission, and they imposed on him their separate secular and clerical punishments. He was fined 10,000 pounds by the former, which also put him in the Tower of London for as long as it pleased the King, and the latter confiscated his two Church incomes. The King was content with that, since Laud's Church policies were his own. Williams was, to that extent, Charles's opponent too.

The Archbishop did not particularly want him kept in prison. He wrote and told me he expected that Williams would offer to resign the Bishopric and the Deanery in return for being released from prison, but the Bishop was made of sterner stuff than that. He put up with being reduced to one main meal a day (which he had to pay for), though he was allowed to have visitors dine with him. The High Commission took away his right to carry out his clerical functions as Bishop and Dean as well, but the law did not allow it to take away his entitlement to those offices.

Laud took over the duties of Bishop of Lincoln, but none of this changed Williams's mind. He stayed in prison fearlessly talking and writing to anyone who would take any notice, and doing everything he could to undermine Laud. As it turned out he was right to think that something would change, that Laud would have to go, and that he would be back in power. When that happened, just before Christmas, it was a disaster for me, because in revenge Williams has removed at a stroke a big block of votes – the Bishops' – which would almost certainly have been mine.

Thomas. 15th March, 1641. The Tower.

An excellent visit today from brother George, and our cousin, Peter Wentworth, who is also an MP. They tell me that the Earl of Essex, on behalf of the Lords, has told the Committee controlling my Impeachment, that the Peers have changed their minds about Article 27. That is the one which says that I, and I alone, ordered the raising of money for the Army in Yorkshire during the Council of Peers six months ago.

When they first saw this allegation they accepted it as true, but they have seen my Answer, and have investigated it, and agree with me that the charge is false; they admit they all agreed in York to the raising of the money in the County!! One Charge has died prior to the start of the Trial. Thank God.

Deliver Me From Evil.

Thomas. 22nd March, 1641. Westminster Hall.

I applied for more time to prepare my Answers at the end of January. I was given a week, and then more. Eventually my servants took them to the Lords on 23rd February. They gave Pym and his friends another month to examine them and get ready for today. I know nothing more of their case than I knew before.

Three days ago I had a message from the Upper House. They discuss my petitions as to the conduct of the Trial with the Commons. When the Commons refused to let me have Counsel the Lords wanted me to be represented; a compromise was reached: I could have barristers for the law only, and must deal with all the evidence myself. I then asked for permission to call my own witnesses, and cross-examine the prosecution witnesses; now I'm told I can do both, but I cannot cross-examine under oath – so lying by them may be quite acceptable! I wanted to call MPs, and the Lords agreed but accepted the Commons' condition that whether they came was up to them.

Two of the basic provisions of the Rules of Law and Natural Justice are being broken: everyone is entitled to representation if he can afford it; everyone is entitled to a fair trial. In any case letting me call my own witnesses is a joke, since I have been told of this right so late in the day, so close to the start of the Trial, that I cannot get any of my Irish witnesses here in time. To make sure that is so, last month the Irish Parliament began the impeachment of my friend Sir George Radcliffe in his absence. Lord Chancellor Bolton, Lord Chief Justice Lowther, and Bishop John Bramhall of Derry are to be impeached too. They are not allowed to give evidence for me at my Trial, but have to stay in Ireland. But then, who said life was meant to be fair?

Early this morning I was rowed here in a barge with many soldiers guarding me. Another five barges followed, also full of soldiers. There were about a hundred soldiers altogether. There were other passengers too; persons ill-disposed towards me, and very partisan in favour of Pym's party. Despite it being broad daylight no-one could attack me in the middle of the Thames, and the guards kept close formation around me as we disembarked. There my guards were joined by some two hundred members of the London Trained Bands carrying their weapons. We all marched up to the Hall, and before I was led to my seat, an officer of the Parliament asked Maxwell whether he should carry the axe into Court before me, as usually happens in treason trials before a jury. Maxwell said that the King had expressly forbidden it in my case, and in any event I was not being tried by jury but by my peers in the Upper House.

I am now sitting in a chair with a desk in front of me, and beyond that the Prosecutors at a bigger desk; I can only see the backs of their heads. Beyond them again are those judges who are members of the Lords, and beyond them a small throne-like chair representing the King. At the sides of the Hall, on the floor in front of me are two rows of seats full of the remaining Lords, and at the sides behind those four rows are many rows full of MPs. These rows are stepped like a gladiators' arena, so that everyone can see the drama unfold below. The Lords have their hats on; the MPs do not. To my surprise I find that the President of the Court (known as the Steward) is not an independent minded Judge or non-partisan Lord, but my antagonist and enemy, Earl of Arundel, dressed in his colours, as though off to war. Is this a guarantee of a fair trial? I think not! He sits alongside the King's chair. Not a single Bishop is to be seen, not even Juxon.

Some boxes have been built behind the dais where Arundel sits. These are somewhat like boxes at the theatre. I am told one is for the King and Queen and Prince of Wales. They will stay secluded in their box, to be able to hear the case. The King has been asked not to sit on his chair on the dais. Several reasons are given. First, if he is seen as part of the trial, will his presence intimidate the process? Secondly, if the King is to be a witness or speak on one side or the other, he should not be seen to be a part of the trial until then. Thirdly, it has not been the practice for the Monarch to sit at a trial since early Plantagenet times.

Behind me, mainly standing, are members of the public, and some of them are seated amongst the MPs.

At a little before nine in the morning John Pym and the Prosecutors enter and sit. The others are Messrs Glyn, Maynard, Whitlock, St.John, Palmer, Earle, Stroud, Selden, Hampden, and Lord Digby. I was brought here at about 8am. I was up before dawn, since before 6. At nine the King and Queen and Prince Charles arrive and take their places in their box; curtains are drawn across. The King calls for me to enter his box, and we confer for about an hour before the case starts. I do not see the Royal couple after that, but the Prince comes out once or twice to the King's chair, which is under a Canopy of State.

Steward. Master Pym, read the charge.

Me. *(I stand to address the Court).* My Lord, before he does so, I notice that none of the Bishops are here today.

Steward. They have excused themselves.

Me. *(I try to look desperate, hoping to propagate sympathy with this, even though I already know about it).* What? Why?

Pym. *(He stands with a sly smile).* They were persuaded that as you will be .... sorry, did I say will? .... may be executed they should avoid having blood on their hands.

Me. *(Sadly).* Then there can be no chance that they would vote to acquit me! In this House the Lords Temporal and Spiritual are the jury. *(I address the Steward).* Some might think this jury has been tampered with!!

Pym. *(Laughing).* None of the Lords, even the Bishops, can be forced to come.

Steward. People can say what they like, but I shall see that your trial is a fair one. I shall not excuse myself from sitting, even if the Bishops do! Master Pym, read the charge.

Pym. *(Rising and addressing the Steward).* If it please the House, My Lord Steward. *(He turns and reads to the jury of peers).* Articles of the Commons assembled in Parliament against Thomas, Earl of Strafford, whereby he stands accused of High Treason. First, that you have traitorously endeavoured to subvert the fundamental laws of England and Ireland, and instead, to introduce an arbitrary and tyrannical government. Secondly, that you have traitorously assumed to yourself regal power ....

He proceeds to read all nine general charges and the twenty eight specific ones. Then Lane is called upon to read my answers to all of them. It seems to take forever. During this interminable process I hear many mutterings of "Shame" from some of the MPs and members of the public at my alleged criminality. By contrast there are only a few expressions of surprise at the completeness of my rebuttal. The Court adjourns for the day at around 2pm, and the guards are ordered to have me back in the Hall at 9am. On my way back to the Tower I am shown more respect by the common folk in the streets and at the wharves than I was shown in the lobby of the Houses of Parliament, yet it is these commoners who are, according to rumour, the source of the general hatred felt toward me.

Thomas. 23rd March, 1641. Westminster Hall.

Today is Tuesday. The King, Queen, and Prince are here again. Pym makes an opening speech, inflaming the allegations out of all proportion, as it seems to me, with the use of amazingly horrifying adjectives and the most extraordinary hyperbole I have ever heard. He tells the Lords that mere words fail to describe the depths of my Treason; that having been given the highest offices in the North, in Ireland, and over the Army, and being raised to the peerage as an Earl, I have repaid the King by abusing his generosity, and placing all His Majesty's nations in peril of losing their liberty, their true religion, their privileges, and even their lives. He crowned this exercise in what he may have thought of as understatement by saying that no punishment anyone could invent would be ghastly enough for me.

I rise to reply, telling myself that I must bear in mind Richard Lane's advice to express myself moderately. I hope I speak professionally, and inwardly thank my Father for having sent me to the Temple to study and practice law. I do not want to sound like Pym, merely raising a rabble. I feel he makes a mistake; some Lords may be no better than villains, but a rabble they are not.

I tell them quietly the services I had rendered to the King on the Council of the North, on the Privy Council, in governing Ireland, and in trying to take charge of the Army against the Scots when in fact the situation was already irredeemable. I express my gratitude to the King for all he has done for me and the honour he has bestowed upon me by the great matters he entrusted to me, and the rank he afforded me. I explain as briefly as I might, reserving detail for later in the trial, how I suppressed bandits in Ireland and pirates in the Irish Sea, restored land and money to the Irish Church so that it was properly maintained, and increased the Royal income there tremendously. At the same time I endeavour to say all this in a humble way, implying that if I had been a more able man, I could have done a better job.

I may be wrong, but I feel that I have made quite a few of those present rather more sympathetic to my cause than they were at the start. That is how I must continue. I thank God for Richard Lane.

As I sit, Pym stands. He makes another speech rebutting, as best he can, some of what I have said. He refers to my Answer to some of the Charges in these words: "My Lord Strafford says: 1) He has maintained Religion. We shall prove that he has promoted innovations and encroachments and usurpations of the clergy on the practice of religion. 2) He says he has striven for the Honour of the King. We say the Honour of the King is to be the father of his people and the fountain of Justice. It is not compatible with his Honour and his Justice to have his government polluted with Tyranny and Oppression. 3) Strafford says he increased the Revenue of Ireland. It is true there may have been some additional sums, but we say there is no addition of strength or wealth, because in those parts of the country where it has been increased, this Earl has taken the greater share himself, and when he has despoiled and ravished the people, he has been content to yield some small part to the King, so that he may enjoy the rest more securely. 4) He says he has worked for the Strength, Honour, and Safety of the Kingdom. My Lords, we say that in a time of Peace he has let loose upon us the calamities of War, Weakness, Shame, and Confusion. 5) He says he has protected the Peace and Quiet of the people. We say he has been an agitator, arming us against each other, and has left us weak and naked in the face of all the World."

This is all a travesty of what I truly did, and I am sure I shall be able to prove it.

He tells the assembly that there are three new charges arising from information obtained and inquiries instituted after the other thirty-seven charges were prepared. I tell the Court this is a terrible shock; that it is passing strange that this should occur when all the preparatory steps have been taken, but I am innocent, and rather than create the impression that may not be so, I am content to hear these new matters, provided I may have adequate time to prepare my answers.

At that, Arundel tells Pym to read them. He does so, then Arundel and the Lords retire to confer, and return to say that as they do not seem to be very meaty, there should be no further delay, and I should give my answers there and then.

"My Lords, I beg you, in that case, to pardon the weakness of my extempore answers, but if it please you I shall hear the new Articles of Charge now."

Pym rises to read these charges, which are, according to my reckoning, numbers thirty-eight, thirty-nine, and forty. He accuses me of taking 40,000 pounds out of the Irish Treasury in the last two years, and keeping it for myself. Next, that when I went to Ireland I made the English Treasury pay for the army garrisons there. Last, that I had given all the plum Church posts in Ireland to 'popish and infamous persons'.

In answer I produce a letter from the King authorising the taking of the money, which was used to help pay the Army in England. Second, the Irish army used to be paid from England because there was no money in the Irish Exchequer to do it, and I raised the income of Ireland and the taxes and customs from that, so that Ireland could pay its own army. Third, that any cleric I had advanced had the full backing and approbation of his fellow clergymen and the King, as being suitable for the post. I tell the Court I accept that the Bishop of Waterford has turned out to be an unfortunate choice, but neither I nor the King could, without divine power, have known in advance of the monstrous impieties with which that Bishop has now been charged.

The whole day is taken up in this way, the King and Prince depart having sat there the while. The Steward commands that I be brought again tomorrow when the witnesses to the First Charge (he calls them Articles) will be heard, and the evidence be examined on oath.

Lucy Carlisle. 23rd March, 1641. Westminster.

I have been at the Hall listening to the case against Thomas. I have spoken to two or three peers and one or two of their ladies. I think the cards are really stacked against him, and the hands unfairly dealt to boot. Some of my friends believe all of these dreadful accusations made against him. Some say that, come what may, he will not lose his life. Others feel that Pym and the Lower House have put their honour, and perhaps their own lives, at risk, to bring him to this vale of tears. They will stop at nothing, no, not the lowest trick, to secure his ruin.

How has he borne all this? Some say he has shown great courage, and carried himself so modestly, that he is to be admired. Certainly, that is how I see it. I clearly recall one exchange. Pym asked the Steward's permission to read the Irish Remonstrance.

Thomas. *(Passionately, he overcomes his weariness with a supreme effort).* I object, My Lord. This Remonstrance was only laid before Parliament after I was charged. I've had no time to answer it.

Pym. He needs no time to answer it. It proves his evil doings in Ireland. He is like the whore in the Book of Proverbs: "he wiped his mouth, and with a brazen face said he had done no evil."

Thomas. The *reading* of the grievances proves nothing. There is no evidence. I hope my protestations of innocence will not be taken for impudence.

Pym. The Commons insist that the Court hears the Irish Remonstrance, Your Lordship.

Thomas. My Lords, I shall, during this trial, give the honourable Houses of this Parliament full satisfaction regarding my life up 'til now. My only present ambition is to retire from all public employment. There is a great conspiracy against me. I hope shortly to clear myself of these foul aspersions laid upon me by my malicious enemies, and ....

Glyn. *(A tall, gangling, man, whose face appears to have been hewn from rock, leaps to his feet with a deafening shout).* Now we see!! Now we see, My Lords. He insults the House of Commons by accusing it of conspiracy and of being his 'malicious enemies'!!

Thomas. *(He steps from behind his desk and falls to his knees, facing the peers and the Commons).* I beg you to pardon my sudden outburst, My Lords. Nothing was further from my mind than to accuse the Commons of anything. I meant only the Irish Lords and others outside the House who have raised these matters against me. If I had been a Member of the Commons and had the information they have had before them, I should have adopted their course. In proving my innocence I do not accuse them.

Steward. The Commons are not on trial, Master Glyn. Do not be so eager to defend yourself.

Denzil Holles. *(Calling from the MPs benches).* Perhaps he will soon have to! *(There is laughter from many).*

In spite of this sort of happening, Pym seems to me an interesting man. He appears to have prepared well, but he is not a ready orator or advocate as Thomas is. He looks at his papers a great deal, as if he were reading them, and indeed, it often sounds as if that is what he is doing. This can make him sound rather boring, even if what he is saying (or reading) is interesting. One thing is clear, however: he is very passionate about his cause, but whether it is righteous indignation or fear of the King and Thomas, I cannot tell.

I have not seen Thomas for some time. He is very much changed. He barely stands upright as he shuffles into Court, he is so stooped. His face is pale and sickly, probably from lack of fresh air, exercise, worry, and his ailments. He wears a grey cloak wrapped tightly about him, and a grey woollen head-cover which comes down over his ears. I imagine these garments match the dull colour of what was once his thick black hair. It is a chilly spring day, and I cannot imagine he can get warm either in the Tower or in this vast hall, where I can see breath rising like steam from all around. It puts me in mind of cattle in a winter barn.

Thomas. Wednesday, 24th March, 1641. Westminster Hall.

Today they lay the first Article against me. The Nine General Articles are supported in each case by one or more of the specific Articles. The First Article is that I tried to subvert the fundamental laws and government of England and Ireland, and introduce tyrannical government contrary to the law, and that that was monstrous Treason. This is put forward by Mr Glyn. I know this man by reputation. He is an able lawyer from Wales. He is about ten years my junior. Currently he is the MP for Westminster. In a long, fiery and exaggerated speech, he says that this is a cumulative crime, for none of the offences on its own amounts to treason, but that I am undoubtedly 'the most wicked and exorbitant traitor' ever brought before the bar of a Court. The proof is in things I had said or done. Several witnesses said I declared in York in March 1633 that 'The King's little finger should be heavier than the loins of the law'.

I believe many in the Hall understand this to mean that the King's tiniest finger is bigger that the law's dick. Glyn calls some witnesses to prove what I am supposed to have uttered. I cross-examine them, and call my own witnesses.

I rise to reply. "My Lords, it strikes me to the heart to be accused of such a wicked crime by honourable men, men such as Messrs Pym, Selden, and Hampden. These are men with whom I sat in the Commons in my youth, when we fought to uphold the liberties of the subject, who now seek judgment against me. Yet it is not guilt, but grief, that troubles me now. The infirmity of my body, and the anguish of my mind, make it almost impossible for me to represent myself, as I must, as I am not permitted a lawyer as to the facts. But God knows I am innocent, and lends me some little ability to tell the truth with a good conscience. Even so, if my memory fails, it is due to my weakness, and that, I trust, you will forgive.

"I ask you to bear in mind that my Accusers, such as Mr Glyn, may be better prepared with their Charges than I am with my Answers, for there are several of them, and only one of me, and they have spent a lifetime in the intricacies of the law. Their rhetoric may present many things to your eyes as though through a magnifying glass, making it look like anything other than what it truly is. Further, they have had far longer to prepare than I was permitted.

"Nevertheless, I shall vindicate my honour here, and then retire to enjoy the privacy I have longed for, having been weary of public service for many years. I wish I had done so earlier, a ripe fruit falling from a tree, rather than a withered branch torn from it untimely, as Macduff was torn from his mother's womb.

"So I turn to this allegation that I said 'The King's little finger is mightier that the loins of the law'. My words have been inverted, and what I did say was said eight years ago, in Court, in York, to some prisoners who were being pardoned by the King, and released. I wanted them to be grateful to His Majesty for his mercy. What I told them was: 'The little finger of the law is heavier than the King's loins, if the King does not grant pardons for penalties inflicted by the law'.

"My Lords, I produce the Court record to show the time and place this occurred. Then I ask you to recall that my witnesses confirm that I did not speak as I am accused of doing, and that when Mr Glyn's third witness was cross-examined, I forced him to admit that he lied. He agreed that he had been rather deaf for over fourteen years, and when he was in Court that day, he was standing twelve yards from me. I showed that he could not hear what was said from only three yards away in this Hall. He then admitted he had not heard me but was repeating what someone told him."

Glyn then calls David Foulis, but he is easily dealt with. I go into no detail here; full details of the trouble I had with him have been given in these pages long ago. I tried to have him excluded as being totally biased against me. That request was rejected, but I doubt that the Lords believed him. It is a sign of the lack of wisdom in the prosecution that they did not check the truthfulness of some of their witnesses and so-called 'evidence' before we got this far.

That is the end of another exhausting day for me, which I end, comfortless and lonely, in the Tower.

Thomas. Friday 26th March, 1641.

Yesterday went much as the day before, arguing about whether I said that 'Ireland is a conquered Kingdom, and the King might prescribe them what law he pleased', or something else. The first phrase could not be denied, I told the Lords, but the other part was that 'the King is the law-giver', and saying that could hardly be treason. I had always tried to have the Liberty of the Subject and the Royal Prerogative run together, as neither could survive without the other, and reminded the Court that Pym, Selden, and Hampden had sat in the Commons with me when I said so.

I tried to call Sir George Radcliffe to give evidence on this sort of point, but Pym objected, and the Lords said they would not let me call him today. Will they ever let him give evidence? Am I supposed to remember to ask again at some unknown date in the future? Just how high are the Commons going to stack the cards against me?

Today is more exciting, and consequently more stressful for me. I am required to answer the Charge that I would not suffer my Ordinances to be questioned by lawyers in lower Courts, and would make Acts of State equal to Acts of Parliament.

"My Lords, I do not dispute that I often said that I should not suffer my Ordinances to be condemned or ignored, and with good reason. What is an Ordinance but a law of the King as to the behaviour of the people? Who is the Lord Deputy of Ireland but the King's deputy for the laying down of laws in Ireland? These laws are made in the King's name, and many are made at His Majesty's express request, or in pursuit of policies laid down by him. Are the King's laws to be condemned or ignored? No, they are not; they are to be obeyed. Then how can it be treason to make it clear that that is so?

"My Lords, I turn to the other part of the Charge, that I said I would make an Act of State equal to an Act of Parliament. I do not deny that either, for it is true that I said it, and the statement that laws, whether Acts of Parliament or State, here or in Ireland, should be obeyed equally, is true also. If such laws are not equally binding, then neither is binding. Is it Treason to say so? No, My Lords, it is not."

As I sit down Oliver St.John rises. He comes from an aristocratic family, and looks it, is a famous lawyer, and the King's own Solicitor General. He calls Lord Cork to give evidence to support this charge in accordance with his Deposition. I then stand to cross-examine him. He sticks to most of his tales about my wickedness towards him, but I believe his manner of answering my questions shows beyond a peradventure that he is my mortal enemy, and I hope that the Lords take into account that one so biased may not be giving an unblemished account of the facts. Then I move on to two particular allegations he makes against me.

Me. My Lord Cork, as I understand it you say that I issued an Ordinance against you? Is that right?

Cork. Certainly it is. It was about handing back rectories to the Church. Don't you remember? You had some of the words which were favourable to me scratched off the parchment, didn't you?

Me. Yes, thank you for that. I was in fact going to ask you to clarify that, as I thought I must have got the wrong end of the stick. So what were the words you say I had erased?

Cork. The words were that 'Lord Cork shall have six months to effect the transfers of the rectories back to the Church'. Or some words very like that; they meant the same anyway. You made it appear I had to give them back immediately.

Me. Did I?

Cork. Yes. Are you saying I'm lying?

Me. I'm supposed to ask the questions, My Lord. Do you know who Sir Paul Davison is?

Cork. Don't you patronise me, Strafford! He's the Clerk to the Irish Privy Council.

Me. Do you know his hand-writing, My Lord?

Cork. I was on the Privy Council in Ireland, wasn't I? I was one of the Lords Justice governing the country before you came, wasn't I? And you've got the nerve to ask me if I know his hand-writing!

Me. I take that to be 'Yes'. Please look at this document. Whose signature is that at the end?

Cork. Davison's, of course.

Me. And what is the heading on the document?

Cork. 'Certified Copy of Ordinance Directed to Lord Cork'.
Me. Very well. Now please turn to clause 3, and read it aloud to the Court.
Cork. Lord Cork shall complete the conveyance to the Church in Ireland of the rectories specified in clause 5 hereof within .... *(Cork's face turns the colour of a beetroot; he splutters to a halt).*
Me. Is something wrong, My Lord? Can someone bring him a glass of water? Please continue reading, My Lord? *(Cork does not look up; he says nothing).* I'm sorry for your indisposition, My Lord. Let me finish the reading for you. '... complete the conveyance of the rectories specified in clause five hereof within six months of the date of promulgation of this Ordinance'. Now, My Lord, are they not the very words you say I scratched out of the Ordinance? *(Cork remains silent).* A little while ago you asked if I was suggesting you were lying. I'll leave it to our peers to decide. Let us move on. You accuse me of having raised one of my grooms to be a Preacher. Is that what you say?
Cork. It is.
Me. What do you know about the man?
Cork. Not much. What do I need to know about him? His name's Daniel Goddard. One day he's a groom in your stables, and the next he's preaching in Church. *(He turns to the Lords).* How ridiculous is that, and that's the sort of thing Strafford does! He thinks he is the King.
Me. Now while you know 'not much' about my groom, he was my groom, and I like to get to know my servants. Shall I tell you what I found out?
Cork. I'm sure you're going to.
Me. Indeed. I found out by talking with him about Jesus that he had an intimate knowledge of Scripture, and spoke eloquently on the Gospels. Did you know he could do that?
Cork. Do you suppose I care about your servants?
Me. I made enquiries about him. I found out that he had been a priest, but had lost his living when the Lord of the Manor appointed his cousin to it. He could not find another living, and having a love and deep knowledge of horses he applied to my Steward for a position. Did you know that?
Cork. Of course I didn't.

Me. But you saw fit to make allegations about the character of this man, did you not?

Cork. I did, but it's you that's to blame. You're just saying he's a priest. It's a lie.

Me. Is it? Would you please look at this document? Where is it from?

Cork. The University of Dublin.

Me. What is the date at the end of it?

Cork. October 1629.

Me. Whose name in the middle of it?

Cork. It's ... it's ... er ... *(almost in a whisper)* Daniel Goddard.

Me. Could you speak a little louder, please? I can see some of their Lordships didn't catch that. And could you tell us what this Certificate is for?

Cork. *(He coughs, takes a drink of water, coughs again, and speaks slightly louder).* It says that Daniel Goddard is awarded a degree of Master of Arts in Scripture.

Me. So let us get this clear. I appointed a man with a degree in Scripture to be a Preacher who, it seemed to me, was extremely suited and qualified for such a post. Do you still say that is I who am lying? *(Silence).* Is that what you are saying? *(Silence).*

Steward. You must answer. My Lord Cork.

Cork. No, I don't say it.

Me. Thank you, My Lord Steward. May I add that I do not understand how, even if My Lord Cork had been telling the truth, the alteration of an Ordinance for the making of which I was responsible, and the appointment of a man who might not have been a priest to be a preacher, can possibly amount to Treason against His Majesty, but that is, of course, for their Lordships to decide.

I bow to the Steward and the peers and sit. St. John rises to his feet to call his next witness. Into the Hall walks Lord Mountjoy. They have brought out what they hope are their big guns today, but Newcastle adjourns until tomorrow.

Thomas. Saturday, 27th March, 1641.

We start with Francis Annesley, Lord Mountjoy. He has to take the oath as he is not an MP. St.John takes him through his evidence from his deposition. It's all about the Court Martial, and is no surprise to me.

It takes the rest of the morning. When it is finished Newcastle adjourns the hearing for lunch. I am exhausted and glad of a break. I am taken to a guarded room where some refreshment is brought to me, as it has been every day. Whether I feel like eating is another matter. The hearing is to resume at 2 o'clock, and does so.

Me. My Lord Steward, Lord Mountjoy was sworn this morning. Is he still under oath?

Steward. He is.

Pym. He should not be.

Steward. He is under oath, Mr Pym. Proceed, My Lord Strafford.

Me. I'm obliged, My Lord. Now, Lord Mountjoy, your case, as I comprehend it, is that I sentenced you to death, contrary to law, contrary to Magna Carta, and contrary to the Bill of Rights, thereby undermining the liberty of every subject in the Kingdom. Is that it?

Mountjoy. Correct. You caused me to be prosecuted more than rigorously, and the sentence was unjust.

Me. And when that sentence was pronounced, didn't I say that was so, and that I would straightway appeal to the King?

Mountjoy. You said you'd rather lose a hand than that I should lose my head, which I thought a very poor jest.

Me. It was no jest my Lord, and it was not what I said. I said I would rather lose a hand than you should lose a hair of your head, but let us not dwell on that, since it is not germane to the issue, which is whether I am guilty of Treason, and whether your death sentence is proof of my guilt. Now let us stick to what is germane. You accuse me of sentencing you under martial law in time of peace, do you not?

Mountjoy. Of course I do, because that's what you did?

Me. Were you then an officer in the Irish Army?

Mountjoy. You know I was.

Me. Sometimes a simple 'Yes' or 'No' will be quite enough. Are you a Protestant?

Mountjoy. Of course.

Me. This Trial of yours was in December 1635, was it not?

Mountjoy. You know it was.

Me. Was Ireland at war with anyone abroad then?

Mountjoy. No. Do you have to go on asking stupid questions?

Me. I am getting to the point, My Lord Mountjoy. So why was a standing Army necessary in Ireland when His Majesty keeps only a very tiny minimum force in arms in England?
Mountjoy. To make sure that the Papists are kept in order, and that they don't rise up calling for a Spanish or French invasion.
Me. So you were an officer in a large Army kept on foot because of a constant threat of rebellion or invasion, or both?
Mountjoy. You can put it like that.
Me. I do put I like that. Now your Trial arose out of this sequence of events, didn't it? Your brother insulted and disobeyed me, his commanding officer, on parade. You expressed approval of your cousin dropping a stool on my foot. You, an officer, said your brother would, in effect, take a tougher revenge than that, and uttered it as a threat. Isn't that right?
Mountjoy. Well, that's what the Court Martial found, but it was wrong to have a Court Martial in the first place.
Me. Armies are normally ruled by Martial Law, aren't they, in peace or war?
Mountjoy. They are.
Me. So here we have an officer in the Army approving of acts of insubordination to the commanding officer, acts of violence to the commanding officer, and uttering threats against the commanding officer, and therefore bound to be tried by Court Martial even in time of peace.
Mountjoy. I should have been tried as a civilian. You just made use of Martial Law to get rid of me.
Me. Would you say that a private or corporal who did what you were convicted of doing should be tried as a civilian in a civil Court?
Mountjoy. Of course not!
Me. So Lords like you and me should be treated differently, should we? Shouldn't be expected to set a good example, or be made an example of? *(Mountjoy says nothing).* Very well, I take it you agree. *(He remains silent, looking very sullen).* You say I made use of Martial Law, as though that had not happened before. Is that right?
Mountjoy. Yes.
Me. My Lord Steward, here are copies of Martial Law Ordinances promulgated by previous Deputies in Ireland, and copies for Lord Mountjoy. You will see, My Lords, that these documents come from the

periods when Lords Wilmot, Chichester, and Falkland were successively Lord Deputy in Ireland, and they go back forty years. I hand in a copy of one issued, when he was Lord Justice in the period between Lord Falkland going and my arrival, by the last witness, Lord Cork himself. Finally, may it please the Court, I hand in the warrant from the King for the holding of a Court Martial, and the King's own letter, authorising me to proceed. Now, Lord Mountjoy, do you allege that in acting on the King's command, I was committing Treason against him?

Mountjoy. No, but I do say that you were prosecutor, judge, and jury in your own cause.

Me. Very well, let us examine that. I do not dispute that I was the prosecutor. After all, the insubordination, the injury from the stool, and the threat from you were directed at me, and I was the complainant to the Court Martial. Do you agree?

Mountjoy. Indeed. And I say you were the judge and the jury.

Me. Was there only one judge?

Mountjoy. No, there were several, but you were the superior.

Me. This Court Martial was in fact the Irish Privy Council, was it not?

Mountjoy. It was, and you, as Lord Deputy, were the Chief Judge.

Me. Can the Privy Council sit, whether as a Council, or as a Court, without its head?

Mountjoy. No, it can't. But you can't be the prosecutor and the Judge.

Me. I accept that. Did I keep my hat on, as the other judges did? Or did I sit uncovered?

Mountjoy. I don't remember.

Me. Well, I do, and if you do not recall, you can hardly contradict me when I say I was uncovered. Now, when the evidence had all been presented, did the judges express their opinions of your guilt or innocence?

Mountjoy. They did. So did you.

Me. I deny that. I shall call witnesses who will say that I made nothe case after I had presented the prosecution case. Do you still say I pronounced judgment on your guilt?

Mountjoy. I do .

Me. Then their Lordships will have to determine which of us they believe. Did I vote for your conviction or sentence?

Mountjoy. No.

Me. If I did not vote on either, how could I have delivered judgment upon you? *(Mountjoy says nothing).* When the verdict was pronounced, what did I say?

Mountjoy. You said you would appeal to the King.

Me. And what happened?

Mountjoy. I was pardoned, and excused the death penalty. But I was held in prison for a long time.

Me. That was because you would not apologise for what you had done, wasn't it, and when you did, you were released, were you not? *(Mountjoy is silent).* My Lords, let me summarise this matter as briefly as I am able. I was not a party to the sentence against his Lordship; I had the power to hold Courts Martial under my commission as Lord Deputy; I did not sit as a judge other than in a purely nominal capacity; I did not exercise that martial power over Lord Mountjoy until I received the King's commission so to do; and I exercised that martial power no more than had been done by previous Deputies, and perhaps not so much. Indeed, it may be thought that my only fault may have been that I was too lenient or remiss in what I did.

Then there are some brief exchanges between me and Mr Glyn. He tells the Court he recalls very well that once I was as passionate for enlarging the liberty of the subject and advocating the Petition of Right as I am now for creating my own arbitrary and tyrannical government. I reply that if ever I had done any service to the House of Commons, I was glad, for it meant my life was well spent, and I was grateful to that House for allowing Mr Glyn to say as much before this assembly of honourable men. I ask that if they find I had committed any slight misdeeds, they would weigh the good I had done against them. I tell them I deny that anything I have done could make me guilty of Treason, unless it is Treason for a man to have no more wit and prudence than the Good Lord has endowed him with.

With that, Arundel adjourns the hearing until Monday. Six days have I sat here, battling alone against eight or more able lawyers, in the face of a hostile Steward, and a largely hostile Court. I have never been so tired in my life. Tomorrow I shall attend the Tower Church, pray a great deal, rest as much as I can, and prepare for Monday. God help me. And I must find time to write to Bess. How I miss her! I could do with her shoulder to cry on and her breast to sleep on.

Thomas. Tuesday, 30th March, 1641.

Yesterday was mainly legal wrangling over some land I was said to have confiscated illegally from Mountnorris. I proved that he had himself come by the land in question with extortion and violence, and I think, and hope, that I satisfied the Court that this whole complaint was ill-founded. There was one almost amusing piece of theatre in this matter. The prosecutors alleged I had taken this land away from Mountjoy in breach of a proclamation of King Charles. I proved that the event in question occurred five years before the King issued his proclamation, and, keen as I am on obedience, even I could not obey it before anyone even knew of it.

Today is another legal battle over land, again in the Irish Privy Council, in October 1635. This was another judicial act, and as in the case with Mountnorris's property, it was not directed to or against the King, so it is difficult to see how it could be Treason. In brief, this land was owned by a member of the Hibbots family. Lady Mary Hibbots acquired this land by what seemed like skullduggery, and the original owner sued her for it.

I sent her to prison for failing to produce documents to the Court. Pym's men say I refused to agree with the majority of my Court who wanted a verdict for Lady Hibbots, and over-ruled them. I denied that and they could not prove it. The land came into the hands of one Sir Robert Meredith. The prosecution say I had arranged this so that Meredith held the land on trust for me. I say that this is false, that they have produced nothing but hearsay to prove it, and that Lady Hibbot had regained her property direct from Meredith. How that could be Treason even if what they said was true, I do not know, but I feel that this matter may have left a bad impression about me. However, the next point dealt with today could, arguably amount to Treason, I suppose.

I had given the Bishop of Down and Connor power to arrest all who were contemptuous of or disobeyed the Ecclesiastical Ordinances. This was true. They say this is an attack on the liberty of the subject. I produce evidence from Archbishop Ussher and two witnesses that this course had been adopted in Ireland many times before I came there. I argue that in a country with many Papists and sects broken away from the Church in Ireland, the clergy need such a power or there would be no respect for the Church, for God, or for the King. I show that I had only issued such a power once, and had soon cancelled it. I did not know how the Bishop might have used this power, and I could not be responsible for how he did so, but the Court could ask him.

Lucy Carlisle. Wednesday, 31st March, 1641. Westminster Hall.

I've been in the Hall again for the last two days, and I'm here again. Thomas looks dreadfully ill and frail. His appearance makes me think of Cardinal Richelieu, *L'Eminence Gris*, though Thomas is only *gris*, and no longer the *eminence* he used to be. He looks shrunken down inside his clothes. Despite this, and the continual agitation to which he is subjected, I hear people on all sides speak quietly and with admiration of his demeanour, and his able defence of himself against many attacks from so many quarters.

Today Mr Glyn is on his feet again. He proclaims, as Article 10, that having established arbitrary and tyrannical government over the King's subjects and their lives, lands, property, and liberties, Thomas desired to do the same to the crown itself, and put his treacherous designs into practice by increasing the public revenue and keeping it for himself. This is all financial, and I'm not sure I understand it, but this is what I think it's all about.

First, they accuse him of something nasty to do with a lease of the Irish Customs farm granted to the late Duke of Buckingham. Thomas says: "How can that be my fault? The Duke was murdered in 1628, and got the Farm before that. I had no government position then apart from the Council of the North, and I wasn't made Deputy in Ireland until 1632 and didn't go there until 1633." That seemed to be the end of that, and I saw many Lords nodding their heads and whispering to each other.

Secondly, Glyn says that Thomas altered the lease in the Duke's widow' favour, and took money away from the Crown by doing so, and got more money for himself. Glyn says there were quite a few alterations. One was said to take the customs on wines away from my late husband, and another to subject all Shipping captured by the navy in Ireland to the Prize Court customs, for the benefit of the Duchess. I knew that was a silly allegation, as this also had happened years before Thomas went to Ireland. In any case, Thomas and my James were friends; why would Thomas do that to us? One of James's relatives, another James Hay, gives evidence about this, and pretty stupid he looks by the time Thomas finishes with him. Again I think many Lords seem to agree with Thomas.

Then Lord Ranelagh goes into the witness box. He's the Earl of Cork's son-in-law, and he and Cork hate Thomas. He says he's examined the Account Books of the Customs. He says Thomas raised the Customs Rates making the yield of Tax much higher. Then he says the amounts collected were 36,000 pounds in 1636, 39,000 in 1637, 54,000 in 1638, and 59,000 in 1639. Glyn makes out that this shows how greedy Thomas was, getting a huge commission on all that, and robbing the King, while saying that he worked hard and diligently for the Crown and the public. In truth he just did it all for himself, and that shows, all on its own, that he is guilty of Treason.

What a magnificent defence Thomas puts up to this! It amounts to this, as I recall: "I'm not going to repeat myself over the 'arbitrary government' allegation, or the work I've done; I've done that already. Let's look at the Book of Rates. Who increased them, and when? Lord Falkland increased the rates in 1628. That was over three years before I was made Deputy in Ireland. And when my Privy Council wished to put them up again, I was worried about the effect on Irish trade, so I wrote to the King expressing my concerns, and here is my copy of the letter.

"I bought the Customs Farm Lease from the Duchess. Was it Treason for me to make a good bargain when I did that?" He cross-examines Ranelagh about this, and wins all his points. Then he calls Lord Cottington and Sir Arthur Ingram to prove that he took on the Customs at the King's request to investigate how they ran and whether they could be improved, and he's done that, which was why the figures went up and up. Actually, I think it pretty brave, or even foolish, to have Sir Arthur as a witness, since he and Thomas are not the best of friends now, and Arthur is known to be such a swindler, but his evidence shows he lost out when he sold out of the Farm, so he has to be believed when he confirms what Thomas says about improving the revenue.

Thomas finishes something like this: "I do not deny that I made money out of the Farm, for that is why men take it on. But as my income increased, so did the money paid to the King. That was what this was all about. I made the Farm and the collection very efficient. I could pay the standing Irish Army, instead of the King having to do it. I could pay for the government of the country instead of the King doing it, and Ireland could send money to England for the English Treasury, a thing never before known to have happened.

"My Lords, I leave it to you whether Mr Glyn's allegation is not mere rhetoric on his part, rather than a serious charge against me." Again I feel that the sympathy of most people is with him.

Then Glyn goes onto Article 11, about a Monopoly on Tobacco. Lord Newcastle says it is time to stop for lunch, and they'll go on with that in the afternoon. I'm quite worn out trying to follow all this evidence and argument. Thomas must be nearly dead, although he looks as though he may be quite pleased with the day so far. I've noticed, though, that he never seems to get excited or show any sense of victory. I think it's clever. He gets more and more people to feel sorry for him, is how I see it. I'm going home.

Thomas. Wednesday, 31st March, 1641. Westminster Hall.

This morning Glyn presented his case about the Customs Farm. I think I disposed of it pretty effectively. I remember saying to someone long ago that if Pym and his gang brought in many of the Irish Remonstrance grievances it would not go well for them. I think I'm being proved right.

Just before the lunch adjournment Glyn asks to bring in Article 11 about the Tobacco Monopoly, but the Steward puts that off until this afternoon, and we're starting on that now. Glyn tells the Court that I started the Monopoly myself and there are five particulars to this Charge. 1) I restrained the import of Tobacco. 2) I imported a lot of it myself and sold it at exorbitant prices. 3) I stopped anyone selling Tobacco unless it had first been examined and put in Bond by my officers. 4) I had a large number of people seized, locked up, whipped, pilloried, and fined on false charges of having broken the Monopoly laws. 5) As a result I had been able to pocket over 100,000 pounds for myself.

Glyn produces my Proclamations stopping the imports and sealing and Bonding the Tobacco. Then he calls witnesses to say ships had been stopped from landing it, and others to say stores of Tobacco had been seized. As to my alleged profit, Glyn relies on the Irish Remonstrance which calculated I had sold 500 barrels of Tobacco at 2s/6d per pound, making 100,000 pounds profit. His case is that this was Treason because I had 'sucked up the blood and eaten the King's loyal people'. By this one activity alone I had made more money for myself than the whole Crown Revenue of Ireland, and broken the peace of the realm by relieving the people, with whose care I had been entrusted, of their goods.

In my defence I produce a quiver full of documents to shoot at him. I admit the truth of the allegation that there was a Monopoly, and that the traders had to pay a tax on the Tobacco. That produces some cries of "There you are!!" and "I told you so!!" These shouts did not last long, for I handed in a decree of King James's imposing a tax of 18 pence per pound, and restraining the import of the weed. I point out that at that time the Tobacco men paid only twenty pounds a year from this tax to the King, and explain how that had now risen to 4000 pounds a year. Five years before I even set foot in Ireland a Petition had been sent from the Irish Parliament to the King to have his tax imposed forever as an Act of State so that it would be a settled part of the Royal revenues. My Proclamations about Tobacco being examined, sealed and put in Bond store were according to the express command of His Majesty, and had in any case been put forward, not by me alone, but by the whole Irish Privy Council.

In a nutshell I argue again that it is a queer sort of Treason that obeys the King's own orders. I swear that as I produce the King's letter ordering the Proclamations I heard a loud chuckle from the Royal box.

As for the Contract for importing and selling Tobacco, I show the Court the papers, a letter from me to the Privy Council in England asking for their approval, and documents from that Council giving consent for the Contract to be used.

Then I turn to the charge that I had seized the traders' stocks, put some of them in the pillory, or had them whipped, and stopped them trading. I'm sure I satisfy the Court that I had only had the customs men seize the stocks when a trader would not pay the tax – after all, that amounted to trying to smuggle – and stopped him from trading for breaking the law. If they lied about whether they had paid the tax, or had smuggled the Tobacco into the country, they were whipped or pilloried for perjury, for those were the usual penalties for that crime.

I tell the peers that I had not done any of this except on the King's orders, and with the agreement of the Council. The King's Tobacco revenue had increased to 4,000 pounds, and in calculating the profit, the Commons had overlooked the cost of buying the Tobacco abroad, the expenses of selling the merchandise, and the tax paid over to the King. As the tax had been started by King James, I submit it was all so far from being Treason as to be no crime at all.

Lucy Carlisle. Thursday, 1st April, 1641. Westminster Hall.

Here I am again, and it is strange and disturbing: strange because Thomas is said to have committed treason by setting up a business of growing flax and turning it into linen, and to have crushed a linen trade carried on by the Irish, so that many of them in Ulster died of starvation. That seems rather far-fetched to me. Lord Ranelagh and Sir John Clotworthy give evidence against him on this matter, but I don't think the way their hatred for him shines out like a beacon helps their case.

Thomas answers that by the time he got to Ireland the linen trade had more or less died out. He noticed that the people were beginning to make woollen clothes, and he knew how important the wool and cloth trades were to England; so important in fact that Irish industry had often been suppressed in the past in favour of the West of England and the sheep counties and cloth towns of the North. He denies making any money out of linen, saying it had cost him 3,000 pounds which had been lost.

As for thousands of people dying in Ulster because of loads of linen being seized, he says that all the prosecution has proved is that one wagon load of unfit linen was confiscated in Connaught. It is difficult to see how that caused the death of thousands in Ulster.

Today is also strange because Mr Glyn charges him with the matters raised in the Irish Remonstrance, but there is no evidence to support it. Thomas says reading a Remonstrance on its own with no evidence proves nothing, so Articles 13 and 14, and a bit of 15, are passed over.

What is disturbing, or I find it so, is the way the prosecution have different men presenting different charges. So far Thomas has had to face Pym and St.John, and Mr Glyn, but this afternoon a Mr Palmer stands up to deal with the other half of Article 15. This alleges that

Thomas issued a warrant to a Sergeant Savil to billet soldiers on members of the public in a military fashion, and that this was, all on its own, enough to convict him of Treason, because when the people did not want to take in the soldiers, they and their possessions were seized.

Palmer calls Sergeant Savil to produce the warrant and to say that he had indeed billetted the soldiers. Thomas proves this is only a copy of the warrant and has not been certified or sworn to be a true copy by comparing with the original, and as an unsworn copy cannot be used, even in a case of debt, in the ordinary Courts, it could not be right to allow such a copy to be used to put a man on the scaffold for Treason.

That is when I get really disturbed, for Mr Glyn gets to his feet to argue this point instead of Mr Palmer. It is just so unfair. The Prosecutors choose different men to argue different points, and poor Thomas has to deal with all the evidence and all these speeches and arguments from different counsel one after the other. Yet he still seems to me to win almost every time. Then the Lords leave the Court to consider their opinion on this matter, and after an hour (of very loud wrangling coming from another part of the building) come back and say they agree with Thomas.

That means Palmer has to call what evidence he has, and this is Lord Ranelagh (again) and a Mr Clare, but their evidence doesn't seem to me to amount to much, just that they had seen such a warrant under Thomas's hand and seal. Palmer also refers to lots of Statutes which he says make billetting soldiers illegal.

Then it's Thomas's turn, but he hands this over to Mr Lane, his barrister. He shows that all those Acts of Parliament were for England, that there is a wholly different set of Acts and customs in Ireland, and that several previous Deputies had billetted the soldiery. I feel his best point is when he produces an Act of Queen Elizabeth making billetting legal in Ireland but Treason in all other parts of the Crown Dominions. Then Mr Lane makes many people laugh by adding: "And in the end, My Lords, this is all about the alleged billetting of five – yes, only five – soldiers."

Pym and Glyn look like thunder, and the other lawyers with them look downcast, but they are more furious still when Thomas gets up again. He looks to me as if he can barely stand, and he leans heavily on the table. His voice, normally strong and loud, sounds rather weak. Politely he asks: "My Lords, might you be good enough to consider adjourning to Saturday? I am feeble and tired almost to the point of dropping where I stand. I need some rest to gather my thoughts and such wits as I have if I am to be fit to continue."

He sits, looking greyer than ever and tired, so very tired. That this is the same man who was a strong and important man, and my very energetic lover not long since is almost beyond belief. There is not a shred of sympathy from Pym, however. He leaps to his feet, and angrily addresses the peers about the necessity for getting on with the trial with no delays, and makes out that Thomas is just play-acting for time and the benefit of the gallery. Some Lords are clearly of the same mind and the argument rages back and forth for quite a while, but in the end what seem to me to be wise counsels prevail, and the case is held over until Saturday. I am so happy for Thomas. I do hope he can get some rest.

Thomas. Saturday, 3rd April, 1641.

The day begins badly. When I wake, the servant who brings my breakfast says he is ordered to tell me that yesterday the King gave his assent to the Graces in Ireland. In a way I can understand it, since in our present difficulties he needs to bring over to his side as many of his enemies, and keep as many of his supporters, as possible. Even so, I feel betrayed, since this act will undo so much of the work he wanted me to do over there, and so much of what I had achieved, or was well on the way to doing.

At the Hall I am faced again by Mr Geoffrey Palmer, of whom I really know very little, save that he is quite handsome, with curly dark-brown hair, but rather short. To say I find it irksome that Pym and his friends can take it in turns to attack me like a pack of hounds baiting a bear at Barnet Fair is to put it very mildly indeed. Still, enough of that.

Palmer's task is to present Article 16. Yes, 16; we are not yet half-way through the list of my crimes!! The general thrust of it is that in Ireland I established a tyranny, and by giving summary Decrees and Verdicts and Punishments, had deprived the King's Irish subjects of all justice. I had done this, he says, by making myself the supreme being in the land, so that no-one could appeal even to the King. In addition, I had made things worse by stopping anyone from leaving the island without my permission.

He offers eight facts to prove this general proposition. First, he reads out the Proclamation stopping men leaving the country.

Secondly, he reads out my Proclamation that no-one who travelled to Ireland could leave there without my licence. Thirdly, I stopped the Earl of Desmond leaving Ireland until judgment in a case between the two of us was pronounced. Fourthly, Lord Roch was prevented from entering Ireland until Star Chamber proceedings in London against him in London were concluded. Fifthly, a Mr Marchatee was refused peremission to travel. Sixth, I was blamed for the Committee of the whole House of Commons of Ireland being restrained from foreign travel by my late friend Kit, because we used to communicate, and because Kit made the order under my Proclamation. Seventh, a Mr Parry left Ireland without my licence, and I fined him 500 pounds when he went back. Lastly, the Irish Remonstrance said this was "the greatest innovation and thraldom put upon Ireland" since William the Conqueror.

Palmer winds up his speech by saying that what I had done was to stop the people communicating with "so just and so gracious a prince," depriving them of the remedies the King might afford them, making myself an independent royal power, and thereby trespassing mightily against the King and the Nation.

The Steward calls upon me to reply, and I stand to do so. "My Lords, I hope I shall show to your satisfaction that I have done nothing which fits those last few remarks of Mr Palmer's except what has been usual, necessary, and just in Ireland for a very long time. By the Grace of God I shall give you a reasonable account of all my conduct, and not just in respect of this Charge currently before you.

"First, permit me to read the Instruction restraining men from leaving the country: 'It would be unjust to complain of injury or oppression done in Ireland until the Deputy's judgment was given, and his integrity had been tested. The King's Ministers in Ireland would be discouraged if every trifling complaint about their government could be taken to England, but if justice were denied to anyone by the Deputy, it should be lawful for any man to go to the King'. This was not my work alone, but that of the King and English Privy Council, so it cannot amount to Treason.

"As to the second point, about stopping men going back to England unless I permitted it, that merely repeats, word for word, the Irish Statute of Henry VI. The Irish Government had petitioned His Majesty for this power again five years before I went to Ireland, and it was issued by Deputy Falkland.

"Thirdly, I have here King Charles' own warrant for me to re-issue the restraint of travel in 1634, but I did not do this until September of the following year, and it was approved by the Privy Council in Dublin. I invite you, My Lords, to consider whether this measure was and is necessary in Ireland. There are many more Papists there than here, and if the ports there are open to all, many will go to the Catholic seminaries in Spain, Douai, Rheims, and St.Omer, and they will return to spread religious and civil discontent throughout the land. Here in England where the King is master, he can stop whom he pleases from going abroad, and it is illegal to go without the King's permit. If that is required here, how much more vital is it in Ireland?

"My Lords, let me now turn to the examples on which Mr Palmer relies. Let us look at the case of the Earl of Desmond. There was no law suit between him and me. He was charged before the Irish Council with Treason for plotting to take the life of Sir Valentine Cooke, and could not be permitted to escape before his trial was concluded. I proffer the Indictment against him as evidence

"The case of Lord Roch was similar. He was already in prison for debt, as the warrant I now hand in shows. It was a source of some amazement to me that he should even contemplate applying for a permit to leave Ireland. If I had granted him one, wouldn't his creditors not now be clamouring for me to be charged with Treason on that account?

"Mr Marchatee did not say, when he applied for licence to travel, where he wished to go, but intelligence I had received indicated he wanted to go to Spain, and I have already told you, My Lords, what my fears were in that respect. Indeed I venture to surmise that many of you would have held similar apprehensions if you had been Deputy, or Lord Lieutenant, in my stead. Had his application, which I now produce, said he wanted to go to England, I should have granted it, as I did with all similar requests by those innocent of any wrong-doing.

"I have little to say about Sir Christopher Wandesford having stopped the Commons Committee coming to England, if he did so, as it was nothing to do with me, and was done when I was here in England, and waiting for this trial, in the Tower." My throat is suddenly very dry,

I cough, and I ask for some water. I sit until it comes, and the Steward waits patiently for me to drink. Then I stand again.

"Thank you, My Lord Steward. Now, the 500 pound fine on Mr Parry. I have here the sentence pronounced against him by the Court. He was not punished for coming to England, but for contempt of the Council in Dublin. As you will see when you read that document, that is precisely what it says. Finally, I am threatened again with what the Irish Remonstrance says, and again I say that without evidence, that is no proof of anything at all, let alone Treason. My Lords, that is all I have to say on the subject of Article 16."

Arundel then adjourns for lunch and I am right glad of a break, and some refreshment. I am expecting Articles 17 and 18 to be levelled against me this afternoon, but when the Court resumes, there are two surprises. First, a new adversary pops up in the shape of a Mr Bulstrode Whitlock. I know him well. He is a very able lawyer indeed, and sits as a judge in Abingdon and Henley. We both sat in the Parliaments of the 1620s under King James and during the early years of Charles's reign. He doesn't look like a bull, and he never strode over anyone, as far as I know. He's a handsome fellow, and wears a beard and moustache like the King – well – like me too, really. He's MP for Marlow in this Parliament. He's the kind of man I was talking about when I told the Lords earlier that it wounds me to be accused of Treason by the friends of my youth.

The second surprise is that he announces no evidence will be offered on Articles 17 (that I encouraged the King to have an Army modelled on my Irish one in England, Wales, and Scotland), and 18 (that I had brought monasteries and friaries and other Roman institutions back to life in Ireland and made the Catholics dependent on me). How they could have thought it worthwhile to put such Charges in the Indictment I do not know. It might make the Prosecution case look overwhelming at first blush, but when no evidence is offered, the folly of their position is manifest. My hopes rise accordingly, but I manage not to give my feelings away.

"May it please this Court," Whitlock begins, "the accused not only wished to take control of the bodies of the subjects of Ireland, but he wished to domineer over their consciences too. He contrived an Oath which the Scots living in Ireland were to be forced to take, that they did not support the Covenant movement in Scotland. The Lieutenant fined most heavily those who refused, as a matter of conscience, to take the Oath. Some of them he banished from that Kingdom. He called all the Scots Traitors and Rebels, and said that if he ever returned to England he would destroy them root and branch.

"In support of these allegations I call four witnesses," and he produces amongst them Sir John Clotworthy. "Only Parliament has the power to cause Oaths to be administered. It was Treason for Lord Strafford to do it."

I cross-examine them all. I do not think their evidence amounts to much. For example, Clotworthy gave the names of several people who, he says, had fled Ireland to avoid taking the Oath, but that did him no favours as they were not supposed to leave the country without permission anyway. None of these people give evidence, so what he says is only hearsay, and worth nothing. The evidence I had called all the Scots Nation "Traitors and Rebels" is given by a Mr Samuels, a small dark man with a swarthy countenance, who tells the Lords that he had heard me say it on 10th October 1639 at a meeting in Dublin, and then starts to leave the witness box.

Me. Kindly remain in the witness box, please, Mr Samuel. It is my turn to ask you a few questions now Mr Whitlock has sat down.

Steward. Yes, Mr Samuel, you must stay where you are for the moment. Lord Strafford?

Me. Thank you, My Lord. Mr Samuel. You say I told the meeting on 10th October, almost eighteen months ago, that all the Scots were Traitors and Rebels, and that if I returned to England I should destroy them all, root and branch. Have I got that right?

Samuel. True enough, that's what I heard you say.

Me. Didn't you think I must have been quite mad to say that?

Samuel. Well, I don't know about that. You looked sane enough to me.

Me. I'm surprised you could see me at all at the meeting, but I'll come back to that. Do you know where our gracious King was born?

Samuel. Of course I do. Scotland.

Me. And what kind of men are born there, Mr Samuel?

Samuel. *(He laughs).* Scotsmen. *(He laughs again; then he blushes to the roots of his hair).*

Me. Yes, Mr Samuel, Scotsmen, and I see you realise you have just alleged that I threatened to destroy the King root and branch, too. If I said it at all, I should not be likely to say it at a public meeting, should I? Would you?

Samuel. *(Very quietly).* No.

Me. Thank you. Now have you heard of Lord Huntly?

Samuel. I have. He's the head of the Gordon Clan.

Me. Yes, the Gordons of Aberdeen. Did you know that he resisted the Covenant of behalf of the King, was supported by his kin and tenants, was arrested, and Aberdeen had to be besieged twice by the Covenanters?

Samuel. Yes, I heard something of that.

Me. Do you accept that Lord Huntly and the Gordons are loyal and true to the King?

Samuel. Of course I do.

Me. Then is it likely that I should say that I wanted to root him and his people out?

Samuel. That isn't what you said. You said 'all Scots'.

Me. Then if Huntly is Scottish I'd have to root him out too, wouldn't I?

Samuel. *(After a pause, and very reluctantly).* Well, maybe you said you'd root out all Traitors and Rebels.

Me. And how can that be Treason against His Majesty, or against England, Mr Samuel? *(He is silent).* Scotland being the birthplace of our Sovereign is a country I honour greatly, Mr Samuel. Is it so for you?

Samuel. It is.

Me. Then we can agree about that. Now, let us look again at the date of the meeting. 10th October 1639, I believe you say?

Samuel. Correct. I'm absolutely certain.

Me. Would you look at this document, please? Would you tell us what it is?

Samuel. It says it's a true copy of a meeting of the Privy Council in London on 25th September, 1639.

Me. Has it been sworn as a true copy? Has it got a judge's seal on it?

Samuel. Yes, at the bottom.

Me. Very well. Mr Samuel, would you kindly read the list of Councillors to their Lordships?

Samuel. Certainly. His Majesty, Secretary Vane, Lord Northumberland, Archbishop Laud, Lord Hamilton, and ....

Me. And, Mr Samuel?

Samuel. Lord Strafford.

Me. Yes, Mr Samuel. I sailed from Dublin on 12th September, I arrived in London on the 21st, and after a short period in the capital, attending Council meetings like that one, I followed the King north to York and the Scots Army. Mr Samuel, everyone in this Hall knows I was in England from September that year until March of 1640 when I went back to Ireland for a couple of months. I could not have been at a meeting in Dublin on 10th October 1639, now could I?

Steward. If you are unable to answer the question Mr Samuel, you may leave the stand.

And that is what he does, his head hanging very low indeed. I finish by saying to the Lords: "If I had not stopped the Scotsmen in Ireland – about 100,000 of them, from going to Scotland - and had not made them take the Oath, they would have flocked to the Covenanter's colours against the King, and that would undoubtedly have been Treason. Far from administering the Oath to control their consciences and their relations with God, I simply gave them the chance to swear their loyalty to their King, and that can be no Treason. If they fled the country to avoid taking the Oath, and they do not come here to give evidence, then this Court can decide what their true intentions were, if they went to Scotland."

The Steward then adjourns until Monday, so I have another day of prayer, a little rest, a chance to write to dearest Bess and the children, and meet with Lane to prepare for Monday.

Thomas. Sunday, 4th April, 1641. The Tower.

Dearest Bess, My Sweetheart,

I hope you are well, and the children too, especially baby Margaret. The Trial is such grinding toil that I am desperately tired, but I have been to the Tower Chapel today to pray, and that is always a comfort. I believe that God helps me, for Pym and his friends seem to be having a hard time of it to make their charges against me stick. It would be an unwise boast for me to say that I am getting the better of the evidence and arguments all the time, but from the murmurings I hear around me, and some of the shouted comments, and some laughter, I am sure that more and more of the people – Lords, the spectators, and even some MPs - are becoming more sympathetic to my plight and my side of these dreadful stories.

I pray fervently that that may be so, that I shall be acquitted, and that I shall soon be home safely with you and the family. Brother George is in London, and he writes to me, but I am not allowed to see him. He says Pym intends to call him to give evidence against me soon.

Thank you for your recent letter. I treasure each one I receive, and read them time and time again until I can almost recite them word for word. They are no subsitute for having you by me, but they buoy me mightily. I wish I had time to write more, but I expect Richard Lane shortly, and we have much work to do, for I fear that the Articles which will be raised against me tomorrow are the most serious of all, though I am confident I can answer them right well.

Pray for me.

As always, my love, I am your own Thomas.

Thomas. Monday, 5th April, 1641. Westminster Hall.

A sledgehammer blow strikes me full force as soon as the Trial opens this morning. I had been expecting that the Prosecutors would proceed with Article 20. That charge was that in the previous two years I had laboured hard to make the King think very ill of his Scottish subjects; had, especially since the Pacification of Berwick, tried to provoke the King to take an offensive war against Scotland; and was the chief incendiary of war and discord between His Majesty and his subjects, both Scots and English. To reinforce these allegations, this Article, when it was first promulgated last November, even relied on my supposedly having said I would 'destroy the Scots root and branch'. I did not think that would do their case much credit, when, as it seemed to me, Mr Samuel's evidence on that point had been entirely exploded on Saturday.

Instead of that expectation, Mr Whitlock rises to tell the Court that he will amalgamate Article 20 with the next four, as they all tend towards the same end, namely to show that I had a plan to subdue the Kingdoms of England and Scotland by force of arms and subject them to the same form of arbitrary government I had introduced in Ireland.

I am so shocked I am, for once, rendered almost dumb. How can I deal with five charges at once, having prepared for one at a time? "My Lords, at the outset of this case, you wisely laid down the procedure to be followed. On this point you stipulated that the Charges would be laid against me one after the other in the order laid down in the Articles of Impeachment. It is on that basis that I am prepared for today. Five Articles at once is too many, the subject of them too meaty, and my memory too treacherously defective to do myself justice at such short notice. Indeed, if you aim to do your duty and minister to justice, you would not allow this request of Mr Whitlock's. In fact, when you examine it, it is not a request; he has simply told you that he is going to present five Charges at once, and over-ride your directive."

I slump into my chair, and Glyn leaps out of his. "If it please Your Lordships, it ill behoves the prisoner to tell us in what way we should present our evidence. The case must proceed as Mr Whitlock has suggested."

Lane's advice not to attack anyone if I can help it comes to mind again. "My Lords," I say as I struggle to my feet, "it may be that if Mr Glyn and Mr Whitlock were in my place, they would crave the same favour, though I accept that their abilities may be so much greater than mine that they could easily deal with five Charges at once. Even so, I am content that they go on in any manner they deem fit, provided always that you, My Lords, will grant me ample time to reply."

The Lords allow them to proceed with all five counts, having given me leave to make my answers.

Then Whitlock resumes the attack. Attack is what he does. He is like a bull-dog, aggressive both in manner and appearance. "My Lords, these five Articles concern the Scots and the English nations. There are five allegations in the Scottish case, and seven in the English. As against the Scots they are that the Lord Lieutenant did the following:

"1) He told the Privy Council that the Scots' Demands in their Petition to the King, and in their Covenant, were sufficiently serious to justify an offensive war;

"2) He said that those Demands did strike at the root and life of the monarchy, and could only be answered by the sword.

"3) He had Scottish goods and ships seized in Ireland.

"4) He enraged the Irish Parliament into a Declaration of War against the Scots.

"5) He laboured to make the King think ill of the Scots, and to create a national quarrel between Scotland and England, which was only avoided by the piety of His Majesty, and the prudent advice of other statesmen.

"As for the prisoner's actions against this, our country – his own country too – they were:

"1) In the presence of his bosom friend, Sir George Radcliffe, he had said to Sir Robert King, who questioned how the King might pay his Armies, that he, the prisoner, had 400,000 pounds in his purse, 30,000 men in the field, and his sword by his side. He added that 'If I need money afterwards, who will refuse me?'

"2) His brother Sir George Wentworth said to Sir Robert Barrington that if the English would not grant the King supplies, they must be weary of peace, and wish to be conquered by the Scots a second time.

"3) The prisoner told Archbishop Ussher, Primate of All Ireland, that he agreed with those Divines who held that, if a King sought the affections and help of his people, and was refused, he might, where the Kingdom were in inevitable and present danger, use his Prerogative to raise money and defend the Kingdom and his subjects.

"4) In May he told Lord Conway that if Parliament should refuse the King adequate money, he was acquitted before God and man, and could use his Royal Authority to take what he needed.

"5) He told the Privy Council that if Parliament would not help the King, he could take any other way he liked to obtain assistance.

"6) He voiced the opinion that the Parliament had forsaken the King, who should not allow himself to be mastered by such forward, obstinate and stubborn people.

"And last, but by no means least, he told the King in Council that if the King wanted to use force he had in Ireland an Army that could reduce this Kingdom."

Whitlock then calls evidence from no fewer than six witnesses on the Scots charges, and eleven about what I am supposed to have said concerning England.

His first witness is none other than Lord Traquair, the King's minister and emissary from Scotland, who brought the Scots Demands to the Privy Council. It is clear to all that he is on my side, and if he says anything to my disadvantage, it is only when Whitlock treats him as if he were pulling his teeth out. He admits that he heard me say that it was high time for the King to make himself ready for war, but adds that that was the opinion of the whole Council, and it was his own opinion too. He tells the Court that the prosecution seem to think that because I said that, I contemplated no other remedy.

There was no point in my questioning him, so I merely stood to thank him for being there. I hope their Lordships realise that by doing so I accept the truth of what Traquair has said, and that, in effect, he has defended me well.

The next witness is sick and not in Court, so Whitlock reads his evidence. I point out to the Steward that as I cannot test the witness by cross-examintaion, his written testimony is worthless, and sit down again. Whitlock seems likely to have apoplexy at that, but his protests amount to nothing, and he calls Sir Harry Vane as his next witness. He says he also heard me call for offensive war, when in his view it should be defensive only. I ask him if he has heard that attack is the best method of defence, and he admits it, and I leave it at that, since Traquair has already put the record straight.

My friend Algie, Earl of Northumberland, is Whitlock's next witness, but he is not present either, so he reads his proof. This is to the same effect as Vane's, that he heard me talk of offensive war when he favoured defence alone. I rise to make the same point about being unable to cross-examine, and I say that if Algie had been there he would have spoken favourably of my part at the Council Board, and I doubt not that that was why Whitlock had kept him away from the Hall.

The Bishop of London, Juxon, now Treasurer of England, is called by Whitlock. He gives evidence almost identical to Lord Traquair's, doing me no harm, so I thank him for coming too. He is followed by an Irishman called Beane, who is to give evidence that I had seized Irish goods and ships, but is a dreadful disappointment to Pym and his allies, for he says that whilst he knew some ships and goods had been taken, he did not know who had authorised it.

Now Whitlock turns to the Charges regarding what I'm alleged to have said about England. He calls Sir Robert King and Lord Ranelagh. He asks them what they heard me say. What they tell him helps him not a jot. They say they heard Sir George Radcliffe say what the Article alleges. He tries to get them to admit that it was I who had spoken, but that is not what they tell the Court. This is so harmful to Pym's case that I do not need to expose Ranelagh as Cork's son-in-law and my enemy, even though Glyn says that Radcliffe is my 'creature' and that my spirit can force him to say what I wish. However, I do make the point to their

Lordships that what Sir George may have said cannot make me guilty of Treason. As so often happens now, I hear murmurs of what sound like assent to my proposition.

Next into the witness box is Sir Robert Barrington to relate what brother George is supposed to have said. The answer to that is the same as in the case of Radcliffe: I cannot be guilty of Treason because of the utterances of others. Whitlock then reads Archbishop Ussher's statement, as he is another witness absent, he says, through illness. Again I make the point that in the absence of cross-examination, the statement is worth nothing, and as with Algie, if he were there, it would be a different story.

I do not need to deal much with Lord Conway, who tells the Court I said: "If Parliament does not give the King enough money, he could take it as he likes." I ask him: "Do you agree that the law is that dangerous times call for dangerous remedies, and that such action is essential to supply and pay armies in such times?" Being an old soldier, he agrees, saying: "If it were otherwise the Kingdom would always be over-run by the invader."

Lord Holland comes into the box to tell the Court I told him the King should not let himself be mastered by Parliament, but his hatred of me is so solid all can feel it. I ask a few questions to make that even plainer, and discredit him. Three others give similar evidence, but a fourth, the Earl of Bristol, minces his words and damages Whitlock's assertions, casting doubt on the Charge.

Now is the most dangerous moment for me. Whitlock calls his evidence on the charge that I said I had an Army in Ireland which could 'reduce this Kingdom'. He tells the Steward he has one witness, Sir Harry Vane. He has no other evidence, yet this is the most vital of the allegations against me. The law is that Treason cannot be proved by the testimony of only one witness!

Sir Harry tells their Lordships of the Council meeting, and of the people present, including the King. I intervene.

Me. The witness should take the Oath, My Lord.

Pym. *(he stands to address the Court).* The Court has already ruled that prosecution witnesses are not to be sworn, especially not Members of Parliament.

Me. But this charge carries with it the death penalty!!

Steward. The ruling will not be changed, My Lord Strafford. Sir Harry will not be sworn.
Pym. I am obliged, My Lord. *(And he resumes his seat).*
Whitlock. *(Rising to continue with Sir Harry).* Sir Harry, you were at the meeting of the Privy Council on 5th May last, I believe?
Vane. I was. The Council discussed the war against the Scots.
Pym. Was the Irish Army mentioned?
Vane. Yes.
Pym. By whom?
Vane. By the accused, the Earl of Strafford.
Pym. And what did he say?
Vane. *(Nervously.)* Never in the whole of my life have I loved to tell an untruth.
Pym. Of course not. What did he say?
Vane. *(In a stuttering, confused manner.)* My Lord of Strafford did say....... Did advise the King...... I really am telling the truth...... He said: "Your Majesty has tried all ways, and in this extreme necessity, and for the safety of the Kingdom, you are acquitted before God and man, and you have an army in Ireland which you may employ here to reduce this kingdom." *(Uncertainly).* Or some words to that effect. *(Querulously).* Is that clear? I am sorry. I must make myself clear. It is true Lord Strafford said these words: "You may," but what he meant by them I cannot say. They were the words he spoke. If this were my last hour, I must say this is the truth.

(I am full of unrevealed glee, since he is now saying he is not absolutely sure what words I actually used. I am not the only one who notices this.)

My nephew, Lord Savile, stands and asks Sir Harry: "Did Lord Strafford say 'there, or 'this', or 'that'?" Sir Harry is flustered and unable to give a very clear answer. At that Savile remarks: "It is very hard to condemn a man for treason upon such petty circumstances," and sits.

At once the Earl of Southampton is on his feet: "Sir Harry, can you swear those words positively or not?" Vane replies: "Positively I say, either them or the like." Some soft laughter can be heard, most of the prosecutors look down at their briefs, or up to Heaven, as if for guidance, and Pym smacks his fist down on the table in rage. His discomfiture does not end there, however, for Arabella's brother, now Earl Clare, rises, and asks Sir Harry:

"What did Earl Strafford mean by 'this kingdom'? I think it means the Kingdom of Scotland, for that was the only kingdom being discussed at the meeting. I am reinforced in that opinion, since I cannot see by what grammatical construction it could be gathered from the prisoner's words that he meant to reduce England, which neither then was, nor is now (thanks be to God) in a state of disobedience or rebellion."

Sir Harry Vane makes no response.

It is my turn to address their Lordships on those charges,
and I have already related how I dealt with them to some extent, but I need to elucidate three matters. First, what was said about offensive and defensive war. "My Lords, I do not dispute what Lord Northumberland and Sir Harry Vane said about offensive and defensive war. I remember the debate very well. I spoke of an offensive and they for a defensive approach to war. This was at a meeting of His Majesty's Privy Council. The purpose of the Council is to offer the King opinions and advice on courses of action that may be open to him, or which, perhaps, he should avoid.

"I do not adhere to my views in the face of contrary argument, as a heretic might in matters of faith. I acknowledge my fallibility, and my weaknesses, and I am ready to correct and amend them. That does not mean that we should be afraid to offer the King our honest counsel for fear that we may be in error. In the end the decisions are his, and he takes them in the light of the advice of his Councillors, but he is not bound by that advice, for the decisions are, as I say, his alone to make.

"You might like to consider what would have been the effect of an offensive war if properly prepared and funded. It might have been expensive, but is it possible that we should not have had the burden of the Scots occupying the six northernmost counties of England, living off the land and the people, and then being paid over 800 pounds per day to stay there? Can anyone put a figure on what might be the difference between the cost of an offensive war, and what has in fact been the cost of the way the Bishop's War was fought, and the amount it still costs daily?

"My Lords, the other point which still needs clarification is the question of the detention of ships and goods in Ireland. I submit that

Mr Beane's evidence on this proves nothing against me personally, but I have no desire to be anything but completely frank with this Tribunal. Therefore I accept that some ships were seized, and were seized on my orders, as I was Vice-Admiral of Connaught. Why did I do this? Because I was ordered to do it by the King. Here is His Majesty's letter instructing me what action to take. Now, if it be Treason against the King to obey the King, my understanding of the law is much mistaken.

"It is also necessary to explain that I have been unable to call some of my own witnesses because they have been impeached or arrested in Ireland, and may not come here. There are others whom I could have called, except that I was not given permission to do so until three days before the Trial started, so the permission was of no use to me

"Finally, My Lords, I must deal with the evidence of Sir Harry Vane that I told the King he could use an Irish Army to 'reduce this Kingdom', the implication being that I meant he should use the Irish Army to conquer England. May I now cross-examine him?" The Steward gives me permission to do so after lunch, but Pym is immediately on his feet.

Pym. *(To the Steward).* My Lord, this is a most serious charge, and we are entitled to a decision.

Steward. There will be no premature findings of guilt, Master Pym. *(Pointedly, and kindly to me).* This trial will not be a farce if I can help it.

After lunch, Sir Harry goes to the witness box.

Me. Now, Sir Harry. You are Secretary to the Council?

Vane. I am.

Me. Your job is to take notes of what is said at the meetings?

Vane. It is.

Me. Now the Court has heard your evidence that I am a traitor because I advised the King that he could bring over the Irish Army, has it not?

Vane. Yes. It was treason.

Me. What is treason, then?

Vane. *(Cupping his ear).* What was your reason?

Me. *(Louder).* No, Sir Harry, I asked you what is treason?

Vane. Ah! What is treason. It is plotting against the King and giving comfort to his enemies.

Me. And who were the King's enemies at that time?

Vane. *(Sheepishly).* The Scots.

Me. The Scots. And what was money from Spain wanted for?

Vane. The King wanted money to pay the Army to fight the Scots.

Me. The King wanted the money to pay the Army to fight the Scots. *(I pause).* To fight the enemy. *(Again I pause).* But the King did not get the money, did he? Why was that?

Vane. Er.... well.... er..... *(He looks at Pym who looks away).* It was... er.... because... er...

(I decide to increase the pace).

Me. It was because someone told the Dutch, who told the King that if he got the money from Spain, he would have to fight them as well as the Scots. Wasn't it?

Vane. I don't know.

Me. I think you do. You and Master Pym did not want the war with the Scots. Did you?

Vane. *(Boldly).* No, we didn't. Neither did most of the Commons.

Me. But it is not treason to defy the Commons, is it?

Vane. *(Reluctantly).* No.

Me. So as Secretary to the Council, you had the information, and you told the Dutch.

Vane. *(Desperately).* I didn't tell them. I told Master Pym.

Me. And –

Vane. - and he told the Dutch.

Me. So when you told the Court you did not know who told the Dutch, that was untrue. *(Vane Says nothing. I pause).* Mr Pym told the Dutch. So you and Pym plotted against the King.

Vane. No! We plotted against you and foiled your scheme!!

Me. But the King didn't get the money he needed?

Vane. No.

Me. *(I slow the pace a little).* Don't you think that gave comfort to his enemy - gave comfort to the Scots? *(Pause).* I take it your silence implies assent. *(Pause).* It looks as though the treason was not mine for arranging the Spanish payment, but yours and Pym's for preventing it.

Pym. *(Rising).* I am not on trial here.

Me. I know very well who is on trial here.

Steward. So do I. *(Was that directed at me or Pym?)* So please get on with it!
Me. As you please, My Lord. *(I turn back to Vane).* Sir Harry, let's go back to the Council meeting. You told the Court that I told the King I could bring over the Irish Army.
Vane. Yes.
Me. So that the Irish Army could conquer England, was what you meant, I think.
Vane. That's what I said. Yes.
Me. *(I increase the pace again).* You have already agreed that it was your job to make notes of what was said at the meeting?
Vane. It was. Yes, I did.
Me. But you have given your evidence entirely from memory, haven't you?
Vane. Yes.
Me. And why is that?
Vane. *(Very Quietly).* My notes are not to be found.
Me. *(I am sarcastic).* My ears must be failing me. Could you say that again?
Vane. The notes are missing.
Me. But you remember word for word what was said a year ago?
Vane. Yes.
Me. Even though I deny using the words you have described?
Vane. Yes.
Pym. What else would you do but deny it?
Me. *(I speak in measured tones to the Steward).* Your Lordship might remind Mr. Pym that it's my turn to ask the questions. May I remind the Court that I do not deny the conversation, nor advising the King to use the Irish Army? What I deny is telling the King to use that Army to overrun England. *(To Vane, resuming the pace).* What were we discussing at the Council, Sir Harry?
Vane. The war. The war with Scotland.
Me. Yes, the war with Scotland. And we spoke of the trouble the King was having raising an Army, did we not?
Vane. Yes. And how to pay the Army.
Me. Correct. How to raise an Army and how to pay the soldiers to fight the Scots.
Vane. Yes.

Me. Did the King speak of fighting his English subjects?
Vane. *(Reluctantly).* No.
Me. No. *(Pause).* The King did not seek advice on fighting his English subjects?
Vane. No.
Me. Bishop Juxon was at the meeting. So were the Earl of Hamilton and Lord Cottington, and the Earl of Northumberland. They all deny that I said anything about using the Irish Army to subdue England. Are they wrong?
Vane. They didn't take the notes. I did.
Me. And the notes have mysteriously disappeared. And you are deaf, are you not?
Vane. I am hard of hearing, yes.
Me. *(Very Quietly).* Can you be certain of what you think you heard?
Vane. *(He uses his ear-trumpet).* I didn't catch that.
Pym. *(Coming to the rescue).* The notes have not disappeared. I have a copy here. *(He hands them to me. I look at them, and hand them to Sir Harry).*
Me. Are these your notes?
Vane. This is not my writing.
Me. Then whose is it?
Vane. I believe..... it is Master Pym's.
Me. *(I am incredulous).* Master Pym's?
Vane. Yes. My son copied my original notes, and I gave them to Master Pym who copied them again. My notes are lost, and my son's copy too.
Me. The words you quoted me as using are, word for word, what is on that paper, are they not?
Vane. They are.
Me. And in the end I am to be convicted - nay - executed - on the basis of one man's memory of a non-existent piece of paper that has been copied out by Master Pym who wants nothing better than to see me die! *(I address the Steward).* My Lord, this is but the evidence of one man, and the law is that no-one is to be convicted of treason on the evidence of one man. As a Privy Councillor I took an oath to give the King the best advice fearlessly. That is what I did, and I do not deny that; indeed, I am proud of it.
King. *(Banging his cane on the ground).* This is the truth.

Steward. This House sits as a Court, Your Majesty, and you may not interrupt.

Queen. The King is not subject to the Law!!

Steward. You may not interfere either, Ma'am. One of the issues in this case is whether the King and his Ministers are under the Law. *(To me).* Go on.

Me. Ask yourselves this My Lords. If I am undone for doing my duty, who would dare fearlessly to advise the King – or any government - in future? Which of you – who may have advised the King in the past - would wish to exchange places with me now?

Pym. *(Rising as I sit).* My Lords, what is this plea? Is it anything more than this, that Councillors may speak treason freely? Is my Lord Strafford's plea not simply that the privilege of a Councillor hides and excuses treason?

Me. *(I am scathing).* Committing treason by talking to the King about the things the King wishes to discuss is a concept I find it difficult to follow! *(I stagger and almost fall. Wearily).* My Lord, I call the members of the Privy Council who were present at the Council Meeting on 5th May, and who are free and able to attend. I cannot call the Archbishop, nor Secretary Windebanke, as the one is in the Tower, and the other has fled the country. I call The Earl of Northumberland, Lord Hamilton, the Lord Treasurer Bishop Juxon, and Lord Cottington.

All of these noblemen come into the witness box in succession, and ask to be sworn, in contrast to Sir Harry Vane. They all deny I had spoken the words related by Vane. Algie says, in addition, that I had spoken with great honour and regard for England. Hamilton, surprisingly as we have not always cared for each other much, denies the words, and adds that he had often heard me say that the King should rule truly, and that it would never be well for England until the Prerogative of the Crown and the Privilege of the Subject went hand in hand, and that Parliaments were the happiest way to achieve this harmony between King and People.

Bishop Juxon and Lord Cottington speak to the like effect. I then tell their Lordships, for the avoidance of any doubt, that there was never the least intention on my part to bring the Irish Army into England, and that it is a marvel that of all these witnesses, only Sir Harry heard what is alleged against me.

"My Lords, if a man is to be convicted of treason for what he says in his home or to his friends, and particularly when they have been sworn on Oath to secrecy, as members of the King's council are, is any man free? Let what is happening to me be a warning to you. Your wise ancestors put bonds and limits on this lion of a crime, Treason. If you remove those restraints, he will at last tear you and yours to pieces.

"Opinions are free, and men may argue the pros and cons of everything. If they could not, then the King would consult them in vain. They may act as Devil's Advocates, to get a better understanding of the point at issue. You may express a point of view, but change it on hearing wiser judgements. We may pitch our arguments too high so as to reach a compromise with our fellows.

"If to give your opinions in political matters should be accounted Treason, who will be willing to serve the King? If you, as Councillors, having taken your Oath, do not speak your mind truthfully, you are guilty of Perjury. But if you do, and if this case goes against me, you will be guilty of Treason. How can the King rule with wise counsel if that be the case?

"My Lords, I do not see how I can be guilty of Treason, unless it be Treason that I am not infallible." At this point I almost fall down again. "The Court has been sitting for ten hours today, My Lords, and I am too sick and weary to last any longer. I beg the Court to adjourn, perhaps for a day."

Pym. I object, My Lord. We must go on.

Steward. Mr. Pym, the prisoner is not the only one who is in need of rest. We shall adjourn until the day after tomorrow when we shall hear the final speeches.

Thomas. Tuesday, 6th April, 1641. The Tower.

It may not be Sunday, but I am allowed to go, escorted, of course, to the Chapel to pray, and the Keeper of the Tower accompanies me on a walk in the grounds within the walls. I feel relieved that yesterday seemed to go so well, and today I have a letter from Elizabeth. What comfort that is!! She gives me news of herself and the children, and of William's progress in his studies. She tells me she misses me dreadfully, and that she loves me eternally.

I must go in and write to her, and I do. Then I have a cheering visit from the Bishop of London, and he helps me pray, and we discuss what occurred yesterday, and he gives me news of my old friend Archbishop Laud, whom I am not allowed to see, and he tells me the prelate is failing in health and seems very, very old.

After lunch, Richard Lane joins me in preparation for tomorrow. It is tiring, but I am more and more confident of a victorious outcome, so I am content.

Thomas. Wednesday, 7th April, 1641. Westminster Hall.

Whitlock starts the day with a highly inflammatory attack on me and 'my most horrid Treason', and flatters his hearers by saying that I should have succeeded with it but for 'the clemency and goodness' of the King and 'the piety and carefulness' of the loyal peers who had with timely foresight prevented it. He adds that the Articles which have already been heard are so important and of so paramount a nature as to need nothing more to prove my Treason, but he will now present Article 25! This charge is that I advised the King: a) to exact Ship Money rigorously and unlawfully; b) to fine and imprison the sheriffs if they did not use their best endeavours to collect it; and c) to fine, ransom, and arrest (or 'lay by the heels', as he put it) City of London Aldermen who had refused to supply a list of those City Magnates who could afford to pay the War Loan the King had sought, and that he should hang some of them.

Bishop Juxon is called to give evidence against me, but sorely disappoints Whitlock. He agrees that I told the King to gather in the Ship Money, but tells the Lords that everyone on the Council did the same, because of the necessities of the times, and because the King was already short of money to pay the Army.

Then Alderman Wiseman gives evidence that when he took a Humble Remonstrance from the City to the Council resisting the taxing of their estates, I said that they ought to be fined, ransomed, and laid by the heels, but he did not hear me say anything about hanging anyone. The Earl of Berkshire tells the Court I said that if the King's command were ignored, they should be fined. Finally, City of London Mayor Garraway was the only witness to allege I had mentioned hanging. Whitlock and his colleagues have told the Court that all these Articles are an 'accumulative Treason'. I tell their Lordships that even if the whole of the Charges were verified against me, they could not conceivably amount in law to Treason if none of the acts were in itself a treasonous one. "A heap of grain is made up of grains, but if it is a heap of something else, it may be a heap, but it cannot be a heap of grain. Likewise here, these Articles may make up a heap of felonies, misdemeanours, and other crimes (which I do deny), but that does not make it a heap of Treason.

"Further, all the witnesses against me are single witnesses each to a single allegation, but it takes two witnesses to each act to prove a Treason."

I do not disagree with Juxon's evidence, but simply emphasise that all the Councillors gave the same advice, and it cannot be treason for a man to speak his mind freely in Council. I do not dispute what I said about imposing fines, but point out that nothing had been done about it, that I spoke impetuously and angrily because the King was being disobeyed, and if angry words were Treason, this Hall would always be full of Treason Trials.

As for Garraway's testimony, I voice admiration at his hearing being so acute that he could hear words about hanging which I denied ever uttering, and again, he was the only one who alleged this, so it proved nothing. I end by advising the Lords to recall that they are the great ones of the nation who were born to wield its great affairs, and if they condemn me for advising the King, they might well finish by being called Traitors themselves.

Thank God we adjourn for lunch at this time.

* * * *

In the afternoon they raise Articles 26 and 27 against me. They are a most odd set of Charges: that I had exhausted the King's Treasury; had desired to debase the coinage; had, as Lord Lieutenant of the Army during the recent war, levied a money charge on the gentry of Yorkshire to pay the Army; and had, at that time, refused to agree to the calling of a Parliament. Finally, they accused me of advising the King to seize the money and bullion in the Mint, but their witness to this, one Skinner, told the Court that at the time it happened I was away sick and had said I said I knew nothing about it. These were not such weighty matters as many of the others, and the answers were fairly simple.

In defence I said I had done nothing to empty the Treasury; I had not been in England when that happened, and had in fact been adding to it from Ireland. There was no evidence at all I had thought of debasing the coin of the Realm, the Council of Peers and the Yorkshire gentry had agreed to pay the levy, and the only reason I did not want a Petition presented to the King calling for Parliament was that the King had already proposed it.

John Pym. Thursday, 8th April, 1641. Westminster Hall.

This case goes much worse than I hoped, and no better than I feared. Much as it pains me to have to admit it, Strafford is very clever, and very persuasive and eloquent. He seems to be getting more and more of the Lords, and even some of my House, and of the public, to sympathise with him. I can feel it in the atmosphere, and gather it from some of the quiet comments I hear. Today only emphasises those impressions.

The Impeachment Committee met in the Commons this morning. A large majority of us were for announcing that we had finished with the evidence on the Articles even though we had not dealt with them all. We felt that the proofs on Article 24 were not enough. Then Sir Walter Earle said that he could strengthen that Article, and the other four about bringing over the Irish Army, raising money by force, and so on, and persuaded us to let him try. I thought he would be able to make a fist of it. I knew he had been to the Inner Temple to train as a barrister, and he ought to have known what he was about, as he is about 55, I think, and must have some experience. Like me, he has a West Country accent, and, again like me, sat with Wentworth in the 1620s Parliaments.

We trooped into the Hall to make a start. It was disastrous. The witnesses Earle called let him down, failing to say what he expected. On Article 22 about landing the Irish Army in England, all he did was to produce and read Strafford's Commission from the King for his command of that Army. His main point, which could have been a good one in the absence of any other documents, was that this Commission enabled Strafford, in effect, to land his forces anywhere in the British Isles. But it wasn't the only document; Strafford produced the previous Commision of the Earl of Northumberland, and read out its almost identical wording meaning the same.

Earle could not prove by this evidence that Strafford had any intent at all to attack England from Ireland. Considering that he has had so much less time to prepare than we have, his preparation is remarkable.

Not for nothing do the best lawyers rely on the six Ps: "Proper preparation prevents piss-poor performance".

If Earle had been properly prepared he would have looked for earlier examples of Commissions to see whether Strafford's was unusual. His failure was made painfully obvious when Lord Digby stood to mimic Sir Walter, nailing the coffin lid down on this Article by proposing that it be overlooked, and nothing more heard on the matter.

Mr Glyn then rose to demand that the prisoner should make his closing speech on the facts of the case, so that we could repeat our case afterwards. Strafford then told the Lords that as we were all lawyers, we should never agree to that if we were in his shoes, and he would not do so either. He said he needed more time. Argument raged over this for a while. Then the Lords sided with him, we were forced to agree, and the hearing adjourned to tomorrow.

I have to concoct another plan.

Lucy Carlisle. Friday, 9th April, 1641. Westminster Hall.

I am at the Hall very early today, hoping to get a quick and quiet word with Thomas, to ask how he really is. I have no chance to have a word with him at all. He is not coming. It is about eight o'clock when the Lieutenant of the Tower comes to the Hall with one of Thomas's servants. They take the oath, and tell the Lords that Lord Strafford has been taken with an exceeding painful attack of the stone, and cannot even get out of bed.

That beastly man Glyn rises, and addresses Arundel, the Steward, most angrily. "This is just a token of Strafford's wilfulness, not his weakness, and he should have sent a doctor to make this report, My Lord."

Arundel replies quite gently, and I am rather amazed by what he says, for he had always seemed to me to be as much an enemy of Thomas's as Pym or Glyn himself. "It may be, Mr Glyn, that a doctor could not be found so early in the morning. After all, these two gentlemen have come all the way from the Tower to tell us this, and it is still early. Besides, I believe a physician cannot diagnose an attack of the stone as there is no visible manifestation of his pain, only sweat and groans or screams."

Glyn was vicious. "If the prisoner does not appear tomorrow morning, Saturday, he should not be allowed to say any more in his defence, but we should be permitted to proceed."

Lord Arundel raised his eyebrows at that, but turned to some of his fellows to confer. "Mr Glyn, My Lords have agreed with me that we shall send four of our number to the Tower to see the prisoner, and see how the land lies. If he is well enough to come tomorrow, then come he must, but if he is not, then common humanity and the rules of equity would excuse his attendance, and so shall this Court."

For an experienced barrister Glyn is barely able to hide his emotions and his rage. Is it just Arundel's refusal to go on regardless, or does he see the danger in the Steward becoming increasingly favourable to Thomas? Perhaps it is both.

After lunch, which I take at an inn with a friend who happens to be in Court as a spectator, too, we return to the Hall. A rumour, which reaches the inn, and, it seems, most of London and Westminster, is that Thomas is dead. However, the four Lords deputed to attend on Thomas in his cell return and tell the Lords that he is likely to be well enough to be here tomorrow.

John Pym. Saturday, 10th April, 1641. Westminster.

Today the Lower House assembles early in the Commons Chamber, the doors are locked, and orders are given that no-one may leave without leave to do so. I have my new plan. I present a Bill of Attainder against the Earl. It is read to the House.

Mr Glyn then tells the House that he has some more proof on Articles 22 and 23, those concerning Strafford's threatening to bring the Irish Army to conquer England. "Some further notes have come into my possession which seem to be a record of the meeting in May when Lord Strafford advised the King to employ the Irish Army in this country. I should like Sir Harry Vane to tell us what he knows about this document."

Sir Harry comes forward, and is handed the notes. Having looked at them he says: "I took notes, but these are a copy of the notes I took on 5th May."

"What do these notes show?"

"That Strafford spoke the words I say he spoke, and that the Archbishop and Lord Cottington also gave the King most pernicious and dangerous counsel, and did speak most slanderously of this House of Commons."

I then propose that we should go into the Hall, and ask for this extra evidence to be heard.

Thomas. Saturday, 10th April, 1641.

I am unbelievably weak after suffering much with the stone on Thursday night and yesterday. Today I am in my seat at the Hall. I wait for the Prosecution to do what they told the Steward they would do at the close on Thursday: namely, recap on their Charges and then I will do so with my Defence. But that is not what happens at all.

The Commons enter the Hall as a body, and Glyn, Pym, and the others take their seats at the prosecution table. As soon as the Steward calls the Hall to order, Glyn rises and asks permission to call further evidence on Articles 22 and 23 about the Irish Army.

I am devastated. "My Lord Steward, on Thursday we were told by Mr Glyn that they were finished with the evidence, and you decreed that today should be given over to the closing speeches on the evidence. I am no way prepared for what Mr Glyn now proposes. Two days ago you closed the business, and it is improper for it to be re-opened now."

Glyn stands. "My Lords, the business is not closed unless there is nothing further to be heard. It ill behoves the prisoner to dictate to the Commons of England how they should proceed."

"My Lords," I say, "it behoves me to fight for my life just as much as it suits Mr Glyn to rob me of it. If it please the Court, I shall not object further to his bringing in further evidence, provided I may have more time to consider and answer it, and to bring in further evidence on any Articles which suit me."

Lord Newark addresses the Steward. "My Lord Arundel, perhaps we should adjourn to our House to consider these matters, and return with our decision."

Arundel consults his colleagues, and adjourns the sitting. They go to the Upper House. They are gone for two hours, during which time the prosecutors talk agitatedly amongst themselves and it is patently obvious that they are as worried about this as I am, even though I may be executed, and they will not. I confer with my faithful Lane, who tells me that if the Lords have any regard for justice, they will exclude the further proofs or grant my request.

Indeed, that is what occurs, but their order is confusing, and a long argument rages about whether they have only given me permission to have more evidence, or Mr Glyn, or both. The Lords go off to their own House again, and are away for yet another two hours. The tension is, for me, unbearable. On their return they say that both sides should forgo further evidence and proceed as was ordered on Thursday, but if we are not willing to do so, they will let me call further evidence too, and in that event, we should both name our witnesses at once.

Glyn is frustrated. "My Lord Steward, we think the prisoner should name his witnesses first."

"With respect to Mr Glyn, My Lord, the prosecution should name theirs first, since you have put them first in the Order."

Glyn says: "My Lord, we have told you and the prisoner on which Article we seek to adduce new evidence. He has not."

"If it please you, My Lord, I shall bring in new proofs on Charges 2, 5, 13, and 15. I call upon Mr Glyn now to nominate his witnesses."

Glyn turns to speak to Pym and the others, and then addresses the Court. "My Lords, we cannot agree to this without consulting the whole of the Commons."

"Withdraw! Withdraw!!" There are deafening shouts from all about me. I look around and can see men shouting in the Lords seats, the Commons benches, and amongst the gentry and ladies who have come as spectators. No-one seems to be looking at me, so I gather that they are calling for the prosecution to withdraw. Does this mean they think the prosecutors are acting unfairly? Or are they worried that Glyn is making a mess of his own case? I cannot tell, but if they were accusing me of playing lawyer's games, surely they would yell at me?

Suddenly there is pandemonium. Lords, Commons, and spectators leave their places as quickly as they may, and rush for the doors as if the Hall were on fire. The prosecutors leave with them.

Arundel rises, signalling the session is ended, but it is a meaningless gesture, as the people have already terminated it themselves. He cannot be heard above the din, and it seems to me that he does not even say when the trial will continue. Before the guards come to take me back to the Tower I can hear in the tumult many frightened comments. Some say there is a breach between the two Houses, and others welcome it (as I do). I am not the only one, for the curtain on the Royal Box is twitched aside, the King looks directly at me, and smiles. I smile back, and then we both laugh.

Thomas. Sunday, 11th April, 1641. The Tower.

Dearest Bess and Sweetheart,

As I told you in my letter last Sunday, I become increasingly confident that the Trial goes more and more in my favour. Mr Glyn, a nasty piece of lawyerly work if ever there was one, seems to be annoying many of the Lords with the legal tricks he tries to play, but I think I have outsmarted him most of the time. He wants to introduce new evidence, but if he can, it seems the Lords will let me do so too. Either that, or neither side will be able to put in more witnesses, and that suits me just as well.

If the case continues like this I have every hope that I shall soon be with you and the children once more. Today is like all the other Sundays. The Lieutenant of the Tower, or one of his officers, take me for a walk in the grounds or on the battlements after I have been to Church. Today the Bishop of London was allowed to take lunch with me, and that is always a great consolation, but nothing compared to the joy I should get from lunching with you!

He tells me that the streets are full of shouting and threats of disaster of one kind or another. Some are saying the Commons will declare me a traitor come what may. Some of the peers who are against me say they will do the same, and insist that I should not be allowed to defend myself in public any longer. Nothing will content them until my head is off. I do not tell you this to frighten you, but because you must know what is going on, so that you can pray for me, as I pray for you and the little ones. I love you with all my heart. Imagine, if you can, the kisses I should rain upon your lovely sweet face if I were there with you. You are my reason to live, and not to give up this fight.

With all my love for ever,
Thomas.

John Pym. Monday, 12th April, 1641. House of Commons.

The Impeachment Committee held a debate in the Commons this morning, and agreed to put three propositions before the Lords. First, that the notes which were read on Saturday should be put before them, and two MPs would swear to them. Secondly, the Commons considered these notes most material to the case against Strafford, but because of the dangers inherent in presenting them to the Court and the time likely to be wasted in debate over whether they could be admitted in evidence now, the Committee would only make a general reply, and set this new evidence on one side for the time being. Thirdly, that the notes should be read to the Lords, showing that at the time the prisoner spoke about using the Irish Army in England, inflammatory words were also spoken to the King by Archbishop Laud and Lord Cottington.

We – that is the Committee – are now before the Lords, who agree to hear the paper read, and the Lord Steward tells us of their decision on this matter. We go back to the Commons, and Mr Glyn tells them the result. "The Lord Steward spoke for the rest of the Lords, and told us they were resolved that the case should go ahead as had been previously ordered, that there would be no new evidence, that Lord Strafford must make his final speech on the facts, and we must then make ours. After that there will be legal argument, and they want the facts finished with by the time the Court rises tomorrow. The hearing will resume in the morning."

I am actually pleased with this. I cannot call new evidence, but the Lords have allowed me to read it to them anyway, and Strafford won't get a chance to question it. Pure prejudice! I should be ashamed of myself. I'm not; I'm very happy.

A great deal of heat and hot air was generated during these discussions. One Lord told us it was quite unnatural for the tail of the Parliamentary dog to wag its superior parts and tell the Lords how to proceed. Many peers agreed with that. I did not clap eyes on Strafford all day.

Thomas. Monday, 12th April, 1641. The Tower.

I was taken early, as usual, to the Hall this morning, but on arrival I was told that the Commons were having a debate, and then there would be a conference of the two Houses. I was brought back here. Late this afternoon Sir Philip Mainwaring is admitted to see me.

He says that the Lords have decided to go ahead tomorrow with final speeches, and have declined to allow the Commons to present more evidence – some new notes of the Privy Council meeting in May –

in the case. Philip says the reading of these notes – about bringing the Irish Army over – created a rather prejudicial impression, but he does not think that too problematical. Indeed, he believes that many Lords are beginning to realise that my misfortune may lead to their own, and if this attack on me hurts the Monarchy it will hurt them too. That, he says, is why the Lords have stuck firmly to their decision not to allow further evidence.

I am encouraged by this. I imagine that Pym must be discouraged to the same extent.

John Pym. Tuesday, 13th April, 1641. Westminster.

I arrive early, and meet Sir Harry Vane as soon as he appears. We take ourselves off into a small room in the Commons, and I shut the door.

Me. The case is going very badly; from bad to worse, in fact. This is your doing.

Vane. Mine? You were the one who planned this case.

Me. You're a fool! Why did you tell them it wasn't your writing, the first time the notes of that meeting came up?

Vane. You're the fool, Pym. I'm Secretary to the Council. Everyone in Parliament knows my handwriting. Every time I wrote to Strafford in Dublin he saw it. There was no point in lying about it.

Me. Well, I cannot argue with that. And my writing is well known too. You're quite right, Harry. We can do nothing about that now.

Vane. So what are we going to do? The Lords have, in the end, been giving him a pretty fair trial. There's no chance they will find him guilty now.

Me. The Lords will think that there, but for the Grace of God, they go too. They're terrified of what Strafford will do if he is acquitted, so they will want to be seen to be on his side.

Vane. As I said before, what are we going to do?

Me. We have to bring the whole business back before the Commons. They are behind us.

Vane. How?

Me. We put the Bill of Attainder before the Commons again and get it passed.

Vane. What?

Me. As I said just now, most MPs are behind us. If they weren't, we would never have been able to impeach him in the first place. Remember, the main issue is curbing the King's power – forcing him to call frequent Parliaments.

Vane. And giving us the power instead.

Me. And giving us the power instead. But we have to get rid of Strafford. Without him the King cannot stop us, but with Black Tom at his side, the King's authority will increase, and Parliament will be powerless.

Vane. If the Lords throw out the Impeachment, why should they pass a Bill of Attainder?

Me. They are different things. With the Impeachment the Lords sit as a Court. The rule of law and the rules of justice come into it. As Strafford has pointed out, in law he could not be convicted of treason on your evidence alone, even on the charge about the Irish Army, and that was the most serious one. And he rubbished most of the evidence anyway.

Vane. Why should an Attainder work if Impeachment doesn't?

Me. Because it won't be a Court of Law, and we don't have to prove Strafford guilty of anything. It will be Parliament sitting to make a new law. Justice will be irrelevant. Parliament will pass a new law simply requiring that Strafford's head be chopped off -

Vane. - that Strafford should die, right or wrong, fair or unfair, just or unjust. *(He nods).* That's politics, not justice.

Me. Precisely! The Commons started this and will want to finish it. Plenty of peers hate Strafford, and will vote for the Bill. Those who won't can be frightened by the mob and the Ship Money Inquiry to leave London.

Vane. But if the evidence won't stand up for the Impeachment, why should it stand up for Attainder?

Me. Because in a Parliamentary debate you don't need evidence. You need lobbying, and pressure, and prejudice. If the Lords are lobbied to vote for us, or pressurised by the mob to run away, or prejudiced to vote purely in their own interests, they will pass the Bill. The House of Commons will declare Strafford a traitor. So will the Lords. Justice doesn't come into it.

Vane. You're right. In the end politicians will always look after their own interests. *(He pauses).* Unfortunately, that's not the end of it.

Me. Why not?
Vane. Because an Act of Parliament is made by the King, Lords, and Commons. The Act of Attainder must be signed by the King, and the King will never sign it. He will never sacrifice Strafford.
Me. We shall see, shan't we? We'd better get into the Hall.

When we enter the Hall and take our seats, everyone is in his place. Wentworth is on his feet. He has abandoned his usual grey attire, and is dressed entirely in black. Even to me he looks a tragic figure, his shoulders bowed, his face pale, in pain, and tired. Yet he manages to dominate the proceedings despite this. Arundel, the Steward, is telling him that the Lords have ordered that all further testimony has been prohibited, and that both sides should make their final speeches on the facts and evidence.

Strafford replies that, humbly and obediently, he submits to that or any other order the Lords make, but he asks whether, as the Commons will speak last, if they put any new matter forward, he should be allowed to deal with it, as his life depends on it. The Steward says that there is every reason in the world why he should. The prosecution bench is unhappy to hear that.

Strafford begins to speak. He makes occasional eloquent, dramatic, and graceful gestures. He speaks to the Lords, but it seems as though he is encompassing everyone in the Hall in his speech. He bows to the Steward very deeply. He has been doing that at the opening of every day of the Trial. No-one who has seen this display of humility, and nothing else, could have any idea just how proud and arrogant he used to be before we reduced him to this pitiful spectacle.

Thomas. Tuesday, 13th April, 1641. Westminster Hall.

Today of all days is my birthday. What a way to celebrate being forty-eight years of age, in fighting for my very existence. I have to make my final speech. God give me strength!

"My Lords, I stand before you charged with High Treason. The charge has been fathered by the House of Commons, and I stand alone against them, David against Goliath." *(I go through all the Articles in as masterly fashion as I can manage, dealing with the evidence and casting as much doubt on it as anyone could. I reach the end).*

"I have always acted out of loyalty to the King. Were it not so I should cast the first stone and pass sentence. *(I pause).* The only charge which could amount to treason is the allegation that I advised the King to bring the Irish Army here to conquer *England.* Dreadful!! Off with his head!! *(I pause again).* "But just a moment. Did this strike you, as it struck me, as nonsense? Mr. Pym says I talked the King into making war on his Scottish subjects. Then Mr Glyn says I advised the King to use the Irish Army to defeat the English. Finally they say I betrayed the English to the Scots at Newcastle and Newburn so that the King would be defeated.

"What a complicated mind he thinks I have! I get the King to start a war against the Scots, which I want him to lose? I believed I was charged with treason, not with being a fool!! If any of that were true, the King *(and I gesture and bow to the Royal Box)* would have laid these charges. *(Yet again I pause).* Perhaps you will ask yourselves how I can be an incendiary for war against the Scots and at the same time a confederate of this Scottish enemy.

"Sir Harry Vane told you that it was Treason for me to talk to the King of an offensive war against the Scots. He talked of a defensive war. But why is it Treason for me to talk of offensive war but not Treason for Vane to talk of defensive war? Either way there is war, and it has to be paid for, and either way we may lose. It was the duty of all Privy Councillors to tell the King honestly what they thought he should do.

"In the end all this turns on the evidence of Sir Harry Vane. If his evidence is not to be believed, then I must be acquitted. Is his evidence believable?

"In law you need at least two witnesses to convict anyone of treason. Sir Harry's evidence alone would barely be enough if I were accused of stealing Five Pounds, let alone Treason. He wasn't even certain of his evidence himself. He could not recall the exact words, and he was not on Oath. How then can you be sure beyond a reasonable doubt? And will you still cut off my head? Sir Harry relied upon a document which turned out to be a copy of a copy of the original, and no-one could produce the original. It proved nothing.

"I deny saying I wanted to bring the Irish Army to fight in England. The other Councillors all gave evidence that I did not say it. Only Sir Harry says I did. *(I burst out passionately).* Those forces were never to be landed in England. They were only ever intended for Scotland.

(I resume as calm and a professional manner as I can achieve). "Let me turn to the charge that I plotted against His Majesty. *(I bow to*

the King). The power of the Crown and the liberty of the subject are dependent one on the other. The excess of power is oppression. The excess of liberty is anarchy and chaos. Power and liberty are inseparable in a well-governed Kingdom, and there is no better way to nourish both than the frequent use of Parliament. This has always been my guiding thought, as God, His Majesty *(I look at the King, who nods),* and all with whom I have sat in Council, can bear witness. *(Once more I am strengthened by passion).* No-one has given evidence to the contrary. Is it likely, then, that I should commit this *(I speak the words with utter contempt)* 'day-dream Treason'? *(I pause and point at Pym).* Master Pym says he speaks in defence of the country against me, but *(and I speak very loudly)* I make my appeal to you in defence of the people against his new Treason!!

(I drop my voice again, and talk quietly). "My Lords, Master Pym and his friends have conjured up this new Treason. None of the things I have done is Treason on its own, yet he says if you add them together, Treason is proved. Have any of you heard of this new Treason? Can you find it in a law book? Then how can it condemn me? Perhaps Mr Pym thinks that by laying all these untreasonable acts together, they will breed, and "Hey Presto," produce an act which is Treason. *(I am gratified when there is a great deal of laughter at that, and I go on passionately again).*

"Where has this fire of cumulative Treason hidden all these years when there has been no smoke? And when it has never appeared in a statute or a case? If it was no law when I performed these actions, how could I know it was wrong? Ignorance of the law is no defence, but can anyone claim to know a law that is not yet passed? And if no-one knows it, how can anyone be ignorant of something which does not exist? I could only have known about this non-existent law by Divine Revelation, and I am not sufficiently close to the Almighty to benefit from that.

"Where are all the bloody and mysterious books of law on this arbitrary and cumulative Treason? My Lords, in the unlikely event you find them, I advise you to throw them on the fire, and stick to the plain words of real Statutes; then you will know where you stand.

"Are you going to – can you afford to – let Mr Pym get away with it? If you let Mr Pym invent new Treasons, one day he'll tear you and your descendants in pieces. Your ancestors chained Treason up in the law. If you vote to kill me you will throw those chains away! No-one has been executed by Attainder for 240 years, and England has not suffered for it. *(I pause again, this time for what seems like an age, looking down at the floor. Then I look up).*

"I have troubled your Lordships a great deal longer than I should, but my children.... My wife and children .....*(I break down, choke, weep; I recover myself).* What I forfeit for myself is nothing, but it wounds me very much that my family should suffer on my account. My Lords, should I die on this evidence, in the eyes of God I should rather be the sufferer than the Judge!! *(There is more shouting; "Not Guilty"; "Acquit him," etc).*

"My Lords, with all humility and a tranquil mind I submit clearly and freely to your Judgments, and whether that righteous Judgment shall be, for me, life or death, Te Deum Laudamus."

My tormentor Mr Glyn takes an hour to consult his notes. Then he gets to his feet to make his final speech for the prosecution. He goes over the Articles in order as I have just done. He tells the Lords that "the prisoner was as cunning in his speech and answers as he had been with his attempts to bring in arbitrary and tyrannical judgment." In effect, he makes much the same sort of speech as that with which the case was opened twenty-three days ago.

Pym then rises to make his speech, which he must have prepared before today, and right embarrassing for him I would have found it if my life had not been at stake. He has clearly not anticipated what I might say. Unlike Glyn and Whitlock, or any other polished advocate, Pym is not as quick-witted as to be able to respond spontaneously to argument. He also fumbles with his papers and cannot easily read his own notes as far I can see..

I am, nevertheless, cast down that the Steward refuses to let me say another word in reply to what Glyn and Pym said. Then he adjourns until tomorrow.

John Pym. Tuesday 13th April, 1641.

As my team of prosecutors leaves the Court Whitlock takes my arm and stops me in the corridor. "You know, John, I'm certain I never saw a man act such a part in such a theatre. No-one ever showed more wisdom, consistency, and eloquence, more fine judgment, use of controlled temper, with a better grace than Strafford has just done. I think he moved the hearts of all those who have heard him."

I am shocked. "How can you say that, Bulstrode? He is a villain. If we haven't proved that, we may soon be standing where he is."

"He moved me, John, and I have hitherto been as much against him as anyone. We'll just have to hope we get your Bill of Attainder through."

"Then you'd better vote for it, no matter how 'moved' you were."

"Oh, yes, I'll vote for it alright. I've no desire to end my days with my neck pillowed on the block, thanks."

Denzil Holles. Wednesday, 14th April, 1641. Westminster.

I have been at Strafford's trial every day, and today is no exception. Apart from anything else, no other business is being done in Parliament, and I'm told even the theatres are having a hard time of it, since it is generally said that the drama in these precincts is better than anything you can expect to see by the footlights.

First thing this morning I turn up at Westminster Hall to take in the action, only to learn that the Commons are in their House, and that I should join the debate. What do I find? A Bill of Attainder against my former brother-in-law has been drafted by John Pym, and brought in by Sir Arthur Haselrigg, having been read in the Commons twice on Saturday.

Argument about this is long and arduous. Three of the most important and well-respected lawyers in the House, Selden, Holborne, and Bridgeman, stoutly oppose the motion that the Commons should pass the Bill.. They say, in effect, that it is not possible in law. Yet Selden is one of those who backed the Impeachment in the first place. He helped draft the final version of the Charges. Has Thomas gained that much sympathy for his case?

Some MPs argue that Treason can only be proved under a 350 year-old Act of Parliament, and the Bill of Attainder doesn't fit. Even some of Thomas's enemies could see no virtue or equity in Attainder, nor could they see any difference between alleging Treason in the Impeachment and alleging it in the Bill, apart from the fact that the former requires a guilty verdict, and the latter does not. One very powerful legal argument is that if the 'cumulative' Treason is only defined by this new

Bill, it is wrong to execute a man for something he did before it was illegal. In fact that is the case Thomas put forward yesterday.

It seems to me that the House of Lords realises that if they go along with this Bill of Attainder, they will be laying a path to their own destruction. I am confirmed in that opinion when we go into the Lords. I am surprised to see that Thomas is not there. The Steward tells the House of Commons that they will not stop the case to deal with the Bill, but will go on tomorrow, letting Thomas's Counsel, Mr Lane, make the legal arguments for the Defence. They intend to stick to the procedure they had laid down days before.

The Commons end the day by returning to the Lower House and passing a resolution which means that any judgment after the Trial is meaningless to them, for in the view of the MPs, Treason has been proved against Strafford.

Sir George Wentworth. Thursday, 15th April, 1641. Westminster.

When the conference of the two Houses re-commences, the Steward tells the Impeachment Committee that the Court will go on with the Trial, and will not stop to let the Commons present their Bill of Attainder against Thomas. They used Impeachment against the old Treasurer, Cranfield, and got rid of him, but he was not to be beheaded. They used it against Buckingham, but the King stopped it. He would hardly have been executed in any event. But for Thomas? His death is what they want. This does not depend on truth or his ability to defend himself, It depends on how well Pym can manage the Commons, and how much pressure he can bring on the Lords. However, it also hangs – unfortunate word – on whether His Majesty will sign the Bill into an Act if it is passed by both Houses.

Arundel is still speaking. He tells Pym and Whitlock that the Peers will follow the steps and procedure they have laid down, and will give full audience to Mr Lane's arguments on matters of law. He then delivers a hefty punch. He tells them that they will not share the passing of the verdict and the sentence with the Commons, but will do that themselves, for they are competent Judges in matters concerning the Lords, and it has never been the practice in English law for the Commons to give sentence of death on a peer, and there was no other course compatible with the laws and statutes of the Kingdom, the safety of the nobility, or with equity and common justice.

Pym replies that the Lower House is resolved to go on with their Bill, and that they fear any rupture of the two Houses would lead to the ruin of the Kingdom. There would be no peace for the King's subjects unless the man who had done so much to destroy their rights (he means Thomas, of course) were branded a Traitor and executed. They add that he has had the fairest hearing possible, since in the last century, the Duke of Norfolk and the Earl of Essex had trials which only lasted a day, and in this, the same with Somerset.

I think that is a specious argument. They were all tried for Treason which was clear from definitely Treasonable acts. No constructive or 'cumulative' Treason was alleged against them!

The Steward then adjourns the case to tomorrow, so that the Lords might consider this submission.

Thomas. Saturday, 17th April, 1641. Westminster Hall.

I am far from feeling well today. I passed the most dreadful, almost entirely sleepless night. Late in the afternoon (I am not permitted visitors after dark) my brother-in-law, Denzil, managed to get permission to see me in my prison quarters. He came with news of what has been going on as I have not been taken to the Hall these last two days.

He told me that on Thursday there was a long argument in a conference between the two Houses. The Commons wanted the Lords to halt my case so that they could all proceed with a Bill of Attainder against me. A Bill of Attainder!! I began to tremble with fear. That would do no good. I recall that the King assured me he will protect me. I told myself to calm down, but is it any wonder I slept badly?

In brief, he said that the Lords refused to stop the Trial, and the Commons said that the people would be unhappy if I were not branded a Traitor and lost my head. The Kingdom would be destroyed if Lords and Commons fell out. The Lords adjourned to yesterday to consider their reply.

When they met yesterday the Steward told them that the Lords did not expect anything from the Lower House but what would preserve the peace of the Realm, and the best way to do that was to stick by established law and practices. The Commons complained much about

'Strafford's innovations', but they now wanted a serious innovation of their own, and the Lords could not agree to that. They took the point about justice to the people, but that could not be secured by injustice to me, and the eyes of the world are on this trial.

They dismissed Pym's argument about Norfolk, Essex, and Somerset, and pointed out that those men had been charged under particular Statutes. Therefore they would hear Mr Lane on law today. It follows the Commons need a new Act for me, or I should be found not guilty.

In response to all that, Pym and Whitlock told the Lords that they would come to hear what my lawyers have to say, but they themselves would say not a word more, because they had already passed the Bill in the Lower House. However, if the Lords wanted to examine any points of law with them, they could do so in a private conference.

"You mean a conference I could not attend?"

"Yes, Thomas, that's what they mean?"

I do not know whether to laugh or cry. "Surely they must think their case against me very weak, if they can abandon it at this late stage? So I should be happy about that. But if they can simply get enough Lords to vote for Attainder somehow, I am doomed."

"That's just how it looks."

So this morning I am in my seat at the Hall, and my lawyers,

Lane, the Prince of Wales' Attorney, the Recorder of London, Mr Gardiner, and Messrs Loe and Lightfoot, are in their places. Richard Lane makes a speech of great length, but very powerful. He says he will only refer to the facts as may be necessary to relate the law to the Articles. Then he goes through each Charge, applying the relevant law and Acts of Parliament, and numerous cases showing how the law has been applied, and how it ought to be used in my case. Many of the Statutes go back hundreds of years to Edward III's reign, and to those of Richard II, and Henry IV, and so do the Treason Trial cases he quotes.

It is a masterly address, and I can see that despite its length, the Lords are not bored, but seem very interested, and, if anything, sympathetic. Then Mr Gardiner makes a fairly short but able speech, asking the Court to determine, first of all, whether they have found the allegations against me proved, and then whether they amounted to

Treason or not, for if the facts were not against me, then neither could the law be.

The lawyers from the Commons say not a word, and the Court is adjourned for their decision, but no date is fixed for the next hearing. I am taken back to the Tower.

Thomas. Sunday, 18th April, 1641. The Tower.

It feels so strange to have no work to do on the case for the time being, and no real reason for Lane to visit me. I go to Church as usual, and am taken for my short interlude of exercise in the grounds and, this time, on the battlements too, by which I am much refreshed.

I write a letter to my daughter Anne.

Dear Nan,

I am as well as can be expected when living in this dismal place. The Tower is not the most comfortable of dwellings, but I get pleasant visits from good friends including your Uncle George, and I can eat well. When I go for my daily walks in the grounds and on the battlements I can see very interesting views of London, and across the Thames into parts of Kent.

I expect you have been wondering how the case is going, for you have written to ask me whether I have been allowed to speak to the Lords on my own behalf. Yes, my dear, I have been allowed to speak, and to ask questions, and my Counsel, Mr Lane, made a wonderful speech for me the other day all about the law. In fact, your Father, as you desired, has been heard to speak for himself now all through these four weeks.

I am very happy with the way the trial is going, and I am sure, and you must be sure, too, that we shall all be together again soon and that we shall have a peaceful and contented life. We may be a tiny bit worse off with money than we have been, but that matters not at all if I am with you and Will, and Arabella, and little Margaret, and of course, with your Mother, my own dear Elizabeth.

Please kiss all the family from me many times, and soon I shall be able to kiss and be kissed by all of you.

Your loving Father.

After lunch Bishop Juxon comes to see me, and so does Richard. We sit in the rather uncomfortable chairs with which my rooms are furnished, and I call my servants to bring some wine. Despite being incarcerated, I am allowed to order reasonable food and drink to be brought in from outside the Tower. I don't always have much of an appetite, but picking at good meals is better than struggling to swallow bad cooking.

We drink each others' health, and then Richard speaks: "Something very odd is going on, Thomas. There is absolutely no indication from the House of Lords as to when they will deliver their judgment."

That makes me give a wry chuckle. "I shan't get too upset about that. As long as they keep quiet, I can still draw breath."

"True, but if my reading of the atmosphere in the Hall over the last few weeks is anything to go by, a majority of them are now minded to find you 'Not Guilty'."

Juxon nods. "I agree with Mr Lane, Thomas. It is definitely strange. The Lords have been pressed over and over again by the Commons to get on with it, by which they mean 'get Strafford hanged'. But the Lower House pushes on with their Bill of Attainder, and say they will take no further part in your Trial."

I get up and amble about, thinking. How I have changed. In this sort of discussion a few years ago I used to march about, big strides, arms swinging, talking loudly. Now I seem to creep about, with hardly a vestige of my old energy. After a little while I get control of my thoughts: "If the Lords are mainly on my side, you'd think they'd bring in a verdict of Not Guilty pretty quickly, since if they do, it would look really terrible for the Commons to take my head off, and worse, with Attainder, when I've been acquitted of any wrong-doing."

Juxon looks puzzled. "What do you mean by 'take your head off or worse'?"

Richard has the answer, of course. "What Thomas means, Your Grace, is that in cases of Treason, and particularly where there are so many allegations, the usual sentence is hanging, drawing, and quartering."

Juxon turns pale. "We must ask the Almighty to help the Lords to vote the Bill down, if the Commons send it up to them."

Richard shakes his head sadly. "I think it has already gone to them, Your Grace. I just hope that enough of them will see that where Thomas is concerned, there but for the Grace of God they go too. It is such a pity that your fellow Bishops allowed themselves to be persuaded by Williams to absent themselves from the Trial."

"Most certainly it is, Mr Lane. Do you know, Thomas, how the mood in the streets, and in the dining halls of the nobility, has changed since the Trial started? How can you, locked up in here? Then everyone was baying for your head. Now a more sombre atmosphere is abroad in the City. Those who are related to you, or are indebted to you for favour or advancement, and all those who have been, or are likely to be, called upon to serve the King in government, are worried that they, too, may be charged with Treason if you are convicted, but that seems less and less likely."

"But those who are still totally against you," Richard offers, "are saying that now it is not what should be done which counts, but what must, and so your head must come off with the Bill of Attainder. The multitudes are saying that it is not a matter of justice that you should die, but a necessity. It will be to assuage the venomous fears of men like Pym should you be freed."

I laugh bitterly. "What an excellent Job's comforter you can be, Richard! No, don't take it unkindly. I jest; if I don't laugh I'll cry."

Richard comes across and puts his arm around my shoulders. "In the last resort the King has the last word; he need not sign the Bill. I pray that he won't."

So do I!! Oh yes! So do I!

John Pym. Wednesday, 21st April, 1641. House of Commons.

The debate on Attainder resumed the day before yesterday. A fair number of short speeches supported the Bill, and one or two wereagainst it, but then Lord Digby stood and was called by the Speaker. I was half-expecting what he would say after some of his interventions in the House and in the Hall lately, but I was astounded at the power with which he addressed the House. His courage was quite remarkable, even if I hated what he said and wished fervently he had kept quiet.

"Mr Speaker, and Honourable Members all, like you I hold it to be true that My Lord of Strafford is the most dangerous minister of the Crown who has ever set foot in Westminster. He is the greatest threat to free subjects as may be imagined.

"None of you will doubt that I was as earnest for his prosecution as anyone could be, but prosecutors deal only in probabilities, and are accountable only for their zeal and industry in seeking a conviction. Judges are different. They are accountable to God, and for their rectitude, for a Judge is the steward of the blood of the parties before him.

"When this case began I believed we could prove Strafford would bring over the Irish Army to England, but we failed. A bad and unreliable copy of Sir Harry Vane's notes produced in dubious fashion harmed rather that helped our cause. In addition, he cannot be convicted of Treason on that Article on the evidence of Sir Harry alone.

"I am not convinced in all conscience, in all my conscience, that we can convict the Lord Lieutenant judicially. I cannot agree to do so by legislation. I shall vote against taking the Earl's life."

There were more speeches, and the House adjourned to Tuesday, when John Selden made another great rhetorical speech against the Bill. I say 'great' purely in the sense of the power of his oratory, not in the sense of the validity of his arguments. I felt the same about those as I did about Digby's. Nothing else of any moment occurred and the house adjourned to today.

The debate draws to a close and a division is called. The doors of the House are locked, and members file into the lobbies. When they return the tellers hand their counts to the Speaker. "Those who say Yea, 204; those who say Nay, 59. The Ayes have it!" The House then orders me to take the Bill up to the Lords.

There is a mighty outburst of cheering and waving of papers and hats. Many hats are thrown in the air, and some are trampled as members leave as soon as the doors are unlocked.

I make my way to the Upper House. I hand the Bill to Lord Arundel, the Steward. I ask for their consideration of it to be expedited, and for the Lords to read and debate it as publicly as possible. Why do I do that? Because lately I have noticed a change in the attitude of much of the public, and there have been fewer riotous gatherings of the apprentices and other mobs clamouring for Strafford's head. I shall stir up the City of London to call for their complaints to be examined, and press those I know who control the apprentices to provoke more rioting in the streets, especially here round the Palaces of Westminster and Whitehall.

I shall also apply pressure to stay away from the Upper House on peers who think as Digby and Selden do, so that my supporters there have it all their own way.

Charles I. Friday, 23rd April, 1641. Whitehall Palace.

My dear Strafford,

I find it difficult to express just how sorry – how dreadfully sorry – I am that Mr Pym and his party should have put before Parliament a Bill of Attainder seeking your life. As you are aware, I attended your Trial every day, and as often as not the Queen and Prince of Wales accompanied me. On the day when Mr Glyn tried to introduce new evidence we were as certain as we could be that Treason could not be proved against you, and it is a great pity that the Lords have yet to make a finding, since if they acquitted you the Bill would, I believe, almost certainly fail.

And fail it must. I noticed that on at least two occasions you told the Court that you would never again seek any kind of public office, and would retire to a quiet family life. I think that is a wise course, for you must understand that, after all that has passed, I can never again employ you in any state business. Not that I believe you guilty of anything, but it would be impolitic of me to do so, and might once more place you in danger if I did.

It is vital that you should be confident that under no circumstances will I permit your life, your honour, or your fortune to suffer. The Lords are, I understand, likely to refuse the Bill, and should they not do so, I shall not give it my assent. I am doing what I can to improve the chances that the Bill will be rejected. I am grateful for all the service you have rendered me so loyally, and if I can say that, it is hard to understand of what Treason you could possibly be guilty.

You are high in my personal regard,

Charles R.

Thomas. Saturday, 24th April, 1641. The Tower.

Brother George comes to visit. I am so glad to see him. He asks if I knew that lately the mobs filling the streets with calls for my head had virtually disappeared. I say I was aware of that. He is very despondent.

"There's been a change in the atmosphere, Thomas. The apprentices are out again; not in big crowds as yet, but they are growing, and the old clamour for you to go to the scaffold is being heard once more. Today I'm told by Lord Henry Clifford that a Petition from the City has been handed in to the Upper House. It's supposed to have been signed by 20,000 'men of rank and quality'."

I cannot help laughing at the vanity of that. "Who says they are of rank and quality? They do, I'll be bound."

"I have no idea, but I think this Petition is very prejudicial to you. It comes before the Lords have decided whether you're guilty or not; it's intended to make them wonder what will happen if they say 'Not Guilty'. It's addressed to the Commons, too, but the City knows the MPs want you dead, so it must be the Lords it is really aimed at."

"What does it say, George, this Petition?"

"It asks Parliament to redress their grievances over many things, but particularly some which are really directed at you. They don't name you, but it's obvious they mean you when they talk about Papists in the Army, and 'plundering of this City' and 'hanging some Aldermen'."

"Somebody's put them up to this."

"That's just what I think, Thomas, and that's why the mobs are back on the streets. They want to frighten everyone into voting for your Attainder."

Whilst George is with me, Henry himself arrives. It is about six, so it is still light and he is allowed to see me. He confirms what George has said about the London Petition, and gives me more unpleasant news.

"I was out in Piccadilly earlier – only an hour or so ago, in fact. I strolled past the bowling green, and everyone I spoke to was talking about you and the Attainder. Then I saw Bedford, Essex and Hertford discussing something with that acolyte of Pym's ..."

"Do you mean Edward Hyde?" George asks.

"That's the man. As I approached, Hyde and Essex acknowledged me with a wave, and walked away, but Bedford and Hertford stayed to talk. I thought Bedford might be unwell. Bedford told me he asked Hyde what he thought about the Attainder, but he didn't say much. Bedford said his view is that the King would do anything to save you, Thomas, so they ought to take advantage of that to get whatever they could from him for their reforms and grievances. He said Essex would have none of that. 'If Strafford lives, he'll still be a power behind the throne, or even in front of it again. Even if he is shamed and out of the King's employ, he'll still be dangerous. Stone dead has no fellow'. Essex laid a wager that if the King wants you alive, Thomas, there must be something behind it."

"Well, Henry, I can hardly thank you for telling me that, but I suppose forewarned is forearmed. I'd better see what support I can drum up for my retirement rather than my beheading!"

"You should. You know that Cottington has resigned the Exchequer?"

"No, I didn't."

George nods. "I knew. I should have told you, Thomas."

Henry is quite excited. "There is a rumour, which Bedford confirmed, that the King may offer Pym the post if he will kill the Bill."

I shake my head emphatically. "I don't think that will happen. The King may offer it, but if I know Pym, he'll see it as a bribe, and it will just strengthen his resolve to be rid of me. I don't like the sound of Hyde being able to go back to Pym and tell him this bribe may be coming his way, either. It will just make matters worse."

When they depart I write a letter to Lord Hamilton.

I am told that the Lords may be inclined to preserve my life and family, for which generous compassion I hope the God of mercy will reward them. All I ask your Lordship is that, divested of all public employment, I should be allowed to go home to my private estates, there to attend to my wife, my domestic affairs, and the education of my children. I should be grateful for any steps my noble and just friends can take to secure this for me, with as few words or marks of infamy attached to me as possible. Please do what you can to persuade the House that this is the course I should be glad they might adopt.

I have had trouble with Hamilton in the past, and he with me, but he gave evidence for me at my trial. I hope this message is not addressed to deaf ears.

Algie Percy. Wednesday, 28th April, 1641. House of Lords.

This week has started with three very busy and worrying days. On Monday a Petition, which came from 20,000 men in the City demanding Thomas's head, was being read by both Houses. Yesterday we had a conference with the Commons about it, and about the Bill of Attainder, which the House read for the second time, and a further conference about the Bill was fixed for tomorrow.

I'm suspicious about what may have prompted the City Petition, and I have noticed there seems to be a resumption of rioting in the streets, especially round Westminster. To cap it all something very strange appeared on a wall in Palace Yard a day or so ago. Fifty-four of the MPs who voted 'No' in the Lower House against the Bill of Attainder are named in a poster stuck up there. These names include Lord Digby and Mr Selden, and Sir George and Peter Wentworth, Strafford's brother and cousin. It's a surprise to me to think that Digby and Selden voted against the Bill; they were both on the Prosecution Committee!

That may be a comfort to Thomas, but it looks very much as though everything is being done to frighten my fellow peers into voting for the Bill.

Today an MP named Edward Hyde came to the Upper House with a report that Strafford may have a design to escape, and has ships at his command. He says that there are not many Guards assigned to Strafford, they should be reinforced, and the prisoner closely confined. Can this rumour be true? He added that Sir William Balfour, the Lieutenant of the Tower, had a visit from an officer who wanted to bring one hundred soldiers into the castle.

Balfour refused to take them in. He suspected a plot to have them take it over and free Thomas. Rumours are all over London and Westminster that Thomas tried to bribe Balfour with 20,000 pounds, but how he could lay his hands on that kind of money when he's locked up in the Tower is beyond me.

What will happen to Thomas? And what is happening to this country of ours?

Thomas. Thursday, 29th April, 1641. Westminster Hall.

I was brought here early this morning to hear Oliver St. John address the Lords on all the legal ramifications of their case of Treason against me, and why they should agree to take my head off with the Bill of Attainder.

I cannot say that I liked the speech. I cannot say it was even professional. It was far too nasty, brutal, full of prejudice, and in no sense moderated by lawyerly qualities. I realise all that was aimed at me, but lawyers should be persuasive rather than bullying and threatening, and he was both.

He was also very longwinded, and spoke for hours and hours. His address was longer than mine and Lane's put together, and they were, when all is said and done, long enough. He went over an enormous number of Statutes and old cases. The burden of his message, in brief, was that the Commons had proved their case, so although the Bill was a legislative thing, my guilt had already been ascertained judicially, so there was nothing objectionable about removing my head with an Act of Parliament.

St. John told the Lords that if there were a Traitor and a Treason, but no judicial way of dealing with him, the remedy could justly be supplied by Attainder. In my case, he said, it is just and necessary to use the supreme power of Parliament if all else should fail.

He made a strange point which I did not understand, and I hope my fellow peers failed to understand it too. He said that old cases showed that levying war and taking the King's Crown were the same thing and couldn't be separated, and that any intention to alter the laws or government of the country is war against the King. But how can that be in my case, where all I ever did was what the King wanted me and had authorised me to do?

He even went back over all the evidence about the Irish Army and my plan to defeat England with it, as though that allegation had not been exposed as falsehood by the forged notes and the evidence of so many witnesses. He tried to make the mud stick by saying that, if I had myself raised the Army, instead of it being the King's Army, I should have been guilty of Treason. I frankly think that a mad argument, for anyone who is asked by the King to raise and take command of one of his armies would then be a Traitor.

Richard Lane raised some objections from time to time, but nothing was going to put Mr St.John off. He finished his speech with numerous examples of men who were executed pursuant to Acts of Attainder, to show that it was a legitimate way of proceeding, but in none of those cases, as I saw it, were those men acting on the King's orders. They were defying him. He told the Peers that he had been commanded by the Commons to declare to the Lords why they believe that in my case, if there were no judicial reason, the use of legislative power and the Bill of Attainder was justified. First, because the nature and quality of my offences were so evil. But how can that be, if no evil deeds have truly been proved? Secondly, since the nature and constitution of Parliament allows that laws such as this can be and are made. And thirdly, because the practices and usages of former times allow it.

No-one else spoke; I did not seek to do so. I raised my arms and my eyes to Heaven in supplication to the Almighty.

Charles I. Friday, 30th April, 1641. My Audience Chamber.

I am sitting on the Chair of State. Queen Henrietta stands, very agitated. I am fairly worn out with the worry of this awful situation concerning Strafford. How long ago was it that I last went hunting? I do not think I have ever worked so hard as I have the last few weeks, and all I have been doing most of the time is attending the Palace of Westminster to listen to Pym and his gang trying to destroy Strafford. How he handled that for so long all on his own with those dreadful things being said about him I cannot imagine. I pray to the Almighty that it never happens to me.

Queen. I am so frightened, Charles. There are mobs outside all the time, and we cannot go out. What are we to do?

Me. Henrietta, you must not worry.

Queen. Why shouldn't I worry? I warned you years ago that you would have trouble with this Strafford. They say twenty thousand Londoners want him dead. How can you save him? And if you do, are you going to be able to save us?

Me. I cannot betray him, and I will not. I shall offer the post of Treasurer to Pym. It is very lucrative, and most of these politicians will do anything for power and money.

Queen. Is that enough to save Strafford? And us?

Me. He just wants to go home to look after his family. I shan't employ him ever again in state affairs. I've told him that I shall not let his life be taken, and that his honour and fortune will not suffer further.

Queen. Why didn't he just leave the country, as others have done?

Me. He was advised to.

Queen. Then why didn't he?

Me. Honour. Do you remember him saying "I shall never stop doing what I believe to be right for fear of the consequences"?

Queen. Yes – it was that first time you gave him an audience.

Me. Well, what he believed to be right was to go to Ireland to bring the Army to Scotland. I made him come to London. In a way, I put him in the Tower, God help me!
(A Servant enters, followed by Pym and Vane).
Servant. Your Majesty, Master Pym and Sir Harry Vane are here.
Vane. We have come at once in answer to your summons, Sire.
(The Servant exits, and I indicate to Henrietta that she should sit, and she does).
Me. Rumours have been started of foreign invasions and Papist plots. The London mob is being incited to violence. You are behind this, Master Pym.
Pym. *(Very angry.)* We have not come this far, I have not done all this, to see the Bill die in the Lords. Rumour says you are prepared to do anything to save Strafford.
Me. I am prepared to offer you the post of Treasurer.
Vane. *(To Pym).* Even if Strafford is out of public life none of us would be safe.
Pym. *(He turns to go, takes a few steps, and turns again to face me).* No bribe on earth could stop me watching Strafford die!
Queen. You are the one who ought to die! *(She speaks to me).* Have him arrested and killed - killed now!
Pym. Hah! He doesn't have the power. We do! Your Majesty.

Pym and Vane go, and immediately the door opens again and the footman announces the Earls of Bristol and Bedford. They come in, saying they have news to impart. I invite the men to do so. They tell me of the latest developments, with a new version of Vane's notes of the meeting last May, and the talk of the Irish Army, what they know of the riots, and much besides.

I tell them that my attempt to put my troops into the Tower failed, and so I have appointed one of Strafford's enemies to be Constable of the Tower, and ordered the guard on his prison to be doubled. Bristol asks why.

"Pym and his friends think I have a plot to use the Army to take over Parliament, and the country. As my plan to seize the Tower did not succeed, I have to make the Commons think that there was no plan."

Bedford, I know, wants to be Chancellor of the Exchequer himself, and is doing his best to ingratiate himself with me and the Commons. "Your Majesty, I believe that, if I were Chancellor, I should have enough authority and credit with Parliament to be able to persuade them to let Strafford live in return for your giving way on many of the grievances of which the Commons complain. In my humble opinion you might go to Westminster tomorrow and tell them this."

"And that would give me, Sire," Bristol adds, "the chance to give reasons why the Bill should be rejected. Your speech should be to the effect that the Lords should not open the door to this sort of Bill, and this retrospective creation of Treasons and other crimes, if I may say so."

"Indeed, Sire," Bedford says, "a sympathetic address striking the right note may deliver the result we all want."

Sir George Wentworth. Friday, 30th April, 1641. The Tower.

"Thomas, Thomas, I'm sorry to come so late, but I had to see you. Something quite extraordinary is going to happen tomorrow."

"George, I'm glad to see you, but I'm amazed the Guards let you in." Thomas sits and waves me to a chair.

"So am I. I know you're not supposed to have any visitors after dark, but I seem to be on good terms with most of them, and it's remarkable what a small purse of gold will do!"

"Indeed. What's extraordinary about tomorrow, then?"

"The King. He's going to speak to the Lords. I think he's going to tell them not to vote for the Bill."

"Is that what he told you? When did you see him?"

"I didn't see him. I was walking home down Whitehall when I saw Lord Bedford come out of the Palace. I thought he looked dreadful, by the way. Anyway, he told me he's asked the King to go to the House and tell the peers that he could never, in all conscience, assent to the Attainder Bill against you, but that he was satisfied that you were unfit ever to hold office under him again, in any capacity at all, or any other employment. He thought that would induce them to refuse the Bill."

"Oh! Sweet Jesus, that is the last thing it'll do. First, some of the Lords are in league with the Commons over this; men like Cork and Mountnorris and Clanricarde dislike me almost as much as Pym does. In fact Cork and Mountnorris hate me more, for I have never actually done Pym any harm at all. He just hates me on principle for helping the King. He cannot tell Parliament what they should and shouldn't do. He mustn't go. He has to leave it to them! Secondly, if he tells them he thinks I'm unfit for office, it sounds as though he agrees with them that I'm a criminal at least, and a Traitor at worst. They'll pass the Bill."

"What can I do?"

"You can go straight back to the King and ask him not to go. Tell him what I just said. See if you can persuade him."

I'm worried. "But it'll be after midnight by the time I get there, Thomas. He may not see me."

"You'll have to make him. Bribe your way in, if necessary. Don't take 'No' for an answer. I don't suppose he'll be in bed with this Bill keeping him and everyone else awake, and the rabble rioting in the street."

Charles I. Saturday, 1st May, 1641. Whitehall Palace.

Last night Henrietta and I were up late talking about what I should tell the Lords today. Sometime after midnight I heard some loud voices downstairs and I looked out to see who it was. Strafford's young brother George was down there telling the servants that he had to see me about my speech to the Lords. I called to the footman to bring him up.

I took him into the Audience Chamber where Henrietta was waiting. "You seem very agitated, Sir George. Do sit down. Shall I call for some wine for you?"

"No, Your Majesty. It's kind of you to see me at this late hour. It's about Thomas, er, my brother."

"I imagined it would be. Has he sent you?"

"Yes, Sire. Earlier on I saw Lord Bedford coming out of here. He told me you are going to speak to the Upper House today."

"Yes. I'm proposing to tell them I won't sign the Bill and Strafford will never work for me again."

"Please, Sire, Thomas says that's the last thing you should do. He says it would be pernicious to him, and he wishes to rely on the honour of the Lords and their consciences."

Sir George explained what Strafford meant by this, and I was persuaded to agree; no speech to the Lords, even though it was what my good friends had suggested I do. If Strafford was saying he didn't like the idea, I won't do it.

First thing this morning, Lord Saye comes to tell me that Lord Bedford is so ill, he's either dying or dead already. He advises me to make the Speech as planned. He clearly wants the Treasurer's job himself if he can get it now Bedford is out of the way, and says that if I take that course it will prevail, but if I do not, he cannot say what the outcome will be, and he will not be engaged in the business then.

So here I am, on my way by carriage to the Lords, to make a speech Strafford would rather I abandoned.

Henry Clifford, Earl of Cumberland. Saturday, 1st May, 1641. House of Lords.

When I arrive at the House this morning someone tells me that the King is expected at 10 o'clock to make a speech about my friend Thomas and the Bill of Attainder. There is such excitement. Those, like me, who are sympathetic to Thomas, are excited at the prospect that the King's intervention may save the day on the Bill. It is clear that Pym could never have got a majority of the Lords to find the Lord Lieutenant guilty of Treason after the Trial, but it is by no means certain what they will do about the Bill.

On the other side, those who follow Pym and want Thomas in his coffin are angrily excited that the King should try to interfere, as they see it, with the workings of Parliament. I cannot understand that attitude. If law is made by Commons, Lords, and Monarch acting together, surely what the King thinks is something the two Houses should know. After all, why should he – or a Queen for that matter – have to sign a new law he doesn't agree with? Pym and St. John themselves say that the King is the Father of the people and his duty is to protect them. How can he do that if he cannot form an opinion of what he is being asked to sign, cannot tell anyone what he thinks, and has to sign it anyway?

If the King can say the important things persuasively, Thomas may be safe.

I am standing about in the lobby, as most people are, circulating, sounding others out, and guessing what the King will do, when he arrives to a fanfare, and happens to pass by me. "Good morrow, Cumberland," he says, "do you know where Lord Bedford might be? I expected to see him here."

I bow. "Good morning, Your Majesty. When I arrived, I was told that Bedford was taken extremely ill last night, and cannot be here. Some say he is dead. Can I help?"

"I fear not. I am to make a speech on which he gave me some advice last night, and I wanted to check some ideas with him. Ah well, I'll just have to do my best without him."

By this time most peers have taken their places in the House, and the King is escorted to his throne. He asks the Lord Keeper to summon the Commons to come to the House. After a few minutes they do so, and the King begins.

"As you will all know, having seen me in daily attendance at the Earl of Strafford's Trial, I have sincerely endeavoured to inform myself about the charges against him. I have also seriously pondered on the Law and the evidence. I have come to help inform your judgments in this matter rather than to clear my own conscience.

"First, there never was any plot, nor has Lord Strafford ever offered me advice, that the Irish Army should be brought to England. In nothing that has been said has he been more misunderstood than in that. The imputation of it is a reflection on me too, suggesting that I intended to make war on my own subjects. No-one could possibly believe that, if they look at the gracious way I have always dealt with my people.

"Secondly, the Lord Lieutenant has never counselled me to set up an arbitrary government, and if he had, he would have been punished for it. No-one could believe I would countenance that either, unless they think me a fool or a tyrant. I am well content with the power and authority I have received from God, and I should never think my Prerogative allowed me to intrude on the property of my subjects.

"For myself and my conscience, I now declare that, in my Judgment, there is nothing in the process against the Lieutenant that deserves the censure of Treason. He was guilty of such mistakes and misdemeanours that I must confess that Lord Strafford will never be worthy from now on to fill any office in my Kingdoms, no, not even of the lowest rank.

"He is answerable for his errors if they are charged against him, and I should support that with alacrity. Nevertheless, I hope none of you will deny me the first voice on this matter, and that is that I can never, in heart or by hand, concur with those who would punish this man as a Traitor. I pray you to think of some other way in which this business may be resolved, for it will never be less important to me to protect the innocent than to punish the guilty, not even if my own blood should pay for it."

I am dumbfounded. Far from making the sort of speech which might sway the Lords, the King has simply told everyone that he will not allow it. He is telling them his conscience matters more than theirs. In a sense he is acting in just the sort of arbitrary way that Thomas is accused of doing, and Thomas was his servant.

Has he dealt graciously with all his subjects always? Didn't he try to have MPs arrested? Did he try to put soldiers in the Tower to rescue Thomas? He says he would 'never think his Prerogative allowed him to intrude on the property of his subjects'. But didn't he enforce payment of Ship Money against the will of the people even if a majority of the Judges agreed with him? Before that, didn't he exact the Forced Loan? How ironic it will be if that is held against Thomas, when he refused to pay it and went to prison for it. Perhaps worst of all, he is telling the Commons that their resolution that they have proved the case against Thomas is quite simply wrong.

That's how I see it, and I'm on Thomas's side! Pym and his cohort must be delighted. My dear friend, my dear dead sister Margaret's husband, may be doomed.

Tomorrow Princess Mary will be married to the Prince of Orange. They are only children. How can anyone know if they will be happy? Does it matter? The people will be happy that it is a Protestant marriage. A Protestant marriage, and the prospect of Thomas's head on a platter.

Lucy Carlisle. Monday, 3rd May, 1641. The Tower.

I have permission from Lord Newport, the new Constable of the Tower, to visit Thomas. I find him sitting at his desk in the Tower, writing.

Thomas. *(He rises and embraces me in a very chaste manner).* Lucy! I..... Oh! I am so happy to see you! But what has happened? Why are you here?

Me. *(I move away)* Thomas! Thomas! I don't know how to bear it any longer. They couldn't prove you guilty with the Impeachment, so they - are going to kill you anyway. Isn't that what this Act of Attainder means?

Thomas. It does.

Me. *(I cannot stand still, I am so agitated).* How can they do this? The evidence against you didn't stand up. The House of Lords would have acquitted you.
Thomas. *(He is very angry).* I know, but that was law and justice, and now it's politics. Politicians like Pym will do anything for power, and woe betide anyone who gets in their way.
Me. Woe betide you, then! Pym is evil. He presses on with the Attainder as fast as he can, and uses every trick he couldn't get away with in Court.
Thomas. He says that if Lane, my lawyer, so much as mentions the possibility that I might be innocent, he is to be arrested for contempt of Parliament.
Me. *(I go to him and take him by the shoulders).* But you are supposed to be innocent until proven guilty!
Thomas. That's the law! Innocent until they prove you guilty! But this is politics. *(He stops, and pulls himself together with an effort).* I was just writing to the children. *(He picks up the letter, moves away, and reads).* 'Dearest Nan, Your letter was such a pleasure to me. You must not worry, for with God's help I'll soon be home, and we shall be happy together. One thing I have learned in the last few months is the wisdom of Jesus' words. Do not lay up treasure on earth where it can be stolen, where the moth eats it and the rust rots it. That is what I have been doing. Lay up your treasure in heaven. That is what I should have been doing, and it would be heaven to be with you laying up that treasure now. Your loving Father".
Me. *(I am moved to tears, and come to him again).* Are you that confident of Heaven, or are you putting on an act for the sake of your family and friends? Aren't you afraid? I'd be terrified!
Thomas. Well, they always say I've never been much good at hiding my feelings. *(He pauses once more).* Yes. I'm afraid. At last, I am afraid. On Saturday the Lords will take the final vote on the Attainder. Someone said they were about to commit murder with the sword of Justice. *(He stops again for a moment, and sighs, despondently).*
Me. *(Rhetorically, as I move away).* Justice doesn't seem to matter in politics, does it? It never has, and it never will.
Thomas. Lord Falkland says I must be guilty because even if you do not know how many inches make a tall man or how many make a short man, you can still tell a short man from a tall man when you see

one. So, you may not know how many acts make treason, but you know it when you see it. *(He looks down at the floor; he looks up at me).* They are such cowards, Elizabeth. *(He's just called me Elizabeth. I say nothing; his mind must be in turmoil, and I know he loves her).* How can it be better for the country to be ruled by such men than by the King? And they call themselves gentlemen? They don't know the meaning of the word! Pym intimidates everyone, but the King still swears he will not sign the Bill.

The Head Jailer comes into the cell. "I heard that, Strafford. Just to set your mind at rest, I have sent a message to the King to tell him that if he doesn't sign the Act of Attainder, I'll execute you myself, whether I get his warrant or not." He goes out, slamming the door, and shouting to the Guards, to keep a careful watch, to frighten Thomas, no doubt. It certainly frightens me.

I am appalled, but I came with more news for Thomas, and I must go on before the Guards throw me out. "Thomas, the streets are buzzing with stories of what has happened in the Commons today. Pym went there and told the Members that there was a plot by the King and the Army to take over the country and the Tower, and to rescue you from here."

"What? I don't believe it. It can't be true. I should never agree to that. I'd be hounded and hunted for the rest of my days. I could have gone abroad before the King ordered me to come to London to manage Parliament, but I stand no chance of escaping now. My family would be made to pay for it if I did."

"They say you offered that ghastly man who came in just now ..."

""Balfour? Offered him what?"

"20,000 pounds to let you escape."

"That is just ridiculous. You saw what he said to me just now. He'll hang me if the King doesn't let them chop my head off!! He's always hated me, and so does Newport. Why should I try to bribe them? In any case, what could I bribe them with? I've only enough money here to pay my servants and get food. I borrowed heavily to help the King with the war, and gave him all my available money. It's ridiculous."

"Maybe Pym is just trying to inflame everyone with fear so that the Lords will pass the Bill and you go to the scaffold."

Henry, Lord Cumberland. Saturday, 8th May, 1641. House of Lords.

It is as I feared. The Lords have passed the Bill against Thomas. I think some who were wavering disliked being told by His Majesty last week that whatever they did, he would not assent to the Bill. They didn't care for it at all. Very few peers were actually in the House. Looking round I came to the conclusion that those who were absent were Thomas's friends, or some of them, at any rate. Many who voted with me in the 'Nay' lobby said that others had told them they were afraid to come because of the violence of the mob. That may be true of some, but I think it likely that many stayed away for fear of what Pym would do to them if they sided with Thomas.

Many of the Bishops were present, but that hypocrite Williams, who is now Archbishop of York, stood to tell them that as they had absented themselves from the Trial and Judgment on the judicial proceedings, they should do likewise now.

As a result the outcome was almost a foregone conclusion, despite the decision being by so narrow a majority. Only forty-five Lords attended, and only twenty-six voted for the Bill. The other nineteen voted to save Thomas's life, refusing to pass the Bill. The House then resolved to send the Bill to the King as soon as possible, with a request that he assent to it as soon as possible.

As we left the House another peer grabbed my arm and whispered that he had only voted for the Bill because he knows the King will not sign it! Seven votes will have killed my friend if the King gives his assent. How can he, after what he told us about his conscience a week ago?

Thomas. Sunday, 9th May, 1641. The Tower.

Your Majesty,

In all my troubles none has been so severe as to be accused of setting you apart from your people. To try to do so would have been the greatest madness, considering all the advantages I have received from you. I could not possibly hope to improve my fortune by any other scheme than staying in the position where you had so graciously and generously put me.

You are well aware that my opinion has always been that you and England would never be happy unless there were a proper understanding between you and your people, and that the only way to achieve that was through Parliament. That is the truth, but it finds little credit, so I am blamed as the cause of the evils between you and your people.

No man can suffer heavier censure than that. I understand the minds of men are more and more incensed against me, despite your Majesty declaring that in your princely opinion I am not guilty of Treason, and that you are not satisfied in your conscience that you should sign the Bill. This puts me in a frightful situation. Before me is the ruin of my innocent children and all the branches of my family. Also before me are the evils which may befall your sacred person and the whole Kingdom, should you and Parliament be dissatisfied with each other. I have before me the two things most feared by mortal men: Life, and Death.

To say that there has been no conflict in my soul about these matters to makes me less of a man than my faults would allow. To call my own destruction upon me and my young children when my intentions were innocent of the offences charged in the Bill, finds no easy consent from my flesh and blood.

But very sadly I am resolved to do what I think will become me best, and to concentrate on what will be best for the prosperity of Your Majesty and the Commonwealth of England, which are infinitely to be preferred to my private interests. Therefore, to be brief, I put myself on the honour and justice of my peers. Just as much as I wish Your Majesty had spared yourself the trouble of making that Declaration on Saturday, and left me entirely to the mercy of their Lordships, so now, to set your conscience at liberty, I do most humbly beseech you to assent to the Bill, to prevent the terrible things which might befall you and the nation if you refuse. By doing so you will remove – praise be to God I cannot say this accursed, but I confess - this unfortunate 'thing' which is an obstacle to peace between you and your subjects.

Sire, my consent shall pardon you more with God than the rest of the world can. To a willing man no injury is done. By God's grace I forgive all the world. With calmness and meekness of infinite contentment in my soul which may be about to be sent elsewhere, I can cheerfully give up this earthly life, and justly acknowledge the manifold favours I have received from you.

I only beg that in your goodness you will cast your gracious regard on my poor wife and son and his three sisters, whether their father appears more or less guilty and so deserves to die like this.

God preserve Your Majesty, your most humble and faithful subject.

Strafford.

Having finished that, I compose a short letter to the Lords asking them to do what they can to spare my children and their inheritance.

Charles I. Monday, 10th May, 1641. My Audience Chamber, Whitehall Palace.

Henrietta is with me. She is in a frantic agitated state, and, frankly, I am little better myself. We could sit on our Chairs of State, but neither of us can stay still for a moment. We must have marched miles in our own home here to try to get away from, or find a solution to, this terrible problem. I have a letter from Strafford giving me permission to sign the Bill, and my conscience battering at my brain telling me I cannot. Henrietta is plainly scared, but in earthly terms, whilst I am terrified of what God will do to me if I break my promise to save Strafford's life. Why should I sacrifice him when I do not believe he has done anything wrong? Unless obeying me, or giving me advice, is wrong!

Queen. The Lords have passed the Bill, Charles. You 'ave to sign it, or we shall all be killed. You must think of the children.

Me. *(I am angry and contemptuous of that remark).* Do you honestly think I might forget about you and the children?

Queen. *(She is tearful, and so distraught her French accent has strengthened).* I am sorry, Charles, but I am so frightened. I 'ave been praying with my ladies. And listen to that mob. It sounds like a 'urricane from 'ell.

Me. *(I am struggling to recover my dignity).* No-one could ignore those rioters, least of all me. If they don't get Strafford's head they will want mine.

Queen. *Et la mienne, probablement!* You must sign this Bill. It is our only chance.

Me. I told the House of Lords only a few days ago that even if they passed the Bill, I could not find it in my conscience to assent to it.
Queen. You are the King, Charles, and I should not speak so, but I think it was not wise to say that.
Me. What should I have said?
Queen. *(Helplessly).* I don't know... *(She sobs heartbrokenly; she recovers).* But you should not 'ave told them that you would not sign the Bill. They do not want to be told what they must do, and what you will not do. Perhaps you could have tried to persuade them, instead of ordering them. That is what this Pym does, *n'est ce pas*?
Me. To some extent, yes. But he also bullies and threatens, and uses that mob to frighten people who oppose him. Like me.
Queen. If the mob breaks in 'ere, we shall be killed. You must sign the Bill. If it is Strafford's life or ours, Strafford must die. You 'ave no choice.
Me. I have a letter from him. *(I hold it up).* He asks me to sign, but I gave him my word I would not.
Queen. What does the letter say?

I read it to her; all of it. It makes me weep. It is so sad, so pathetically kind and generous. How, why, did I never really like this man? He is a statesman from the sole of his boots to the top of his hat. He has given his all for me, and now he is prepared to lay down his life for me and the country. He took up his cross and will bear it to the very end. "I promised him Henrietta. How can I break that promise?"
Queen. *(Desperately).* But he is releasing you from your promise. You must sign.

(A servant enters and bows).
Servant. Your Majesty, Archbishop Williams of the York Diocese, Archbishop Ussher of Ireland, and Bishop Juxon of London ask if you will grant them an audience.

"Then please show them in," and the servant goes. "We shall see them sitting down, my dear. Williams has been a difficult man with me and Laud over Church reform. He talked the Bishops out of taking part in the Trial, and from voting on the Bill, and God alone knows what he wants with me now. Still, I asked the others to come and advise me."

The servant comes back. "His Grace the Archbishop of York, Sire, the Archbishop of Ireland, and the Bishop of London." He stands aside to let the prelates in, and goes, closing the doors. I thank them for coming at my request and on such short notice. I tell them that I want their advice on the religious aspects of this Attainder, and to know what my conscience should direct me to do. I add that I have seen some of the Judges to discuss the Law of Treason in this matter, but I did not get much enlightenment from them.

Ussher is, as usual, ponderous and forthright. "Your Majesty should do whatever your conscience tells you. For what it is worth, mine would not allow me to assent to this Bill if I were, in this terrible situation, to have the misfortune to be the Monarch."

Juxon speaks much to the same effect.

Williams is more subtle. "Sire, it seems to me that for a King there are two types of conscience. One is the personal conscience of the King as a man, and he should do what is right from that personal point of view. The other is the public conscience of a man as King, whose conscience must direct him in what he believes to be the best interests of the country he governs. It may be that the public, Kingly conscience, can set aside the private one. The question is not whether you should save the Earl of Strafford, but rather what will happen to you and your people if you do. Will you perish with him, Sire? Will doing so preserve the Kingdom, and protect your Queen and children?

"Do those considerations not outweigh the private conscience which may wish to save a friend and servant? If you look at it in that light, might it not be better, for conscience sake, to turn the Bill into an Act by giving your assent?"

I do not know whether to be angered, dejected, or demoralized by that advice, or grateful for it. Whatever I feel, I cannot resist saying: "I'm obliged to you. Of course, if you had not persuaded your fellow clerics to abstain from voting on this Bill in the first place, I should not now be faced with signing the Bill, your advice would have been unnecessary, and Strafford would live."

Smoothly as a serpent Williams misses not a beat: "Perhaps, Sire, but that is not the position we are now in, and my advice is directed to that. You must take or ignore it, as you see fit."

Ussher and Juxon look embarrassed, but soon all three Bishops depart. As soon as they are gone, Henrietta is on her feet and comes to me, wrapping her arms about my neck. "You 'eard what Bishop Williams said, Charles. You 'ave to protect me and the children. You 'ave to protect everyone in England, not just this one man. Please Charles, you 'ave to do this!"

"Very well, my dear. You should go to bed. I need to read the Bill again, and think about the advice I have had. If I can bring myself to sign, I shall do it. I shall write to the Lords asking them to spare his life anyway, even if he has to spend the rest of it locked up in prison, or confined to his own home. Go to bed, Henrietta."

I kiss her, disentangle her arms, and she does as she's told. I sit down to read the Bill again. It recites very shortly all the evil things Strafford is supposed to have done, and even says that they have been proved sufficiently on his Impeachment, despite the Lords, who were his Judge and his Jury, having never made a finding of guilt. Then it says it is enacted by me, the Lords and Commons in Parliament assembled that Strafford 'shall suffer the pain of death, and the forfeiture of all his goods and land and estates'. They won't even let his children inherit anything. And I have to put my name to this?

But do I really have a choice? I'm not worried about my own neck, but listen to that mob outside. Can I - could any husband and father - leave his family at their mercy? So I sign the Bill. It is now an Act, and Strafford's head will come off.

I write the letter I told Henrietta I should, asking for his life to be exchanged for imprisonment, and I date it tomorrow. I also ask, in a PS, that if he is to die, perhaps it could be put off until Saturday. I shall also tell the Lords who come to collect the Bill and my letter that: "My Lord of Strafford's condition is happier than mine."

The Prince of Wales shall deliver my letter to the House of Lords for me. He is such a winning, personable young man, and they will find it harder to deny him than they would me, even if I am the King. I have been flouted enough already.

Thomas. Tuesday, 11th May, 1641, The Tower.

My dearest Will,

These are the last lines you will receive from a father who loves you tenderly. I wish there were more time to share my mind with you, but our merciful God will supply all things by His Grace, and guide and protect you in everything you do, and I bequeath you to Him.

Be sure you show every respect to my wife, who has ever had a great love for you. Never let your love and care for your sisters be wanting, but let them always be dear to you, and have the same regard for your youngest sister. Indeed you owe it to her for her mother and father's sake.

I trust the King will deal graciously with you, and restore to you those honours and fortune which these awful times have deprived you of, together with the life of your father. Be sure to avoid, as much as you can, inquiring after those who have been sharp in their judgments of me, and I charge you never to suffer any thought of revenge to enter your heart.

May Almighty God of His infinite goodness bless you and your children's children, and your sisters in the same manner. May He perfect you in every good work, and give you to understand rightly in all things.

You must not fail to behave yourself towards my Lady Clare your grandmother with every duty and faithfulness, for she loves you most tenderly, and has been more than kind to me. God reward her for her charity. And once more I do, from my very soul, beseech our gracious God to bless and guide you in all, and join us again in communion with His saints, where we shall find fullness of joy and bliss for ever more.   Amen.

Amen.

Your loving father.

William Laud. Tuesday, 11th May, 1641. The Tower.

I am in my cell – well, perhaps that is an exaggeration, for it is a not uncomfortable room, but it is definitely a prison – writing, when a jailer announces that Archbishop Ussher wishes to see me. I ask for him to be admitted. Like me he is an old man. Unlike me he is free. He was, of course, more tolerant as Primate of Ireland towards Puritans than I have ever been, so he is not in the bad books of the likes of John Pym.

Thomas is incarcerated somewhere else in the Tower, and we are not allowed to see each other. That is a hardship for both of us, as we are great friends, and I am sure Thomas would be glad if we could pray together. That proves to be the reason for Ussher's visit.

"I've been visiting My Lord Strafford lately,' he says. "He's in a very placid state for a man who is to have his head lopped off tomorrow, but he asked Blount, the Lieutenant of the Tower, if he could see you."

"What was his answer?"

"Blount told him he could not unless Parliament authorised it."

"That is just ridiculous, Ussher. He is to be executed soon. What chance is there of getting Parliament to agree to anything today?"

Ussher is sad, which is surprising considering the trouble he has had with me and Thomas in the past. "I know. Strafford told Blount that he could be present in the room to hear what the two of you talk about. He said: 'This not a time for Laud to plot heresy or for me to plot treason'. Blount repeated that he couldn't see you and again told Thomas to apply to Parliament, and Thomas told him that he already knew what Parliament was prepared to let him have. He wouldn't petition them again."

Ussher sits down, and looks me straight in the face. "Then Strafford said something which shows just how calm and philosophical he is about his fate. 'I am now petitioning a higher court, where neither partiality can be expected, nor error feared.'

I am moved. "He meant the Almighty."

Ussher nods. "He did, and he asked me to come to you with his best wishes, and to tell you that whilst you will be in his prayers, he would be grateful if you will, likewise, pray for him tonight, and stand at your window as he passes on his way to the block tomorrow, to give him your blessing."

"How did he learn that the King had given his assent?"

"One of the King's secretaries carried the message to him last night."

"Of course. The same man came to tell me, and said that Thomas cried out: 'Put not your trust in Princes!' "

"Did you believe that, William?" "

No, I did not. I don't think Thomas has ever felt sorry for
himself in his life, except when his Margaret and Arabella died. Even then he was sorrier for them than for himself."

Ussher sits in contemplation for a moment. "He's worried about them, of course - I mean his wife and children - and the rest of his family, and many others who depend on him, such as Wandesford's children, and George Radcliffe. He's heavily in debt for money he borrowed to give the King, and the guarantee he gave for Army pay in Yorkshire last year. Still, at least with the aid of his brothers-in-law, Henry Clifford and the Hollises, the King will try to ensure that his estates will go to his children no matter what the Attainder may say."

I am pleased. "Well, that's something, at any rate." He hesitates. "Do we know when he is to die?"

"Yesterday Prince Charles took a letter from the King to the House of Lords asking them to spare his life, or at least give him until Saturday, so that he could do more to set his affairs in order. He told me he'd written to the Lords with his own request to be allowed to live for the rest of the week. They said 'No' to him and to the King. The headsman will be waiting for him on Tower Hill tomorrow morning."

I choke back my tears. I promise to pray for Thomas, and then the tears roll, unstoppable, down my face. I mumble that I hope, when I am executed, as I am likely to be, the world will perceive that I regret the loss of Lord Strafford's life more than my own. He has served the Church - let alone the King - more than I have done, or any other clergyman. I add that Thomas is the wisest, the strongest, and in every way the most able subject the country has produced for many a year. He has faults. His poor health is one. Another is his refusal to pander to or place himself under obligation to anyone. Finally, he is envied by the nobility, and serves a Prince who trusted false and perfidious men to serve him in the North and in Scotland, and who knows not how to be, nor be made, great.

Ussher agrees, and adds: "As you know, Traitors are normally hanged, drawn, and quartered, and some think this Attainder provides for that, but it will not. He will be beheaded. The King would not tolerate anything else."

Ussher says no more. He blesses me, says he will pray for Thomas and for me, and departs.

Thomas. Wednesday, 12th May, 1641. Tower Hill.

I was brought out of my prison at about eleven of the clock this morning by my Guards and the Lieutenant of the Tower, Balfour. As we walked past the window of Archbishop Laud's prison, I looked up and saw him standing there, as I had asked him to do. I bowed to him, and called: "My Lord, your prayers and your blessing." The Guards did not stop me doing this. I saw Laud lift up his hands as though to pray and bless me, as he might do in his Cathedral, but he fell back, away from the window, and I saw him no more. I thought he must have passed out. He looked so frail and ill and old. I called to him again; "Farewell, My Lord, and God protest your innocence."

The Guards then asked me to walk on, and as we went, I thought, as I have done many times since I was arrested, that I have never seen my dear Elizabeth and my lovely children since I left Ireland for the last time this month last year, and I shall never see them again on this Earth. I have not wanted them to come here, for fear that they would be in more danger from the mob, and that somehow Pym's gang would use them as a weapon against me, but that does not reduce the pain and sadness I suffer from their absence.

As we approached the gates to leave the Tower, Balfour asked me to go by coach for fear the mob would tear me to pieces, but I told him: "No, Master Lieutenant. I dare look death in the face, and, I hope, the people too." I laughed. "Have a care that I do not escape! I don't care how I die, whether by the hand of the executioner, or by the madness and fury of the people, if that will make them more content; it's all one to me".

We walked out of the gates, towards Tower Hill and the huge scaffold I could see had been erected for me, and the even larger platforms and enclosures which had been put up for spectators. Balfour told me that it was said that 100,000 people had come to see me die, and they had been gathering all night. Certainly I could see there was a multitude.

I walked as upright as my weakness and my gout would allow, with my head held high, and as we passed some of the people, I heard one man say to his neighbour: "Just look at Black Tom; even now he marches more like a general at the head of his army than a condemned man".

When I mount the scaffold with my Guards and Balfour, I find my dear brother George and old Ussher there already, with many others. George is racked with sobbing, and tears stream down his cheeks. I take him in my arms: "Brother, what do you see in me to deserve these tears? Does any indecent fear betray any guilt? Do I seem to be bold with atheism as if I do not have to face my Maker? No, of course not. Imagine that you are accompanying me a third time to a marriage, and that I have never before thrown off my clothes more freely than I do to prepare for my grave. That block is to be my pillow, and here I shall rest from all my labours.

"No envious thoughts, no nightmares about Treason, no worry for the King's matters, affairs of State, nor even my own, will disturb the easy sleep I'm about to take. Instead, George, thank those who have made me happy this way, and pity them, for I am happy, and I am innocent."

Sir George Wentworth. Wednesday, 12th May, 1641. Tower Hill.

I am unable to say whether it is the fact that Thomas's bearing is so regal as he climbs the steps to the scaffold, or that he looks so ill and old, that shocks and upsets me more, but I am reduced to the most shameful burst of weeping I have experienced since I was a boy. Thomas embraces me like the loving brother he is, and has always been, and tells me to dry my tears.

Then he kneels down, and addresses the Irish Primate and the Lords and others with him on the scaffold: "I hope, Gentlemen, that you do not think that either the fear of loss or the love of reputation will suffer me to lie to God and my own conscience at this time. I am now at the door to Heaven or Hell, and my next step will take me from here to an eternity of peace or pain. Therefore I solemnly declare before God and call Him to witness before all of you, that I am not guilty of the great crime laid at my door. I have never had the slightest intention of doing anything to harm or prejudice the King, this State, the Laws, or the religion of this country. My only aim has been to serve and support all of them. So may God have mercy on my soul."

Thomas stands up, and says he will speak to the crowd, tells us his voice may not be heard, and kneels down again, this time at the block. It seems as though he is trying it for size, for he rises again. He makes a very long speech, but is calm and seems at peace. I do not have the feeling that he is speaking to delay the inevitable. I am unable to take it all in and recall it for this account, but I think the main points are these, as near as I can say, in his own words.

"My Lord Archbishop of Ireland, My Lords, and all of you noble people, I come here to die at the hands of Parliament, and to submit to that Judgment which has been passed against me. I do it with a quiet and contented mind, and at the will and pleasure of Almighty God, and to pay the debt we all owe to sin, which is death. Even so, I hope through the blessings of God and the merits of Jesus, to rise to eternal life." *(At this point there are shouts from the crowd of 'Not much hope of that for you, Black Tom', and similar yells. One or two even shout*

'God Bless you', but they are drowned out by louder calls of 'Take his head off now!')

"I have no bitter thought against any man. I thank God that I strove only for the prosperity of the King and his people, and England's happiness. Maybe those who live by politics deserve to die by politics; certainly, that is what is happening to me. I am being killed as the result of a political - some may say a democratic – process, and I was one of the highest in the land. I'm not the first man to suffer in this way and I shan't be the last. Righteous judgment is in heaven; here on earth we misjudge one another. But I cannot let this pass without saying yet again that I have never been against Parliaments. I always thought that English Parliaments were the happiest constitution any nation lived under, and the best means, under God, to keep King and people happy. *(Thomas pauses).* I acquit all the world of my death, and beg God to forgive those who contrived it, despite knowing in my heart I am not guilty of what I die for.

"My Lord Primate, it is a great comfort to me that His Majesty considers that I do not merit that most heavy of punishments which this sentence usually carries. I beseech God that he, too, will find mercy when he most stands in need of it. I wish this kingdom every prosperity and happiness, but I ask you all to think whether the beginning of happiness and reform for a kingdom should be written in blood, for I fear you have taken the wrong path.

"I profess that I die a true and obedient son of the Church of England, and deny that I have ever inclined to Popery. I have never doubted the Church of England and no man has had the courage to say to my face that I have. I beg the forgiveness of everyone for any rash or ill-advised words I may have uttered, and any wrong I have done. I thank God I go from a corruptible world to an incorruptible Paradise. God bless this Kingdom, and may Jesus have mercy on my soul. *(He calls on all of us on the scaffold to join him in prayer, and he prays for some minutes. Then he stands and embraces me).* Brother, remember me to our sister Anne, and to my dear wife Elizabeth, and the children. Give my blessing to my son Will, tell him to fear God, be loyal to the Church of England, and to bear no grudge or thought of revenge against any man.

"Give my blessings also to my daughters Anne and Arabella, and to dear little infant Margaret, who barely knows me, and knows nothing of good or evil.

(He turns to the Executioner, forgives him, and hands him a purse. He takes off his doublet and fastens his hair up. He kneels at the block once more, and prays with Ussher on one side and Juxon on the other). I shall pray a while; then I shall give you a sign.

Thomas rests his head on the block, and raises his eyes and hands to heaven in prayer briefly. As soon as he does so there is a roar of kettle drums and the Executioner retrieves the axe from the pile of straw, and stands holding it in both hands ready to strike. Thomas, whose arms are at the side of the block, stretches them out to the side, palms up, and the Executioner swings the axe up ready to strike. Thomas drops his hands, and the axe swipes up and down in a flash of light. Thomas's head comes off with that one stroke, thank the Lord. His blood gushes forth.

The Axeman lifts this head by the hair, and holds it up for the people to see. He shouts: "God Save the King." The crowd thunders out the loudest sound I have ever heard. "His head is off!! Black Tom's head is off!!"

Epilogue.

Charles I. 30th January 1649. The Banqueting Hall of Whitehall Palace.

This morning I was brought here from St James's Palace by a column of guards. Did they feel sorry for me? I doubt it, but they were not marching fast enough for my liking so I asked them to step out more quickly. I was brought here to the Banqueting Hall. At first I was agitated, and paced up and round and back and forth, but after a while I felt more tranquil, sat down, and incredibly, fell asleep. I had the most peculiar dream. A servant came to the door and announced that the Bishop was here. That was no surprise, even in a dream, since I was expecting Juxon to come and pray with me and give me his blessing before I walk out on to the scaffold.

Me. *(I nod, but I do not look up).* Admit him. Is there any news of my children?

Bishop. *(The Bishop wears a long black gown over a full-length white surplice. He wears a floppy type of square black cap, the corners of which hang down, partially obscuring his face. He stands to the side of my chair).* Princess Elizabeth and Prince Henry are safely at Syon House.

Me. Thank God the House of Commons let me see them before it's too late; two sunbeams to pierce the gloom.

Bishop. England's a gloomy place now Master Cromwell and the Army rule it. Dancing is banned, music is banned. The theatres have been shut down....

Me. ....and the stained glass in the churches is being smashed along with statues and carvings hundreds of years old. Yes, My Lord Bishop, I hear about it all. I thank Christ I can't see it all!!

Bishop. I suppose even being a prisoner has its consolations at times like these, Sire.

Me. *(I answer with an ironic laugh).* That's one way of looking at it, I suppose. Your Grace, this palace is hardly my home. Still, I offer you what welcome I can.

Bishop. *(He kneels and kisses my hand).* I trust I find Your Majesty well. *(He rises)*

Me. Well? Happier, maybe. Two of the children coming to see me yesterday lightened my mood – for a time. *(I gesture to the Bishop to* *sit. He does so).* The prospect of death isn't as painful as being robbed of my family.

Bishop. And the Queen, Sire? It must be – what - eight years since you saw her? Is there news of her?

Me. Eight years. Yes. She writes to me. I think the Government, if that's what you can call it, has the letters opened. She's in Paris. The Prince of Wales is in Holland. Cromwell would execute my family unless one of the children agreed to be his puppet.

Bishop. None of them would accept the crown from Cromwell.

Me. I pray God you are right, but the tyranny of this "Parliament," this "People's Government," is hard to bear. We fought two civil wars because Parliament dubs me a tyrant, yet at my trial I wasn't allowed to speak before sentence was passed. Even the lowliest of my subjects was not denied that right.

Bishop. Your Majesty shouted "I am not allowed to speak; what justice can other people expect?"

Me. Parliamentary justice! They convened a Court to convict me. Was there any chance I might be acquitted? *(I stop for a moment).* Still, it's the separation from my Queen and my family which has been so dreadful. More so than today's appointment with Death.

Bishop. The Prince of Wales will be Charles II, God willing.

Me. God may be willing, but will Master Cromwell? *(I pause again).* Dear Charles. *(I sigh).* Not yet nineteen. What has he learned from me except the art of unsuccessfully waging war against this tyrannous Parliament?

Bishop. When Your Majesty ruled without Parliament, England enjoyed ten of its most peaceful and prosperous years.

Me. Monarchs and Parliaments do not make prosperity. The people make their own. Governments merely interfere with their efforts.

Bishop. You ruled the kingdom with a mere million pounds a year. Parliament now taxes the people three times as much, and they will be taxed more to pay for the Army.

Me. *(I chuckle, and shake my head sadly).* I, the condemned tyrant, had no Army before the Bishop's War, yet Parliament now has one, cannot control it, and taxes the people to pay for it to an extent I never dreamed possible. And for this I am to be beheaded? *(I fall silent again).* Your Grace, I am in need of blessing - God's Blessing.

Bishop. Let us kneel together and say Our Saviour's Prayer, and then I shall hear your confession.

(We kneel together and say)

Me and Bishop. Our Father, Which art in Heaven, Hallowed be thy name; Thy kingdom come, Thy will be done, on Earth as it is in heaven. Give us this day our daily bread, and forgive us our trespasses as we forgive them that trespass against us; and lead us not into temptation, but deliver us from evil. Amen.

(In this dream we rise and I sit, but Bishop Juxon remains standing. Suddenly, he removes the black gown and hat, and metamorphoses in a few seconds into a ghost of Wentworth in the white surplice. He no longer looks grey and ill as he did during his trial. His hair is black, as it used to be when I first knew him, and he is fit and upright, six or more inches taller than I. But it is a dream, and I do not react as if I had seen the change. To me he still seems to be the Bishop, as though this is just what I should expect).

Wentworth. Which trespasses does Your Majesty wish to confess? *(He smiles).* At your trial, you were compared to the Emperor Caligula.

Me. I never governed according to whim and caprice.

Wentworth. Nor did you appoint your horse to your Council. Your court was a model of God-fearing sobriety, Your Majesty.

Me. Perhaps; God will judge me and my works. Nevertheless, there is one matter which oppresses my soul unbearably.

Wentworth. What is that, Sire?

Me. "Greater love hath no man than this, that he lay down his life for his friends." I let the most loyal, the most fearless, of my servants lay down his life for me. I'd promised that I should protect him, and I could have saved his life.

Wentworth. You speak of the Earl of Strafford? He was Your Majesty's Servant, but was he your friend? *(During this speech he moves round to sit in another chair).*

Me. God help me, no. I never liked him. Despite all his years of loyal service, I never called him "friend." Oh! I honoured him. I made him a Baron, and a Viscount, and then Earl of Strafford, but I never liked......
(As I speak I look at Wentworth and recognize him for who he is for the first time. I am shocked but not frightened). **....** never liked .... you.

Wentworth. Perhaps you couldn't overlook my period in opposition. I was the Duke of Buckingham's fiercest critic, and the Duke was your

closest friend. I was one of those who, to put it charitably, was not displeased when he was stabbed to death.
Me. Buckingham's assassination nearly broke my heart. I hated anyone who rejoiced at his death! You were one of them.
Wentworth. True, Sire, but I was never opposed to you or the Crown. I always strove for a strong monarchy. Buckingham only strove for a strong Buckingham! My loyalty to you was total.
Me. I know. Yet, in my weakest, darkest hour I permitted Parliament –
Wentworth. Ably led by John Pym!
Me. – I permitted them to cut off your head. The people rejoiced at your execution, and the crowd was the biggest the country had ever seen - a hundred thousand people.
Wentworth. *(He smiles again, and speaks gently).* I was there.
Me. They called you Black Tom Tyrant. They feared you. I'm not sure the people ever loved me, but I don't think they feared me.
Wentworth. Yes, Black Tom. They feared what you might do with my help. We were so different, you and I.
Me. No, Thomas, we weren't, or you might be alive today, and I might be alive tomorrow. No. Our tragedy wasn't that we were different, but that we were too much alike. You were arrogant; so was I. But I had another flaw. I believed in the Divine Right of Kings. I always thought I was right even when I was wrong, and I wouldn't listen. I wouldn't even listen to you. Not even to you. Not until it was too late. And then even when you were so ill, you fought, might and main, for me and for what you believed in. When the final test came, you released me from my promise, and signed your life away. They say you died courageously. *(I am too overcome for a moment to continue).* I must do likewise. Which reminds me, Thomas. They say that when you heard I had signed your death warrant, you cried "Put not your trust in Princes!" Is it true?
Wentworth. *(He gives a wry laugh).* Why should I write telling you to sign it and then blame you for doing so? No, Sire, it is not true. It was a rumour. I had many faults, but I trust hypocrisy and inconsistency were not among them.
(I wake at this point to find I am wiping away real tears, and that the real Bishop Juxon stands before me. I take off my doublet, and point to a shirt on a chair). Help me on with that. *(I continue speaking as*

Juxon helps me put the shirt on over the one I'm already wearing, and then I resume my doublet). These January days are bitter cold. My people must not see me shiver – they will think I am afraid.

Juxon. When I came in, Sire, you seemed to be talking in your sleep.

Me. I was dreaming of talking with Strafford. And praying with him. Pray with me now. *(We kneel and pray, and Juxon puts his hand on my head and blesses me, and gives me absolution. I rise, and go towards the large window which opens onto the scaffold. I stop and turn back to Juxon).* I should have honoured my promise. When the axe severed Strafford's head from his body it severed me from my wisest and most trusted adviser. How ironical! Having sacrificed his head to save the Monarchy, in ten minutes I am to lose my head and the Monarchy. *(I walk to the door, stop, and look back again).* I can never forgive myself. *(I walk out onto the scaffold. There is a roar of kettle drums).*

In Memoriam.

None were so high but would comply with me and my commands,
For else they were forc'd to obey, and perish in my hands.
None durst devour the widow poor, nor seize another's right,
But I brought in to scourge his sin, and crush him with my might.

But what's all this? I did amiss, for so the Commons say;
All this did tend to my own end and profit every way.
My Port advanc'd, my State enhanc'd, and my revenues too,
The common laws I did dispose and wrest them God knows how.

First I did fleece our merchandise and grievous imposts raise,
For private gain I trucked with Spain, and with injurious lays
Impair'd men's state t'increase their hate, no pity did I render;
Thus with all ill I'm twitted still; my good deeds none remember.

An Excerpt from *Strafforiados: the Lieutenant's Legend* (1652).

Four Hundred Years later, Thomas looks back.

I was buried in the Church at Wentworth Woodhouse, much of which is now a ruin. My parents are buried there too.

After I was beheaded it was not long before Lucy Carlisle became the Mistress of John Pym, thereby proving that his being a Puritan was no guarantee that he could not be a hypocrite. Lucy certainly knew how to be on the right side at the right time. Mind you, neither of them enjoyed their fling for long, as he died of cancer a couple of years later.

It is said that she was the source of the Parliamentarians learning of King Charles's plan to come to the House of Commons to arrest the five members. She allegedly knew of the plot because of her friendship with the Queen and her ready access to the Palace, and told her brother Robert, the Earl of Essex, who was on the parliamentary side in the Civil war.

I recently came across a poem by Sir John Suckling about Lucy. I think he may have been an admirer of hers at one time, despite being some nine or ten years her junior, though by the time he wrote this, he seems to have been somewhat disillusioned. He was not her only troubadour of the pen. Robert Herrick was another. What Suckling wrote may seem rather scurrilous, but in a way it does sum up what she was like and the effect she had on men. He called it "Upon Lady Carlisle's walk in the Garden"; here are the last two Stanzas:

JS. Alas! Tom, I am flesh and blood,
And was consulting how I could
In spite of masks and hood descry
The parts denied unto the eye,
I was undoing all she wore,
And had she walked but one turn more,
Eve in her first state had not been
More Naked or more plainly seen.
Tom. "Twas well for thee she left the place,
There is great danger in that face.
But hadst thou viewed her leg and thigh,
And upon that discovery,
Searched after parts that are more dear
(As fancy seldom stops so near)
No time or age had ever seen
So lost a thing as thou hadst been.

I do not know who Tom is supposed to have been, but it wasn't me. I certainly wasn't JS either; no-one could have seen Lucy more naked nor more plainly than I had been lucky enough to do, but I certainly was not lost. Alternatively perhaps the poet thought that I was a peeping Tom who had unsuccessfully sought to uncover 'those parts that are more dear', and had had to be content, as in the poem, with trying to strip her bare in my imagination as she took a stroll.

My erstwhile mentor and, latterly, opponent in some respects, Sir Arthur Ingram, died in 1642, a year after me, but very much older, and his was not a violent death; he died in bed. If I had learned to trim my sails as he did, maybe I could have died in bed too.

Poor old William Laud, Archbishop of Canterbury, was kept in the Tower of London for two years after my death, and then he, too, was beheaded at the behest of Parliament.

One of my bêtes noirs, Francis Annesley, Lord Mountnorris, became Viscount Valentia in 1642, and also sided with Parliament in the war. He held various offices in the Revolutionary Regime, and died in 1660, just in time, probably, to avoid having his head chopped off for treason when Charles II came to the throne at the Restoration of the Monarchy.

My chaplain, John Bramhall, who was appointed by me to the Bishopric of Derry, sided loyally with Charles during the Civil War and had to go into exile when Parlaiment won. He came back in 1660 with the Restoration of Charles II, and became Archbishop of Armagh, Primate of All Ireland. He died in 1663.

My friend James, Earl of Ormonde, went on successfully to keep – just – on the right side of Cromwell and Parliament, and became an honoured and important member of the political scene in England and Ireland after Charles II came to the throne, dying full of years in 1688.

My dear wife Elizabeth stayed in Ireland until after my death, then returned to England. She, too, died in 1688, in Hooton Roberts. She is said to have been buried in the Church there next to the dower house in which she lived. Hooton Roberts is not far from Wentworth Woodhouse. My son William went on to become 2nd Earl of Strafford at the Restoration in 1660, when Charles II's government restored the family titles and inheritance, which had been confiscated by Parliament after all, but William died childless. The wealth I had worked so hard to accumulate, already depleted by the vicissitudes of my trial, my death, and the debts my early termination left, passed out of my immediate family. Not the least of these debts was the cost to me of the tobacco monopoly, on which I had spent a fortune. I had a huge stock of the weed in warehouses in Dublin at my death, and some of it went to the Crown to pay my debts to the Revenue.

The rest was used to pay the Irish Army, as once I was dead, no money was being raised for the soldiers' wages.

The plantation of Galway did not go ahead because not long after it was to be implemented there was a threat of war with the Habsburgs, which I strongly advised the King against undertaking, and not long after that, there was an actual war with the Scots. All I had achieved in Connaught, then, for the most part, was to annoy the De Burghs, Earls of Clanrickarde, father and son, for nothing.

The Old English nobility, like the De Burghs of Clanricarde, were ignored in the charges which were laid against me at my trial. Those of them who had helped to get rid of me found, to their cost, that all they had done was to strengthen the hand of the Protestant New English and the Ulster Scots against them and the Catholics generally, and thus there was a rebellion in the island soon after my death, and war raged there for nine years until Cromwell put an end to it, and to many thousands of the people.

Can I claim that if I had lived and been allowed to complete my task in Ireland, all would have been peaceful there? I doubt it. You cannot force people who do not like or even tolerate each other, to do so. If there is no sense of a common interest, and if one or more sections of the people feel that they are oppressed by a minority, all that can be done is to keep the lid on the outbreak of strife for a while. I cannot be sure that I could even have held that lid on for much longer, and looking back I do not think I even realised just how fiercely the pot was boiling.

Thomas. 12th December, 1632. Wentworth Woodhouse.

I was writing about the King's attempt to rule without Parliament from 1629. What I wrote was:

"If the actions the King and his ministers take are just and fair, and aim at pleasing the people rather than negligently alienating them, a few years of going alone without Parliament could set the country on a safe course."

It is odd, in a way, that I should think of pleasing and alienating like that then, on the King's behalf, when I could not see the necessity for it later on, for myself in Ireland, as far as the rich and powerful were concerned. I did not set out to alienate the middle and lower classes and the poor Irish, though that may have been the effect of some of my policies for some of them. However, in the case of the "proud and insolent," as I called them, I adopted a "no holds barred" attitude. Unfortunately for Charles, his own policies as King of England and Scotland alienated most of the population.

I also wrote about making government without Parliament work for a number of years, and then calling Parliament and managing it in the country's interests:

"To do all this I need – the King needs – a loyal band of servants who will implement our policies. He has nothing like enough, and too many are only interested in their own pockets. I think that my fellows in the Lords, and the gentlemen who are the backbone of the judiciary as Justices of the Peace, with all the functions the law and government impose upon them, will happily enforce the King's laws when they are seen to be fair, and lead to stability and prosperity. I believe they will work as hard as I do. I believe that if the King's officials had proper and adequate salaries so that bribery and corruption could be reduced, government would be more efficient, and stronger."

I was wrong. The system could only be changed by very drastic action, and I did not take it far enough. I misjudged the King's willingness to take strong steps. He still thought his will and his word was enough. Did he ever learn? He took the status of kingship seriously, but not the business that went with it. He wanted to spend his time on his art collections and polite conversation on gentile matters with friends such as the Duke of Lennox and the Marquis of Hamilton. He could be persuaded by them to take the wrong course, as he had with Buckingham, though he made the decisions now, whereas Buckingham had made them for him.

Thomas. 23rd March, 1635. Dublin Castle.

I wrote about the City of London's land grant in Ulster being confiscated.

I have always wondered to what extent this Ulster disaster for the City of London helped turn the Lord Mayor, Aldermen, and Council against King Charles when the Civil War started in 1642. Whoever had London had nearly all the money, and most of the shipping and trade - the Port of London was the biggest and most important in the country - and was almost bound to win the war.

Of course, the City did not know what my views were, and what advice I had given. They simply saw that I was the man on the spot at the time, and laid a lot of the blame at my door. I would not have confiscated its land; I would just have made sure it paid properly. But at the end of 1640, these events became just another stick to beat me with.

Thomas. 16th August, 1636. Secretary Coke's House, London.

I wrote about my reluctance to make life easier for Clanricarde.

That really was a good example of the sort of stupid decision I was capable of making. As things turned out the plantation of County Galway did not get under way properly, as other more important matters in England – namely trouble with Scotland - began to take up more and more of everyone's time, and especially mine, two or three years later. Clanricarde was again complaining to me a year later that he still could not afford to pay his debts and his dues, without mortgaging his land.

I placed his loyalty to the King at risk, and he would have known that this was a policy approved by the King. Yet seven years later, when Charles was at war with Parliament, Clanricarde, in his other role as Earl of St Albans, sided with the Royalists against the Parliamentary forces. My tussle with him was not my greatest hour.

Thomas. 30th August, 1636. Secretary Coke's house, London.

The plantation of the province of Connaught was a project on which I worked very hard as Deputy. It is in the West of Ireland, comprising the counties of Galway, Roscommon, Sligo, and Mayo. I had very little trouble making the legal arrangements that should lead settlers to take up land in the last three, but the one that gave me most difficulty was Galway. Looking back, it was one of the least successful and most harmful of the efforts I made in Ireland.

I didn't see that at the time. Either that or I wilfully blinded myself to the obvious. The omens were there before I started, and the evidence became clearer and clearer as time went on that I was probably doing the wrong thing. Like Lear with his vanity, Macbeth with his ambition, Hamlet with his indecisiveness, and Othello with his jealousy, my source of ill fortune was my desire to impose my will regardless of the cost, and take little or no notice of the storm I was creating for myself. You might say I was even more of an absolute monarch believing in my own Divine Right than Charles was.

That's enough psycho-babble. What was the background to this trouble with Galway? As I've said before, the Old English had been there since Plantagenet times. They were Catholic, as everyone was in both England and Ireland in the Thirteenth Century. Why didn't I see that would be a problem? Or was I just too arrogant to care?

Thomas. 29th December, 1640. House of Commons.

On this date John Pym recorded that my great friend George Radcliffe was impeached for Treason. In fact his trial never took place.

Impeachment proceedings started in February, but were not pursued, and in 1642 he was set free. He joined the King's side in the Civil War. He became an adviser to the Duke of York in exile for a time. He died in 1657 in the Low Countries.

Author's Thoughts.

Thomas's Comment on the Irish, 10th August, 1633.

In these days of political correctness it a hard to believe how an intelligent person thought about some things at the time. What Thomas wrote about the Irish on 10th August, 1633, is such a moment. It is trite to say that 'history never repeats itself', and it is untrue into the bargain.

His description of the Irish in 1633 reads just like a 19th Century description of the American Red Indian and the Aborigine in Australia. (I cannot bring myself to put 'Native American', when in some contexts the word native is a term of abuse or contempt, as in the phrase 'Arthur went native'. The Canadians call their aborigines 'First Nation, which is better, but 'The Nation' would be better, and then all the immigrants **since** 1600 could be 'The Second Nation'). These peoples had their own civilizations, and the thing that 'the white man' didn't - and doesn't - like about it is that their way of life interferes with our way. So to make our way work in those countries, we try to extinguish their way of life and impose our own, and expect them to adapt, or we wipe them out, or herd them onto Indian reservations or Aboriginal reserves.

And one very odd aspect of that process is that the Irish and the Scots, so many of whom fled their native land to escape the depredations of the English, turned up in America and Australia and did exactly the same thing to the real owners of the land they found there. The settlers turned them off their hunting grounds and away from the good water and land by the rivers, and drove them out into deserts and very much less habitable places. Then they said the natives lived in such appalling conditions, and in such a wild and uncivilised way. Finally, if the immigrants found gold, or silver, or coal, or iron ore, oil, or anything else they could dig up, or grow crops or raise cattle on, they evicted the indigenous folks even from the uninhabitable places.

Is it any wonder these poor people had such mean and awful lives, and still do? How could the Irish and Scots do that to anyone else, when they complain and sing so many laments about what was done to them?

Still, there may be progress of a kind. There was much talk of black rights from 1950 onwards, and the USA has had a coloured President, but how about a Red Indian President? How many of that unfortunate race have been Congressman, or Senators? How many are in Congress now?

In Australia at least the Northern Territory had a part indigenous State Premier. Whether he was any good is beside the point. How many politicians are any good? How many Australians look forward to their first Aborigine Prime Minister?

Acknowledgements.

The portrait used for the cover of this book shows "Thomas, Viscount Wentworth, later 1st Earl of Strafford, and his Hound," by Sir Anthony Van Dyck. For its use I am indebted to the Trustees of the Rt. Hon Olive, Countess Fitzwilliam's Chattels Settlement, by Permission of Lady Juliet Tadgell.

At Sir Walter St John's Grammar School, Battersea, England, I had one particularly history teacher, Johnny Walker. Under him I studied 17th Century history. I was entranced by Strafford. At that time (1958-1961) he had usually been written up as a hero and a martyr. In 1961 C.V.Wedgwood revised her original biography of Wentworth in **1961 following** H.F.Kearney's book, "Strafford in Ireland," and J.P.Cooper's study "The Fortune of Thomas Wentworth Earl of Strafford." I am greatly indebted to those works. I have read Miss Wedgwood's books, "The King's Peace," "The King's War" and "The Thirty Years War."

I also used: Trevor-Roper's Archbishop Laud, Upton's Sir Thomas Ingram, McElwee's "England's Precedence," Watson's "The Life and Times of Charles I," and Mackie's "A History of Scotland," a copy of the transcript of the trial of Strafford from the British Library, copies of original documents from Sheffield City Library, and Wikipedia with regard to many of the characters. I obtained a copy of an old memoir about Sir John Reresby, and of what is believed to be Wentworth's own account of the 1621 Parliament in which he sat.

James Hogan of Oberon Books gave me some help with dialogue, as did Peter Matheson, the Australian dramaturg.

The staff of the Wingham Library, New South Wales, Australia, and their colleagues in the Taree branch, have tracked down all sorts of books and articles for me, including Rushworth's very full account of the trial published in 1700. I had help from Jennifer Allison, Town Guide of Northallerton, Yorks, the Staffordshire Record Office, The National Gallery of Ireland, William Derham at Dublin Castle, Liz Street at The National Gallery of Ireland, Tim Kneble at Sheffield City Library.

I cannot claim that this work is totally accurate, because many of the authorities on which I relied do not make it plain when some events occurred, and without the help I have had, the errors would have been legion. Even great historians leave out dates, and divide their story into separate topics, making piecing together the sequence of events almost impossible. Further, in Strafford's time an old calendar was used which started the year on 1st April, rather than 1st January. I have used today's calendar.

I thank my friends Peter and Philippa Cocks, Joe Shevlin, Eric Blyth, Jean Burden, and Phil Hewitt, journalist and author, my cousin Loretta for all their help with the first drafts and the guide staff of Wentworth Woodhouse for a truly entrancing tour. My readers would find a visit to this magnificent stately home very rewarding.

Michael Davies of the Mickie Dalton Foundation has edited, formatted, and published this work with great skill, and incredible expedition. His help was and is invaluable.

Finally, I thank my wife, Christine, for her patience during the hours I have spent researching and writing, and for reading and helping me correct the book.

I dedicate the book to her.

Terry Stanton.
February, 2017.

68999177R00399

Manufactured by Amazon.com
Columbia, SC
04 April 2017